P9-DVO-316

THE COLLECTED STORIES OF
BENEDICT KIELY

THE COLLECTED STORIES OF

BENEDICT

KIELY

DAVID R. GODINE · *Publisher*

BOSTON

Published in 2003 by
David R. Godine, Publisher
Post Office Box 450
Jaffrey, New Hampshire 03452
www.godine.com

Originally published in the United Kingdom in 2001
by Methuen Publishing Ltd., London

Text design by Byrony Newhouse

LIBRARY OF CONGRESS
CATALOGING-IN-PUBLICATION DATA

Kiely, Benedict.
[Short Stories. Selections]
The collected stories of Benedict Kiely.
p. cm.
ISBN 156792-248-1 (alk. paper)
1. Ireland—Social life and customs—Fiction. I. Title.
PR6021.I24A6 2003
823'.914—dc22 2003063062

FIRST U.S. EDITION
Printed in the United States of America

To Frances

CONTENTS

INTRODUCTION

Henry James, to whom we all must sometimes listen, said that the art of fiction was in telling not what happened but what should have happened. My father, who, as a member of an Order now extinct but then known as the Leinster Regiment, had found himself in many strange places and could tell strange stories of the places he had been and seen, put it more simply. He said 'Never spoil a good story for the sake of the truth.'

Antoninus Pius (and my father in the course of all his wanderings never did encounter him) said 'Whatever happens is as common and well known as a rose in the spring or an apple in autumn. Everywhere up and down, through ages and histories, towns and families are full of the same stories.'

I now find that looking back, or walking or stumbling back over more than fifty or so years of living and trying to tell stories, can be a disturbing experience. What happened? What should have happened? What was the good story? What exactly was the truth? Who were the real people? Did you transform or disfigure them? Would they speak in a friendly way to you if you ever encountered them again, in this world or the next? If, that is, there is a next?

For instance: there was in my home town a man who was so well read in the literature of what we used to call the Wild West, from Fenimore Cooper to Zane Grey and even W. C. Tuttle, that at times he half-imagined he had been there. He simply wished intensely that he had, and the wish fathered thoughts and dreams and words. It was harmless dreaming. He never fired a shot; and he entertained himself and many others with his stories. He belonged to an imaginative and literary family: his brother was a notable authority on, and performer of, traditional music.

So remembering him some years after he had gone to God, or Manitou, I wrote a story inspired, if that's the word, by that man. A schoolfriend who had actually seen the carter stun the white animal ('The White Wild Bronco') was embarrassed. By that time, although he was still my friend, that schoolfriend had become an eminent banker, and with the caution of his profession he could not approve of coming too close to the truth in a work of fiction. My idea was that the story-teller stumbled over an idea; somebody told you something and it stayed in your head, or you saw something and remembered it. After all, the man who thought, or pretended he thought, that he had been in the Wild West had only been telling short stories.

But a nephew of that imaginative man said something to me that made me feel a lot less guilty. He was a liberal and pleasant man, that nephew, a famous boxer and amateur actor. He said 'Who, anyway, would remember Uncle Jamie if you had not written that story?'

Then there is haunting me still that business about the heroes and/or the old man in the dark house. Back in the 1940s I wrote a book about the novelist William Carleton (1794–1869). I was back celebrating in my native town of Omagh, County Tyrone, when I got a message from a man called Robert Bratton in the neighbouring village of Seskinore; he would have been what was then in the north-east of Ireland called a Liberal Unionist: that is, a Unionist of the type that went back to before the Carsonite and High Tory agitation against Home Rule for Ireland destroyed Gladstone's great movement. Bratton had also known that Andrews, the man who built the *Titanic* and sank with it. He (Bratton) told me that he would be in Omagh if I were on holiday, and I met him in a restaurant, where he told me that he had also written a book about William Carleton. I took the typescript of his book away with me and tried hard to find a publisher for it, to no avail. Nobody at that time was much interested, and if it weren't for the help of two friends, Robert Farren, the poet, and Francis MacManus, novelist, my own book would never have seen the light of day, or whatever.

Then that fine man, Robert Bratton, told me a sad story.

He had been carrying another book, a collection of folk-tales that he had heard from old country-people, around with him for some time. Then someone told him (this was in the war years in the 1940s) that there was in Belfast City a Major McCutcheon, U. S. Army Cultural Relations, who might be interested. So he brought the book up to the Major, who looked at it and was delighted. But that night in Seskinore, Robert Bratton was awakened by the thunder of trucks on the road and in the morning the U. S. Army was gone. It was D-Day and the book of folk-tales was never published. So I tried to build a story around that. I changed the locale and placed it down south, near Campile in the County Wexford, a place I knew well and liked at that time. I put another man in the place of Robert Bratton. The ancient folk-heroes, breaking rocks and climbing mountains and all that, seemed to belong.

Then there was a tall, stern, puritanical, and most admirable clergyman to whom some lady had once, in Scotland, presented a copy of that
poem in which William Morris speaks of a 'Great God's Angel Standing'.
He, the clergyman, passed the poem on as a gift to me. I tried to write
about him and myself, all together, but it would not work. Then in the
town of New Ross, in Wexford, I met a rake of a fellow who was notorious for being a menace to all the maidens of the countryside. A little later
in Dublin City I heard stories about a similar type of fine young man.
I rolled the two of them into one and made that one man the friend
of the tall priest; and that gave the story the springboard that I felt it
needed.

The place of the original giving of the book I moved from Scotland
to the Peaks of Otter and the Blue Ridge Mountains of Virginia, U.S.A.
I had recently been around that way and I felt it necessary to mention
that wonderful land.

So, you see, that's how stories get made.

Then there was a man, a friend of mine, who when he was a young
fellow used to climb up to the top of the great tree on the green of
Duleek village in County Louth. He could spend half a day up there
quite happily, viewing the world from his treetop. On the green under
that tree Father Theobald Mathew, the nineteenth-century Franciscan
and advocate of temperance (keep the Irish sober), had preached and
Johnny Patterson, the great circus-clown, had performed. The river
Boyne was down there below, and the place where William and James
had disputed the Crown of England.

At the time when my friend was up that tree the village schoolmaster
was a man by the name of Brennan. I had the honour of knowing him
and walking with him along the battlefield of the Boyne. Then away to
the west in Aughrim, County Galway, there was another schoolmaster.
His name was Joyce. He was a sound historian and even kept a schoolhouse museum containing relics of the fatal Williamite-Jacobite Battle
of Aughrim. With him I walked the fatal field. And it was true that some
of his pupils stole relics of the battle out of the school museum.

So for the sake of a story I rolled those two gentlemen, and those two
battlefields, into one. May all the ghosts forgive me.

Where then does the stealing, or borrowing, from life end and where
does invention begin? It differs from story to story, and from story-teller
to story-teller. There are some elect spirits who live completely in their
own imaginations and are quite proud of that. And, often rightly so.

Yet, re-reading my own stories, I find that faces peep out, voices are
heard. Are they, or are they not, frowning faces, accusing voices?

But you, my reader, need have no such worries. Perhaps the story-teller is, in the end, only searching to find himself or herself: a face and/or a spirit in the crowd. He, or she, may even be trying to laugh at himself, or herself, and frequently succeeding.

BENEDICT KIELY

A JOURNEY
TO THE SEVEN STREAMS

THE WHITE WILD BRONCO

At the age of five, when asked what he wanted to be when he grew up, Isaac said he wanted to be a German. He was then blond and chubby and not at all pugnacious. Because he stuttered, he pronounced the word, German, with three, sometimes with six, initial consonants. He had heard it by his father's bedside where, propped most of the day on high pillows, the old fusilier remembered Givenchy and Messines Ridge in the hearing of his friends: Doherty the undertaker; Mickey Fish, who sold fish on Fridays from a flat dray and from door to door, and who stopped young women – even under the courthouse clock – to ask them the time of evening; Pat Moses Gavigan who fished pike and cut the world's best blackthorns; and the Cowboy Carson, the only man in our town who lived completely in the imagination. Occasionally the old fusilier read aloud out of one or other of the learned anthropological tomes dealing with the adventures of Tarzan the ape man, but mostly the talk was about Germans. Isaac, quiet on his creepie stool, liked the sound of the word.

Bella, the loving wife of the old fusilier, had received her husband home from the war, we were told, in a glass case, the loser by a stomach shot away when – all his superior officers dead – he, the corporal, gallantly led an action to success, carried the kopje or whatever it was they carried in Flanders, and stopped just short of advancing, like the gallant Dublins, into the fire of his own artillery. Back home, stomachless in his glass case, he cheated the War Office on the delicate question of expectation of life, collected a fine pension and lived at ease until the world was good and ready for another war. No crippled veteran, left to beg at the town's end, was the old fusilier. Secure in his bed, in his lattice-windowed room in his white cottage that was snug in the middle of a terrace of seven white cottages, he talked, read about Tarzan, told how fields were won and, on big British Legion days, condescended to receive homage from visiting celebrities, including, once, Lady Haig herself. On the creepie stool, chubby Isaac absorbed the wonder of half-comprehended words, pondered the girth of the undertaker, the lean, loveless face of the fish merchant who thought that only beauty could tell him the time on a June evening, watched the hands of Moses as they cut a thorn or measured the monstrousness of an escaped pike, studied the cowboy's eyes that squinted, by way of twopenny paper-covered books, back to the Texas Panhandle and the Old Chisholm Trail.

The undertaker, or the pike fisherman, or the fish merchant, or the Cowboy would say, 'Isaac, what do you want to be when you grow up?'

Isaac would say, 'I want to be a German.'

Then the four visitors would laugh. His father, pale on his pillows, would laugh – forgetting Germans once seen in the sulphurous haze as he charged roaring through shot and shell to become a hero. His father would read the next instalment:

'When Tarzan of the Apes realised that he was in the grip of the great jaws of a crocodile he did not, as an ordinary man might have done, give up all hope and resign himself to his fate. . .

'His body trailed out beside the slimy carcass of his captor, and into the tough armour the apeman attempted to plunge his stone knife as he was borne to the creature's horrid den. . .

'Staggering to his feet the apeman groped about the reeking, oozy den. . .'

In the moonlight the Cowboy walked home, pulling imaginary guns and talking in admonitory tones to Wyatt Earp, 'Stand there, Earp. You may be a big man, but I'll cut you down. Do I have to push you into slapping leather?'

Alone in the moonlight on the hill that went down to the red-and-white creamery, the brook, the Cowboy's hut, the fields beyond, he pulled and whirled and fired three times. With satisfaction he listened to the echoes dying away at the town's last fringe of shabby, sleeping terraces, over the tarred iron roofs of Tansey the carter's stableyard, over the railway-engine shed and the turntable. On green-and-white moonland beyond the Dublin railway a mystic, white bronco galloped in circles as, noiselessly, the Cowboy slipped the smoking Colt back into the holster. He turned then and went on down the hill to Tansey, the carter's, and supper. Every day he worked, carrying bags of meal to clumsy four-wheeled drays, in the warehouse of Dale, the grain-merchant, nicknamed Attention, who was an amateur astronomer and had a telescope installed in a beehive-shaped structure at the back of his store. Every night after the fusilier's reading the Cowboy ate his supper of yellow Indian porridge and buttermilk in the huge coppery kitchen where Tansey the carter was a smiling extrovert Buddha in the middle of six stout sisters who had never shown the least inclination towards matrimony.

'Every day, Cowboy, Attention's back is stiffer and stiffer,' Tansey said.

'He sat on a poker,' said the third sister.

The sisters were all red-faced and brown-haired. The fourth one cooked the porridge.

'I hear he got drunk on wine gums in Devlin's sweetie shop in Bridge Lane,' Tansey joked. 'The sergeant had to wheel his bicycle home for him.'

Seriously resenting the imputation, the Cowboy, thumbs in the armholes of his patched and darned grey vest, drawled, 'The Big Boss is a fast man on the draw. He never touches hard likker.'

'We heard he can stare the sun in the face up in that spinning beehive of his,' said the second sister.

The carter said, 'It takes a good man to stare the sun in the face.'

On a hook behind the broad oak door the first sister considerately hung the Stetson that a rope juggler in a travelling circus had once given to the Cowboy.

'What goes on between the sun and himself is his own business,' said the Cowboy reverently. 'There was a cattleman in Wyoming had as big a spyglass. Could spot an Injun or a stray ten miles off.'

'You and Wyoming,' gently said the sixth sister.

'The Big Boss reaches me my wad. At the door of the bunkhouse. Your pay, Michael, he says. Count it. I counted one pound, nineteen and eleven pence. A penny short, boss, says I. One penny deducted, Michael, for a box of matches purchased on credit last Tuesday at eleven ah em. He misses nothing.'

'Your porridge,' said Tansey the carter, 'and give us another bit of the story.'

'The place I was in at that time,' said the Cowboy. 'Down Deep South. There was a river. Alligators. As plentiful as trout in the brook. This day I went for a swim. Just the way you'd go for a swim above the salmon leap by the hospital on the Camowen River.'

'Showing off and strutting before the nurses,' said the third sister. 'For shame, Cowboy.'

'And what should happen when I was out in deep water but an alligator. Silent-like he grabs me by the arm. I could show you the marks still. But cute enough, he doesn't take the arm off. He needed it, you see, to drag me down.'

'In this life you'll always get somebody to drag you down,' said the second sister.

'Down to where?' asked the carter.

'Not down the town to a pub or the pictures, anyway. Down to his cave. They live in caves in that river.'

'No homes to go to,' said the third sister.

'Was he big?' asked the carter. 'Would he be the size now of the last pike Pat Moses Gavigan caught at Blacksessiagh?'

'Size! Ten times the size. A mouth that wide. And the growls of him. Well, there was I. My body beside the slimy carcass of my captor. But I had a knife. A stone knife. Never swam without it. Wouldn't be safe in those parts. And as I was borne to the creature's horrid den I attempted to plunge my knife into the tough armour of the reptile.'

'Cowboy,' said the carter, 'you're the lucky man to be alive and eating porridge there this blessed night.'

'Lucky! Quickness: that's what does it. An ordinary man might have given up all hope and resigned himself to his fate.'

From the stables came a wild volley of hooves on cabbining wood, then a second volley, then a slow thud – thud – thud and one mad, high, equine scream.

'That savage you bought,' said the fifth sister. 'He'll never cart.'

'He'll cart,' said Tansey. 'More India-buck porridge, Cowboy?'

That was the time when Isaac desired – as every child, male or female, sometimes desires – a pony. It was, of course, long before he found his vocation and in a green lane above the engine shed – the town's unroofed gymnasium – learned to become the best fighter our town ever had. Poise and stance, dynamite right and cunning left, footwork, speed, quick eye, cool head and iron muscles, the fusilier's son was a natural champion. And, graduating from the green lane, he brought belts, cups, medals, honour and glory home with him from every part of the country. We were proud of him.

But in the days of his desire for the pony there were no blows struck but one. Where would a boy go who wanted a pony or a stable to house him but to Tansey's yard where the great carthorses stamped with the assured gravity of savants, where the Taggarts, the horse dealers, displayed the shaggy, sullen-eyed animals they brought in droves from the mountains away to the south-west, even from tinker camps in the province of Connacht. Roosted high on the shaft of an idle dray, Isaac was there the day Tansey bought the wild, white horse. In among the brown, shaggy brutes he was white-limbed Tarzan among the ape people of Akut and, until he felt on his quivering flanks the confining shafts, he concealed horror in docility. Then he reared to the perpendic-ular, assaulted the heavens, came down again and lashed out backwards, did the rounds of the yard like a Derby winner while old and young, Isaac among them, ran for shelter. With great Tansey swinging from the reins the horse went round and round and round until the cart was in firewood and broken shafts trailed the ground.

'Powerful God,' said Tansey to the Taggarts, 'where did you get this one?'

'In Ballinasloe in the County Galway,' they said.

As if that explained everything.

'Take him back to Ballinasloe,' said Tansey.

'But no, linger now,' he said. 'There's life in him. He'll cart. I'll coax him.'

Dreaming at a safe distance, Isaac saw himself coaxing the savage with gently-proffered lumps of sugar, and all through the white one's novitiate under Tansey, Isaac was in constant, reverent attendance. But no coaxing, no lump sugar, no whispers or magic hands, could reconcile the untamed tinker-spirit of Ballinasloe to the base servility of the shafts of a dray.

'He has good blood in him,' Tansey said. 'I'll try him in a trap.'

Some of the fragments of the trap, they say, were found fifty yards away on the railway line, and the great white creature stood shivering as if, if it were human, it would burst into hysterical sobs. For a whole fortnight, with Isaac perched on high walls or drays or snug on the hay in the hayshed, the wooing went on, and it was one evening in the stable that Isaac said: Give him to me, Mr. Tansey. I'll tame him for you.

For one half second while the carter, distracted, turned and laughed, the horse lunged and snapped, the razor teeth grazing the back of Tansey's skull and gashing the lobe of his left ear. The blood came out like a spout and Tansey dyed his hand in it. Then, disregarding it, he looked sadly at the animal. With no sign of temper he went to the back of the stable, picked up a crowbar from a heap of rusting metal and, with the deliberation of God, struck the animal between the eyes and stunned it. When it woke up an hour later it went, almost of its own accord, to the shafts. Isaac's sugar lumps were never needed.

By the fusilier's bedside that evening the Cowboy was sitting straddle on a stool, knees in, feet out, hands wide, showing how he had held the reins and stayed in the saddle when lesser men had bitten the dust of the rodeo ring. Isaac chewed toffee. He said, 'Tansey the carter broke a bronc today. I saw him.'

He told his story.

'Tansey's a brute,' said Doherty the undertaker. 'He'd slay his six sisters before he'd lose two pounds sterling.'

'You'd benefit,' said Pat Moses Gavigan. 'Six coffins.'

'They're six fine big girls,' said Mickey Fish.

'Not a watch between them,' said the fusilier. 'Time doesn't count in Tansey's.'

The fusilier read: Screaming with terror the Maoris were dragged from their lofty perches. The beasts, uncontrolled by Tarzan, who had gone in search of Jane, loosed the full fury of their savage natures upon the unhappy wretches who fell into their clutches . . . Sheeta, in the meanwhile, had felt his great fangs sink into but a single jugular . . .

Afterwards when the guests had gone Isaac said, 'The Cowboy Carson had a ranch once on the Rio Grande. He told me he had seventy pinto ponies.'

'Son,' said the fusilier, 'I hate to rob you of your fancy. But better for your father to do it than for the hard world and the black stranger. The Cowboy Carson was never out of this town except perhaps to carry Pat Moses Gavigan's bag as far as the pike-water at Blacksessiagh. It all comes out of the wee books you see in the paper-shop window: Deadwood Dick and Buffalo Bill, and Hit the Tuttle Trail with Hashknife and Sleepy.'

'But he was a gun-slinger, da, in Texas.'

'Guns, he never saw guns,' said the fusilier – musing for a minute and remembering Flanders and the roar of the iron monsters.

In the dusk the Cowboy walked home, spurs jingling, stiff and stilted on high heels, bowlegged from the saddle, left to right and right to left practising the cross-draw and remembering with affection his deceased friend, Buck Duane, the Lone Star Ranger. He was light and elated. There was no pressure of crushing bags of grain on his old, bony shoulders. Melodious with beeves, a freight train from the West truckled on towards Belfast. The Cowboy made his customary crooked way to the kitchen of Tansey the Carter.

'You broke the bronc today, I'm told,' he said to Tansey.

'I broke the bronc, Cowboy, the only way my father taught me. If I buy a horse to cart he has to cart. Or a woman to cook.'

'He never bought a woman,' said the third sister, and the six sisters laughed.

'Your porridge, Cowboy.'

'Did I ever tell you about the time I was in New Zealand?'

'You never did,' said Tansey the carter.

When the Americans came to our town on their way to meet Hitler somebody told them about the Cowboy and one of them, meeting him, said, 'Haven't we encountered you before?'

'Was it in Tucson?' said another.

'More whisky,' said a third, 'it was in Tombstone.'

'Not there,' said the Cowboy. 'I guess and calculate it might have been in Deadwood.'

'Deadwood it was,' said the three of them. 'Well, we'll be doggone darned.'

'Tell us about Deadwood, Cowboy,' said the man behind the bar.

'I was riding shotgun at that time,' said the Cowboy. 'Stiff knee, you see. Couldn't mount a bronc.'

For corroborative purposes he displayed his stiff knee. They listened with a little laughter. They weren't cruel. They were, in fact, kind, because the worst thing you could have done was to tell him he was never there.

By that time the old fusilier was dead, and buried by Doherty the undertaker; Attention Dale had been succeeded by a nephew who couldn't face the sun and sold the telescope; Mickey Fish was confined to a mental home for chasing young girls to ask them the time of evening; and arthritis prevented Pat Moses Gavigan from fishing pike or cutting blackthorns. And Isaac the fusilier's son had realised that he would never be a German. He came like a bird as a paratrooper into Narvik, came out again alive, and possibly helped the three Americans who had listened to the Cowboy to storm the French shore. Until he was killed at the Rhine crossing he remained the best fighter our town ever had.

THE HEROES IN THE DARK HOUSE

'They were gone in the morning,' the old man said.

His name was Arthur Broderick, and the young folk-tale scholar sat quietly, listening for the story that had been promised him.

'Lock, stock and barrel,' said the old man. 'The whole U.S. garrison, off for the far fields of France. Jeeps, guns, and gun-carriers. In the dump behind the big camp at Knocknashee Castle the handful of caretakers they left behind slung radio sets and bicycles and ran a gun-carrier with caterpillar wheels over the lot, and as good as made mash of them. Very wasteful. War's all waste. Those bicycles would have kept every young boy in the county spinning for the next five years.'

Like the plain girl that nobody wanted Mr Broderick's nine-times rejected manuscript-folk-tales set down with such love and care in high-spined script lay between them on an antique drawing-room table. The table's top, solid oak and two inches thick, was shaped like a huge teardrop pearl with the tip abruptly nipped off.

'Oak,' Mr Broderick said through the smoke. 'Solid oak and two centuries old. In 1798, in the year of the Rising, it was the top of a bellows in a smithy. Look here where the British yeomanry sawed the tip off it so that the rebels could no longer use it for the forging of the pikes. When I was the age of yourself I converted it into a table. Sixty years ago last July.'

Around them in the ancient, musty, tapestried room the wreathing smoke might have come from the fires of 1798. Birdsong outside, sunshine, wind in the creepers were as far away as Florida. The greedy, nesting jackdaws held the flues as firmly as ever at Thermopylae or the Alamo or Athlone, or a score of other places all around the battered globe, unforgotten heroes had held passes, bridgeheads or gun-burned walls. And unforgotten heroes had marched through the smoke in this room: Strong Shawn, the son of the fisherman of Kinsale, triumphant, with the aid of white magic, crossed the seven-mile strand of steel spikes, the seven-mile-high mountain of flames, the seven miles of treacherous sea, and came gloriously to win his love in a castle courtyard crowded with champions and heroes from the four sides of the world; the valiant son of the King of Antua fought with Macan Mor, son of the King of Soracha, in the way that they made rocks of water and water of rocks, and if the birds came from the lower to the upper world to see wonders it was to see these two they came.

Mr. Broderick went on with his tale. All night long through the village below the old, dark, smoky house that had once been a rectory the lorries had throbbed and thundered on the narrow, twisted street and above, in the upper air, the waves of planes had swept east towards Europe.

'They were gone in the morning,' he said. 'Lock, stock and barrel. There was never a departure like it since the world was made. For quick packing, I heard afterwards, they drove the jeeps up the steep steps of the courthouse below. It reminded me of the poem about the three jolly gentlemen in coats of red who rode their horses up to bed.'

'They were gone,' he said, 'like snow off a ditch.'

It was as much as the young scholar could do to see him for smoke. But with an effort that would have done credit to Macan Mor or Shawn of Kinsale he managed to control his coughing.

In the old dizzy chimney the jackdaws were so solidly entrenched that at times Mr. Broderick had found it hard to see the paper he transcribed the folk-tales on. The smoke no longer made him cough, but at eighty-five his eyes were not as keen as they had been when he was in his prime and from the saddle of a galloping hunter could spot, in passing, a bird's nest in a leafy hedgerow. Lovingly he transcribed the tales in the high, spidery handwriting that – like himself, like his work for Sir Horace Plunkett in the co-operative creameries, his friendship with Thomas Andrews who had built the Titanic and gone bravely with it to Wordsworth's incommunicable sleep – belonged to a past, forgotten time. For years of his life he had followed these tales, the people who told them, the heroes who lived in them, over miles of lonely heather-mountain, up boreens that in rain became rivulets, to crouch in mountain cabins by the red hearth-glow and listen to the meditative voices of people for whom there was only the past.

Peadar Haughey of Creggan Cross had sat on the long, oaken settle with his wife and three daughters and dictated to him the adventures of the son of the king of Antua, as well as the story of the giant of Reibhlean who had abducted from Ireland a married princess. Giants as a rule preferred unmarried princesses. Peadar told the story in Irish and English. His wife and daughters understood only English but together they rocked in unison on the settle and sang macaronic songs in a mixture of both languages. That simple world had its own confusions.

At times in his smoky house he found it hard to separate the people in the tales from the people who told them.

Bed-ridden Owen Roe Ward, in a garret in a back-lane in the garrison town ten miles away, had told him the story of the King of Green Island and other stories that were all about journeys to the end of the earth in search of elixirs that could only be won by herculean labours. Hewing trees for hire in a tangled plantation whose wood had once paid for the travels and other activities of D'Orsay and Lady Blessington, Owen had brought down on his hapless spine a ton-weight of timber. Paralysed in his garret he travelled as he talked to find life-giving water in the well at the world's end.

A woman of eighty by the name of Maire John (she still sang with the sweet voice she had at twenty and displayed the fondness for embracing men that, according to tradition, had then characterised her) had told him of the three princesses who sat in the wishing chair. One wished to marry a husband more beautiful than the sun. The second wished to marry a husband more beautiful than the moon. The third stated her honest but eccentric preference for the White Hound of the Mountain. It was a local heather-flavoured version of the marriage of Cupid and Psyche, and Maire John herself was a randy old lady who would, in the days of silver Latin, have delighted Apuleius.

The stories had come like genii, living, wreathing from holes in the wall behind smoky hearths, or from the dusty tops of dressers, or from farmhouse lofts where ancient, yellow manuscripts were stored. By Bloody Bridge on the Camowen River (called so because of no battle, but because of the number of fine trout killed there) he had heard from Pat Moses Gavigan a completely new version of the story of Fionn MacCumhail and the enchanted Salmon of Wisdom.

Plain and mountain and river-valley, the places he knew were sombre with the sense of family, and folk-tales grew as naturally there as grass. Heroes, princesses, enchanters good and bad, he had marshalled them all, called them to order in his own smoky room, numbered them off right to left, made his roll-call, described them in that high-spined handwriting he had studied so laboriously in the old manuscripts. Properly thus caparisoned they would go out into the twentieth century. He made his own of them. He called them his children. He sent them out to the ends of the earth, to magazine editors and publishing houses. They came back rejected to him, as if being his children they could have no life when torn away from him. Then one day in the smoky room under the power of the squabbling enchanters of jackdaws he had the bitterness of discovering that his children had betrayed him. In a Dublin newspaper he read the review of the young scholar's book:

'The scholar who has compiled, translated and edited these folk-tales has a wise head on young shoulders. Careful research and a wide knowledge of comparative folklore have gone into his work. He has gleaned carefully in the mountainous area ten miles north of the town where he was born. He presents his findings with an erudite introduction and in an impeccable style. . .'

The smoke wreathed around him. The reviewer's weary sentences went on like the repetition of a death-knell:

'His name is worthy to rank with that of such folklorists as Jeremiah Curtin. Particularly notable is his handling of the remarkable quest tale of the King of Green Island. . .'

Mr. Broderick couldn't blame the three princesses for leaving the wishing chair and making off with a younger man. That scholar, wise head on young shoulders, could be Cupid, more beautiful than the sun and the moon: he might even be that enigmatic character, The White Hound of the Mountain. But Shawn of Kinsale could have been kinder to old age, and so could all those battling heroes or venturesome boys who crossed perilous seas, burning mountains and spiked strands.

He wrote to the young scholar at the publisher's address: 'While I am loath to trade on your time, I have, it would seem, been working or wandering about in the same field and in the same part of the country. We may share the acquaintanceship of some of the living sources of these old tales. We certainly have friends in common in the realms of mythology. Perhaps my own humble gatherings might supplement your store. So far I have failed to find a publisher for them. If you are ever visiting your home town you may care to add a few miles to the journey to call on me. My congratulations on your achievement. It gratifies me to see a young man from this part of the country doing so well.'

A week later he took up his stick one day and walked down the winding, grass-grown avenue. An ancestor was rector here long years ago, he thought, as in the case of William Yeats, the poet, who died in France on the eve of this war and who had an ancestor a rector long years ago in Drumcliffe by the faraway Sligo sea. Mr. Broderick's house had been the rectory. When the church authorities judged it a crumbling, decaying property they had given it to Mr. Broderick for a token sum – a small gesture of regard for all that in an active manhood he had done for the village. Crumbling and decaying it was, but peace, undisturbed, remained around the boles of the trees, the tall gables and old tottering chimneys, the shadowy bird-rustling walks. Now, as he walked, yews gone wild and reckless made a tangled pattern above his head.

Weeks before, from the garrison town in the valley, war had spilled its gathering troops over into this little village. Three deep, burdened with guns and accoutrements, they slouched past Mr. Broderick on the way down the hill to their courthouse billet. Dust rose around them. They sang. They were three to six thousand miles from home, facing an uncertain future, and in reasonably good humour. A dozen or so who knew Mr. Broderick from the tottering house as the old guy who made souvenirs out of blackthorn and bog oak, waved casual, friendly hands. Beyond and behind them as they descended was the blue cone of Knocknashee Hill where the castle was commandeered and where a landlord had once stocked a lake with rainbow trout that like these troops had been carried across the wide Atlantic. The soldiers' dust settling around him in wreaths and rings, Mr. Broderick went down the road to collect his mail at the post-office. There had been no troops in this village since 1798 when the bellows had been mutilated and the soldiers then, according to the history books, had been anything but friendly.

The long red-tiled roofs and white walls of the co-operative creamery, the sheen of glasshouses from the slopes of the model farm were a reminder to Mr. Broderick of the enthusiasms of an active past. People had, in his boyhood, been evicted for poverty in that village. Now every year the co-operative grain store handled one hundred and fifty thousand tons of grain. An energetic young man could take forty tons of tomatoes out of an acre and a quarter of glasshouses, and on a day of strong sunshine the gleam of the glasshouses would blind you. Crops burst over the hedges as nowhere else in that part of the country. It was good, high, dry land that took less harm than most places from wet seasons and flooding, and the cattle were as heavy and content as creamy oxen in French vineyards.

Over the hedge and railings by the parish church the statue of the old Canon, not of Mr. Broderick's persuasion, raised a strong Roman right arm. The pedestal described the Canon as a saintly priest and sterling patriot and to anybody, except Mr. Broderick, that raised right arm might have been minatory. To Arthur Broderick it was a kind memory of hero and co-worker, it was an eternal greeting in stone.

'Arthur,' the statue said, 'yourself and myself built this place. There was a time when you'd have clambered to the top of a telegraph pole if somebody'd told you there was a shilling there would help to make the village live. You did everything but say mass and I did that. You got little out of it yourself. But you saw they were happy and strong. Look around you. Be proud and glad. Enjoy your dreams of lost heroes in the mist. No young man can steal from you what you want to give away.'

High above the dead stone Canon the Angelus bell rang. Before him, down the cobbled footwalk, so steep that at times it eased itself out with a sigh into flat, flagged steps, went a tall soldier and a small young woman. Mr. Broderick knew her. She was one of the eighteen Banty Mullans, nine male, nine female, all strawheaded and five feet high, the males all roughs, and the females, to put it politely, taking in washing for the Irish Fusiliers in the town below. She was ill-dressed, coarse-tongued and vicious. She carried in her left hand a shiny gallon buttermilk-can. Stooping low, the tall warrior eased the handle of the can from the stumpy, stubborn fingers and, surprised at a gentlemanly gesture that could never have come from a pre-war fusilier trained in the old Prussian school and compelled in public to walk like clockwork, she asked with awe, 'Aren't you feared the sergeant will see you?'

'In this man's army,' he said.

He could be a Texan. It was diverting to study their accents and guess at States.

'In this man's army, sister, we don't keep sergeants.'

Suddenly happy, Arthur Broderick tripped along behind them, kicked at a stray pebble, sniffed at the good air until his way was blocked by the frail, discontented figure of Patrick who kept the public house beside the post-office and opposite the courthouse, and who sold the bog oak and blackthorn souvenirs to thirsty, sentimental soldiers.

'Lord God, Mr. Broderick,' said Patrick. 'Do you see that for discipline? Carrying a tin can like an errand boy.'

'But Patrick, child, it's idyllic. Deirdre in the hero tale couldn't have been more nobly treated by the three Ulster brothers, the sons of Uisneach. Hitler and Hirohito had to bring the doughboys over here before one of the Banty Mullans was handled like a lady.'

'Mr. Bee,' said Patrick, 'we all know you have odd ideas on what's what. But Mr. Bee, there must be a line of demarcation. Would you look across the street at that for soldiering?'

In sunshine that struggled hard, but failed, to brighten the old granite walls and Ionic columns of the courthouse the huge, coloured sentry had happily accepted the idea that for that day and in that village he did not have to deal with the Wehrmacht. Unlike the courthouse he looked as if he had been specially made by the sun. He sat relaxed on a chair, legs crossed, sharing a parcel of sandwiches with a trio of village children. Behind him on a stone ledge, his weapon of war was a votive offering at the feet of a bronze statue of a famous hanging judge who, irritated by the eczema of the droppings of lawless, irreverent birds, scowled like the Monster from Thirty Thousand Fathoms. Then clattering down the courthouse steps, came fifty young men, very much at ease. Falling into loose formation they went jauntily down the hilly street to the cookhouse at the bottom of the village. To the rhythm of their feet they played tunes with trays and table utensils.

'Their morale is high,' said Mr. Broderick.

Dark, hollow-cheeked, always complaining, persecuted by a corpulent wife, Patrick resented the young warriors with every bone in his small body. Some local wit had once said that he was a man constitutionally incapable of filling a glass to the brim.

'Those fellows, Mr. Bee, are better fed than yourself or myself.'

'They're young and growing, Patrick. They need it more. Besides, doesn't the best authority tell us an army marches on its belly?'

'They're pampered. Starve the Irish, Lord Kitchener said, and you'll have an army.'

'Ah, but Patrick the times have changed. I had the pleasure of serving under Lord Kitchener. But he never impressed me as a dietician.'

'Soft soles on their boots,' said Patrick, 'and their teeth glued together with chewing gum and all the girls in the country running wild since they came.'

'Life,' said Mr. Broderick, 'we can't suppress. Every woman worth breathing loves a warrior who's facing death.'

'Once upon a time,' Patrick said, 'your old friend, the Canon, made a rake of a fellow kneel at the church gate with a horse collar round his neck to do public penance for his rascalities with the girls.'

'Lothario in a leather frame, Patrick.'

Mr. Broderick laughed until his eyes were moist, at the memory and at the unquenchable misery in the diminutive, unloved, unloving heart of hen-pecked Patrick.

'Today, Patrick, there wouldn't be enough horse collars to go round. The horse isn't as plentiful as it was. The Canon had his foibles. He objected also to tam o'shanters and women riding bicycles. That was so long ago, Patrick. We'll drink to his memory.'

Everything, he thought as he left the public house and stepped on to the post-office, was so long ago. Patrick could hardly be described as part of the present. His lament was for days when heroes went hungry, when the fusiliers in the town below were forbidden by rule to stand chatting on the public street, were compelled to step rigidly, gloves like this, cane like that under the oxter – like a stick trussing a plucked chicken in a poulterer's shop. Patrick in his cave of a pub was a comic, melancholy, legendary dwarf. His one daring relaxation was to brighten

THE HEROES IN THE DARK HOUSE · 17

the walls of his cave with coloured calendars of pretty girls caught with arms full of parcels and, by the snapping of some elastic or the betrayal of some hook or button, in mildly embarrassing situations. With startled but nevertheless smiling eyes they appealed to Patrick's customers.

'Your souvenirs sell well, Mr. Bee,' Patrick said. 'The pipes especially. But the sloe-stone rosary beads too. Although it puzzles me to make out what these wild fellows want with rosary beads.'

'They may have mothers at home, Patrick, who like keep-sakes. They're far from home. They're even headed the other way.'

At the post-office the girl behind the brass grille said, 'Two letters, Mr. Broderick.'

He read the first one. The young scholar said that he had read with great interest of Mr. Broderick's interest in and his collection of folk-tales. He realised that folk-tales were often, curiously enough, not popular fare but he still considered that the publishers lacked vision and enterprise. He had only had his own book published because of the fortunate chance of his meeting a publisher who thought that he, the young scholar, might some day write a book that would be a moneymaker. The young scholar would also in the near future be visiting his native place. He thanked Mr. Broderick for his kind invitation and would take the liberty of calling on him.

The second letter came from an old colleague in the city of Belfast. It said: 'Arthur, old friend, yesterday I met a Major Michael F. X. Devaney – it would seem he has Irish ancestry – who has something or other to do with cultural relations between the U.S. troops and ourselves. He's hunting for folk-tales, local lore, to publish in book-form for the army. I thought of you. I took the liberty of arranging an appointment and of loaning him a copy of some of the stories you once loaned me.'

Mr. Broderick went to Belfast a few days later to keep the appointment. From the window of the major's office the vast, smoky bulk of the domed City Hall was visible. He turned from its impressive Victorian gloom to study the major, splendidly caparisoned as any hero who had ever lived in coloured tales told by country hearths.

'Mr. Broderick,' said the major, 'this is real contemporary.'

'Old tales, major, like old soldiers.'

'This spiked strand and burning mountain. I was in the Pacific, Mr. Broderick. This seven miles of treacherous sea. A few pages of glossary, Mr. Broderick. A few explanatory footnotes. How long would that take you?'

'A month, major. Say a month.'

'We'll settle for a month. Then we'll clinch the deal. These tales are exactly what we want, Mr. Broderick. Tell the boys something about the traditions of the place.'

He took the train home from the tense, overcrowded city to the garrison town in the valley. The market-day bus brought him up over the ridge to his own village. All that warm night the lorries on the steep street robbed him of his sparse, aged sleep as the troops moved; and they were gone in the morning, lock, stock and barrel, and on the far French coast the sons of the Kings of Antua and Soracha grappled until they made rocks of water and water of rocks, and the waves of the great metal birds of the air screamed over them.

High in the sky beyond Knocknashee one lone plane droned like a bee some cruel boy had imprisoned in a bottle to prevent it from joining the swarm. At his hushed doorway sad Patrick the publican looked aghast at the newspaper headlines and more aghast at the cold, empty courthouse that once had housed such thirsty young men.

'You'd swear to God,' he said, 'they were never here at all.'

Arthur Broderick left him to his confusion. He walked home under twisted yews, up the grass-grown avenue to his own smoky house. The heroes had gone, but the heroes would stay with him for ever. His children would stay with him for ever, but, in a way, it was a pity that he could never give his stories to all those fine young men.

'Come in,' Mr. Broderick said to the young scholar, 'you're welcome. There's nothing I'm prouder of than to see a young man from these parts doing well. And we know the same people. We have many friends in common.'

'Shawn of Kinsale,' the young scholar said, 'and the son of the King of Antua.'

'The three princesses,' said Mr. Broderick, 'and the White Hound of the Mountain.'

He reached out the hand of welcome to the young scholar.

'Publishing is slow,' the young man stammered. 'They have little vision. . .'

'Vision reminds me,' Mr. Broderick said. 'Do you mind smoke?'

He opened the drawing-room door. Smoke billowed out to the musty hallway.

'My poor stories,' he said. 'My poor heroes. They went away to the well at the world's end but they always came back. Once they came very close to enlisting in the U.S. army. That's a story I must tell you sometime.'

The manuscript of his tales lay between them on the table that had once been part of the rebel's bellows. Around them in the smoke were the grey shadows of heroic eighteenth-century men who, to fight tyranny, had forged steel pikes. And eastwards the heroes had swept that earth-shaking summer, over the treacherous mined sea, over the seven miles of spiked strand, over the seven and seventy miles of burning mountain.

TEN PRETTY GIRLS

Andrew Fox still talks about that visit to Belfast. Listening to his recitals, now one fragment of the story and now another, hearing him repeat himself, reassert himself, occasionally contradict himself, the sequence of events has become more part of me than it ever was of Andrew Fox.

He had a running greyhound, a mouse-coloured bitch called Ballyclogher Comet. She won all before her at the Saturday night dog-track in Ballyclogher where, Jack MacGowan once said, you could see the best dog-racing in Ireland when the machine that moved the hare was working and the poteen and adrenaline convenient for gingering the dogs. But Andrew, to be unusual, ran the mouse-coloured bitch as honest as daylight, won every prize he or she could win, looked around him like Alexander and saw beyond Ballyclogher the distant dog-tracks of Belfast. He set off one morning early, sitting in a dusty box-carriage, with Ballyclogher Comet as comfortable as a queen in a corner of the guard's van.

At Portadown he changed into the fast train that runs between Dublin and Belfast, found himself a seat in the corner of a crowded compartment. Sitting directly opposite him, apologising when in moving she accidentally kicked his foot, looking up to smile at him out of grey quiet eyes, was the first girl. By her side sat a pert little red-faced woman with a black coat, a black skirt, a high cornucopia of a hat, knitting needles that knitted rapidly at something green, and a tongue that, talking at the girl, chattered ten times as rapidly. When the girl had a chance she made a remark, always sensible, always with a suggestion of that grey smile, and with a voice quiet like her eyes with the quiet of the sea on a calm evening singing the shore to sleep.

'He was once only a special constable,' the little woman said. 'But now he's high and mighty as a full-blown member of the Royal Ulster Constabulary.'

With a nod of her busy fantastically-crowned head she indicated a black-uniformed policeman who sat a few yards away.

'I mind the time,' she said, 'he was smuggling sugar across the border with the best smuggler of the lot of them. He was never out of our wee shop. It's three miles south of the border, you know. We did a roaring trade in sugar.'

She was a friendly little woman. She readily took it for granted that everybody knew the exact, advantageous location of her little shop. She was solidly convinced that the centre of the world wasn't very far from the door of that shop. She gathered the whole compartment into her conversation. She would have gathered the nations of the earth to her in the same way if they had all understood English with a Monaghan accent, if they had all been within comfortable hearing distance. Now and again the girl looked across at Andrew and Andrew was seldom looking at anybody else but the girl. Even when her face was thin and set and serious her eyes were quietly smiling. Her hair was somewhere between the colour of ripe hazel-nuts and the colour of good straw. Her hands were slender and delicate and beautifully made. Her voice was rich, easy and even, the accent of Munster when it ceases to be eccentricity and becomes the loveliest sound on God's earth. Once when an accidental movement brought one shapely knee into contact with Andrew's leg he knew in his soul that the train no longer ran evenly on iron rails between the two prosaic linen towns of Lisburn and Lurgan. It was flying high in the blue air with the soaring, swooping speed and grace of a swallow.

She smiled at Andrew, encouraged the little woman, replied graciously to her questions. It seems she was a native of Cork city and a member of the British A.T.S. It seems that at Dundalk the customs officer had made her take off her shoes until he examined them. He had suspected her of smuggling new shoes across the border. Remembering that minor indignity she was half-angry and half-amused. But Andrew was on fire with fury, seeing all customs officers as infamous excrescences on God's green Ireland, seeing one particular customs officer as a degraded, decadent creature whose every word was blasphemy, whose most casual action was a symptom of unnatural vice.

At the station in Belfast he carried her heavy case out to the bus-stop on the rattling street. He wanted to take a taxi to have her driven off to her billet in high state. But then he remembered Ballyclogher Comet, her sleek supple limbs, her nervous feet, waiting patiently in the guard's van. He couldn't see the girl, the greyhound, the big suitcase and himself all together in one taxi. He didn't want to lose the girl. He couldn't afford to abandon the greyhound. The rattle of the street confused him. The complications of the situation left him tongue-tied. Before he could sort out ideas or words the bus was moving away from him, the girl standing and waving, her face lonely and no smile to be seen. He didn't know her name. He didn't know where she lived in Cork or where she lodged in Belfast. And she was possibly the only girl Andrew Fox had ever loved.

Jack MacGowan always says you can't mix girls and greyhounds.

When the racing was over, with Ballyclogher Comet a good first in her own class, Andrew strolled, taking the air, around by the City Hall and up Royal Avenue. It was Charity day with the students of Queen's University. At Castle Junction the weirdly-dressed, half-dressed, fantastically-painted boys and girls had blocked the whole central city traffic. The pavements were black with people. The trams stood in long, immovable, unmanoeuvrable lines. A tall young man, his face painted black, clad in a black bathing suit and a pair of wellington boots, climbed to the roof of one tram and danced a hornpipe. A policeman climbed up to dislodge him. The dancer jumped to the roof of another tramcar. The crowd jeered the policeman. Under the circumstances, Andrew thought, it was a good hornpipe.

Then somewhere in the crowd a student threw into the air a roll of toilet paper. As it went up it unwound to drape itself around a trolley cable. In two minutes the air was thick with soaring and unwinding and descending rolls of toilet paper, the streets rustled like a beechwood, black Belfast roared with laughter at the indecorous scheme of municipal decoration. The trams moved with a heave and a great effort. The moving trolleys set the paper burning and falling. Andrew laughed along with Belfast.

Behind him in the crowd a girl said, 'Andrew Fox, you're a disgrace to Ballyclogher. Laughing at the like of that.'

She was a brown-haired girl linked arm-in-arm to her brown-haired sister who was, in turn, linked to a taller dark-haired girl. Andrew knew the three of them. They were all girls from our part of the country and they had steady teaching jobs in Belfast. They were handsome girls. They were smiling, friendly girls. It was good to meet them in the middle of that daft, shouting, laughing crowd. It was good to meet them on the streets of that hard, stony city.

All together they edged their way out to a quiet side-street, chatting in a way that dissolved into nothing the trams, the high houses, buses, lorries and automobiles, and showed Andrew as plain as the nose on his face the little town he came from, the old, humpy roofs, the two or three spires, and all around the blue circle of quiet hills.

'You'll all be coming home soon for the holidays,' he said.

The dark-haired girl said, 'We won't be going to Ballyclogher at all this summer.'

'At most we'll only be stopping there for a few days on our way through to the new Gaelic college in Donegal,' said the elder of the brown-haired sisters.

The younger one said, 'Come with us, Andrew.'

'Is it me? Learn Irish? For a holiday? That's a joke and a half.'

'But it's a lovely holiday. Perhaps it is a wee bit more strict than the other colleges. You get up and go to mass every morning. There's compulsory drill. The tricolour is hoisted every morning and we all salute the flag and sing in Irish one verse and the chorus of The Soldier's Song.'

'It's a fine stirring song,' said Andrew. 'It's a beautiful bright flag. Still, I think I'll go to the ocean waves at Bundoran where they stay in bed in the morning. Or go west to Galway for the races where they don't go to bed at all.'

They talked about scores of things as he walked with them up the steep Falls Road to the house where they lodged. They were friendly girls. They were modest girls. In the lapels of their neat costume jackets they wore shining gold rings to show that they spoke Irish as well as they spoke English.

He said goodbye to them at a street corner. Their steep street went up like a stairway under the shadow of Cave Hill. Above the high dark hill the sky was red with the falling sun.

A bumping bus carried him back to the centre of the city. The streets were cleared of crowds and trailing paper. The traffic was moving normally up and down Royal Avenue, around and around the monstrous Victorian City Hall. He moved aimlessly with the traffic, up and down and around and around, looking into shop windows, looking at the people on the pavements. The darkness came quietly. Suddenly around him windows and street lamps were golden. He liked looking at people and looking into windows. He was also hoping that somewhere in the anonymous crowd he would see again that thin, sensitive face, those grey eyes. Then he would speak to her and she would answer him and the noisy street would be a splendid orchestra around the melody of her voice. Every time he saw a girl in uniform he stared hard. A certain number stared back, some haughtily, some curious, some inviting. The majority didn't even notice his stare.

He walked down Royal Avenue for the twentieth time, crossed the tram-tracks at Castle Junction, saw the tram lumbering up above him and stepped back hurriedly to safety, dragging with him a girl who had walked herself into a similar predicament. The tram sailed past. The conductor looked back wrathfully. The girl waved a hand and called, 'Cheerio, granda, mind your eye.'

Then she looked at Andrew and Andrew looked at her and they laughed.

He said, 'I thought you were gone that time.'

She said, 'Not so easy to kill a bad thing.'

They crossed to the safety of the pavement, fell into step and walked together towards the City Hall. She was well-dressed: a green skirt showed under a sort of fur coat. Dark hair piled up in shiny, complicated coils on the crown of her head. Her face was pretty in a plump good-humoured way, with lips artificially widened into expansive and inviting redness. He could guess at soft, generous curves under the loose coat, keeping the beauty of things soft and generous until between her knees and the ground she thickened into unattractive calves and ankles.

'Do you live here?' Andrew asked.

'Born and bred here.'

'Do you like it?

'Like it? Hell. I like it so little I'm getting out to Australia. As far as I can go. As soon as I can get away.'

'Did you marry an Australian?'

'Did I marry a dingo dog?' she said.

She looked sideways at him. The outsize crimson mouth twisted in a good-humoured, pitying smile.

'You're telling me,' she said. 'Did I marry an aborigine or a bushranger? Did I marry a kangaroo?'

Her voice was soft. The words, like the curves of her body were rounded elegantly, a little too elegantly, a little too obviously refined by imitation of English accents and American accents, any accents native to people who were not poor and didn't belong to Belfast.

'Not me,' she said. 'I'd marry no man from the other end of the earth. Some of the girls thought every American soldier was a millionaire or a movie-star. They thought his people back home lived in a palace. Were they cheesed when they found out.'

They passed the City Hall. The curves, the soft voice, the red, friendly mouth comforted Andrew and drove the loneliness from streets of strangers where his eyes might search for ever but never see the thin girl from the south with an accent that belonged to her as liquid song belonged to the skylark.

'Come and have supper with me,' he said.

'I'd only be wasting your time. I had a date. The girl-friend and myself. Her boy was there. I was stood-up. I'm going home now. It's too late to go anywhere.'

'It's not too late to eat.'

'All right, stranger. But don't say I didn't warn you.'

They passed two cinemas and a railway station and found a bright noisy restaurant, smelling of fish, warm and smoky and comfortable. Andrew thought how pretty she was when she was sitting with those fat legs hidden under the table, how pleasant, friendly and confidential she was once she was assured that he wasn't a wolf on the prowl for succulent innocence. She was a factory girl. Her friend was another factory girl. She knew a boy in Bangor was the living image of Andrew Fox. She and the girl-friend were going to Australia together. They didn't intend to remain factory girls. Somebody had told her the boarding-house business was good in Melbourne. So Andrew gave her the home address of his brother who had gone to his uncle in Melbourne when he was a boy.

He was proud of her ambition to be something more in Melbourne than she had been in Belfast. Australia was a big country, a new world, a new life.

When a group of half-drunken soldiers and three A.T.S. girls took possession of the neighbouring three tables Andrew paid his bill and they left the restaurant. At the risk of provoking a brawl he had a quick look at the three girls. But she wasn't there. He hadn't really expected to find her in that company.

He left the girl with the fat legs as far as her bus-stop. She was gone from his mind almost as soon as the bus was out of sight. Once again the crowded streets were painful with loneliness. Friendliness was all very well as far as it went. But there was the wide world of difference between grey, quiet beauty, sensitive shapely hands, a voice that spoke softly and naturally, and a round friendly girl with a dozen false accents who was pretty only when her legs were hidden under a table.

The crowds bursting out from cinemas swept around him like a flood. Buses packed with people set off with strain and effort, pulling up the bumpy slopes that led out of the city. Faces swept past him, white patches against darker backgrounds. The nightmare that can overtake men in the middle of unknown, uncaring crowds made him weak and dizzy, showed him the hopelessness of walking up and down and around looking for a face that he would never see again. Leaning against a street-corner he watched the heedless people hammering past, the crowds decreasing, the traffic thinning and growing quiet. Somewhere above the buildings a clock struck midnight. Three women came slowly out of a dark side-street, eyed him speculatively, stopped in a group a few yards away.

The youngest of the three looked at him steadily until she caught his eye. Then she said: 'Who are you looking at?'

He didn't in the least mind being accosted. But he didn't like the way the girl did it. He didn't like the look of the young brat. She was pretty. Her face was shiny and brazen. Her wandering eyes showed no indication of either brains or good feeling. He didn't like the way her stockings wrinkled. He didn't like the way she tightened the belt of her brown coat or the way her flaxen hair hung untidily about her head. He stared at her stonily, then looked away up the street to show her he had seen nothing worth looking at a second time. She muttered something to the other couple, then walked away by herself along the pavement.

'Don't mind her, mister,' said the elder of the two. 'She has no more manners than a pig.'

'Five months up from the country,' said the other, 'and all the polis in the place are after her for the way she carries on in the street.'

They had a high sense of decorum and dignity, a precise knowledge of the way a possible friend or patron should be spoken to. They were outraged by the uncouth, ill-mannered approach of the flaxen-haired hussy. Andrew struck a match to light a cigarette for the elder woman. She was stout and not unhandsome, her hair grey in middle-age. The younger woman didn't smoke. She was bony, wistfully pretty, pregnant, red-headed, friendly and exceedingly coarse-tongued. They studied the slow, stately progress of two helmeted policemen on the far side of the street.

'They're not after us anyway,' said the red-headed girl. 'They're out to get Blonde Margaret. Big Joe the taximan nearly lost his licence over her when a cop halted his taxi on the Antrim Road. Only the cop was a fella Joe knew, Margaret woulda been in the clink. But Joe threw herself and the Yankee sailor was with her out on the road. Said he'd pull the white hair outa her head if she ever came near his taxi again.'

'She's as bold as brass.'

'She's as ignorant as sin.'

'She oughta get jail.'

'Jail's too good for her. I'm only out myself and, honest to God, I liked it. I get along all right in there.'

'You would, Mary,' said the red-head. 'You're the contented, mother-ly type. But I did my fourteen days an' God it was awful. They'd take the skin off Margaret in there.'

Andrew smoked his cigarette and listened. They had accepted him as part of their company. Common dislike of the uneasiness created by

Margaret's rudeness drew them together. He was a friend. They didn't seem to think of him as a possible customer. They may have sensed that he was searching for something they couldn't offer. The contented motherly woman sucked her cigarette, puffed out smoke in the direction of the two policemen.

'They're not so bad, the cops,' she said. 'That big fellow over there helped me home one night I was down on Royal Avenue too drunk to put one foot past the other.'

Margaret came back along the pavement with three rough, dirty, cap-wearing, scarf-wearing young fellows. They pushed each other about and shouted and laughed, and used every dirty and doubtful word under the moon. Margaret, in one scuffle, lost an ear-ring and groped for it on the stone setts of the street while her companions, hands in pockets, looked at her and chatted to her derisively.

'She has her own sort there,' Mary said.

'Not much money between them,' said the red-head.

The noisy group, abandoning the ear-ring, moved on down the street. On the opposite pavement the two policemen strode impassively in the same direction.

'What did I tell you,' said Mary.

'They'll get her yet,' said the red-head.

'She lost another ear-ring the other night round at the City Hall.'

'She must have a big stock of ear-rings,' said Andrew.

'When I got my three months,' Mary said, 'it was with a fellow like you. He was younger, even. The cop that caught us said: What are you at there, mister? Having a pee, constable, he said. A quare pee, said the constable, hitting him down like that, a sore blow. He got off with forty shillings on account of he wasn't married, and was respectable.'

Respectability, Andrew thought, can be at times useful and at times both embarrassing and perilously precarious.

He offered Mary a cigarette, lighted it for her. He bade the pair of them farewell and walked away. Margaret was standing at another street corner. Her entourage had swollen to a dozen or more, all loud and shouting, and in the middle of them Margaret as proud as a princess in a circle of courtiers. Across the street the two policemen had patiently taken up their position.

Beyond the City Hall the streets were completely deserted. He walked on without any particular objective, with no definable hope. Even if she had been in the city at a picture or a play or a concert or a dance she would have gone back by this time to her lodging or her barracks or her billet or wherever in heaven she slept at night. The thought that some other man might have left her at the doorstep or the barrack gate gave him momentary pain. But he soothed it with a great effort of deliberate hope. He walked on slowly, expecting, who knows, the dead streets to reawaken, the little comical two-legged symbols of life to go hurrying up and down the pavements and in and out among hooting, ridiculous traffic. Then he would find her, not hurrying comically, but moving with graceful deliberation, not a symbol or a fragment of life but the whole fullness thereof, the essence and meaning of all the living.

An hour later when his feet were tired and the streets had grown cold, and he had smoked his last cigarette, he knew that hope was folly and hope was a dream. He leaned for rest against the parapet of a railway bridge and a girl came walking up from the centre of the city. She stopped and asked him for a cigarette. He fumbled through all his pockets.

'Smoked my last,' he said.

But he wasn't anxious to lose the comfort of her company.

He said, 'You're late out tonight.'

She was a plain girl, nothing notable in figure, feature or dress. She was a decent girl. But she was lonely and inclined to be trusting and innocently confidential. Her name was Minnie. She worked in the kitchen in a big city restaurant. She lived in Bangor. Her boy-friend was a soldier. She came up on the train every morning to her work. It wasn't easy being in time. Once a week she went down to a military camp on the outskirts of the city to see her boy-friend. Usually after that weekly assignation, she got the last train back to Bangor. Tonight, when she had separated herself from her boy-friend and returned to the city, she was just in time to see the tail-end of the last train to Bangor vanishing out of the station. There was a fix to find yourself in. She had to get a night's sleep somewhere so as to be able to work in the morning. Her father in Bangor was as cross as hell.

In sympathy for the plain girl without a bed to lie on or a roof over her head Andrew for a moment forgot his own despair.

'Do you know nobody in Belfast?'

'My sister's in digs up this way. If I could get her to let me in quietly. But her bitch of a landlady would write to my father about me being out at this time of the night.'

'On our way,' said Andrew.

They walked for a mile along hard pavements, through narrow streets lined with small kitchen-houses. To Andrew who loved running dogs and sport on windy uplands it was all a nightmare of men, women and children sweating away the night in rooms as small as coffins, sweating away the day in factories and mills as big as palaces, as comfortable as prisons and as noisy as nine bedlams. He waited at the corner of one narrow street while she walked fifty yards ahead and surveyed the house her sister lodged in. There was only one lighted window in the whole street, one small room where people were still alive in this city of death. The rest of the city, the rest of the world was dead. Andrew Fox and the homeless girl called Minnie were two people forgotten and left to exist through all eternity on the back of an abandoned desolate globe. Perhaps the light was shining in that room only because somebody was sick there, coughing up blood, dying in pain. When death would go into the room the window would be as dark as all the other windows in the street. Outside in the withering, chilly night there would be homeless Minnie and Andrew Fox looking hopelessly for something he would never find.

There would also be the policemen, as black as the devil and six feet high, looking suspiciously at Andrew Fox.

The policeman said, 'Are you waiting on somebody?'

No policeman in Belfast or in the world could have appreciated exactly what he was waiting for and hoping for.

'For that girl,' he said.

The policeman peered up the street. He said, 'What in the name of God is she doing?'

Andrew explained. He explained with the extravagant good humour, the exaggerated, detailed politeness of the civilised, sensible, law-abiding man caught in a position that savours even ever so slightly of law-breaking. The policeman was partially convinced. He continued to peer up the street. The light in the one window was suddenly extinguished. The policeman said, 'Why doesn't she knock?'

Andrew explained further. He explained about the landlady and the cross father. He was beginning to feel annoyed with the policeman's curiosity. After all he wasn't a thief. He wasn't an I.R.A. man. He was Andrew Fox, the owner of Ballyclogher Comet who had seen for a moment a thin girl from Cork and lost his heart, his peace of mind and his night's rest.

Minnie came back down the street. The people of the house were in bed. Her sister was in bed. For the benefit of the policeman Minnie commenced her own explanation. The policeman was completely convinced. He was even anxious to help. He would knock on the door himself and waken the people. If they wouldn't heed a girl then they would heed a member of the force. Minnie's honest, pimpled face went grey with unaffected horror. Suppose her da in Bangor heard she had turned up at two in the morning escorted by a policeman. Her da, mind you, had been a policeman himself. There was nothing he didn't know.

'Get me a taxi,' said Andrew. 'I'll take you to the house of a friend of mine in Ballyhackamore.'

He didn't have a friend in Ballyhackamore. But for his own sake and for the sake of the terrified girl he wanted to see the end of that hellish, helpful constable. He led the way to a telephone kiosk, rang a taxi rank, chatted amicably until the car arrived, pushed Minnie in ahead of him, thanked the policeman with high, firm politeness, and was driven off to no particular destination. Somewhere in a select, fashionable suburb he dismissed the taxi, having first bought a packet of cigarettes from the driver, and sitting on a seat between the respectable road and a row of shadowy tennis-courts, Minnie and himself chain-smoked the cigarettes. No policeman passed to molest them. They were miles away from the rough, narrow places where the poor lived. They were high above the terrible pavements where the abandoned sold their bodies. In the sky above the streets there was the reflection of light. But there was no sound, absolutely no sound.

Down there, Andrew thought, she is resting her head on a pillow and sleep has closed the grey eyes and she will not smile again until morning. Or, possibly, she smiles in her sleep, seeing the bright curves of Patrick Street in Cork and hearing the soft voices of her Southern people. Or does she lie awake and restless wondering why the fool of a fellow who sat facing her in the train didn't ask her to meet him again? Or, perhaps, she hears the voice and sees the face of somebody who wasn't so slow nor so foolish, who hadn't a valuable greyhound bitch waiting for him in the guard's van.

When the last cigarette was smoked he telephoned another taxi, paid the fare in advance and sent simple Minnie careering proudly back to the house where her sister lodged. The policeman would certainly be gone. She could knock quietly at her sister's window.

Then he walked slowly down to his hotel. It was that strange time, about four or five on a summer morning, when you realise that suburban gardens are alive with loudly-singing birds.

Stretching himself on his bed he thought that, if it was a story in the pictures, he would be awakened by a heavy knock on his door, there would be two policemen to arrest him and tell him that Minnie had been found murdered and horribly mutilated in a back alley. But the knocking on the door that did awaken him was merely the night porter hammering loudly to arouse him for the early train. He wasn't sure whether he was glad or sorry. Notoriety could have its uses and, anyway, he would be innocent and she might be standing there to welcome him out of the court, smiling at him out of quiet grey eyes.

When Ballyclogher Comet was safe in the guard's van he found himself a seat. Sitting across from him was a fat, heavily-breathing man with a red face and a black moustache.

When the last houses of Belfast melted into the flat green fields he went up to the dining-car and ordered breakfast. He ate slowly, ruminating, reading the paper casually, and when he folded up the paper and laid it aside he saw the girl in uniform facing him across the table. Her face was thin and sun-tanned and for half a minute he tried to bludgeon himself into believing that this was the girl he had spoken to twenty-four hours previously, the girl whose features were already fading and becoming vague in his memory. Cold with fear he realised that if in days to come he did meet her somewhere, on the street or in a train or coming out of a cinema, he mightn't even recognise her, might confuse her with any one of a thousand uniformed girls.

The girl across the table looked at him over the rim of her raised cup. The letters on the shoulder of her jacket told him, as he returned to a sensible acceptance of reality, that she came not from Cork but Canada. When she spoke her voice was quiet enough but it drawled lazily and easily with accent, intonation and pronunciation known neither in Cork nor Ballyclogher. She had been on a holiday in Dublin and a friend had advised her to go north and see Belfast. She had seen Belfast and was very glad to be returning to Dublin. Her father and mother were English and somewhere in her blood there was a trace of Pennsylvania Dutch. But Ireland was the country of her choice. The people were so friendly. Almost everybody had a relative somewhere in Canada or the U.S.A., and they expected you to be fairly well acquainted with their relatives even though you lived thousands of miles away from the places mentioned. She found that very amusing. The men in Ireland, she said, were handsomer than the men in most other countries; an opinion that gratified Andrew. And there weren't many wolves about. Leastways, she hadn't met them. The men didn't seem to want to push you around.

She talked with the easy assurance of a girl who had travelled and been around and seen things. She judged people easily and humorously, with a charity as wide as the wide plains of Canada. Andrew found it easy to talk to her, easy to be friends with her, to forget that she had come over vast distances and would return again for ever to distant places.

When the train pulled into Portadown they shook hands like old friends. She said, 'You're not a bad scout, Andrew Fox. It's been nice knowing you.'

She leaned from the window and waved as he went racing up the platform to the guard's van and the greyhound bitch. He had her name and address written down on the back of an envelope.

There's the poem about the fellow who, using a berry as a bait, fished in a stream and caught a little silver trout. Then when he was greasing the pan and kindling the fire the trout changed into a lovely girl who ran from him, calling his name. He followed her through hollows and over hills, growing old in the chase, keeping his aged limbs supple with hope for the day when he would find her and kiss her and live with her in an enchanted land.

We all know the poem. We learned it at school, those of us who learn anything at school. Our greatest poet wrote it. It's a lovely poem. We should be proud of it. We are – those of us who know enough to be proud of anything.

Then there are ninety-nine poems, good, bad and indifferent, about poets pursuing ideal and evasive beauty.

I wonder do they ever find it. I wonder did that old fellow keep up the pursuit as long as he said, searching over hills and through hollows for the girl that had once been a silver trout. Perhaps he grew tired, kissed somebody with a real father and mother and with money in the bank: somebody with fat legs, somebody as trite as three school-teachers learning languages, as stupid as a pimply girl missing her train and living in mortal terror of a father who had been a policeman. Perhaps he went down into the dark night of mercenary misery and forgot his vision. Or could it be that men can realise their visions in the strangest ways and places?

Andrew Fox still writes letters to that Canadian girl. He signs them, 'Your sincere friend, Andrew Fox, Canonhill Road, Ballyclogher.' He shows them to me. They're mostly about the dogs he's breeding and the books he's reading. He reads a lot and he's lucky with dogs. He doesn't show her letters to me but the whole town knows that they arrive regularly. He tells me he's not in love with her, yet something may come of it. If anything does it will be the sensation of Ballyclogher, for Andrew is generally regarded as a prosaic person unlikely to rush out to far horizons. The girls in Ballyclogher would be annoyed. So, for all I know, would the boys be in a little town somewhere in Ontario.

All I do know for certain is that when he got into the train in Belfast, Andrew was determined to go to Cork as soon as possible, to walk around the streets and make enquiries of the friendly, talkative people. He was determined, too, that every time he went to Belfast he would ask every A.T.S. girl he met if she knew a girl from Cork who looked this way and talked that way, and so on.

But when he had left the Canadian girl at Portadown and changed into the Ballyclogher train he went down to the guard's van, sat chatting with the guard and admiring his own greyhound: the quivering thin nose, the strong legs, the nervous electric feet.

He has never gone to Cork. He doesn't talk to A.T.S. girls any more than to any other girls.

A VIEW FROM THE TREETOP

There were two famous trees in the village: the cork tree and the lime tree. Strangers used to travel miles just to look at them. The cork tree was a decrepit foreign character who stood guiltily and raggedly, as if he knew he was an intruder, on the unkempt slope below the railway station. Nobody knew who had planted it, but the Old Master had the theory that some mysterious brown man, passing that way, had taken a seed out of his pocket and blown it from the palm of his hand to seek shelter and mercy from our soft earth.

'In Portugal,' the Old Master once read out in the course of a geography lesson, 'the freshly cut trunks of the cork oaks are in July deeply flushed with red.'

It was a long way from Portugal to the scrubby slope below the station where the bark hung loosely, half-on and half-off, our poor, leprous cork-oak. There was no view worth talking of from the top of it and, even if there had been, nobody could climb it in comfort, because you couldn't get a grip on it; the bark came off in your hands. But from the top of the lime tree, on the triangular green in the centre of the village, you could see the world. Nobody knew that better than Paddy Sheehan. Paddy spent a whole August morning in the lime tree. As he told me himself, long afterwards, it was worth being hungry and thirsty, lost and missing for an August morning, just to see what he saw and to realise himself as he did.

'I was never the same after that morning,' he said. 'I knew I was a bit of a god.'

Down the road from his father's large, square, stone house to the double bridge over the river two damson trees from one wild orchard grew out over a straggling hedge. This sunny morning Paddy galloped to the double bridge, plucking, on the way, two damsons, one from each tree, not for himself but for his invisible horse who, unaccountably, liked damsons. Horses you invented need not diet on grass or oats or hay particularly when you did the eating for them. Because there was a white horse in training in the long field by the railway, and because this horse was in his mind, the horse he ate the two damsons for was a racehorse. At the double bridge he unsaddled and unbridled it, smacked its flank and sent it off to graze on the wide field in the loop of the river where his father, a big grazier and the village butcher, said was the best fattening land in Ireland.

The bridge had to be a double bridge because the river, one time in high flood, had changed its course. The older half of the bridge now spanned a muddy sunken ditch lined with reeds and willows, where water had once flowed. In every subsequent flood the water tried unavailingly to return to its ancient channel. That struggle between restless river and solid grazing land was one of the topics the Old Master loved to talk about when he wasn't talking – which he mostly was – about the wonders of the battlefield on the far side of the village.

'On that black plain,' he would say, 'nearly three centuries ago, two kings played at pitch-and-toss for the crown of England.'

The Old Master was as much part of the village as the ancient battlefield was: born and reared there he had come back to take over the school and talk to generations of boys about the history of the place.

Sunlight danced on glittering water. Wagtails darted and dipped over the wide salmon pool above the bridge. Heavy cattle churning in the mud of the old channel sought the shade of the willows and fortified themselves against the day's heat. When Paddy's horse was contentedly grazing he went back homewards, bent on breakfast.

To the left of the road was a high, ivy-grown wall. It was part of the morning game to clamber up a few feet, clutching the ivy, and to peer through a hole in the wall at the mad major who had suffered sunstroke in India. Most mornings he worked in the gardens at the back of his big house. Nobody in the village could afford for shame to wear clothes as tattered and dirty as the major wore. He affected an ancient battle-dress held together by strings and pins, and a wide straw hat and furious red whiskers. Nobody in the world talked so loudly or took such long strides or could shoot snipe better or was more given to fits of high-pitched laughter. It was exciting to peer through a hole in the wall at this wonder of a man talking to himself as he worked, and sometimes talking to the plants and blossoms. The only thing in the village that was at all like him was the rare and alien cork tree.

Before Paddy's eyes then, as he peered through the hole in the wall, the major became the cork tree. It was as real to Paddy as if he had been dreaming. The magic of sunlight on flowers in the old walled garden dazzled him and set him playing a new game: Close my eyes, open them, I see the major; Close them again, open them again, I see the cork tree. To vary the fun he made the cork tree talk with a high foreign voice, and made the battle-dress peel like brown, crumbling bark off the hapless major. That was why, when he looked sideways and saw the Old Master coming towards him from the direction of the bridge, and the station and the cork tree, he panicked and ran. He couldn't think of the cork tree and the Old Master at one and the same time without sharp feelings of guilt. Because when he thought of the cork tree he had also to think of the seventeen musket balls he had abstracted from the school museum. They were hidden in a tin box in a hole under the roots of the cork tree.

The Old Master, he hoped, was yet too far away to see him. So he dropped from the wall and ran, up the slope and around the corner into the main street of the village and across the triangular green; and, having come so far, it seemed as natural to run up the great lime tree as to run further along the ground. There was nobody to be seen except the parish priest who, fifty yards away and with his back to Paddy, was reading his breviary. Up and up Paddy went and then on a broad branch, his back to the trunk, he rested straddle, soothed by the sound of morning air in the leaves and the gentle, swaying motion of high timber. He looked down on his world and began to examine his conscience.

In school the previous day things had come to an embarrassing point of discovery when the Old Master had been proudly displaying his museum to the schools inspector with the white moustache who talked half in Irish and half in English, quoted poetry most of the time, breathed out whisky all the time, and was for ever jingling money in the pockets of his trousers. The Master and the Inspector had known each other since college days in Dublin. Old friends together, they talked and jingled round the room. The Inspector was a big man and bulky in tweeds. The Old Master, small, mild, and stooped, his left ear wired for hearing, went ahead of him like a tug before a liner, around the senior schoolroom which, with glass cases filled with relics of that battle long ago, was a miniature museum.

'About here where this school stands, James,' the Inspector bellowed, 'the last shots were fired on that black day three hundred years ago.'

He intoned in Irish some mournful verse about a lost battle and a broken cause.

'Boys,' he roared at us, 'you should be able to feel history and you going to school here. Not Gettysburg nor Mons were more renowned than this place. That stream across the road there, that you catch pinkeens in, more than likely ran red with blood.'

We listened. The stream was in a brown fresh that day after a cloudburst in the hills and we could hear it rushing down the slope to join our river below the double bridge. Perhaps the more imaginative of us could hear above the sound of the falling water the echo of the last salvoes, the agony of the last cries.

'They're strong on history,' said the Old Master.

He was proud of us, God knew why.

'And they were as industrious as beavers, these good pupils of mine going on all fours over the battlefield, searching with fine combs for relics of the battle. The things we found.'

'Turn a sod and start the muse of history,' said the Inspector.

'Take a look at our glass cases.'

'Didn't I read in the papers,' the Inspector roared and jingled, 'about the things you found? Wonderful, James. A credit to you and these good boys. The children of decent parents, I'll be bound.'

They studied a brutal-looking lump of wood so long buried in the black earth that it looked as if it had been turned into stone.

'A digging wedge,' said the Old Master.

'The oldest digging instrument in the world,' said the Inspector. 'The Hottentots used it.'

'And the South Sea islanders.'

They moved from glass case to glass case. They studied a stone with the mark of a fossil on it. Concerning that stone, Paddy told us, he used to have nightmares. He was an imaginative, red-headed, bony-kneed, hard-knuckled boy of thirteen. Every stone in the world, he said, even the stones in the walls around the mad major's house and gardens, might be just waiting to burst open to let monsters, part fish, part bird, part reptile, fly out. The major himself was a fossil cased in stone.

The Old Master and the Inspector studied two muskets, and a blunderbuss it would have taken a giant to raise to shooting level. They studied an old clay pipe with a slender stem and a long bowl, and stamped on the bowl, a heart and a hand and the name of Parnell. They examined brass five-shilling pieces made from the broken, melted metal of old guns.

'Payment in kind,' said the Inspector, 'from greedy kings to needy soldiers.'

He jingled his own coins.

'Do you know, when I set the boys searching the battlefield we dug up musket balls as plentiful as blackberries or those edible nuts the pigs grub for?'

'How many of them,' moralised the Inspector, 'might have accounted for a good man's life.

''Twas a great work to collect all these things, boys,' he said. 'It's a pity that any relic of the past should be lost. Didn't the Lord himself say: Colligite quae superaverunt fragmenta ne pereant.'

We sat in horror in case he might ask us to translate but, gentleman that he was, he did the dirty work himself: 'Gather up the fragments that remain lest they be lost.'

'And furthermore, James, don't you think as a reward we could give them a holiday tomorrow?'

Our cheering rattled the objects in the glass cases. When the tumult had subsided the Old Master said, 'I'll give you one of these musket balls as a keepsake, Matthew. You can rattle it with your ha'pence.'

'My mother always said a rattler would never be a spender. I wish I could say she was right. I'd be a rich man today.'

In Irish too fast and idiomatic for us to follow the two old men talked together, then laughed loudly, until the Old Master choked and the Inspector turned purple.

From the junior room next door, separated from us only by a glass-and-wood partition, the voice of the Young Teacher haranguing his misfortunate pupils rose high in strident envy. He wasn't a very good teacher. If it hadn't been for the Old Master, whose assistant he was, the Inspector would have given him bad reports. He was a most dislikeable man: thin-lipped, ill-tempered, pointy-eyed, with a sideways beak of a nose and oiled, black hair pasted down flat and shining like a polished floor. His only virtue, if it could be counted a virtue, was that he was almost as good a sporting shot – snipe, duck, grouse, or pheasant – as the Mad Major, but it was said of him that, like a Frenchman, he'd shoot the sparrows in the hedges. He envied and elected to despise the Old Master who treated him with the charity of God.

Once peering and eavesdropping at the back window of one of the village pubs, Paddy and myself had caught the Young Teacher in action among the scruff who were his familiars.

'I could instruct him about real guns,' he said. 'Guns that shoot. Like this.'

Imaginary gun to shoulder he pivoted on his left heel, and sighted, followed and pinked an imaginary fowl. His claque applauded – he was paying for their drink.

'Living in the past like a mole in the ground,' he said. 'His guns are stopped up with clay like his deaf ears.'

Now, enraged by our cheers and delight, and by the camaraderie of the two old men, his voice, berating some boy, rose an octave higher.

The Old Master led the Inspector to the last of the glass cases and opened it, then looked long and sadly at the empty corner where the musket balls had been.

'Somebody,' he said quietly, 'seems to have removed them.'

There was a horrified silence. Every boy in the room looked fixedly at the digging wedge as if he expected it to give tongue and name the culprit.

'I suppose we are lucky that all the muskets are still with us,' the Old Master said.

'I'd put up a notice, James,' said the Inspector, 'warning all travellers: Heads down when passing this village. A clever boy could be a David and use those balls as slingshots.'

'When I was young,' said the Old Master, 'I was a dab hand with the sling myself.'

He closed the glass case slowly. He said, 'Boys, you found them once. I'll expect you to find them again.'

That was all, but to Paddy Sheehan it was worse than brutal words and birchings.

He was a sailor high in the swaying crow's nest. Close my eyes, open them again, and all around is the heaving limitless Pacific and, far on the skyline, the dark green palms of a coral island like a thumb-smudge on a painted wall. Close them again, open them again, the tattered mad major is bent over the begonias in his garden, the morning sun still glitters on the salmon pool above the double bridge and the Old Master, as small as a rabbit, is walking along the street towards his house.

On the green at the foot of the tree the story had it that Johnny Patterson, the famous clown, had once pitched his tent and joked and danced and sang. Because of that hallowed memory an old, broken-down clown, performer once at fairs and rural football games and now no longer fit for the road, had parked his caravan there to spend his last days under the shelter of the lime tree. He was unshaven and witless. The village was kind to him. No children mocked him – possibly because the illustrated bible-history used in the school had one vivid, exemplary picture of bears eating up boys who had mocked just such a man. For a few coppers he could paint, with some talent, gaudy landscapes and portraits that came fairly close to the originals, or play the fiddle by holding the bow in his teeth and sawing the instrument backwards and forwards or rattle bone-clappers in each hand and play a whistle with one side of his mouth and sing with the other, and simultaneously dance the Irish Washerwoman. The old horse that had drawn his caravan to haven was, like himself, no longer fit for journeying, so it idled and grazed on the commonage that was part of the battlefield and slept at night, like a dog, by the steps at the caravan door. When the clown emerged for his morning wash in a bucket of water, he roused the horse, gave him a sniff of oats in a basin and, as the Old Master said, day had officially begun in the village.

The clown washed. The Master talked to him and tapped the hide of the horse gently with his blackthorn. Paddy, masthead-high and swaying with the gentle wind, looked down on them and felt like Judas and wondered what the Master would say to the Inspector, his guest for a few days, when he returned from his morning walk and they breakfasted together. Would they talk of the missing musket-balls and of skill with the sling?

Part of the agony was that Paddy was an expert with the sling, and the whole world and half the windows in the parish knew it. His father used to say not without a certain pride, that half the profits of his shop went in putting back the panes Paddy smashed. One evening, when it was his turn to stay behind and tidy the senior room, he had fallen to thievery simply because, in a blinding flash of inspiration, he had realised that, while muskets were out, slings, for the adept, were still in. Then walking home, his trouser-pockets weighed down, his braces creaking with the strain, shame and guilt had overtaken him. How could he have done this to the Old Master? It was far worse than stealing. How could he make restitution? Restore them openly and admit his shame? Restore them as he had taken them: secretly? But suppose he was caught in the act and the effort at restoration mistaken for crime? To gain time he had buried them under the cork tree.

The Mad Major was running around his garden clapping his hands and leaping in the air. Chasing a butterfly?

The clown's old spavined horse tottered off towards the commonage.

The Old Master tapped on up the street and vanished into his house.

Smoke and the smell of cooking came up from the section of discarded rainspout that made a chimney for the caravan. Hunger and guilt in the high tree were miserable companions and, ironically, the blue innocence of the morning heaven seemed only grasping distance away.

Far on the fringe of the commonage the Young Teacher fired his last morning shot and, Paddy fervently hoped, missed. That year was too mild for early duck although the Bully Cryan, and he was probably telling lies, said that one morning when he was out with the Young Teacher he saw a flight of at least four hundred passing – well out of range. Now, through a framework of leaves, Paddy watched the slow, homeward plodding of the Young Teacher and the Bully Cryan, his stupid, faithful Sancho Panza, one of the few boys in the school who, if civil war had been declared, would have gone with the Young Teacher against the Old Master. He was a surly steam-roller of a boy with close-cropped black hair and porcine features, a terror to the smaller boys because of his weight, but no skilled fighter and unwilling ever to try conclusions with Paddy, a quick mover and a leader of men. The Young Teacher, perhaps sensing the slavish weakness behind the bullying heaviness or, less likely, pitying a boy whose existence seemed so pointless, used him as a body-servant.

Bearing bag and gun he trudged along behind the Young Teacher. He was born to be a gilly. Paddy loftily surveyed their progress: from the open common into the fruit-bearing area where apples from bending branches sank to orchard grass or even plopped into small slow streams; through a maze of lanes and by higgledy-piggledy cottages bowered in laden trees, then round the corner by the church and across the green to halt at the foot of the lime tree.

'Run home now, Cryan,' said the Young Teacher.

'Yes, sir.'

'We had poor luck for duck.'

Paddy was delighted to hear it.

'But we'll do better next time.'

'Yes, sir.'

'Call to my house at twelve-thirty post meridiem.'

'Yes, sir.'

'My wife wants to send across a cooked pheasant to brighten the luncheon table for the Inspector.'

'Yes, sir.'

'Give him for once a taste of good cooking.'

'Yes, sir.'

'He's not likely to get it where he is.'

'No, sir.'

Among the leaves Paddy seethed. But then the thought of the Bully Cryan as an authority on cooking, good or bad, was so comic, and so sad, that his resentment rapidly melted. The Young Teacher went one way. Relieved of bag and gun and very likely without two pennies to clink in his pocket the Bully Cryan descended to the riverside lane where he lived. We could more easily have believed that the Young Teacher was being kind to the Bully and not merely using him if, as a recompense for all the gillying, any coin of the realm had ever changed hands.

The village was alive now.

From the byre behind his house Soldier Sweeney, the shoemaker, drove his one cow and two goats out to graze and depredate on roadside hedges and insufficiently-fortified gardens. Back in the days of World War One, when the soldier had been clinked for drink, a sympathetic fellow-soldier and sentry had funnelled porter to him through the lock-up window and down the barrel of a rifle.

The pimply Badger Smith who worked for Paddy's father and in his spare time taught the village boys to use foul language was taking down the shutters from the butcher's shop.

One old voteen of a woman, dark in widow's weeds, was first into the church for mass, then three girls, the doctor's daughters, in light summer frocks and with coloured handkerchiefs, in obedience to Saint Paul, covering their heads.

At the door of the post-office a postman straddled a bike and pushed off towards the station to meet the train.

Window blinds went up wearily in lazy households. The tall tree swayed with a lulling gentle motion and, now that the first attack of hunger was over, he decided he'd stay aloft a little longer. His mother would assume that he had gone to mass. Besides he was growing fond of tree-living and he knew that once he put his foot back on the grass he would again assume the guilty weight of the cached musket-balls. Nearly three centuries ago they had whizzed through the air and the battlesmoke over the common, bringing death and destruction with them. Ill-luck, he felt, had followed them since.

Molly, the doctor's maid, neat and black-and-white, ran across to the newsagent's, her high heels clicking as clearly as castanets. Thoughtfully, the Badger rested on the block a cleaver he had raised and looked after her.

The mad major was gone from the garden and Paddy knew why. For the train was pulling out of the station and all of a sudden the glorious white racehorse the major owned was in the long, narrow, rising limestone field that went parallel with the railway track for a resounding four hundred yards. Glued by nature to the silver back the major raced and paced the horse against the train and, swaying on the tree, Paddy felt in his blood the thud of every marvellous hoofbeat.

'On the day of the battle,' the Old Master had said, 'legend has it that a chieftain from the Midlands was shot dead off his war-horse. And, riderless, the noble steed, stirrups and reins swinging wild, galloped halfways across Ireland to fall dead with a broken heart at the gate of its master's castle. You see, it knew that the day was lost.'

For ever in Paddy's mind a white horse, proud bitter messenger of defeat, hammered on and on across a darkening land.

His father in his gleaming new Austin pulled up at the shop, issued some instructions to the Badger, then drove away out of the village. There was a cattle-fair in a town twenty miles away.

The worshippers had long gone home from mass. On the gravel

outside the church the parish priest was talking to the doctor. By now his mother would be beginning to wonder what was keeping him from his breakfast. But there was euphoric contentment, ease, exaltation in being up so high and swaying so gently as if you moved with the deep breathing of the earth and, although he knew he should descend and go home, his limbs wouldn't obey him.

With an empty potato-sack over his hunched shoulders Grandfather Cryan set off to pick cinders in the dump at the railway station. Ten minutes later the Burglar Cryan, one of the Bully's many uncles, set off with an iron rod in his hand and a wooden box containing a ferret, strapped to his back to catch rabbits. A gaunt, tubercular man, he was notable for three things: his skill in rabbit-catching; his having done time for breaking and entering; and once, at the corner of Brennan's smithy where he spent his spare time seated on an antique mounting-block whittling sticks, for having arisen patiently to knock down his virago of a mother-in-law because she had tavered him even beyond the endurance of a man who had uncomplainingly suffered much.

Ten minutes later the Poacher Cryan, the Bully's father, went by in another direction. He had once, by day, given his expert knowledge to help a group of fishery conservators stock a stretch of the river with fingerlings and then, by night, when the fish were grown, he had removed them illegally to barter them for drink or to feed them to his own brood.

The two small Cryans, one male, one female, each bearing two iron buckets, went from door to door collecting kitchen scraps for pig-swill. Behind them grandly strode the Bully wheeling a wooden handcart into which the buckets were emptied, and making certain, since he only played the servitor to the Young Teacher, that his smaller relatives did all the work. They could be a brother and sister. Or they could be cousins. There were, Paddy knew, scores or hundreds of Cryans. Nobody knew for certain how many because they were never seen all together in public. There were three generations of them living in the one lane in the one row of whitewashed cottages and it was suspected that they even had the great-grandfather, dead but stuffed, in the boarded-up cottage at the end of the lane. It was commonly accepted, too, that there had been so many Cryans in the British Army that, in spite of official histories and the alien names of Foch, Haig and Pershing, it was the Cryans all the time who had won the war. And once when a brother of the Burglar had died it was true that at the funeral one old shawled woman had said to another: God sees, Mary, that's the first of the Cryans ever died.

The Badger downed tools and, wiping big hands in apron, came to the door of the shop to teach the three Cryans a few more bad words, as if they didn't know enough already.

Two loafers emerged from a lane to join the Badger. The Bully moved on rapidly when he saw the Young Teacher's wife, strong in breasts and buttocks, vivid in high-piled, ash-blonde hair, orange sweater, tartan slacks, red shoes, coming with her shopping-basket down the street. She was the first woman in the village ever to wear trousers. She was fast, violent and dominating, and she drank, and it would seem that the Young Teacher had his own troubles: dirty shirts, an occasional black eye, and now and again a claw mark on his jaw that might have meant love but was scarcely the signature of domestic bliss. So as we grew up we learned that there were reasons for the Old Master's protective leanings towards his assistant.

Down the street she sailed, a stately ship of Tarsus bound for the isles of Javan or Gadire, with all her bravery on and tackle trim, sails filled and streamers waving. She addressed a few words to the Badger: admonitory words, Paddy guessed, because not the best beef ever grazed on the fat ground where Paddy had that morning set his dream-horse on grass was good enough to satisfy that woman. The Badger, standing in an obsequious crouch, listened attentively. The two loafers withdrew to a cowardly, diffident distance. But when she had dismissed the Badger and walked off down the street the three of them came together again like vultures over a delectably-decayed corpse, and studied the retreating movement of her swaying rear, radiant in ersatz tartan, and whispered and sniggered.

Paddy, if you can believe him, says that at that moment he saw all life like maggots on bad meat. Below his eyes the Badger and the two loafers swayed backwards and forwards as if they were on strings and, again if you can credit Paddy, an imaginative boy, straddle on a strong branch, his back to the trunk, he fell asleep. He will admit though that if he had really been asleep he could have fallen out of the tree. But if it wasn't true sleep, he says, it was a trance, and the world was all white horses and tartan women, and the acrid smoke of battle rolled over the black commonage and vicious musket-balls chipped the apples off the trees. The remote earth was his easy cradle.

When the trance had passed he looked down and saw the Bully Cryan, covered tray in hands, stepping out of the Young Teacher's doorway. There and then he knew why inexorable destiny had sent him up the tree.

The Young Teacher's wife who, in spite of her faults, was a good cook and very proud of her cooking had gone to great trouble about that particular Phasian bird.

Chestnut brown and cream and black, iridescent with specks of green and purple, its sad gentle face bright red and featherless, its spurs short and blunt, to tell of youth and tender flesh, the bird had given beauty to the woods beyond the battlefield and by the big river to which our river was but a tributary. Then the proud woman had sent forth her husband, the sharp-faced, mean-eyed hunter, and the hunter's gilly had gone like a retrieving hound to gather the soft bleeding body from the crushed grass.

The hanging, plucking, drawing of entrails, the trussing and roasting, could all have been part of a necromantic rite designed to mortify the Old Master and his kind, silver-haired wife, plain people who were content with plain fare. It was known that the Inspector was fond of his stomach.

The Young Teacher's wife didn't stuff the bird with two snipe as Brillat Savarin recommended, but she did ornament the cooked stern with a few tail feathers – a practice disapproved of, possibly on grounds of propriety, by Mrs. Beeton. She made the hollow, where the entrails had been, delicious with molten butter. She tied rashers over the breast before roasting. She prepared the fried breadcrumbs with which to serve it. She laid the savoury brown morsel, now devoid of life, that once had carried colour through the woods, on one of her best willow-pattern platters. She circled it with little rashers, crisp and rolled and pierced by toothpicks and coy as any Gallic escargots. She placed above it her most gleaming dish-cover and her whitest linen cloth. She steadied the tray in the gilly's hands and said, 'Cryan, don't waste one second. Are your hands clean? Go directly across the green. Don't trip or stumble. You clumsy fool.'

'Yes, ma'am.'

Then she went back to her husband and cold with triumph and drawn together by a common malice they drank gin and tonic for half an hour.

The first of Paddy that the Bully saw was his feet in the air as he swung like a pendulum for his leap to the grass. They were aggressive feet. They came so close to the precious tray that the Bully backed a step and almost stumbled. On the caravan steps the Clown was seated swabbing with a crust his midday meal, a greasy mess, from an iron pan.

'Mind your big feet,' said the Bully.

Then he saw Paddy crouching on the grass before him.

'They're looking for you, Sheehan,' he said. 'You'll be killed. Get out of my way.'

There was, as clearly he gripped the tray, the crack of panic in his voice.

'Who's looking for me?'

'Your mother asked me where you were.'

'In Mars,' said Paddy. 'I'm just back. I'm Jack the Giant-Killer. I was up the beanstalk.'

He touched the white linen. He knew his Shakespeare. He said, 'What find I here?'

'You'll be killed for this, Sheehan.'

'Who'll kill me?'

He lifted off the cloth and dish-cover and dropped them on the grass. The brown body, bedecked with feathers, ringed with rashers, was exposed, and the very air under the tree was as good as edible. To look and sniff, the clown moved closer. Transfixed with horror at the incredible event the Bully was helpless: his hands were bound to the tray.

'The Teacher,' he said, 'will slay you.'

'Sucks to the Teacher.'

'I'll tell him you said sucks.'

'Sucks to you, too. Yum yum.'

The first rasher was gone. He gave the second to the clown.

'Yum yum,' said the clown.

He rubbed his belly and smacked his lips.

'Eat up,' said Paddy.

To the appreciative Clown he gave the left leg of the pheasant. When the Bully, with tears in his eyes, opened his mouth again to protest Paddy popped a rasher into it and, sizzling hot as it was, it went down in one agonised gulp. With the trembling of the Bully's hands the platter rattled on the tray.

'Careful with the delph,' said Paddy, 'or Daisy Coloured Trousers will smack hims iddle bottom.'

He took four splendid bites of pheasant. He restored the mangled corpse and the dish-cover and the cloth, on which he delicately wiped his fingers.

'Go thy way in peace, B. Cryan Esquire,' he said. 'Sin no more.'

He went back up the tree. It seemed the only place to go. Where did David go after he had eaten the loaves of sacrifice?

And the Bully who hadn't the wit or the courage to turn back went on at a trot to lay the half-burnt offering between the Old Master and the Inspector.

There was hell to pay afterwards of course, because Daisy Coloured

Trousers cried to heaven for vengeance and Paddy's parents had to take punitive measures and the Old Master had to pretend that he did. But the days of the Bully Cryan were numbered and Paddy was the hero of the school. He had discovered, too, that he could really think and size things up and get control of life by sitting up in the lime tree and meditating. So a fair share of his boyhood and youth was spent up that tree. Man, at times he felt, was meant to live in trees; and one sullen, clouded afternoon when the white horse had flashed like a star along the narrow field, and when the last puff of the pacing train had faded away towards the coast, he heard the Old Master call him from the Green.

'The Lord called to Zaccheus,' said the old man. 'Come down, Paddy Sheehan, come down. Are you a boy or a bird?

'By eating a bird, Paddy,' he said, 'it may be that you became a bird. A condign punishment. According to a maxim in civil law, Paddy, qui non habet in aere luat in pelle, or he who can't pay in coin will have the price taken out of his hide. Come for a walk with me. Be the staff of my old age.'

By lanes twisting around orchards they walked towards the common. That was a rich year for apples and in the dark day, under the heavy sky, the fruit glowed like gems. Shuffling along with short steps – he had the arthritis bad in the feet – the Old Master leaned on Paddy's shoulder and now and again gave him a shrewd, sideways look from under the wide brim of a black hat that he wore in memory of a fashion of his youth.

'And talking of birds, Paddy, history has it that the men of this village were once geniuses at the netting of plover. 'Twas said they could even take them out of the air. A feat only possible, believe me, if the netter is the extreme expert. Most bird-catchers have to wait until the bird actually lodges before springing the net. But then we have had many famous men in this place. Did you ever know that the major swam on a line under the waters of the Nile and, in spite of an encounter with a crocodile crossed safely from bank to bank. A travelled, amazing man. They say he'd have been knighted by the King of England only he'd never use his handkerchief. Perhaps it was in the dust of the lining of his coat-pocket that the seed of the cork tree came home to us.'

High in the lime-branches Paddy could escape from the cork tree and its grisly secret, but down on the ground the leprous monster followed him about: a crooked, accusing, many-armed ghost.

Ahead of them the common-land, once a part of the place of battle and death, was black under rolling seaward clouds.

'There's a fury in the skies and clouds now, Paddy, wasn't in them in my youth. Or perhaps as the years pass you read more meaning into the colours and the motions of the clouds. But, young or old, I always thought that this little stream here made the sweetest of all sounds.'

Bearing with it a few apple-droppings from the orchards that fringed the common the stream went onward placidly to fall down the slope by the schoolhouse. Strong water-cress grew thickly where the water splayed out below a one-arched bridge. Retrieving a few apples, Paddy plucked also for the Master some cress with its metallic burning flavour, and munching apples and cress, they went on together. From somewhere, far away and unseen on the great plain, came the pop-popping of sportsmen's guns: faint echoes of a lost battle.

'I wasn't much older than yourself, Paddy, the day they dug the skeleton of the soldier out of the Black Trench ahead of us there. Clutching his gun just the way he fell two hundred years before. They dug themselves into the trench and fought to the last. There were a lot of old guns and bones, and coins scattered among the bones. Did they plan to spend them when the day was done? Did they rattle them in their pockets the way the Inspector does?'

The Inspector, deprived of the musket-balls, was, like the cork tree, an accusing ghost.

'Some day I'd like to see a stone raised here, Paddy, by the Black Trench and in memory of all the dead.'

'Would the big tree have been there on the day of the battle, Master?'

'It could well have been.'

'If a man was up there could he have seen it all?'

'The cavalry. The foot. The cannon. The camp-followers. The dead and dying.'

'The war-horse that went home alone.'

'Or just glimpses through gaps in the smoke, Paddy. Old-time battles were smoky affairs.'

'If men lived in trees they'd see a lot more, Master, wouldn't they?'

'You're a great lad for the trees, Paddy?'

'I like trees, Master.'

'Climbing up on high, Paddy, a man comes closer to himself. The saints and the sages and the Lord himself proved that. There's that mountain in the West of Ireland where Saint Patrick climbed up to pray. You'll go to it sometime on the pilgrimage. Thousands of people and lots of them fasting and barefooted going up like saints or goats over sharp stones in the early morning. Then the sun comes out and the mist breaks and down below you see the hundreds of islands in Clew Bay, the islands of the blest, and spread out beyond them the whole ocean, infinity, eternity. That's what Saint Patrick was after. People climb up, Paddy, to repent of their sins.'

'Yes, Master.'

'When you were up the tree, Paddy, did you ever find out why you broke the sweeping-brush and the floorboards?'

'Yes, Master,' he said.

It had been an evening of brown fresh in the river, and the trout below at the double bridge gaping their mouths wide for bait-feeding, and Paddy and the Bully Cryan and two others had been detailed as a punishment for lessons missed to stay behind and clean and dust the entire school. Taut with vexation Paddy had suddenly, and only imperfectly knowing why, started to hammer the floor with his brush until he made bits of the brush and smashed a hole in the floor-boards.

'It was to frighten Bully Cryan, Master.'

'Did it succeed?'

'A bit, I think. Coming down the tree frightened him more.'

'It would. The violent are seldom really frightened by violence. But they would be by a blinding light on the road or by a descent from above. And did you ever discover, Paddy, why you ate the pheasant?'

'I hate the taste of pheasant, Master. Nobody should ever eat those lovely birds. And it drives you mad with thirst.'

'Not an act of greed so, or even of hunger. But perhaps an act of repentance.'

'It was to make up for the musket-balls, Master. The musket-balls are in a box in a hole under the roots of the cork tree.'

'That I know, Paddy. Like yourself, I'm a great man for trees. But too old and stiff to go on the branches now, Paddy, I content myself with poking among the roots.'

'You knew all the time, so.'

'No, Paddy. Only since the morning I saw you running up the tree. The day of the pheasant.'

'You knew all the time I was up the tree? Even when I was missing?'

'What goes up must come down, Paddy. I knew you weren't lost or drowned. I knew you couldn't go far astray if you were merely closer to heaven than anybody else in the village: thinking your own thoughts.'

'We'll walk as far as the cork tree, Paddy,' he said, 'and reclaim that box of musket-balls. Nobody but ourselves need be any the wiser.'

They walked to the cork tree and back to the schoolhouse and the museum was complete again.

'And some day, Paddy, when you've a particularly good speckled trout, make a present of it to the Young Teacher's wife. I hear she's great on fish sauces. And even if her husband's a fine shot he still isn't so good with the rod and line. Not patient enough, perhaps.'

'Yes, Master.'

As it happened the next good fish Paddy got was a spring salmon which Daisy Coloured Trousers gratefully accepted and expertly cooked. She sent ample savoury cuts to the Old Master's wife and to Paddy's mother. On his next visit, too, the Inspector got his portion of the musket-balls, one of which, to the day of his death, ornamented his watch-chain.

The white horse went to the Curragh and the Phoenix Park, Baldoyle, Tramore, Galway, Listowel and, in the end, to Newmarket and won all before him. But as the mad major, who increased his fortune, by stake-money and the lavish laying of bets, said, 'It was to be expected. It was on the cards. It was in the stars and in signs in the heavens. Was there ever in history another horse that was trained by a steam-engine?'

THE PILGRIMS

Blue was the colour of the rosary, the colour of the Mother of God, of the hot steam screaming up from the black engine, of the sky arched over the morning town and the tiny station. Long before the train started the pilgrims were saying the rosary, a separate rosary in each carriage, blue voices swelling out, falling and rising, to the blue morning. Then with five decades finished the pilgrims rested from praying and talked about the world they lived in, about the town they were leaving and the town they were going to, about the journey before them to the holy place where the brown skull of the martyr dead for centuries was kept as a sign and a memorial in a glass box.

Listening to the talk, he looked out of the window at the coloured advertisements nailed to the railings on the opposite platform. He put his hands on his bare knees, his own flesh touching his own flesh, and shuddered with self-pity at the ignominy of short pants. He thought of the greater ignominy of dry shaves to sandpaper from his cheeks and chin the white cat-hairs that were less like a man's beard than they were like the fluff that gathered around what the cat left in the coal-hole. George had long trousers, good grey flannels with a fine crease in them. But then George was a man with seven years' experience of shaving and the brown wisdom of twenty-one in his eyes. George sat facing him and taking a part in the conversation.

The advertisements slowly moved away from him. Wheels clanked, gathering speed, over the metal of a bridge. He looked down at narrow backyards and small windows with blinds still drawn. That was a Protestant part of the town and Protestants didn't make pilgrimages and stayed in bed on Sunday mornings reading the English newspapers. When his ma and da reached for their rosaries a second time he made a sudden excuse-me noise that could mean only one of two things. He slipped out of the compartment into the empty swaying corridor. He watched the humpy ridges of the roofs going away from him to be swallowed up in the fields. George joined him.

'Your mother sent me out to see were you sick or something.'

He said, 'I'm not sick or anything.'

'They've got praying on the brain in there,' George said. 'They'll say the fifteen decades of the rosary if the Lord himself doesn't halt them. I can tell by the look in their eyes.'

A slow river curved through the green fields.

He said, 'Isn't that what a pilgrimage is for? All praying. An excursion is all drinking and fighting.'

'And a wee bit of coorting,' George said. 'But you wouldn't know about that.'

'I heard tell of it.'

'I was a year in a seminary,' George said. 'You can't tell me anything about pilgrimages.'

'You know everything.'

'I know that the people who go on excursions go on pilgrimages too. The only difference is they don't fight and there isn't much drink.'

Green was the colour of the fields on both sides of the railway, the colour of childhood and fun and the first kiss.

'Come on up the train,' said George. 'There might be card-playing somewhere.'

From end to end the train was blue with the rosary. They waited in a corner of the corridor outside a lavatory and gave the people time to tire of praying. Then they slipped into another compartment and sat down side by side. The old lady sitting opposite them manoeuvred her newspaper with the awkwardness of one unaccustomed to reading a newspaper in a moving vehicle. It was a local newspaper with wide clumsy pages and black blotchy print. She was a small, stout stump of a woman, her long black skirt billowing outwards and downwards to meet the shiny blackness of buttoned boots of patent leather, her solemn black bonnet almost sitting beside her, its ribbons dangling over the edge of the seat like two thin legs. She sighed loudly behind the newspaper. She folded the newspaper into very small folds. It crackled like a fire catching in weeds and dry sticks. Her face was fat with a hard square fatness and two black moles on her forehead were like the tops of screwnails holding the tough yellow skin in place and preserving it from wrinkles.

She sighed again and said loudly: 'It's a terrible thing to read a third cousin's name in the newspaper in connection with something as terrible as a wilful murder.'

She was as black as the soot up the chimney, he thought, and her face was as yellow as goose grease. But inside in her mind she was meditating on murder, and red was the colour of blood and murder, and of martyrdom, and the colour of the vestments the priest wore reading the mass in memory of a man or woman who died for the love of Christ.

The other people in the carriage sighed sympathetically. George was curious. George was always curious. Curiosity was stamped all over his thin, freckled face and sharp question-mark of a nose. It set his round protruding eyes shining like headlights. He leaned across the compartment and tapped the old lady on the knee. She was long gone past the time of life when a stranger's tap on the knee could be interpreted as anything other than courtesy. George said, 'Was it that your third cousin murdered somebody, ma'am?'

'He was murdered,' she sighed. 'Had his poor head battered clean off. On the threshold of his own barn. The motive was robbery.'

Her face wrinkled suddenly, the yellow skin defying for a moment the tightening pressure of the moles. It might have been the grimace of great grief or mental agony. It might just as readily have been the satisfied smile of a princess among her courtiers or an actress surrounded by her admirers, of any man or woman becoming for a moment the centre of interest and attention. For everybody in the compartment had suddenly sat up to listen. The case was in all the papers. When she spoke again it was not only to George but to her alert audience, to the whole world of prosaic people who had never a murdered relative.

'God rest the poor man,' she said. 'He was civil and innocent all the days of his life. Too trusting, by far. Very unlike his half-brother who two years ago had his name in the papers for something similar.'

'Was he murdered as well?' said George.

She blessed herself. She said, 'God between us and all harm it was worse. Farandaway worse. He murdered a poor girl and, by all accounts, marrying instead of murdering would have been better for both of them.'

The compartment shuddered.

'They were an unfortunate family,' she said. 'Those of you that are old enough might remember the time the servant man murdered the three unmarried sisters.'

Nobody seemed to remember it. She was queen and mistress of a horrified silence that absorbed everybody except George.

'Colm here heard his grandfather talking about it,' lied George.

He indicated Colm by putting his left hand upon Colm's right knee so that Colm for a moment forgot about murder and remembered the mortifying lack of long trousers.

'Well, the granduncle of this poor fellow that cut the girl's throat. . .'

'Was he the servant man that killed the three unmarried sisters?'

'No. But he found the bodies. And wasn't the murderer his best friend. They say the shock of the discovery affected the creature's mind.

He never did a day's good afterwards. He ended his life by jumping into a canal in England.'

George leaned back in his seat and breathed out slowly and audibly. Brown was the colour of freckles and of curiosity and even the brownest curiosity had to come sometime to the point of satiety. Green was the colour of the first kiss given and taken in the quiet corner of a field, and red was the colour of a man murdering a girl that he should have married, and black was the colour of the devil and of the clothes of a woman who knew too much about murder.

'May God have mercy on all their souls,' said George – with a panache of piety.

He raised his round eyes to the white ceiling of the compartment and beyond the ceiling was the blue heaven.

'That they may share in all the graces of the pilgrimage,' said the woman.

She whipped out a rosary as long as a measuring tape and with each individual bead the size of a schoolboy's marble, and before George or Colm could escape, the gentleness of prayer was around them as blue as the air, and red murder was forgotten and martyrdom and green kisses, and the prayers they said were set like jewels around the mysteries of the resurrection, the ascension, the descent of the Holy Ghost, the assumption, and the crowning of the Mother of God in the blue courts of heaven.

Grey was the colour of age, the colour of the hair of old men and women, of old streets and high tottering houses and ancient towers, the colour of history.

His mother said, 'Where were you all the time, boy?'

'Got stuck in the crowd far up the train, ma.'

'Did you say your rosary?'

'We said several,' George replied. 'Isn't there a great crowd on the pilgrimage?'

Colm's mother smiled and said there was surely. She always smiled when George spoke politely to her and George always spoke politely to elderly ladies who, for some reason surpassing Colm's comprehension, always liked George.

And there most certainly was a great crowd on the pilgrimage. The pilgrims jammed the exits from the platform. The sun was shining. Outside on the roadway a brass band was slowly, solemnly, playing the music of a hymn. Some of the pilgrims began to sing with the band. George and Colm waited cautiously on the edge of the crowd. A thin monkish man coming from behind caught George by the arm. He said, 'George. The right man in the right place, the very man I want.'

'Hello, Mr. Richards,' George said. 'Hello, Rosaleen.'

Rosaleen stood at a little distance and smiled sweetly. Her father was baldheaded and blackavised, as solemn, in his dark suit, as the high grey houses of the antique town, but Rosaleen was plump, pretty, yellow-haired, and her little body curved attractively. George had one eye on the father and one on Rosaleen. Colm had one eye on Rosaleen and one on George. Green was the colour of the first kiss but the colour of the second kiss and afterwards, or the colour of warm curves, could easily be the yellow colour of ripening corn.

'You're an educated young man, George,' said Mr. Richards.

He handed George a short length of red ribbon.

'Tie this ribbon around your left arm and that'll make you a steward.'

George tied the ribbon around his left arm.

'I'm a steward,' he said. 'What happens now?'

'You stand outside the station and help to direct the people to the church.'

'I was never in this town in my life.'

'We'll soon mend that,' said Mr. Richards.

He sketched with a pencil on the back of an envelope. He handed the sketch to George.

'That's the town,' he said.

George glanced at the sketch, then put it into his breast pocket with what seemed to Colm a pantomime of carefulness. In the background Rosaleen was laughing silently at the antics of George. The solemn man was looking solemnly at the struggling crowd. He said, 'Tell them to go straight down the hill, turn right over the bridge, turn left in the centre of the town and stop at the first church on the right.'

George beating time with the index finger of his right hand, repeated the words as if he was memorising them. George was a card. When he had repeated his instructions twice he gave a military salute and said, 'Aye, aye, sir.' The solemn man didn't even know he was being fooled. Rosaleen was laughing quietly behind her father's back. Yellow and gold were the colours of her laughter and the colours of the strengthening sunshine. Colm wished to God that he could be a card like George.

Headed by the band the pilgrims were going in a shapeless mass down the slope towards the centre of the town. Colm hesitated. He said, 'What about directing the people?'

George laughed.

'Would you pay any attention to that holymary of a man? I wouldn't mind directing his wee daughter.'

'She's a nice girl.'

'She's all that and something else too,' George said.

He looked sideways at Colm. He patted Colm's shoulder. He said, 'Take the advice of an older man. Don't worry your head about her or the likes of her. She's bad medicine for the young.'

'She's only three years older than I am myself.'

George halted to lean on the wall at the side of the road, to look down on the town, streets and houses and factories, on the wide river with two steamers moored at the quayside, and to look across the river at grey steeples that could chime and grey towers that were always silent.

'A girl of sixteen is a lot older than a boy of thirteen,' he said. 'Especially when the girl is Rosaleen and the boy has short pants.'

Colm said nothing. His soul was weak with the bitter shame of those bare knees. The old suit he wore going to school had long pants but his mother wouldn't allow him to wear his old suit on a Sunday and his father wouldn't buy him a new Sunday suit until the one he had was worn out. For a moment, walking in the blinding sun, he understood the colours of anger and murder.

'What I want now,' George said, 'is something to eat.'

They turned to the right over the bridge. The pavements were crowded with pilgrims gulping down the salt air that came blowing in cool from the sea. In the middle of the bridge a girl called to George. She was tall and sunburned and darkheaded and she wore a blue coat. Her voice had all the round, rough, friendly vowels of country places. The blue coat had about it the musky odour of turf smoke and faintly from her clean skin Colm smelled the smell of plain, unscented soap. She said, 'George, it's generations since I've seen you.'

George eyed her calmly. He said mechanically, 'Go straight down the hill, turn right over the bridge, turn left in the centre of the town and stop at the first church on the right.'

She wasn't easy to snub. She laughed. She said, 'You're as daft as ever, George. You never come to the crossroads now.'

'I'm a steward now,' he said. 'I haven't a minute. I'm run off my feet directing people.'

A passing crowd of pilgrims swept between them. Colm saw George moving away speedily across the bridge and he followed as fast as he could, looking back once or twice for a sight of the tall girl. But the crowd had swallowed her and her coat that was the colour of the rosary and the colour of the sea and of the wide river flowing down to the sea.

The smell of her washed skin troubled his senses and he marvelled at the greatness of George who could afford to despise such riches.

The big event of the day was the procession and the procession was all the colours of the rainbow: no less than seven bands blaring golden music; the Children of Mary dressed in blue-and-white; the silken banners of all the confraternities; the Sunday clothes of all the marching men and women; the white surplices of the priests and altar-boys; the brown Franciscans and the white Dominicans, and always the yellow sunlight pouring out of a blue sky and brightening the walls that were grey with age.

Colm liked the procession, the slow solemn movement, the music of the bands, the wind flapping the banners, the watching crowds lining the street that led up to the church where the shrine was. He liked it because, in spite of the indecency of short pants, he walked with the men who walked strongly and steadily and four deep. He was a man moving in a world of men and for a while he forgot the girl with the blue coat and the girl with the yellow hair.

The bands stopped playing as they approached the church. The bandsmen stood in silence at the sides of the street while the procession turned to the right through wide iron gates and went up steps and through a high-arched doorway. Candles burned on a distant altar. Organ music accompanied shuffling steps as the pilgrims filed into the pews. A priest stood waiting in the pulpit, motionless as a statue, until the shuffling ceased and the pews were filled. Then he crossed himself with the crucifix of his rosary beads and commenced the rosary. The voices of the pilgrims rose in the responses, swelling upwards and outwards, filling the church up to the carved wooden angels on the high rafters.

Colm and George knelt side by side at the outer end of a pew in the aisle to the right of the pulpit. It was a pleasant enough place to be. The breeze blew cool in through an open doorway. You could look out through the doorway at green trees and sunshine. Colm would have looked out through the doorway all the time but his mother was sitting two seats behind him and he could feel her eyes boring into the small of his back.

The rosary ended. The pilgrims rose from their knees and sat down on the hard seats. The priest said in a loud voice, 'The souls of the just are in the hand of God and the torment of death shall not touch them. In the sight of the unwise they seemed to die and their departure was taken for misery; and their going away from us for utter destruction: but they are in peace.'

George leaned towards Colm and whispered something unintelligible, then rose from his seat, genuflected, and was gone into the sunshine.

The priest was saying, 'As gold in the furnace he hath proved them, and as a victim of a holocaust he hath received them, and in time there shall be respect had to them.'

George might be back in a minute. He might have been feeling ill. He might merely have wanted to go out for a mouthful of air. But for some reason that he could not yet quite understand Colm was nervous and fidgetty. He listened uneasily to the priest, 'The just shall shine, and shall run to and fro like sparks among the reeds. They shall judge nations, and rule over people, and their Lord shall reign for ever.'

The space on the seat left by George was cold and empty. He felt it with his left hand. But he didn't risk a sideways look that his mother might consider a yielding to distraction. He kept his eyes on the priest in the pulpit. The priest said, 'Words taken, my dearly beloved brethren, from the Book of Wisdom, the third chapter.'

Then he led the pilgrims in making the sign of the cross. He cleared his throat, steadied himself by resting the palms of his hands on the edge of the pulpit, and was off into the sermon. He was good for an hour at least, thought Colm, looking at the size of him and listening to the sound of him, and George was gone like a spark among the reeds, but not in the least like one of the just. For the just who had in the sight of the unwise seemed to die had hardly bothered much about maidens with yellow hair, and Colm's instinct, shivering on the threshold of knowledge, told him that Rosaleen was gone also, like a yellow flame between grey, ancient walls. He rested his hands on his bare knees and gritted his teeth. George had known that he couldn't follow because his mother's eyes were nailing him to his place on the hard wooden seat. That thought set a red mist before his eyes and the priest and the pulpit and the pilgrims faded away and the words of the sermon thundered in his ears as if God were speaking to him alone.

Afterwards, searching the town for George, the words came back to him and fragments of the ceremony that followed the sermon.

He leaned on the parapet of the bridge, losing his own identity in the movement of the blue water going in one mass and glittering with the sun to the neighbouring sea.

After the text the preacher had said, 'These words apply most appropriately, dear brethren to the martyr whose memory we celebrate today.'

So many centuries had turned the town grey, all the time the river flowing down to the sea, since the martyr had lived the life of a wandering hunted man. The preacher had preached about those wanderings, about the journey to Europe and the quiet years spent there in studious and cloistered preparation, about the return to Ireland in a small ship sailing precariously over stormy seas. The preacher had gone into great detail about the perils of stormy seas. Studying the smooth movement of the river, Colm tried to imagine what a stormy sea looked like: dark water rising and falling under dark skies.

The preacher had gone into greater detail about the wandering years that followed the martyr's return to Ireland: the minister of a proscribed religion going from house to house with a price on his head, celebrating mass in open places when the hills were white with snow. White was the colour of silence and of eternity. The preacher had grown red in the face and loud with anger when he came to the capture, the betrayal by false friends, the lying charges, the torture and brutal execution.

With his left hand Colm felt the cold empty seat where George had sat: the false friend gone with a girl whose hair was yellow like gold, the yellow gold of the lifted monstrance, the gold of the flames of the candles burning on the altar, the golden voices of the choristers singing Latin words in praise of God, chanting Latin words as the pilgrims filed one by one past the shrine of the martyr and out again into golden sunshine.

Once in the course of his search for George he saw his father and mother at a distance along a crowded street. He was hungry and he guessed they were on their way to have tea before the train left. But he stifled his hunger and avoided them, running along a side street that narrowed to a lane and along the lane until it changed into a path that went by the side of the river and away from the town. He followed the path, the gossiping water to his right and a whispering meadow to his left, until the town was far behind him, and the sunlight weakening, and shadows gathering in corners of distant fields.

He found George and Rosaleen sitting on the grass by the edge of the path. George had his legs crossed like a tailor squatting. He was chewing a piece of grass and saying something to Rosaleen out of the corner of his mouth. Rosaleen was combing her yellow hair, her arms raised, her soft mouth fenced with hairpins, her breasts and shoulders disturbed with laughter at the humour of what George was saying.

'Fancy meeting you here,' George said.

'It's a free country, isn't it?'

'It's all that and heaven too,' George said.

He stood up and stretched himself lazily.

'Is the praying all over?'

'It is.'

'My apologies for deserting you,' George said. 'But I couldn't wait to hear about the martyr's sufferings. It would have broken my heart.'

Rosaleen, standing straight while George dusted fragments of grass from the back of her skirt, tinkled with merriment. George grinned. Colm smiled weakly. Slowly and silently they walked back towards the town, Rosaleen walking between George and Colm, Rosaleen and George holding hands and now and again pressing against each other. The river went gossiping beside them and the whispering of the meadow-grass died away into shadows.

In the crowded street near the big bridge they came so suddenly on his father and mother that he had no time to run or dodge. His mother said, 'Where were you all the time, boy? We searched the town for you.'

'We went walking after the devotions,' George said. 'Wasn't it a fine sermon?'

A lie no matter how shameless, was never the least trouble to lucky George.

'It was indeed,' his mother said. 'But you'd want to hurry to get something to eat before the train goes.'

'I'm waiting for the late train,' George said.

'Can't I wait too?' he asked.

'Indeed you can't,' his mother said. 'It's all very well for George. George is a grown man.'

She looked at George and George looked at her and they laughed with understanding.

Walking away between his father and mother he didn't speak a word, didn't look back once over his shoulder. He knew that George and Rosaleen were going somewhere hand-in-hand and that they had already forgotten about him.

There was no room for him in the compartment so his mother sent him up the train to find a seat for himself. From end to end the train was blue-black with the rosary. He stumbled along the swaying corridor looking into compartment after compartment, seeing quiet hands holding rosary beads and quiet faces with eyes staring into infinity. Nobody noticed him, a pale face passing the glass, a small boy staggering along the corridor, weak and shivering and ready to cry with the overpowering force of his anger. The train was crowded. There was no room for him in any compartment.

He went on until a doorknob refused to turn in his hand and he knew that there was nothing but the engine, steel and coal as black as night and the devil. Holding the doorknob in his two hands he sobbed painful dry sobs. What had the martyr suffered that was worse than this: the shame and ignominy and humiliation, the bullying and the betrayal. He turned back down the corridor, looking mechanically into compartment after compartment, looking suddenly into one pair of eyes that did not stare into infinity. It was the girl with the blue coat and the sight of her renewing his agony he fled, hiding for a while in a dimly-lighted water-closet, watching his pale reflection in a dirty, spotted mirror. When he opened the door and came out into the corridor she was standing patiently waiting.

'Hello,' she said. 'You left George behind you.'

'George left me.'

The light in the corridor was blue, a lighter shade than the blue of her coat. The rocking of the train bumped them suddenly against each other, he steadied himself, his right hand on her shoulder.

'That's a way George has,' she said bitterly. 'Leaving people behind him.'

Looking over her shoulder into the darkness he knew how she had been hurt when George snubbed her, hurt painfully somewhere behind her loud talk and careless laughter.

'A person like George always meets his match,' she said. 'He won't leave the girl with the yellow hair.'

They stood side by side in the corridor looking out into the black world that was spotted now and again with the light in the window of some farmhouse. Their shoulders touched. He pressed closer. His nose was once again troubled with the odour of skin scrubbed clean with plain, unperfumed soap. Her left arm was around his shoulders, the way two friendly boys might walk home from school.

'Do you ride a bike?' she asked.

'I do.'

'Then you should cycle out to the crossroads.'

'What for?'

'We have great fun there in the evenings. Dancing to the bagpipes and everything.'

He didn't like dancing. He didn't like the bagpipes, but he knew that dancing and the bagpipes could be the beginning of something. Sitting in loneliness and anger could only be the end of everything: sitting in loneliness and anger remembering George and yellow-haired Rosaleen walking hand-in-hand beside the smooth river and the lovely shadowy evening going behind them and gathering in the old streets and around the towers and spires. Remembering was death. Cycling and dancing to bagpipes and smelling the smell of plain soap was life.

'I'll go out surely,' he said.

Her arm tightened about his shoulders. He turned towards her and kissed her. He had to raise himself a little on tiptoes in order to reach her lips. She had to steer her own mouth carefully down to his. He had never kissed a girl before and, anyway the train was jolting wildly from side to side. He smelled and tasted the cigarettes she had been smoking.

From end to end the train was blue-black with the rosary. Blue was the colour of the rosary, the colour of the mother of God, of the light in the corridor and the coat that covered the body of the laughing, sunburned girl. Black was the colour of the night all around them, of mouth finding mouth in the darkness and making a beginning and an end.

THE HOUSE IN JAIL SQUARE

When my mother went to school as a day pupil in the Mercy Convent in the town of Clonelly she lodged in Jail Square in the house of a respectable widow who had two daughters aged between twenty and thirty. Thirty years later when my mother sent me down from the mountains to the Brothers' School in the same town, she lodged me in the House in Jail Square with two stranded, derelict, time-worn, desiccated beldames aged somewhere between fifty and sixty. They were happier people, I soon found out, when my mother knew them, or perhaps in her days they had hope and things seemed different. Or perhaps, as I had reason to think, they just didn't like males. I was twelve years old, a timid biddable boy, at least as far as elderly ladies were concerned, and for two school terms I lived in slavery to Maryanne and Ellen. During the Christmas holidays I was unable even to begin to reveal to my mother the depth of my servitude to those two female dragons. In their cold grey stone mansion I was message-boy, gardener, waiter, scavenger, scullery-maid, chamber-maid, butler, duster, polisher, and something to scold, abuse and lecture. They would have had no life without me and, to give the situation its irony, my mother underwrote their tyranny to the extent of thirty shillings weekly.

'Aloysius, you will run home punctually at lunch hour.'

That was practically my morning greeting.

Sleep still in my eyes, the sour prospect of school before me, I would feebly protest, 'Half-hour. We don't get an hour.'

'Aloysius, don't quibble. At lunch hour you must go for the daily paper and do another message.'

'Give me the penny now and I'll get the paper on the way home. That'll save time. I'll be biffed if I'm late for afternoon school.'

'We will give you the penny at the fit and proper moment.'

'What other message?'

'Never mind, Aloysius. Just you do as we say. That's what your dear mother would wish you to do. We still have to decide about the other message.'

So my lunch half-hour went into sprinting. In Clonelly, a hilly town,

Jail Square was at the top of one high hill. To get to the Brothers' School you descended and ascended again along Old Castle Street. The school was halfway up that street and the shops of the town were all at the top of it. I found it was easier on the wind and sinews if I pelted up the steep blue pavement of Old Castle Street to the rhythm dreamed up by that Wizard of the North and bore of the schoolroom, Sir Walter Scott. With my lips compressed and breathing through my nose as somebody had told me the supreme athletes did, I repeated in my mind, 'Fleet foot on the corrie, sage counsel in cumber, red hand in the foray, how sound is thy slumber.' It was rubbish, but it helped me to run, swept me ultimately back to school in time, and diminished the aggregate of corporal punishment.

On days when Walter Scott wouldn't work in harness with me I thought, to speed my stride, of the great running horses of that season. As I'll point out shortly, I had good and sufficient reason to know their noble names and, although I should have hated them, I didn't. There was Ramtapa who had hard luck at Newmarket where Flares gave a fine performance; Corofin who was fancied for the Irish Cesarewitch in spite of the claims of Spion Hill, Lady Ellen, Call Him, Silver Salt, Ringwood Sun, Yellow-dine, Gorgia, Glen Levin. There was the slinky femme fatale, Serpolette, and Statarella, lovely as a poppy, who was headlined as the best of the fillies; and Speakeasy II, who in spite of the bibulous habits of himself and his sire, got the vote for the chief event in Naas; and Eastern Ford and Foxy and Port Lester. They were all allies in my sprint. It saddens me to think that by now they may all be dead.

Clutched in one hand I would have the penny that Maryanne had given me for the day's paper. Clutched in the other hand I would have the two sixpenny bits – sixpence each way – wrapped in paper, that Ellen had given me for the bookie. The name of the chosen runner was written on the paper. Idling on the steep slope of Old Castle Street my free-and-easy school companions, who had no lunchtime chores to do, would click their tongues or catcall or whistle rhythmically to the beat of my feet. As well as I could, and that wasn't completely, I closed my eyes and ears to their presence.

'Run, Alo, run.'

'You'll never have the bet laid in time.'

'He couldn't run so well up hill if we hadn't put the shoes on him the day he came down from the mountains.'

'Nothing but bare feet up where he comes from.'

'Run, Alo, run rabbit, run, run, run.'

The House in Jail Square looked solid from the outside. It was one of

eight grey stone houses in which the higher officials of the prison had
lived when there had been a prison high on a hill where the river
escaped from the last red metal bridge and curved northwards away
from the town. But, in spite of its appearance of dry stone solidity, that
house was musty with dry rot and when you moved in it everything
rattled or jingled. There were hundreds of things to rattle and jingle.
Maryanne and Ellen had accumulated the years around them in
whatnots congested with china ornaments, pictures of officers in
antique dress-uniforms or noble ladies standing languidly where
smooth marble steps descended to smoother artificial water, in useless
creaking furniture, clocks that didn't work, stones shaped fantastically
by some remote ocean, sea-shells on mantelpieces, family portraits by
the score, and coloured glass balls used as floats by trawler fishermen.
The most cluttered, clinking room in the house was the museum of a
drawing-room where the ritual of choosing the horse of the day was
observed with unholy solemnity. On Saturday mornings when I was
free from school, and provided I was sufficiently advanced with my
housework, I was allowed or compelled to witness it.

'Have you the hatpin, Ellen?'

'I have. The Lord direct us, Maryanne.'

'Pray, Aloysius, pray.'

Maryanne's right hand enclosing Ellen's left and both their hands
grasping a hatpin, long and bent like a sabre, they would sneak up on
the previous day's evening paper where it lay prostrate and helpless on a
couch.

'Sacred Heart guide our hand.'

Plunge and then stab and the broad couch was pierced and the horse
or mare impaled. It was a savage rite, and when I watched it I waited to
hear the whinnying scream of a noble animal wounded by witchcraft.
For I loved horses just because they were horses, and I loved old sporting
prints and photographs of horses, and fast-galloping horses in the acrid
dust of western films, and the noise of the hooves of carthorses on the
old streets of the town, and the sound of a trotting horse pulling a trap
on a country road on a June evening. Maryanne and Ellen, you'd know
to look at them, may have seen but never loved a horse.

Maryanne – tall, scrawny, brown-skinned, ribbed like the skeleton of
a salt sea-herring, as prickly as a blossomless whin bush, with black,
brooding eyes and a nose like a beak and a distinct moustache – would
inspect the mutilated newspaper and read out the name of the
perforated horse, 'It's a nice name today.'

'It could be a lucky name.'

Small, round-faced, with soft, rubicund cheeks that bore no relation to her hard black nut of a heart, Ellen would write the name on a slip of paper, wrap the paper around the two sixpenny bits, never, oh God never, not even once by accident or error, around a single shilling. Times I thought they must be minting their own sixpennies.

'The boy's day-dreaming, Maryanne.'

'Arouse yourself, Aloysius. Thinking long never buttered bread.'

'Here's the money for the message. The name's on the paper.'

'And don't dare to turn back on the way. It's bad luck to turn back. Did you put on your left or your right shoe first this morning?'

'My right.'

'We hope you're truthful. It's bad luck to put on the left shoe before the right.'

'Saint Colmcille was being pursued by enemies,' said Ellen, 'and they caught him because he put on the left shoe first.'

'And the saint put an everlasting curse on anyone after him who would ever put on the left shoe before the right.'

I always left unexpressed my sceptical feeling that Saint Colmcille, like the Franciscans a mile outside the town, would have worn sandals. Yet such is the power of early conditioning that, as God is my judge, to this day I always put the right shoe on before the left.

'And don't waste a second,' said Maryanne, 'even if it is Saturday morning.'

'You have the potatoes to scrub and the hall-floor to polish.'

'Your pocket money will have to go to help to replace the flower-pot you knocked off the pedestal and down the basement stairs last Saturday.'

'Sheer vandalism. Boys are destructive demons.'

'The good flower-pot our mother left us with the Saint Joseph's lily. The lily will never bloom again.'

'And when you come back you can run out again for the morning paper.'

'Couldn't I do the two messages together?'

'Do as we say, Aloysius. You have an idle day from school.'

'The devil and idle hands, you know.'

'Think of Montgomery,' said Maryanne, 'the man who was hanged for murder in the days of the Old Jail. In the death cell he cursed the idle hours and companions that led him to the scaffold.'

In Maryanne's stygian cosmos both saints and sinners spent a lot of time cursing things and people.

'Run now. Stop to speak to nobody. Idle words never sowed corn.'

It was at least a momentary relief to run from them, steeply up Old Castle Street, shutting my agonised soul to the vision of the freedom other boys enjoyed on Saturday morning. I was fleet-foot on the corrie, whatever that was. I was a horse, I was a jockey, I was a centaur, I was Pegasus, Bucephalus, and Tipperary Tim who won the Grand National at a hundred to one. The town's blue, grain-picking pigeons scattered before my galloping hooves. I was cossacks, I was United States cavalry, I was cowboys and Indians and the Light Brigade. I was Ascot and Aintree and the Curragh of Kildare and the Dublin Horse Show, and the colour and the paddocks, the cheers, the satin sheen of bay mares and black stallions. For a few galloping moments the silence and gloom of the musty old house were as remote as the death-cell with its curses and repentant statements before hanging.

My most satisfactory release from Maryanne and Ellen – they couldn't deny me fresh air – led, in my odd moments of leisure, out of the Square through the arched gateway of the Old Jail. Once through the gateless arch, the echoes of your feet clanking on the flagstone like metal, you were out into complete freedom on a windy escarpment high above the looping river. By constant quarrying for other building the strong walls of the Jail had been reduced to an archaeological pattern, and the seasons had mercifully half-clothed the grey remains in nettles, dock-leaves and parched yellow grass. On the dusty flagstone, where prisoners had once stood to hear bolts barred behind them and to know despair, I stood and sensed liberation and saw far away the blue curves of my own mountains. The best and longest time I ever spent there was the sunny day of the horse-jumping and the military tattoo in the flat holm beyond the river. There went the wonderful horses, curvetting, rising and descending in the most graceful of jumping dances, taking or refusing walls or fences, displaying dressage, melting their own sensitive moods into the skills of the riders. No daft old women in a dark house could prick them with a hatpin. I wanted so badly to be across the river and down on the flat land with the crowds, but that week my pocket money had gone down the drain to compensate for two soup plates that had slipped to destruction when I was washing the dishes; and those two hags made the confiscation of the pocket money my mother sent me appear in the light of a favour.

'Aloysius, when will you learn to be careful?'

'We don't really like making you pay for the damage you do.'

'But we don't want to let your mother know you're so destructive. It would break her heart.'

The day of the horse-jumping, too, was the day I first saw the inscribed stone. A rustle in the weeds, a rat, set me hunting and poking, stick in hand, through the ground-pattern of small, coffin-narrow shapes that had once been cells. Insects scurried away from the stick into mazes of yellow sun-starved stems, and there lay the damp, fallen stone sharply-lettered to do honour to justice: Thomas Henry Montgomery was hanged here for the murder of William Glass. My first chill thought was that it was a bitter thing to hang any man in such a corner of weeds and crawling desolation. But then my imagination couldn't help rebuilding the confining walls, the cell, the scaffold, the trap, the dangling rope. The morning knell tolled. Towards this corner the slow, heavy steps approached. The parson prayed the last prayer. The blindfolded body dropped like lead. The neck cracked. The helpless pinioned feet swinging in a pendulum could have cut the air just where my head and shoulders were.

The relief it was to find that the walls were not really around me, that I could be an Indian on a pony and trot back to the bluff above the river and, hand shading eyes, look down on the pale-faces at their capers in the showgrounds and see the smoke signals of my own people spiralling and puffing up from blue hills that seemed as far away as Montana. Out there in the evening behind those curved hills the old men would be walking to the forge at the crossroads. Old men were my favourite people. They were complete, and alive like bushes; and for three of the old men of our mountains I had a particular veneration.

Old Paddy Horish had made his son a priest and, in the process, spent two hundred pounds. In those days on the mountain, where cautious men had the heart in twopence, that was big money. For ever after he judged the magnitude of any enterprise by whether or not it cost two hundred pounds. At Taggart's smithy, outside in summer, inside in winter by the glowing forge, Paddy, silent and thoughtful, his life's great work accomplished, listened while Chuck Taggart, the smith, and the other men talked of the news of the world. The Germans were to build the biggest airship the world had ever seen.

'Do you think now, Chuck, would it cost two hundred pounds?'

The Yankees were putting up in New York a building would scrape the stars.

'Do you think now, Chuck, would it cost two hundred pounds?'

Next week the British would launch on Belfast Lough a liner a mile long.

'Do you think now, Chuck, would it cost two hundred pounds?'

Nobody ever laughed. Paddy's standard of measurement was no more comic than the twelve inch-rule or old Peter Scott's one and only known way of judging the desirability of a woman. From as high on Broughderg Mountain as human life could exist Peter Scott rode bareback on a white jennet to the smithy to punctuate the fine talk with lament for mischance in marriage: I always thought I would marry a fine, healthy, red-cheeked girl.

The wife the Lord had allowed him was yellow-faced and ailing, a drain on his resources in doctor's bills, a valiant sufferer but no great bearer of sons and no use at all in a heavy harvest or at carrying pots of spuds to the pigs. As the women of the two worlds of Erin were, by the power of the Dagda, the father of the gods, paraded in vision before the eyes of the lovesick Aengus, the sun-god, so, through the mind of old Peter Scott, all the strong girls he had never possessed passed like a procession of buxom, dancing village maidens in a festival in Faust: 'I always thought I would marry a fine, healthy, red-cheeked girl.'

The talk would always touch on a consideration as profound as the nature of the First Cause: When would Big Joe Gormley, who was bedridden, allow his son-in-law to move the five-gallon keg of poteen embedded in the thatch since the day of wrath when the bishop of the diocese made the distilling, and transporting or consuming of illicit whisky a reserved sin. On the bed from which he would never arise, Joe, once the mountain's best distiller and most furious drunkard, had developed religious scruples. It was a sight to see him haul himself to a sitting position with the aid of a rope tied to the foot of the bed and look in love and horrors of remorse at that symbol of past sin, the brown protruding belly of the keg.

'We'll drink it at his wake,' Chuck the smith would say. 'We'll drink the bishop's health.'

And Chuck, who sang bass in the parish choir, would roar out to the rhythm of swinging hammers and flying sparks the words of a randy old Limerick ballad:

> 'And there, by my sowl, were the priests in a bunch
> Round a big roaring fire drinking tumblers of punch,
> Singing Ballinamona, ho ro,
> And the juice of the barley for me.'

'There was a robber in London yesterday,' somebody reading the paper would say, 'stole a jewel as big as your fist from the flat of a film actress.'

'Do you think now, Chuck, would it cost two hundred pounds?'

Those were my mountains and those my beloved old men, and out there was the happy holiday freedom of my home: hedges, laughter, hay-making, strong tea on the windy, sunny, upland bog at the saving of the turf, running on white roads, and the Rooskey river wriggling for ever down its long valley. There was a grey heron always haunted the one pool in the Rooskey river. His day-long meditation, broken only by an odd lightning dart at the sweetness of a speckled trout, was my perfect symbol of content and peace. The world, as he saw it, was water like moving crystal, clean sand and silver gravel. Looking down now, from my height, on the deep soiled river escaping from the town's sprawling limbs my heart made my eyes transfer the heron from the happy mountains to that tired, ravished water and, seeing the heron, I saw home and heard the Rooskey river and the wind in rowan trees and whin bushes, and the contented garrulity of men as old as the Fenians, and the melodeon at a mountainy dance and the laughter of the young – until the shriek of round-faced Ellen, with the voice of barbed wire, recalled me to the shades of the prison house.

'Aloysius. Stop idling, boy. It's time and more than time to prepare for tea.'

Then back through the gateway, where happy men had once passed to freedom, I went to dust and polish, wash dishes, peel potatoes. Times, meditating on my life in Jail Square, I'd think also the fine thing it could be to be hanged decent and have it all over with.

I told them about my discovery of the murder stone.

'To think of it lying there all those years,' said Maryanne, 'as a lasting testimony to the wickedness of man.'

'Like the Ten Commandments graven in stone,' said Ellen.

I was rash enough to ask them who Thomas Henry Montgomery had been.

'He was a policeman,' Maryanne said.

'What would a policeman be doing murdering?'

'Don't contradict, Aloysius. He was a policeman, as we said. A high officer. He was a wicked man and he's damned in hell. He cursed the hour that ever he was born.'

'Idleness and evil companions,' said Ellen.

In bits and scraps of sombre dialogue I heard from them, by way of homily, the story of the famous case. It had been a good old-fashioned Irish murder, direct as dynamite. 'Twas with the sharpened point of a file Montgomery did it, striking Glass in the ear, as he stooped, totting and computing, over his banker's desk.

'Pretending all the while to be his friend,' said Ellen. 'Oh, the rascality of men.'

'Glass was no better,' said Maryanne. 'There was something at the trial that he knew about his sister and Montgomery.'

'Poor woman. Betrayed between two villains.'

'There was that in it too, as well as money. Drink and gambling, debts and evil passion.'

'And there was a coward of a man from your part of the country, Aloysius, a farmer who saw the murder with his own two eyes and was afraid to say a word about it.'

'He feared the police would say he did it.'

'The police would say anything.'

'He drove past the bank standing up in his cart at the very moment Montgomery struck the fatal blow. He could see in through the top half of the bank window.'

'Years afterwards, on his deathbed, he confessed what he saw.'

'And Montgomery rifled the safe and hid the money in a wood.'

'And didn't the flood come and wash the notes down the stream, and a little boy saw them and told his father.'

'The hand of God.'

'Working in mysterious ways.'

'Grinding slowly, but exceedingly small,' said Ellen.

'Drink and gambling.'

'And sin and idleness, Maryanne.'

'Indeed, yes. Let his fate be a warning to all young men.'

My discovery of the stone enabled them for days to dwell happily, all the time pointing morals for my benefit, in the shadow of the murder. If I was dilatory in rising in the morning or in my lunchtime gallop, or slovenly in washing, scrubbing or polishing, or merely happily absent with my own thoughts and the heron in the Rooskey river, I was reminded of the fate of Thomas Henry Montgomery. They quoted, or invented, his death-cell speech of repentance, his bewailing of bad company, his renunciation of the world – which meant, according to Maryanne, all his fellow males. The thought of the accident, the hand of God, that had betrayed him, disturbed even my moments of contemplation above the big river. For every tiny island of foam struggling away from the weir became a pound note, eloquent of robbery and murder, drifting on for ever to find some horrible, eternal sea. Then home from school I came one day to find the stone enthroned on the broken lily's pedestal in the narrow polished hallway. With washing soda and hot water they had scoured it in a big zinc bath. The lettering stood out sharp and harsh as a recrimination. The daily dusting of the stone became part of my duties. It was the mercy of God, I thought, whatever about his vengeful hand, that they demolished the scaffold after the hanging of Montgomery. Dusting and scrubbing a scaffold would be uphill work.

'That there's a historic stone,' Maryanne said. 'He was the last man ever to get the rope in the Old Jail.'

'The very last,' said Ellen.

'Not but that there were many since in this town,' said Maryanne, 'would have benefited from similar treatment.'

'We could name their names,' said Ellen.

It was Red Cunningham and the new lodger who in their different ways sowed within me the seeds of revolt. Left to myself I'd have been a sheep for ever. Red Cunningham was a mountain ram. He was small, snub-nosed and freckled, with baggy tweed pants that were too long for him, and a blue serge jacket too tight for him and spotted like an archipelago with assorted stains and straining to snapping point at one brown incongruous button. Sharp blue eyes peeped out like the eyes of an animal watching from under a burning bush of red, red hair. There never was hair as red as his. The nailed boots he wore were made for hard usage in rough places. They rattled like castanets on the blue pavement of Old Castle Street. They were too big for him, and the square black toes that would never take a shine turned up like the toes of Dutch clogs. But the first day a town boy made, in his presence, the inevitable joke about the short length of time it was since the barefooted country boys had been shod, Red Cunningham used the dull, ungainly boots to doleful effect. It was against all rules of the ring and fair fighting, but the display was awesome. The offending town boy, tall, athletic, a bit of a boxer, struck time and again at the wild red head but, with all his height, reach and science, he might as well have been playing a tin whistle. Like mechanical hammers, and with merciless precision the boots worked over his shins and knees, and when Red had him howling, and marked so that he limped for a week, Red made his only tight-lipped comment, 'Damme, you'll know more about boots the next time.'

He was the only man I ever knew who said damme, but long afterwards I heard it was common usage in his part of the country.

But, savage as he could be when roused, he was to me, first, a well of sympathy and then a shining example. He never jeered or whistled when I galloped up Old Castle Street. Sharing a desk with me in school he, with cunning kindness – he never looked more like a compassionate ferret than at that moment – drew from me the true story of my life in the house in Jail Square.

'Damme, they say in the town that when that Maryanne one go to a whist-drive she cheats with one hand and has the rosary beads under the table in the other.'

He made me laugh. He knew all the talk of the town about my two dragons.

'Damme, I wouldn't stand for that treatment.'

'What can I do?'

'Tell them.'

I told him about the gullibility of my mother.

'Damme, your mother's a fool. Tell her the truth.'

'She'd never credit it. Nobody would.'

'I do. I'd do something. I'd take the boot to that Maryanne one.'

He made me laugh again.

'Up and tell them you're no skivvy. Tell them, damme, to wash their own spuds.'

Then one momentous evening he came clattering up the flagged garden pathway to the door of the house in Jail Square, to borrow my *Elementa Latina* – he was always mislaying or losing his own books. Visitors were as rare as laughter in that house, very likely because normal human beings were repelled by the claw-like curiosity, the glittering eyes, the drilling, searching questions of Maryanne. She was on fire to know everything about everybody and Cunningham was welcomed like a bird into a trap and, to his mystification, put sitting with a cup of tea in his hand, on a hard chair, in the exact geographical centre of the dungeon of a kitchen. Around him there was, as always, the effluvium of cigarette butts for he and all his many brothers, and possibly his many sisters, had been chain smokers from about the age of four. In hands stained with nicotine up to the wrists, and devoid of any but the merest chewed stumps of finger-nails, he clutched cup, saucer and spoon and a slice of seed-cake no thicker than a tram ticket. The knot on his twisted rope of a necktie was no bigger than a dried pea.

'You're a studious young boy, I'd say,' said Maryanne.

'I do my best, ma'am.'

'Very fond of his Latin,' said Ellen.

She was like somebody saying that the dog liked bones.

'There's worse than Latin,' Cunningham conceded.

'What part of the country would you come from?' said Maryanne.

'Ardstraw, ma'am.'

'Any relation of the Master Cunningham who taught school there?'

'He's my father, ma'am.'

'Goodness, how interesting,' said Ellen. 'That's where the boy gets the love of the learning.'

'How many brothers and sisters have you?'

Unless you knew the red man as well as I did you wouldn't have noticed the twitching of his feet that told his blood was rising.

'Twenty-two of us. All on the baker's list, thank God, and all well fed.'

'Goodness, what a lot of children to have. Your poor mother,' said Ellen.

'She's quite well-off and happy, ma'am, thank you.'

'Are they all as red in the head as you?' said Maryanne.

'Half red and half black.'

'What colour are your parents?'

'My mother's as grey as a badger and my father's as bald as a coot.'

'But the poor woman,' said Ellen. 'All those children.'

'Damme, more than you'll ever have by the look of you,' said Red Cunningham.

The descending body of Montgomery the murderer jerked no more fearfully when the neck snapped than did the bodies of Maryanne and Ellen in response to that statement.

'How dare you,' said Ellen.

'That's no way to speak to ladies,' said Maryanne.

'It's a good way, damme, to teach pokenoses to mind their own business.'

'You're a vile boy,' said Ellen.

'Leave this house,' said Maryanne.

'Observe me dust, ma'am, and thanks for the tea and the cake.'

Although to this day I can hardly believe it, he left the house unscathed and in triumphant possession of the last word. Perhaps the continuing roll and clog-rattle of his boots would have made mockery of any attempt to reduce him by a valedictory reproof. But the storm burst as we heard the door closing.

'Aloysius, you are never again to speak to that boy.'

'If I told your mother the company you keep.'

'But I sit beside him at school.'

'The vile odour of nicotine,' said Maryanne.

'I could have swooned,' said Ellen.

'And his language,' said Maryanne.

'We'll speak to the Brothers. We'll have him put to sit somewhere else.'

'We could have him expelled. We could write letters about him to the parish priest.'

But somehow they never did speak to the Brothers or, if they did, the Brothers paid no heed to them and, if they wrote to the parish priest, he too disregarded their complaints. Red Cunningham and myself went on sailing the same ship and by degrees the seeds of sedition took root in my soul. All that was needed for open revolt was the new lodger in Jail Square.

The new lodger came in the spring at the same time as the frenzy of preparation began for the annual whist-drive in the pillared courthouse – a benefit for the school's athletic club. The tidings of the new arrival were simply, if indirectly, announced to me when in the basement scullery I was scrubbing the mud off the nine potatoes allotted for Saturday's lunch.

'Aloysius,' Maryanne called down the stairs, 'have you scrubbed the nine?'

'Yes, miss. Almost.'

'Then scrub another three.'

The new lodger was a schoolgirl, the child of some rich relation of Maryanne and Ellen.

Red Cunningham said, 'Somebody to share the skivvying with you.'

It didn't turn out that way for, although Red Cunningham knew about boots, cigarette butts, and the tickling of brown trout, he still had a lot to learn about the oddities of women. The new lodger meant more than three more potatoes to scrub, for, since I was the official bootblack, there were also more shoes to polish. She did help at the dish-washing, but even at that her superior airs made her so obnoxious that her aid was an aggravation. She was plump and bespectacled. She was two years older than me. She went to school to the Mercy nuns and Maryanne and Ellen told me time and again, was highly regarded by them. She was a brilliant scholar, they said, she was a paragon of learning and of all the graces, virtues and accomplishments. She carried off prizes and scholarships by the cartload. She played the piano, and she sang, and one of my new duties was to sit and listen.

'Divine,' said Ellen.

She was, in fact, a pampered, overbearing brat, and why I'm not the world's meanest misogynist I'll never know. She also made a fourth for whist in the practice games in which Maryanne and Ellen were engaged as desperately and viciously as they were in the daily stabbing of the horses; for when they went to a whist-drive they went all out to win.

'Whist, I'm sick of whist,' I said to Red Cunningham. 'I loathe the sound of the word.'

He mocked me. He said, 'Up in Freddy the Shoemaker's select boarding house we don't even know what it means. Poker's the game for men.'

'I missed my Latin today and got bashed because I had no time to learn anything. It's as much as they'd do to give you time to go to sleep.

They stay awake all night, whispering to each other, planning crooked deals.'

'Leave the place. Come down to Freddy's and join the boys. Damme, go on strike. Be a blood.'

'I wish to God I could.'

'Fourteen of us staying there, as well as a journeyman carpenter with a red face, and two commercial travellers. Food plain, but wholesome and plentiful. Damme, fights, morning, noon and night. The best of fun. It's the only place in the town for a fellow to lodge in.'

'It's easy for you to talk.'

'Freddy has a Lee Enfield rifle he's not supposed to have. Last night he showed us how the self-ejector worked.'

'Better than whist anyway.'

'And the company. Damme, Punjab pedlars with bags full of chemises and silk scarves. And tramps and tinkers and travelling people come into the shop. Damme, Freddy knows the world.'

'Whist,' I said, 'and that fat girl.'

'And one night a few of the senior boys, real hard chaws, sipped methylated spirits. Not to get drunk or anything, but just to see what it tasted like. And the other night Jim Ring put seidlitz powder in the journeyman carpenter's chamber-pot. He thought he was done for when it fizzed.'

Freddy the Shoemaker's sounded like heaven, but it seemed just as far away.

'But cheer up,' said the Red Man. 'I hear the whist-drive's the best of gas. The boys do all the serving at the refreshment interval.'

'A lot of use that'll be. I'll be in the madhouse by then.'

'Cakes and lemonade for all, and all for free.'

'Whist. I haven't even time to look at the mountains or the river. I can see nothing but hearts, clubs, diamonds and spades dancing before my eyes.'

'Last year, Jim Ring, they say, drank twenty-seven pint bottles of sarsaparilla.'

Red Cunningham's prophecy of the delights of the night of the annual whist-drive was no exaggeration. So it came to pass that in the course of the splendid chaos of the catering I found myself, flatulent with lemonade to the point of intoxication, on the second-floor landing of the Courthouse with Red Cunningham and three other kindred spirits. We leaned on the bannisters. We looked down the stairway.

'I couldn't drink another drop,' I said.

In my hand was a pint tumbler, full and sparkling to the brim.

'Pour it over them so,' said Red Cunningham.

Ascending the stairs from the ladies' powder-room came Maryanne and Ellen and between them that pudgy, piano-playing girl. A boy may, I suppose, do in lemonade the sort of thing men might do in hard liquor. Yet if Cunningham, who was a superb mimic, had not just then called to Maryanne in the voice of Ellen, and thus added the intoxication of laughter to the effervescence of the lemonade, I might never have struck my blow for liberty. It was all so simple. Maryanne, startled, looked up. When I was quite sure she saw me leaning over the bannister I gave her in the face, and fled, the contents of my glass. If I couldn't convince my mother that Maryanne and Ellen were mean I'd convince her that I was evil or, at any rate, a walking menace to the peace of two lone, lorn women.

It was the end of term and the end of my imprisonment. There could be no going back to Jail Square and for my last night in the town before the Easter holidays I sought refuge in Red Cunningham's lodgings. Then, without my luggage and with the money for my fare borrowed from Freddy the Shoemaker, I headed for the mountains and home. The story, in a special letter hand-delivered by the postman, was there before me.

Blessedly my mother was no believer in corporal punishment but she had a weakness for trying to find out the why of things, and all through the holidays the dreary inquisition went on and on.

'Aloysius, whatever came into you?'

I said nothing.

'How could you, Aloysius, throw slops over two old ladies?'

'They're not that old. They stole my pocket-money. It was lemonade anyway.'

'They say it was slops.'

'If they do I wish it had been slops. It was good lemonade. They made a skivvy and a message boy out of me.'

'They were only trying to teach you discipline, Aloysius. You had it too easy at home.'

After that I gave up. I sought sweet silence. My mother, as Red Cunningham said, was a fool: a nice fool, but a fool.

'You had such nice lodgings, Aloysius. Now I'll have to send you to a common boarding house.'

I said nothing. To a common boarding house was, after heaven itself, exactly where I wanted to go.

'There's only one other place in the town and the accommodation there is most unsatisfactory.'

I said nothing. My mother would never understand the meaning of that splendid freedom in which brotherly battles were of common occurrence nor could she be expected to appreciate the delights of the company, in Freddy's club for young gentlemen, of tramps, travelling people and Punjab pedlars. For her the inner workings of a Lee Enfield would hold no poetry, nor would she be edified by the sight of senior boys – real hard chaws – sipping experimentally at methylated spirits, or swapping tall tales about the travels and amorous adventures of Paddy the Irishman. But for me, the accommodation would be most satisfactory.

'What will become of you, Aloysius?'

I said nothing. Wonders I knew would become of me. I'd be an outlaw and one of a noble band of outlaws. I'd fight with the fists as well as Red Cunningham fought with the turned-up toes of his boots. I'd be a man among men. I'd be on my way to the admired contentment and completion of old age. With a flick of the wrist and a splash and splatter of lemonade I had proved my manhood. When I went back to school after the holidays I proved it still further by taking my thrashing without even attempting to defend myself. That was generally considered the manly thing to do. Afterwards I was to hope that my silence was a subconscious admission of guilt, an act of reparation to childless ageing women whose way of life was charted in loneliness and shadows. After all, my mother had thought well of them and they had been good to the new lodger. They would never know of my repentance. When, a month later, I went to their house to apologise they refused to open the door. Like pig-tailed girls refusing to come out to play they called to me through the keyhole to go away. But whether they knew or not, the divine balance would be readjusted. What more could a gentleman do?

THE ENCHANTED PALACE

Every week that God sends, Renato the Italian hangs up in his shop a long, rectangular three-coloured poster telling our town the names of the three films on that week's programme in Peterson's new cinema. For Peterson and his corrugated iron and concrete palace that's the best available publicity. Most of the people in our town go to the pictures. When the missionary father last month stood up in the pulpit and said at the top of his voice that the pagan, godless and immoral cinema had now more influence over the people than the angels of God, nobody was quite certain whether he was aiding or damaging Peterson's box-office. Some of the older people did stop going to the pictures. But then a lot of the older people wouldn't go anyway. Some parents told their children that they weren't to go any more and the children used their pocket-money or cadged odd pennies and slipped quietly into the fourpenny matinées on Saturday afternoons. Most of the people just went on going to the pictures as soon as the fortnight's mission had ended and they were free in the evenings between teatime and suppertime.

And everybody who comes into Renato's place to eat fish-and-chips in winter or ice-cream in summer is either going to or coming from Peterson's picture palace. They lean over the counter, read out aloud the names of the films and the stars and the days and dates of showing. They speculate innocently about the possibilities of this or that film, trying to divine its content from the sound of its name. Mick McCrumlish, the parish clerk, has a most unecclesiastical preference for murder and horror. John Hamilton of the garage wants the days of the great wild west and keeps telling Renato about the time he was on his honeymoon in Dublin and there was a western film in one cinema and real Red Indians walking up and down on the marble steps outside. An old shawly woman from the lane called the Rat's Pad, taking home her parcel of chips for supper, sighs and says there never was a picture like the *Life of the Little Flower* that a travelling priest showed once in the town hall with the devil sneaking out from behind the altar in the convent chapel to frighten the poor little nun back to the pleasures of the world. Then Renato holds the door open for the shawly woman, smiles and bows in a way that all the school-children can imitate, bids her a gentle good night in a whispering Italian as strange as the songs of angels in our rough-vowelled world.

Jack McGowan of the town's amateur dramatic society plants his elbows on the counter, his head between his twitching, sensitive hands, and tells Renato confidentially that the Irish people are mentally decadent, that a healthy people reared on the land should be ashamed to sink into and wallow in the slough of commercial amusement designed only for the intellectually-exhausted populations of the great industrial cities. Jack gets it all out of a Dublin weekly newspaper written by people who would all like to be writing for *The Tablet*, and nobody pays the least attention to him. Most of the time Renato doesn't even know what the words mean.

For Renato the Italian never made a success of the English language as we speak it. When the doors have closed for the night and the shop is shadowy, quiet, fragrant with the smell of spilt vinegar and fried chips, Renato unrolls his sleeves and reads out aloud and very slowly the three-coloured poster. I'm always with him then. We discuss the possibilities of the next picture. Renato desires mystery. My own preference is for unalloyed murder. Any night Renato can trust the shop to his assistant we slip across to the picture palace. Renato gets two free passes every week as a reward for the publicity he gives Peterson by pinning up the poster in his shop.

The picture on this particular night was called *The Enchanted Cottage*.

If it hadn't been for the word enchanted Renato would never have gone within a mile of it. Where there is enchantment, he reasoned, there may also be mystery. Jack McGowan had talked for a week ahead about the elusive mysticism, the symbolic suggestion in the dramatic writings – Jack never said plays – of Sir Arthur Wing Pinero. Jack, I suspected, knew as much about Pinero as any of us. Vaguely, somewhere at the back of my mind, Pinero equated himself to Dion Boucicault, purely by some accidental association. Across the brown counter Jack handed out to us what he had read in that weekly newspaper. But who paid any attention to Jack and who cared whether he was talking about Pinero or Pindar? I went to the picture not because of Pinero but because Renato liked my company and I liked his and because where there was mystery and enchantment there could also be an exciting murder.

There was just love, spelled out in capital letters as high as the stars. It poured over us in warm, suffocating waves as constant but not as sparkling as the waves of the sea by the shores of which the enchanted cottage stood. There was this American airman knocked all sideways and half-paralysed when his plane crashed over Java. Home he comes all twisted like that and, heaven help him, not feeling very happy. There was this cottage by the deep blue sea that somebody with a doubtful sense of humour had left rent free to honeymoon couples for ever and ever. There was a girl living quietly there as a self-sacrificing domestic servant because she was so ugly that she never got a chance at dances, but Renato whispered to me that if her little mother had ever put her wise to the wonderful uses of soap and water she'd have passed in the right place as well as the next girl. The airman and the girl saw each other. They fell in love. They saw each other again with eyes transformed by love. All ugliness was gone. The twisted face was smooth. The crooked limb was made straight. Love did what soap and water had never been allowed to do. The girl was beautiful in his eyes. Until mother-in-law came motoring with her fancy man and nearly succeeded in bringing the enchanted cottage down around the ears of the happy couple.

Long before that Renato was fast asleep. He slept quietly, breathing evenly, no snoring, no noise. There was no need to disturb him. He worked hard all the week. I said to myself: What does it matter anyway, what does prettiness matter, or ugliness, or bodily beauty? Every day in the year ugly people marry ugly people, and handsome people marry ugly people, and ugly people manage to marry beautiful people and nobody worries. Why should it worry Sir Arthur Wing Pinero or the people who made a film out of his play or the millions who saw the film or me or Renato the Italian sleeping as gently as a baby on a free pass on one of the best seats in Peterson's picture palace in Ireland in the small town of Ballyclogher.

Then Katy came in and sat down on the seat in front of me. Then the little, black-headed fellow with a narrow skull, and a prominence between his shoulder blades, who had already been sitting exactly in front of Renato began to make passes at Katy. Then the couple sitting in the seats behind us introduced themselves to each other and began to talk quite audibly about their lives and the worlds they lived in. They were from the mountainy country to the south of the town. They had never been in a cinema before. When he came in he sat down in the dark on the rim of the tipped-up seat. There were muttered curses from the back row where somebody could see nothing but his broad bucolic back. She showed him how the seat worked. That was how they came to know each other. Her name was Bridget. His name was Hughie. Hughie, Bridget and Katy seemed to me to be three interesting people.

So I nudged Renato into wakefulness. He came out of his sleep like a soft, fat, gentle child and perhaps thought for a moment that he had been dozing in the shadow of some Roman wall lively with lizards. But what he saw was our Katy and the wee fellow with the hump, what he heard were American voices talking about love, and the slow flat voice of Hughie telling Bridget about the green acreage of his arable land, about his cattle, pigs, horses, barns, byres, and brown turbary.

The odd thing about Katy was that she resented the advances of the boy with the hump.

Two years ago she had come to the town to work as a domestic servant in a big house on the Belfast road. She was nineteen years of age, tall and strongly-built, with long black hair and brown brooding eyes and a handsome face with high cheek-bones, and only two moods. One mood was sullen and solitary. The other was bold, aggressive, daring enough to outface the virtuous world and his virtuous mother, to outface even the outraged domestic instincts of her mistress in the big house on the Belfast road.

The boy with the hump opened the campaign by offering Katy a cigarette. She took it. He fumbled in his pocket for matches. Calmly she lighted her own cigarette with her own lighter and puffed grey smoke upwards into the half darkness. He held her hand unnecessarily while he bent forward to light his cigarette. His crooked, pointed face, with the nose slanted to the left, swivelled round in the circle of light and looked at her cunningly. She snapped the lighter shut, went on calmly looking at the story of love and more love and of ugliness transformed by love. It wasn't easy to disturb her.

She wasn't disturbed in the least the time she lost her job. The man of the house protested his innocence to his wife and to anyone he knew anywhere in the town. The town didn't care much. The man and his wife were foreigners, imports from Portadown, planted mysteriously in our midst in government jobs, living in a swanky house, playing golf and tennis and drinking like bedammed. Nothing better could be expected of them. Anyway what was there to get excited about in the shrieking accusations of a childless, faded woman about some unspecified and unproven carryings-on. Ballyclogher, in its time on this weak and sinful world, had seen more tangible evidence of wickedness.

The town, indeed, was all on Katy's side and didn't credit one fraction of the accusations made by that import in the grand house on the Belfast road. The town gave Katy another job and any God's amount of good advice. She took the job, but when her new employer came suddenly on six sheepish young men waiting for Katy behind the apple orchard the town realised that Katy hadn't paid much attention to the good advice. So the town withdrew itself, leaving Katy to exist in a shabby room in a side-street, she herself as shabby as the room and her face sullen and suffering.

The wee fellow with the hump offered Katy a second cigarette. She took it and waited until he had found his matches then, ignoring his proffered flame, she lighted her own cigarette from her own lighter. On the screen the ugly girl was running from the dance hall where she was nobody's darling to the sacred refuge of the enchanted cottage.

Katy never completely belonged to us. We have our frailties and our vices, but her tall body, long legs, thick black hair, reckless challenging ways, belonged to a bigger, less cautious world, to a roaring world where badness or foolishness or whatever it is went with a swing and a gesture, jumping in the light of day: to London, New York, Paris. She might have been half at home even in Dublin with its polished lounge bars inset to shabby faded Georgian.

Even the sheepish fellows with half-crowns in their sweaty palms felt that she despised them, and one day she had a chance to show it. Katy couldn't move out to become part of the whirling madness that was part of her, but, on that day of opportunity, the world came to her and to Ballyclogher. It came in military lorries roaring recklessly up the street. It cheered and shouted and waved oddly-shaped khaki caps, and slouched up and down the pavements wolf-whistling at girls, and played football in the streets and got drunk and fought in the streets, and scrambled fistfuls of coins for the urchins of the town. It occupied Knockduff Hall that had lain desolate for years in the middle of green lands on a loop of the river a mile below the town. It was one small portion of the United States Army but to Ballyclogher it was the whole population of the United States, it was the war and madness and mortal sin, it was the big, bad world.

'Them seats,' Hughie said to Bridget, 'are a complete cod.'

Bridget giggled. She said, 'It's hard in the dark to see how they work. You're blinded as blind as a bat coming in out of the light.'

'I suppose you come here often.'

'No I don't then. This is the first time I ever entered the place.'

She repelled the suggestion that she frequently attended the cinema as sharply as if she had been accused of drinking herself hoarse and blue in the face every night in the week.

'Are you a towney?' he asked.

'Indeed and I'm not. I'm from near Dromore. My father and mother live a mile from Blacksessiagh Creamery.'

'That's a brave bit from this town.'

'But I'm working here for the last week in Miss Murtagh's restaurant.'

'The eating-house,' he said. 'How does that suit you?'

'Very well, indeed.'

There was a precise, needle-like quality about her use of the emphatic word. I tried to imagine what her face was like: thin, quiet, patient, the skin tanned with turf-smoke and sun and wind. Her hands would be bony and nimble with knitting needles, or deftly gentle at polishing eggs or apples for the market, or accurate and capable when washing, cleaning and arranging in Miss Murtagh's eating-house, which she called a restaurant, or surprisingly sinewy at tying sheaves in the autumn or forking hay to the man building the cock when the grass meadows were down in June.

He said, 'Are you never lonesome after Blacksessiagh?'

'Seldom. Except on Sunday mornings when it's quiet and the people are going up the street to mass.'

Her eyes could be pleasantly blue like the June sky over the meadows or thoughtful and black as the slow stream that flowed past Blacksessiagh Creamery.

'I'm from the country myself,' he said. 'I've a farm two miles to the Newtownstewart side of Gortin.'

'Are you for home all that road tonight?'

'No fear. I'll sleep comfortable in the town. I'm off on the train in the morning to Belfast to a brother's wedding.'

'Good to be you. You'll have great fun. I never saw Belfast. I never was further away than the town here.'

'It's a big, busy place. But I don't like it the way I like Dublin.'

'Were you in Dublin too?'

'I went up one year on an excursion to see the big match in Croke Park. We had a great day. It's a brighter place than Belfast. Belfast's as black as your boot. The people are that bitter and divided. You never know, I declare to my God, when they'll go for each other with the stones pulled up from the streets.'

'How can your brother live in a place like that?'

'The same boy made well out of it. He went into the spirits trade. Bought his own licensed premises. And the girl he's marrying on has as many uncles priests as there are in the Vatican City.'

'Are there that many priests in Belfast?'

'You'd never think it from the name the place has.'

'Is there nobody going up with you to the wedding?'

'I'm the only brother he has. There were no girls in the family. The old people are dead. I'm on my own now.'

'You'll have to get married yourself.'

'I would, like the shot of a gun. If I could meet the right girl. A sensible girl like yourself.'

Bridget giggled. She whispered, 'You never even saw my face. You don't even know if I have a face.'

'You'd be surprised,' Hughie said.

He moved in his seat, closer, possibly, to Bridget.

'I've eyes like a cat that can see in the dark. Anyway this place isn't so dark once you get used to it.'

There was a long, warm, contented silence. Then Bridget said, 'Do you like this picture?'

On the screen the face of the twisted man and the face of the ugly girl came close to the camera and close, for kissing, to each other.

'Their faces are too big,' Hughie said. 'He must think he's kissing a five-acre field.'

Bridget giggled, was silent, giggled again, then sighed in long, sweet content.

Every night the jeeps went up the street and down the street and out along the roads leaving the girls home. Some of the fun was decent and some of it, naturally, wasn't. Some of the girls kept their heads and played cautious with men who might have been married twenty times over on the other side of the Atlantic. Some of the girls went on living their own lives and kept as far from the strange men as the ancient Israelites were enjoined to keep from strange women. Some of the girls got themselves husbands, good, bad and indifferent. Some just lost their heads. Others lost anything they had to lose. Two wild country lassies who were skivvying in the town were found one morning in the corner of a hayfield, destitute of their customary inner and outer coverings but warmly and chivalrously wrapped up in American overcoats and sleeping off over-exhaustion and the effects of unfamiliar cocktails.

Renato the Italian leaned over his counter and said, 'We have a say in Italy. It is everywhere the same. When the world goes to war the women go mad.'

Harry Mahoney, the town's coy, heavy comic, said, 'Do you mind the song about did your mother come from Ireland? We'll make a new one about did your da come from America.'

But tall, bold Katy was never seen careering up the street or out the road on the bumping back of a jeep. She knew her business better. She drove mostly in one of the Donnegan's hackney cars and in the company of splendidly-dressed officers. She drank, but moderately, and not in the dark corners of fields but in the best hotel we had. She moved to a house of her own, a neat little bungalow on the Belfast road. She dressed in fine clothes and went like Mother Ireland with the walk of a queen.

The lad with the hump put his arm along the back of the seat and around Katy's shoulders. She looked sideways at him for a moment, searching perhaps for young men in grand uniforms who had drawled their words and spent money like princes before moving eastwards into terrible battle. Then she whispered something into the hunchback's ear. He withdrew his arm and sat humbly smoking his own cigarettes and offering none from that to the end of the picture.

The war burst again on the French shore. Within two days there wasn't a soldier to be seen in Ballyclogher. In the woods and shrubbery surrounding Knockduff Hall the barbed wire rusted and snapped and trailed on the ground, empty tin cans lay in a pile in one place, in another place the stench of a never-efficient urinal died gradually away.

Before the picture ended Hughie and Bridget had bumped and clattered their way across the row of seats. I did my best to see Bridget's face but all I saw as the door opened and closed was that Hughie was a big man, slightly-stooping, and with wide amiable shoulders.

'One day,' said Renato, 'they will be married and happy on the farm that is two miles to the Newtownstewart side of Gortin.'

As clear as daylight the river came down the valley from Gortin to Newtownstewart, silver gravel and salmon trout, and went on northwards by Strabane and Derry City to the sea.

Then across my dream of green places and running water Katy moved. She stood up insolently, a tall woman in a red coat. She swept rudely past the little hunchback. He looked after her, looked over his shoulder to see had his ignominy been observed, then settled down miserably to wait for the final kiss of the film.

'She has gone,' said Renato, 'to her enchanted cottage.'

But next day the bungalow on the Belfast road was empty. The town never saw Katy again. A certain element in Ballyclogher waited eagerly for the day when her body would come up, shapeless and bloated, out of the black hole in the river below the railway bridge or out of the bog-lake by the Derry road, where there had been suicides as far back as anybody could remember. The more prosaic said that she had moved her shop to Derry or Belfast or Dublin. The more imaginative – and they weren't too plentiful in Ballyclogher – thought that, torn with anger and loneliness, she had followed the boys to London or Paris or Berlin, finding peace only where the world had war and rest only in the prickly disquiet of men.

But, barring myself, nobody from our town ever saw her again.

Twelve months later, coming back from a cycling holiday in Connacht, I pushed for a short-cut up over a mountain road on the Fermanagh border. It was in the evening and Katy went before me driving the milch-cows to her father's byre. I walked with her behind them, for the narrow road was blocked with their slow, fragrant bodies. She had rough boots on her feet, a bag-apron tied tightly about her strong hips, her black hair cabbined in a man's cloth cap, her hands rough and reddened with farm-work. I had tea at the open hearth in her father's house and chatted with her mother and the hired man milking in the byre.

When I told Renato he said it was a mystery, a real one, the sort no detective would ever solve, and he attempted to translate for me the words of some Italian song about love gone right and love gone wrong, about the world quiet and the heart at peace, about the world gone mad, the body burning, the heart in pain.

Then we read out the name of the next night's picture. Renato wanted mystery and I wanted murder. It turned out to be a Technicolor musical but Renato likes noise and wasn't disappointed. Through the ersatz radiance I saw all the time the quiet, brown bogland and the soft pasture and a dark, sullen hermit of a girl herding home her father's cattle.

RICH AND RARE WERE THE
GEMS SHE WORE

He was exactly as Monica had described him. The tall, potted palm drooped over him like a sun-umbrella over a great white chief. The slim girl in the black dress in the bright little glittering little reception office put her soft round chin in her perfumed crimson-clawed hands and looked at him with admiration through the palm's drooping leaves. Well-dressed people criss-crossed the lounge to the dining-room or the lift or the cocktail bar. Fanny walked slowly across the deep carpet, circling to avoid the long, stretched legs of an old clergyman half-asleep in an armchair. She fingered in the pocket of her pale grey jigger-coat the smooth creamlined paper of Monica's letter. His description was written there but she didn't need to read it again. She knew it by heart. Monica had a prim, precise way of describing people, writing so that when you read you could hear her talk, each word neatly nipped into separate existence by the firm lips of a small pretty mouth.

'He's six feet. His shoulders are broad but his waist looks quite slim in the very smart uniform of an American major. His skin is dark like an Italian or an Indian. Actually his father was Italian and his mother Irish and when the States went to war he was in the Pacific. And he comes from California – which all helps to add to his natural tan. He's in Belfast on some important business and one isn't supposed to ask him what he's doing there. (That little hint was so like Monica. As if Fanny went about asking American majors what they were doing in Belfast.) His hair is dark and well oiled. His jaws are just a little hollow and his chin always a little shadowed from the razor. A Grecian nose, a wide, high forehead, very white teeth, a flashing smile and of course an American drawl. A real Latin glamour boy but a very nice fellow. You'll love him.'

The flashing smile went on suddenly as if the girl in the glass box had touched her dainty shoe to a concealed switch. He was on his feet before Fanny reached him.

'I bet,' he said to the whole lounge, to the slim girl in reception, to the criss-crossing people, to the dozing priest, 'I bet this is Fanny.'

They clasped and held hands. She said, 'It's Fanny all right. How on earth did you recognise me so quickly?'

He steered her across the carpet towards the cocktail bar and with his free hand slipped from his hip-pocket a bill-fold of tooled blue leather, opened it, still using one hand, and, like a juggler, took from it a folded letter, cream-laid notepaper, and all the time using one hand, restored the bill-fold to his pocket. His dark face had the conscious impassivity of the professional conjuror.

'The clues are all right here. Written down in the neatest orthography in this cute little island.'

He waved the letter in the air. She could – feeling a little uneasy at the familiar way in which his left hand crooked and rested, like a bird home to roost, just above her left buttock – smell when he waved the letter the perfume that Monica used. But he didn't unfold the letter until they faced each other across two drinks and the inevitable, tiny, glass-topped table that didn't come up to his knees. He read snippets from Monica's description of Fanny, glanced across drinks and table after each snippet like a policeman verifying a passport description, smiled dazzlingly when the reality corresponded, as it always did, to Monica's neat words.

He said, 'That Monica girl sure has both eyes on the ball.'

He read, 'Tall for a woman. Dark hair, razor cut and curling beautifully. Oval face, a little lonely looking. Large grey eyes. Slim. Walks very gracefully with head high.'

He said, 'I spotted that as you came in.'

'Somebody should tell Monica I'm not a racehorse.'

'I will if you like.'

He dropped his eyes, laughing, to the letter, 'She'll wear by arrangement if the day is wet, a white mac with cape lined with white fur and carry a green umbrella, and if the day is dry a three-quarter-length jigger-coat in pale grey with large sailor collar trimmed with red.'

His eyes checked across the table, meeting and, for a moment, holding her large grey eyes.

'So that's what they call a jigger. She doesn't say a word about your skirt. I suppose you normally wear one.'

'Except when in bed. All the girls do here, you know. The climate isn't like California.'

'It's swell today, though.'

He raised his eyes to the imitation Georgian ceiling as if he could see through its falsity and through layers of hotel bedrooms, spotless from the morning efforts of chambermaids, to the blue sky and the sunlight over the city.

His eyes were again on the letter, 'I hope you two will get on well together. And that Fanny will show you all the beauties of Dublin.'

Slowly he raised his glass, his handsome face serious, 'Well here's to Monica's good wishes. And to the first beauty I've laid eyes on in dear old Dublin.'

Fanny wasn't embarrassed. She was quite accustomed to people telling her she was beautiful. But this splendidly-uniformed man had been in so many places and seen so many women that a girl couldn't but be pleased when a compliment, sober, and hard with sincerity came from his lips. So, smiling, she raised her glass and gently clinked it against his and later when they walked for lunch to the dining-room she no longer felt uneasy at the touch of his crouching, caressing left hand.

The dozing priest as they passed opened his eyes and took one pastoral disapproving look at the spectacle of an American officer walking in a public place with his arm around an Irish girl.

The girl in reception studied her red claws. Her impossibly pretty face could have concealed anything from envy to contemplative thought on crossword puzzles. Monica, teaching in a schoolhouse in another city, checked on her watch to satisfy herself that her two letters of introduction had done their work.

Over an excellent lunch and a bottle of good wine they began to get on well together. Fanny had always prided herself on being an easy mixer.

His name was Eddy. His dark eyelashes were long and silken and his eyelids drooped when he talked, lazily drawling. That droop of the eyelids he must have inherited from his Latin father. It reminded Fanny of the face of a fiddler in Simonian's in Paris when Monica and herself had been on holidays: a sallow inscrutable face, eyelids drooping to suggest uneasy mystery; a fiddler with white shirt, red sash, tight black trousers, playing odd Hungarian dance tunes around and around your table. Monica had intensely admired the poise and the playing of that fiddler with the disturbing, sphinx-like face.

'Have you visited Paris?' Fanny asked.

'Sure I have. A swell town.'

She couldn't expect him to say more and to manage his soup at the same time yet, from a Latin-visaged man in a magnificent uniform his brief description didn't seem fair to Paris. She tried to raise the conversation to a clearer air.

'I know a man who lived there for twenty years. He came back recently. He was a friend of James Joyce.'

'Gee, that's mighty interesting. James Joyce was that fellow who wrote all those books.'

'Not very nice books I'm afraid.'

It wouldn't do to let a stranger out of the country with the impression that young Irishwomen unreservedly approved of James Joyce.

'Back home,' he said, 'where I went to college, everybody seemed to think his books took a lot of licking. A friend of mine came all the way over here to write a thesis about him. But from what he told me subsequently I think he wrote his thesis on Paddy Flaherty's whisky, instead.'

Fanny was mildly amused. He said, 'I'm not really a literary fellow myself. But I know a guy called Lefty whose uncle is an author.'

'Which author?'

'That I don't know. I reckon he can't be much of an author or Lefty'd have told me. Lefty's apt to talk big about his folk.'

Over braised ham and chicken there was the inevitable lull in the conversation. Then, sweetening her mouth with three short sips of wine, she said, 'What are your first impressions of this place?'

'Swell town. Not as big as London and not as bright as Paris.'

'I think myself it's dowdy.'

'Oh, well, dowdy's a hard word. Granted I've only seen what you see coming in from the airport. And this hotel. And yourself. It all looks swell to me. Especially yourself.'

The difficulty about talking to men, Fanny reflected, was that – Irish or English or American and worst of all, French – they had a most irritating way of continually forcing the conversation away from interesting general topics to embarrassing, and possibly insincere, personalities. She didn't smile. She refused to look embarrassed. She was here to show a stranger the beauties of the capital city of Ireland, not to welcome, like a tittering adolescent, silly compliments.

'Are you staying in Dublin for long?'

'Want rid of me already?'

There he went again. Say the day was wet or fine or cold or hot and a man always made the remark a personal issue.

'I'll be pushing off tomorrow. This is only a flying visit.'

She almost said, 'What do you expect me to do? Weep?'

Instead she skimmed away from personalities like a wild duck skimming lake water, cunningly avoiding the clump of bushes that concealed the gun.

'The man I mentioned, the friend of James Joyce, always said the quays in Dublin reminded him slightly of Paris.'

'The Paris quays are swell.'

'But I know another man who's lived here all his life who says the Liffey reminds him of one of the greater Paris sewers.'

'You know a heap of men.'

She sighed, 'A few.'

Leaning across the table with its two glasses of potent Gaelic coffee he held a lighter to her cigarette, and suddenly seeing under the drooping eyelids she realised that he was amused, that he was quietly laughing at her and James Joyce and the cobbled quays of Paris and Dublin's dirty river. For one instant she was angry. After all she was doing her best to be entertaining. But she couldn't afford to be angry because anger made her blush and blushing was idiotic and if he noticed her cheeks reddening his amusement would only be increased. She sipped her Gaelic coffee: rich cream and sugar and Irish whisky and black, black coffee. With the strong taste in her mouth, with cigarette smoke wreathing before her face, she smiled at him and he smiled in return. Then they laughed together at the unspoken, undefined joke. The initial awkwardness was over.

'So we see the quays,' he said, 'and decide for ourselves.'

And after lunch they saw the city. They climbed laboriously to the sight-seeing platform on the top of Nelson Pillar, counting the steps as they ascended, losing count and laughing and holding hands in the darkness on the steep, spiral stairway. He was Monica's friend, and holding his hand as a means to ascend those interminable stairs seemed to be something that, without shame or scruple, a girl-friend of Monica could do. Out on the dizzy, windy platform she could also shelter and support herself in the crook of a muscular, uniformed arm while they looked down on pedestrians swarming like comical ants, on buses like long beetles, on the Liffey cutting straight through Georgian houses to the rattling docks; or lifting their eyes they could look southwards to round-backed mountains like a crowded herd of blue cattle, or eastwards to flat, sandy coastline and a graceful headland lying long on the water.

'That's Howth Head.'

'It looks heavenly.'

'It is. Up on the summit there's just heather and gorse and grazing goats. On a clear day you can look north to the Mountains of Mourne and south to Wicklow Head.'

On the high platform at Nelson's stone feet, dizzily high above beetles and clockwork ants, he chanted, 'But for all that I found there I might as well be where the Mountains of Mourne sweep down to the sea.'

An elderly couple looking north towards the statue of Father

Theobald Mathew, apostle of temperance, and towards the monument to Charles Stewart Parnell, who loved his country and his lass, smiled encouragingly when they heard the American voice singing a song about Irish mountains.

'My mom sang that song,' he explained generally. 'She came from County Down. I'd love to go to Howth to see the heather and the gorse.'

She promised, 'We'll go there when we see the centre of the city.'

Guiding her all the way down the steep, winding stair he held her hand again, but once out in the street, in the crowds and the dazzling sunshine, she gently, ever so gently, disengaged herself. She didn't want to hurt his feelings or to set him thinking that Irish girls were impossibly rigid, stiffly and uncompromisingly proper, but she had to live in the city and if any of her acquaintances saw her hand-in-hand in O'Connell Street with a Yankee officer she'd never hear the end of it. So, primly separate and apart, they walked the crowded pavement as far as the bridge, stood there while she pointed to the graceful dome of Gandon's eighteenth-century Customs House, to the towers of a Norman cathedral, to the greatest brewery in the world, to the slim distant obelisk built in the Phoenix Park to honour the Victor of Waterloo. From the bridge southwards their progress was according to the guide-book, their talk was of cities and famous men. (The Bank of Ireland had in the eighteenth century housed a parliament. And there was Trinity College founded by Queen Elizabeth. And there on pedestals were Thomas Moore, Oliver Goldsmith, Edmund Burke and Henry Grattan.) She warmed towards him more and more, discovering behind his active, continually-threatening glamour and his nonchalant assumption of ignorance, a sound knowledge of books and places. (And there sitting on his pedestal beside the Trinity campanile was William Hartpole Lecky, the famous historian.) He liked her, too, she thought. He seemed to enjoy her conversation. He held her hand again at the door of Trinity library and she closed her fingers on his firm, dry palm. After all, Trinity students didn't count as people. (And there secure in its protecting case was the wonderful Book of Kells, burning with colour, intricate with whorled illuminated capitals drawn by holy men who had a hand in heaven.) And that last bit, she explained, was a quotation from a modern Irish poet and, to her surprise, he named the poet. Americans could at times be most unexpected.

By a side-gate opening into a byway they came out into the streets and once again, being aware of the eyes of people who might know her, she disengaged her hand. He patted his lips with fingers warm from her fingers, mentioned thirst and the heat of the sun, suggested a quick one and, thinking she should really say no, she said yes. In a cellar where brawny, blazered students were sitting on barrels or playing darts he drank iced lager and she drank iced orange. She wasn't, she assured him, when they were out again in the streets and out of the hearing of the students, really a drinking woman: she drank wine at meals when possible because she had lived in Paris and contracted a liking for some French habits.

'Not all French habits?'

She didn't answer that question. It had been put to her so often by men who thought that because an Irish girl taught school for a while in Paris she must therefore be an abandoned woman. (And there was Leinster House where Lord Edward Fitzgerald once lived and where the Dail – pronounced Doll – now talked about politics, partition and the price of bacon. And there was the historical museum. The zoological museum was in another street. And there was the place where there had once been a hideous statue to Queen Victoria: she had turned green before they finally removed her. And here now was the National library sacred to the memory of James Joyce and here was the green marble bannister that had reminded Joyce of smooth-sliding Mincius crowned with vocal reeds.) What a pity, she said sternly, he hadn't censored his own books just a little more thoroughly. There were some words to be found in his pages that just shouldn't be written down and the younger Irish writers had been affected by his bad example.

Of course, she explained to his wondering Californian ears, the Irish people were inclined to extremes: in politics, bad language and drink. They needed literary censorship and much more rigid licensing laws. You never saw in Paris the hordes of drunkards you saw at closing time in Dublin.

He said yes – doubtfully. He pointed out that the French didn't worry their pants about closing time.

'But that would never do here. The people would run wild.'

Again he said yes. He held her right elbow tightly in the intensity of the argument. They leaned against smooth-sliding Mincius crowned with vocal reeds.

He said, 'Now tell me about the Irish colleens. Do they share the national wildness?'

She was looking away from him towards the hideous, stained-glass window, centred by the representation of a dirty, old, bearded man supposed to be Leonardo, so he didn't notice how she winced at the mention of colleens. Nor did she notice how his eyes twice considered her, ankles to buttocks to bust to lips to dark glossy crown and slowly curving back again. She said, 'Irish women have always been a steadying influence. That's our national tradition. I think we keep ourselves to ourselves better than the women of most nations except, perhaps, the English who are very reserved. I can't speak for the United States.'

'I can.'

His dark face was the face of a man made suddenly melancholy by memories of lost youth and past pleasures, by fears for the arid and unrewarding present.

The Howth bus was blue and waiting outside a cream-coloured cinema on the windy, sunny quays. When they climbed the stairs to the upper deck he was still inclined to be silent and melancholy, she was still excited by her consciousness of spiritual union with generations of heroically-aloof women. (And there once again as the bus went north was Gandon's graceful Custom House, and the track of mud called the river Tolka, and Clontarf where Brian Boru beat the Danes.) He began to talk again when, through the gaps between neat suburban houses, they could see the sunlight bright on green fields. He shouted when he saw the sea. He draped his left arm around her shoulders. There wasn't much she, or any heroic woman, could do to curb his enthusiasm. His left hand fondled her left ear. Thank God they were sitting in the back seat. Thank God there were none of her acquaintances on the bus. Her heart was beating rapidly. (And there, she said with trembling voice, her right hand pointing across the water, was Lambay Island and the rock called Ireland's Eye.) His left hand pinched the lobe of her left ear. She'd always heard Americans were over-familiar. When his pincering fingers closed for the second time she stiffened herself away from him so noticeably that he withdrew the encircling arm. He stayed quiet then, listening to her breathless description of the beauties of the coast, the arms of the harbour curving around the bobbing, anchored boats, the gradual ascent of the cliffs until the path they walked on was high above the screaming gulls, the burning yellow of the hillside furze, the lighthouse white as snow and set on a promontory that was like the end of the world. That day the cliff-path was crowded with holiday visitors. It was so narrow that they had to walk slowly and in single file. So keeping always a few paces ahead she could guard herself against embraces and pinches – until they sat down for a rest on a green, crumbling, wooden seat and, without a word or the least preliminary, he bent over her and kissed her full on the lips.

She could have screamed. She would have screamed. She would have slapped his olive-coloured face. But two, flabby, elderly women came along the curving path, talking loudly in Glasgow accents about Leopardstown Races. They wore black silk dresses and they perspired.

By the time they had slowly waddled out of sight she had remembered that even if he was rude he was Monica's friend. She couldn't, because of that, reply to rudeness by rudeness, couldn't slap, couldn't rise and run away. She said weakly, annoyed by the unsteadiness of her breathing, 'You shouldn't do that.'

'Why not?'

'We've only known each other a few hours.'

'Is that the only reason?'

'It's so common.'

'Not common enough.'

He sighed, and against her will she smiled until he spoiled it all by saying, 'You're so uncommon. I've never seen a model like you before.'

'You don't mean that.'

'Test me and see.'

Since the argument was going so hopelessly against her she thought the best thing to do was to stand up, look at her watch, say, 'Time we were going back to the hotel.'

She did all that and said that and he agreed amiably. All the way back along the cliff-path she walked as fast as she could, feeling awkward, feeling his eyes perched like bats on a wall somewhere about her lumbar spine, hearing him coming easily, soft-footedly behind her. He talked about the cliffs and the distant northern mountains, about the speed of a steamer coming out from the port and curving round the headland to face across the water towards Liverpool. Now and again he complimented her on the lovely way she walked.

Two violins, a violoncello, a piano, two tall fiddling women in black evening dress, a red-headed male 'cellist, and a fat woman at the piano.

Their table was in the corner of the dining-room furthest away from the orchestra, but waiters and diners, like the shaded lights, were muted, and their ears were washed against and filled with the sound of rich strings, slowly beginning, a cool Grieg wind blowing over lakeside reeds in some brief northern summer. The reeds quiver, bend, sway apart like silken dancers to show a lake sometimes placid like a pure soul, sometimes glimmering like an untouched virgin body. She said nervously, feeling her way, 'I adore Grieg.'

'Some music. Swell,' he said. 'But too Scandinavian for my own personal taste.'

'It's all rocks and forests and lakes and fast-flowing streams.'

'Not enough about wine and the sun,' he said, 'and dancing girls, castanets, tarantellas, the lot.'

Forgetting his soup he talked excitedly, hands gesturing, about flamenco. If it hadn't been for his emblemed uniform and his slight nasality she could have imagined she was listening to some Spaniard or Italian in whom a hatred of cold northern places had smouldered all day like a banked fire. He spoke with passion. He knew a great deal about music. No longer had she the uneasy feeling that he was looking at her under drooping eyelids and laughing a little. His eyes were now wide open. Monica, too, was musical and Fanny imagined that a common love for beauty in sound must be the basis for the friendship between Monica and this forward, foreign man. All through the soup and the fish and the joint he talked music, then relaxed with a self-deprecatory sigh and a shrug, his palms flat on the table-cloth, his mouth softening into a smile.

'Father Abraham,' he said, 'how I do run on.'

'I like you when you talk like that.'

She really meant it. He laughed and, forgiving his impertinent kiss, she laughed with him. Later when they sat side by side in the lounge he said, 'Thanks a lot, Fanny. That was a lovely day.'

'I think so too.'

'I had no idea that I'd find such a sweet person to show me the sights.'

'I never thought I'd find such a . . .'

There she stopped. She didn't as a rule talk like that and, thinking back, she tried to remember how many drinks she had taken that day. But his shoulder was against her shoulder, his inbreathing just a little slower than hers, and she couldn't count beyond five.

'Such a what?' he asked.

Turning towards her. He said, 'A drip? A dope? A heel?'

She could only smile and play with her glass and feel foolish and then, to shatter the silence, spreading out like a damp mist from the central swamp of her foolishness, whisper, 'What a pity such a day has to end.'

'It doesn't have to.'

She thought that over, her thinking confused. She shouldn't have allowed herself to take so much drink. Determinedly she put her glass down on the glass-topped table, bringing down the curtain on the lovely day, quenching the light, drowning the sun in the sea, saying, 'But every day must end.'

'When the day ends, dear Fanny, the night begins.'

He was leaning sideways, whispering to her. His breath was pungent with whisky. His left hand was covering her right hand and pressing some hard metal object against her dry palm. The words, the pressure, the unseen but felt shape of the hard metal made her sober and cold with realisation, made her withdraw her hand, open it, look at the key, then drop it suddenly on the seat between them, in horror that some acquaintance might be sitting in the lounge, watching her with an American officer and a bedroom key.

'Good God,' she said. 'Do you seriously mean that you want me to . . . go up to your room?'

He was, to do him justice, startled. He said, 'I'm offering you hospitality.'

Then rather weakly, 'You were so sweet to me.'

'What do you think I am?'

'A wonderful girl.'

'Every time you meet a wonderful girl do you offer her . . . this?'

Her fingers touched quickly on, then leaped away from the metal of the evil key.

'Not every time, Fanny. I have my likes and dislikes.'

'How big of you. I suppose you think I ought to feel complimented.'

'After that, Fanny,' he said (or he drawled wearily) 'you'll ask me haven't I any respect for you or for women in general or don't I remember my mother.'

'What would you think if some other man made that suggestion to your sister?'

That touched him. He wasn't sprawling sleepily any more, but sitting upright, talking rapidly, his hands as active as they had been when he talked of the rhythms of the south, flamenco and tarantella.

'Listen,' he said. 'I've three sisters. Great kids. Good to look at. What they do is strictly their own business. I don't like big brothers.'

'I can imagine why.'

She picked up her handbag, her net gloves, seldom worn because her hands were generally clean and cool. She said, 'You shock me.'

He laughed with high good humour. He said, 'What do you do to me, Fanny? What do you do to me? You're so lovely. Hasn't any man ever? Ever even tried?'

She would have stood up but that would have meant louder speaking and heaven only knew who was watching and listening. She was afraid to look directly at the faces lined like white masks around the walls of the lounge.

'No. Nobody ever.'

'Never even tried.'

There had been one or two slight incidents in Dublin and in Paris but she saw no reason why she should go into explanatory details. So she said, 'No. No. No.'

'Well, strike me!'

He rubbed his palms on his thighs, smoothly rubbing downwards towards his kneecaps. It was a bawdy gesture of gleeful surprise.

'Are all the men around here paralysed?'

Then indignantly she stood up. She said, 'They have some respect for their women.'

'Oh, that!'

He walked beside her across the lounge and the outer lounge and through the swinging glass doors. The slim girl in the black dress in the bright little glittering little reception office had been relieved by a pretty, plump, redheaded girl also in a black dress who cupped a dimpled chin in warm hands and looked mistily after the major.

To one of the porters he said, 'Call a cab.'

When they were crossing the pavement, he said, 'Okay, Fanny. No hard feelings. It's been a lovely day and I hope I didn't offend you. But I sure do wish you could have told me earlier in the night the sort of nice girl you were.'

'I think that should have been clear enough. I didn't have to tell you I'm not a . . .'

She couldn't say the horrible word. She should have been devastatingly angry but instead her voice trembled and she wanted to cry. Men were rotten. He was so unperturbed, so politely ready to put her into a taxi and see the end of her.

'I'm only passing through,' he said.

His voice was mock apologetic. But she knew he didn't mean to be apologetic. His hand was on the door-handle of the taxi.

'I've no time to waste. You get that way with a war on and the habit sticks. I like constant company and I bet you, Fanny, ten dollars that before the night is out. . .'

She couldn't listen to any more. She caught the door and slammed it and in a stifled voice gave the taxi man the secure address of her father's house.

In the corner of the taxi she sat shivering for several minutes, shrinking away from somebody or something. Then, courage returning, she moved to the middle of the seat. What was it to her if a strange man had proved himself a contemptible blackguard?

At her father's gate she fumbled in her handbag. The driver said, 'Gentleman paid, miss.'

She felt hot all over, angry, ashamed, humiliated, an empty carton returned carriage-paid to the factory. And he was Monica's friend?

It wouldn't be so bad if he hadn't up to that moment been such a pleasant fellow. She had forgotten about the kiss on the Hill of Howth, a foray of a kiss, unexpected, undesired, unremembered. He had seemed well-read. He did know about music. And underneath he was rotten, no different from a diseased creature, hopefully, suggestively whispering in a dark alley or from a maniac chasing young girls along badly-lighted suburban roads. They were all after the one thing. And he was Monica's friend?

Well Monica, she supposed, her hand again fumbling in her bag, Monica was capable of looking after herself. But the feel in her hand of the key of her father's door renewed the awful revelation of that moment in the hotel. She felt again the hard metal pressed against her palm in evil, corrupting invitation. How could Monica escape such moments if she went on being his friend? Or was Monica above and superior to such degradation and was she, Fanny, just the sort of woman who made a man feel the castle was conquered, the gate flung open and the drawbridge down?

In her bed the cold shivering returned and with it, as in the taxi, the tendency to move away from something.

She clutched her rosary beads and prayed for sleep and was then afraid that sleep might come not unaccompanied. When she did fall into an uneasy slumber it was only to be awakened by the shrilling of a bell, the telephone, once, twice, three times, and warned by some instinct she raced barefooted, her nightdress slipping off her left shoulder, before her father or mother could come out of their decent rest. Over the wire his nasality was more pronounced. He said, 'Hallo! Hallo! Is that you, Fanny? Apologies for butting in on your repose.'

'What do you want?'

'Monica gave me a parcel, a book or something, to give to you. I've just recollected. If I leave it here at the hotel perhaps you could pick it up sometime.'

'Thank you. Good night.'

'No hard feelings, Fanny?'

'Good night.'

'I'm a brash boy but I wouldn't want to be more than necessarily offensive.'

More than necessarily?

'Good night.'

'Just one thing, Fanny. You remember I was about to lay a little bet when you slammed the door of the cab in my face. Well here she is to say hallo. Say hallo to Fanny, honey, Fanny's a nice girl.'

Deliberately prolonging and intensifying the horror she listened until she heard a woman's voice, husky, probably with drink, saying, 'Hello, hello, Fanny, hello, hello.' Then quietly she put down the phone.

Her rumpled bed was as inviting as a rack. Slipping on a heavy dressing-gown she went into her father's study, sat in his chair at his desk before his black-and-white crucifix, tried with his pen and on his notepaper to write to Monica, tore up three attempts, ceased to try any more. The quiet of the house invited a scream. Her rosary beads sprawled black on her pillow. Tomorrow she'd take the train and go to Belfast and warn Monica. But perhaps Monica already knew. Perhaps Monica didn't mind. Monica? Monica? Monica?

At any rate she couldn't go to Belfast tomorrow because he'd be on the train.

THE WILD BOY

We grew up in the same town myself and Lanty whose left-handed luck made his life a continual procession of events, accidents, things happening. He was a few years older than me and lived only a few doors away from the yellowstone house I was reared in, and we spent much of our boyhood together in spite of my mother's disapproval of our friendship. She used to warn me: He's a wild unbiddable boy. He's no company for the like of you.

The trouble was that I was an only child guarded by my parents as carefully as they'd guard a pet canary, and Lanty was one of a crowd of brothers and sisters of all ages and as plentiful as tinker children around roadside caravans. They went to school or evaded school in droves, played, laughed, and fought together, and at times the life and sound of them shook the town. My mother regarded their noise, their multiplicity, their ecstatic lawlessness with distant disfavour. For some strange reason Lanty, on occasion, detached himself from the herd to give me the benefit of his leadership and life wisdom. He may simply have liked me, or at times the noise may have been too much even for him.

By the time he was twelve Lanty had fallen down every climbable tree within a three mile radius of our town. When we played football on the convent field – two dozen ragged, half-jerseyed trespassers – Lanty was the only one of the lot who ever fell on the place where a wicked fragment of metal protruded from the ground. The fall left him with a permanent mark on his left knee. It was matched by a jagged scar around his left eye – a reminder of his first day at the seaside. Once a year the children of our town led, as the young ones of Hamelin had once been led by the Pied Piper, by an old Crimean veteran in white beard, baggy breeches, crimson jacket and an enormous busby hat, headed off to the railway station to travel the thirty miles to the sands of Rossclara for a free day at the seaside. This hilarious event – they called it the Kiddies' Excursion – was the result of the benevolence of a group of veterans of the First World War. It was my star-crossed friend Lanty who had to complicate proceedings by rushing wildly to get his head out of the carriage window for a view of sand, surf, blue sea and the sentinel chain of table mountains that guard Rossclara. He forgot to open the window. The old Crimean veteran, known for no reason as Joe the Lamb, bore him in his gnarled arms to the local doctor who, on the side, ran a shebeen and sampled his own wares. The scar was the work of his unsteady hand. The tale of Lanty's boyhood was written in mishaps and scars.

At the gable end of the house I lived in there was a patch of grassless earth used by the young of the neighbourhood for games of marbles, cricket, cowboys and Indians, and primitive football encounters with a ball made of paper. A road ran beside it, a road so steep it could never be properly surfaced, for the rivulets after the rain tore it as they'd tear a mountain side, and the town council considered anyhow that a rough surface gave better purchase for the hooves of toiling dray horses. It also saved money on macadam. Across that road there was a corresponding gable and patch of earth – not however grassless, but transformed into a garden by the green-fingered energy of McCaffrey the cattle-dealing man who lived there. On a June evening while Lanty and myself casually bowled and batted, the cattle-dealer's child played in the garden.

'Watch me,' said Lanty.

He clutched the cricket-ball.

'I'll send it spinning within an inch of the skull of young McCaffrey. I'm the champeen skimmer.'

He was, too, at that wonderful game of skill: the sending of flat pebbles dancing like demented water-birds along the still, deep reaches of the Camowen River.

The cricket ball rose in the air like a bird. It made its graceful parabola across the wrinkled road and neatly dropped on the head of the child exactly as the cattle-dealer, six feet high, wattle in hand, a man who had driven hard bargains in fairs that were worse than fights, turned the corner of his house. That sort of thing was liable to happen to Lanty even when he had the most harmless intentions in the world, and if you were in his company you could share the consequences.

Then there was the case of Lady Bob, who kept a huckster shop and who was part of our boyhood and our growing-up to be young men with shameful cat-hairs on our chins and voices swinging uneasily between falsetto and double bass. Lady Bob had his own painful experience of Lanty's earlier escapades – in this way:

His house, with the huckster shop at the front, stood at the bottom of a brief, steep hill. Behind the house there was a diminutive garden, half flowers, half vegetables, which Lady Bob tended with loving care. In the centre of the garden stood a weird scarecrow. Rising up from the back of the garden there was a precipitous green slope and, on top of the slope, a high fence of tarred, corrugated tin. At one end of that fence stood Lanty and myself gazing on Lady Bob who, with his back towards us, was bending down, assiduously cultivating his garden.

'Just look at that scarecrow,' I said to Lanty.

I had, unfortunately, a voice that carried.

Now, one of Lanty's weaknesses was that he could never resist and seldom missed, a target. The brutal crack of sharp-edged stone on soft, broad, grey-flannelled buttocks is in my ears to this day, and the whinnying scream of pain from Lady Bob as he straightened up and rose with a salmon leap into the air. We were gone like hares behind the black tin fence but my fatal remark had reached the ears of the victim and when, still smarting with insult and injury, he told my father that I had miscalled and assaulted him, I was soundly thrashed. My only defence, which seemed to me then sweetly reasonable, was to say over and over again, 'I didn't call Lady Bob a scarecrow. I called the scarecrow a scarecrow.'

When Lanty found out about the thrashing it was too late for him to go, as the conventional noble boy might have gone, to tell the truth to my father and Lady Bob. He had a more practical turn of mind. Because I had suffered for his sins he compelled me for a month, to take his pocket-money.

'Compensation,' he said. 'It was in the Sunday papers about a man who was jailed in the wrong and they had to give him millions when he got out.'

When Lanty was twelve he went with his blond, slow-witted cousin to the great horse-chestnut tree near the Lynn Bridge, in the smooth pastures by the Drumragh River. The leaves were in their autumn beauty. The cattle grazed as quietly as the water flowed. God's peace was all around the place. Lanty climbed the tree. He slung down chestnuts to the cousin. Then, looking down, he saw on the roadway a local policeman. Like some tree-imp he danced out along a swaying branch.

'Flatfoot,' he called, 'flatfoot.'

And the branch broke.

'Thirty feet he came down,' the policeman said, 'spinning like a propeller every time he hit a branch.'

'He's dead,' said the slow-witted cousin. 'What'll I tell my uncle?'

For a fortnight Lanty lay unconscious in the hospital, white screens around him, and death was close to all of us in our hushed classroom. He was a distinguished person. We spoke about him in whispers. At school the Brothers asked us to pray that he would live. He lived. He was proud of the dent on the back of his head. For twopence you could have the privilege of groping in the shiny dark hair and exploring the depth of the dent. He had, as I said, a practical turn of mind.

It was the summer after this that the freedom of bare feet and the possession of an empty jam jar apiece put the vagrant idea into our minds, and Lanty and myself set off one morning early to catch what we called minnows but what were, in reality, three-spined sticklebacks. The more aristocratic ten-spined stickleback, native to the complicated island of Britain, is not known in the waters of Ireland.

On the way to the Creevan Burn, where the sticklebacks were, there were a thousand waylaying delights. Sparse, hardy chickweed growing on the cracked, sun-baked fair-green tickled our toes, and the saffron tiny tops of the weed were pleasantly edible. Our scientific curiosity was never fully satiated by the brownness of the flies banqueting on cow-pats left behind after the fair-day, and by the speculation as to whether they were or were not, identical with the blue-back houseflies.

'I love fair days,' Lanty said. 'I could stand all day looking at a cow.'

The bars of the cattle-pens by the weighbridge were a source of endless delight.

'We're acrobats,' he claimed, 'in Buffalo Bill's circus.'

So I had to be an acrobat with him and twist in and out of the bars, and balance, as a tightrope man, on the topmost.

We moved on towards the railway station. Leaning over the wall above the Station Brae was a sycamore tree from which Lanty had once fallen, his fall broken, not too comfortably, by crushed stone that workmen surfacing the road had piled against the wall. He climbed the tree again to show me the exact branch he had fallen from.

The musical shunting and buffeting of trucks in the goods-yard below the station delighted us for a whole half-hour until a workman slung a piece of coal at us and Lanty, with unerring aim, returned it. Clutching our jam jars we fled through narrow bright streets. Sunlight dazzled back at us from whitewashed walls. Breathless, but safe from pursuit, we came to the bridge over the Creevan Burn.

It was the toy stream in which every boy in our town caught his first trout. It twisted away from us through deep meadows where the tops of the grasses were ripe but the mowing had not yet begun. It curved around the base of the rugged green heights we called Gormley's Quarries. Above the bridge a rippling run of shallow water smoothed out into a wide pool and sunlight on the still water revealed the tiny, frisking sticklebacks. We brooded over them where brown stepping-stones, bearded with weeds, crossed the stream. But it so happened that for that day they were safe from our intrusion. For bending forwards, foot on the first stone, Lanty slipped, tottered, recovered his balance with admirable agility but, in doing so, dropped his jar with a shattering explosion on the second stone. The curious thing about him was that his disasters were always partial, never complete. Like bursting bubbles of light the startled sticklebacks vanished. The water laughed at us. Fragments of broken glass, uncomfortable and fragile aliens, settled down among the pebbles on the bottom of the pool. We sat on the bank in a long, melancholy silence. Somewhere behind a hedge bees were buzzing.

'We'll chase bees,' he said.

'I have a jar, Lanty.'

'One jar's no good for minnows. We'll chase bees.'

It was at any rate a new sport, yet my heart bled for him. He could have had my jar for the asking and he knew it, but he was too noble to ask. I was the first person who ever understood his nobility.

'We'll chase bees,' he said again. 'It's great fun chasing bees.'

We left the sunlit stream and the lurking sticklebacks behind us and, although I was doubtful about the fun to be found in chasing bees, so elusive and, unlike sticklebacks, possessed of stings, I followed him on and on through tangled grass fragrant with meadowsweet. When we saw our first bee we pursued it, cavorting like buffaloes. It was a doomed bee, too brightly coloured to escape the searching eye, too heavy with sleep and summer to rise more than a few feet from the tops of the grasses. We stalked him slowly and relentlessly, great white hunters closing in on the game. He was no busy black honey-bee but a doddering bumble that obviously had not found his direction in life. He waited on a wild red blossom and breathlessly we watched him. No alerted senses, no movement in the still air warned him of the descent of the glass trap. Closer and closer it came and, when it wasn't more than a foot away from the prey, excitement proved too much for Lanty.

'Quick! Quick!' he shouted. 'It'll effect its escape.'

He had an odd choice in phrases.

Then, lunging forwards to help, he knocked me off balance, and the jar that should have closed neatly over blossom and bee, instead crushed the poor, bumbling, lazy loiterer, and death was with us in the meadow. Far away, somewhere, the buzzing of bees was loud and, to our ears, hostile.

'We should bury him,' I said, 'I suppose.'

'What we should do is make our getaway, quick.'

'Why?'

'You kill one bee and all the bees come after you.'

'How do they know?'

'They know all right. Listen.'

Undeniably, the buzzing of the distant bees seemed louder. Could it be the metallic angry sound of a mustering army?

'Run for it,' Lanty shouted. 'Smash the jar. Bees can trail you. Like bloodhounds.'

He was racing and jumping away across the meadow heading for the wild earth of Gormley's Quarries, and I followed him as well as I could – he was a champeen runner as well as a champeen skimmer.

'This,' he said, 'is Injun country. Keep your eyes skinned and your ear to the ground.'

At that time when I read in the National Geographic Magazine about the Badlands of Dakota, or the wonders of the Grand Canyon, I thought, relativity being what it is, of Gormley's Quarries. All in all they roughened about twenty acres of the ground of Ireland and their highest hump might have struggled up a hundred feet higher above sea-level than the top of the Boer War monument in the main street of our town.

But they were our Badlands, our Grand Canyon. They had the added attraction of being dangerous. A boy had been drowned there once by accident. An old woman had drowned herself. Like Lanty they were wild company for a good boy like me.

Once upon a time, before my memory, the Quarries had been a range of low green hills crowned by an ancient windmill. The armless, disembowelled torso of the old mill still stood on the high centre of the wilderness. The greedy needs of metalled roads, of house-building and church-building, had sent stone-cutting men and dynamiting men in to open up the earth. There were sharply-ridged terraces where the old-style stone-cutters had cut the stone from the naked rock-face. There were slopes of shale where gelignite had torn away the last serviceable fragment. As in all worked-out, abandoned quarries, springs had burst forth to create chill dark pools of uncertain depth, fringed with green reeds and the tall furry-topped canes we called blackheads. What their proper botanical name was I never knew. Once I heard a Scotsman call them bulrushes, but of course they weren't bulrushes. In the old days country people used to plait baskets out of them. In their season they were prized collector's items with the children of our town.

We lay down to rest in the coarse grass by the old mill. No vengeful bees had pursued us.

'We threw them off the scent,' Lanty said, 'by seeking refuge in the Quarries.'

Down the slope we saw the ridged roofs of the town, the two limping imitation-Gothic spires of the Catholic church, the single plain steeple of the Protestant church and, blue behind them, like a giant's blue cattle on a fair day for mammoths, the Sperrin Mountains.

'We'll go scouting,' he said.

So we went scouting. He was Hawkeye. I was Kit Carson. Several times we almost spotted Indians but, as he said, the varmints preferred to evade us.

'The critters are lurking,' he explained. 'There's no fight in them at this season of the year.'

Never before or since did I hear that there was a close season in Indian fighting as in grouse shooting or, in the old days in Ireland, in the shooting of landlords – the season began with the dark nights. Yet since no bedaubed brave dared to show himself above grey scutch-grass, benweed or bedraggled furze, it is just possible that Lanty's explanation was the true one. We found, fair enough, the places they had camped in: circles of flattened grass littered with crushed and wrinkled newspapers. At nine years of age and reared in our quiet town, it had never occurred to me that lovers in the evening might seek out the peace and solitude of the Quarries. Indians were then to me more imaginable than lovers. So we scouted for hours. We crawled on our bellies to the tops of precipices of shale and terraced rock and, looking down on black unfathomable tarns, waited for a hunting party or, perhaps, even a party on the warpath to bring their long-tailed pinto ponies to the water. We saw no life, short of bearded chewing goats who stared at us with grave and learned disapproval. We saw the waterlogged quarryhole where the boy gathering blackheads had been accidentally drowned. We looked down solemnly on the ebony surface that had closed over the sorrows of the mad old woman.

Lanty said, 'Those are smashing blackheads down there. It's God's gospel truth that her ghost comes dripping up out of the water twice a year. Peter McGovern the breadman saw her waving once.'

Then, noticing my awed silence, he said, 'Look, did you ever see this? This is the way a cow lies down.'

It was a complicated acrobatic manoeuvre and it set me laughing long enough to forget about the old woman.

Moving westwards – there had been an article on the Santa Fe Trail, Path to Empire, in the National Geographic Magazine – we looked down from a dizzy height on definite signs of human activity.

'A white settlement,' Lanty said. 'It could be Fort Laramie.'

Unseen we settled ourselves in the grass to watch the colourful life of the frontier outpost: Traders coming and going, Indians in radiant blankets, an occasional intoxicated cowboy whooping and shooting into the air, a detachment of boys in blue riding out on a punitive expedition. The noise of the drill the quarry-workers were using was made by cavalry recruits on the firing-range. The high Ford motor-car approaching in a cloud of dust was the stage-coach rattling in with the Apaches in headlong, shrieking pursuit. But the sight of the owner of the ancient Ford was sufficient to dispel my fantasy. He was Gormley who owned the Quarries and he was a close friend of my father. His appearance reminded me that I had not been home since early morning and that evening shadows were now lengthening over the grass. He was a big man with red bushy eyebrows, the far sight of a hunting hawk and a voice like thunder. His eyes swept the face and rim of the quarry and, hidden as we were, spotted us as quickly as any Red Indian could. Then he raised his voice in violent language, all the louder and more startling because the chatter of the drill had ceased. He waved his fists. He shouted, 'Run for your bloody lives.'

Left to myself I might have failed to realise his meaning but Lanty was more perceptive. Before I knew what it was all about he was pulling me by the arm and we were running and running and then he was hurling me on the ground and throwing himself down beside me while, behind us, the Irish earth from which we had so recently surveyed Fort Laramie went skywards with a swoosh, stayed poised for a while in the air and then, as if tired with the wild skywards effort, settled slowly down again, stony crash succeeding stony crash and dying away at last into the growl of sea on a pebbly place. A few yards away from where we lay breathless some vagrant stones crashed to the grass, rolled towards us, then gave up the struggle and lay still.

'We'd be wise to evacuate before they track us,' he said. 'We're technically trespassers.'

He walked back as far as the nearest stones. He picked up one. He said solemnly, 'They could have blown us up.'

Then he tossed the stone carelessly into the air and laughed.

'That's as good as war,' he said. 'It's better than the film about Mons that was in Millar's Picture House. Because all they had behind the screen was Barney Hunt, the operator, rattling sheets of tin to pretend it was guns.'

He was the sort of boy who saw through every deception.

Ghost or no ghost, the smashing nature of the blackheads growing along the edge drew us back to the pool where the boy and the old woman had drowned and it was there, in the whispering, haunted evening, that the search-party found us. I was sitting disconsolately on the steep bank while Lanty, trousers rolled up to his hips, was dipping his feet carefully into the cold water. The blackheads moved gently and rattled in the evening wind. They were close to the bank, but the menace of such sombre waterholes was their rapidly shelving way of gaining depth.

'Stay where you are,' he had said almost fiercely. 'You can't swim. This is dangerous work if you slip.'

Humiliated, yet still with the warm feeling of being protected from unknown dangers, I sat on dry land while he uprooted the most adjacent blackheads and handed them back to me. Then my mother spoke from the ridge above us. Great Gormley was with her.

'Come on home, boy,' was all she said.

Expecting slaughter, I climbed up to the ridge but, instead of slaughter, affection met me and a warm embrace so that I felt bold enough to ask, 'Isn't Lanty coming with us?'

'Lanty,' my mother said, 'is quite capable of looking after himself.'

When I looked back he was lingering on a jagged skyline, the blackheads high above him like slender spears. He seemed lonely and forlorn, yet what could I do but wade on obediently homewards through deep grass already damp and chill with the coming night.

'You could have been blown to Bulgaria, boy,' Gormley roared.

He was a kindly man but he couldn't talk low. Back on the main road to the town we clambered into the ancient Ford. No longer was it a stage-coach.

'You could have been drowned, boy, wading into that quarryhole,' he bellowed.

I said piteously, 'I wasn't wading. Lanty wouldn't let me.'

All my mother said was, 'He's an unbiddable wild boy. He's no company for the like of you.'

All night long I tossed on my bed, feverish with worry for Lanty left alone by the haunted quarry where, when the shadows came, the ghost of a mad old woman would move, crouching like an animal, out of the rustling reeds and the canes of the blackheads. No sun was ever more splendid than the sun that shone the next day when I saw him, barefooted and alive, reading in one of the lurid periodicals of our day about the adventures of an unbeatable goalkeeper by the name of Cannonball Sam.

Lanty ran away from home and joined the Royal Artillery the day he was eighteen: a spring morning five years before Munich. Lady Bob told me. Lady Bob who kept open house in a room behind the huckster shop where, on winter nights, the works of Robert W. Service were read aloud, was a gentle, companionable soul and had grown to like Lanty.

When Bob was afflicted with rheumatism Lanty helped him to run the shop. He smiled sadly at me. He said, 'Lanty's gone a-soldiering.'

My mother said when she heard the news, 'I never expected better.'

'Kind father for him,' said my own father.

He meant, 'He's the same as his father before him and how could he be different.'

'His father fought at Mons,' said my father. 'Now and again his wounds still bleed.'

Years later, long after I had left my native town, and when the smoke of the war had settled down as the quarrystones that day had settled down in the grass, I went one afternoon to visit my mother who was a patient in a big city hospital.

'Guess who's here,' she said. 'Your old schoolmate, Lanty. He's an up-patient.'

'Is that so,' I said.

'He comes round to see me often. A perfect gentleman, like his father before him.'

'Is that so,' I said. 'I heard he was wounded in the war.'

'In the heart of the African desert, God help us. He suffered a lot. But his life was miraculously preserved.'

There had been twelve to twenty of them in a lorry in Libya when they struck a land mine. His comrades were killed outright but Lanty, flung to a distance, lived with a leg and a half. He lay for seven hours, now conscious, now unconscious. When they found him he had torn off his shirt and wrapped it around the shattered, bleeding stump. But he lived.

'By a blessed miracle,' said my mother.

He came stiff-legged towards us down the slippery floor of the women's ward. He was meticulously dressed in dark cloth as, vaguely, I remembered his father, the veteran of Mons, had always been. He was tall and straight, carried no stick, and his dark glossy hair was parted exactly up the middle and well-oiled. He enquired after my mother's health. He shook hands with me.

'The old wound bleeds now and again,' he said. 'I came in for a check up.'

'Your father, God rest him, suffered a lot,' my mother said.

'I often think of the old days,' he said. 'We had great times then.'

When he walked away from us up the ward I could see, so clearly that I was in pain, the forlorn wild boy with the handful of blackheads on the edge of the sullen ebony water where the old despairing woman had stumbled in to her death. My own wound bled.

'I always knew he was a gentleman,' I said truculently. 'Ever since the day he wouldn't let me wade in after the blackheads.'

'What day was that?' she asked. 'And whatever are blackheads?'

'They are tall things like canes that grow in watery places. They have long black furry heads. I never knew what their proper botanical name was. I once heard a Scotsman call them bulrushes, but of course they're not bulrushes. In the old days people used to plait baskets out of them.'

'Poor boy,' she said. 'You always did ramble so.'

She smiled. She said, 'I always thought blackheads were nasty spots that destroyed complexions.'

Then after a pause she said, 'You could settle my pillows. Isn't it wonderful the way his wound bleeds? Just like his father before him. His father, God be good to him, was a fine man.'

BLACKBIRD ON A BRAMBLE BOUGH

I only knew one poet in my life. The day before yesterday I saw his photograph, two columns wide, on the literary page of the American newspaper that Jim O'Neill, the publican, gets from his aunt who went to Philadelphia to marry Jack Kane from Drum. From the reading matter on the page it appeared that the poet went to the United States shortly after he met me. Not, I imagine, that I had anything to do with his emigration. He published a book of poetry after his arrival in the United States. The critics in America, or at least one of them, thought the poems great poems altogether or, should it be, entirely. The reviewer in this particular paper had a whole lot to say about the brown bogs of Ireland, about a note of lyrical freshness like the song of the blackbird on the bramble bough, about a warm wet wind from the land of song and shamrock. Yet I suspect that that same poet had never seen a bog, black, brown, or deceptively emerald green, until I introduced him to the one at the back of the town; and never in all my days of bird-nesting did I see a man who looked less like a blackbird on a bramble bough.

The picture in the paper wasn't a particularly good one. It looked as if it was reproduced from a photograph taken for a passport or a driving-licence, giving the subject either the drawn, hollow-cheeked look of someone dying in a decline or the unsocial look of somebody wanted for murder – or even murder with nasty complications. Success, perhaps, had thinned the man, or the high-life they live in American cities. The face wasn't as wide and smooth. The eyes had a little narrow loneliness. For half a minute I was pitying him and thinking of the apology I owed him, an apology he would never get. But then Jim O'Neill came round behind me, polishing a tall tumbler, looking over my shoulder, seeing the picture and saying, 'So that's the lad in question.'

He rested the tumbler and the white cloth on the counter, took up the paper and studied it carefully.

'You'd never think he was that kind. Clip it out,' he said, 'and send it up to the holy nuns. They might want to write a letter to the editor about his poetic gifts.'

Then we saw our faces reflected between rows of bottles and lines of gilt lettering in the long mirror behind the counter and we laughed until my drink went with my breath and I coughed and spluttered over the American paper and the picture of the poet.

The nuns never forgave me. That didn't worry me much. If it hadn't been for my cousin, Tommy Mack, who was going for the priesthood at that time, but who left the college afterwards and made a pile out of insurance and greyhounds, I wouldn't have been invited to the thing in the first place. Tommy was on holidays then, convalescing, spending his weekends in our house in the town where he was convenient to the new cinema. One morning after breakfast he opened a neat white envelope forwarded to him from his father's house in the country. He read the letter.

'Poetry,' he said. 'The curse of mankind. The Egyptian darkness. The eighth and dirtiest of the seven deadly sins.'

'Don't be so bitter, Tommy,' said my brother.

'Nuns,' said Tommy. 'They mean well. But, God help them, what do they know.'

'Not much,' said my brother, 'about some things. As much as is good for them about others.'

'They don't know, for instance,' said Tommy as he tore the white letter into tiny pieces, 'that the night they invite me to listen to a lecture on poetry in the convent's aula maxima is the one night before I'll be immured in Maynooth again that I've a chance of hearing Betty Grable as Sweet Rosie O'Grady.'

'Seeing,' I suggested.

'Hearing and seeing,' he conceded. 'Two senses are involved. And the worst of it is that this Sister Margaret Mary who invites me went to school with my mother.'

'There's no escape,' said my brother.

'Not a loophole,' said Tommy. 'The letter says, though, I can bring a friend.'

With a calculating eye he looked from me to my brother and back again to me.

'It'll be experience for you,' my brother said to me. 'The life of a big convent boarding school is one interesting aspect of all life. It is about three hundred different approaches to the same small problem.'

'We know well,' I said, 'that you don't want to go.'

'The problem of the young and the pure looking forward with much longing and a soupçon of suspicion to the fullness of life,' he said. 'Guiding and directing them are those chosen ones who have willingly turned their backs on the song and the dalliance in the sunshine. I would gladly go with you, Tommy. But on that particular night a young lady who, incidentally, had all her problems, or almost all, of approach to life solved within those sacred walls has persuaded me to take her to a dance in a certain rural house of amusement. Not select but lively.'

'Dalliance,' I said sourly, 'in the moonshine.'

But as Tommy Mack was a decent fellow even if he was a relation and a damned odd clerical student I went to the convent with him to the lecture.

There was the poet sitting on a high chair and propped up with his elbows on a desk and lecturing like the hammers of hell about the poetry of Alice Meynell.

'It could have been worse,' Tommy whispered. 'It could have been Francis Thompson or Gerard Manley Hopkins. It could have been Chesterton. I'd have given you ten to one the field on the certainty of it's being Chesterton.'

The poet was as big as a house. He went up from and out from the chair on which he sat and his great body was dressed in reverent and decorous black. He inclined forwards over the desk that supported his elbows and gestured with hands that were white and wide and hairless and as bulky as heavy hams. The great head, completely bald, tilted slightly backwards. His voice was thin, piercing, incredibly refined. He told the nuns and the rows of nice little girls that she walked, the lady of his delight, a shepherdess of sheep.

'Her flocks are thoughts,' he read out of a little blue book.

Then he waited until the noise of our late entry had rippled along all the rows of loose chairs and died into silence against the walls of the aula maxima.

'She keeps them white,' he read. 'She guards them from the steep.'

The aula maxima was full of them, white flocks of white thoughts, idle thoughts, possibly a few scarlet thoughts, rows and rows of young ladies who would some day be somebody's delight, two rows of quiet nuns hoping for delight in meadows beyond this world. We sat, timidly enough, at the end of the second row of nuns. As far as I could see there wasn't another man in the place except the poet who thundered on and on, reading quotation after quotation with a line now and again of straight speaking that may or may not have been his own invention. After every such passage of prose he smoothed the wide forehead slowly with the ham of a hand, then tenderly with finger and thumb felt the bridge of his nose and, assured that his brain container was standing up to the strain, on he swept. It all sounded hellishly familiar, but then one time I had read a whole book about Alice Meynell and few people in our town could say the same. Sister Margaret Mary, who wrote religious verse in the local paper, may also have read that book. If she had then her thoughts as she listened to the poet must have been as bleak and forbidding as a bare cell. She had a name for economy. It would have been cheaper for her to buy the book and read it to the girls.

After the lecture there was tea, the nuns presiding, for the poet and ourselves and for a half-dozen or so of the senior girls. There were introductions all round. I got the feeling that, in spite of Tommy's black coat, in spite of his miraculously-sudden interest in the works of Don Columba Marmion and the retreats given by some famous Dublin Jesuit, the shepherdesses looked with grim faces on the introduction of Tommy's cousin into the sheepfold. Perhaps I had a bit of a reputation about the town and the gossip of the town always came in the end to the convent, like lost ships in that film long ago to the centre of the Sargasso Sea. Perhaps it was mistaken politeness to say, when I was introduced to a well-developed redheaded member of the flock: 'Oh, we've met already.'

By the look on Sister Margaret Mary's face she clearly wanted to ask, 'When? Where? How often? For what purpose? Under what circumstances?'

In the isolation in which I was left for the rest of the party I took malicious pleasure in speculating on the possible reaction if I upped and gave Sister Margaret Mary all the splendid details.

The poet was as bald as a coot. He had a clammy handshake that would have warned off any decent girl who knew the difference between fun and danger. But he wore a dignified black suit. He wrote poetry. He talked poetry. He lectured about the poetry of Alice Meynell. He was old enough to be the father of any girl in the school. So the poet was Sister Margaret Mary's whiteheaded boy. The girls of the party and most of the nuns gathered around him. He ate cakes and drank tea with a burning consuming ability. Sister Margaret Mary talked to Tommy. An old nun with a sharp face and a rheumatic left hand talked to Tommy's cousin. She was detailed, I knew, to keep an eye on me, to keep me at a distance from the circle of white thoughts, from that well-developed redheaded prize-lamb. Yet once in a while the redhead gracefully and slyly swivelled around to give me the full glowing benefit of her amused, devil-may-care eyes. Once she made a lightning gesture with her right arm, pouted her underlip and with a nod of the head indicated the poet. How was Sister Margaret Mary to know, even if she had witnessed the pantomime, that the girl was comparing the poet to

Charles Boyer and enjoying the comparison, or contrast, as only the thoughtlessly, recklessly happy can enjoy anything in our town, or in any other town.

This carry-on continued for the best part of an hour. Outside it was a heavy moonless night, warm and soft after long days of rain.

The old nun was telling me about her childhood in some part of the County Waterford. The taste of sweet cakes and sweet tea was like wet ashes in my mouth. Mirages, visions of tall beakers of strong, black fluid, appeared before my eyes, white foam spilled viscously over smooth brims. Sister Margaret Mary, cloistrally dry – even though she walked through my dripping visions – came towards me with the semi-clerical cousin, Tommy, in her wake. He looked weary.

'Our lecturer,' she said, 'doesn't know the way to his hotel. I suppose you could show him where it is.'

She spoke as if she had learned the sentences by heart and as if she doubted my ability to make my way from any one given point to another.

'I want to keep Tommy for a while,' she said. 'I want to talk to him about his mother.'

Seeing Tommy's face I laughed, I couldn't help laughing. But Sister Margaret Mary didn't laugh with me and neither did Tommy. It was a long, long way to Sweet Rosie O'Grady.

In the slippery, polished hallway where a visiting monsignor had once fallen and broken his hip, I helped the poet into his overcoat, a black astrakhan business weighing about seventy pounds and with a Chestertonian cape. He lighted a cigar and watched me struggle into my battered, belted covering of cheap tweed. Swinging a black cane he paraded down the curving stone steps.

Sister Margaret Mary pointed to a large two-handled object on the hallway floor. She said, 'This is his bag. Good night now and God bless you. Tell your mother Tommy will be down in thirty minutes. I want him to meet Sister Benigna.'

About Tommy or Sister Benigna I couldn't at that moment have cared less. I hobbled down the steps and followed along the avenue the crunch of his monstrous feet on the gravel and the beacon-like glow of his cigar. The bag was twice as heavy as the overcoat. At the end of the long avenue he took the cigar out of his mouth and with curiosity rather than compassion studied my struggling, muscle-strained progress. He said, 'I carry so many books with me. Tools of the lecturer's trade. That bag must weigh a lot. Perhaps we'd better take a taxi.'

Donnegan's hackney place was fifty yards down the road from the convent gates. Dragged forwards and given, by the weight of the bag, the staggering, perilous momentum of a sufferer from Saint Vitus' dance, I kept the lead all the way. He came regally behind me and the wind, puffing up the street, swept around my nostrils the exotic eastern odour of scented tobacco burning sweetly in the darkness.

'Take it carefully,' he said. 'I've something there more fragile than books.'

He laughed a high thin laugh.

'Books and bottles,' he said. 'Almost but not quite the complete secret of graceful living.'

Jimmy Donnegan backed his old Ford out of the cobbled entry-way and we drove down the long straggle of a town to the hotel. Jimmy is a small dark man with a sideways nose and two shiny black eyes not very well balanced in the general layout of his face. Every bone in his little body is brittle with understandable suspicion of the outsize, in human bodies, hearts or minds, in motor-cars, horses, dogs or stall-fed cattle. So when the poet had gone into the hotel, leaving me to struggle with the bag, Jimmy whispered conspiratorially in my ear: 'Is yon big brute of a fellow paying for the car?'

'He's a poet, Jimmy.'

'Poets,' said Jimmy, 'are odd boys. Are they all as big as yon fellow?'

'They come in pocket editions too,' I said.

I rattled two shillings and six pennies into Jimmy's little left hand. It wasn't a lot to pay for the privilege of riding in the back-seat of Donnegan's Ford with a real poet who was as big and wide as a mountain.

In the hotel the poet had already made his way to the lounge and was sitting in the height of comfort with a glass of brandy in his fist.

'Is the bag all right?' he asked.

'Grand,' I answered, remembering that while paying Jimmy his fee I had forgotten to continue the struggle that would have brought the bag safely to the pavement. But my arms, my shoulders and back-muscles were crying out to their creator against any renewal of the struggle with that burden of books and bottles. Anyway Jimmy was halfway back to the garage in the cobbled entry. The bag would be safe there till morning and the poet would be none the wiser until I was gone beyond recall.

'Books and bottles,' said the poet. 'Thirsty work lecturing. But the sisters adore it. The girls lap it up. Bless their little poetical hearts.'

He was fluid. He was a fountain of oil.

'Won't you join me in a drink, young man?'

I ordered a pint. I paid for my pint and for the poet's brandy.

'So you like long large drinks,' he said dispassionately.

He ignored splendidly the lingering slowness with which I pocketed my diminishing small cash.

'It's a northern habit. If you'll allow me to say so, a barbarous habit. Overloading the kidneys and depressing the stomach. Now in the southern countries, in the Latin lands. As Chesterton says, the secret of the sun. This.'

He held up the brandy to the light. He said, 'Small. But exquisite. Concentrated.'

'Good goods,' I said, 'in small parcels.'

'Chesterton you should read,' he said. 'On Chaucer. And in his veins the secret of the sun. I envy a young man like you the wealth of good reading that still lies ahead of you. My America. My Newfoundland.'

We drank and I paid for another brandy and another pint.

'Books and bottles,' said the poet. 'Two-thirds of life. Never complete until the missing one-third is added. Beauty and form. Shapeliness. We do not understand in this country. But the French. The French are the people. They have so perfectly understood human nature.'

He steadied his glass on the table and with his free hand cut the air with curving gestures that showed to me as plainly as day from night the legs and figure of the nameless abstraction in the man's warm mind.

'You understand,' he said.

'I understand.'

'You are a man of the world,' he said. 'Shall we have another drink? Thank you, sir. A man of the world. And men of the world can be the exceptions in the virtuous towns of the Irish provinces. I observed, sir, the glad eye given to you by that so charming creature with the golden hair. So charming. I said to myself: A man of the world. We understand each other.'

'We do.'

'This hotel now. A fine hotel, sir. A credit to a prosperous, commercial, historic town. A quiet hotel, I suppose.'

'As quiet as a graveyard.'

Over the counter I explained the position to Ned the barman. My credit was good. I watched the poet drink three more glasses of brandy as if he was entitled to them and as if it was my man-of-the-worldish privilege and duty to buy them for him. We talked, or he did, about Belloc and Maurice Baring, about Christian men and wine.

'There is,' I hinted, 'another hotel. Four or five miles from the town and doing a big after-hours trade with singsongs and all that.'

'All that,' he said.

'The best of company,' I said.

'A man of the world,' he said. 'A man in a thousand.'

'Have another brandy?'

He had three more. Altogether it cost me a lot of money. He leaned on my shoulder as we made our way out to the side-door where, Ned the barman had whispered to me, Jack the boots was waiting with the hotel Austin. He needed a little support and a little careful steering. For a big man he had a poor head. But by that time he was feeling brotherly, affectionate and trusting; and in his eyes I was a man in a thousand.

Jack the boots drove us three times around the town, keeping out of sight of the houses, turning and twisting and leaving one road for another with marvellous and unmonotonous skill. He halted the car at last on the back road that runs from the flax scutching mill through Beatty's black bog. In the distance I indicated for the poet's benefit the shadowy bulk of the long building but it was doubtful if his brandy-blinded eyes could see further than the low-clipped hedge at the side of the road. But he was in a hopeful and a credulous mood.

'It's the back entrance,' I said.

I pointed to the path that led down across the black bog and up the slope to the rear of the long building.

'You know the way people in a place like this talk.'

He punched my ribs and laughed and belched enough brandy fumes to deflower a total abstainer.

'Sly dog,' he said. 'Sly dog.'

I led the way along the path across the bog. It wasn't more than seventy-five yards but the path twisted, the ground was soft and slippery and spotted with puddles. He fell once and it was no easy business putting him back on his feet, and the black substance of Beatty's bog was no addition at all to his splendid overcoat.

The little iron gate in the grey wall has been on the latch night and day since Molly, the caretaker's daughter, declared her independence and took to going to late dances. I closed it quietly behind us and led the way, tiptoeing along the concrete path between the lime trees. There was the back door of the building and not a light in any window.

'Knock the three quiet knocks,' I said, 'that are known the world over. They keep open house. I'd go with you myself only I'm not *persona grata* there just at the moment. There was a fight one night over a woman.'

He was already moving eagerly but unsteadily towards the door.

'Everything you want is there,' I said, 'if you can get it.'

'Leave that to me,' he said gallantly.

Attempting a swagger he tottered and just barely managed to recover his balance.

Going back in the car with Jack the boots I realised that the poet hadn't even said thanks for what he believed he was about to receive. That annoyed me more than anything else. So I walked across the town to Donnegan's and paid Jim another two and sixpence to drive the big bag as far as the metal bridge over the Fairywater. Possibly little Jim, too, became annoyed when he studied the outsize bag. At any rate he willingly helped me to raise it to the red parapet and to push it outwards and downwards to watery darkness. Afterwards Jim and myself had a long talk about the night in the troubled times when the boys blew up the predecessor of the metal bridge and Butt Kelly, their leader, was the last to withdraw in good order, leaving his coat on the river-bank with seven letters in the pocket of it as well as the military plans of his column for the next six months and the names, addresses and records of all revolutionary personnel.

Yesterday a Dublin paper reprinted on its literary page the article from the American paper. The photograph that went with the reprint was only a single column in width but the face was fatter than in the American picture and the eyes had no loneliness. Ireland, said the Dublin paper, is proud of his poems: he has spoken to thousands of exiles and sons and daughters of exiles of the Ireland of their childhood or the Ireland of their dreams and of the faith of their fathers.

I wonder did Sister Margaret Mary read the article. And did she recall the night she had to telephone the police to take him away from battering and cursing at the back-door of the convent? He told the police next day about a valuable bag that had been stolen. But he had no proof, no witnesses, not even Sister Margaret Mary. He was a foreigner in the town. He was a poet. He was drunk and disorderly.

But America's a big place and there's room in it for poets and all classes.

HOMES ON THE MOUNTAIN

The year I was twelve my father, my mother, my brother and myself had our Christmas dinner in the house my godmother's husband had built high up on the side of Dooish Mountain, when he and she came home to Ireland from Philadelphia.

That was a great godmother. She had more half-crowns in her patch pockets than there were in the Bank of England and every time she encountered me which, strategically, I saw was pretty often, it rained half-crowns. Those silver showers made my friend Lanty and myself the most popular boy bravados in our town. A curious thing was, though, that while we stood bobby-dazzler caramels, hazelnut chocolate, ice cream, cigarettes and fish and chips by the ton to our sycophants, we ourselves bought nothing but song-books. Neither of us could sing a note.

We had a splendid, patriotic taste in song-books, principally because the nearest newsagent's shop, kept by an old spinster in Devlin Street, had a window occupied by a sleeping tomcat, two empty tin boxes, bundles of pamphlets yellowed by exposure to the light, and all members of a series called Irish Fireside Songs. The collective title appealed by its warm cosiness. The little books were classified into Sentimental, Patriot's Treasury, Humorous and Convivial, and Smiles and Tears. Erin, we knew from Tom Moore and from excruciating music lessons at school, went wandering around with a tear and a smile blended in her eye. Because even to ourselves our singing was painful, we read together, sitting in the sunshine on the steps that led up to my father's house, such gems of the Humorous and Convivial as: 'When I lived in Sweet Ballinacrazy, dear, the girls were all bright as a daisy, dear.' Or turning to the emerald-covered Patriot's Treasury we intoned: 'We've men from the Nore, from the Suir and the Shannon, let the tyrant come forth, we'll bring force against force.'

Perhaps, unknown to ourselves, we were affected with the nostalgia that had brought my godmother and her husband back from the comfort of Philadelphia to the bleak side of Dooish Mountain. It was a move that my mother, who was practical and who had never been far enough from Ireland to feel nostalgia, deplored.

'Returned Americans,' she would say, 'are lost people. They live between two worlds. Their heads are in the clouds. Even the scrawny, black-headed sheep – not comparing the human being and the brute beast – know by now that Dooish is no place to live.'

'And if you must go back to the land,' she said, 'let it be the land, not rocks, heather and grey fields no bigger than pocket handkerchiefs. There's Cantwell's fine place beside the town going up for auction. Seventy acres of land, a palace of a dwelling-house, outhouses would do credit to the royal family, every modern convenience and more besides.'

For reasons that had nothing to do with prudence or sense, Lanty and myself thought the Cantwell place an excellent idea. There were crab-apple trees of the most amazing fertility scattered all along the hedgerows on the farm; a clear gravel stream twisted through it; there were flat pastures made for football and, behind the house, an orchard that not even the most daring buccaneer of our generation had ever succeeded in robbing.

But there were other reasons – again nostalgic reasons – why my godmother's husband who was the living image of Will Rogers would build nowhere in Ireland except on the rough, wet side of Dooish, and there, on the site of the old home where he had spent his boyhood, the house went up. There wasn't a building job like it since the building of the Tower of Babel.

'Get a good sensible contractor from the town,' said my mother, 'not drunken Dan Redmond from the mountain who couldn't build a dry closet.'

But my godmother's husband had gone to school with Dan Redmond. They had been barefooted boys together and that was that, and there was more spent, according to my mother, on malt whisky to entertain Dan, his tradesmen and labourers, than would have built half New York. To make matters worse it was a great season for returned Americans and every one of them seemed to have known my godmother and her husband in Philadelphia. They came in their legions to watch the building, to help pass the bottle and to proffer advice. The acknowledged queen of this gathering of souls fluttering between two worlds was my Aunt Brigid, my mother's eldest sister. She was tiny and neat, precise in her speech, silver-haired, glittering with rimless spectacles and jet-black beads. In the States she had acquired a mania for euchre, a passion for slivers of chicken jelled in grey-green soup, a phonograph with records that included a set of the favourite songs of

Jimmy Walker, and the largest collection of snapshots ever carried by pack mule or public transport out of Atlantic City.

Then there was a born American – a rarity in our parts in those days – a young man and a distant relative. Generous and jovial, he kissed every woman, young or old, calling them cousin or aunt; but it was suspected among wise observers that he never once in the course of his visit was able to see the Emerald Isle clearly. For the delegation, headed by my Aunt Brigid, that met him in Dublin set him straight away on the drink and when he arrived to view the building site – it was one of the few sunny days of that summer – he did so sitting on the dickey seat of a jaunting car and waving in each hand a bottle of whisky. The builder and his men and the haymakers in June meadows left their work to welcome him, and Ireland, as the song says, was Ireland through joy and through tears.

Altogether it was a wet season: the whisky flowed like water, the mist was low over the rocks and heather of Dooish and the moors of Loughfresha and Cornavara, the mountain runnels were roaring torrents. But miraculously the building was done; the returned Americans with the exception of Aunt Brigid, my godmother and her husband, went westwards again in the fall; and against all my mother's advice on the point of health, the couple from Philadelphia settled in for late November. The house-warming was fixed for Christmas Day.

'Dreamers,' my mother said. 'An American apartment on the ground-walls of an old cabin. Living in the past. Up where only a brave man would build a shooting lodge. For all they know or care there could be wolves still on the mountain. Magazines and gewgaws and chairs too low to sit on. With the rheumatism the mountain'll give them, they'll never bend their joints to sit down so low.'

Since the damp air had not yet brought its rheumatism we all sat down together in the house that was the answer to the exile's dream. Lamplight shone on good silver and Belfast linen. My godmother's man was proud to the point of tears.

'Sara Alice,' he said to my mother.

Content, glass in hand, he was more than ever like Will Rogers.

'Sara Alice,' he said. 'My mother, God rest her, would be proud to see this day.'

Practicality momentarily abandoned, my mother, moist-eyed and sipping sherry, agreed.

'Tommy,' he said to my father, 'listen to the sound of the spring outside.'

We could hear the wind, the voices of the runnels, the spring pouring clear and cool from a rainspout driven into a rock-face.

'As far as I recollect that was the first sound my ears ever heard, and I heard it all my boyhood, and I could hear it still in Girard Avenue, Philadelphia. But the voices of children used to be part of the sound of the spring. Seven of us, and me to be the youngest and the last alive. When my mother died and my father took us all to the States we didn't know when we were going away whether to leave the door open or closed. We left it open in case a travelling man might pass, needing shelter. We knocked gaps in the hedges and stone walls so as to give the neighbours' cattle the benefit of commonage and the land the benefit of the cow dung. But we left the basic lines of the walls so that nobody could forget our name or our claim to this part of the mountain.'

'In Gartan, in Donegal,' said my father, 'there's a place called the Flagstone of Loneliness where Saint Colmcille slept the night before he left Ireland under sentence of banishment. The exiles in that part used to lie down there the day before they sailed and pray to the saint to be preserved from the pangs of homesickness.'

My Aunt Brigid piped in a birdlike voice a bit of an exile song that was among her treasured recordings: 'A strange sort of sigh seems to come from us all as the waves hide the last glimpse of old Donegal.'

'Our American wake was held in Aunt Sally O'Neill's across the glen,' said my godmother's husband. 'Red Owen Gormley lilted for the dancers when the fiddlers were tired. He was the best man of his time at the mouth music.'

'He was also,' said my father, 'the first and last man I knew who could make a serviceable knife, blade and haft, out of a single piece of hardwood. I saw him do it, myself and wild Martin Murphy who was with me in the crowd of sappers who chained these mountains for the 1911 Ordnance Survey map. Like most of us, Martin drank every penny and on frosty days he would seal the cracks in his shoes with butter – a trick I never saw another man use. It worked too.'

'Aunt Sally's two sons were there at our American wake,' said my godmother's husband. 'Thady that was never quite right in the head and, you remember, Tommy, couldn't let a woman in the market or a salmon in the stream alone. John, the elder brother, was there with Bessy from Cornavara that he wooed for sixty years and never, I'd say, even kissed.'

The old people were silently laughing. My brother, older than myself, was on the fringe of the joke. As my godmother came and went I sniffed fine cooking. I listened to the mountain wind and the noise of the spring and turned the bright pages of an American gardening magazine. Here were rare blooms would never grow on Dooish Mountain.

'All dead now I suppose,' my father said to end the laughing.

'Bessy's dead now,' said my Aunt Brigid. 'Two years ago. As single as the day she was born. Like many another Irishman John wasn't overgiven to matrimony. But in the village of Crooked Bridge below, the postman told me that John and Thady are still alive in the old house on Loughfresha. Like pigs in a sty, he said. Pigs in a sty. And eight thousand pounds each, according to all accounts, in the Munster and Leinster Bank in the town.'

'God help us,' said my mother. 'I recall that house as it was when Aunt Sally was alive. It was beautiful.'

My father was looking out of the window, down the lower grey slopes of Dooish and across the deep glen towards Loughfresha and Cornavara.

'It won't rain again before dark or dinner,' he said. 'I haven't walked these hills since I carried a chain for His Majesty's Ordnance Survey. Who'd ever have thought the King of England would be interested in the extent of Cornavara or Dooish Mountain.'

'Get up you two boys,' he said, 'and we'll see if you can walk as well as your father before you.'

The overflow of the spring came with us as we descended the boreen. Winter rain had already rutted the new gravel laid by drunken Dan Redmond and his merry men. Below the bare apple-orchard the spring's overflow met with another runnel and with yet another where another boreen, overgrown with hawthorn and bramble, struggled upwards to an abandoned house.

'Some people,' said my father, 'didn't come back to face the mountain. Living in Philadelphia must give a man great courage.'

He walked between us with the regular easy step of an old soldier who, in days of half-forgotten wars had footed it for ever across the African veldt.

'That was all we ever did,' he would say. 'Walk and walk. And the only shot I ever fired that I remember was at a black snake and I never knew whether I hit or missed. That was the Boer war for you.'

Conjoined, innumerable runnels swept under a bridge where the united boreens joined the road, plunged over rock in a ten-foot cataract, went elbowing madly between bare hazels down to the belly of the glen. White cabins, windows already lamp-lighted and candle-lighted for Christmas, showed below the shifting fringe of black grey mist.

'This house I knew well,' he said, 'this was Aunt Sally's. The Aunt was a title of honour and had nothing to do with blood relationship. She was stately, a widow, a great manager and aunt to the whole country. She had only the two sons.'

By the crossroads of the thirteen limekilns we swung right and descended the slope of the glen on what in a dry summer would have been a dust road. Now, wet sand shifted under our feet, loose stones rattled ahead of us, the growing stream growled below us in the bushes. To our left were the disused limekilns, lining the roadway like ancient monstrous idols with gaping toothless mouths, and as we descended the old man remembered the days when he and his comrades, veterans all, had walked and measured those hills; the limekilns in operation and the white dust on the grass and the roadside hedges; the queues of farm carts waiting for the loading. Fertilisers made in factories had ended all that. There was the place (he pointed across a field) where a tree, fallen on a mearing fence, had lain and rotted while the two farmers whose land the fence divided, swept away by the joy of legal conflict, had disputed in the court in the town the ownership of the timber. The case never reached settlement. Mountainy men loved law and had their hearts in twopence. And here was Loughfresha bridge. (The stream was a torrent now.) The gapped, stone parapet hadn't been mended since the days of the survey. And there was the wide pool where Thady O'Neill, always a slave to salmon, had waded in after a big fish imprisoned by low water, taken it with his bare hands after a mad struggle and, it was said, cured himself by shock treatment of premature arthritis.

Once across the bridge our ascent commenced. Black brooding roadside cattle looked at us with hostility. On a diagonal across a distant meadow a black hound dog ran silently, swiftly up towards the mist, running as if with definite purpose – but what, I wondered, could a dog be doing running upwards there alone on a Christmas Day. The thought absorbed me to the exclusion of all else until we came to the falling house of John and Thady O'Neill.

'Good God in heaven,' said my father.

For a full five minutes he stood looking at it, not speaking, before he led his two sons, with difficulty, as far as the door.

Once it must have been a fine, long, two-storeyed, thatched farmhouse, standing at an angle of forty-five degrees to the roadway and built backwards into the slope of the hill. But the roof and the upper storey had sagged and, topped by the growth of years of rank decayed grass, the remnants of the thatched roof looked, in the Christmas dusk, like a rubbish heap a maniacal mass-murderer might pick as a burial mound for his victims.

'They won't be expecting us for our Christmas dinner,' said my brother.

To reach the door we went ankle-deep, almost, through plashy ground and forded in the half-dark a sort of seasonal stream. One small uncurtained window showed faintly the yellow light of an oil-lamp.

Knock, knock, knock went my father on the sagging door.

No dogs barked. No calves or cocks made comforting farmhouse noises. The wind was raucous in the bare dripping hazels that overhung the wreck of a house from the slope behind. An evil wizard might live here.

Knock, knock, knock went my father.

'Is there anybody there said the traveller,' said my brother, who had a turn for poetry.

'John O'Neill and Thady,' called my father. 'I've walked over from the Yankee's new house at Dooish and brought my two sons with me to wish you a happy Christmas.'

He shouted out his own name.

In a low voice he said to us, 'Advance, friends, and be recognised.'

My brother and myself giggled and stopped giggling as chains rattled and slowly, with a thousand creaks of aged iron and timber in bitter pain and in conflict with each other, the door opened. Now, years after that Christmas, I can rely only on a boyhood memory of a brief visit to a badly-lighted cavern. There was a hunched decrepit old man behind the opening door. Without extending his hand he shuffled backwards and away from us. His huge hobnailed boots were unlaced. They flapped around him like the feet of some strange bird or reptile. He was completely bald. His face was pear-shaped, running towards the point at the forehead. His eyes had the brightness and quickness of a rodent's eyes. When my father said, 'Thady, you remember me,' he agreed doubtfully, as if agreement or disagreement were equally futile. He looked sideways furtively at the kitchen table half-hidden in shadows near one damp-streaked yellow wall. For a tablecloth that table had a battered raincoat and when our knock had interrupted him Thady had, it would seem, been heeling over onto the coat a pot of boiled potatoes. He finished the task while we stood uncertainly inside the doorway. Then, as if tucking in a child for sleep, he wrapped the tails of the coat around the pile of steaming tubers. A thunderous hearty voice spoke to us from the corner between the hearth and a huge four-poster bed. It was a rubicund confident voice. It invited us to sit down, and my father sat on a low chair close to the hearth-fire. My brother and myself stood uncomfortably behind him. There was, at any rate, nothing for us to sit on. The smoky oil-lamp burned low but the bracket that held it was on the wall above the owner of the voice. So it haloed with a yellow glow the head of John O'Neill, the dilatory lover of Bessie of Cornavara who had gone unwed to the place where none embrace. It was a broad, red-faced, white-haired head, too large and heavy, it seemed, for the old wasted body.

'It's years since we saw you, Tommy,' said John.

'It's years indeed.'

'And all the wild men that had been in the army.'

'All the wild men.'

'Times are changed, Tommy.'

'Times are changed indeed,' said my father.

He backed his chair a little away from the fire. Something unpleasantly odorous fried and sizzled in an unlidded pot-oven. The flagged floor, like the roof, had sagged. It sloped away from the hearth and into the shadows towards a pyramid of bags of flour and meal and feeding stuffs for cattle.

'But times are good,' said John. 'The land's good, and the crops and cattle.'

'And the money plentiful.'

'The money's plentiful.'

'I'm glad to hear you say it,' said my father.

'The Yankee came back, Tommy.'

'He came back.'

'And built a house, I hear. I don't go abroad much beyond my own land.'

'He built a fine house.'

'They like to come back, the Yankees. But they never settle.'

'It could be that the change proves too much for them,' said my father.

Then after a silence, disturbed only by the restless scratching of Thady's nailed soles on the floor, my father said, 'You never married, John.'

'No, Tommy. Bessy died. What with stock to look after and all, a man doesn't have much time for marrying.'

'Thady was more of a man for the ladies than you ever were,' said my father to John.

Behind us there was a shrill hysterical cackle and from John a roar of red laughter.

'He was that. God, Tommy, the memory you have.'

'Memory,' said my father.

Like a man in a trance he looked, not at John or Thady, but into the red heart of the turf fire.

'There was the day, Thady,' he said, 'when Martin Murphy and myself looked over a whin hedge at yourself and Molly Quigley from

Crooked Bridge making love in a field. Between you, you ruined a half-acre of turnips.'

The red laughter and the cackle continued.

'Tommy, you have the memory,' said John. 'Wasn't it great the way you remembered the road up Loughfresha?'

'It was great,' said my father. 'Trust an old soldier to remember a road.'

The odour from the sizzling pot-oven was thickening.

'Well, we'll go now,' said my father. 'We wouldn't have butted in on you the day it is only for old time's sake.'

'You're always welcome, Tommy. Anytime you pass the road.'

'I don't pass this road often, John.'

'Well, when you do you're welcome. Those are your two sons.'

'My two sons.'

'Two fine clean young men,' said John.

He raised a hand to us. He didn't move out of the chair. The door closed slowly behind us and the chains rattled. We forded the seasonal stream, my brother going in over one ankle and filling a shoe with water.

We didn't talk until we had crossed the loud stream at Loughfresha Bridge. In the darkness I kept listening for the haunted howl of the black hound-dog.

'Isn't it an awful way, Da,' I said, 'for two men to live, particularly if it's true they have money in the bank.'

'If you've money in the bank,' said my brother, who suffered from a sense of irony, 'it's said you can do anything you please.'

With a philosophy too heavy for my years I said, 'It's a big change from the house we're going to.'

'John and Thady,' said my brother, 'didn't have the benefit of forty-five years in Philadelphia.'

My father said nothing.

'What, I wonder,' I said, 'was cooking in the pot-oven?'

'Whatever it was,' said my brother, 'they'll eat it with relish and roll into that four-poster bed and sleep like heroes.'

The black brooding roadside cattle seemed as formidable as wild bison.

'Sixty years,' said my father to himself. 'Coming and going every Sunday, spending the long afternoons and evenings in her father's house, eating and drinking, and nothing in the nature of love transpiring.'

Like heroes I thought, and recalled from the song-books the heroic words: 'Side by side for the cause have our forefathers battled when our hills never echoed the tread of a slave; in many a field where the leaden hail rattled, through the red gap of glory they marched to their grave.'

Slowly, towards a lost lighted fragment of Philadelphia and our Christmas dinner, we ascended the wet boreen.

'Young love,' soliloquised the old man. 'Something happens to it on these hills. Sixty years and he never proposed nothing, good or bad.'

'In Carlow town,' said the song-books to me, 'there lived a maid more sweet than flowers at daybreak; their vows contending lovers paid, but none of marriage dared speak.'

'Sunday after Sunday to her house for sixty years,' said the old man. 'You wouldn't hear the like of it among the Kaffirs. It's the rain and the mist. And the lack of sunshine and wine. Poor Thady, too, was fond of salmon and women.'

'For I haven't a genius for work,' mocked the Humorous and Convivial, 'it was never a gift of the Bradies; but I'd make a most iligant Turk for I'm fond of tobacco and ladies.'

To the easy amusement of my brother and, finally, to the wry laughter of my father I sang that quatrain. Night was over the mountain. The falling water of the spring had the tinny sound of shrill, brittle thunder.

After dinner my godmother's husband said, 'Such a fine house as Aunt Sally O'Neill kept. Tables scrubbed as white as bone. Dances to the melodeon. I always think of corncrakes and the crowds gathered for the mowing of the meadows when I recall that house. And the churning. She had the best butter in the country. Faintly golden. Little beads of moisture showing on it.'

'We'll have a game of euchre,' said my Aunt Brigid.

'Play the phonograph,' said my godmother's husband.

He loathed euchre.

So on the gramophone, high up on Dooish, we heard that boys and girls were singing on the sidewalks of New York.

I wondered where the hound-dog could possibly have been running to. In a spooky story I had once read the Black Hound of Kildare turned out to be the devil.

My godmother asked me to sing.

'But I can't sing,' I said.

'Then what do Lanty and yourself do with all the song-books?'

'We read them.'

Laughter.

'Read us a song,' said my brother.

So, because I had my back to the wall and also because once when visiting a convent with my mother I had sung, by request, 'Let Erin Remember,' and received a box of chocolates from the Reverend Mother, I sang: 'Just a little bit of Heaven fell from out the sky one day, and when the angels saw it sure they said we'll let it stay; and they called it Ireland.'

That spring, following my heralding of the descent from Elysium of the Emerald Isle, there was a steady downpour of half-crowns.

MON AMI, EMILE

Emile and myself left Paris in a hurry the year the war broke out. For as many francs as would make a florin he became mine not five minutes' walk from the bright stalls of food, fruit and fish in the Rue de Seine. Strong and tall, solemn as John Knox, he stayed with me under my arm when my luggage was stolen or mislaid in the crowd, already beginning to show signs of panic, at the Gare du Nord. My firm companion, he crossed with me the narrow seas, lay flat on the counter when the last of my money went on beer in a boozer at Victoria, was with me when I borrowed from a fellow-countryman who practised in Fleet Street the craft of journalism, the taxi-fare to Euston. Then with Emile by my side I set my course westwards by Crewe, Chester, the lions of Menai, Holyhead and the Irish mail to the far, fair city of Dublin.

My total wealth, the remnants of my Fleet Street borrowing, was carefully calculated to purchase on the mail-boat one steak with garnishings and one bottle of nourishing stout, and my first embarrassment was with the two fat women who had been all the way to Rome to see the Holy Father. They told me about it: how he looked and what he said. They ordered tea and scones. They asked me to join them.

'No thanks,' I said. 'I never touch tea.'

To allay their suspicions I went on, 'I haven't tasted tea in years, not since I was in hospital with orthopaedic trouble.'

I never, as it happens, was.

'A spine,' said one of them.

She revealed herself as a hospital matron.

'A hip,' I said – with a vague feeling that I was being at least indelicate.

We discussed Whitman frames, hip frames, reverse beds, back splints, spinal grafts and other amenities and I was able to keep my end up because once a second cousin of mine did have the misfortune to be afflicted with a tubercular spine: lumbar region. Carefully, behind the well-placed barrage of medical terms, I concealed my craving for tea and scones, for how could I join the ladies without being a gentleman and paying the bill, and I preferred by far the prospect of steak and stout to the business of being a gentleman. Mutely beside me, mon ami Emile said never a word, but once when the two ladies had shyly withdrawn for private purposes I consulted him and he said, 'Toutes les capitales se ressemblent, tous les peuples s'y mêlent, toutes les moeurs s'y confondent; ce n'est pas là qu'il faut aller étudier les nations. Paris et Londres ne sont à mes yeux que la même ville.'

'You'd be lost as a tourist courier,' I said. 'A poor hero you'd be to meet on the street, Emile, if a man wanted to find his way to Longchamps or to an Irish Saturday night dance in a hall in a lane off Hammersmith Broadway.'

Emile, to that one, had no satisfactory answer. Later the two nice ladies and myself talked about Lourdes which, in spite of Emile, is not the same town as Pau.

At Crewe junction the upper halves of two white men, Cobden and Bright, joined us, borne proudly and on high by the members of a Dublin rugby football team returning in triumph from a game in Manchester.

'They insisted on coming with us,' said the full-back.

'They couldn't bear to see us go,' said the scrum-half back.

'Nothing,' said the monstrous man of a hooker, 'could keep them away from Ireland. They wanted to see it all their lives.'

'I considered,' said the right-wing-three-quarter-back, who had removed from a hotel foyer the two immobile busts of the noble nineteenth-century men who had done so much towards the repeal of the iniquitous Corn Laws, 'that they would look well in my lonely bachelor flat. The mantelpiece is bare. I have no statuary even if I have the finest collection of public house glassware in Europe. And the most representative collection of railway-company dining-car napkins.'

'And two No Parking signs,' said the doleful left-centre-three-quarter-back who had sprained his right ankle. 'And I regret to say a slot machine for chewing gum, once the property of a Fun Palace.'

'A well-furnished flat,' said the fly-half-back.

'We're declaring them at the customs as team mascots,' said the fatherly trainer. He was as proud as a rooster of his bouncing boys.

They were big hilarious fellows. They filled the whole train. They were red with drink and victory. They bellowed for joy. They wore club scarves and blazers. Pale in righteous marble, Cobden and Bright, remembering beloved Argos, looked back towards Manchester.

At the customary unearthly hour of four in the morning we came in mizzling rain to slate-grey, Welsh Holyhead and the Irish sea, and like lost souls on the shore of Styx filed up for the customs. Cobden and Bright escaped unscathed.

The north-west prevailing wind blew thunderously against our faces and with malevolent deliberation the high, long breakers trampled towards us. The effect on a ship, in case you don't know that sea-route, is that gradually the bow ascends and pointing towards the stars the vessel proceeds, deceptively steadies itself, then with a sickening lurch leaps the ridge and descends into the next salty trough. The effect on the stomach, whether you know the sea-route or not, can readily be imagined, and the weakness of the stomachs of strong men is one of the wonders of creation before which we can only bow in faith. Before my eyes they went down like stalks before the scythe. Still hilarious in the dining-room, while we were sheltered by the harbour mole, they ordered meat and wine to fill a regiment. Pale and abstemious, Cobden and Bright were enthroned on the centres of two tables. Still hilarious the footballers sang their club song – it mentioned the other sex more than seemed wise if they were to stay in training. They slapped each other on broad shoulders. They drove every diner except myself to seek the refuge of cabins or the lounge. But there on my table before me was the reward of my long abstemiousness: my stout, my steak savoury with splendid onions, and when the ship, for the seventeenth time, shuddered like a nervous horse, myself, the catering staff, and Cobden and Bright had the dining-room all to ourselves. Never in my life had I been seasick. So with the exact artistic delight of a potentate of Cathay or Turkestan treating a foreign, diplomatic representative to the death of the thousand cuts, I sliced and ate. The steak was tender. The juice ran red and warm. The cutlery could have been forged in ancient Solingen. Wind and sea were music in my ears and the lack of money, like death (as the poet said) in relation to first love, could only be a little thing. I drank the first quarter-pint of my half-pint of stout. I repeated to myself that I had never been seasick. The frolicsome ship played seesaw. So did the meniscus of the remaining quarter-pint of stout. I repeated again to myself that I had never been seasick, but you cannot, with impunity, play seesaw with a meniscus, so I withdrew briefly to the humming bowels of the ship and there, listening to the groans of my companions in travail, was gently deprived of my steak and was instantly well again but cold and absolutely moneyless and as empty as a whistle. Cobden and Bright, left alone when their protectors retired, gazed at me without passion. For safety's sake I placed them side by side on the floor where they wouldn't have far to fall and placed before them, as a propitiatory offering to a Britain who ruled unruly seas, the remnant of my stout. I never saw them after nor met their gentle kind.

With my friend Emile I sought my cabin where, in a lull of wind and sea and creaking ship, he said to me, 'Il y a un excès de rigueur et un excès d'indulgence, tous deux également à éviter.'

'Emile,' I said as I fell asleep, 'you have your finger on the pulse. You are probing to the heart of the matter.'

The excess of rigueur came at eight-thirty a.m. in the mizzling rain in Dublin's fair city.

Traveller, have you ever stood in sunshine on a high Alpine pass, the eternal snows glistening above you, and around you, and contemplated before you and below you the vast plains of . . .?

But, traveller, have you ever stood with one shilling, in coppers and halfpennies, in your pocket, on a rainy morning outside a boat-train railway station in a broken-down wreck of a Georgian city? The higher windows of the old brown houses are blank as blind eyes, when they are not actually hostile. They resent the futile attempt to brighten and modernise by turning the ground floors into shops and offices. People, of both sexes, and replete with breakfast, are hurrying to work. It is one mile and a half to the only hotel in the city where you are well enough known to eat on credit and you can't afford a cab or even bus-fare because if the attempt to obtain credit should fail, the coppers and halfpennies mustered together would be just about, and no more, exchangeable for one bottle of beer. A wet traveller without luggage reaching a hotel on foot at such a time on such a morning does not command respect, particularly when the old waiter he has known for years has, because of death which ends all things including hotel-waiting, been replaced by a brisk, impudent young fellow with glossy black hair, parted exactly in the middle, and a most offensive way of flicking with his napkin not only crumbs from tables but impurities out of the air.

He said, 'A soft morning, sir.'

He meant: You look shabby, wet, tired and broke.

I said, 'Breakfast, if you please.'

He said, 'Are you a resident, sir?'

I said, 'I am a schoolteacher from a remote part of rural Ireland. There are bears on the mountains there still and wolves in the woods but the stranger is always, in the homes of the people, received with traditional Irish hospitality which means cold chicken and ham washed down by, at the visitor's choice, whisky and/or black porter: a meal that would constipate an ox. I have travelled many miles from the fair land of France. Here beside me is my friend, Emile, an authority on educational theory. A man besides who has a word or phrase for every occasion. And furthermore, I am known, and my father before me, to the management. I want in this order, a large portion of John Jameson's ten-year-old whisky for warmth, breakfast for filling, and forty cigarettes for nervous relaxation. Then a room for washing-up and a bed for sleeping.'

Breakfast, with whisky and cigarettes, was served, but afterwards as I am whistling my way up to my couch I am approached by this fellow, busily flicking.

'The whisky and cigarettes, sir.'

'They were excellent, thank you.'

'We do not serve wines and tobacco on account, sir.'

'You did not serve wines.'

'I have my orders, sir.'

'Then have a few more. Ascertain from the manageress that my credit is good. I am now going to sleep. See that I am aroused half an hour before noon and not until then. Afterwards I will walk a short distance to the building – a noble pile – that houses the Department of Education, to collect two months' salary waiting for me since shortly after I set out for France. Then, and not sooner, will I pay you for the whisky, not wines, and cigarettes. Good morning, fellow.'

No longer whistling, but seething inwardly, I ascended.

'That flunkey, I know his type. He'll own seven hotels before he's forty. He'll marry the dark girl in the bar solely because she knows the business. Returning change on his tray he will always with exactitude isolate one silver shilling, as who would say: this sir, is mine by right and in addition to the ten per cent service charge. He will possibly even fiddle the till.'

There is the following anecdote, which you may or may not consider amusing. It concerns a dialogue in the city of Dublin between two prosperous publicans or tavern keepers.

First publican to second publican, 'I hear your barman, John, has bought his own public house.'

Second publican, 'That is so.'

First publican, 'How did he do it?'

Second publican, 'How did we do it?'

Festooned by prosperous publicans and fiddling flunkeys I fell asleep.

The girl behind the grille in the office in the Department building was ugly. It seemed therefore less possible to blame her than if she had been beautiful. Moreover it was not her fault but the fault of some pimpled, bespectacled male clerk who was skulking behind her dowdy skirts. What she had to say she said respectfully, seriously, modestly, 'There has been an error, sir. Instead of retaining your two monthly cheques here, to be called for, they have been forwarded to your school in the country. It is also contrary to the regulations to issue substitute cheques until the whereabouts and safety, or otherwise, of the original issues have been ascertained and verified. We are sorry for the error and hope it will not lead to undue inconvenience.'

Outside, for the record, it was past noon. The rain had ceased. The September sun was promenading westwards. People in normal circumstances of life were limbering up for, or eating, or digesting, lunch.

'Even now,' I reflected, 'that westering sun gilds the latticed windows of my beloved, familiar schoolhouse and sends a holy blush along the Virginia creeper. Even now from perfumed meadows arise the silver voices of my pupils set free by the holidays to help their parents with the harvest. Even now in the silent schoolroom the finger of the sun touches the spot, scorched earth, where once in my absence the Grampians were forcibly removed from the map of the British Isles. Even now a lonely mouse scampers from the orifice in my dusty, untrampled rostrum to the empty, wire wastepaper basket and, hungry and deprived of crumbs fallen from the pupils' lunch parcels or of discarded, greasy crusts slyly wrapped in brown paper, wonders sadly where all those happy young voices, all those hobnailed feet have gone. Even now secure from his nibbling, rodent teeth, but, oh so far from me, two official envelopes lie side by side in the letterbox, while even now an infuriated flunkey awaits my return to recompense him for forty cigarettes and a large whisky. Westward the sun will fall over the Burren of Clare and Galway Bay and the far island of Inishmore to drown in the soft Atlantic.

'There in the corner behind my rostrum, mon ami Emile,' I said, 'there's a warm welcome place for you. May we live to see it.'

'Il importe,' he said, 'que la peau s'endurcisse aux impressions de l'air et puisse braver ses altérations; car c'est elle qui défend tout le reste.'

When the halfpennies and coppers were mustered wheel to wheel, like the guns of El Alamein, I purchased in a public house a bottle of beer. It was a place frequented by county footballers and hurlers and by the followers of football and hurling. The walls were ornamented with pictures of the great teams or sporting individuals of past years. On the shelves behind the bar were three silver cups, two small, one gigantic, and five shields. Yet the six drinkers and the barman were discussing not sport but literature. They talked about the quality of the books sold in a certain select bookshop. Sipping my beer, unheard and almost unseen, I became a humble but attentive member of the community.

'It's a disgrace to Ireland,' said one man.

'Magazine covers,' said another, 'would make a brewery drayman blush.'

They were clean, open-air men who played games or admired those who did.

'That Amusements Palace of his,' said the first speaker, 'is only a screen for an unsavoury racket.'

'It might pass unnoticed,' said another, 'at Charing Cross in London or in America.'

'He'll never get away with it,' said the barman. 'Not in a quiet country like this.'

'Public opinion just won't stand for it,' said a thin man in a bowler hat and a pin-striped suit.

'We should have a vigilance committee,' said the second speaker.

'Wreck his shop for him,' said another, 'and his slot machines, his one-armed bandits. Burn those books before his eyes.'

'Lurid,' said a small, shabby man with a striped knotted scarf, a cloth cap and an outsize raincoat. He gave the matter further thought. Then he said, 'Positively lurid.'

Guiltily I ended my pallid beer and, with Emile, slipped quietly away.

A sandwich man with a pig's head on him stood at the door of the Amusements Palace. He jingled a handbell. The pig's head was made of cardboard. The message fore and aft, on the sandwich said, 'Meet the best people at the Amusements Palace.'

There is also this anecdote which you may or may not consider in good taste. There was a certain rural Irish lawyer who made a habit of spending one fortnight of his annual vacation in the lively town of Douglas on the Isle of Man. He was a gay bachelor and his devoted clerk was an elderly, settled man of conservative habits. Now it so happened in one year, a fortnight or thereabouts after the lawyer had returned from his relaxation in Douglas, Isle of Man, that the quiet clerk was methodically paper-knifing his way through the morning's correspondence and, most unusual for him, neglected to read meticulously the address on one envelope. Slit open, it delivered itself, like a silver run of salmon, of a series of snapshots of personable young ladies happy on sunny beaches and in other places and dressed, more or less, in the least cumbersome of holiday or sportive clothing. The clerk closed his eyes, sighed for the folly of youth and tapped the snapshots back into the envelope as quickly and gently as if they would burn his fingers, and said, 'It would appear, sir, that inadvertently I have opened an envelope addressed to you personally.'

'It is no matter, James,' was the generous, offhanded response.

But later when the lawyer's turn came to inspect the correspondence he allowed the silver stream to trickle through his fingers, laughed as a man with pleasant memories would, and said, 'James.'

'Yes, sir.'

'Have you ever holidayed in the Isle of Man.'

'No, sir.'

A long busy silence.

'Sir.'

'Yes, James.'

'I am told you meet the best people in the Isle of Man.'

'James.'

'Yes, sir.'

'You don't go to the Isle of Man to meet the best people.'

Neither did I enter the Amusements Palace to meet the best people, but with steps bound towards evil I went forwards to betray a friend and make money. On either side of me like hawk-headed, dog-headed gods in an Egyptian palace of the dead, the one-armed bandits stood silent. Business was slack at that time of day. Nobody even cared to see what the butler saw. But beyond the palace of the dead was the inner sanctum, the chamber of delights that had caused such indignation among the healthy men and, surely, I thought not even the Sultan Medjid, father of Abdul, whose household hearth was brightened, if confused, by nine hundred odalisques and kadines and who with their aid, and that of drugs and machines, died at an early age, could have surrounded himself with so much fascination. The colours and shapes of a colony of nudist magazine cover-girls brightened the walls. Such pictures, I thought, as Tiberius took from Elephantis and dull Aretine but coldly imitated. Behind the counter was the Turk himself, six feet six in height, twenty stone in weight, genial, with four fine chins, red in the face and full of welcome, not, one would say, a man of great subtlety or book-learning, yet a noble figure of a man who in another walk of life might have stood happily before the door or behind the bar of his old English inn on a May morning on a Malvern hillside.

'Do you buy books,' I said.

'That I do, lad. On special occasions. It depends. Let me see your wares.'

One after the other I reached him the three volumes. He fondled them. He held them as if they were hot. He looked at the title page. This is what he saw: Oeuvres Complètes de J.-J. Rousseau avec des éclaircissements et des notes historiques par P. P. Auguis Emile: Tome I.

'Rousseau,' he said, 'was, they say, a rare one.'

'He was all that. He was French.'

'So I see,' he said. 'Is this good?'

'This,' I said, 'is the last word. For connoisseurs. For those who know.'

'It's French,' he said thoughtfully. 'How much?'

Bravely I said, 'Two pounds.'

'Thirty shillings,' he said.

Inevitably he paid me in shillings, my thirty pieces of silver. It was one of the times of the year when the Gas Company collectors were doing their rounds of the slot meters and setting free for circulation long-imprisoned shillings and pennies.

So I sold my friend and took the coins. The moment of betrayal and parting was as brief and simple as that. Behind me as I retreated through the palace of the dead the lost, sad voice of Emile reproached me: 'Conseillez-nous, gouvernez-nous, nous serons dociles: tant que je vivrai j'aurai besoin de vous. J'en ai plus besoin que jamais, maintenant que mes fonctions d'homme commencent. Vous avez rempli les vôtres; guidez-moi pour vous imiter: et reposez-vous, il en est temps.'

A telegram to my cleaner ordered her to open the school, find the envelopes, cable me money immediately. The flunkey I paid and, with studied contempt, tipped him sixpence: my small share in those seven hotels he would some day own. Sadly I drank and waited for the money and thought of the empty place on my schoolroom shelves and knew that never again, in any shape or form, could I face my betrayed Emile. But what, I wondered, would the four-chinned Sultan of the Amusements Palace, or those people, the best of the best, who slyly sought delight from his under-the-counter stock, ever make out of the following exchange of ideas: 'Voici la formule à laquelle peuvent se reduire à peu près toutes les leçons de morale qu'on fait et qu'on peut faire aux enfants:

> LE MAITRE Il ne faut pas faire cela.
> L'ENFANT Et pourquoi ne faut-il pas faire cela?
> LE MAITRE Parce que c'est mal fait.
> L'ENFANT Mal fait! Qu'est ce qui est mal fait?

While master and pupil talked I thought of Emile, bewildered in the palace of delights, and drank more whisky, and sadly recalled Cobden and Bright, and slept in the chair I sat in. Mal fait, indeed.

SOLDIER, RED SOLDIER

For Padriac Colum
whose poem provided the title

Nobody could ever have imagined that awkward John, the milk-man, was the sort to come between a husband and his wife. There was no badness in him and he was anything but handsome. To think of John was to think of easy, slow-moving, red-faced good nature, of the jingle of harness bells and the clip clop of hooves in the morning, of the warm breath of milk fresh from the udder in the byres of Joe Sutton's place out in Coolnagarde. John was one of Sutton's several hired men.

He would enter singing with his morning delivery into our informal town. He was the harbinger of day, as punctual as an alarm clock but by no means as minatory. He was closer to the birds than to any time-machine because he came, simple and melodious, from fresh, awaken-ing fields and warm byres to arouse and refresh the leaden mechanical streets. This was long before bottling and pasteurisation took the flavour of life, and the cream, out of the milk; and the vehicle that John drove, and the well-combed, long-tailed, grey pony pulled, was as splendid as a chariot; and no dull array of shelves stacked with squat bottles. Heavy on his heels, leaning slightly backwards, managing the pony with the gentlest touches of finger-tips on the strap-reins, the huge, crimson, flaxen-haired, innocent youth stood up as high as a statue. There were two large silvery milk-cans to his right and two to his left. The pint and half-pint measures dangled and rattled on hooks in front of him. The taps of the cans were gleaming brass. You turned a lever and the milk flowed out. If you were up early enough in the morning, and if you were young and a favourite of his, you could fill your own measure. It was nearly as good as milking a cow.

And he was fond of the young and the young fond of him, so that in school-holiday time it was a common sight to see two or three boys travelling with him as volunteer assistants, and a hilarious flight of six or seven racing behind the cart to snatch a quick mouthful of milk from the brass taps. John, laughing loudly and not bothering to look back, would scatter them by flicking his whip over their heads, harmlessly, but with a crack that could be heard all over the town. He was a star performer with that whip.

As I said, it was an informal town. In High Street and Market Street where the rich shopkeepers lived, and in Campsie Avenue where the doctors and professional people lived, a white-aproned maid might, in some of the more staid houses, meet John at the side-door and present a jug for the milk. More often, he whistled his way affably into the kitchen, found the jug himself, filled it, made a harmless glawm at the maid, and went on his way contentedly.

But every door was open to him in the working-class kitchen houses that stood in parallel rows on Gallows Hill. The kitchen houses indeed, were brown brick ramparts against any sort of formality. The architectural pattern came over to us from the industrial areas of Scotland and Northern England: an entrance hall, about five feet square, opening into a kitchen-cum-living-room; a steep twisted stairway ascending from the kitchen; two doors opening from the far end of the kitchen, one via a pantry and scullery to the backyard, the other into a diminutive parlour or drawing-room or what you will – it was never described as anything grander than The Wee Room. They were small intimate, cosy nests of houses and, if the next-door neighbour had a row you could, if you were curious, learn all about it and, in exceptional circumstances even offer your services as arbitrator.

It was an honest town and nobody bothered much to bolt doors so that in the mornings Awkward John was king of the kitchen houses. He might waken the family with a healthy shout up the crooked stairs. Or he might quietly put a match to the ready-laid fire in the range and proceed to the cooking of breakfast for the family and himself. The sleepers would be aroused not by sound but by the wispy, drifting odour of rashers and eggs on the pan and, dressing and descending the stairs, would find the fire blazing, the food cooking, and John at his ease in a chair, reading the paper – which he did with difficulty, big, blunt forefinger following the line of print – or chanting a fragment of a song he had picked up from Joe Sutton who was a great traditional man. (His favourite fragment went something like this: 'I wonder how you could love a sailor. I wonder how you could love a slave. He might be dead or he might be married or the ocean wave might be his grave.') It was reckoned that, on an average, John ate three full English breakfasts a morning, discounting casual collations and cups of tea or, in the more select houses, coffee, to show that he had nothing against continental customs. But he was a big, healthy, amiable youth, slightly stooped in the shoulders because he was too tall and heavy to carry himself straight, and nobody grudged him his excessive provender.

He also seemed as happy in his way of life as the lark in the clear air.

That was why my mother was so startled when he told her one morning over his rashers, 'Missus, I'm thinking of 'listing in the British Army.'

'God look to your wit,' she said. 'Are you an Irishman at all?'

'The barracks is full of Irishmen,' he said. 'Some of them from as far away as Wexford. The two full-backs on the depot team are from Sligo.'

'More shame for them,' she said. 'They worked to earn it. The army's a place for disobedient boys. They wouldn't obey their mother at home so God punished them by delivering them into the hands of the sergeant major.'

'Wasn't your own husband, missus, a soldier?'

'He was,' she said. 'And he rued the day he 'listed. And he'd be the last man to encourage you to follow in his foolish footsteps. You're not cut out for the army.'

'Amn't I as strong as any sergeant in the barracks?'

'Tisn't strength, but rascality, counts in the army, boy. You're too soft, John, too used to easy ways. The good life you had of it with Joe Sutton.

'My own girlhood,' she said, 'was spent in Coolnagarde.'

'That I know. Mr. Sutton often mentions your name.'

'I had the greatest regard for his lately-deceased mother. A lady if ever there was one. In that great place of Sutton's the servant-boys led the lives of princes. I'm sure her son treats them no differently.'

'He's easy on us, true enough.'

'The long warm evenings at the hay,' she said. 'The taste of strong tea in the bog at the saving of the turf. Tea anywhere else never tasted like that. And the boys on their hunkers in the heather or stretched chewing among the bilberry bushes. And always a bit of music and a song. The heavenly taste of the bilberries and the lovely wine you could make from them. And the wicked bites of the grey midges as the evening came on.'

'True enough, missus, the little cannibals would stand on their heads to get a better bite at you.'

'You've thick, healthy skin, John, that they'd never puncture. 'Twas different for soft young girls. And at Ballydun Foresters' Hall the dances.'

'Mostly poker or pitch-and-toss nowadays, missus. Times must be changed. There's no life in the country for the young people. And little money or adventure.'

'You'll have adventure in the army. Up at dawn to scrub out the latrines.'

But there was another, different prospect before John's big, blank, blue eyes. He saw a vision that altered, dissolved, reshaped itself, was now an eastern palace with towers like twisted, beckoning fingers, now a half-circle of laughing girls, and now a field of sport or of battle where Awkward John was transformed into the lithe, powerful hero. The warnings of an old woman, or her rhapsodies about the simple joys of her girlhood when, it seemed, every day had been summer, had no power against that compelling dream.

The tall talk of Yellow Willy Mullan who was a storyteller, or a liar, of the first order had brought the vision to John all the way from the garrisons of India. Twelve to fifteen years previously Yellow Willy, a pale-faced Irish boy, brown scapular and a chain of holy medals round his neck, had marched away with the Inniskilling Fusiliers. Six months previously he had marched home again: a gaunt, sallow-faced, sinful-looking man who had been but once to confession all the time he was in the East, and only then because he was ambushed, as he put it, by an aggressive Irish padre in Bombay. Seeing him in the home-coming parade, his aged mother burst into tears: weeping, perhaps, for the boy who had marched away for ever or, as the gossip of the kitchen houses cynically said, judging from the lean, lined face and wolfish eyes of him, how much it would take to feed him. At Kane's public house corner he was king of the Indian Army reservists, the toughest old sweats the Empire had, and his tales, lies or truth, of brothels in Bombay or bullets on the Khyber Pass made the story of the lives of the Bengal Lancer read like a white paper on social welfare. For John, the whirling words of Yellow Willy gave life and truth and all the needed corroborative detail to the coloured recruiting posters outside the courthouse and the post office, and all along the grey stone wall in Barrack Lane where he drove to deliver milk to the married quarters. On some of the posters a fine, brown-faced fellow in white knickers and red jersey leaped up to head a flying football, or came running in first at the end of a race, or went diving and swimming – ringed with the faces of admiring girls. Another poster showed a smiling soldier pointing to the Taj Mahal as if he had just bought it at a sacrifice price from an estate agent who was retiring from the business.

John could never grow weary of listening to Yellow Willy telling how he had actually seen the Taj Mahal.

'It was big, John, and shining. Six times as big as the courthouse and the town hall together. As big nearly as the mental hospital. Palaces, John. India's full of them. But you'd soon be fed up looking at palaces. Give me the brown girls and the wiggles of them, and the perfume – I can smell it still.'

To captivate John's ears, by bringing girls and palaces into the same tale, Yellow Willy told how he had spent a holiday with a prince who was a friend of his and how the prince, squatting, like Paddy MacBride the tailor, on a pile of silken cushions, waved his beringed, bejewelled hand at the glittering dancing-girls and said, 'Fusilier Mullan, pick the six you fancy and keep them for a week.'

Later, a tender affection developed between Yellow Willy and the prince's daughter who wanted to elope with him, but Willy, treating her as he'd wish another man to treat his own young sister, dissuaded her. 'She wasn't a Catholic, John, you see. And what life would it be in a kitchen house on Gallows Hill for a girl was used to palaces and plenty.'

After all that romancing, it was little use to talk to John about the good life at Coolnagarde, or about the kind heart and sweet songs of Joe Sutton; or for my mother to point out that Yellow Willy was just the biggest boaster in an unemployable group of misfits who never stirred their arses from Kane's Corner except to go to bed at night, or to go into Tom Kane's to get drunk on stout and cheap red wine – Red Biddy – when the army reserve money came up once a month.

My mother said, 'John, what did Joe Sutton say when you told him you'd 'list?'

'He said nothing, missus. He said a verse of poetry: "And soldiers, red soldiers! You've seen many lands. But you walk two and two and by captain's commands".'

'Very true,' said my mother. 'He has a verse to meet every need.'

But no verse had Joe Sutton to halt John in his career. The day he headed up Barrack Lane, not to deliver milk but to offer his services to the King of England, Yellow Willy made the nasty joke, 'They'll never take him, not with the crouch he has in his shoulders. Men for India they want, not camels for Egypt.'

Yellow Willy was wrong, and all through the houses on the hill mornings were not real mornings any more. No other milkman could be found to equal Awkward John.

Sergeant Cooper, at that time, was the brutal, blackavised, tyrannical ruler of the barracks gymnasium. We knew that, to our cost, because our own school had no gymnasium and, by arrangement between the commanding officer and the superior of the school, the boys who played football went twice a week to the barracks to be put through their paces. That could have been fun if it hadn't been for Sergeant Cooper.

He was a man, not heavily nor largely built but perfectly-proportioned, with chest muscles that extended to the limits of endurance the fabric of the red-and-black barred football jersey he wore in the gymnasium. In tight serge trousers and slippers he was as light on his feet, on the polished wooden floor of his athletic torture-chamber, as the most sylph-like of ballet dancers. He had dark hair cropped to stubble, a Roman nose, a full mouth, a mole to the left of his chin, and grey, quite motionless eyes. To anyone except ourselves, the school-boys, and the raw recruits, the rookies, in the barracks he would have been a mighty handsome man particularly when, in dress uniform, he stepped out with his olive-skinned, opulent, brunette wife. She was taller and heavier than her husband and a sight, fore and aft, to observe when she walked the town.

'By Mahomet,' said Yellow Willy, 'she's something to think about. There's Indian blood in her. Such a woman to be wasted on the like of that man.'

Yellow Willy, to do his line of talk justice, had a lot more remarks, highly technical and speculative, to make about the scandalous squandering of such material.

But to the schoolboys and still more to the rookies – those shapeless youths from barns and back-streets who had to be licked into the semblance of soldiers – the sergeant was a monster. At least he couldn't assault us with the sweat-hardened flat palm of a boxing glove as he could and did assault, or discipline, the rookies. We weren't in the army – not yet. We hadn't, according to my mother's fatalistic morality, advanced far enough in disobedience to our parents to be doomed by avenging heaven to the mercy of Sergeant Cooper. What morbid cul-de-sac in North London had reared him? From what sulphurous Rillington Place, with the corpses of unfortunate women decaying in every alcove, had he paced forth to work off his venom on things green and fresh, things young and happy? Everything and everybody who looked rustic – that word was his favourite abusive adjective, and his sharp London voice could make it sound viler than sin – were anathema to him: grass, blue skies, birds on the bushes, clean water flowing otherwise than through pipes, unsurfaced, dusty side-roads, and unspoiled children of nature like Awkward John.

Twice a week, then, forty or fifty of us would troop apprehensively up Barrack Lane, under the long grey wall and the radiance of the same recruiting posters that had enticed and deluded John, to keep our assignment with the satanic sergeant. Some boys take better than others to the challenge of the horse, the wall-bars and the parallel-bars. Some men like war and climbing Everest. But even those of us who might have loved the gymnasium machines and rituals were put off by the sergeant's manners. For he had a way of making horse and bars and punch-balls, mats, skipping ropes, clubs and boxing gloves, his allies against the crowd of us. They were all civilised Londoners together and we were the benighted children of brambles and hayseed.

'Up, up, up boys,' he would snap – prancing east to west and west to east like something made out of steel springs.

'Up, up, up. You're not just going to market and you haven't all day.'

Like a flight of demented bats we would go at the wall, clamber up the bars with varying degrees of speed, skill and grace, swing face outwards at the crack of command and at the grave risk of losing both arms at the shoulders, and descend, like birds to a mesmerising bird-catcher, in obedience to that prancing man, 'Down, down, down boys. Back to good old Mother Earth. Back to the friendly soil of Mother Erin.'

To welcome us back to the friendly soil of Mother Erin there stood the sergeant's most obedient servant: the monstrous, headless, legless, tailless horse, an insult and a blasphemy against the beauty and goodness of living horses. One look at it, with the sergeant by its side, and you could think of nothing but of strong men being held face down, legs and arms straddle across its smelly leather padding, and flogged to the drumbeat until they broke down and yelled. We suffered so much from our compulsory assaults on its slothlike obscenity, and Cooper obviously enjoyed himself so much as he impelled us on, that we suspected some unholy compact between them; and one sour wit went so far as to say that in the dead of night the master of the gymnasium came out, bucket in hand, to talk to the brute, stroke it down, and feed it oats. For over and above all things, he believed in the horse, and his greatest joy in life – if the name of joy could for anything be applied to him – was to see its ravenous appetite fed by a flying file of boys.

'On the toes. Off we go. Hit the board. On your toes. Up. Touch. Splits over. Hit the mat. Fast out of the way, boy. This isn't the place to say your prayers. Up and Out. Keep the line revolving. On the toes. Hit the board. Splits over.'

Fear of the mockery of that voice, in the case of clumsiness or failure, made antelopes out of boys who, under normal circumstances, wouldn't have moved so fast or jumped so high to save their lives. Through desperation we all became masters of the horse. There are scientific experiments in which caged rats are set running up tiny circular flights of steps which descend as the rats attempt to ascend. The creatures just keep turning wheels until they drop from exhaustion. Cooper's stage-army of half-terrified boys had its cheerful resemblance to that rat race, and perhaps, in moments of a special cold frenzy, he may really have been trying to discover the secret of perpetual motion. Round and round we went and over and over, and the process more closely resembled an eternity of punishment because there was no clock visible in the gymnasium. It was only when he pulled one dried-up boxing glove onto his left hand that we knew for us the respite had come and a deeper, hotter hell was about to commence for the rookies. By the barrack time-table the sad souls who wouldn't do what their mothers told them were doomed, immediately after the sergeant had disposed of us, to an hour's instruction in some elementary methods of defence and offence. For most of that hour they were very much on the defensive. He was a boxer and wrestler of some note, that sergeant.

From the dressing-room as we steamed with perspiration and sighed with relief we could study in awe what was liable to happen to us if we showed an habitual disregard for the fourth commandment. High in his pride, that arrogant son of Greater London was master of thirty or so pairs of simultaneously-performing game-cocks and, down there on the sand of the bloody pit, it must have grieved him to think that he couldn't fit them out with flesh-rending spurs. He set them hammering each other, or throwing each other, and egged them on until he brought out the bestial or the demoniacal, or both, in every one of them.

'Put your heart in it, hayseed. Hit him. Think it's a bloody Boche you've got, if you can think.'

The blows, the grunts, the sound of falling bodies resounded, punctuated by the steel-like crack of the dry, open glove on the head of some recalcitrant performer. It was hammer your opponent or be lacerated by the glove.

Cooper was the emperor, and reserved the gladiatorial contests all for his own cruel delight. He rested his dulcet voice more with the rookies than with us, and let his viper of a left hand, fanged by the glove, supply the word of command: bull-whips were frowned on in the British Army.

'Give me any day the galleys in Ben Hur,' said the voice of that sour wit.

And so pitifully unprotected the rookies were – in black shorts, sleeveless green singlets, slippers and short socks. Chain mail would not have been excessive for what they were called upon to encounter.

To demonstrate the more delicate points of throwing or buffeting he'd pick on one guinea pig; and, in some black book in the lowest caverns of Gehenna, it was written in pitch that five times out of ten Awkward John should be his choice. The size and shape, or lack of shape, of John would have aggravated any well-formed soldier. The width of John's stooping shoulders stretched the green singlet to the transparency of sheer nylon. The seeming nakedness of his torso was made more provokingly pitiful by the real nakedness of his white-blond head, as good as scalped by the barracks barber. His slow-moving body was the focal point of all confusion, and in three minutes he could have transformed a dress-parade of the Irish Guards into Keystone Comedy: turning left when the rest went right, by-the-left-quick-marching a half minute too late and halting a half minute too early, affronting even those military virtues which the sergeant undeniably possessed, making to his vices the perverted appeal helpless innocence makes to the heart of corruption. A perfect sawdust-stuffed dummy was John for the expert application of the subtleties of wrestling: Chancery back heel, cross buttock and waist hold, the half Nelson, quarter Nelson, full Nelson; and not Milo of Croton, supreme among the Greeks, nor the deified Sukune of Japan, nor the Great Danno Mahony of Ballydehob in the County Cork, was more adept than Sergeant Cooper. Patiently, John accepted every shattering fall. Ox-like he waited, for the next experiment, resigned, it would seem, to the misery and humiliation, if others could by his tumbles learn how to keep their feet.

'There's styles and styles of wrestling,' the sergeant would say. 'Cumberland and West Country, and catch-as-catch-can as is practised in Lancashire and many foreign parts. But take it from me, if you go on a man, disregarding styles, and squeeze his kidneys down he has to go.'

Panting, and clearly in some pain, down John went. When he was bent enough and low enough, the sergeant rested his right leg over the bowed neck and shoulders – a gallant captain and his heathen slave – and, for one fatal moment, relaxed as he explained the technicalities of his triumph to the gaping, breathless throng. At the same moment, possibly without any malice in the world, John decided to straighten up, and the loudest noise heard that day was the clump of the sergeant's head on the gymnasium floor. There was no laughter. One does not laugh when the lightning strikes and the earth opens. He didn't curse or shout or call names as a normal man might have done. He sat on the floor and shook his head once, twice, thrice – methodically. It almost seemed as if we could hear his brain tick, not like a clock but a time bomb. Spluttering apologies, John stepped forward and stooped to pick him up, when with the force and exactitude of a skilled dirty fighter, Cooper shattered the big fellow's mouth with a foul blow of the right elbow.

As he staggered back, spitting out and swallowing blood and teeth, John, I'd say, abandoned without regret his dream of ever seeing the Taj Mahal.

For myself and the other observers in the dressing-room that blow was the end of boyhood, of mornings chiming with harness bells and flowing with creamy milk. John was lost for ever to us in a heartless world where, with the regularity of monastic bells and the viciousness of dropping guillotine blades, strident bugles dismembered the day.

What happened about a month after that was, to begin with, a slightly altered version of the hoary story of the sergeant who asked for four volunteers who knew something about music and, when four innocents had stepped out, roared at them to carry a grand piano four hundred yards from the O.C.'s residence to the officers' mess.

Cooper never roared. His voice was sharp, level, penetrating and exact as a chisel, and his face was never flushed. He surveyed twenty or thirty possible victims. He said, 'You're all experts on hay. Reared on grass by the look of you. Your fathers kept the sons at home and sent the donkeys to the army.'

A little, fearful laughter acknowledged his traditional army witticism.

'But which of you is the best hand with the scythe, the bleeding scythe – you know, favourite weapon of Old Father Time. One pace forward. Four men or what passes for men in this 'ere barracks.'

Awkward John was out in front before Cooper had finished speaking. Every man has his moments of power and poetry, and it was common knowledge out in Coolnagarde that with a scythe in his hand and his feet well-spread to balance his great body on Antaean earth, and the razor-sharp blade shearing the roots of good meadow-grass and, in delicate curves, shaving the ground, Awkward John was no longer Awkward.

Reluctantly, and fearing the worst, three other martyrs stepped out beside him.

'By the left quick march,' the sergeant said. 'Shoulder scythes. Step forward the merry farmers' boys. To the swamp. Left. Right. Left.'

The laughter of the fortunate ones who had escaped that fatigue followed the four victims as he herded them across the interminable barrack square. It was a hot sultry day in late summer and the black flies and horse flies in the swamp were a bloody torment. The barracks stood on a high hill with the town to the south and a river running northwards from the town below the eastern wall of the barracks, then faltering in its course and looping, first west, then south, before turning again to the north. The wide acres that the looping river enclosed were known as The Soldiers' Holm, and held playing-fields, firing ranges and jumps for exercising horses. Lovely green land that Holm was, except for one scabrous spot of sour marsh where the river made its final northward turn. There, rushes and brambles grew in unholy profusion and, at intervals, an attack had to be made on the swamp to preserve a pathway leading to an iron foot-bridge. Half-eaten alive by the pestering flies and attempting to swing jagged-edged scythes that no stone could sharpen or no skill balance, John and the other hapless three suffered under the sergeant's flinty, unrelaxing eye. He wore his tight serge trousers, his black-and-red jersey and a pair of running shoes. He left the four labourers at intervals and coursed like a thoroughbred over the velvet levels of the Holm and thus evaded the torment of the flies.

The sweat blinding him, soaking his yellow canvas fatigue suit, making puddles in his army boots, the black flies crawling all over him, the horse flies drawing blood, John swung the wobbly scythe at rasping brambles and leathery rushes that lay down and then stood up again to mock the blunt, hacked blade. He saw the sweet, scented meadow-grass of Coolnagarde. He heard the singing of good well-sharpened blades. He saw the servant girls carrying food and strong tea across the mown land. Then with one last swing he sent the hopeless scythe spinning to the deep middle of the river. The sergeant, raising his knees high like a runner in track-training, was half a mile away across the Holm. But he turned, when he heard the clang of nailed boots on the metal bridge, to see the big youth cross the river and head north for open country, freedom and the haven of Coolnagarde. Like the wind he crossed the Holm and started in pursuit. Happy at any excuse to escape from the flies the three mowers downed tools and followed them – a good ways behind and steadily losing distance, for John was a good runner even if he was ungraceful and the sergeant had style and could travel like a springbok.

John was a better jumper than he was a runner. It was a wonder to the world at jumping contests at rural sports how high he could ascend before gravity claimed him and he began to come down again.

'Well I knew,' he said long afterwards, 'the hoor would be too fast for me on the flat. But I could beat him at the jumps. So I steeplechased him over bog-holes and ditches until there wasn't a puff of wind left in his body.'

He echoed an old racing-song from Joe Sutton's repertoire, 'Over hedges and ditches and bogs I was bound.'

'I drew the map of Ireland for him,' he said, 'around three swampy, low-lying townlands.'

It was the season of the year when the flax-crop had been pulled by hand and lay retting in the water of the dams, the softening fibres stinking to the sky above.

A week previously a doctor's wife out riding in all her grandeur had been thrown and badly injured when her horse shied at the stench of a flax-dam near a crossroads a mile outside the town; and, to anyone who has ever given the matter thought, it is quite miraculous that decaying vegetable matter, breathing out from filthy water an almost visible smell, should ever have been part of a process leading to beautiful tablecloths or to gentlemen in Cuba dressing themselves in gleaming suits of Irish linen.

Panting heavily, and with the inexorable pursuit closing in on him, Awkward John, running like a gingered mule, came to a wide flax-dam and crossed it with a tremendous leap, then on the far side of the scummy vaporous water he stood at bay.

Afterwards, as he told the tale, he said, 'I waited for him with my fist in a ball.'

He struck a pose like Cuchullain at the ford. An enormous ball of a fist it was.

'I could never face him in the ring, but thon slippy mucky bank was no ring. And I swung when he jumped, and struck when he touched the ground and he went down like a duck. The gas and the dirty water came up like steam.'

Then with an élan, and a brutality, that he had never before displayed and with the massive hitting power of his heavy boots, John jumped on the fallen man's stomach, recrossed the dam, and headed off at a canter across country to Coolnargarde. Doubled in agony, waterlogged and stinking, the sergeant, after several efforts crawled out of the mire and made, back to the barracks, the broken-backed movement of a man disgraced for ever.

No more than a month later the long yellow Rolls Royce took to calling to the sergeant's house, in a quiet road on the fringe of the town, at times when even the nuns in the convent knew that the sergeant, by duty, was confined to the barracks. That splendid woman would emerge dressed in the best, and while a uniformed chauffeur held the door of the car would survey the small street and the mean houses with their twitching window-blinds half-concealing curious eyes. Then she would wave the daintiest of white handkerchiefs to the watchers, and step in and be driven away. The owner of the Rolls – the watchers at the windows soon found out – was the son of a family who lived in a town ten miles away and out of sawmills in World War One had made a fortune which the son was scattering as a gentleman should. In later years he was to be seen through a hole in the hedge, in the park before his house, being supported by two male nurses while he restudied the art of walking. Brandy had made him bowlegged and reduced him to a curious staccato movement.

Yellow Willy, who always defended her, implied that she had fallen on reckless ways because she could not stand the odour of ridicule and retting flax.

In the evening when the Rolls Royce had delivered her back to her door she would stand on the sidewalk until it had driven away, then wave that tiny handkerchief to the eyes behind the twitching curtains and say with great gaiety, 'You can go to bed now. He's gone away. Sleep tight.'

She seemed to know that she was talking to people who had nothing to do but peep out from their own lives: they possessed no big rooms that could engage their attention.

There were other whisperings about her. There were tales of muffled tappings and visits by night and, as Kipling said, knocks and whistles round the house, footsteps after dark; and a legend of one grey-headed, dignified solicitor whose sprained ankle, which kept him from taking his usual place in the Corpus Christi procession, was the result of the nocturnal necessity of making a hasty departure over the back-garden wall.

So in the end off she went one day in the Rolls and didn't come back, and the watchers behind the window-curtains waited in vain, and the sergeant took to living a lonely life in the barracks until he got the transfer he applied for – back to the part of England to which the false one had flown.

'What else could you expect,' said Yellow Willy, 'if you let the like of Awkward John into the army.'

In an abandoned chest of drawers in the house she left behind her the new inhabitants found bundles of letters, each bundle tied in differently coloured ribbon, addressed to her by her many admirers. A fine, poetic anthology, it was circulated for many a day among the town's careful readers: and wry humour was added to the glowing sentiments by the fact that one of the contributing authors was a highly respectable and wealthy member of the urban district council. It could at least be said of her as Yellow Willy, who to the end admired her from afar, said, that she didn't go in for blackmail. But since one graphologist said that some of the letters were in her own handwriting her purpose may even have been more humorous and subtle.

In the Second World War, we heard, the sergeant distinguished himself by many wounds and much promotion and his wife rejoined him, turning the blades of her shapely shoulders on the liquefying sawmills.

The day that John, like the hare whom hounds and horn pursue, panted home to Coolnagarde, Joe Sutton, a man of persuasion and influence, went to the barracks and saw the commanding officer, a man of humanity and understanding. For thirty pounds Joe bought the runaway soldier back from the King of England who probably never missed him anyway. The Commanding Officer may also have considered that in those halcyon days of peace the Army was better off without Awkward John. And when John had his false teeth – paid for by Joe Sutton – he was able to sing as well as ever and recount his army experiences like a veteran of the field. The milk trade and the early mornings were the better of it all, and the Taj Mahal remained as far away as India.

THE BRIGHT GRAVES

The sun shone on the church and the churchyard, on the rockery and forest of tombstones, on the meditative living, some of them kneeling and praying, who were paying their Sunday afternoon respects to the sunless dead. It seemed to shine with a special brilliance on two new graves, on the white marble headstones, on the small white stones that decently covered the brown clay, on the white marble that boxed and defined the stones. That radiant candour seemed to draw the sunshine away from the greens and browns and greys, or the faded weatherworn off-whites, that covered the rest of the churchyard. Light concentrated on those two graves, light that was blindingly white but deprived utterly of heat: as cold as the decaying matter the marble and clay concealed.

Elizabeth didn't pay much attention to the burning coldness of the marble. The pillars in the parish church felt like that and the high altar, the altar steps and rails where communicants knelt. Her duties as one of the members of the parish altar society, burnishers of brass, washers of linen, providers and arrangers of flowers, gave her the opportunity and privilege of sensing and understanding, although she was only a woman, the meaning of the chill, holy solidity of those things. Coldly and sorrowfully they had laid Christ in the tomb. But on a Sunday when the sun shone she was always impressed by how white the graves were, and how radiant. They leaped at the eyes, shining against the brown-and-green background like frozen fragments of the sun. They were separate and apart from the other graves. They were patricianly superior to rustic green and plebeian brown. It consoled her to know that he had been buried so nobly.

She – once again, because of her duties as a member of the altar society – was more than a mere Sunday visitor to those graves. For every evening she stepped up the crunching gravelled path from the churchyard gate to the door of the sacristy: in the light of summer, in the evening sunlight with the soft grass long and shining around the rowed graves, in the blackness of winter, in the rain, with the wind swishing in the trees and bellowing about the granite corners of the church. Her hands clipped and arranged the flowers for the altar, placed the vases at carefully judged intervals, until the abrupt lines of marble melted into soft curves of colour. The other teachers in the convent school looked sideways on her activity and listened with a feigned interest, that was part hostility, to her talk. They were noisy, vigorous, forceful women who looked forward through chattering wearisome days of school-teaching to their eight weeks of summer freedom. Her placid reserved lack of colour was a reproach to them. They suspected her quietness, her decorative activity in the parish church, her life as steady as the flame of the small lamp before the holy picture in her bed-sitting-room above a draper's shop in the Market Street.

Rita Gallagher was the most offensive of her colleagues. She was tall, redheaded, good-looking and clever, too. But there was more than the instinctive reaction of one type against its opposite in the way she resented Elizabeth and in the way Elizabeth – among the flowers she blushed for her own uncharity – resented Rita Gallagher. They knew why they continually rubbed each other raw, and under white stones and shining marble he also knew.

Out of the sacristy door turning left to avoid stepping over one grave and right to avoid stepping over another, kneeling for a few moments by the bright graves, then crunch-crunch down the gravel and out to the quiet road that led over the hill into the town. The grass, the stones and the little houses were asleep in the June sun. It was a small town: a Diamond with a pillared, porticoed courthouse and four banks; four streets reaching out north, south, east and west; a tangle of narrow cobbled lanes where whitewashed cottages clung to the hill that sloped down to the river. It was as small as all that, yet she didn't know who the man was who knelt so often to pray by the other white grave. He was a quiet respectable sort of man who dressed in good heavy mourning cloth. He had a serious, thoughtful face, a long round chin and dark eyes sheltered behind heavy black-rimmed spectacles. When he was kneeling, head uncovered, at the grave her eyes were fascinated by the spot where years of methodical brushing had thinned his dark hair and extended his bony solemn forehead. She could see the brush passing over it morning after morning just as regularly as his alarm clock summoned him out of timed and regulated sleep. He was that sort of man: neat, clean, methodical.

He interested and distracted her. When he knelt at one grave her prayers for the soul of the poor deserted body that lay in the other grave were inclined to stop and start again like the ancient projector in the town's one draughty cinema. He prayed. He was in mourning. Some-times he looked at her with a vague air of recognition or, perhaps, it was that he simply recognised in her another person who mourned. But although they looked at each other, often twice in the week over the narrow width of two graves, he never smiled, never spoke, never allowed the faint glimmer in his dark eyes to brighten into acquaint-anceship.

She had a tender heart. She pitied the seriousness in his face, the slightly-weary droop in his shoulders. The sound of his feet on the gravel as he walked away slowly, deliberately, sorrowfully, went to the rhythm of the tolling of a knell. She was susceptible and had an imaginative mind. She had seen him so often, wondered about him so curiously that he had become part of the routine of her life, loved, almost, because familiar, like the rocking chair in her room, or the great potted lily at the window, or her few favourites in class. She painted in behind him a dozen varying backgrounds complete with pathetic, interesting detail.

The lettering on the tombstone merely mentioned the loving memory of Maria, some dates and figures and a surname that meant nothing to her. It wasn't much to go on but it was enough to set her imagination moving. His wife, Maria. She saw him in love, serious and honourable, timid about proposing. She saw him ruffled by the surprising ritual of the honeymoon. She saw him assuming, as deliberately and steadily as he walked, the responsibilities of a husband. She saw him shaken by the first awful blow of sorrow. The end of the story was before her eyes: the visit twice a week to the grave of the loved one, the slow solemn steps over the gravel, the uncovered head, the incipient baldness, the sad end – as in her own case, except that the symptoms were different – of a broken love.

Traffic went with sleepy leisure up and down the Market Street. In the evening she moved the great lily to one side and, sheltered by the heavy hanging curtains, looked almost tearfully out at the life of the town: the occasional car or cart, the loaded lorry painfully steaming, and tugging its trailer against the slope, the straggling, whistling schoolboys, the groups of people going down the slope to dare the draughts and the hard seats in the corrugated-iron cinema. At such moments she forgot altogether the quiet man at the graves. He was alien to that picture of sleepy, sunshiny street. Somewhere – she didn't know where – he had a totally different background; in some house, some street where the presence of the dead Maria was still felt. Had she been dark or fair, or oval-faced or plump and rosy, or beautiful or pretty or – the thought was almost disrespectful to the dead – ugly?

She was too proud to sink to a vulgar questioning curiosity that in her small town would certainly be misinterpreted. A weakness for readily attributing motives was common to all the people of that town. You asked somebody who somebody else might be. The town whispered and whispered, then said openly that the wind was blowing from a stated point of the compass, that Miss Elizabeth Nolan, for all her grand airs, was cocking her cap in a specified direction. The dreadful power of the whispering gallery to change a casual remark into a public declaration terrified her, sent her in silence to nurse her own quite painful curiosity. Someday he would speak to her, quietly, seriously, sorrowfully.

Meanwhile, seated in the curve of her window, she washed him out of her mind. The view of quiet street, the soft feel of the curtains, the vague creamy scent of the lily, evoked another and an opposing presence. No weight of white marble could crush that big man down into utter banishment: his close-cropped red hair, his great active limbs, his ruddy healthy face, his boisterous laugh that had somehow taken her unawares and faded for ever into silence. Honestly, she had been a little afraid of him when he was alive, afraid of his vigour and of the tremendous laugh that might thunder suddenly on the street or the tennis-court, in the garage that he owned or in the town hall in the middle of some stuffy parochial concert. That fear made her dubiously say no when he asked her at intervals during three years or so to marry him. He was like a steam-roller or a grizzly bear.

But now that he was dead he appealed as pitifully to her as might a tender little child. She had forgotten the way she had once feared his laughter and how, in a fanciful, literary moment, she had compared herself to an escaped convict who runs, crouching and dodging, waiting for the ravenous yell of the hounds. She had forgotten more than that. At times it needed an effort, with closed eyes and sedulous enquiring mind, to piece together the features of his honest radiant face. One evening she had had to cross to the dainty oaken bureau to take his photograph back with her to the window and to study it there under the last thin fingers of the sun.

It was a typical photograph: really an enlarged snapshot. He had worn grey flannels, a white shirt open at the neck, the cloth as tight as the hide of a drum over his tremendous shoulders. They had spent a lovely summer's afternoon around the deep black lakes in the quietness of the hills seven or eight miles from the town. That had been their last afternoon together.

He leaned towards her out of the photograph. He said, 'Time to go home, Liz. It gets very cold up here in the evening.'

Sitting on a rock by the edge of the water she had been taking the used film out of the camera. Below her feet the black lake stretched away to the foot of a jagged pyramidal cliff. The shadow of the cliff lay clearly across the steady water. She felt the first chill wind of evening come cunningly out of the heather, making her shiver suddenly, depressing her with a weary sense of dusk, darkness, the end of things. Together they walked up and down with the heathered curves of the hills, along the rutted crumbling cart-pass to the cottage where they had left their bicycles. Clumsily he held her hand as they walked. He was good-natured, like a kind father or a generous brother. But she knew that the shy woman at the mountain cottage, and her affable, unshaven, pipe-smoking man, were amazed at his bigness, at the width of his shoulders and the great roll of his limbs. Her precise neat nature was hurt. She felt as if their eyes, kindly but just a little amused, were accusing her of some breach of etiquette.

The wheels of their bicycles whirred down the sloping road into the town. He leaned sideways and said, 'I suppose it's no use, Liz.'

'What's no use?'

'Asking you again to marry me.'

She said thoughtfully, 'I like you. But you know what I think.'

'That we wouldn't suit each other.'

'Not that exactly. But, yes, I suppose.'

Around the corner of the road the first houses were in view. He spun his pedals violently backwards and for no visible reason twirled the bicycle bell loudly.

'Then you shouldn't have allowed me to continue going about with you, Liz. I'm a marrying man.'

She said, 'I didn't encourage you.'

The effort to be superior and distant failed. She knew she hadn't encouraged him. But then she had so easily taken him for granted: bulky, permanent, as solid as the ancient monument before the courthouse. No leap of imagination could have told her that he would turn and shamble out of her life like a great, tamed, amiable bear wounded by mistake.

At the first street corner he dismounted. He said, 'Good night, Liz.'

Puzzled, a little alarmed, she said good night. He had always, like a perfect gentleman, left her all the way to the door of her lodgings. She saw his lips twisting like the lips of a beaten child biting down tears. She was weak with a sickening, surprising feeling of guilt. Then he mastered himself. He said goodbye roughly and abruptly. He rode off down the street.

For a week she waited for his heavy knock on the door, his heavy stride passing along the hallway to the parlour common to all the boarders. When he moved in the old leather armchair the little ornaments on the oaken whatnot jingled and nodded like a family of comical, mechanical puppets. He didn't come. She told herself that he was ill, that she should go to see him, bring him consolation and charity fragrant as the flowers on the altar. But pride kept her a prisoner in her own room, waiting for the knock and the step along the hallway. She never had mixed with people as a young woman should. In a crisis she sank back into herself, suspicious, doubting, afraid to make the one generous gesture.

Then one day she met him face-to-face in the porch of the post office. Had he been ill? Why, no. He'd never felt better. He was awkward, embarrassed, obviously anxious to escape. Momentarily vexed, she forgot her sense of guilt and allowed herself the luxury of feeling slighted and hurt. She showed it in her looks and words. But he didn't appear to be in the least affected. A passing acquaintance nodded. He took his chance, called after the passer-by, excused himself to her, ran down the steps from the door of the post office and walked heavily away. The feeling of hurt increased, then died as she studied the view of his great back and legs moving from her down the slope of the street. Perhaps this was the best way. She went over to the assistant, caged behind the counter, bought three stamps and posted two letters and one postcard.

When his engagement was announced a month later she wasn't surprised. But she was hurt in her pride and in her motherly pity for his poor gigantic swaddled spirit that the girl should be Rita Gallagher. The redheaded one had snapped him up, looking around and beyond him to the big prosperous garage with the horde of hired mechanics and the shining petrol pumps, the lavish new bungalow at the edge of the town, the two motor cars, the servants, the cottage by the sea in summer. Elizabeth wasn't uncharitable. But she knew that girl inside out. She pitied him, and was angry with him for his incredible folly. The way Rita Gallagher fondled her sparkling ring and looked at her when they met in corridor or common-room made little spasmodic shivers go up and down her spine. She told herself she wasn't proud. But she longed wickedly to face the redheaded effrontery of that girl and say, 'I could have worn that ring. But I didn't choose to.'

Something restrained her: a horror of sinking to the level of those who couldn't conceal their feelings. When she read to the children the line in which the ancient Roman advises conspiracy to hide it in smiles and affability she found herself wondering at the wisdom that over the centuries could give such solid excellent advice. At any rate, Rita Gallagher would only laugh at her and ask her why she hadn't wished to wear that ring. She could ask herself that question and give herself a satisfactory answer. But how could she make other people understand?

One windy night about a week after his engagement had been headlined in the local paper – he was an important man – he went down to his garage for some purpose or other. The garage was built on a flat space thirty feet above the river. A tiny side-door led over a single-plank bridge to the back of the building. It could have been the wind or his weight or drink or all together. Poor creature. The two hours he spent on the rocky shallows at the edge of the deep water, his limbs broken, the wind shrieking in heartless derision in the crevices of the rock-bank, would surely take him quickly through the flames of Purgatory. Then there were three anxious days with Rita Gallagher in hysterics dramatising herself before the whole town and running to Elizabeth Nolan for consolation. He lay half-conscious in hospital until the life was crushed out of him by its own inert weight.

One grey Sunday afternoon she looked across the width of the two graves at the serious man taking off his hat, exposing his incipient baldness, going down carefully on his knees on a spread handkerchief to pray, she assumed, for Maria. Every Sunday and every Wednesday now he was there, as regular as a factory bell, saying his prayers with thoughtful devoutness, his eyes half-closed behind the thick black-rimmed spectacles. This time, when he stood up and delicately dusted the knees of his dark pin-striped trousers, he scrutinised the rectangle of white stones, plucking here and there a thin green tongue of hungry invading grass. She crossed herself and stood up, then saw on the grave at which she had just been praying an occasional spot of delicate green. He came to her assistance. His voice was smooth and deep. It was a voice that accompanied by music might ascend a few notes to a strong sweet tenor.

He said, 'The parish clerk seems to be neglecting his job.'
'It's not his fault, poor man. He's had a death in the family.'
'Well everyone has his troubles. So have we.'
'Yes, we have our troubles.'
'Deaths in the family too.'
They straightened up suddenly and simultaneously. The tip of the long feather in her hat flicked his eye. She apologised earnestly. He stood with his hand shading the wounded eye. She saw, half-hidden behind his fingers, his deliberate smile. That little blundering collision had in an instant made them something a little more than mere

acquaintances, and made her like him on the first quick impression as she liked the small number of people she counted as friends. They crunched down the main walk – she always wore flat-heeled sensible shoes for the deep gravel – and past the cool porch of the church. He didn't, she noticed, raise his hat.

'The death wasn't in my family,' she said. 'That's the grave of a friend.'

'I noticed that you didn't wear mourning.'

Only in my heart, she thought. She said, 'I noticed that you did.'

'So we've been noticing each other.'

They laughed together. The bond strengthened. When you had laughed with somebody else at the same joke and almost bumped your head against somebody else's head you had genuinely become a part of their life. They could never completely forget you.

They walked down the road towards the town. The hedges and the June grass smelt warm and fragrant.

'It was in my family,' he said. 'Poor Maria.'

'You loved her very much.'

'She was a good soul. But she had her own opinion of me. She thought I was too staid. There were some things she could never imagine me doing. She told me often what they were.'

'That sounds intriguing.'

'Poor Maria.'

She smiled in a way that was meant to be motherly and consoling, telling him as plainly as she could without the aid of words that she understood his sorrow. Two little pig-tailed girls that she taught in school met them, accepted docilely her smiling and patting and looked after her with surprised curiosity. She didn't often stop to pat her pupils on the head.

He said, 'Are you a teacher?'

'In the convent school.'

'Is it a big school?'

'Big enough for a town like this.'

'My father belonged here,' he said. 'That's why Maria's buried here. But we've lived in Ballyclogher for years.'

'Ballyclogher's a lovely town.'

'It has its qualities.'

At the bus-stop in the Diamond he stretched out his hand to her. She looked at him steadily, the motherly feeling in her heart, wishing foolishly that he were pig-tailed and about three feet high and pattable on the head. She wanted to comfort him.

'You shouldn't mourn too much,' she said. 'When you over-do it you don't honour the dead.'

'Thank you so much. Perhaps we'll meet again, Miss . . .'

'Nolan.'

He went sideways and upwards into the shiny green bus, smiling and raising his hat. Her heart expanded with pity and with joy, too, that she had been given this opportunity of dispensing the charity of kind words.

Pity, she told herself primly, remembering another line of Shakespeare, was not even a step, no, not a grise, on the way to . . .

She recoiled timidly from the very name of the strange shattering thing that, according to the poet, was not brought any nearer by the feeling of pity. In the pigeon-holes of her precise disciplined mind she searched for the higher motive that would make pardonable all the strangeness, all the warm melting power. Suppose that a woman's love for a man could help him to forget some sorrow, could fill up the emptiness left by some loss. Nobody could find fault with that motive.

She painted in yet another background behind his serious pathetic figure: the empty house that, for a year or two years or three or ten, had been his home when the work of the day ended. Now the voices of children – there were certainly some children – sounded so hollow and lonely in that emptiness. He looked at them, remembered their mother and was crushed under the weight of sorrow. They wondered, children always did, why mother had gone on such a long, long journey. They asked plaintively when she would come back to them. Poor, pitiful, puzzled orphans. Poor man.

She realised suddenly that the thought of him had followed her from the white graves through the easily moving traffic of Market Street, up the stairs to her room and into the sheltered world of the hanging curtains and of the chaste significance of the tall potted lily. In that quiet place two men met and battled in the heart of a woman. It was a conflict beginning before clothes or recorded history, as fierce as the writhings of two male monsters in some primeval swamp. Dark and mysterious and serious and slightly bald, one man was standing in the doorway of a departing bus and raising his hat in respectful salute. Shoulders and hips extending even the width of the brown shroud, laughing tremendously and terrifyingly, the second man was rising up out of the grave, bursting brown earth and white marble, shaking white stones from his shoulders to rattle like hail on the grass. She sat quietly looking out of the window, the book she had been reading idle and unattended on her knees. She was sheltered by the curtains from passing, inquisitive eyes.

But all the time her body was trembling and uneasy, torn with curiosity and desire, with regret and hope. She could but she would not cross to the oaken bureau to go back through an enlarged snapshot to a windy day by a black lake on the side of the mountain. She could but she would not go back through the issues of the local newspaper, piled neatly in one corner of her room, to unearth, perhaps, further details about the death of Maria who had left behind her in lovely Ballyclogher the loneliness of an empty home. She could but she would not walk downstairs to the landlady who had a friend who came over once a week from Ballyclogher. But any one of those three actions would be corrupt with the suggestion of surrender. So she sat quietly in her room. She talked and taught in the school-room. All the time she felt that her spirit was like a sapling in a high wind, bent and straining but still unbroken. For a long fortnight the dead struggled with the living. The serious man was not seen praying by Maria's grave.

A whole tortured, indecisive fortnight. Then one day Sister Mary Francesca said, 'Miss Nolan, Jim has got himself into trouble again.'

She clucked sympathetically. She said, 'I'm sorry to hear that. The poor man.'

'Poor man indeed,' said Sister Mary Francesca.

She fingered her rosary beads. She said, 'He's nobody's enemy but his own. But then he was the only boy. My poor parents spoiled him out of all imagining.'

The tragedy and the contradiction Elizabeth thought: the sister praying in the cloister, the brother with monotonous regularity getting into difficulties with the police.

'I had a letter from a solicitor in Ballyclogher. He gave me some friendly information about Jim's case. It isn't easy answering him in writing. I was wondering, Miss Nolan. You see, I trust you so.'

Elizabeth went to Ballyclogher to see the solicitor. She went like a hero in an ancient tale going bravely to some foretold end in a brave battle. She had a feeling of destiny about that journey. For this had Jim's parents spoiled their only son. For this had their daughter entered the convent and become Sister Mary Francesca. For this had Jim ruined his own life and befouled his father's name: that Elizabeth should go in a bus to the town of Ballyclogher and talk across a desk in an orderly office to the grave methodical man of law that she had first seen kneeling at his prayers beside that second bright grave.

'I don't understand,' she said. 'This isn't the surname on the tombstone.'

'I bought the practice. An old established one. We kept the old name.'

He was business-like but courteous. He explained with charity the tragedy and the enormity of Jim. Then he invited Elizabeth to tea in his own home to kill the two hours until her bus left and, he said, to meet his mother, a widow, and his sister. There was no mention of the children of the dead Maria and as she walked with him along a tree-lined avenue to his large detached house she was saddened by the additional sorrow of a childless marriage, broken by death and leaving behind it nothing more tangible than fading memories, nothing more lasting than the snapshot she herself kept in the drawer of her bureau.

Going up the avenue to the house she said, 'She must have been very happy here.'

He asked absently, 'Who?'

'Maria.'

He thought for a moment before answering, 'Happy? I suppose she was happy. She was the sort could make her own contentment anywhere.'

Turning his key in the lock he said, with unexpected bitterness, 'But her contentment wasn't the happiness of other people.'

Through an uneasy half-hour of conversation across teacups, that edge of bitterness in his voice troubled her with a sense of deeper tragedy: the unhappy home, the slighted husband, the unloved wife. Nobody mentioned Maria. But Maria was with them in that room, a stern enigmatic presence, a restraint on the corpulent good-nature of his grey-haired mother, on the round-limbed vitality of his brown-haired sister.

Back in his office she sat with him near the window where they could look down the street to see the approaching bus.

She risked saying, 'Do you feel lonely now?'

'I've always been lonely,' he said. 'Until I saw you praying in the graveyard.'

She blushed and her heart thumped as no contiguity of great limbs had ever made it thump. When he bent down over her chair and kissed her until her lips hurt she didn't know whether to laugh or cry or scream or suffocate or burst.

Breathlessly she said, 'Maria?'

'Her,' he said. 'The bitch. That killed her.'

He was even more out of wind than the panting woman he had kissed. He wasn't used to kissing and moreover he had had to stoop down at an awkward angle.

'She wouldn't die,' he said. 'She could never forget she was the eldest of us and my father's favourite child. You see my father was a tyrant and she was the image of him and she knew that and rejoiced in it. We thought her wedding would keep her away from us. But she came back. Her husband ran away from her. Nobody could live with her. She taunted me always. With a tongue like poison. She used to keep saying that our father had never been afraid of women.'

He kissed her again, quite fiercely for so decorous a man. She saw the grave, and the white stones and marble and the weight of clay crushing down on the dead defeated Maria. With every kiss of the seven he gave her the weight of stones, marble and clay grew heavier. She saw as in a vision the tombstone falling with a crash and the name and memory of Maria passing for ever from the earth.

Going back in the bus she knew that whatever it might be it wasn't love. Sitting in her window above the lazy traffic of the street she looked again at the enlarged snapshot, at the great limbs resting easily by the edge of the black lake. It was all tenderness and sunshine and good nature wounded by mistake. From the shining white grave he reached out and held her as she had held him for so long during life. She could not battle with the dead as the serious man could, trampling on the memory of the dead with a kiss that was wicked with a little passion and with a good deal of exulting, triumphing revenge.

But she no longer feared the living and fear was her only protection. She put the picture back in the bureau. She sat by the heavy curtain and the tall lily wondering what she would feel when she saw his dry figure crossing the street and heard in the hallway the metronomical regularity of his steps.

THE DOGS IN THE GREAT GLEN

The professor had come over from America to search out his origins and I met him in Dublin on the way to Kerry where his grandfather had come from and where he had relations, including a grand-uncle, still living.

'But the trouble is,' he said, 'that I've lost the address my mother gave me. She wrote to tell them I was coming to Europe. That's all they know. All I remember is a name out of my dead father's memories: the great Glen of Kanareen.'

'You could write to your mother.'

'That would take time. She'd be slow to answer. And I feel impelled right away to find the place my grandfather told my father about.

'You wouldn't understand,' he said. 'Your origins are all around you.'

'You can say that again, professor. My origins crop up like the bones of rock in thin sour soil. They come unwanted like the mushroom of merulius lacrimans on the walls of a decaying house.'

'It's no laughing matter,' he said.

'It isn't for me. This island's too small to afford a place in which to hide from one's origins. Or from anything else. During the war a young fellow in Dublin said to me: "Mister, even if I ran away to sea I wouldn't get beyond the three-mile limit".'

He said, 'But it's large enough to lose a valley in. I couldn't find the valley of Kanareen marked on any map or mentioned in any directory.'

'I have a middling knowledge of the Kerry mountains,' I said. 'I could join you in the search.'

'It's not marked on the half-inch ordnance survey map.'

'There are more things in Kerry than were ever dreamt of by the Ordnance Survey. The place could have another official name. At the back of my head I feel that once in the town of Kenmare in Kerry I heard a man mention the name of Kanareen.'

We set off two days later in a battered, rattly Ford Prefect. Haste, he said, would be dangerous because Kanareen might not be there at all, but if we idled from place to place in the lackadaisical Irish summer we might, when the sentries were sleeping and the glen unguarded, slip secretly as thieves into the land whose legends were part of his rearing.

'Until I met you,' the professor said, 'I was afraid the valley might have been a dream world my grandfather imagined to dull the edge of the first nights in a new land. I could see how he might have come to believe in it himself and told my father – and then, of course, my father told me.'

One of his grandfather's relatives had been a Cistercian monk in Mount Melleray, and we went there hoping to see the evidence of a name in a book and to kneel, perhaps, under the high arched roof of the chapel close to where that monk had knelt. But, when we had traversed the corkscrew road over the purple Knockmealdowns and gone up to the mountain monastery through the forest the monks had made in the wilderness, it was late evening and the doors were closed. The birds sang vespers. The great silence affected us with something between awe and a painful, intolerable shyness. We hadn't the heart to ring a doorbell or to promise ourselves to return in the morning. Not speaking to each other we retreated, the rattle of the Ford Prefect as irreverent as dicing on the altar-steps. Half a mile down the road the mute, single-file procession of a group of women exercitants walking back to the female guest-house underlined the holy, unreal, unanswering stillness that had closed us out. It could easily have been that his grandfather never had a relative a monk in Mount Melleray.

A cousin of his mother's mother had, he had been told, been a cooper in Lady Gregory's Gort in the County Galway. But when we crossed the country westwards to Gort, it produced nothing except the information that apart from the big breweries, where they survived like birds or bison in a sanctuary, the coopers had gone, leaving behind them not a hoop or a stave. So we visited the woods of Coole, close to Gort, where Lady Gregory's house had once stood, and on the brimming lake-water among the stones, we saw by a happy poetic accident the number of swans the poet had seen.

Afterwards in Galway City there was, as there always is in Galway City, a night's hard drinking that was like a fit of jovial hysteria, and a giggling ninny of a woman in the bar who kept saying, 'You're the nicest American I ever met. You don't look like an American. You don't even carry a camera. You look like a Kerryman.'

And in the end, we came to Kenmare in Kerry, and in another bar we met a talkative Kerryman who could tell us all about the prowess of the Kerry team, about the heroic feats of John Joe Sheehy or Paddy Bawn Brosnan. He knew so much, that man, yet he couldn't tell us where in the wilderness of mountains we might find the Glen of Kanareen. Nor could anybody else in the bar be of the least help to us, not even the postman who could only say that wherever it was, that is if it was at all, it wasn't in his district.

'It could of course,' he said, 'be east over the mountain.'

Murmuring sympathetically, the entire bar assented. The rest of the world was east over the mountain.

With the resigned air of men washing their hands of a helpless, hopeless case the postman and the football savant directed us to a roadside post office twelve miles away where, in a high-hedged garden before an old grey-stone house with latticed windows and an incongruous, green, official post office sign there was a child, quite naked, playing with a coloured, musical spinning-top as big as itself, and an old half-deaf man sunning himself and swaying in a rocking-chair, a straw hat tilted forwards to shade his eyes. Like Oisin remembering the Fenians, he told us he had known once of a young woman who married a man from a place called Kanareen, but there had been contention about the match and her people had kept up no correspondence with her. But the day she left home with her husband that was the way she went. He pointed. The way went inland and up and up. We followed it.

'That young woman could have been a relation of mine,' the professor said.

On a rock-strewn slope, and silhouetted on a saw-toothed ridge where you'd think only a chamois could get by without broken legs, small black cows, accurate and active as goats, rasped good milk from the grass between the stones. His grandfather had told his father about those athletic, legendary cows and about the proverb that said: Kerry cows know Sunday. For in famine times, a century since, mountain people bled the cows once a week to mix the blood into yellow maize meal and provide a meat dish, a special Sunday dinner.

The road twisted on across moorland that on our left sloped dizzily to the sea, as if the solid ground might easily slip and slide into the depths. Mountain shadows melted like purple dust into a green bay. Across a ravine set quite alone on a long, slanting, brown knife blade of a mountain, was a white house with a red door. The rattle of our pathetic little car affronted the vast stillness. We were free to moralise on the extent of all space in relation to the trivial area that limited our ordinary daily lives.

The two old druids of men resting from work on the leeward side of a turf-bank listened to our enquiry with the same attentive, half-conscious patience they gave to bird-cries or the sound of wind in the heather. Then they waved us ahead towards a narrow cleft in the distant wall of mountains as if they doubted the ability of ourselves and our conveyance to negotiate the Gap and find the Glen. They offered us strong tea and a drop out of a bottle. They watched us with kind irony as we drove away. Until the Gap swallowed us and the hazardous, twisting track absorbed all our attention we could look back and still see them, motionless, waiting with indifference for the landslide that would end it all.

By a roadside pool where water-beetles lived their vicious secretive lives, we sat and rested, with the pass and the cliffs, overhung with heather, behind us and another ridge ahead. Brazenly the sheer rocks reflected the sun and semaphored at us. Below us, in the dry summer, the bed of a stream held only a trickle of water twisting painfully around piles of round black stones. Touch a beetle with a stalk of dry grass and the creature either dived like a shot or, angry at invasion, savagely grappled with the stalk.

'That silly woman in Galway,' the professor said.

He dropped a stone into the pool and the beetles submerged to weather the storm.

'That day by the lake at Lady Gregory's Coole. The exact number of swans Yeats saw when the poem came to him. Upon the brimming water among the stones are nine and fifty swans. Since I don't carry a camera nobody will ever believe me. But you saw them. You counted them.'

'Now that I am so far,' he said, 'I'm half-afraid to finish the journey. What will they be like? What will they think of me? Will I go over that ridge there to find my grandfather's brother living in a cave?'

Poking at and tormenting the beetles on the black mirror of the pool, I told him, 'Once I went from Dublin to near Shannon Pot, where the river rises, to help an American woman find the house where her dead woman friend had been reared. On her deathbed the friend had written it all out on a sheet of notepaper: "Cross the river at Battle Bridge. Go straight through the village with the ruined castle on the right. Go on a mile to the crossroads and the labourer's cottage with the lovely snapdragons in the flower garden. Take the road to the right there, and then the second boreen on the left beyond the schoolhouse. Then stop at the third house on that boreen. You can see the river from the flagstone at the door."

'Apart from the snapdragons it was exactly as she had written it down. The dead woman had walked that boreen as a barefooted schoolgirl. Not able to revisit it herself she entrusted the mission as her dying wish to her dearest friend. We found the house. Her people were long gone from it but the new tenants remembered them. They welcomed us with melodeon and fiddle and all the neighbours came in and collated the long memories of the townland. They feasted us with cold ham and chicken, porter and whisky, until I had cramps for a week.'

'My only grip on identity,' he said, 'is that a silly woman told me I looked like a Kerryman. My grandfather was a Kerryman. What do Kerrymen look like?'

'Big,' I said.

'And this is the heart of Kerry. And what my grandfather said about the black cows was true. With a camera I could have taken a picture of those climbing cows. And up that hill trail and over that ridge is Kanareen.'

'We hope,' I said.

The tired cooling engine coughed apologetically when we abandoned it and put city-shod feet to the last ascent.

'If that was the mountain my grandfather walked over in the naked dawn coming home from an all-night card-playing then, by God, he was a better man than me,' said the professor.

He folded his arms and looked hard at the razor-cut edges of stone on the side of the mountain.

'Short of too much drink and the danger of mugging,' he said, 'getting home at night in New York is a simpler operation than crawling over that hunk of miniature Mount Everest. Like walking up the side of a house.'

He was as proud as Punch of the climbing prowess of his grandfather.

'My father told me,' he said, 'that one night coming home from the card-playing my grandfather slipped down fifteen feet of rock and the only damage done was the ruin of one of two bottles of whisky he had in the tail-pockets of his greatcoat. The second bottle was unharmed.'

The men who surfaced the track we were walking on had been catering for horses and narrow iron-hooped wheels. After five minutes of agonised slipping and sliding, wisdom came to us and we took to the cushioned grass and heather. As we ascended the professor told me what his grandfather had told his father about the market town he used to go to when he was a boy. It was a small town where even on market days the dogs would sit nowhere except exactly in the middle of the street. They were lazy town dogs not active, loyal and intelligent like the dogs the grandfather had known in the great glen. The way the old man had described it, the town's five streets grasped the ground of Ireland as the hand of a strong swimmer might grasp a ledge of rock to hoist himself out of the water. On one side was the sea. On the other side a shoulder of mountain rose so steeply that the Gaelic name of it meant the gable of the house.

When the old man went as a boy to the town on a market day it was his custom to climb that mountain, up through furze and following goat tracks, leaving his shiny boots, that he only put on, anyway, when he entered the town, securely in hiding behind a furze bush. The way he remembered that mountain it would seem that twenty minutes active climbing brought him halfways to heaven. The little town was far below him, and the bay and the islands. The unkempt coastline tumbled and sprawled to left and right, and westwards the ocean went on for ever. The sounds of market-day, voices, carts, dogs barking, musicians on the streets, came up to him as faint, silvery whispers. On the tip of one island two tall aerials marked the place where, he was told, messages went down into the sea to travel all the way to America by cable. That was a great marvel for a boy from the mountains to hear about: the ghostly, shrill, undersea voices; the words of people in every tongue of Europe far down among monstrous fish and shapeless sea-serpents that never saw the light of the sun. He closed his eyes one day and it seemed to him that the sounds of the little town were the voices of Europe setting out on their submarine travels. That was the time he knew that when he was old enough he would leave the Glen of Kanareen and go with the voices westwards to America.

'Or so he said. Or so he told my father,' said the professor.

Another fifty yards and we would be on top of the ridge. We kept our eyes on the ground, fearful of the moment of vision and, for good or ill, revelation. Beyond the ridge there might be nothing but a void to prove that his grandfather had been a dreamer or a liar. Rapidly, nervously, he tried to talk down his fears.

'He would tell stories for ever, my father said, about ghosts and the good people. There was one case of an old woman whose people buried her – when she died, of course – against her will, across the water, which meant on the far side of the lake in the glen. Her dying wish was to be buried in another graveyard, nearer home. And there she was, sitting in her own chair in the chimney corner, waiting for them, when they came home from the funeral. To ease her spirit they replanted her.'

To ease the nervous moment I said, 'There was a poltergeist once in a farmhouse in these mountains, and the police decided to investigate the queer happenings, and didn't an ass's collar come flying across the room to settle around the sergeant's neck. Due to subsequent ridicule the poor man had to be transferred to Dublin.'

Laughing, we looked at the brown infant runnel that went parallel to the path. It flowed with us: we were over the watershed. So we raised

our heads slowly and saw the great Glen of Kanareen. It was what
Cortez saw, and all the rest of it. It was a discovery. It was a new world.
It gathered the sunshine into a gigantic coloured bowl. We accepted it
detail by detail.

'It was there all the time,' he said. 'It was no dream. It was no lie.'

The first thing we realised was the lake. The runnel leaped down to
join the lake, and we looked down on it through ash trees regularly
spaced on a steep, smooth, green slope. Grasping from tree to tree you
could descend to the pebbled, lapping edge of the water.

'That was the way,' the professor said, 'the boys in his time climbed
down to fish or swim. Black, bull-headed mountain trout. Cannibal
trout. There was one place where they could dive off sheer rock into
seventy feet of water. Rolling like a gentle sea: that was how he
described it. They gathered kindling, too, on the slopes under the ash
trees.'

Then, after the lake, we realised the guardian mountain; not rigidly
chiselled into ridges of rock like the mountain behind us but soft and
gently curving, protective and, above all, noble, a monarch of mountains, an antlered stag holding a proud horned head up to the highest
point of the blue sky. Green fields swathed its base. Sharp lines of stone
walls, dividing wide areas of moorland sheep-grazing, marked man's
grip for a thousand feet or so above sea-level then gave up the struggle
and left the mountain alone and untainted. Halfways up one snow-
white cloud rested as if it had hooked itself on a snagged rock and there
it stayed, motionless, as step by step we went down into the Glen.
Below the cloud a long cataract made a thin, white, forked-lightning
line, and, in the heart of the glen, the river that the cataract became,
sprawled on a brown and green and golden patchwork bed.

'It must be some one of those houses,' he said, pointing ahead and
down to the white houses of Kanareen.

'Take a blind pick,' I said. 'I see at least fifty.'

They were scattered over the glen in five or six clusters.

'From what I heard it should be over in that direction,' he said.

Small rich fields were ripe in the sun. This was a glen of plenty, a
gold-field in the middle of a desert, a happy laughing mockery of the
arid surrounding moors and mountains. Five hundred yards away a
dozen people were working at the hay. They didn't look up or give any
sign that they had seen two strangers cross the high threshold of their
kingdom but, as we went down, stepping like grenadier guards, the
black-and-white sheepdogs detached themselves from the haymaking
and moved silently across to intercept our path. Five of them I counted.
My step faltered.

'This could be it,' I suggested with hollow joviality. 'I feel a little like an early Christian.'

The professor said nothing. We went on down, deserting the comfort of the grass and heather at the side of the track. It seemed to me that our feet on the loose pebbles made a tearing, crackling, grinding noise that shook echoes even out of the imperturbable mountain. The white cloud had not moved. The haymakers had not honoured us with a glance.

'We could,' I said, 'make ourselves known to them in a civil fashion. We could ask the way to your grand-uncle's house. We could have a formal introduction to those slinking beasts.'

'No, let me,' he said. 'Give me my head. Let me try to remember what I was told.'

'The hearts of these highland people, I've heard, are made of pure gold,' I said. 'But they're inclined to be the tiniest bit suspicious of town-dressed strangers. As sure as God made smells and shotguns they think we're inspectors from some government department: weeds, or warble-fly or horror of horrors, rates and taxes. With equanimity they'd see us eaten.'

He laughed. His stride had a new elasticity in it. He was another man. The melancholy of the monastic summer dusk at Mount Melleray was gone. He was somebody else coming home. The white cloud had not moved. The silent dogs came closer. The unheeding people went on with their work.

'The office of rates collector is not sought after in these parts,' I said. 'Shotguns are still used to settle vexed questions of land title. Only a general threat of excommunication can settle a major feud.'

'This was the way he'd come home from the gambling cabin,' the professor said, 'his pockets clinking with winnings. That night he fell he'd won the two bottles of whisky. He was only eighteen when he went away. But he was the tallest man in the glen. So he said. And lucky at cards.'

The dogs were twenty yards away, silent, fanning out like soldiers cautiously circling a point of attack.

'He was an infant prodigy,' I said. 'He was a peerless grandfather for a man to have. He also had one great advantage over us – he knew the names of these taciturn dogs and they knew his smell.'

He took off his white hat and waved at the workers. One man at a haycock raised a pitchfork – in salute or in threat? Nobody else paid the least attention. The dogs were now at our heels, suiting their pace politely to ours. They didn't even sniff. They had impeccable manners.

'This sure is the right glen,' he said. 'The old man was never done talking about the dogs. They were all black-and-white in his day, too.'

He stopped to look at them. They stopped. They didn't look up at us. They didn't snarl. They had broad shaggy backs. Even for their breed they were big dogs. Their long tails were rigid. Fixing my eyes on the white cloud I walked on.

'Let's establish contact,' I said, 'before we're casually eaten. All I ever heard about the dogs in these mountains is that their family tree is as old as the Red Branch Knights. That they're the best sheepdogs in Ireland and better than anything in the Highlands of Scotland. They also savage you first and bark afterwards.'

Noses down, they padded along behind us. Their quiet breath was hot on my calves. High up and far away the nesting white cloud had the security of heaven.

'Only strangers who act suspiciously,' the professor said.

'What else are we? I'd say we smell bad to them.'

'Not me,' he said. 'Not me. The old man told a story about a stranger who came to Kanareen when most of the people were away at the market. The house he came to visit was empty except for two dogs. So he sat all day at the door of the house and the dogs lay and watched him and said and did nothing. Only once, he felt thirsty and went into the kitchen of the house and lifted a bowl to go to the well for water. Then there was a low duet of a snarl that froze his blood. So he went thirsty and the dogs lay quiet.'

'Hospitable people.'

'The secret is touch nothing, lay no hand on property and you're safe.'

'So help me God,' I said, 'I wouldn't deprive them of a bone or a blade of grass.'

Twice in my life I had been bitten by dogs. Once, walking to school along a sidestreet on a sunny morning and simultaneously reading in *The Boy's Magazine* about a soccer centre forward, the flower of the flock, called Fiery Cross the Shooting Star – he was redheaded and his surname was Cross – I had stepped on a sleeping Irish terrier. In retaliation, the startled brute had bitten me. Nor could I find it in my heart to blame him, so that, in my subconscious, dogs took on the awful heaven-appointed dignity of avenging angels. The other time – and this was an even more disquieting experience – a mongrel dog had come up softly behind me while I was walking on the fairgreen in the town I was reared in and bitten the calf of my leg so as to draw spurts of blood. I kicked him but not resenting the kick, he had walked away as if it was the most natural, legitimate thing in heaven and earth for a dog to bite me and be kicked in return. Third time, I thought, it will be rabies. So as we walked and the silent watchers of the valley padded at our heels, I enlivened the way with brave and trivial chatter. I recited my story of the four wild brothers of Adrigole.

'Once upon a time,' I said, 'there lived four brothers in a rocky corner of Adrigole in West Cork, under the mountain called Hungry Hill. Daphne du Maurier wrote a book called after the mountain, but divil a word in it about the four brothers of Adrigole. They lived, I heard tell, according to instinct and never laced their boots and came out only once a year to visit the nearest town which was Castletownberehaven on the side of Bantry Bay. They'd stand there, backs to the wall, smoking, saying nothing, contemplating the giddy market-day throng. One day they ran out of tobacco and went into the local branch of the Bank of Ireland to buy it and raised havoc because the teller refused to satisfy their needs. To pacify them the manager and the teller had to disgorge their own supplies. So they went back to Adrigole to live happily without lacing their boots, and ever after they thought that in towns and cities the bank was the place where you bought tobacco.

'That,' said I with a hollow laugh, 'is my moral tale about the four brothers of Adrigole.'

On a level with the stream that came from the lake and went down to join the valley's main river, we walked towards a group of four whitewashed, thatched farmhouses that were shining and scrupulously clean. The track looped to the left. Through a small triangular meadow a short-cut went straight towards the houses. In the heart of the meadow, by the side of the short-cut, there was a spring well of clear water, the stones that lined its sides and the roof cupped over it all white and cleansed with lime. He went down three stone steps and looked at the water. For good luck there was a tiny brown trout imprisoned in the well. He said quietly, 'That was the way my grandfather described it. But it could hardly be the self-same fish.'

He stooped to the clear water. He filled his cupped hands and drank. He stooped again, and again filled his cupped hands and slowly, carefully, not spilling a drop, came up the moist, cool steps. Then, with the air of a priest, scattering hyssop, he sprinkled the five dogs with the spring-water. They backed away from him, thoughtfully. They didn't snarl or show teeth. He had them puzzled. He laughed with warm good nature at their obvious perplexity. He was making his own of them. He licked his wet hands. Like good pupils attentively studying a teacher, the dogs watched him.

'Elixir,' he said. 'He told my father that the sweetest drink he ever had was out of this well when he was on his way back from a drag hunt in the next glen. He was a great hunter.'

'He was Nimrod,' I said. 'He was everything. He was the universal Kerryman.'

'No kidding,' he said. 'Through a thorn hedge six feet thick and down a precipice and across a stream to make sure of a wounded bird. Or all night long waist deep in an icy swamp waiting for the wild geese. And the day of this drag hunt. What he most remembered about it was the way they sold the porter to the hunting crowd in the pub at the crossroads. To meet the huntsmen halfways they moved the bar out to the farmyard. With hounds and cows and geese and chickens it was like having a drink in Noah's Ark. The pint tumblers were set on doors lifted off their hinges and laid flat on hurdles. The beer was in wooden tubs and all the barmaids had to do was dip and there was the pint. They didn't bother to rinse the tumblers. He said it was the quickest-served and the flattest pint of porter he ever saw or tasted. Bitter and black as bog water. Completely devoid of the creamy clerical collar that should grace a good pint. On the way home he spent an hour here rinsing his mouth and the well-water tasted as sweet, he said, as silver.'

The white cloud was gone from the mountain.

'Where did it go,' I said. 'Where could it vanish to?'

In all the wide sky there wasn't a speck of cloud. The mountain was changing colour, deepening to purple with the approaching evening.

He grasped me by the elbow, urging me forwards. He said, 'Step on it. We're almost home.'

We crossed a crude wooden stile and followed the short-cut through a walled garden of bright-green heads of cabbage and black and red currant bushes. Startled, fruit-thieving birds rustled away from us and on a rowan tree a sated, impudent blackbird opened his throat and sang.

'Don't touch a currant,' I said, 'or a head of cabbage. Don't ride your luck too hard.'

He laughed like a boy half hysterical with happiness. He said, 'Luck. Me and these dogs, we know each other. We've been formally introduced.

'Glad to know you dogs,' he said to them over his shoulder.

They trotted behind us. We crossed a second stile and followed the short-cut through a haggard, and underfoot the ground was velvety with chipped straw. We opened a five-barred iron gate, and to me it seemed that the noise of its creaking hinges must be audible from end to end of the glen. While I paused to rebolt it he and the dogs had gone on, the dogs trotting in the lead. I ran after them. I was the stranger who had once been the guide. We passed three houses as if they didn't exist. They were empty. The people who lived in them were above at the hay.

Towards the fourth thatched house of the group we walked along a green boreen, lined with hazels and an occasional mountain ash. The guardian mountain was by now so purple that the sky behind it seemed, by contrast, as silvery as the scales of a fish. From unknown lands behind the lines of hazels two more black-and-white dogs ran, barking with excitement, to join our escort. Where the hazels ended there was a house fronted by a low stone wall and a profusion of fuchsia. An old man sat on the wall and around him clustered the children of the four houses. He was a tall, broad-shouldered old man with copious white hair and dark side whiskers and a clear prominent profile. He was dressed in good grey with long, old-fashioned skirts to his coat – formally dressed as if for some formal event – and his wide-brimmed black hat rested on the wall beside him, and his joined hands rested on the curved handle of a strong ash plant. He stood up as we approached. The stick fell to the ground. He stepped over it and came towards us. He was as tall or, without the slight stoop of age, taller than the professor. He put out his two hands and rested them on the professor's shoulders. It wasn't an embrace. It was an appraisal, a salute, a sign of recognition.

He said, 'Kevin, well and truly we knew you'd come if you were in the neighbourhood at all. I watched you walking down. I knew you from the top of the Glen. You have the same gait my brother had, the heavens be his bed. My brother that was your grandfather.'

'They say a grandson often walks like the grandfather,' said the professor.

His voice was shaken and there were tears on his face. So, a stranger in the place myself, I walked away a bit and looked back up the Glen. The sunlight was slanting now and shadows were lengthening on mountain slopes and across the small fields. From where I stood the lake was invisible, but the ashwood on the slope above it was dark as ink. Through sunlight and shadow the happy haymakers came running down towards us; and barking, playing, frisking over each other, the seven black-and-white dogs, messengers of good news, ran to meet them. The great Glen, all happy echoes, was opening out and singing to welcome its true son.

Under the hazels, as I watched the running haymakers, the children came shyly around me to show me that I also was welcome. Beyond the high ridge, the hard mountain the card-players used to cross to the cabin of the gambling stood up gaunt and arrogant and leaned over towards us as if it were listening.

It was moonlight, I thought, not sunlight, over the great Glen. From house to house, the dogs were barking, not baying the moon, but to welcome home the young men from the card-playing over the mountain. The edges of rock glistened like quartz. The tall young gambler came laughing down the Glen, greatcoat swinging open, waving in his hand the one bottle of whisky that hadn't been broken when he tumbled down the spink. The ghosts of his own dogs laughed and leaped and frolicked at his heels.

THE SHORTEST WAY HOME

The first school I ever went or was sent to was full of girls and that wasn't the worst of it. We were taught by big black nuns who had no legs or feet but who moved about as if, like the antediluvian chest of drawers in my mother's bedroom, they went on concealed casters. They used to haunt my dreams, moving uncannily about in thousands, their courses criss-crossing like the navigational lines on the maps on the classroom walls, bouncing off each other and spinning around like bumper cars at a fancy fair, holding aloft white canes like witch's wands. They didn't teach us much. All I remember is making chains by tearing up and intertwining thin strips of coloured paper, and rolling plasticine which we called plaster seed, into sticky balls. I can smell the turpentiny smell of it still.

At any rate the wells on my path to learning in that harem of a school were poisoned by the affair of the school-reader and by the blow Sister Enda caught me on the knuckles with her cane when I was absorbed drawing funny faces, with spittle and finger tip, on the glossy brown wooden desk.

'Wipe the desk clean this instant,' she said. 'You naughty little boy.'

The offending funny faces – they were a first effort at recapturing the fine careless rapture observed, in a newspaper strip, on the faces of Mutt and Jeff – I wiped out or dried off with my handkerchief fastened with a safety pin to my white woollen gansey. That was a precautionary measure taken against loss of linen by my mother who for years preserved a snapshot of me pennant-come-nosebag flying, a surly freckled boy with uncontrollable hair who looked as if he had just murdered nine reverend mothers. In more select schools, I've heard tell, they had in those days an inhuman device by which gloves too were ensured against loss. An elastic string passed around the back of the young victim's neck and then down the insides of the sleeves and from each extremity of the string a glove depended: so that when not in use, the gloves retreated up the sleeves like mice into holes. Fortunately, we were never grand enough for gloves. The worst we had was this pinned-on wiper with which I extinguished Mutt and Jeff, and I looked for sympathy towards Big May, and hated Sister Enda, as the long Act of Charity said, with my whole heart and soul and above all things.

At that time Big May was the only woman I loved and, great-hearted queen that she was, it wasn't Big May betrayed to the nun that I already had at home a duplicate copy of the coloured school reader, the first book that I, a born collector of books, ever possessed. She was nine and a half, four years older than me, her protégé, and big even then so that she might, in the words of the poet, with her great shapely knees and the long flowing line, have walked to the altar through the holy images at Pallas Athene's side, or been fit spoil for a centaur drunk with the unmixed wine. She was big and wild and lovely and never could take the straight road to school nor the straight road home, so that to be in her company was always an unguessable adventure. She ran messages for my mother and undertook to chaperone me to school when my sister, who was thirteen and a half, was too busy and superior and too absorbed in her own companions to be pestered with the care-taking of a toddler of a brother. May was lithe, laughing-eyed and dark-headed and could box better than most boys and climb trees like a monkey. She was an adorable woman and a born mother, so with my knuckles smarting, I turned my moistening eyes towards her for sympathy.

But the morning that martinet, Sister Enda, tried to commandeer my second copy of the school reader, Low Babies Edition, I wasn't looking for any woman's sympathy. Sister Enda said precisely, 'Your sister tells me you have one of these at home.'

It was a lovely reading-book: sixteen pages of simple sentences, big print, coloured pictures. It told the most entrancing stories. This one, for instance: My dog Rags has a house. He has a little house of his own. See, his name is over the door.

Or this one: Mum has made buns for tea. She has made nice hot buns.

Or yet another: When the children went to the zoo they liked the elephant best of all. Here is the elephant with happy children on his back.

Or breaking into verse: When the old owl lived in the oak never a word at all he spoke.

To have one copy, which my mother had bought me, at home, and another copy, supplied by regulations, in school, gave that miracle of coloured picture and succinct narrative the added wonder of twins or of having two of anything. So when Sister Enda, soaring to the top of her flight in the realms of wit, said one reader should be enough for such a little boy, and when all the girls except May giggled I saw red and grabbed, leaving Sister Enda momentarily quite speechless with shock and turning over and over in her hand a leaf that said on one side: Here comes the aeroplane, says Tom; and on the other: When the children came home from town they had much to tell Mum.

Gripping the rest of the reader I glared at the nun who was white in the face with something – fright or fury – at this abrupt confrontation with the male forces of violence and evil. She looked at me long and thoughtfully. Fortunately for me she was perambulating without benefit of cane. She said, 'You naughty boy. Now your poor mother will have to pay for the book you destroyed. Stand in the corner under the clock with your face to the wall until home-time.'

Which I did: tearless, my face feverish with victory, because that onset with Sister Enda had taught me things about women that some men never learn and, staring at the brown varnished wainscotting in the corner of the room, I made my resolve. On the homeward journey I told May all about it.

I said, 'As long as I live I'm not going back to that school. It's all women.'

'Not till tomorrow morning.'

'Never. Never, if I die.'

'Where will you go?'

'To the Brothers with the big boys.'

'You're too little.'

'I'll go all the same.'

'They mighn't take you.'

'They'll take me.'

'What will your mother say?'

'I don't care what she says.'

Which was true, because I knew if I could best Sister Enda I could best my mother. It was a man's world.

'You're a terrible boy,' May said. 'But I'll miss you.'

She believed me, I felt, and knew in her heart that that was our last day at school together, and she was proud of me. So with my hand in hers we went on the last detour of my career at the female academy, leaving Brook Street and Castle Street, our proper route, and wandering into the cosy smelly crowded world of the gridiron of lanes of one-storeyed whitewashed houses below and at the back of the towering double-spired Catholic Church; Fountain Lane, Brook Lane, The Gusset, St. Kevin's Lane, Potato Lane, and the narrowest of all, which was a cul-de-sac called the Rat's Pad. Previously we had prudently passed it by because even to May, the narrow roofed-over entry opening out into a small close that held only four houses was a little daunting. Besides, you could not go through it and come out the other end and, as

May saw things, a place of that sort did not constitute a classical diversion.

It was a dog's walk, she said. You came back the way you went.

But on this day the Rat's Pad attracted us because a woman in one of its four houses was shouting her head off and outside her half-door a dozen or so people had gathered to find out what all the noise was about. Skillfully May worked her way in to a point of vantage, carrying me pick-a-back, both to save space and to give me enough altitude to study the domestic interior. The woman, in blouse and spotted apron, was gesticulating with a long knife. Of all the words or sentences only one remained with me, 'I'll cut the head off you, you lazy gazebo.'

The man saying nothing, his head bowed as if meekly to accept the blade, sat on a low stool by an open, old-fashioned grate. The fire burned brightly.

'May,' I whispered, 'will she really and truly cut the head off him?' I wasn't sure whether I did or did not want to witness the spectacle.

'From what they say,' said May, 'she couldn't cut a slice of bread.'

So since there was nothing happening but shouting we rejoined our main route homewards and May bought for me, as a special treat to mark the ending of the first phase of my scholastic career, a toffee apple in Katy McElhatton's huckster shop in Castle Street. Those toffee apples were a noted home-made delicacy, and Katy was a woman, old as the Hag of Beare, who lived in the end to be one hundred and eight and only died of a stomach disorder that came on her when she mistook a bottle of Jeyes fluid for a bottle of stout she kept always on a shelf behind the counter. But her toffee apples were something to savour and remember, and the flavour of thick golden syrup toffee and roasted green apple was still in my mouth when I fell asleep that night to dream of a severed head held aloft by the hair in the hand of an irate wife. There was no blood neither from stump nor severed neck, nor any jagged dangling sinews. When, for purposes of demonstration, the vengeful spouse turned the head and neck around and around, the cross-section of the neck was solid and shiny like the corned beef when it had been subjected to the slicer in James Campbell's big shop. That was the way you were when your head was cut off. It was also true that husbands and wives could work themselves into such a state that they threatened each other with knives and decapitation. My last day at the school for girls had taught me a lot and I owed it all not to any organised institutional education but to my own assertion of manly independence and to the divagations of my amazonian love and protectress, that queen among women, Big May. Henceforth I would be a man and would bear my expanding satchel into the world of the big boys. Farewell, farewell for ever to first love and all it had given me.

'The only Brother I'll go to,' I dictated to my mother, 'is the Wee Brother.'

Having won my battle against any return to the monstrous regiment of women I was advancing to invest new positions.

The six black Brothers of the Christian Schools emerged from their monastery every morning to kneel in the top pew, to the left of the nave and under the marble pulpit, at eight o'clock mass. A wide-eyed study of their movements, kneeling, sitting, standing, praying, yawning, genuflecting, reading missals, blowing noses, had for some time been for me a substitute for any form of worship: latria or dulia.

The Grey Brother, whose place was on the extreme right of their pew, was Brother Superior. His bush of grey hair was clipped and shaved in an exact straight line dead level with the tops of his ears. He had a fine Roman nose and a trumpet style of blowing it that never since have I seen or heard surpassed. His production of handkerchief from a slit in his black habit, his preliminary flourish of white linen, added up to a ritual fascinating to watch. He never produced the handkerchief with his right hand. He always flourished before he trumpeted and, when he blew, even the two old voteens, one man and one woman, who prayed out loud and talked over their affairs with God for all to hear, were momentarily startled out of the balance and rhythm of their recitative.

To the left of the Grey Brother stood or knelt or sat, according to the stage of the celebration, Brother Busto and Brother Lanko, for even then I knew them according to the nicknames the boys bestowed on them, and had to that extent my instruction in the lingua franca of the world of men. They had the same soothering Munster accents and the same surnames and were distinguished from each other only, as the nicknames so subtly indicated, by the robust girth of one and the handsome height of the other. The Beardy Brother was unusual because beards were rare among Brothers, but the phenomenon was satisfactorily explained by the boys saying that the Beardy Brother had been in China, and later in life it came as a shock to me to find that beards were comparatively as rare among Chinamen as among Brothers. The Red Brother, true to the colour of his hair and the close, disciplined army cut of it, was the terror of the school and the legend went so far as to say that on one of his punitive forays he had trapped the shoulders of a delinquent boy under a window sash and thumped him on the buttocks with a hurling stick. To my extreme relief he had withdrawn from the religious life, possibly to devote more time to hurling, before I had advanced as far as the grade he so robustly instructed.

But it would have been clear to me, even if the opinion of the grown up people had not already been there to confirm my intuitive judgement that the Wee Brother was an angel descended from above. The children adored him. They ran messages for him, swept the schoolrooms and the schoolyard for him, and in the season, under his direction, shook the trees and picked up the fallen apples in the monastery orchard. They banded themselves at his behest into groups of all sorts, from paper and comb orchestras to football teams, or went walking with him in crowds in the country learning the names of birds and trees, and not too often wandering off in small foraging parties to rob orchards or egghouses. In spite of the vow of poverty he always clinked with small coins to reward them for their more meritorious efforts. He was good to the poor and his favourite pupil was Packy Noble, a shuffling albino boy too big for his grade and mentally incapable of advancing further or of mastering more than the alphabet. Grown men admired the Wee Brother because he had been a famous amateur horse jockey before religion claimed him, and – although this was something I did not then understand – the girls, looking at him, sighed heartbroken resignation to the inscrutable ways of the Lord who claimed such a paragon for the cloister.

It was his waving fair hair and the way the light reflected on his pince-nez that caused me first to worship him, and shining pince-nez seemed to me the clearest of all marks of the angelic nature manifesting itself in mortal shape. Even still I'm inclined to think that the world is the way it is because not half enough people wear pince-nez.

So I said to my mother, 'The only Brother I'll go to is the Wee Brother.'

It was autumn, and the schoolyard was the best place in our world for horse-chestnuts. The yard was triangular with the apex pointing up a slope towards the schoolhouse, an oblong cut-stone building of two storeys. Access to the second storey, because of the oversight of the builder who forgot the stairs originally planned for, was by an iron outside stairway. The long branches of the chestnut trees overhung the walls of the yard and with a little encouragement from sticks and stones readily dropped their thorny green fruit. Wonder was all around my mother and myself as we ascended towards the school. Ten million boys, it seemed to me, were playing conkers, swinging the seasoned chestnuts scientifically on lengths of string, slashing at and bashing their opponents' chestnuts. Fragments of the casualties of a myriad battles crackled under our feet like cinders. Surrounded by an excited crowd a tiny fellow called Tall Jimmy Clarke was bending down with his hands behind his back and picking ha'pence off the ground with his teeth. He did it for the price of the ha'pence he picked up and prospered by it because the fascination of what's difficult always proved overpowering, even for boys who had seen and paid for the trick a dozen times over. In a corner by the concrete lavatories and washrooms a crowd of hydromaniacs were having the time of their lives pumping the handles of the drinking fountains and covering each other and the ground around them with water. This was life, this was a battlefield, this was the wonderful world of school and apart from my mother, there wasn't a petticoat to be seen.

Then a whistle blew and in shuffling hordes the boys ascended, to be swallowed up by the old stone building. The slamming of doors, the clatter of iron-tipped heels on the iron stairway were wonderful to hear; then we were alone, my mother and I. Dust still rose from the yard. It steamed in the sun on the damp patch left by the water-sprites. Beyond a row of chestnut trees the gardens kept by the Brothers were well-ordered and radiant. Variously-regulated chants arose from various classrooms and we listened to them, my hand in hers, until the Grey Brother came to us from the monastery beside the schoolhouse and said, 'So this is the little man who doesn't like the girls.'

The Grey Brother I took to from the start for he was a fellowman and he saw my point.

'And what book shall we put him into,' he said. 'He's so far under the admittance age.'

Book, I thought, I have my own books. In the satchel on my back there was one jotter, slightly scribbled on, one pencil, two school readers even if one of them, due to the villainy of woman, was lacking a leaf. There was also my lunch of bread and butter sandwiches, a small bottle of milk, two biscuits and one piece of cake.

'He wants nobody but the Wee Brother,' my mother said.

'Then the Wee Brother it shall be.'

He waved his arm at a window on the second storey and on the landing of the stairway at the corner of the building the vision appeared, fair hair like a halo blowing around its head, the sunlight shining through the halo, the sun beaming out of its glass eyes, truly an angel descending to walk with us. He took me up the stairs again with him and that was how I came to meet the Four Horsemen of the Apocalypse who, after Big May and the Wee Brother, were the greatest teachers I ever had.

Sometimes the Wee Brother called them the Twelve Apostles because he said any one man of them was as good as three. Other times he called them simply the Four Just Men. But mostly, and I think merely because they ran most of his messages for him – carrying despatches all over the town, from errands of charity to admonitory notes to parents who weren't sending their boys to school – he called them the Four Horsemen of the Apocalypse. They sat, or knelt at prayer time, on the bench nearest to the door, making sure in winter that the door was securely closed against draughts, enjoying in summer a high green view of the neighbouring convent field where the nuns, for some symbolic devotional purpose, grazed a small black donkey; the happiest laziest donkey in the world, the Wee Brother said. That big bench by the door was the highest and oldest in the classroom. Even by the standards of those days it was a museum piece. It had survived several changes of school furniture. It was battle-scarred with the names of boys now grown to be men. It towered over the other desks like a Spanish galleon over the dogged little ships of Elizabeth's gunners. It creaked with age every time one of its occupants moved. It had space, the Wee Brother said, for four and a quarter men, so he lifted me up, seated me at one end of it, my legs dangling, beside Packy Noble, told me I was the image of an artistic mantelpiece ornament in a modern house, and placed me thus under the Tutelage of the Four Horsemen; Packy himself, Tall Jimmy Clarke, Jinkins Creery and Tosh Mullan who later in life was to become a boxer and to acquire by a painful accident the pseudonym of Kluterbuck.

My two school readers opened before me, I studied the pictures and listened to the drone of learning all around me and sometime in the afternoon fell asleep. For no lullaby ever sung soothingly by loving peasant mother could equal the power of the simple addition table to induce slumber: One and one are two, one and two are three, one and three are four. Before my eyes radiant woolly balls rolled up and down hills and I slept and as I learned afterwards, was gently lifted by the snowheaded Packy and under the direction of the Wee Brother, laid to rest on the broad bottom shelf of a brown press used as a wardrobe on dry days for the scholars' coats and caps. Comfortably cushioned, I slumbered until it was time for the litany of the Blessed Virgin and the journey home and then, thumbing the sleep out of my eyes, I boarded the galleon again and balanced on my knees for a prayer so soothing that I would have fallen asleep again except that, just as the Wee Brother said Tower of Ivory and we sang out Pray for Us, the old desk gave up the ghost and collapsed with a crash, and the litany dissolved in the laughter of boys and when the Wee Brother saw that nobody was hurt he laughed too. That was a day's learning I'll remember when I've forgotten – as I have already – sines, cosines and declensions and the fine poem about the Latin prepositions that govern the accusative case.

The Four Horsemen, taking the place of Big May, conducted me home. Tall Jimmy Clarke, by stooping and lifting, acquired on the way four halfpennies and bought sweets and shared them out. Jinkins Creery held me up on the parapet of the bridge over the Strule and showed me where he had caught a river lamprey a mile long and promised to show me the seven baby lampreys he had in a glass jar at home. He explained to me how he had caught them by holding a tennis-ball in among a maze of them in a foot of water in the Killyclogher Burn and how the stupid, vicious creatures had clung on to it so tightly with the suckers they had instead of mouths that he was able to lift seven of them out of the water. Packy, who was Master of All, and Tosh Mullan put on, for my instruction, a display of the noble art of self-defence which was great fun because Packy was huge and white-headed and his battered boots were too big for him and his toes turned up and he could imitate a dancing bear he had once seen in John Duffy's travelling circus.

Packy's greatest weakness was that he could never be in time for school in the morning. His mother or, to be more charitable, his aunt, went by the strange name of Pola and was the proprietress of what we knew bluntly as a tramp lodging-house where, it was rumoured, the itinerant patrons cooked over candles and slept on their feet, elbows hooked on a common rope, so that inexorably they were all roused together when the rope was slackened at reveille. Cooking conditions may not have been so primitive nor sleeping conditions so arbitrary in Pola's caravanserai, but certain it was that the mixed clientele of sallow-faced oriental bagmen, pedlars, vagrant musicians, buskers and downright beggars who patronised it did not go to bed until the small hours and then only to the accompaniment of a pretty consistent bedlam. So, shuffling in late, morning after morning, Packy would wearily rub red eyes that had around them rims of sleep, like grey mud around a weeping flowering marsh; and the back of his white poll was never devoid of a tiny pillow-feather or two. Every morning the prolegomena to his day's study followed the same pattern.

'He who rises late must gallop all day. Do you know what that means, Packy?'

'Yes, sir.'

'What, Packy?'

'It's in the headline copy, sir.'

The headline copy with its incomprehensible maxims in stiff old-fashioned copperplate, in elegant lines and curves that no young inexperienced hands could ever imitate, was the master-work on which we were supposed to model our handwriting.

'Packy, you're right. I suppose one way or another the sum total of wisdom is in the headline copy.'

'Yes, sir.'

'Packy, I must buy you an alarm clock.'

'Yes, sir.'

'Diluculo surgere saluberrimum est, Packy. To rise early is most healthful.'

Tenderly, with his finger-tips, the Wee Brother would pick the feathers of the night before from the close-cropped white head.

'Yes, sir,' said Packy.

'Early to bed and early to rise makes a man healthy, wealthy and wise, Packy.'

With those gentle finger-tips he would drum out on Packy's shoulder a rhythm to go with the words.

'That's in the headline copy too, Packy.'

'Yes, sir.'

The early bird catches the worm was also in the headline copy and it struck me as a brutal saying because the early worm was the head of a fool to be out at that hour. The only saying I liked at all in the headline copy was about violets: I would give you some violets but they withered when my father died. Not one of us, not even John MacBride, a clean boy who was clever and was taught by his musical mother to sing Moore's melodies at parochial concerts, knew what it meant or who said it or who died or who wanted to give violets to whom. But, regardless, we copied out the words painfully and with all the intensity of faith: slope lightly up, slope heavily down, curve at the top and curve at the bottom, Packy peering so closely at the page that his nose was as good as in the inkwell, the tip of Tall Jimmy Clarke's tongue peeping out like a moist pink rodent.

Packy, being as he was and doomed to an early grave could only in some heavenly fields ever have discovered the coy beauty of the modest flower. Here on this earth his peering eyes discovered more about nettles than violets for Pola was a great believer in the health-giving powers of nettle tea, nettle soup or nettles as a vegetable and it was Packy's task to gather, in the spring, the soft succulent young nettles before age had soured them and forced them to show their stings. The other three horsemen went along to help and I went with them.

Because of the four oblong fields that belonged to Big James Campbell, the butcher, and the engine shed and Spyglass Hill and the grass wigwam and the cave at the spot where four hedgerows joined and the Ali Baba's treasure house of a town dump and the roaring bull in Mackenna's meadow, gathering the nettles was not as prosaic a business as you might readily imagine. Three of the fields were gently-rising slopes and the fourth was a dome of a hill overlooking the bull's deep meadow, and the four of them lay just beyond the straggling fingers of houses at the edge of the town.

You crossed the town dump, a grey-black wasteland, smoking with an occasional volcano where discarded cinders had refused to die. There were always a few old people, sacks in hands, shoulders hunched and eyes on the ground, wandering slowly about, gathering the makings of a fire and hoping for treasures of scrap. Since the most extraordinary relics of careless housekeeping came to that island of lost ships the aged searchers were quite frequently rewarded and the curious schoolboy could find there, too, objects to delight the heart: shining biscuit tins, discarded motor wheels and tyres, bicycle frames that could be refurbished and made useful. Tosh Mullan who was lucky at finding things had once come upon a handsome point-twenty-two rifle that would do everything but shoot.

The best nettles were always found on the fringe of the dump just before you ascended the slope, climbed a fence and crossed the railway line to the turntable and the engine shed.

'Nettles for measles and pimples,' Packy would say. 'That's what my aunt Pola says.'

In the murk of the one-night lodging house for wandering men who had no parish of their own Pola managed to maintain a flawless olive complexion.

'Boil them in water, she says, and drink the tea. She says if you drink nettle tea you'll always have a clear skin.'

'Tosh could do with it,' said Tall Jimmy Clarke.

For Tosh, with a hanging lower lip and a squint and a recurring rash of pimples was not the most beautiful of boys. Yet even then he had in his social relations the tolerant mildness of the natural professional fighter who never, outside the ring, feels called upon to prove his prowess; and the pummellings with which he responded to Tall Jimmy's witticisms were perfectly good-natured.

One day – if I can distinguish one day from another over a period of years – Tosh flourished in his hand a full-grown dead lamprey that Jinkins had caught and given to him. He carried it as proudly as if it had been a policeman's truncheon, until the stench became too much. Waving it in his hand he pursued Jimmy with warlike whoops towards the railway line and the engine shed. Jinkins, carrying his fishing rod, ran after them and I ran after Jinkins because, bright ferret-eyes glistening in his turnip of a head, he had promised to show me how he caught fish and how, incidentally, he had acquired the nickname we called him by. I never knew his Christian name.

From the fence on top of the railway embankment we looked back at Packy the Herbalist on hands and knees among the rank green growth at the fringe of the wasteland. Even if he was never to know much about violets it could just be part of the irony of living that he knew more than any of us about the meaning of growing things. He was so close to them because, being half-blind, he had to kneel to see them, their shapes and colours, and when the rare flowering nettle showed its fragile white bloom through the red mist of his eyes it must have meant something miraculous to him. He was the herbalist gathering plants from the ground to make messes and potions to keep blood pure and a woman beautiful.

'Come on Packy,' Tosh called. 'We have nettles enough to sink a battleship.'

Packy rose, clutching his herbs, and to excite our laughter, did his bear's gallop towards us.

'We'll cross over the engine shed and grease our boots.'

'We'll wait for the goods first. We always wait for the goods.'

Swinging on the wire fence we watched with a wonder that never lessened the variety of cargo on the interminable lumbering goods train. We counted the trucks. Cattle on their last sad journey looked out at us morosely. The wind blew towards us smells of dung and good timber, the sour smell of scrap metal, the wet milky smell of farm produce. The tick-tock of wheels over joints and fish-plates was delightfully soothing. We cheered the guard in his van at the end of the train as a crowd in a theatre might cheer the author. He waved his flag to us as he always did before the embankment and the round mouth of a bridge devoured him.

'Big Mick O'Neill, the railway porter, can turn the turntable with one hand and an engine and a coal-wagon on it.'

'He's farandaway the strongest man in this town.'

'He's the strongest man in Ireland.'

We had never you see, heard of the bragging man who said: 'Give me a lever and I'll move the world.'

'There was a stronger man in Dublin once,' said Tall Jimmy Clarke. 'My father told me about him.'

Tall Jimmy's father, a roadworker, was admittedly a man of great knowledge as all makers and menders of roads come, by dint of their occupation, to be. All day long they watch the world, unaware of their observation, passing them by.

'He was a policeman. His name was Patrick Sheehan. He caught a mad bull by the horns once and when people asked him was he afraid he said he was only afraid the horns would break.'

In the middle of the railway track we stopped and listened, each one of us thinking that far away across the four fields we could hear our own private bull roaring in Mackenna's meadow.

'He went down a manhole once,' said Tall Jimmy, 'to rescue a workman was stuck in a pipe and he rescued the workman and he was smothered dead by the gas. He was so strong that was the only way he could be killed. My da says there's a monument to him in Dublin.'

'We'll grease our boots,' said Packy.

It was a thick yellow suet-like grease kept in little iron boxes on the sides of the freight trucks. It was meant to soothe and cool the friction of axles and wheels and not to be applied to any leather ever hammered out of an animal's hide. But in ritual fashion, like savages daubing on war paint, we greased our boots with it before we entered the four fields. Its one beneficial quality was that it could withstand moisture and, if the grass was wet, the beads of rain or dew danced like jewels on the dulled leather. Leather treated with that yellow grease could defy for ever all shine and polish and cause quarrels between mystified parents and indignant bootsellers about the quality of the material they put in footwear nowadays.

With our feet anointed we slipped through a well-worn hole in a high hawthorn hedge and trod the holy grass of the first field. Tall Jimmy was in the lead, dancing a dance that was halfway between his idea of an Indian war-dance and his slightly more accurate idea of a sailor's hornpipe. Packy came in the rear, beaming like a bride over his bouquet of nettles. Pola, who never had had a wedding, white or coloured, or a groom from whose arm she could dangle, was an assiduous spectator at every wedding in the parish church, and Packy could simper like any lace-clad virgin just as well as he could prance like a circus bear.

In the middle of a clump of rushes a tall unheeded wooden pole carried a notice saying trespassers would be prosecuted. We regarded it as the dissolute members of an aristocratic family would regard a family ghost who had become an old-fashioned bore. No longer even did we use it as a cockshot for cinders carried from the engine shed.

'Tony,' Tall Jimmy shouted, 'Tony.'

Running away from us he called back, 'Watch me. I'm Tom Mix.'

For the old horse grazed or wearily sucked the grass in the first field. Nothing less like the renowned Tony ever shuffled along on four shaky feet. He was an old saddle-backed bay left out there to die in peace. There were white spots of age on his hide like stabs of lichen on old stone. He was just about able and no more, to bear the featherweight of agile Jimmy and it was Jimmy's delight to straddle on the sunken back that seemed almost to creak like a worn iron bedstead, to hammer his heels as if they were spurred against the withered flagging flanks, to hang from the scraggy neck as if he was a Red Indian, to wind up the exhausted slack-springed body to a trot in which every leg seemed to limp away in a different direction.

'Look at him now. Hasn't he the lovely smile.'

He pulled the lips apart to show great green and yellow teeth lazily floating in saliva. They weren't bright or beautiful, yet the expression was more like a smile than it was like anything else.

He was an amiable old animal and to him and Tall Jimmy I owe it that I was never afraid of the long heads of horses, and that, later in life I was able to find myself in agreement with the Tipperary trainer who at the Curragh of Kildare races smacked the tight-skirted titled lady on her prancing buttocks and cried out for all to hear, 'Women, the best things God made – after horses.'

Tall Jimmy on horseback leading us, we went in procession through the gapped hedge and up the slope to the grass wigwam on Spyglass Hill. From the Wee Brother's public readings we knew about Long John Silver, Jim Hawkins and the fifteen men on a dead man's chest so, although the dome-shaped hill that was the highest of the four fields offered no view of the blue Pacific, that was still the only name we could give it. From the wigwam that Tosh and Tall Jimmy had lovingly plaited from branches, rushes and long grass you could see the traffic on the road to Clanabogan, the long scimitar-shaped meadow where our bull fed, Pigeon Top Mountain where the sportsmen went for grouse, the town's three steeples, the deep Drumragh River where Jinkins fished and the clanking metal structure called the Lynn Bridge which carried the railway over the river. So we called the place Spyglass Hill. The wigwam was a magic restful place. Green light filtered down into it. The air was sweet with the smell of warm grass. The particoloured branches, peeled in strips by Tosh who had a clasp-knife as long as a sabre, seemed, if you lay flat on your back and looked up at them long enough, to move and writhe like serpents. Although that big man James Campbell who owned the fields went to the trouble of putting up notices banning trespassers, neither he nor his foreman nor working men ever tampered with the grass wigwam and, when Tosh had built around it a circular palisade of strong sticks to protect it from the curiosity of cows, it lasted for a whole summer.

All together we lay in the green light and Tall Jimmy's exhausted discarded mount lay thinking the thoughts of age on the grass outside the palisade. From the tired horse to the roaring bull was no distance at all because the wigwam was our halfway house to the cave that wasn't a cave. It was a sort of unfinished tunnel that cattle seeking shade from the sun had made under branches at the meeting place of four hedgerows. Smaller than the cattle we could penetrate further into gloom and then, parting a few branches, peer down into the meadow where the big red bull grazed. The game was to roar at him until he roared back. He never failed to oblige us. He would delight us still further by rooting at the ground with his horned head and sometimes even drive us into sheer ecstasy by racing around in circles and kicking his hind legs in the air as a horse would. He was a fine performer. He was our own menagerie: a giant red bull alone like a king in his private park.

'They'll kill him some day,' Jimmy said sadly. 'They'll kill him and make Bovril out of him. That's what they do with bulls.'

Our roaring done – Packy who could dance like a bear was also the best of us to roar like a bull – we wandered aimlessly across the grass thinking sadly of all the noble roaring bulls, black and red, who had gone down to the doom of being melted to fill small bottles with meat extract. To brighten our mood Tall Jimmy seized one of a pair of pitchforks, left stuck in a hedge by some of Campbell's men, and shouted, 'We'll play "Ninety-Eight".'

It wasn't a card game. It was a by-product of the Wee Brother's fervent lecturing on the long sad history of Irish Rebellion. The pitchforks, one in the hands of Packy and one in the hands of Tall Jimmy, became the pikes the boys of Wexford carried in 1798. Before their glistening points hordes of redcoats fell back at Camolin, Enniscorthy, Tubberneering; and Tosh with the dead lamprey was beating an invisible big drum and Jinkins with his fishing rod was a galloping lancer, and the high town of New Ross and Three Bullet Gate were about to be stormed and taken, when Big James and his foreman appeared through a gap in a hedge and roared at us and we ran.

'They'll prosecute us, sure as God,' said Jinkins who had a natural horror of the law.

So we ran faster and the two men for the hell of it ran after us. For my age and the length of my legs I could run well but the Four Horsemen were bigger and better athletes and I was losing ground badly: confused, too, with the awesome thought that I was a trespasser, one of a group referred to specifically in the Lord's Prayer. Staggering under the weight of that thought I stumbled and fell and was resigning myself to prosecution and prison when I was picked up by Packy and carried through a narrow gap between two trees to the covert of a terraced whindotted slope above the river. Concealed by green thorn and yellow blossom we sat whispering for half an hour and looking at, and listening to, the water. It came rattling down over the shallows, curved and spread out to make a deep pool that went on under the railway and the girders of the Lynn Bridge.

'That's where I catch my fish,' Jinkins said.

'Where you catch the jinkins you should throw back,' said Tall Jimmy. 'Some day Robert McCaslan, the water bailiff, will get you.'

On our river the salmon fry and the tiny trout were called jinkins and our friend, the great hunter, had earned his name from his passion for catching, cooking and eating them against all the laws ever made for the conserving of game fish.

Packy held his nose. He said, 'Jinkins always stinks like a fish.'

'No. It's this,' said Tosh.

He dangled the hideous, headless, mouthless lamprey under Packy's nose.

'Come and watch me catch them,' Jinkins said to me.

So when we thought the coast was clear and our pursuers gone Jinkins mounted his rod and readied his dry flies and in single file we marched out from the shelter of the whins, to be greeted with gales of friendly laughter from Big James and his foreman. They waved at us through our escape gap between the two trees.

'They were only fooling all the time,' said Packy.

'They're funny men,' said Tall Jimmy with scorn.

'Don't kill all the fish in the river,' the foreman shouted.

And when Tall Jimmy, never at a loss for an answer, cried back that we'd cut them up and use them for bait they laughed even louder and went back laughing towards Spyglass Hill.

Far away our lonely doomed bull roared on his own demesne.

With a light breeze at his back Jinkins let the long line float out easily. Packy, on his bended knees peering at the earth, might have been the image of the ancient herbalist half-blind from searching the fields and from concocting in his magic cellar, but Jinkins by the river bank was for sure the natural hunter. The stiff hair stood up on him like the bristles on a hedgehog. His ferret eyes pierced the water for the first white flash of soft under-belly. The small hook struck with deadly accuracy and Jinkins chuckled to himself as he unhooked the tiny, silvery, fluttering bodies and strung them through the gills on a looped, peeled ash-twig. It was methodical massacre; and if the salmon are not in that water as they were of old then the cause of their absence, under God and new land-drainage systems, is the Herod-complex that impelled Jinkins Creery to his slaughter of the innocents. As Tall Jimmy taught me never to fear horses, so the sight of Jinkins at work taught me to pity fish: fish on the hook, fish in aquariums gazing sadly through the frustrating glass, pinkeens imprisoned in jam jars, fish sacrificed on slabs in shops and doomed to the fire and the knife and fork.

When the killing was all done we walked the railway line to the middle of the Lynn Bridge, opened a metal trap door between the rails and descended a ladder to a plank walk that workmen used when inspecting or painting the girders. The deep water was quite still below us. Packy held me by the shoulders but, in spite of his protection, I had, that night, my first falling nightmare.

'Long Alex Nixon,' Tosh said, 'drowned himself in that pool.'

'He didn't drown himself,' said Packy. 'He just sank.'

'He couldn't sink.'

'He wasn't cork, was he?'

'I saw them dragging the river for his body,' Tall Jimmy said. 'There was a man diving all the time from a boat looking for him.'

'We all saw that,' Jinkins said. 'They were at it for days.'

'He was the best swimmer in the world,' Tosh said. 'He just held his nose and sank and drowned himself. He was always fighting with his wife.'

'That doesn't prove he drowned himself,' Packy said. 'You couldn't drown yourself just by holding your nose.'

He released my shoulder and holding his nose with his left hand, did, on the swaying plank a few steps of his bear's shuffle. But our laughter between the unanswering black water and the metal girders, was hollow. Awed by the sound of it we climbed back up the ladder and gratefully closed the clanking door on the mystery of Long Alec Nixon.

The possibility or otherwise of drowning by holding the nose was a topic that kept us talking all the way back along the rusted branch-line to the town's auxiliary goods station, where the coal-wagons were lined up with the supplies for the lunatic asylum, and halfway up the town's main street where shops were closed and the tea-time hush had descended. Thought and remembrance came with the hush and we heard the agonised voice of Packy, 'Mother of God, I've lost my nettles.'

Red and blue shop-blinds carefully drawn made the town look like a place of the dead. Not a nettle grew on the cruel pavement. With guilt I remembered that I had seen Packy's nettles fall to the grass when he redeemed me, the trespasser. With the folly of youth I said, 'We'll go back for more.'

'We wouldn't have time. We're late already. She'll murder me.'

Generously Jinkins the hunter said, 'Give her a couple of fish.'

'She never eats fish. She says they're greasy.'

'Give her my ampor eel,' said Tosh.

Ampor eel was our mispronunciation for lamprey.

But sick to the soul, we all knew that this was no joke for Pola put great faith in nettles.

Then as we stood sadly thinking, the angel came to our rescue. She came, tall, wild-haired and ragged. She came as she always came, from a side street of shabby, brown-and-yellow brick houses. She bore in her arms a jungle profusion of wild nettles and, bending her ear to the sorrowful tale, she said simply to Packy, 'One of the women I work for is mad about nettles. But take half of mine. I have enough to physic the town let alone one old woman.'

She patted my head. She said, 'How do you like the big boys?'

She took the lead as if she was the biggest boy of all and we followed her up the street for fifty yards until, being Big May, she left us to make her own detour along another side street.

The day the Wee Brother would no longer close me in the press to slumber my way to learning on the piled coats and caps I knew sorrowfully that life had begun. What happened was that one of the scholars, for reasons known only to himself and which he was never sufficiently articulate to explain, had a pocket of his coat full of broken glass. Turning over in my slumber I lacerated my left hand – I still have a faint scar. I emerged, when awakened, dripping blood. The Wee Brother looked as if he and the class were guilty of murder. He staunched the flow, sent Jinkins to buy me a bag of hard sweets, then sent me home in the company of shambling Packy. It wasn't a serious wound but it was the beginning of the end. Thereafter there was nothing for me but the common lot, the hard reality of wooden desks and, as I mentioned – Life; and Life remorselessly was to take me away from Big May and the Wee Brother and the Four Horsemen, my six favourite teachers.

The Wee Brother is with the Saints and Packy is more than likely his favourite pupil still, for Packy died young. Short of dancing like a bear and roaring like a bull, being late for school and being kind to me, and gathering nettles to preserve Pola from pimples, he never accomplished much in life that I ever heard of. But he had a splendid funeral paid for by the subscriptions of the Wee Brother's numerous clients and led by Pola and the Wee Brother as chief mourners.

Tosh took to boxing and retained his professional amiability except for one unfortunate moment when he was engaged in conflict with a fighter who had the provoking name of Kluterbuck. Every just man loses his composure at least once and Tosh struck Kluterbuck very much and very severely below the belt, lost the fight and gained a new name. Never afterwards was he known as Tosh. The change of name may have altered his character. He gave up boxing. He left the town and never came back. He was last heard of just before the war, working in a bicycle factory in Coventry. In occasional dreams I see him grown larger but otherwise unchanged, swinging a bicycle tyre around his head as once he swung the dead and odorous ampor eel.

Jinkins had a mental breakdown and went for treatment to the asylum whose coal supply we walked past the day Packy lost the nettles. He remained there as a trusted patient, working around the grounds and fishing in the river that flows just outside the walls.

Tall Jimmy Clarke became a jockey but took to drink, put on weight, descended to truck-driving and became a wealthy owner of trucks. No longer as supple or as close to the ground as he was that day under the chestnut branches he makes no money by picking ha'pence up with his teeth. But then as he told me himself, he now has other ways of earning his living.

Big May went off to London and, if you could believe on their Bible oaths the people in the town I came from, went on thinking the longest way round was the shortest way home. Her thick dark hair, the outline of her strong jawbone is still visible to me. She holds me pick-a-back. Together we peer at the flashing knife and the raving woman and the slave of a man in the dim kitchen, and May says, 'From what they say she couldn't cut a slice of bread.'

By the tone of her voice then, she never put much weight on what people said. She gave generously. What violets she had she shared them with Packy.

A JOURNEY TO THE SEVEN STREAMS

My father, the heavens be his bed, was a terrible man for telling you about the places he had been and for bringing you there if he could and displaying them to you with a mild and gentle air of proprietorship. He couldn't do the showmanship so well in the case of Spion Kop where he and the fortunate ones who hadn't been ordered up the hill in the ignorant night had spent a sad morning crouching on African earth and listening to the deadly Boer guns that, high above the plain, slaughtered their hapless comrades. Nor yet in the case of Halifax nor the Barbadoes where he had heard words of Gaelic from coloured girls who were, he claimed, descended from the Irish transported into slavery in the days of Cromwell. The great glen of Aherlow, too, which he had helped to chain for His Majesty's Ordnance Survey was placed inconveniently far to the South in the mystic land of Tipperary, and Cratloe Wood where the fourth Earl of Leitrim was assassinated, was sixty miles away on the winding Donegal fjord called Mulroy Bay. But townlands like Corraheskin, Drumlish, Cornavara, Dooish, The Minnie-burns and Claramore, and small towns like Drumquin and Dromore were all within a ten-mile radius of our town and something of moment or something amusing had happened in every one of them.

The reiterated music of their names worked on him like a charm. They would, he said, take faery tunes out of the stone fiddle of Castle Caldwell; and indeed it was the night he told us the story of the stone fiddle and the drowned fiddler, and recited for us the inscription carved on the fiddle in memory of the fiddler, that he decided to hire a hackney car, a rare and daring thing to do in those days, and bring us out to see in one round trip those most adjacent places of his memories and dreams.

'In the year 1770 it happened,' he said. 'The landlord at the time was Sir James Caldwell, Baronet. He was also called the Count of Milan, why, I never found anybody to tell me. The fiddler's name was Dennis McCabe and by tradition the McCabes were always musicians and jesters to the Caldwells. There was festivity at the Big House by Lough Erne Shore and gentry there from near and far, and out they went to drink and dance on a raft on the lake, and wasn't the poor fiddler so drunk he fiddled himself into the water and drowned.'

'Couldn't somebody have pulled him out, Da?'

'They were all as drunk as he was. The story was that he was still sawing away with the bow when he came up for the third time. The party cheered him until every island in Lough Erne echoed and it was only when they sobered up they realised they had lost the fiddler. So the baronet and Count of Milan had a stone fiddle taller than a man made to stand at the estate gate as a monument to Dennis McCabe and as a warning for ever to fiddlers either to stay sober or to stay on dry land.

'Ye fiddlers beware, ye fiddler's fate,' my father recited. 'Don't attempt the deep lest ye repent too late. Keep to the land when wind and storm blow, but scorn the deep if it with whisky flow. On firm land only exercise your skill; there you may play and safely drink your fill.'

Travelling by train from our town to the seaside you went for miles along the green and glistening Erne shore but the train didn't stop by the stone fiddle nor yet at the Boa island for the cross-roads' dances. Always when my father told us about those dances, his right foot rhythmically tapped and took music out of the polished steel fireside fender that had Home Sweet Home lettered out on an oval central panel. Only the magic motor, bound to no tracks, compelled to no fixed stopping places, could bring us to the fiddle or the crowded cross-roads.

'Next Sunday then,' he said, 'as certain as the sun sets and rises, we'll hire Hookey and Peter and the machine and head for Lough Erne.'

'Will it hold us all,' said my mother. 'Seven of us and Peter's big feet and the length of the driver's legs.'

'That machine,' he said, 'would hold the twelve apostles, the Connaught Rangers and the man who broke the bank at Monte Carlo. It's the size of a hearse.'

'Which is just what it looks like,' said the youngest of my three sisters who had a name for the tartness of her tongue.

She was a thin dark girl.

'Regardless of appearance,' he said, 'it'll carry us to the stone fiddle and on the way we'll circumnavigate the globe: Clanabogan, and Cavanacaw, Pigeon Top Mountain and Corraduine, where the bare-footed priest said Mass at the Rock in the penal days and Corraheskin where the Muldoons live . . .'

'Them,' said the third sister.

She had had little time for the Muldoons since the day their lack of savoir faire cost her a box of chocolates. A male member, flaxen-haired, pink-cheeked, aged sixteen, of those multitudinous Muldoons had come by horse and cart on a market day from his rural fastnesses to pay us a visit. Pitying his gaucherie, his shy animal-in-a-thicket appearance, his outback ways and gestures, she had grandly reached him a box of chocolates so as to sweeten his bitter lot with one honeyed morsel or two or, at the outside three; but unaccustomed to towny ways and the mores of built-up areas the rural swain had appropriated the whole box.

'He thought,' she said, 'I was a paleface offering gifts to a Commanche.'

'But by their own hearth,' said my father, 'they're simple hospitable people.

'And Cornavara,' he said, 'and Dooish and Carrick Valley and your uncle Owen, and the two McCannys the pipers, and Claramore where there are so many Gormleys every family has to have its own nickname, and Drumquin where I met your mother, and Dromore where you' (pointing to me) 'were born and where the mail train was held up by the I.R.A. and where the three poor lads were murdered by the Specials when you' (again indicating me) 'were a year old, and the Minnieburns where the seven streams meet to make the head waters of the big river. Hookey and Peter and the machine will take us to all those places.'

'Like a magic carpet,' said my mother – with just a little dusting of the iron filings of doubt in her voice.

Those were the days, and not so long ago, when cars were rare and every car, not just every make of car, had a personality of its own. In our town with its population of five thousand, not counting the soldiers in the barracks, there were only three cars for hire and one of them was the love-child of the pioneer passion of Hookey Baxter for the machine. He was a long hangle of a young fellow, two-thirds of him made up of legs, and night and day he was whistling. He was as forward-looking as Lindbergh and he dressed like Lindbergh, for the air, in goggles, leather jacket and helmet; an appropriate costume, possibly, considering Hookey's own height and the altitude of the driver's seat in his machine. The one real love of his young heart was the love of the born tinkerer, the instinctive mechanic, for that hybrid car: the child of his frenzy, the fruit of days spent deep in grease giving new life and shape to a wreck he had bought at a sale in Belfast. The original manufacturers, whoever they had been, would have been hard put to it to recognise their altered offspring.

'She's chuman,' Peter Keown would say as he patted the sensitive quivering bonnet.

Peter meant human. In years to come his sole recorded comment on the antics of Adolf Hitler was that the man wasn't chuman.

'She's as nervous,' he would say, 'as a thoroughbred.'

The truth was that Peter, Hookey's stoker, grease-monkey and errand boy, was somewhat in awe of the tall rangy metal animal yet wherever the car went, with the tall goggled pilot at the wheel, there the pilot's diminutive mate was also sure to go. What living Peter earned he earned by digging holes in the street as a labouring man for the town council's official plumber so that, except on Sundays and when he motored with Hookey, nobody in the town ever saw much of him but the top of his cloth cap or his upturned face when he'd look up from the hole in the ground to ask a passer-by the time of day. Regularly once a year he spent a corrective month in Derry Jail, because his opportunities as a municipal employee and his weakness as a kleptomaniac meant that good boards, lengths of piping, coils of electric wire, monkey wrenches, spades, and other movable properties faded too frequently into thin air.

'A wonderful man, poor Peter,' my father would say. 'That cloth cap with the turned up peak. And the thick-lensed, thin-rimmed spectacles – he's half-blind – and the old tweed jacket too tight for him, and the old Oxford-bag trousers too big for him, and his shrill voice and his waddle of a walk that makes him look always like a duck about to apologise for laying a hen-egg. How he survives is a miracle of God's grace. He can resist the appeal of nothing that's portable.'

'He's a dream,' said the third sister. 'And the feet are the biggest part of him.'

'The last time he went to Derry,' said my brother, 'all the old women from Brook Street and the lanes were at the top of the Courthouse Hill to cheer him as he passed.'

'And why not,' said my mother. 'They're fond of him and they say he's well-liked in the jail. His heart's as big as his feet. Everything he steals he gives away.'

'Robin Hood,' said the third sister. 'Robbing the town council to pay Brook Street.'

'The Council wouldn't sack him,' said my eldest sister, 'if he stole the town.'

'At the ready,' roared my father. 'Prepare to receive cavalry.'

In the street below the house there was a clanking, puffing, grinding tumult.

'God bless us look at Peter,' said my father. 'Aloft with Hookey like a crown prince beside a king. Are we all ready? Annie, Ita, May, George, yourself ma'am, and you the youngest of us all. Have we the sandwiches and the flasks of tea and the lemonade? Forward.'

A lovelier Sunday morning never shone. With the hood down and the high body glistening after its Saturday wash and polish, the radiator gently steaming, the car stood at the foot of the seven steps that led down from our door. The stragglers coming home from early mass, and the devout setting off early for late mass had gathered in groups to witness our embarkation. Led by my father and in single file, we descended the steps and ascended nearly as high again to take our lofty places in the machine.

There was something of the Citroen in the quivering mongrel, in the yellow canvas hood now reclining in voluminous ballooning folds, in the broad back-seat that could hold five fair-sized people. But to judge by the radiator, the absence of gears, and the high fragile-spoked wheels, Citroen blood had been crossed with that of the Model T. After that, any efforts to spot family traits would have brought confusion on the thought of the greatest living authorities. The thick slanting glass windscreen could have been wrenched from a limousine designed to divert bullets from Balkan princelings. The general colour-scheme, considerably chipped and cracked, was canary yellow. And there was Hookey at the wheel, then my brother and father, and Peter on the outside left where he could leap in and out to perform the menial duties of assistant engineer; and in the wide and windy acres of the back seat, my mother, myself and my three sisters.

High above the town the church bell rang. It was the bell to warn the worshippers still on their way that in ten minutes the vested priest would be on the altar but, as it coincided with our setting out, it could have been a quayside bell ringing farewell to a ship nosing out across the water towards the rim of vision.

Peter leaped to the ground, removed the two stones that, blocked before the front wheels, acted as auxiliaries for the hand brake. Hookey released the brake. The car was gathering speed when Peter scrambled aboard, settled himself and slammed the yellow door behind him. Sparing fuel, we glided down the slope, back-fired twice loudly enough to drown the sound of the church bell, swung left along John Street and cleared the town without incident. Hands waved from watching groups of people but because this was no trivial event there were no laughs, no wanton cheers. The sound of the bell died away behind us. My mother expressed the hope that the priest would remember us at the offertory. Peter assured her that we were all as safe as if we were at home in bed. God's good green Sunday countryside was softly all around us.

Squat to the earth and travelling at seventy you see nothing from cars nowadays, but to go with Hookey was to be above all but the highest walls and hedges, to be among the morning birds.

'Twenty-seven em pee haitch,' said Hookey.

'Four miles covered already,' said Peter.

'The Gortin Mountains over there,' said my father. 'And the two mountains to the north are Bessy Bell and Mary Grey, so named by the Hamiltons of Baronscourt, the Duke of Abercorn's people, after a fancied resemblance to two hills in Stirlingshire, Scotland. The two hills in Stirlingshire are so called after two ladies of the Scottish court who fled the plague and built their hut in the wild wood and thatched it o'er with rushes. They are mentioned by Thomas Carlyle in his book on the French Revolution. The dark green on the hills by Gortin Gap is the new government forestry. And in Gortin village Paddy Ford the contractor hasn't gone to mass since, fifteen years ago, the parish priest gave another man the job of painting the inside of the sacristy.'

'No paint no prayers,' said the third sister.

'They're strange people in Gortin,' my mother said.

'It's proverbial,' said my father, 'that they're to be distinguished anywhere by the bigness of their backsides.'

'Five miles,' said Peter. 'They're spinning past.'

'Running sweet as honey,' said Hookey.

He adjusted his goggles and whistled back to the Sunday birds.

'Jamie Magee's of the Flush,' said my father.

He pointed to a long white house on a hill slope and close to a waterfalling stream.

'Rich as Rockefeller and too damned mean to marry.'

'Who in heaven would have him,' said the third sister.

'Six miles,' said Peter.

Then, with a blast of backfiring that rose my mother a foot in the air, the wobbling yellow conveyance came to a coughing miserable halt. The air was suddenly grey and poisoned with fumes.

'It's her big end Hookey,' said Peter.

'She's from Gortin so,' said the third sister.

The other two sisters, tall and long-haired and normally quiet girls, went off at the deep end into the giggles.

'Isn't it providential,' said my mother, 'that the cowslips are a glory this year. We'll have something to do, Henry, while you're fixing it.'

Hookey had been christened Henry, and my mother would never descend to nicknames. She felt that to make use of a nickname was to remind a deformed person of his deformity. Nor would she say even of the town's chief inebriate that he was ever drunk: he was either under the influence or he had a drop too many taken. She was, my mother, the last great Victorian euphemiser.

'We won't be a jiffy, ma'am,' said Hookey. 'It's nothing so serious as a big end.'

The three sisters were convulsed.

The fields and the roadside margins were bright yellow with blossom.
'Gather ye cowslips while you may,' said my father.

He handed the ladies down from the dizzy heights. Peter had already disembarked. Submitting to an impulse that had gnawed at me since we set sail I dived forwards, my head under Hookey's left elbow, and butted with both fists the black, rubber, punch-ball horn; and out over the fields to startle birds and grazing cattle went the dying groan of a pained diseased ox.

'Mother of God,' said my father, 'that's a noise and no mistake. Here boy, go off and pick flowers.'

He lifted me down to the ground.

'Screw off the radiator cap, Peter,' said Hookey.

'It's scalding hot, Hookey.'

'Take these gauntlet gloves, manalive. And stand clear when you screw it off.'

A geyser of steam and dirty hot water went heavenwards as Peter and my brother, who was always curious about engines, leaped to safety.

'Wonderful,' said my father to my brother, 'the age we live in. They say that over in England they're queued up steaming by the roadsides, like Iceland or the Yellowstone Park.'

'Just a bit overheated,' said Hookey. 'We won't be a jiffy.'

'Does it happen often?' said my father.

Ignoring the question, descending and opening the bonnet to peer and poke and tinker, Hookey said, 'Do you know a funny thing about this car?'

'She's chuman,' said Peter.

'You know the cross-roads at Clanabogan churchyard gate,' Hookey said. 'The story about it.'

'It's haunted,' said my father.

'Only at midnight,' said Peter.

As was his right and custom, my father stepped into the role of raconteur, 'Do you know that no horse ever passed there at midnight that didn't stop – shivering with fear. The fact is well attested. Something comes down that side road out of the heart of the wood.'

Hookey closed over the bonnet, screwed back the radiator cap and climbed again to the throne. He wiped his hands on a bunch of grass pulled for him and handed to him by Peter. Slowly he drew on again his gauntlet gloves. Bedecked with cowslips and dragging me along with them the ladies rejoined the gentlemen.

'Well, would you credit this now,' Hookey said. 'Peter and myself were coming from Dromore one wet night last week.'

'Pouring rain from the heavens,' said Peter, 'and the hood was leaking.'

'A temporary defect,' said Hookey. 'I mended it. Jack up the back axle, Peter, and give her a swing. And would you credit it, exactly at twelve o'clock midnight she stopped dead at the gate of Clanabogan churchyard?'

With an irony that was lost on Hookey my mother said, 'I could well believe it.'

'She's chuman,' said Peter.

'One good push now and we're away,' said Hookey. 'The slight gradient is in our favour.'

'Maybe,' he said to my father and brother, 'you'd lend Peter a hand.'

Twenty yards ahead he waited for the dusty pushers to climb aboard, the engine chug-chugging, little puffs of steam escaping like baby genii from the right-hand side of the bonnet. My father was thoughtful. He could have been considering the responsibilities of the machine age particularly because when it came to team pushing Peter was more of a cheer leader, an exhorter, a counter of one two three, than an actual motive force.

'Contact,' said Hookey.

'Dawn patrol away,' said Peter. 'Squadron Leader Baxter at the joystick.'

He mimicked what he supposed to be the noises of an aeroplane engine and, with every evidence of jubilation, we were once again under way; and a day it was, made by the good God for jubilation. The fields, all the colours of all the crops, danced towards us and away from us and around us; and the lambs on the green hills, my father sang, were gazing at me and many a strawberry grows by the salt sea, and many a ship sails the ocean. The roadside trees bowed down and then gracefully swung their arms up and made music over our heads and there were more birds and white cottages and fuchsia hedges in the world than you would readily imagine.

'The bride and bride's party,' sang my father, 'to church they did go. The bride she goes foremost, she bears the best show...'

'They're having sports today at Tattysallagh,' said Hookey.

'But I followed after my heart full of woe, for to see my love wed to another.'

We swept by a cross-roads where people and horses and traps were congregated after the last mass. In a field beside the road a few tall ash plants bore fluttering pennants in token of the sports to be.

'Proceed to Banteer,' sang my father, 'to the athletic sporting and hand in your name to the club comm-i-tee.

'That was a favourite song of Pat O'Leary the Corkman,' he said, 'who was killed at Spion Kop.'

Small country boys in big boots, knickerbockers, stiff celluloid collars that could be cleaned for Sunday by a rub of a wet cloth, and close-cropped heads with fringes like scalping locks above the foreheads, scattered before us to the hedges and the grass margins, then closed again like water divided and rejoining, and pursued us, cheering, for a hundred yards. One of them, frantic with enthusiasm, sent sailing after us a half-grown turnip, which bounced along the road for a bit, then sought rest in a roadside drain. Looking backwards I pulled my best or worst faces at the rustic throng of runners.

'In Tattysallagh,' said my father, 'they were always an uncivilised crowd of gulpins.'

He had three terms of contempt: Gulpin, Yob and, when things became very bad he became Swiftian, and described all offenders as Yahoos.

'Cavanacaw,' he said, 'and that lovely trout stream, the Creevan Burn. It joins the big river at Blacksessiagh. That there's the road up to Pigeon Top Mountain and the mass rock at Corraduine, but we'll come back that way when we've circumnavigated Dooish and Cornavara.'

We came to Clanabogan.

'Clanabogan planting,' he said.

The tall trees came around us and sunlight and shadow flickered so that you could feel them across eyes and hands and face.

'Martin Murphy the postman,' he said, 'who was in the survey with me in Virginia, County Cavan, by Lough Ramor, and in the Glen of Aherlow, worked for a while at the building of Clanabogan Church. One day the vicar said to him: "What height do you think the steeple should be?" "The height of nonsense like your sermons," said Martin, and got the sack for his wit. In frosty weather he used to seal the cracks in his boots with butter and although he was an abrupt man he seldom used an impolite word. Once when he was aggravated by the bad play of his wife who was partnering him at whist he said: "Maria, dearly as I love you there are yet moments when you'd incline a man to kick his own posterior".

'There's the church,' my father said, 'and the churchyard and the haunted gate and the cross-roads.'

We held our breath but, with honeyed summer all around us and bees in the tender limes, it was no day for ghosts, and in glory we sailed by.

'She didn't hesitate,' said Peter.

'Wonderful,' said the third sister.

It was more wonderful than she imagined for, as the Lord would have it, the haunted gate and cross-roads of Clanabogan was one of the few places that day that Hookey's motor machine did not honour with at least some brief delay.

'I'd love to drive,' said my brother. 'How did you learn to drive, Hookey?'

'I never did. I just sat in and drove. I learned the basic principles on the county council steamroller in Watson's quarries. Forward and reverse.'

'You have to have the natural knack,' Peter explained.

'What's the cut potato for, Hookey?' asked my brother.

'For the rainy day. Rub it on the windscreen and the water runs off the glass.'

'It's oily you see,' said Peter.

'Like a duck's back,' said the third sister.

'Where,' said my father – sniffing, 'do you keep the petrol?'

'Reserve in the tins clipped on the running board. Current supply, six gallons. You're sitting on it. In a tank under the front seat.'

'Twenty miles to the gallon,' said Peter. 'We're good for more than a hundred miles.'

'Godalmighty,' said my father. 'Provided it isn't a hundred miles straight up. 'Twould be sad to survive a war that was the end of better men and to be blown up between Clanabogan and Cornavara. On a quiet Sunday morning.'

'Never worry,' said Hookey. 'It's outside the bounds of possibility.'

'You reassure me,' said my father. 'Twenty miles to the gallon in any direction. What care we? At least we'll all go up together. No survivors to mourn in misery.'

'And turn right here,' he said, 'for Cornavara. You'll soon see the hills and the high waterfalls.'

We left the tarred road. White dust rose around us like smoke. We advanced half a mile on the flat, attempted the first steep hill and gently, wearily, without angry fumes or backfiring protests, the tremulous chuman car, lying down like a tired child, came to rest.

'We'll hold what we have,' said Hookey. 'Peter . . . pronto. Get the stones behind the back wheels.'

'Think of a new pastime,' said the third sister. 'We have enough cowslips to decorate the town for a procession.'

With the sweet face of girlish simplicity she asked, 'Do you buy the stones with the car?'

'We'd be worse off without them,' Hookey muttered.

Disguised as he was in helmet and goggles it was impossible to tell exactly if his creative soul was or was not wounded by her hint of mockery, but my mother must have considered that his voice betrayed pain for she looked reprovingly at the third sister and at the other two who were again impaled by giggles, and withdrew them out of sight down a boreen towards the sound of a small stream, to – as she put it – freshen up.

'Without these stones,' Peter panted, 'we could be as badly off as John MacKenna and look what happened to him.'

'They're necessary precautions,' said Hookey. 'Poor John would never use stones. He said the brakes on his car would hold a Zeppelin.'

The bonnet was open again and the radiator cap unscrewed but there was no steam and no geyser, only a cold sad silence, and Hookey bending and peering and probing with pincers.

'She's a bit exhausted,' Peter said.

'It's simple,' Hookey said. 'She'll be right as rain in a jiffy. Going at the hill with a full load overstrained her.'

'We should walk the bad hills,' Peter explained.

'Poor John MacKenna,' Hookey said, 'was making four fortunes drawing crowds to the Passionist monastery at Enniskillen to see the monk that cures the people. But he would never use the stones, and the only parking place at the monastery is on a sharp slope. And one evening when they were all at devotions doesn't she run backways and ruin all the flower-beds in the place and knock down a statue of Our Lord.'

'One of the monks attacked him,' said Peter, 'as a heathen that would knock the Lord down.'

'Ruined the trade for all,' said Hookey. 'The monks now won't let a car within a mile of the place.'

'Can't say as I blame them,' said my father.

'Poor John took it bad,' said Hookey. 'The lecture he got and all. He was always a religious man. They say he raises his hat now every time he passes any statue: even the Boer War one in front of the courthouse.'

'So well he might,' said my father.

Suddenly, mysteriously responding to Hookey's probing pincers, the very soul of the machine was again chug-chugging. But with or without cargo she could not or, being weary and chuman, would not assault even the first bastion of Cornavara.

'She won't take off,' said Hookey. 'That run to Belfast and back took the wind out of her.'

'You never made Belfast,' said my father, 'in this.'

'We did Tommy,' said Peter apologetically.

'Seventy miles there and seventy back,' said my father incredulously.

'Bringing a greyhound bitch to running trials for Tommy Mullan the postman,' said Hookey.

'The man who fishes for pearls in the Drumragh river,' said Peter.

They were talking hard to cover their humiliation.

'If she won't go at the hills,' my father said, 'go back to the main road and we'll go on and picnic at the seven streams at the Minnieburns. It's mostly on the flat.'

So we reversed slowly the dusty half-mile to the main road.

'One night in John Street,' Peter said, 'she started going backways and wouldn't go forwards.'

'A simple defect,' Hookey said. 'I remedied it.'

'Did you turn the other way?' asked the third sister.

Artlessly, Peter confessed, 'She stopped when she knocked down the schoolchildren-crossing sign at the bottom of Church Hill. Nipped it off an inch from the ground, as neat as you ever saw. We hid it up a laneway and it was gone in the morning.'

My father looked doubtfully at Peter. He said, 'One of those nice shiny enamelled pictures of two children crossing the road would go well as an overmantel. And the wood of the post would always make firewood.'

Peter agreed, 'You can trust nobody.'

Hurriedly trying to cut in on Peter's eloquence, Hookey said, 'In fact the name of Tommy Mullan's bitch was Drumragh Pearl. Not that that did her any good at the trials.'

'She came a bad last,' burst out the irrepressible Peter.

'And to make it worse we lost her on the way back from Belfast.'

'You what?' said my father.

'Lost her in the dark where the road twists around Ballymacilroy Mountain.'

My mother was awed, 'You lost the man's greyhound. You're a right pair of boys to send on an errand.'

'"Twas the way we stepped out of the car to take the air,' said Hookey.

By the husky note in his voice you could guess how his soul suffered at Peter's shameless confessions.

'And Peter looked at the animal, ma'am, and said maybe she'd like a turn in the air too. So we took her out and tied her lead to the left front wheel. And while we were standing there talking didn't the biggest brute of a hare you ever saw sit out as cool as sixpence in the light of the car. Off like a shot with the bitch.'

'If the lead hadn't snapped,' Peter said, 'she'd have taken the wheel off the car or the car off the road.'

'That would have been no great exertion,' said my father. 'We should have brought a greyhound along with us to pull.'

'We whistled and called for hours but all in vain,' said Peter.

'The hare ate her,' said the third sister.

'Left up the slope there,' said my father, 'is the belt of trees I planted in my spare time to act as a wind-breaker for Drumlish schoolhouse. Paddy Hamish, the labouring man, gave me a hand. He died last year in Canada.'

'You'd have pitied the children on a winter's day,' my mother said, 'standing in the playground at lunchtime taking the fresh air in a hilltop wind that would sift and cut corn. Eating soda bread and washing it down with buttermilk. On a rough day the wind from Lough Erne would break the panes of the windows.'

'As a matter of curiosity,' my father said, 'what did Tommy Mullan say?'

'At two in the morning in Bridge Lane,' said Peter, 'he was waiting for us. We weren't too happy about it. But when we told him she was last in the trials he said the bloody bitch could stay in Ballymacilroy.'

'Hasn't he always the pearls in the river,' my mother said.

So we came to have tea and sandwiches and lemonade in a meadow by the cross-roads in the exact centre of the wide saucer of land where seven streams from the surrounding hills came down to meet. The grass was polished with sunshine. The perfume of the meadowsweet is with me still. That plain seemed to me then as vast as the prairies, or Siberia. White cottages far away on the lower slopes of Dooish could have been in another country. The chief stream came for a long way through soft deep meadowland. It was slow, quiet, unobtrusive, perturbed only by the movements of water fowl or trout. Two streams met, wonder of wonders, under the arch of a bridge and you could go out under the bridge along a sandy promontory to paddle in clear water on a bottom as smooth as Bundoran strand. Three streams came together in a magic hazel wood where the tiny green unripe nuts were already clustered on the branches. Then the seven made into one, went away from us with a shout and a song towards Shaneragh, Blacksessiagh, Drumragh and Crevenagh, under the humpy crooked King's Bridge where James Stuart had passed on his way from Derry to the fatal brackish Boyne, and on through the town we came from.

'All the things we could see,' said my father, 'if this spavined brute of a so-called automobile could only be persuaded to climb the high hills. The deep lakes of Claramore. The far view of Mount Errigal, the Cock of the North, by the Donegal sea. If you were up on the top of Errigal you could damn' near see, on a clear day, the skyscrapers of New York.'

In his poetic imagination the towers of Atlantis rose glimmering from the deep.

'What matter,' said my mother. 'The peace of heaven is here.'

For that day that was the last peace we were to experience. The energy the machine didn't have or wouldn't use to climb hills or to keep in motion for more than two miles at a stretch, she expended in thunderous staccato bursts of backfiring. In slanting evening sunlight people at the doors of distant farmhouses shaded their eyes to look towards the travelling commotion, or ran up whinny hills for a better view, and horses and cattle raced madly around pastures, and my mother said the country would never be the same again, that the shock of the noise would turn the milk in the udders of the cows. When we came again to the crossroads of Tattysallagh the majority of the spectators, standing on the road to look over the hedge and thus save the admission fee, lost all interest in the sports, such as they were, and came around us. To oblige them the right rear tyre went flat.

'Peter,' said Hookey, 'jack it up and change it on.'

We mingled unobtrusively with the gulpins.

'A neat round hole,' said Peter.

'Paste a patch on it.'

The patch was deftly pasted on.

'Take the foot pump and blow her up,' said Hookey.

There was a long silence while Peter, lines of worry on his little puckered face, inspected the tube. Then he said. 'I can't find the valve.'

'Show it to me,' said Hookey.

He ungoggled himself, descended and surveyed the ailing member.

'Peter,' he said, 'you're a prize. The valve's gone and you put a patch on the hole it left behind it.'

The crowd around us was increasing and highly appreciative.

'Borrow a bicycle Peter,' said Hookey, 'cycle to the town and ask John MacKenna for the loan of a tube.'

'To pass the time,' said my mother, 'we'll look at the sports.'

So we left Hookey to mind his car and, being practically gentry as compared with the rustic throng around us, we walked to the gateway that led into the sportsfield where my mother civilly enquired of two men, who stood behind a wooden table, the price of admission.

'Five shillings a skull missus, barring the cub,' said the younger of the two. 'And half a crown for the cub.'

'For the what?' said my mother.

'For the little boy ma'am,' said the elder of the two.

'It seems expensive,' said my mother.

'I'd see them all in hell first – let alone in Tattysallagh,' my father said. 'One pound, twelve shillings and sixpence to look at six sally rods stuck in a field and four yahoos running round in rings in their sock soles.'

We took our places on the roadside with the few who, faithful to athletics and undistracted by the novelty of the machine, were still looking over the hedge. Four lean youths and one stout one in Sunday shirts and long trousers with the ends tucked into their socks were pushing high framed bicycles round and round the field. My father recalled the occasion in Virginia, County Cavan, when Martin Murphy was to run at sports and his wife Maria stiffened his shirt so much with starch it wouldn't go inside his trousers, and when he protested she said, 'Martin, leave it outside and you will be able to fly.'

We saw two bicycle races and a tug-of-war.

'Hallions and clifts,' he said.

Those were two words he seldom used.

'Yobs and sons of yobs,' he said.

He led us back to the car. Peter soaked in perspiration had the new tube on and the wheel ready.

'Leave the jack in and swing her,' Hookey said. 'She's cold by now.'

There was a series of explosions that sent gulpins, yobs and yahoos reeling backwards in alarm. Peter screwed out the jack. We scrambled aboard, a few of the braver among the decent people, rushing into the line of fire to lend a hand to the ladies. Exploding, we departed, and when we were a safe distance away the watchers raised a dubious cheer.

'In God's name, Henry,' said my father, 'get close to the town before you blow us all up. I wouldn't want our neighbours to have to travel as far as Tattysallagh to pick up the bits. And the yobs and yahoos here don't know us well enough to be able to piece us together.'

Three miles further on Peter blushingly confessed that in the frantic haste of embarkation he had left the jack on the road.

'I'll buy you a new one, Henry,' my father said. 'Or perhaps Peter here could procure one on the side. By now at any rate, they're shoeing jackasses with it in Tattysallagh.

'A pity in a way,' he said, 'we didn't make as far as the stone fiddle. We might have heard good music. It's a curious thing that in the townlands around that place the people have always been famed for music and singing. The Tunneys of Castle Caldwell now are noted. It could be that the magic of the stone fiddle has something to do with it.

'Some day,' he said, 'we'll head for Donegal. When the cars, Henry, are a bit improved.'

He told us about the long windings of Mulroy Bay. He explained exactly how and why and in what year the fourth Earl of Leitrim had been assassinated in Cratloe Wood. He spoke as rapidly and distinctly as he could in the lulls of the backfiring.

Then our town was below us in the hollow and the Gortin mountains, deep purple with evening, away behind it.

'Here we'll part company, Henry boy,' said my father. "Tisn't that I doubt the ability of Peter and yourself to navigate the iron horse down the hill. But I won't have the town blaming me and my family for having hand, act or part in the waking of the dead in Drumragh graveyard.'

Sedately we walked down the slope into the town and talked with the neighbours we met and asked them had they heard Hookey and Peter passing and told them of the sports and of the heavenly day it had been out at the seven streams.

My father died in a seaside town in the County Donegal – forty miles from the town I was reared in. The road his funeral followed back to the home places led along the Erne shore by the stone fiddle and the glistening water, across the Boa Island where there are no longer crossroads dances. Every roadside house has a television aerial. It led by the meadowland saucer of the Minnieburns where the river still springs from seven magic sources. That brooding place is still much as it was but no longer did it seem to me to be as vast as Siberia. To the left was the low sullen outline of Cornavara and Pigeon Top, the hurdle that our Bucephalus refused to take. To the right was Drumlish. The old schoolhouse was gone and in its place a white building, ten times as large, with drying rooms for wet coats, fine warm lunches for children and even a gymnasium. But the belt of trees that he and Paddy Hamish planted to break the wind and shelter the children is still there.

Somebody tells me, too, that the engine of Hookey Baxter's car is still with us, turning a circular saw for a farmer in the vicinity of Clanabogan.

As the Irish proverb says: It's a little thing doesn't last longer than a man.

A Ball of Malt
and Madame Butterfly

A GREAT GOD'S ANGEL STANDING

Pascal Stakelum, the notorious rural rake, and Father Paul, the ageing Catholic curate of Lislap, met the two soldiers from Devon by the bridge over the Camowen River and right beside the lunatic asylum. It was a day of splitting sunshine in the year of the Battle of Dunkirk. Pascal and the priest were going to visit the lunatic asylum, Father Paul to hear confessions, Pascal to bear him company and to sit at a sealed distance while the inmates cudgelled what wits they had and told their sins. The two soldiers, in battledress and with heavy packs on their backs, were on their way home from Dunkirk, not home to Devon exactly but to Sixmilecross, to the house of two sisters they had married in a hurry before they set off for France. It was, as you may have guessed, six miles from our garrison town of Lislap to the crossroads village where the two sisters lived, and it was a very warm day. So every one of the four, two in thick khaki, two in dull black, was glad to stop and stand at ease and look at the smooth gliding of the cool Camowen.

The bridge they rested on was of a brownish grey stone, three full sweeping arches and, to the sides, two tiny niggardly arches. In a blue sky a few white clouds idled before a light wind, and beyond a wood at an upstream bend of the river a two-horse mowing-machine ripped and rattled in meadow grass. The stone of the bridge was cut from the same quarry as the stone in the high long wall that circled the lunatic asylum and went for a good half-mile parallel with the right bank of the river.

—In France it was hot, said the first soldier.

—He means the weather was hot, said the second soldier.

The four men, priest and rake and soldiers two, laughed at that: not, Pascal says, much of a laugh, not sincere, no heartiness in it.

—Hot as hell, said the second soldier. Even the rivers was hot.

—Boiling, said the first soldier. That canal at Lille was as hot as a hot bath.

—Ruddy mix-up, said the second soldier. The Guards, they fired at the Fusiliers, and the Fusiliers, they fired at the Guards. Nobody knew who was what. Ruddy mix-up.

They took the cigarettes Pascal offered.

—Boiling hot and thirsty, said the second soldier. Never knew such thirst.

Father Paul said: You could have done with some Devon cider.

—Zider, said the first soldier. There were zomething.

—Zomerzet you are, said the second soldier.

They all laughed again. This time it was a real laugh.

The Camowen water where it widened over gravel to go under the five stone arches was clear and cool as a mountain rockspring. Upstream, trout rings came as regularly as the ticks of a clock.

The two soldiers accepted two more cigarettes. They tucked them into the breast-pockets of their battledress. They hitched their packs, shook hands several times and knelt on the motorless roadway for Father Paul's blessing. They were not themselves Arcees, they said, but in camp in Aldershot in England they had been matey with an Arcee padre, and they knew the drill. Blessed after battle, they stood up, dusted their knees as carefully as if they'd never heard of mud or blood and, turning often to wave back, walked on towards the two sisters of Sixmilecross.

—Virginia, Father Paul said, was the best place I ever saw for cider.

Just to annoy him, Pascal said: Virginia, County Cavan, Ireland.

They were walking together on a narrow footwalk in the shadow of the asylum wall.

—Virginia, U.S.A., Paul said. The Old Dominion. Very well you know what Virginia I mean. They had great apple orchards there, and fine cider presses, around a little town called Fincastle under the shadow of the Blue Ridge Mountains. That was great country, and pleasant people and fine horses, when I was a young man on the American mission.

It was a period out of his lost youth that Paul frequently talked about.

In those days of his strange friendship with Pascal he was thin and long-faced and stoop-shouldered with the straining indignant stoop that is forced on tall people when the years challenge the power to hold the head so high. That day the sun had sucked a little moisture out of his pale cheeks. He had taken off his heavy black hat to give the light breeze a chance to ruffle and cool his thin grey hair, but the red line the hat rim had made was still to be seen and, above the red line, a sullen concentration of drops of sweat. He was though, as Pascal so often said, the remains of a mighty handsome man and with such dignity, too, and stern faith and such an eloquent way in the pulpit that it was a mystery to all of us what the bishop of the diocese had against him that he had never given him the honour, glory and profit of a parish of his own.

—In the mood those two boyos are in, Pascal said, it will take them no time at all walking to the sisters at Sixmilecross.

That was the way Pascal, in accordance with his animal nature, thought; and Sixmilecross was a village in which, as in every other village in our parts, Pascal had had some of the rural adventures that got him his dubious reputation, and that made us all marvel when we'd see a character like him walking in the company of a priest. In Burma, I once heard an old sweat say, adulterers kill a pig to atone for their crime, so it was only apt and proper, and even meet and just, that Pascal should be a pork butcher. When he went a-wooing in country places he'd never walk too far from his rattly old Morris Cowley without bringing with him a tyre lever or starting handle, for country girls were hell for having truculent brothers and if they didn't have brothers they had worse and far and away worse, male cousins, and neither brothers nor male cousins, least of all the male cousins, had any fancy for Pascal rooting and snorting about on the fringes of the family. That's Pascal, for you. But at the moment, Paul is speaking.

—A man hungers to get home, he said. The men from Devon won't count the time or the number of paces. Time, what's time? They've come a long walk from the dreadful gates of eternity. Once I told you, Pascal boy, you were such a rake and run-the-roads you'd have to live to be ninety, to expiate here on this earth and so dodge the devil.

Complacently Pascal said: The good die young.

—Ninety's a long time, Father Paul said. But what's time? Here in this part of my parish . . .

They were walking in at the wide gateway. He waved his black wide-brimmed hat in a circle comprehending the whole place, as big almost as the garrison town itself, for all the crazy people of two counties, or those of them that had been detected and diagnosed, were housed there.

—This part of my parish, he said. As much happiness or unhappiness as in any other part of the parish. But one thing that doesn't matter here is time. As far as most of them know, time and eternity are the same thing.

They walked along a serpentine avenue, up sloping lawns to the main door. The stone in the walls of the high building was cut from the same quarry as the stone that bridged the river, as the stone in the encircling wall. The stone floor in the long cool corridor rang under their feet. They followed a porter along that corridor to a wide bright hospital ward. Unshaven men in grey shirts sat up in bed and looked at them with quick bright questioning eyes. The shining nervous curiosity of the ones who sat up disturbed Pascal. He preferred to look at the others who lay quietly in bed and stared steadily at points on the ceiling or on the opposite wall, stared steadily but seemed to see neither the ceiling nor the opposite wall, and sometimes mumbled to nobody words that had no meaning. A few men in grey suits moved aimlessly about the floor or sat to talk with some of the bright curious men in the beds. Beside the doorway a keeper in blue uniform dotted with brass buttons sat and smoked and read a newspaper, raised his head and nodded to the priest, then returned to his pipe and his newspaper.

Father Paul moved from bed to bed, his purple stole about his neck. The murmur of his voice, particularly when he was at the Latin, was distinctly audible. His raised hand sawed the air in absolution and blessing. Once in a while he said something in English in a louder voice and then the man he was with would laugh, and the priest would laugh, and the man in the next bed, if he was a bright-eyed man, would laugh, and another bright-eyed man several beds away would start laughing and be unable to stop, and a ripple of laughter would run around the room touching everybody except the staring mumbling men and the keeper who sat by the door.

Pascal sat beside an empty bed and read a paperbacked book about a doctor in Germany who was, or said he thought he was, two men, and had murdered his wife, who had been a showgirl, by bathing her beautiful body in nitric acid. That sinful crazy waste of good material swamped Pascal in an absorbing melancholy so that he didn't for a few moments even notice the thin hand gripping his thigh. There, kneeling at his feet, was a man in grey clothes, misled into thinking Pascal was a priest because Pascal wore, as did the gay young men of that place and period, a black suit with, though, extremely wide and unclerical trousers. Pascal studied, with recognition, the inmate's grey jacket, the scarce grey hair, the spotted dirty scalp. The kneeling man said. Bless me, father, for I have sinned.

—Get up to hell Jock Sharkey, Pascal said. I'm no priest. You're crazy.

He was, he says, crimson in the face with embarrassment. The keeper was peeking over his newspaper, laughing, saying Jock sure was crazy and that, in fact, was why he was where he was. The keeper also blew smoke-rings from thick laughing lips, an irritating fellow. He said: Fire away, Pascal. It'll keep him quiet. I hear him two or three times a week.

—It wouldn't be right, Pascal said. He had theological scruples, the only kind he could afford.

Only once in my life, he was to say afterwards, did a man ever ask me to listen to him confessing his sins and, fair enough, the place should be a lunatic asylum and the man, poor Jock Sharkey, that was put away for chasing women, not that he ever overtook them or did anybody any harm. They walked quick, he walked quick. They walked slow, he walked slow. He was just simply fascinated, the poor gormless bastard, by the sound of their feet, the hobbled trot, the high heels, you know, clickety-click, thigh brushing thigh. Poor Jock.

—What he'll tell you, said the keeper, is neither right nor wrong. Who'd anyway be better judge than yourself, Pascal? Even Father Paul doesn't know one half of what you know. You, now, would know about things Paul never heard tell of.

The man on his knees said: I suppose you'll put me out of the confession box, father. I'm a terrible sinner. I wasn't at mass or meeting since the last mission.

—Why was that? said Pascal the priest.

—The place I'm working in, they won't let me go to mass.

—Then it's not your fault, said Pascal. No sin. Grievous matter, perfect knowledge, full consent.

He did, he said afterwards, remember from his schooldays that impressive fragment of the penny catechism of Christian doctrine: the stud-book, the form-book, the rules for the big race from here to eternity.

—But when I go to confession, father, I've a bad memory for my sins. Will you curse me, father, if I forget some of them?

—By no means, Jock. Just recite what you remember.

The keeper, more offensive as his enjoyment increased, said that Pascal wouldn't know how to curse, that he didn't know the language. The head of the kneeling man nodded backwards and forwards while he mumbled the rhythmical words of some prayer or prayers of his childhood. Now and again the names of saints came clearly out of the confused unintelligible mumble, like bubbles rising from a marshy bottom to the surface of a slow stream. Then he repeated carefully, like a child reciting, these words from an old rebel song: I cursed three times since last Easter Day. At mass-time once I went to play.

Pascal was seldom given to visions except in one particular direction, yet he says that at that moment he did see, from his memory of school historical pageants, the rebel Irish boy, kneeling in all innocence or ignorance at the feet of the brutal red-coated captain whose red coat was, for the occasion, covered by the soutane of the murdered rebel priest.

The keeper said: You should sing that, Jock.

—I passed the churchyard one day in haste, Jock said, and forgot to pray for my mother's rest.

—You're sure of heaven, said the keeper, if that's the sum total of your sins. The Reverend Stakelum himself, or even Father Paul, won't get off so easy.

The penitent looked up at Pascal and Pascal looked down at stubbly chin, hollow jaws, sorrowful brown eyes. Poor Jock, Pascal thought, they put you away just for doing what I spend all my spare time, and more besides, at: to wit, chasing the girls. Only you never even seemed to want to catch up with them.

For poor Jock was never more than what we called a sort of a mystery man, terrifying the girls, or so they claimed, by his nightly wanderings along dark roads, his sudden sprints that ended as sharply and pointlessly as they began, his shouted meaningless words provoked perhaps by a whiff of perfume in his nostrils or by that provocative tap-tippity-tap of high hard heels on the metalled surface of the road. A child might awaken in the night and cry that there was a man's face at the window. A girl might run home breathless and say that Jock had followed her for half a mile, suiting his pace to hers, like a ghost or a madman. He couldn't be a ghost, although he was as thin and as harmless as any ghost. So we put him away for a madman.

He stared long and hard at Pascal. His thin right hand tightly grasped Pascal's knee.

—David Stakelum's son, he said. I'd know you anywhere on your father. Thank God to see you in the black clothes. Your father was a decent man and you'll give me the blessing of a decent man's son.

He bowed his head and joined his hands. Behind the newspaper the keeper was gurgling. Pascal said afterwards that his father wouldn't be too pleased to think that his hell's own special hell-raker of a son bore him such a resemblance that even a crazy man could see it. But if his blessing would help to make Jock content then Jock was welcome to it. So he cut the sign of the cross over the old crazy dirty head. He touched with the tips of the fingers of both hands the bald patch on the dome. He held out those fingers to be kissed. The most fervent young priest fresh from the holy oil couldn't have done a better job. Pascal had so often studied the simple style of Father Paul. The keeper was so impressed that he folded the newspaper and sat serious and quiet.

Father Paul walked slowly towards them, along the narrow passage between the two rows of beds. Walking with him came a fat red-faced grey-headed inmate. The fat inmate talked solemnly, gestured stiffly with his right hand. The priest listened, or pretended to listen, turning his head sideways, stretching his neck, emphasising the stoop in his shoulders. He said: Mr. Simon, you haven't met my young friend, Pascal.

The fat man smiled benevolently at Pascal but went on talking to the priest. As you know, sir, I am not of the Roman Catholic persuasion, yet I have always been intrigued by the theory and practice of auricular confession. The soul of man, being walled around and shut in as it is, demands some outlet for the thoughts and desires that accumulate therein.

He had, Pascal says, a fruity pansy voice.

—The child, he said, runs to its mother with its little tale of sorrow. Friend seeks out friend. In silence and secrecy souls are interchanged.

It was exactly, Pascal was to say, as if the sentences had been written on the air in the loops and lines of copper-plate. You could not only hear but see the man's talk: A Wesleyan I was born, sir, and so remain. But always have I envied you Roman Catholics the benefits of the confessional, the ease that open confession brings to the soul. What is the Latin phrase, sir?

Paul said: Ad quietam conscientiam.

—Ad quietam conscientiam, Simon repeated. There is peace in every single syllable. There is much wisdom in your creed, sir. Wesley knew that. You have observed the spiritual similarity between Wesley and Ignatius of Loyola.

The keeper said: Simon, Doctor Murdy's looking for you. Where in hell were you?

—He asks me where I have been, sir. Where in hell.

Father Paul said: He means no harm, Simon. Just his manner of speaking.

Simon was still smiling. From elbow to bent wrist and dangling hand, his right arm was up like a question mark. He said to Father Paul: Surveillance, sir, is a stupid thing. It can accomplish nothing, discover nothing. If I were to tell this fellow where I had been, how could he understand? On this earth I have been, and beyond this earth.

He shook hands with the priest but not with Pascal nor the keeper nor Jock Sharkey. He walked with dignity past the keeper and back down the ward.

—There goes a travelled man, Pascal said.

Father Paul was folding his purple stole. He said: There are times when religion can be a straitjacket.

—It's not Simon's time yet for the straitjacket, the keeper said. When the fit takes him he'll brain the nearest neighbour with the first handy weapon.

At the far end of the ward where Simon had paused for a moment, there was a sudden noise and a scuffling. The keeper said: Too much learning is the divil.

He thumped down the passage between the beds.

—Now for the ladies, Father Paul said. You'll be at home there,

Pascal. They say all over the town that no man living has an easier way with the ladies.

Pascal was to report to myself and a few others that if Paul had wanted to preach him a sermon to make his blood run cold and to put him off the women for the rest of his life, he couldn't have gone about it in a better way.

Is it true that, as the poet said, you never knew a holy man but had a wicked man for his comrade and heart's darling? Was it part of Paul's plan to pick Pascal as his escort and so to make an honest boy out of him or, at least, to cut in on the time that he would otherwise spend rummaging and ruining the girls of town and country? The thing about Pascal was that, away from the companionship of Paul, he thought of nothing but women when, of course, he wasn't butchering pork, and perhaps he thought of women even then. Like many another who is that way afflicted he wasn't big, violent, handsome, red-faced or blustering. No, he went about his business in a quiet way. His hair was sparse, of a nondescript colour, flatly combed and showing specks of dandruff. He wore horn-rimmed spectacles. He was one of those white-faced fellows who would, softly and secretly and saying nothing about it to their best friends, take advantage of their own grandmothers. The women were mad about him. They must have been. He kept himself in fettle and trim for his chosen vocation. When the two soldiers and Paul were, in the sunshine on the Camowen Bridge, talking of Devon cider, Pascal was thinking, he says, of sherry and raw eggs, and oysters, porter and paprika pepper.

On the day of Paul's funeral he said to me: A decent man and I liked him. But, my God, he had a deplorable set against the women or anybody that fancied the women.

—Except myself, he said. For some reason or other he put up with me.

—That day at the female ward, he said, at the geriatrics you call 'em, I cheated him, right under his nose, God forgive me. And may Paul himself forgive me, since he knows it all now.

Pascal stood at the threshold of this female ward while Father Paul, purple stole again around his neck, moved, listening and forgiving with God's forgiveness, from bed to bed. Pascal wasn't much of a theologian, yet looking at the females in that female ward he reckoned that it was God, not the females, who needed forgiveness. They were all old females, very old females, and as such didn't interest Pascal. He had nothing, though, against old age as long as it left him alone. His father's mother was an attractive, chubby, silver-haired female, sweet as an apple forgotten and left behind on a rack in a pantry, wrinkled, going dry, yet still sweet beyond description. But these sad old females, a whole wardful of them, were also mad and misshapen, some babbling like raucous birds, some silently slavering.

He couldn't make up his mind whether to enter the ward and sit down or to walk up and down the cool echoing corridor. He always felt a fool when walking up and down like a sentry, but then he also felt a fool when standing or sitting still. He was just a little afraid of those caricatures of women. This was the first time he had ever been afraid of women, and afraid to admit to himself that these creatures were made in exactly the same way as women he had known. He was afraid that if he went into the ward and sat down he would see them in even greater detail than he now did from the threshold. He was young. Outside the sun was shining, the Camowen sparkling under the sun, the meadow grass falling like green silk to make beds for country lovers. But here all flesh was grass and favour was deceitful and beauty was vain. It was bad enough looking at the men. To think what the mind could do to the body. But it was hell upon earth looking at the women. Jock Sharkey, like a million lovers and a thousand poets, had gone mad for beauty. This, in the ward before him, was what could happen to beauty.

He stepped, shuddering, back into the corridor and collided with a tall nurse. He apologised. He smelled freshly-ironed, starched linen and disinfectant, a provoking smell. A quick flurried glance showed him a strong handsome face, rather boyish, brick-red hair bursting out over the forehead where the nurse's veil had failed to restrain it. He apologised. He was still rattled by his vision in the ward. Contrary to his opportunist instinct he was even about to step out of the way. But the nurse didn't pass. She said: It is you, Pascal Stakelum, isn't it? Did they lock you up at last? A hundred thousand welcomes.

He had to do some rapid thinking before he remembered. There were so many faces in his memory and he was still confused, still a little frightened, by those faces in the ward. She didn't try to help. She stood, feet apart and solidly planted, and grinned at him, too boyish for a young woman but still fetching. She was, if anything, taller than he was. Her brother, then he remembered, had gone to school with us, a big fellow, as dark as she was red, very clever but capricious, making a mockery of things that he alone, perhaps, of all of us could understand and, in the end, throwing the whole thing up and running away and joining the Royal Air Force. So the first thing Pascal said, to show that he knew who she was, was to ask about the brother, and when would he be coming home. She said: He won't be coming home.

—Why for not?

She said he had been killed at Dunkirk.

Coming right after the prospect of the mad old women, that was a bit of a blow in the face, but at least, he told himself, clean death in battle was not madness, deformity, decay; and the moment gave Pascal the chance to sympathise, to get closer to her. He held her hands. He said he was sorry. He said he had always liked her brother. He had, too. They had, indeed, been quite friendly.

She said: It's war. He would always do things his own way.

She seemed proud of her brother, or just proud of having a brother dead at Dunkirk.

—This is no place to talk, Pascal said. And I'm with Father Paul. Meet me this evening at the Crevenagh Bridge.

That was the old humpy seventeenth-century bridge on the way to a leafy network of lovers' lanes and deep secret bushy ditches.

—Not this evening, she said. I'm on duty. But tomorrow.

—Eight o'clock on the dot, said Pascal.

That was his usual time during the summer months and the long warm evenings. And he was very punctual.

She walked away from him and towards Father Paul. He looked after her, no longer seeing the rest of the ward. She was a tall strong girl, stepping with decision and a great swing. Jock Sharkey would have followed her to the moon.

Father Paul, the shriving done, was again folding his stole. He joked with a group of old ladies. He told one of them that on his next visit he would bring her a skipping rope. He told another one he would bring her a powderpuff. He distributed handfuls of caramels to the whole crew. They cackled with merriment. They loved him. That was one bond between Pascal and himself. The women loved them both.

—But if he meant to preach to me that time, Pascal said to us, by bringing me to that chamber of horrors, I had the laugh on him.

In the sunshine on the lawn outside, the superintending doctor stood with his wife and his dogs, three Irish setters, one male, two female. The doctor and his wife stood, that is, and the setters ran round and round in erratic widening circles.

Those smart-stepping Devon men were by now approaching Sixmilecross, and the two sisters, and rest after battle and port after stormy seas.

The doctor was a handsome cheery fellow, even if he was bald. He wore bright yellow, hand-made shoes, Harris tweed trousers and a high-necked Aran sweater. The wife was small and dainty and crisp as a nut, and a new wife; and the two of them, not to speak of the three setters, were as happy as children. They talked—the doctor, the woman, Paul and Pascal—about the war, and about the two soldiers from Devon and their two women in Sixmilecross. Then Father Paul wished the doctor and his wife many happy days, and he and Pascal stepped off towards the town. At the gateway they met a group of thirty or forty uniformed inmates returning, under supervision, from a country walk. One of them was gnawing a raw turnip with which, ceasing to gnaw, he took aim at Pascal and let fly. Pascal fielded the missile expertly—in his schooldays he had been a sound midfield man—and restored it to the inmate who was still chewing and looking quite amazed at his own deed. All this, to the great amusement of the whole party, inmates and three keepers. But, oddly enough, Paul didn't join in the merriment. He stood, silent and abstracted, on the grass at the side of the driveway. He looked at the sky. His lips moved as though he were praying, or talking to himself.

Pascal gave away what cigarettes he had left to the hiking party and he and the priest walked on, Paul very silent, over the Camowen. When they were halfways to the town, Paul said: Some men can't live long without a woman.

Pascal said nothing. He remembered that there was a story that Paul had once beaten a loving couple out of the hedge with a blackthorn stick. He remembered that Paul came from a stern mountainy part of the country where there had been a priest in every generation in every family for three hundred years. He thought of the red nurse and the hedge ahead of her. So he said nothing.

—That new wife of his, Paul said, was American. Did you notice?

—She dressed American, Pascal said. But she had no accent.

—She comes from a part of the States and from a class in society where they don't much have an accent, Paul said. At least not what you in your ignorance would call an American accent.

Pascal said: The Old Dominion.

—You're learning fast, Paul said.

The town was before them.

—Three wives he had, Paul said. One dead. Irish. One divorced. English. And now a brand new one from Virginia. Some men can't go without.

Pascal made no comment. He contented himself with envying the bald doctor his international experience. He resolved to travel.

—Most men, said Paul, aren't happy unless they're tangled up with a woman. The impure touch. But the French are the worst. Their blood boiling with wine. From childhood. How could they keep pure?

Pascal hadn't the remotest idea. So he made no comment. He didn't know much about the French but he reckoned that just at that moment in history they had enough and to spare on their plates without also having to worry about purity.

—But pleasures are like poppies spread, Paul said.

He was a great man always to quote the more moralising portions of Robert Burns. Pascal heard him out: You seize the flower, its bloom is shed. Or like the snow falls in the river—a moment white, then melts forever. Or like the borealis race, that flit ere you can point their place. Or like the rainbow's lovely form, evanishing amid the storm.

—Burns, said Father Paul, well knew what he was talking about. Those, Pascal, are the words of wisdom gained through sad and sordid experience.

Pascal agreed. He was remembering the nurse's dead brother who had been a genius at poetry. He could write parodies on anything that any poet had ever written.

When Pascal met the nurse at the Crevenagh Bridge on the following evening she was, of course, in mourning. But the black cloth went very well with that brilliant red hair. Or like the rainbow's lovely form. There was something about it, too, that was odd and exciting, like being out, he said, with a young nun. Yet, apart from the colour of her clothes, she was no nun. Although, come to think of it, who except God knows what nuns are really like?

Pascal, as we know, was also in black but he had no reason to be in mourning. It had rained, just enough to wet the pitch. Otherwise the evening went according to Operation Pascal. When he had first attacked with the knee for the warming-up process he then withdrew the knee and substituted the hand, lowering it through the band of her skirt, allowing it to linger for a playful moment at the bunker of the belly button. Thereafter he seemed to be hours, like fishermen hauling a net, pulling a silky slip out of the way before the rummaging hand, now living a life of its own, could negotiate the passage into her warm drawers. Pascal didn't know why he hadn't made the easier and more orthodox approach by laying the girl low to begin with and then raising skirt and slip, except it was that they were standing up at the time, leaning against a sycamore tree. The rain had passed but the ground was wet, and to begin his wooing by spreading his trenchcoat (Many's the fine rump, he boasted, that trenchcoat had kept dry, even when the snow was on the ground) on the grass, seemed much too formal. Pascal Stakelum's days, or evenings or nights, were complex with such problems.

Later came the formal ceremonious spreading of the trenchcoat on a protective mattress of old newspapers, and the assuming by both parties, of the horizontal. By that time the big red girl was so lively that he swore she'd have shaken Gordon Richards, the King of them All, out of the saddle. She kept laughing and talking, too, so as to be audible, he reckoned, thirty yards away but fortunately he had chosen for the grand manoeuvre a secluded corner of the network of lanes and ditches. He had a veteran's knowledge of the terrain and he was nothing if not discreet.

He was not unmindful of the brother dead in faraway France. But then the brother had been such an odd fellow that even in Pascal's tusselling with his strong red sister he might have found matter for amusement and mockery. As Pascal bounced on top of her, gradually subduing her wildness to the rhythmic control of bridle and straddle and, in the end, to the britchen of his hands under her buttocks, he could hear her brother's voice beginning the schoolboy mockery of Shelley's soaring skylark: Hell to thee, blithe spirit. Pascal and the splendid panting red girl moved together to the poet's metre.

That was one brother Pascal did not have to guard against with starting handle or tyre lever. Working like a galley slave under the dripping sycamore he was in no fear of ambush.

Paul got his parish in the end, the reward of a well-spent life, he said wryly. He died suddenly in it before he was there for six months. That parish was sixty miles away from Lislap, in sleepy grass-meadow country where the slow River Bann drifts northwards out of the great lake. Pascal missed Paul's constant companionship more than he or anybody else would have believed possible and began, particularly after Paul's sudden death, to drink more than he had ever done before, and went less with the girls, which puzzled him as much as it did us. It worried him, too: for in the house of parliament or public house that we specially favoured, he asked me one day was he growing old before his time because he was growing fonder of drink and could now pass a strange woman on the street without wondering who and what she was.

—You're better off, Pascal, I said. What were you ever doing anyway but breaking them in for other men? You never stayed long enough with any one woman to be able in the long run to tell her apart from any other woman.

He was more hurt than I had imagined he would be. But he sadly agreed with me, and said that some day he hoped to find one real true woman with whom he could settle down.

—Like with poor Paul that's gone, he said. Some one woman that a man could remember to the last moment of his life.

—No, I'm not crazy, he said. Two days before his death I was with

Paul in his parish, as you know. We went walking this evening after rain, by the banks of a small river in that heavy-grass country. That was the last walk we had together. The boreen we were on went parallel with the river bank. We met an old man, an old bewhiskered codger, hobbling on a stick. So Paul introduced us and said to Methusaleh: What now do you think of my young friend from the big garrison town of Lislap?

—The old fellow, said Pascal, looked me up and looked me down. Real cunning country eyes. Daresay he could see through me as if I was a sheet of thin cellophane. But he lied. He said: Your reverence, he looks to me like a fine clean young man.

—That was an accurate description of me, Pascal Stakelum, known far and wide.

Pascal brooded. He said: A fine clean young man.

—Then that evening, he said, we sat for ages after dinner, before we knelt down to say the holy rosary with those two dry sticks of female cousins that did the housekeeping for him. One quick look at either of them would put you off women for time and eternity. There's an unnerving silence in the houses that priests live in: the little altar on the landing, you know, where they keep the sacrament for sick calls at night. Imagine, if you can, the likes of me on my bended knees before it, wondering would I ever remember the words when it came my turn to lead the prayers. But I staggered it. Closed my eyes, you might say, and took a run and jump at it, and landed on the other side word perfect. It would have been embarrassing for Paul if I hadn't been able to remember the words of the Paterandave in the presence of those two stern cousins. One evening one of them sat down opposite me in a low armchair and crossed her legs, poor thing, and before I could look elsewhere I had a view of a pair of long bloomers, passion-killers, that were a holy fright. You wouldn't see the equal of them in the chamber of horrors. Six feet long and coloured grey and elastic below the knee. But when the two cousins were off to bed, and good luck to them, we sat and talked until all hours, and out came the bottle of Jameson, and Paul's tongue loosened. It could be that he said more than he meant to say: oh, mostly about Virginia and the Blue Ridge Mountains and the lovely people who always asked the departing stranger to come back again. Cider presses near Fincastle. Apple orchards. Dogwood trees in blossom. He went on like that for a long time. Then he got up, rooted among his books, came back with this one book covered in a sort of soft brown velvet with gold lettering and designs on the cover and, inside, coloured pictures and the fanciest printing you ever saw, in red and in black. He said to me: Here's a book, Pascal, you might keep as a memory of me when I'm gone.

—So I laughed at him, making light of his gloomy face, trying to jolly him up, you know. I said: Where, now, would you be thinking of going?

—Where all men go sooner or later, he said.

—That was the end of my laughing. That's no way for a man to talk, even if he has a premonition.

—Keep the book as a token, Paul said to me. You were never much for the poetry, I know. But your wife when you find her might be, or, perhaps, some of your children. You've a long road ahead of you yet, Pascal, all the way to ninety, and poetry can lighten the burden. That book was given to me long ago by the dearest friend I ever had. Until I met yourself, he said. Long ago in a distant country and the wench is dead.

—Those were the last words I ever heard Paul speak, excepting the Latin of the mass next morning, for my bus passed the church gate before the mass was rightly over, and I had to run for it. But bloody odd words they were to come from Paul.

—Common enough words, I said. Anybody could have said them.

—But you didn't see the book, Pascal said. I'll show it to you.

He did, too, a week later. It was an exquisite little edition, lost on Pascal, I thought with some jealousy, both as to the perfection of the bookmaker's art and as to the text, which was William Morris telling us, there in a public house in Lislap, how Queen Guenevere had defended herself against the lies of Sir Gauwaine, and a charge of unchastity. Fondling the book, I was not above thinking how much more suitable than Pascal I would have been as a companion for old Paul. So that I felt more than a little ashamed when Pascal displayed to me with what care he had read the poem, underlining here and there in red ink to match the rubric of the capitals and the running titles on the tops of the pages. It was, almost certainly, the only poem to which he had ever paid any particular attention, with the possible exception of that bouncing parody on Shelley's skylark.

—It's like a miniature mass book, he said. Red and black. Only it was by no means intended for using at the mass. See here.

He read and pointed with his finger as he read: She threw her wet hair backward from her brow, her hand close to her mouth touching her cheek.

—Coming from the swimming-pool, Pascal said, when the dogwoods were in blossom. You never knew that Paul was a champion swimmer in his youth. Swimming's like tennis. Brings out the woman in a woman. Arms wide, flung-out, breasts up. Oh, there were a lot of aspects to Paul. And listen to this: Yet felt her cheek burned so, she must a little touch it. Like one lame she walked away from Gauwaine.

—Time and again, Pascal said, he had heard it said that lame women had the name for being hot. Once he had seen on the quays of Dublin a one-legged prositute. The thought had ever afterwards filled him with curiosity, although at the time he wouldn't have risked touching her for all the diamonds in Kimberley.

—And her great eyes began again to fill, he read, though still she stood right up.

That red nurse, he remembered, had had great blue eyes, looking up at him like headlamps seen through mist.

—But the queen in this poem, he said, was a queen and no mistake. And in the summer it says that she grew white with flame, white like the dogwood blossoms and all for this Launcelot fellow, lucky Launce-lot, and such a pansy name. One day, she says, she was half-mad with beauty and went without her ladies all alone in a quiet garden walled round every way, just like the looney bin where I met that nurse. And both their mouths, it says, went wandering in one way and, aching sorely, met among the leaves. Warm, boy, warm. Then there's odd stuff here about a great God's angel standing at the foot of the bed, his wings dyed with colours not known on earth, and asking the guy or girl in the bed, the angel has two cloths, you see, one blue, one red, asking them, or him or her, to guess which cloth is heaven and which is hell. The blue one turns out to be hell. That puzzles me.

It puzzled both of us.

—But you must admit, said Pascal, that it was a rare book for a young one to be giving a young priest, and writing on it, look here, for Paul with a heart's love, by the Peaks of Otter in Virginia, on a day of sunshine never to be forgotten, from Elsie Cameron. Usually the women give breviaries to the priests, or chalices, or amices, or albs, or black pullovers. She must have been a rare one, Elsie Cameron. Would you say now that she might have had a slight limp? It's a Scottish name. Paul was forever talking about what he called the Scots Irish in Virginia and the fine people they were. All I know is that Scottish women are reputed to be very hot. They're all Protestants and don't have to go to confession.

Pascal had known a man who worked in Edinburgh who said that all you had to do to set a Scotswoman off was to show her the Forth Bridge, the wide open legs of it. That man had said that the Forth Bridge had never failed him.

When I said to Pascal that all this about Paul could have been as innocent as a rose, he said he was well aware of that: he wasn't claiming that Paul had done the dirty on the girl and left her to mourn out her life by the banks of the James River. But that it may all have been innocent for Paul and Elsie only made it the more mournful for Pascal. Fond memories and memories, and all about something that never happened.

—Any day henceforth, Pascal said, I'll go on a journey just to see for myself those Blue Ridge Mountains. Were they ever as blue as Paul thought they were? Cider's the same lousy drink the world over. What better could the orchards or women have been in Virginia than in Armagh? You see he was an imaginative man was old Paul, a touch of the poet, and soft as putty and sentimental away behind that granite mountainy face. Things hurt him, too. He told me once that one day walking he met that mad Maguire one from Cranny, the one with the seven children and no husband, and tried to talk reason to her, and she used language to him the like of which he had never heard, and he turned away with tears in his eyes. He said he saw all women degraded and the Mother of God sorrowful in Nancy Maguire who was as bad as she was mad. An odd thought. He should have taken the stick to her the way I once heard he did to a loving couple he found under the hedge.

But pleasures are like poppies spread, as Paul would say, walking the roads with Pascal ad quietam conscientiam, looking at mad Nancy and listening to her oaths, seeing Elsie Cameron under the apple trees under the Blue Mountains in faraway Virginia. Once I wrote a story about him and it was printed in a small little-known and now defunct magazine. That story was all about the nobility of him and the way he used to chant the words of Burns; and then about how he died.

He came home to his parochial house that morning after reading the mass and sat down, one of the cousins said, at the breakfast table, and sat there for a long time silent, looking straight ahead. That wasn't like him. She asked him was he well. He didn't answer. She left the room to consult her sister who was fussing about in the kitchen. When she came back he had rested his head down on the table and was dead.

Looking straight ahead to Fincastle, Virginia, and seeing a woman white with flame when the dogwood blossomed, seeing the tall angel whose wings were the rainbow and who held heaven, a red cloth, in one hand, and hell, a blue cloth, in the other.

There was no place in that story of mine for Pascal Stakelum, the rural rake.

THE LITTLE WRENS AND ROBINS

Cousin Ellen wrote poetry for the local papers and was the greatest nonstop talker you, or anybody else, ever listened to. The poetry was of three varieties: religious poetry, love poetry and nature poetry that went like this, the nature poetry, I mean:

> Farewell to the dreary Winter,
> Welcome to the days of Spring
> When the trees put on their coats of green,
> And the birds with joy will sing.
> The daffodils put on their gowns,
> How proudly they stand up,
> To shake their dewy golden coats
> On the smiling buttercups.

After reading the poem of which that was the opening stanza, I was ever afterwards somewhat in awe of Cousin Ellen: her daring in rhyming only one little up with all those buttercups, her vision of the daffodils as tall fashion models swaying and pirouetting in extravagant golden gowns, of the smirking of those sly little gnomes and peeping-toms, the buttercups, who were so delighted that the stately ladies should shake the dew of their coats to be caught in and savoured from the yellow cups. No one could deny that Cousin Ellen had a poetic mind and a special vision, except my father who loved quietude, and long calm silent days, and a garden growing, and who was driven out of all patience by Ellen's ceaseless clickety-clack when, once a month, she travelled twenty-five miles by train from Hazelhatch to visit us.

—And Uncle Tommy, did you hear that Peter McQuade of Lettergesh sold that bay mare he had at an unimaginable high price, I don't know what the exact sum was, but it was, I hear, absolutely over the moon and out of sight, he ran her at the Maze Races and won all before her and he brought her south to the Curragh of Kildare, and some rich American saw her and brought her on the spot and flew off with her to Hialeah in Florida, that was a travelled mare, they say Florida's lovely,

America that's where the money is, not that money's everything if you haven't happiness, get out there to America, Ben boy, before it's too late, as I left it too late and this, Aunt Sara, is an American fashion magazine I brought for you to look over, the styles will absolutely blind you, you should have been at Hazelhatch last Sunday when the Reverend Dr. Derwent preached the most divine sermon about the Sacred Heart, I wrote a poem in my head on the way home from church and sent him an autographed copy, you see he clips every one of my poems out of the papers and pastes them into one big book, he says that he'll be the first person ever to possess my collected works, he's just divinely handsome, too handsome for a priest as they say although personally I see no harm at all in a priest being handsome, Our Divine Lord himself was the handsomest person that ever lived and exactly six feet in height, and very much the favourite man of the bishop at the present moment, he's leading the diocesan pilgrimage to Lourdes, Fatima, Rome and home by Lisieux this year, an all-rounder, and I have every intention of going, I never saw Lisieux and I have always adored Saint Thérèse, they may call her a little flower but she was in her own quiet way a warrior, as Dr. Derwent says, and she wrote the divinest book, solid as a rock just like Mamma who's in the best of health, nothing shakes her, all plans to make the business prosper, we're expecting such a passing rush of tourists this year on the way to West Donegal, they all stop to stock up with food and drink at Hazelhatch Inn, that old picturesque thatch and the diamond-paned latticed windows, particularly those high cosy dormers, catch the eye, you'd be amazed the number of people who stop to take pictures and then come in and buy, beauty and business mixed . . .

Like Molly Bloom she was no great believer in punctuation which is really only a pausing for breath, and Cousin Ellen's breath always seemed as if it would last for hours. My father said that after half-an-hour or less of her monologue, in which she needed no assistance except seemingly attentive faces, he always felt that he was drowning in a warm slow stream, drifting slowly, sinking slowly, brain and body numb, faraway bells in his ears, comfortable, but teetotally helpless. That talk, he claimed, threatened the manhood in a man, which was why all men had escaped, while there was still time, from Cousin Ellen, except Dr. Derwent who was sworn celibate and thus safe, and except for one other wretch whom she talked into matrimony and who lasted for a year and then vanished mysteriously: dead by asphyxiation, my father said, and buried secretly under the apple trees at the back of the old house at Hazelhatch.

Those were lovely apple trees.

Drowning in what deep waters of constant talk was I, the Saturday I walked her through the marketing crowds in from the country, from brown mountains and green river valleys, to our town? We went along John Street and High Street and Market Street, by the Catholic church with the high limping spires that could be seen for miles, by the eighteenth-century courthouse with Doric columns that was once admired by no less a person than Tyrone Guthrie who said that if you tilted the long sweep of High Street and Market Street the other way, the courthouse steps would be the perfect stage on which to produce a Passion Play. Church and courthouse were our architectural prides. Cousin Ellen, as far as I can remember from my drowning swoon, talked about love. Being all of eighteen I was still interested.

—Your sister, Dymphna, in Dublin, she said, is very happy, Edward and myself called to see her two months ago, not rich but happy and happiness is all, I said to her if only Edward and myself can be as happy as yourself and your husband, you know, Ben, Edward and myself are to be wedded shortly and I do hope everything turns out for the best, and I hope that suitcase isn't too heavy, but oh you're so young and strong and athletic, and they really shouldn't allow these fruit-stalls on the open street any more, not with modern traffic and all that, although you have to admit that they're most colourful and picturesque but they really belong to the Middle Ages, and see me safely now on to the bus for Dromore, the crowd here is just fearful, and oh this letter I forgot, do drop it in the post office for me, it's for Edward, love is all, just a perfect understanding between people and when human love fails there is always the love of the Sacred Heart which I wrote in a poem that Dr. Derwent read out from the pulpit, there is nothing on earth we may cling to, all things are fleeting here, the pleasures we so oft have hunted, the friends we've loved so dear . . .

Then off she went not, as it happened, to Dromore where she had wanted to visit some other relatives, but to Drumquin, because in the confusion into which she had talked me, I deposited herself and her suitcase on the wrong bus. To the casual observer there isn't much difference between Drumquin and Dromore, but one is twenty miles from the other, and it's a bind to be in one when you want to be in the other. But Cousin Ellen found some obliging commercial traveller who drove her to Dromore, and God help him if he had to listen to her for the time it took to drive twenty miles. She wrote me a most amusing letter about it all. She was easier to read than to listen to. The accident about the buses had really tickled her, she said, for life was just like that: you headed off for somewhere and ended up somewhere else. She bore no grudge and we would be better friends than ever, wouldn't we? We were, too.

About that time I headed off for Dublin to go through the motions of a university education, and didn't see Cousin Ellen again, although we constantly exchanged letters, until the husband had come and gone, and she herself was in hospital close to Hazelhatch with some rare ailment that was to stop her talk forever, and her poetry.

The letter to Edward that that day she gave me to post I found two weeks later when, pike-fishing on the Drumragh River, I had a little leisure and used it to clear out my pockets. Since it then seemed too late to send it to where it should have gone I tore it up into tiny pieces and cast it on the running water. My mother always said that you should never burn letters from friends or, indeed, anything that had to do with friendship. Fire destroyed. Water did not. So she was constantly making confetti out of letters and flushing them down the john.

The deep pike-water of the Drumragh, still patterned with froth from the falls at Porter's Bridge, bore away northwards the words of love that Ellen had meant for Edward. Life, she might have said had she then known, was also like that. Our friendship, at any rate, remained unaltered. After all, she was the only other writer in the family.

> Ah, yes! And the tiny little lambs,
> They, too, will play and skip
> In the fields just decorated
> With the daisy and cowslip.
> The blackbird and the thrushes
> They are glad to see you here,
> The little wrens and robins
> To all you bring good cheer.

She was, as you may remember, addressing the Spring. Her favourite picture hung on a wall of the old oak-timbered country kitchen at Hazelhatch. It was called: Springtime on an Ayrshire hillside, or, the Muse of Poetry descends to Robert Burns while at the plough.

But those words were a paltry effort to describe that picture and, out of respect for the memories of Burns and Cousin Ellen and, of course, of the Muse, I will try to do better.

The poet in the picture wears the height of style: a blue tailed-coat, knee-breeches a little off-white, strong woollen stockings and stout buckled shoes. He has taken one hand, the right, from the plough and is using that hand to raise with a sweep a tall hat of a type that in nobler times may have been general issue for ploughmen, or poets. His profile is noble, his head held high to escape extinction in an ample cravat. He salutes a plump girl in a white revealing nightgown sort of costume of the period, perhaps, of the French Directorate, and who is standing on a cloud about two feet above the backs of two patient and unnoticing horses. The girl on the cloud carries a wreath and it is clearly her intention to put the wreath where the tall hat has been. In the bottom left-hand corner a fieldmouse is playing the part of a wee sleekit cowering timorous beastie yet is clearly, to judge from the glint in her eyes, an intent observer of the coronation ceremony and, in the words of another poet, is confidently aware that a mouse is miracle enough to stagger sextillions of infidels. In the background, for it is spring in Ayrshire and a little late for ploughing the birds are plentiful on the branches and in a pale blue sky.

That picture, I feel, had its influence on Ellen:

> The man whose work is in the field
> From you his joy can't hide,
> As he treads along at break of day
> With two horses by his side.
> He whistles all along his way
> And merrily will sing.
> This is a birthday once again,
> Each morning of the Spring.

That picture, too, is always very much present to me. When the Empress of Hazelhatch, as my youngest sister called Ellen's mother, our grass-widowed aunt by marriage, died, and Hazelhatch passed into the hands of strangers, she left me the picture. Ellen and myself, she said, had liked it, and each other. Was the old lady remembering, too, one sad lulled day of sunshine when we sat in the kitchen at Hazelhatch and looked at the picture and she told me what I had already partly guessed that morning, that Ellen would die in hospital?

All around us in the old kitchen were cases of brown stout just freshly bottled in a careful and religious ritual at which I had been allowed to assist, along with a new girl who was there, from the County Mayo, to work in the bar and grocery and learn the trade. A long procession of girls had come and gone and benefited, perhaps, from the strict wisdom of the Empress, even if they had most certainly sighed and writhed and groaned under her discipline. She still decanted her own port, a good Graham, black as your boot—and solid, but that decanting she did on her own, no assistants, no encouragement even to spectators. Certain things were just too sacred.

That port was famous.

—It fixed her marriage, my father said, good and proper. Your good mother's brother could think of nothing but port and running horses. Never left the bar except to go to Punchestown or the Maze or Strathroy Holm or Galway or Gowran Park or Tramore or Bellewstown Hill or the Curragh itself, or the horsefairs of Ballinasloe or Cahirmee. When he ran away to the States and never came back he was both bow-legged and purple in the face.

—He couldn't come back, said my mother.

She felt very sore about the whole story. He had been her favourite brother. She explained: He went to Canada, not the States, and then jumped the line at Buffalo and could never again get his papers in order. He got in but couldn't get out. There were hundreds like him.

—I often wondered why he ran away, said that youngest sister with the thin face and the dark hair and the whiplash of a tongue. Then I met the Empress of Hazelhatch with her long black gown and her hair mounted high on a Spanish comb, and dyed horse-chestnut as sure as God, and her pince-nez, sitting behind the bar all right to speak to the better sort of people, but never demeaning herself by serving a customer, and I knew then why he would run to Alberta, or farther if he could get without beginning to come home again round the world.

Because that sister was herself an embryo empress she was never happy at Hazelhatch. For myself, as easy-going as my father or a wag-by-the-wall clock, I loved my visits to the place, the picture of the poet, the strong drone of the old lady's voice, the odour of good groceries and booze, the glow of old oak, the high bedroom with slanted ceiling and dormer window and an angled criss-crossed vision of the road west to Mount Errigal and the Rosses and the ocean, the apples in the orchard, the procession of young, discontented and frequently sportive girls. Memories of those visits stay with me, stilled, separated from all else, not frayed by time. That particular day the Empress said to me: How did Ellen look when you saw her this morning?

Nobody except her mother could have considered or enquired how Ellen looked. She talked so much you didn't see. So, to answer, I had to think back painstakingly. That was all the more difficult to do because we had left the kitchen and gone, rather sadly, out to the orchard where it seemed unkind and even sinful to think how somebody looked who was going to die, and who had loved that orchard.

> Oft times I sit and think,
> And wonder if God sends
> This season, Spring, so beautiful

To all his city friends.
Ah no! there are no green fields
There are no little lambs to play . . .

For one thing, that morning Ellen had not been in the least like the Muse of Poetry descending to salute Robert Burns at the plough. She had always dressed modestly, mostly in browns or mother-of-god blues with the breast-bone well covered in white frills and lace and such; and there had never been a pick on her bones. Never before had I noticed that she was so freckled, scores of tiny dark-brown freckles around her eyes and down the slopes of her nose. The paleness of her ailing face, perhaps, made them more than ever noticeable. Freckled people are always great talkers and even illness could not stop her tongue: only death or the last gaspings that preceded it.

—It must be heavenly for you, she said, to feel that you are really and truly walking the paths of learning, and in a city that has been ennobled by the footsteps of so many great scholars and poets, how I envy you, I always so wanted to get to the university, but when I'm up and about again and out of this bed I promise you a visit in Dublin and you must show me all the sights and famous places, promise, you'll find my mother very quiet and brooding these days, I can't think what's wrong with her, but sometimes she gets like that, it may be that the new girl and herself do not get on so well, a strange girl from the County Mayo, a great singer, she came to see me several times, and sometimes I think she resembles me, she wants to sing just as I write poems, a lovely voice, too, but it's so sad, such clean regular features and an exquisite head of dark hair, but that purple discolouration on one side of her face, God help her, she would have to sing always with one side of her face away from the audience . . .

Because there was winter and the end of things in the room, even if it was high summer outside the window, I told her about the letter forgotten, then torn into fragments and sent sailing on the Drumragh. I told her about my mother and her opinions on fire and water. She said that, perhaps, it would have been better for both of them, meaning the vanished husband and herself, if it had ended the way the letter did: gone peacefully on the easy water. She said my mother had always been kind. She stepped out of bed and walked with me as far as the door of the room. She wore a heavy blue dressing-gown. She kissed me. We never met again.

Ah no! there are no green fields,
There are no little lambs to play,

But walk out in the country
On any fine spring day . . .

So I in the orchard, all alone and sad, am fixing a puncture in the back wheel of the lofty ancient bicycle on which the Empress of Hazelhatch is wont to cruise forth in deep-green drowsy summers, her skirts high above the dust, her head high above the hedges, surveying the labour of the fields, occasionally saluting the workers. To me, and softly singing to herself for she is proud of her voice and the old lady flatters her about it, comes the Mayo girl with the face, flawless and faultless in shape but discoloured on the left cheek. She stands beside me, at my left hand. Our hands touch as we run the bicycle tube through a basin of water so as to raise a bubble and locate the puncture. The birds in the orchard trees are silent because it is the sultry month of least song. But the girl for a while sings in a sort of sweet whisper about, of all things, moonlight in Mayo. Then she says: It isn't my day off, and I want to get to Strabane.

—Why?
—What do you think? A fella.
—Ask her for the evening off.
—She's hell on fellas. You ask her. She'd grant you anything.
—I'm a fella.
—You're the white-headed boy around here. Say you want to take me to the pictures.
—What picture?
—Any picture. No picture.

But walk out in the country
On any fine spring day.
And there you'll find what art can't paint
Nature's gifts so fair:
The trees, the flowers, the streamlets
And the many birds so rare.

The road is dusty and the hedges high. Had Ellen never written a poem about summer? The girl sings as she walks. It is four miles to the village of Lifford, old houses shaggy with flowering creepers, then across the great bridge where the Mourne River, containing the water of the Drumragh, from Tyrone, meets the Finn River from Donegal to form, between them, the spreading Foyle; then half a mile across level water-meadows to the town of Strabane. She sings about the bird in the gilded cage. But walking through Lifford, curious faces looking out over half-doors, she stops singing and says: Mrs. Lagan is dying, isn't she?

Ellen's married name takes me by surprise. She says: You needn't talk about it if you don't want to. It's just that I like her.

—So do I.

—She's very clever. She's a great poet.

—Not exactly great.

—She gets printed.

—In local papers.

—Nevertheless.

We lean on the bridge and watch the mingling of the Mourne and the Finn, and the wagtails darting and diving over a shining triangle of sand and gravel. She says: The old lady is kindly but very strict. Mrs. Lagan is generous but very sad. They say there never was a man, but one, who could listen to her or talk her down. She should have lived in a world where men talked more.

—Like where?

—New York or Dublin or London or Milan. Big singing cities. Her soul's mate was a flowery preaching priest. They should have been allowed to marry, the old lady says. They'd have made a perfect couple. She'd have made a perfect minister's wife. Did you ever look at a minister's wife? They're all like that. All poetry and bazaars.

—She could have preached better than anyone.

We follow the level road across the water-meadows. There is a raised footwalk designed to keep pedestrians dry-shod in time of flood. The clock has stopped forever on that still day in Strabane. She says: She likes me to sing when I go to see her.

She sings: Ah, sweet mystery of life at last I've found you.

When she has finished singing I declaim:

> You may have your city pleasures
> And its praises you may sing,
> But there's naught on earth that can compare
> With the country's dales in spring.

—What's that?

—The voice of Cousin Ellen.

—I could sing that.

She sings it to a slow sweet tune I never heard before or since. Under the apple trees had Ellen's poetic soul taken possession of the girl?

We sit on the quiet river bank to pass the time until my train departs for Dublin or until her fella arrives. She sits at my left hand. When I hold her chin and try to turn her lips towards me she stiffens her neck, then looks away towards the town. So, when I hear the train whistle, I leave her unkissed there by the Mourne River, waiting for the fella. Often afterwards in Dublin I wonder what song she sings for him, what side of her face does she turn towards him.

A ROOM IN LINDEN

One day in the dark maze of the yew-hedges Sister Lua, who has arthritis, looks up at him from her wheelchair which he's pushing, and says: Tell me the truth. Don't be modest about it. Are you Nanky Poo?

Since he is a bookish young man it is an exciting thing for him to have history living along the corridor. The poet he's reading just before he leaves his room writes that there's a wind blowing, cold through the corridor, a death-wind, the flapping of defeated wings from meadows damned to eternal April. The poet has never seen it, but he could have been writing about this corridor. On its dull green walls, a mockery of the grass and green leaves of life, the sun never shines. All day and all night the big windows at the ends of the corridor, one at the east wing of the house and one at the west, are wide open, and from whichever airt the wind does blow it always blows cold. The rooms on the north side of the corridor are, as one might expect, colder and darker than the rooms on the south side, or would be if their light and heat depended totally on the sun.

Before the nuns got here and turned the place into a convalescent home it was lived in by a family famous for generations for a special brand of pipe tobacco. The old soldier who is reluctantly, vociferously fading away in a room on the north side of the corridor, says: This house was built on smoke. Just think of that. Smoke.

The old soldier himself belongs to some branch of the family that emigrated to South Africa and made even more money out of burgundy than the people who stayed at home made out of smoke, and there was always as much soldiering as smoke in the family; and big-game hunting, too, to judge by the fearful snarling mounted heads left behind and surviving, undisturbed by nuns or convalescents, in the entrance hall.

—You'll be nice to the old man, won't you, Mother Polycarp had said to him. He'll bore you to death. But he needs somebody to listen to him. He hasn't much longer to talk, in this world at any rate.

So he talks to the old soldier in the evenings and, in the afternoons, to the old priest and historian, dying as methodically and academically as he has lived, checking references, adding footnotes, in a room on the south side of the corridor. At other times he reads in his own room, or has visitors, or wheels Sister Lua's wheelchair in the ample bosky grounds, or leaves the grounds on his own and goes through quiet suburban roads to walk slowly, tapping his stick, in the public park that overlooks, across two walls and a railway, the flat sand and the bay. It is not an exciting life, but it's not meant to be.

He wheels Sister Lua round and round the dark cloisters of the yew-hedge maze from the corner where Jesus is condemned to death to the central circle where he is laid in the tomb. He tells her that he is not Nanky Poo.

—Well, I heard you had poems in that magazine. And I didn't see your name. And there is this poet called Nanky Poo. And he's very good. About the missions.

—Not me, alas, sister. I was never on the missions.

—Know you weren't. A university student.

Although she is always sitting down and being wheeled she is also always breathless and never quite begins or finishes a sentence, and it is necessary to fill in her words and meanings as she goes along. Bird-like, he knows, isn't much of a description, but she is bird-like, little hands like claws because of the arthritis, of course, a little nose like a beak peeking out from under the nun's pucog. To the left corner of her pale unvarnished little mouth, so often twisted with patience in pain, there's a mole with two hairs. She loves the dark green maze that grew up, like the house, out of smoke and was used by the nuns as a setting for a via dolorosa with life-size figures; and backgrounds of good stone columns and arches robbed from the wreckage of some eighteenth-century mansion. His first faux pas with the old historian had to do with those stations of the cross. One dull evening when the talk wasn't going so well he had, just to make chat, said: Don't they have a big day here once a year? People coming in hundreds to do the stations of the cross. What day does that happen on?

The old man pulls the rug more tightly around his long legs. His feet are always cold. In large bodies, Edmund Burke held, circulation is slower at the extremities, but the coldness of the old man's feet is just the beginning of death. He snuffs black snuff expertly from the hollow between thumb and forefinger, he sneezes, he says with crushing deliberation: Good Friday, my good young man. Even the younger generation should be aware that the Lord was crucified on Good Friday.

He's a carnaptious old bastard and even for the sake of Mother Polycarp, the kindly reverend mother, who is always thanking God for everything, it's sort of hard to suffer him at times. But he has both made and written history, and poems, too, of a learned sort, and collected folksong, and the best people have written about him and discovered an old-world courtesy and all the rest of that rot behind his rude exterior: the old-world courtesy of a Scandinavian sea-rover putting the full of a monastery of shaven-pated monks to the gory hatchet. By comparison the old soldier who has actually killed his man in far-away wars, is a gentleman. But then the old soldier is simply fading away, all battles fought and won, all comrades gone before him, all trumpets sounding from the other side. The old priest, still trying to work, has his last days aggravated by a mind that remembers everything and by the pain of a stomach cancer.

He leaves Sister Lua in the charge of a big red-headed nurse and walks down the main avenue towards suburbia and the park by the sea. The old white-haired vaudeville entertainer who has some sort of shaking paralysis, which he says is an occupational disease, waves to him from his seat by the grotto under the obelisk and gives him three letters to post at the postbox outside the gate. They are, he notices, all addressed to well-known celebrities of screen, stage and television: one in Dublin, one in London, one in New York. Out there is the world of healthy living people.

Life and playing children are, of course, all around him in the park by the sea but it isn't quite the same thing. There isn't enough of life there to help him to stop thinking of old men dying. He is very much on his own either because of his sullenness, or because he thinks that while he may be of interest to himself he couldn't possibly be of interest to anybody else. Nothing humble about that, though. In that park he's really a visitor from a special sort of world, from a cold green corridor damned to eternal December: sort of exclusive, though, a rich old soldier, a famous old historian, the artist who is still in touch with the best people; and only the best die in that corridor.

One old man who sits on a green wooden seat, close to the play-hall where the children run when it rains, talks to him as if he would gladly talk longer. He discourages that old man with abrupt sentences for he has, at the moment, enough of old men. He walks on beyond him and along by the tennis courts. A stout bespectacled girl with strong tanned legs plays awkwardly with a tall blond handsome fellow who wins every set and enjoys his superiority, while she seems to enjoy being beaten. A stranger from a strange land, he enjoys, as he passes or rests for a while on a seat and watches, the leaping of her legs. So everybody is happy and the park is beautiful. The blond boy isn't even good at the game and he, the stranger, knows that if it wasn't for the stiff hip, still slowly recovering, he could challenge him and beat him easily. But then the stout girl, legs excepted, isn't really interesting.

He himself is blond and doesn't take too well to the sun. So his favourite seat is in a shady corner under dark horse-chestnuts whose white candles are fading. He likes the place also because nobody else sits there. Strollers seem to accelerate as they walk past. Once in a while children run shouting, hooting through the dark tunnel, from one shire of sunshine into another. Through a fence of mournful laurels and copper beeches he sees the glitter of the sun on the lake. Out of the corner of his left eye he sees a well-built girl in white shorts flat on her back on the sunny grass. Sometimes she reads. Sometimes she raises her legs and, furiously with flashing thighs, pedals an invisible bicycle, faster and faster until it seems as if she has seven or seventeen legs, until the flash of her thighs takes the shape of a white circle. Her belly muscles must be jingling like springs. The joints in her hips, unlike his own, must be in perfect lubricated condition. She is at the moment one of the five women in his life: Polycarp thanking God for the rain and the sunshine, for the hail and the snow; Lua, twisted in her chair; she who, nameless, cycles on her back on the grass; the strong-legged tennis player whose name, he has heard the blond fellow shout, is Phyllis; and A. N. Other.

To the rear of his shady corner there is a privet hedge and a high wooden fence and a gate with a notice that says no admission except on business. That's exactly the way he feels. Adam in Eden must have had just such a corner where he kept his tools and experimented with slips and seeds. But then before Adam and Eve made a pig's ass out of a good arrangement the garden must have looked after itself and needed none of that sweat-of-the-brow stuff. What would old Thor the thunderer, brooding in his room, biting on his cancer, think of that?

Belloc, says the old priest, was a big man who looked as if all his life he had eaten too much and drunk too much. The best way to learn French is to read cowboy and injun stories. They hold the interest better than Racine.

Aware of his own inanity, he says: translations.

Before that face, oblong, seemingly about twelve feet long, like a head cut out of the side of some crazy American mountain, he is perpetually nonplussed into saying stupidities.

—Cowboys and injuns, my good young man, are not indigenous to the soil of France.

—There's a city called Macon in Georgia, U.S.A.

—There's a city called everything somewhere in the States. Naturally they mispronounce the names.

So it goes on. You can't win with the old bastard.

—Darlington, he says, used to call on Hopkins to take him out for walks. Hopkins was for ever and always complaining of headaches. What else can you expect, Darlington would say to him, immured up there in your room writing rubbish. I'm not so sure that Darlington wasn't right.

He is at that time just entering his Hopkins phase and if he wasn't afraid of that granite face, eyes sunken and black and burning, jawbones out rigid like a forked bush struck by lightning, he would defend the poet, quoting his sonnet about the windhover which, with some difficulty, he has just memorised. Yet it still is something to hear those names tossed about by a man who knew the men, and was a name himself. He feels grateful to Mother Polycarp who, as a friend of his family, has invited him to this place for a while, after his year in orthopaedic, so that he can read his books and learn to walk at his ease. In all that green cold corridor, which is really a place for old men, he is the only person who is going to live. He searches for something neutral to say: Wasn't Hopkins always very scrupulous about marking students' papers?

—He was a neurotic Englishman, my good fellow. They never could make up their minds between imperialism and humanitarianism. That's what has them the way they are. Darlington was English, too, of course, the other sort, the complacent Englishman, thinking that only what is good can happen to him, and that all his works are good. Then a young upstart called Joyce put him in a book. That should have been a lesson to Darlington, if they have books in heaven or wherever he went to.

He should, as Mother Polycarp says, be taking notes, thank God, except he feels that if he did so, secretly even in his room, the old lion might read his mind and take offence. The old man laughs seldom, but he's laughing now, perhaps at some memory of two English Jesuits marooned in Ireland, or at some other memory surfacing for a second in the dark crowded pool behind his square forehead. He has kept his hair, a dirty grey, standing up and out as if it had never encountered a comb. The long bony hands tighten the rug about his knees. The cold is creeping upwards.

In the green corridor he kneels for a while at the prie-dieu before the shrine, not praying, just thinking about age and death, and looking up at the bearded face of St. Joseph, pure and gentle, guardian of the saviour child. With a lily in his hand. Another old man and, by all accounts, very patient about it. What in hell is St. Joseph, like Oscar Wilde or somebody, always doing with a lily in his hand? An awkward class of a thing for a carpenter to be carrying.

Before his hip betrayed him he has had a half-notion of being a priest, but a year in orthopaedic, bright nurses hopping all around him, has cured him by showing him that there are things that priests, in the ordinary course of duty, are not supposed to have.

—You're too young, the old soldier says, to be in this boneyard.

He's a small man with a red boozy face, a red dressing-gown, a whiskey bottle and a glass always to his right hand. The whiskey keeps him alive, thank God, Mother Polycarp says. He is, like St. Joseph, gentle but not so pure, rambling on about dirty doings in far-away places, Mombasa and Delhi are much mentioned, about Kaffir women, and about blokes who got knocked off in the most comical fashion. He laughs a lot. He doesn't need a considered answer or a balanced conversation, just a word now and then to show he's not alone. He shares the whiskey generously. He has bags of money and, when he dies, he'll leave the perishing lot to the nuns.

—They do good, you know. Keep perky about it, too. Who else would look after the likes of me? Ruddy boneyard, though. Elephants' graveyard. Get out of here and get a woman. Make sons. Before it's too late. Would get out myself only nobody would have me any more, and I couldn't have them. Only whiskey left. But I had my day. When I was your age I laid them as quick as my batman could pull them out from under me. Three women shot under me at the battle of Balaclava and all that. Fit only for the boneyard now and the nuns. They don't want it and I can't give it. But there's always whiskey, thank God, as the mother says. A field behind the barracks where old wind-broken cavalry mounts went on grass with the shoes off until they died. At least we didn't eat them like the bloody Belgians. Smell of slow death around this place.

He sniffs the whiskey and laughs and then coughs. By night the coughing is constant. Lying awake and listening, the young man has a nightmarish feeling that they are all in prison cells, all dying, which is true, all the living are dying, and after one night the sun will never rise again on the park, and every time the cycling girl spins her legs she's another circle nearer to the grave. His own healthy youth has already collapsed in illness. Life is one collapse after another. The coughing goes on and on. To be a brave soldier and to end up coughing in a lonely room. Let me outa here. No, Sister Lua, I am not Nanky Poo.

—But every day that passes, Mother Polycarp tells him, brings you a day nearer to getting back to your studies, thank God. You made a great recovery in orthopaedic.

She is a tall woman with a long flat-footed step and more rattlings of keys and rosary beads than seem natural even in a nun. When he tells her that, she laughs and says, of course, that she has the keys of the kingdom, thank God. She has a good-humoured wrinkled mannish face, and she is famous everywhere for her kindness and her ability to gather money and build hospitals.

Does she say to the old men: Every day that passes brings you a day nearer heaven, thank God?

She naturally wouldn't mention death as the gate of heaven.

He has a feeling that none of them want to go any farther forward, they look backward to see heaven: on the day a new book was published or a new woman mounted or a new show went well. Heaven, like most things, doesn't last, or could only be an endless repetition of remembered happiness, and would in the end be, like dying, a bloody bore.

In her chair as he wheels her, Sister Lua, chirping like the little robin that she is, prays a bit and chats a bit and, because of her breathlessness and the way she beheads her sentences and docks the tails off them, he has to listen carefully to know whether she is chatting or praying. The life-size figures in the maze of dark yews—fourteen Christs in various postures, with attendant characters from jesting Pilate to the soldiers by the tomb—have acquired a sombre existence of their own. Do they relax at night, yawn, stretch stiff limbs, mutter a curse, light a cigarette, say to hell with show business? He must try that one out on the vaudeville man, shaking his way to the grave, on the seat by the grotto under the obelisk.

—Weep not for me, Sister Lua prays, but for yourselves and for your children.

The lord is talking to the weeping women of Jerusalem and not doing a lot to cheer them up. Some anti-semitical Irish parish priest must have written the prayers that Lua reels off. He didn't think much either of the kind of recruitment that got into the Roman army: These barbarians fastened him with nails and then, securing the cross, allowed him to die in anguish on this ignominious gibbet.

From the prayer book she has learned, by heart, not only the prayers but the instructions that go with them. She says, as the book instructs: Pause a while.

He pauses. The yew-hedges are a dark wall to either hand. Twenty paces ahead, the lord, in an arbour, is being lowered from the cross. The dying has been done.

—Nanky Poo. Nanky Poo.

—Sister, I am not Nanky Poo.

—But I call you Nanky Poo. Such a lovely name.

—So is Pooh Ba.

—Pooh Ba is horrible. Somebody making mean faces. Nanky Poo, you must write a poem for Mother Polycarp's feast-day. So easy for you. Just a parody. Round Linden when the sun was low, Mother Polycarp the Good did go.

—There's a future in that style.

—You'll do it, Nanky Poo?

—At my ease, sister. Whatever Nanky Poo can do, I can do better.

By the laying of the lord in the tomb they encounter A. N. Other. She tries to escape by hiding behind the eighteenth-century cut-stone robbed from the old house, but Sister Lua's birds-eye is too quick and too sharp for her.

—Nurse Donovan, Nurse Donovan, the French texts have arrived.

—Yes, Sister Lua.

—When can you begin, Nanky Poo?

—Any time, sister.

—So useful to you, Nurse Donovan, French, when you're a secretary.

She is a small well-rounded brunette who has nursed in the orthopaedic hospital until something happened to her health. He is in love with her, has been for some time. Nothing is to come of it. He is never to see her again after he leaves the convalescent home. The trouble is that Sister Lua has decided that the girl must be a secretary and that Nanky Poo must teach her French, and it is quite clear from the subdued light in the girl's downcast dark eyes that she doesn't give a fiddler's fart about learning anything, even French, out of a book. Worse still: on the few occasions on which he has been able to corner the girl on her own he hasn't been able to think of a damn thing to talk about except books. How can he ever get through to her that pedagogy is the last thing in his mind?

She wheels Sister Lua away from him to the part of the house where the nuns live. Between the girl and himself Sister Lua has thrown a barbed-wire entanglement of irregular verbs. No great love has ever been so ludicrously frustrated.

A white blossom that he cannot identify grows copiously in this suburb. Thanks be to God for the thunder and lightning, thanks be to God for all things that grow.

No, Sister Lua, I am not Nanky Poo, am a disembodied spirit, homeless in suburbia, watching with envy a young couple coming, white and dancing, out of a house and driving away to play tennis, am a lost soul blown on the blast between a green cold corridor of age and death, and the children running and squealing by the lake in the park.

Beyond the two walls and the railway line the sea is flat and purple all the way to Liverpool. He envies the young footballers in the playing fields close to where the cycling girl lies flat on her back and rides to the moon on her imaginary bicycle. He envies particularly a red-headed boy with a superb left foot, who centres the ball, repeating the movement again and again, a conscious artist, as careless as God of what happens to the ball next, just so that he drops it in the goalmouth where he feels it should go. The footballer is on talking terms with the cycling girl. He jokes and laughs with her when the ball bounces that way. She stops her cycling to answer him. From his shadowy corner under the chestnuts Nanky Poo watches and thinks about his latest talk with the vaudeville man on his seat by the grotto under the obelisk.

The obelisk has also been built on smoke to celebrate the twenty-first birthday of a son of the house who would have been the great-grand-uncle of the old soldier.

—Vanished somewhere in India, the poor fellow. There was a rumour to the effect that he was eaten by wild beasts. A damn hard thing to prove unless you see it happen. Anyway he did for a good few of them before they got him. Half of the heads in the hallway below are his.

The obelisk stands up on a base of a flowering rockery, and into the cave or grotto underneath the rockery the nuns have, naturally, inserted a miniature Lourdes: the virgin with arms extended and enhaloed by burning candles, Bernadette kneeling by a fountain of holy water that is blessed by the chaplain at its source in a copper tank.

—The candles, says the vaudeville man, keep my back warm.

He wears a faded brown overcoat with a velvet collar. His white hair is high and bushy and possibly not as well trimmed as it used to be. The skin of his shrunken face and bony Roman nose has little purple blotches and, to conceal the shake in his hands, he grips the knob of his bamboo walking-cane very tightly. When he walks his feet rise jerkily from the ground as if they did so of their own accord and might easily decide never to settle down again. The handwriting on the envelopes is thin and wavery as if the pen now and again took off on its own.

—You know all the best people.

—I used to.

He is never gloomy, yet never hilarious. Somewhere in between he has settled for an irony that is never quite bitter.

—You still write to them.

—Begging letters, you know. Reminders of the good old days. They almost always work with show people. I never quite made it, you know, not even when I had the health. But I was popular with my own kind. This one now.

He points to a notable name on one envelope.

—We met one night in a boozer in London when I wasn't working. He stood me a large Jameson straight away, then another, then another. He asked me to dine with him. We talked about this and that. When we parted I found a tenner in the inside breast pocket of my overcoat. While we were dining he had slipped into the cloakroom. No note, no message, just a simple tenner to speak for itself. He wasn't rich then, mark you, although as the world knows he did well afterwards. But he remembers me. He promises to come to see me. Do you know, now that I think of it, this was the very overcoat.

The cycling girl has stopped cycling and is talking to the red-headed footballer. He stands above her, casually bouncing the ball on that accurate left foot. Whatever he's saying the girl laughs so loudly that Nanky Poo can hear her where he sits in gloom and broods on beggary. She has a good human throaty sort of a laugh.

The night there is no coughing, but only one loud single cry, from the next room, he knows that the old soldier has awakened for a moment to die. He rises, puts on slippers and dressing-gown, and heads down the corridor to find the night nurse. But Mother Polycarp is there already, coming stoop-shouldered, beads and keys rattling, out of the old man's room.

—Thank God, she says, he died peacefully and he had the blessed sacrament yesterday morning. He wandered a lot in his time but he came home in the end.

He walks down the stairway to the shadowy main hall. Do the animals in the half darkness grin with satisfaction at the death of a man whose relative was eaten by one or more of their relatives? The front door is open for the coming of the doctor and the priest. Above the dark maze of yew-hedge the obelisk is silhouetted against the lights of the suburb. The place is so quiet that he can hear even the slight noise of the sea over the flat sand. This is the first time he has been out of doors at night since he went to orthopaedic. Enjoying the freedom, the quiet, the coolness, he walks round and round in the maze until his eyes grow used to the blackness and he is able to pick out the men and women who stand along the via dolorosa. They are just as motionless as they are during the day. When he comes back Mother Polycarp is waiting for him in the hallway.

—Now you're bold, she says. You could catch a chill. But every day that passes brings you nearer to freedom, thank God, and you can walk very well now.

She crosses herself as she passes the shrine in the corridor. She says: One thing that you could do now that you are up, is talk to himself. Or listen to him. He's awake and out of bed and lonely for somebody to talk to.

He is out of bed but not fully dressed; and, in a red dressing-gown that must have been presented to him by Mother Polycarp, he doesn't seem half as formidable as in his black religious habit. There is an open book on the rug that, as usual, covers and beats down the creeping cold from his thighs and knees. He is not reading. His spectacles are in their case on the table to his right hand. Above the light from the shaded reading-lamp his head and shoulders are in shadow. For once, since he is red and not black and half invisible, Nanky Poo feels almost at ease with him.

From the shadows his voice says: Credit where credit is due, young man. The first Chichester to come to Ireland was certainly one of the most capable and successful robbers who ever lived. He stole most of the north of Ireland not only from its owners but even from the robbers who stole it from its owners. Twice he robbed his royal master, James Stuart, the fourth of Scotland and the first of England. The man who did that had to rise early in the morning. For although King James was a fool about most things he was no fool about robbery: it was he who got the Scots the name for parsimony. Chichester stole the entire fisheries of Lough Neagh, the largest lake in the British Isles, and nobody found out about it until after he died. *Age quod agis*, as the maxim says. Do what you do. At his own craft he was a master. I dealt with him in a book.

—I read it.

—Did you indeed? A mark in your favour, young man.

—As a matter of fact, sir, the copy of it I read had your name on the flyleaf. Father Charles from your monastery loaned it to me when I was in orthopaedic.

As soon as the words are out he knows he has dropped the biggest brick of his career, and prays to Jesus that he may live long and die happy and never drop a bigger one. He has never known silence to last so long and be so deafening. Even the bulb in the reading-lamp makes a sound like a big wind far away. Blood in the ears?

—They're not expecting me back, so.

—What do you mean, sir?

—You know damned well what I mean. In a monastery when they know you're dead and not coming back they empty your room. There's another man in it now. They were kind and never told me. That room was all I had, and my books. They have sent me to the death-house as they so elegantly say in the United Sates. This here is the death-house. What do you do here, young man?

He is asking himself that question. So far no easy answer has offered itself.

—Books you build around you, more than a house and wife and family for a layman, part of yourself, flesh of your flesh, more than furniture for a monk's cell, a shell for his soul, the only thing in spite of the rule of poverty I couldn't strip myself of, and my talents allowed me a way around the rule, but man goeth forth naked as he came, stripped of everything, death bursts among them like a shell and strews them over half the town, and yet there are men who can leave their books as memorials to great libraries. . .

Sacred Heart of Jesus, he thinks, up there in the shadows there may be tears on that granite face.

—I'm sorry, sir.

—You didn't know, young man. How could you know?

—You will be remembered, sir.

—Thank you. The old must be grateful. Go to bed now. You have reason to rest. You have a life to live.

In his room he reads for what's left of the night. He has a life to live.

Through a drowsy weary morning he feels he wants to leave the place right away. Never again will he see the old soldier. Never again can he face the old scholar.

—Nanky Poo, Nanky Poo, you won't see your old friend again.

—No, sister. He died last night.

—Not him. Your old friend on the seat by the grotto.

Flying from French, A. N. Other cuts across their path through the maze. But she's moving so fast that not even Lua can hail her. Somewhere in the maze and as quietly as a cat she is stealing away from him for ever. Dulled with lack of sleep his brain is less than usually able to keep up with the chirpings of Lua.

—Is he dead too?

Let them all die. Let me outa here. I am not Nanky Poo.

—A stroke, not fatal yet, but, alas, the final one.

—I'll go to see him.

But Mother Polycarp tells him there's no point in that: all connection between brain and tongue and eyes is gone.

—He wouldn't know whether you were there or not.

—Couldn't he see me?

—We don't know. The doctor says, God bless us, that he's a vegetable.

—I wondered had he any letters to send out. I used to post them for him.

—He can't write any more.

A silence. So he can't even beg.

—It's a blow to you, she says. You were his friend. He used to enjoy his talks with you. But it'll soon be over, thank God. Pray for him that he may pray for us. For some of us death isn't the worst thing and, as far as we can tell, he's content.

A vegetable has little choice. Refusing to lie down and rest in that green place of death he walks dumbly through the suburb. The white blossoms blind him. When he leaves this place he will do so with the sense of escape he might have if he was running on a smooth hillside on a sunny windy day. But later he knows that the place will be with him for ever: the cry in the night, the begging letters sent to the stars, the pitiful anger of an old man finding another man living in his room. Crucified god, there's life for you, and there's a lot more of it that he hasn't yet encountered. He expects little, but he will sit no longer expecting it alone in any dark corner.

He would like to be able to tell the cycling girl a really good lie about how he injured his hip. The scrum fell on me on the line in a rather dirty game, just as I was sneaking away and over: that's how it happens, you know.

Or: An accident on a rockface in Snowdonia, a bit of bad judgment, my own fault actually.

Or: You've heard of the parachute club that ex-air force chap has started out near Celbridge.

He would prefer if he had crutches, or even one crutch, instead of a stick which he doesn't even need. A crutch could win a girl's confidence for no harm could come to her from a fellow hopping on a crutch unless he could move as fast as, and throw the crutch with the accuracy of, Long John Silver.

There he goes, thinking about books again. He'd better watch that.

The red-headed footballer is far-away and absorbed in the virtues of his own left foot. For the first time Nanky Poo notices the colour of her hair, mousy, and the colour of her sweater, which today is mauve, because when she lay flat on the grass and he watched from a distance, she was mostly white shorts and bare circling thighs.

He sits down, stiffly, on the grass beside her. She seems not in the least surprised. She has a freckled face and spectacles. That surprises him.

He says: I envy the way your hips work.

If he doesn't say something wild like that he'll begin talking about books and his cause is lost.

—Why so?

—I was laid up for a year with a tubercular hip. I'm in the convalescent over there.

—Oh I know who you are. Sister Lua told me. You're Nanky Poo. You write poetry.

He is cold all over.

You know Sister Lua?

—She's my aunt. I write poetry too. Nobody has ever printed it though. Yet. Sister Lua said that some day she'd ask you to read some of it.

—I'd be delighted to.

—I watched you sitting over there for a long time. But I didn't like to approach you. Sister Lua said you were standoffish and intellectual.

She walks back with him as far as the obelisk and the grotto. They will meet again on the following day and take a bus into a teashop in the city. They may even go to a show if Mother Polycarp allows him—as she will—to stay out late.

He suspects that all this will come to nothing except to the reading of her poetry which as likely as not will be diabolical. He wonders if some day she will, like her aunt, be arthritic, for arthritis, they say, like a stick leg, runs in the blood. But with one of his three friends dead, one estranged and one a vegetable, it is something to have somebody to talk to as you stumble through suburbia. He has a life to live. Every day that passes brings him a day nearer to somewhere else.

So thanks be to God for the rain and the sunshine, thanks be to God for the hail and the snow, thanks be to God for the thunder and lightning, thanks be to God that all things are so.

MAIDEN'S LEAP

The civic guard, or policeman, on the doorstep was big, middle-aged, awkward, affable. Behind him was green sunlit lawn sloping down to a white horse-fence and a line of low shrubs. Beyond that the highway, not much travelled. Beyond the highway, the jetty, the moored boats, the restless lake-water reflecting the sunshine.

The civic guard was so affable that he took off his cap. He was bald, completely bald. Robert St. Blaise Macmahon thought that by taking off his cap the civic guard had made himself a walking, or standing, comic comment on the comic rural constable, in the Thomas Hardy story, who wouldn't leave his house without his truncheon: because without his truncheon his going forth would not be official.

Robert St. Blaise Macmahon felt like telling all that to the civic guard and imploring him, for the sake of the dignity of his office, to restore his cap to its legal place and so to protect his bald head from the sunshine which, for Ireland, was quite bright and direct. Almost like the sun of that autumn he had spent in the Grand Atlas, far from the tourists. Or the sun of that spring when he had submitted to the natural curiosity of a novelist, who was also a wealthy man and could afford such silly journeys, and gone all the way to the United States, not to see those sprawling vulgar cities, Good God sir no, nor all those chromium-plated barbarians who had made an industry out of writing boring books about those colossal bores, Yeats and Joyce, but to go to Georgia to see the Okefenokee Swamp which interested him because of those sacred drooping melancholy birds, the white ibises, and because of the alligators. Any day in the year give him, in preference to Americans, alligators. It could be that he made the journey so as to be able at intervals to say that.

But if he talked like this to the bald guard on the ancestral doorstep the poor devil would simply gawk or smirk or both and say: Yes, Mr. Macmahon. Of course, Mr. Macmahon.

Very respectful, he would seem to be. For the Macmahons counted for something in the town. His father's father had as good as owned it.

The fellow's bald head was nastily ridiculously perspiring. Robert St.

Blaise Macmahon marked down that detail for his notebook. Henry James had so wisely said: Try to be one of those on whom nothing is lost.

Henry James had known it all. What a pity that he had to be born in the United States. But then, like the gentleman he was, he had had the good wit to run away from it all.

The bald perspiring cap-in-hand guard said: Excuse me, Mr. Macmahon. Sorry to disturb you on such a heavenly morning and all. But I've come about the body, sir.

Robert St. Blaise Macmahon was fond of saying in certain circles in Dublin that he liked civic guards if they were young, fresh from the country, and pink-cheeked; and that he liked Christian Brothers in a comparable state of development. In fact, he would argue, you came to a time of life when civic guards and Christian Brothers were, apart from the uniforms, indistinguishable. This he said merely to hear himself say it. He was much too fastidious for any fleshly contact with anybody, male or female. So, lightly, briefly, flittingly, trippingly, he now amused himself with looking ahead to what he would say on his next visit to town: Well if they had to send a guard they could have sent a young handsome one to enquire about the . . .

What the guard had just said now registered and with a considerable shock. The guard repeated: About the body, sir. I'm sorry, Mr. Macmahon, to disturb you.

—What body? Whose body? What in heaven's name can you mean?

—I know it's a fright, sir. Not what you would expect at all. The body in the bed, sir. Dead in the bed.

—There is no body in my bed. Dead or alive. At least not while I'm up and about. I live here alone, with my housekeeper, Miss Hynes.

—Yes, Mr. Macmahon, sir. We know Miss Hynes well. Very highly respected lady, sir. She's below in the barracks at the moment in a terrible state of nervous prostration. The doctor's giving her a pill or an injection or something to soothe her. Then he'll be here directly.

—Below in the barracks? But she went out to do the shopping.

—Indeed yes, sir. But she slipped in to tell us, in passing, like, sir. Oh it's not serious or anything. Foul play is not suspected.

—Foul what? Tell you what?

—Well, sir.

—Tell me, my good man.

—She says, sir, there's a man dead in her bed.

—A dead man?

—The very thing, Mr. Macmahon.

—In the bed of Miss Hynes, my housekeeper.

—So she says, sir. Her very words.

—What in the name of God is he doing there?

—Hard to say, Mr. Macmahon, what a dead man would be doing in a bed, I mean like in somebody else's bed.

With a huge white linen handkerchief that he dragged, elongated, out of a pants pocket, and then spread before him like an enveloping cloud, the guard patiently mopped his perspiration: Damned hot today, sir. The hottest summer, the paper says, in forty years.

The high Georgian-Floridian sun shone straight down on wine-coloured swamp-water laving (it was archaic but yet the only word) the grotesque knobbly knees of giant cypress trees. The white sacred crook-billed birds perched gravely, high on grey curved branches above trailing Spanish moss, oh far away, so far away from this mean sniggering town and its rattling tongues. It was obvious, it was regrettably obvious, that the guard was close to laughter.

—A dead man, guard, in the bed of Miss Hynes, my housekeeper, and housekeeper to my father and mother before me, and a distant relative of my own.

—So she tells us, sir.

—Scarcely a laughing matter, guard.

—No, sir. Everything but, sir. It's just the heat, sir. Overcome by the heat. Hottest summer, the forecast says, in forty years.

That hottest summer in forty years followed them, panting, across the black and red flagstones of the wide hallway. A fine mahogany staircase went up in easy spirals. Robert St. Blaise Macmahon led the way around it, keeping to the ground floor. The guard placed his cap, open end up, on the hall stand, as reverently as if he were laying cruets on an altar, excusing himself, as he did so, as if the ample mahogany hall stand, mirrored and antlered, were also a Macmahon watching, or reflecting, him with disapproval. It was the first time he or his like ever had had opportunity or occasion to enter this house.

In the big kitchen, old-fashioned as to size, modern as to fittings, the hottest summer was a little assuaged. The flagstones were replaced by light tiles, green and white, cool to the sight and the touch. She had always held on to that bedroom on the ground floor, beyond the kitchen, although upstairs the large house was more than half empty. She said she loved it because it had french windows that opened out to the garden. They did, too. They would also give easy access for visitors to the bedroom: a thought that had never occurred to him, not once over all these years.

Earlier that morning she had called to him from the kitchen to say

that she was going shopping, and had made her discreet escape by way
of those windows. They still lay wide open to the garden. She was a
good gardener as she was a good housekeeper. She had, of course, help
with the heavy work in both cases: girls from the town for the kitchen,
a healthy young man for the garden. All three, or any, of them were due
to arrive, embarrassingly, within the next hour. Could it be the young
man for the garden, there, dead in the bed? No, at least, thank God, it
wasn't her assistant gardener, a scape-grace of a fellow that might
readily tempt a middle-aged woman. She hadn't stooped to the servants.
She had that much Macmahon blood in her veins. This man was, or had
been, a stranger, an older man by far than the young gardener. He was
now as old as he would ever be. The hottest summer was heavy and
odorous in the garden, and flower odours and insect sounds came to
them in the room. The birds were silent. There was also the other
odour: stale sweat, or dead passion, or just death? The guard sniffed. He
said: He died sweating. He's well tucked in.

Only the head was visible: sparse grey hair, a few sad pimples on the
scalp, a long purple nose, a comic Cyrano nose. Mouth and eyes were
open. He had good teeth and brown eyes. He looked, simply, surprised,
not yet accustomed to wherever he happened to find himself.

—Feel his heart, guard.

—Oh dead as mutton, Mr. Macmahon. Miss Hynes told no lie. Still,
he couldn't die in a better place. In a bed, I mean.

—Unhouselled, unappointed, unannealed.

—Yes, sir, the guard said, every bit of it.

—I mean he died without the priest.

With something amounting almost to wit—you encountered it in the
most unexpected places—the guard said that taking into account the
circumstances in which the deceased, God be merciful to him, had
passed over, he could hardly have counted on the company of a resident
chaplain. That remark could be adopted as one's own, improved upon,
and employed on suitable occasions and in the right places, far from this
town and its petty people.

—Death, said the guard, is an odd fellow. There's no being up to him,
Mr. Macmahon. He can catch you unawares in the oddest places.

This fellow, by heaven, was a philosopher. He was, for sure, one for
the notebook.

—Quite true, guard. There was a very embarrassing case involving a
president of the great French Republic. Found dead in his office. He had
his hands in the young lady's hair. They had to cut the hair to set her
free.

—Do you tell me so, sir? A French president? 'Twouldn't be the present fellow, De Gaulle, with the long nose would be caught at capers like that.

—There was a Hemingway story on a somewhat similar theme.

—Of course, sir. You'd know about that, Mr. Macmahon. I don't read much myself. But my eldest daughter that works for the public libraries tells me about your books.

—And Dutch Schultz, the renowned American gangster, you know that he was shot dead while he was sitting, well in fact while he was sitting on the toilet.

—A painful experience, Mr. Macmahon. He must have been surprised beyond measure.

Far away, from the highway, came the sound of an automobile.

—That, said the guard, could be the doctor or the ambulance.

They waited in silence in the warm odorous room. The sound passed on and away: neither the doctor nor the ambulance.

—But that fellow in the bed, Mr. Macmahon, I could tell you things about him, God rest him.

—Do you mean to say you know him.

—Of course, sir. It's my business to know people.

—Try to be one of those on whom nothing is lost.

—Quite so, sir, and odd that you should mention it. For that fellow in the bed, sir, do you know that once upon a time he lost two hundred hens?

—Two hundred hens?

—Chickens.

—Well, even chickens. That was a lot of birds. Even sparrows. Or skylarks. He must have been the only man in Europe who ever did that.

—In the world, I'd say, sir. And it happened so simple.

—It's stuffy in here, Robert said.

He led the way out to the garden. The sound of another automobile on the highway was not yet the doctor nor the ambulance. They walked along a red-sanded walk. She had had that mulch red sand brought all the way from Mullachdearg Strand in County Donegal. She loved the varied strands of Donegal: red, golden or snow-white. To right and left her roses flourished. She had a good way with roses, and with sweetpea, and even with sunflowers, those lusty brazen-faced giants.

—He was up in Dublin one day in a pub, and beside him at the counter the mournfullest man you ever saw. So the man that's gone, he was always a cheery type, said to the mournful fellow: Brighten up, the sun's shining, life's not all that bad. The mournful one says: If you were a poultry farmer with two hundred hens that wouldn't lay an egg, you'd hardly be singing songs.

—The plot, said Robert St. Blaise Macmahon, thickens.

—So, says your man that's inside there, and at peace we may charitably hope, how much would you take for those hens? A shilling a hen. Done, says he, and out with two hundred shillings and buys the hens. Then he hires a van and a boy to drive it, and off with him to transport the hens. You see, he knows a man here in this very town that will give him half-a-crown a hen, a profit of fifteen pounds sterling less the hire of the van. But the journey is long and the stops plentiful at the wayside pubs, he always had a notorious drouth, and whatever happened nobody ever found out, but when he got to this town at two in the morning, the back doors of the van were swinging open.

—The birds had flown.

—Only an odd feather to be seen. And he had to pay the boy fifteen shillings to clean out the back of the van. They were never heard of again, the hens I mean. He will long be remembered for that.

—If not for anything else.

—His poor brother, too, sir. That was a sad case. Some families are, you might say, addicted to sudden death.

—Did he die in a bed?

—Worse, far worse, sir. He died on a lawnmower.

—Guard, said Robert, would you have a cup of tea? You should be writing books, instead of me.

—I was never much given to tea, sir.

—But in all the best detective stories the man from Scotland Yard always drinks a cup o' tea.

—As I told you, sir, I don't read much. But if you had the tiniest drop of whiskey to spare, I'd be grateful. It's a hot day and this uniform is a crucifixion.

They left the garden by a wicket-gate that opened through a beech-hedge on to the front lawn. The sun's reflections shot up like lightning from the lake-water around the dancing boats. Three automobiles passed, but no doctor, no ambulance, appeared. Avoiding the silent odorous room they re-entered the house by the front door. In the dining-room Robert St. Blaise Macmahon poured the whiskey for the guard, and for himself: he needed it.

—Ice, guard?

—No thank you sir. Although they say the Americans are hell for it. In everything, in tea, whiskey, and so on.

Two more automobiles passed. They listened and waited.

—You'd feel, sir, he was listening to us, like for a laugh, long nose and all. His brother was the champion gardener of all time. Better even than

Miss Hynes herself, although her garden's a sight to see and a scent to smell.

—He died on a lawnmower?

—On his own lawn, sir. On one of those motor mowers. It blew up under him. He was burned to death. And you could easily say, sir, he couldn't have been at a more harmless occupation, or in a safer place.

—You could indeed, guard. Why haven't I met you before this?

—That's life, sir. Our paths never crossed. Only now for that poor fellow inside I wouldn't be here today at all.

This time it had to be the doctor and the ambulance. The wheels came, scattering gravel, up the driveway.

—He was luckier than his brother, sir. He died in more comfort, in a bed. And in action, it seems. That's more than will be said for most of us.

The doorbell chimed: three slow cathedral tones. That chime had been bought in Bruges where they knew about bells. The guard threw back what was left of his whiskey. He said: You'll excuse me, Mr. Macmahon. I'll go and put on my cap. We have work to do.

When the guard, the doctor, the ambulance, the ambulance attendants, and the corpse had, all together, taken their departure, he sprayed the bedroom with Flit, sworn foe to the housefly. It was all he could think of. It certainly changed the odour. It drifted out even into the garden, and lingered there among the roses. The assistant gardener and the kitchen girls had not yet arrived. That meant that the news was out, and that they were delaying in the town to talk about it. What sort of insufferable idiot was that woman to put him in this way into the position of being talked about, even, in the local papers, written about, and then laughed at, by clods he had always regarded with a detached and humorous, yet godlike, eye?

He sat, for the sake of the experience, on the edge of the rumpled bed from which the long-nosed corpse had just been removed. But he felt nothing of any importance. He remembered that another of those American dons had written a book, which he had slashingly reviewed, about love and death in the American novel. To his right, beyond the open windows, was her bureau desk and bookcase: old black oak, as if in stubborn isolated contradiction to the prevalent mahogany. She had never lost the stiff pride that a poor relation wears as a mask when he or she can ride high above the more common servility. She was a high-rider. It was simply incomprehensible that she, who had always so rigidly kept herself to herself, should have had a weakness for a long-nosed man who seemed to have been little better than a figure of fun. Two hundred hens, indeed!

The drawers of the bureau-bookcase were sagging open, and in disorder, as if in panic she had been rooting through them for something that nobody could find. He had seldom seen the inside of her room but, from the little he had seen and from everything he knew of her, she was no woman for untidiness or unlocked drawers. Yet in spite of her panic she had not called for aid to him, her cousin-once-removed, her employer, her benefactor. She had always stiffly, and for twenty-five years, kept him at a distance. Twenty-five years ago, in this room. She would have been eighteen, not six months escaped from the mountain valley she had been reared in, from which his parents had rescued her. He closes his eyes and, as best he can, his nose. He remembers. It is a Sunday afternoon and the house is empty except for the two of them.

He is alone in his room reading. He is reading about how Lucius Apuleius watches the servant-maid, Fotis, bending over the fire: Mincing of meats and making pottage for her master and mistresse, the Cupboard was all set with wines and I thought I smelled the savour of some dainty meats. Shee had about her middle a white and clean apron, and shee was girdled about her body under the paps with a swathell of red silk, and shee stirred the pot and turned the meat with her faire and white hands, in such sort that with stirring and turning the same, her loynes and hips did likewise move and shake, which was in my mind a comely sight to see.

Robert St. Blaise Macmahon who, at sixteen, had never tasted wine except to nibble secretively at the altar-wine when he was an acolyte in the parish church, repeats over and over again the lovely luscious Elizabethan words of Adlington's translation from the silver Latin: We did renew our venery by drinking of wine.

For at sixteen he is wax, and crazy with curiosity.

Then he looks down into the garden and there she is bending down over a bed of flowers. She is tall, rather sallow-faced, a Spanish face in an oval of close, crisp, curling dark hair. He has already noticed the determination of her long lithe stride, the sway of her hips, the pendulum swish and swing of her bright tartan pleated skirt. For a girl from the back of the mountains she has a sense of style.

She has come to this house from the Gothic grandeur of a remote valley called Glenade. Flat-topped mountains, so steep that the highest few hundred feet are sheer rock-cliffs corrugated by torrents, surround it. One such cliff, fissured in some primeval cataclysm, falls away into a curved chasm, rises again into one cold pinnacle of rock. The place is known as the Maiden's Leap, and the story is that some woman out of myth—Goddess, female devil, what's the difference?—pursued by a savage and unwanted lover, ran along the ridge of the mountain, and when faced by the chasm leaped madly to save her virtue, and did. But she didn't leap far enough to save her beautiful frail body which was shattered on the rocks below. From which her pursuer may have derived a certain perverse satisfaction.

All through her girlhood her bedroom window has made a frame for that extraordinary view. Now, her parents dead, herself adopted into the house of rich relatives as a sort of servant-maid, assistant to the aged housekeeper and in due course to succeed her, she bends over a flower-bed as Fotis had bent over the fire: O Fotis how trimely you can stir the pot, and how finely, with shaking your buttocks, you can make pottage.

Now she is standing tall and straight snipping blossoms from a fence of sweetpea. Her body is clearly outlined against the multi-coloured fence. He watches. He thinks of Fotis. He says again: We did renew our venery with drinking of wine.

When he confronts her in this very room, and makes an awkward grab at her, her arms are laden with sweetpea. So he is able to plant one kiss on cold unresponding lips. The coldness, the lack of response in a bondswoman, surprises him. She bears not the slightest resemblance to Fotis. It was the done thing, wasn't it: the young master and the servant-maid? In the decent old days in Czarist Russia the great ladies in the landed houses used to give the maids to their sons to practise on.

The sweetpea blossoms, purple, red, pink, blue, flow rather than fall to the floor. Then she hits him with her open hand, one calm, deliberate, country clout that staggers him and leaves his ear red, swollen and singing for hours. She clearly does not understand the special duties of a young female servant. In wild Glenade they didn't read Turgenev or Saltykov-Schedrin. He is humiliatingly reminded that he is an unathletic young man, a pampered only child, and that she is a strong girl from a wild mountain valley. She says: Mind your manners, wee boy. Pick up those sweetpea or I'll tell your father and mother how they came to be on the floor.

He picks up the flowers. She is older than he is. She is also taller, and she has a hand like rock. He knows that she has already noticed that he is afraid of his father.

This room was not then a bedroom. It was a pantry with one whole wall of it shelved for storing apples. He could still smell those apples, and the sweetpea. The conjoined smell of flower and fruit was stronger even than the smell of the insect-killing spray with which he had tried to banish the odour of death.

That stinging clout was her great leap, her defiance, her declaration of independence but, as in the case of the Maiden of Glenade, it had only carried her halfways. To a cousin once-removed, who never anyway had cared enough to make a second attempt, she had demonstrated that she was no chattel. But she remained a dependant, a poor relation, a housekeeper doing the bidding of his parents until they died and, after their death, continuing to mind the house, grow the roses, the sweetpea and the sunflowers. The sense of style, the long lithe swinging stride, went for nothing, just because she hadn't jumped far enough to o'erleap the meandering withering enduring ways of a small provincial town. No man in the place could publicly be her equal. She was part Macmahon. So she had no man of her own, no place of her own. She had become part of the furniture of this house. She had no life of her own. Or so he had lightly thought.

He came and went and wrote his books, and heard her and spoke to her, but seldom really saw her except to notice that wrinkles, very faint and fine, had appeared on that Spanish face, on the strong-boned, glossy forehead, around the corners of the eyes. The crisp dark hair had touches of grey that she had simply not bothered to do anything about. She was a cypher, and a symbol in a frustrating land that had more than its share of ageing hopeless virgins. He closed his eyes and saw her as such when, in his writing, he touched satirically on that aspect of life in his pathetic country. Not that he did so any more often than he could help. For a London illustrated magazine he had once written about the country's low and late marriage rate, an article that had astounded all by its hard practicality. But as a general rule he preferred to think and to write about Stockholm or Paris or Naples or Athens, or African mountains, remote from everything. His travel books were more than travel books, and his novels really did show that travel broadened the mind. Or to think and write about the brightest gem in an America that man was doing so much to lay waste: the swamp that was no swamp but a wonderland out of a fantasy by George MacDonald, a Scottish writer whom nobody read any more, a fantasy about awaking some morning in your own bedroom, which is no longer a bedroom but the heart of the forest where every tree has its living spirit, genial or evil, evil or genial.

At that moment in his reverie the telephone rang. To the devil with it, he thought, let it ring. The enchanted swamp was all around him, the wine-coloured water just perceptibly moving, the rugged knees of the cypress trees, the white priestly birds curved brooding on high bare branches, the silence. Let it ring. It did, too. It rang and rang and refused to stop. So he walked ill-tempered to the table in the hallway where the telephone was, picked it up, silenced the ringing, heard the voice of the civic guard, and then noticed for the first conscious time the black book that he carried in his right hand.

The guard said: She's resting now. The sergeant's wife is looking after her.

—Good. That's very good.

It was a ledger-type book, eight inches by four, the pages ruled in blue, the margins in red. He must, unthinkingly, have picked it up out of the disorder in which her morning panic had left the bureau-bookcase. For the first time that panic seemed to him as comic: it wasn't every morning a maiden lady found a long-nosed lover, or something, cold between the covers. It was matter for a short story, or an episode in a novel: if it just hadn't damned well happened in his own house. What would Henry James have made of it? The art of fiction is in telling not what happened, but what should have happened. Or what should have happened somewhere else.

The guard was still talking into his left ear, telling him that the doctor said it was a clear case of heart failure. Oh, indeed it was: for the heart was a rare and undependable instrument. With his right hand he flicked at random through the black book, then, his eye caught by some words that seemed to mean something, he held the book flat, focused on those words until they were steady, and read. The hand-writing was thick-nibbed, black as coal, dogged, almost printing, deliberate as if the nib had bitten into the paper. He read: Here he comes down the stairs in the morning, his double jowl red and purple from the razor, his selfish mouth pursed as tight as Mick Clinton, the miser of Glenade, used to keep the woollen sock he stored his money in when he went to the market and the horsefair of Manorhamilton. Here he comes, the heavy tread of him in his good, brown hand-made shoes, would shake the house if it wasn't as solid on its foundations as the Rock of Cashel. Old John Macmahon used to boast that his people built for eternity. Thud, thud, thud, the weight of his big flat feet. Here he comes, Gorgeous Gussie, with his white linen shirt, he should have frills on his underpants, and his blue eyeshade to show to the world, as if there was anybody to bother looking at him except myself and the domestic help, that he's a writer. A writer, God help us. About what? Who reads him? It's just as well he has old John's plunder to live on.

The black letters stood out like basalt from the white, blue-and-red lined paper. Just one paragraph she wrote to just one page and, if the paragraph didn't fully fill the page, she made, above and below the paragraph, whorls and doodles and curlicues in inks of various colours, blue, red, green, violet. She was a lonely self-delighting artist. She was, she had been, for how long, oh merciful heavens, an observer, a writer.

The guard was saying: She said to the sergeant's wife that she's too shy to face you for the present.

—Shy, he said.

He looked at the black words. They were as distinct as that long-ago clout on the side of the head: the calloused hard hand of the mountainy girl reducing the pretensions of a shy, sensitive, effeminate youth.

He said: She has good reason to be shy. It is, perhaps, a good thing that she should, at least, be shy before her employer and distant relation.

—It might be that, sir, she might mean not shy, but ashamed.

—She has also good reason for being ashamed.

—She says, Mr. Macmahon, sir, that she might go away somewhere for a while.

—Shouldn't she wait for the inquest and the funeral? At any rate, she has her duties here in this house. She is, she must realise, paid in advance.

So she would run, would she, and leave him to be the single object of the laughter of the mean people of this town? In a sweating panic he gripped the telephone as if he would crush it. There was an empty hungry feeling, by turns hot, by turns cold, just above his navel. He was betraying himself to that garrulous guard who would report to the town every word he said. It was almost as if the guard could read, if he could read, those damnable black words. He gripped the phone, slippy and sweaty as it was, gulped and steadied himself, breathed carefully, in out, in out, and was once again Robert St. Blaise Macmahon, a cultivated man whose education had commenced at the famous Benedictine school at Glenstal. After all, the Jesuits no longer were what once they had been, and James Joyce had passed that way to the discredit both of himself and the Jesuits.

—Let her rest then, he said. I'll think over what she should do. I'll be busy all day, guard, so don't call me unless it's absolutely essential.

He put down the telephone, wiped his sweating hand with a white linen handkerchief, monogrammed and ornamented with the form of a feather embroidered in red silk. It was meant to represent a quill pen and also to be a symbol of the soaring creative mind. That fancy handkerchief was, he considered, his one flamboyance. He wore, working, a blue eye-shade because there were times when lamplight, and even overbright daylight, strained his eyes. Any gentleman worthy of the name did, didn't he, wear hand-made shoes?

On the first page of the book she had pasted a square of bright yellow paper and on it printed in red ink: Paragraphs.

In smaller letters, in Indian black ink, and in an elegant italic script, she had written: Reflections on Robert the Riter.

Then finally, in green ink, she had printed: By his Kaptivated Kuntry Kusin!!!

He was aghast at her frivolity. Nor did she need those three exclamation marks to underline her bitchiness, a withdrawn and secretive bitchiness, malevolent among the roses and the pots and pans, overflowing like bile, in black venomous ink. She couldn't have been long at this secret writing. The book was by no means full. She had skipped, and left empty pages here and there, at random as if she dipped her pen and viciously wrote wherever the book happened to open. There was no time sequence that he could discern. He read: He says he went all the way to the States to see a swamp. Just like him. Would he go all the way to Paris to see the sewers?

—But the base perfidy of that.

He spoke aloud, not to himself but to her.

—You always pretended to be interested when I talked about the swamp. The shy wild deer that would come to the table to take the bit out of your fingers when you breakfasted in the open air, the racoon with the rings round its eyes, the alligators, the wine-coloured waters, the white birds, the white sand on the bed of the Suwannee River. You would sit, woman, wouldn't you, brown Spanish face inscrutable, listening, agreeing, with me, oh yes, agreeing with me in words, but, meanly, all the time, thinking like this.

Those brief words about that small portion of his dreamworld had wounded him. But bravely he read more. The malice of this woman of the long-nosed chicken-losing lover must be fully explored. She was also, by heaven, a literary critic. She wrote: Does any novelist, nowadays, top-dress his chapters with quotations from other authors? There is one, but he writes thrillers and that's different. Flat-footed Robert the Riter, with his good tweeds and his brass-buttoned yellow waistcoat, has a hopelessly old-fashioned mind. His novels, with all those sophisticated nonentities going nowhere, read as if he was twisting life to suit his reading. But then what does Robert know about life? Mamma's boy, Little Lord Fauntleroy, always dressed in the best. He doesn't know one rose from another. But a novelist should know everything. He doesn't know the town he lives in. Nor the people in it. Quotations. Balderdash.

He found to his extreme humiliation that he was flushed with fury. The simplest thing to do would be to let her go away and stay away, and then find himself a housekeeper who wasn't a literary critic, a secret carping critic, a secret lover too, a Psyche, by Hercules, welcoming by night an invisible lover to her bed. Then death stops him, and daylight reveals him, makes him visible as a comic character with a long nose, and with a comic reputation, only, for mislaying two hundred hens, and with a brother, a great gardener, who had the absurd misfortune to be burned alive on his own lawn. Could comic people belong to a family addicted to sudden death? Somewhere in all this, there might be some time the germ of a story.

But couldn't she realise what those skilfully-chosen quotations meant?

—Look now, he said, what they did for George MacDonald. A procession of ideas, names, great presences, marching around the room you write in: Fletcher and Shelley, Novalis and Beddoes, Goethe and Coleridge, Sir John Suckling and Shakespeare, Lyly and Schiller, Heine and Schleiermacher and Cowley and Spenser and the Book of Judges and Jean Paul Richter and Cyril Tourneur and Sir Philip Sidney and Dekker and Chaucer and the Kabala.

But, oh Mother Lilith, what was the use of debating thus with the shadow of a secretive woman who was now resting in the tender care of the sergeant's wife who was, twenty to one, relaying the uproarious news to every other wife in the town: Glory be, did you hear the fantasticality that happened up in Mr. Robert St. Blaise Macmahon's big house? Declare to God they'll never again be able to show their faces in public.

Even if she were with him, walking in this garden as he now was, and if he was foolish enough thus to argue with her, she would smile her sallow wrinkled smile, look sideways out of those dark-brown eyes and then go off alone to write in her black book: He forgot to mention the Twelve Apostles, the Clancy Brothers, and the Royal Inniskilling Fusiliers.

All her life she had resisted his efforts to make something out of her. Nor had she ever had the determination to rise and leap again, to leave him and the house and go away and make something out of herself.

He read: He's like the stuck-up high-falutin' women in that funny story by Somerville and Ross, he never leaves the house except to go to Paris. He doesn't see the life that's going on under his nose. He says there are no brothels in Dublin. But if Dublin had the best brothels in the long history of sin . . .

Do you know, now, that was not badly put. She has a certain felicity of phrase. But then she has some Macmahon blood in her, and the educational advantages that over the years this house has afforded her.

. . . long history of sin, he'd be afraid of his breeches to enter any of them. He says there are no chic women in Dublin. What would he do with a chic woman if I gave him one, wrapped in cellophane, for Valentine's Day? He says he doesn't know if the people he sees are ugly because they don't make love, or that they don't make love because they're ugly. He's the world's greatest living authority, isn't he, either on love or good looks?

On another page: To think, dear God, of that flat-footed bachelor who doesn't know one end of a woman from the other, daring to write an article attacking the mountainy farmers on their twenty pitiful acres of rocks, rushes, bogpools and dunghills, for not marrying young and raising large families. Not only does he not see the people around him, he doesn't even see himself. Himself and a crazy priest in America lamenting about late marriages and the vanishing Irish. A fine pair to run in harness. The safe, sworn celibate and the fraidy-cat bachelor.

And on yet another page: That time long ago, I clouted him when he made the pass, the only time, to my knowledge, he ever tried to prove himself a man. And he never came back for more. I couldn't very well tell him that the clout was not for what he was trying to do but for the stupid way he was trying to do it. A born bungler.

The doodles, whorls and curlicues wriggled like a snake-pit, black, blue, green, red, violet, before his angry eyes. That was enough. He would bring that black book down to the barracks, and throw it at her, and tell her never to darken his door again. His ears boomed with blood. He went into the dining-room, poured himself a double whiskey, drank it slowly, breathing heavily, thinking. But no, there was a better way. Go down to the barracks, bring her back, lavish kindness on her, in silence suffer her to write in her book, then copy what she writes, reshape it, reproduce it, so that some day she would see it in print and be confounded for the jade and jezebel that she is.

With deliberate speed, majestic instancy, he walked from the dining-room to her bedroom, tossed the book on to her bed where she would see it on her return and know he had read it, and that her nastiness was uncovered. He had read enough of it, too much of it: because the diabolical effect of his reading was that he paused, with tingling irritation, to examine his tendency to think in quotations. Never again, thanks to her malice, would he do so, easily, automatically, and, so to speak, unthinkingly.

Coming back across the kitchen he found himself looking at his own feet, in fine hand-made shoes, his feet rising, moving forwards, settling again on the floor, fine flat feet. It was little benefit to see ourselves as others see us. That was, merciful God, another quotation. That mean woman would drive him mad. He needed a change: Dublin, Paris, Boppard on the Rhine—a little town that he loved in the off-season when it wasn't ravished by boat-loads of American women doing the Grand Tour. First, though, to get the Spanish maiden of wild Glenade back to her proper place among the roses and the pots and pans.

The guard answered the telephone. He said: She's still resting, Mr. Macmahon, sir.

—It's imperative that I speak to her. She can't just take this lying down.

That, he immediately knew, was a stupid thing to say. On the wall before him, strong black letters formed, commenting on his stupidity.

There was a long silence. Then she spoke, almost whispered: Yes, Robert.

—Hadn't you better get back to your place here?

—Yes, Robert. But what is my place there?

—You know what I mean. We must face this together. After all, you are half a Macmahon.

—Half a Macmahon, she said, is better than no bread.

He was shocked to fury: This is nothing to be flippant about.

—No, Robert.

—Who was this man?

—A friend of mine.

—Do you tell me so? Do you invite all your friends to my house?

—He was the only one.

—Why didn't you marry him?

—He had a wife and five children in Sudbury in England. Separated.

—That does, I believe, constitute an impediment. But who or what was he?

—It would be just like you, Robert, not even to know who he was. He lived in this town. It's a little town.

—Should I have known him?

—Shouldn't a novelist know everybody and everything?

—I'm not an authority on roses.

—You've been reading my book.

She was too sharp for him. He tried another tack: Why didn't you tell me you were having a love affair? After all, I am civilised.

—Of course you're civilised. The world knows that. But there didn't seem any necessity for telling you.

—There must be so many things that you don't feel it is necessary to tell me.

—You were never an easy person to talk to.

—All your secret thoughts. Who could understand a devious woman? Far and from the farthest coasts . . .

—There you go again. Quotations. The two-footed gramophone. What good would it do you if you did understand?

—Two-footed, he said. Flat-footed.

He was very angry: You could have written it all out for me if you couldn't say it. All the thoughts hidden behind your brooding face. All the things you thought when you said nothing, or said something else.

—You really have been reading my book. Prying.

The silence could have lasted all of three minutes. He searched around for something that would hurt.

—Isn't it odd that a comic figure should belong to a family addicted to sudden death?

—What on earth do you mean?

Her voice was higher. Anger? Indignation?

—That nose, he said. Cyrano. Toto the Clown. And I heard about the flight of the two hundred hens.

Silence.

—And about the brother who was burned.

—They were kindly men, she said. And good to talk to. They had green fingers.

It would have gratified him if he could have heard a sob.

—I'll drive down to collect you in an hour's time.

—He loved me, she said. I suppose I loved him. He was something, in a place like this.

Silence.

—You're a cruel little boy, she said. But just to amuse you, I'll give you another comic story. Once he worked in a dog kennels in Kent in England. The people who owned the kennels had an advertisement in the local paper. One sentence read like this: Bitches in heat will be personally conducted from the railway station by Mr. Dominic Byrne.

—Dominic Byrne, she said. That was his name. He treasured that clipping. He loved to laugh at himself. He died for love. That's more than most will ever do. There you are. Make what you can out of that story, you flat-footed bore.

She replaced the telephone so quietly that for a few moments he listened, waiting for more, thinking of something suitable to say.

On good days, light, reflected from the lake, seemed to brighten every nook and corner of the little town. At the end of some old narrow winding cobbled laneway there would be a vision of lake-water bright as a polished mirror. It was a graceful greystone town, elegantly laid-out by some Frenchman hired by an eighteenth-century earl. The crystal river that fed the lake flowed through the town and gave space and scope for a tree-lined mall. But grace and dancing light could do little to mollify his irritation. This time, by the heavenly father, he would have it out with her, he would put her in her place, revenge himself for a long-ago affront and humiliation. Body in the bed, indeed. Two hundred hens, indeed. Swamps and sewers, indeed. Bitches in heat, indeed. She did not have a leg to stand on. Rutting, and on his time, with a long-nosed yahoo.

The Byzantine church, with which the parish priest had recently done his damnedest to disfigure the town, struck his eyes with concentrated insult. Ignorant bloody peasants. The slick architects could sell them anything: Gothic, Byzantine, Romanesque, Igloo, Kraal, Modern Cubist. The faithful paid, and the pastor made the choice.

Who would ever have thought that a lawnmower could be a Viking funeral pyre?

The barracks, a square, grey house, made ugly by barred windows and notice-boards, was beside the church. The guard, capless, the neck of his uniform jacket open, his hands in his trouser pockets, stood in the doorway. He was still perspiring. The man would melt. There was a drop to his nose: snot or sweat or a subtle blend of both. Robert St. Blaise Macmahon would never again make jokes about civic guards. He said: I've come for Miss Hynes.

—Too late, Mr. Macmahon, sir. The bird has flown.

—She has what?

—Gone, sir. Eloped. Stampeded. On the Dublin train. Ten minutes ago. I heard her whistle.

—Whistle?

—The train, sir.

—But the funeral? The inquest?

—Oh, his wife and children will bury him. We phoned them.

—But the inquest?

— Her affidavit will do the job. We'll just say he dropped while visiting your house to look at the roses.

—That's almost the truth.

—The whole truth and nothing but the truth is often a bitter dose, sir.

—As I said, guard, you are a philosopher.

He remembered too late that he hadn't said that, he had just thought it.

—Thank you kindly, sir. Would you chance a cup of tea, sir? Nothing better to cool one on a hot day. Not that I like tea myself. But in this weather, you know. The hottest day, the forecast says.

Well, why not? He needed cooling. The bird had flown, sailing away from him, over the chasm, laughing triumphant eldritch laughter.

In the austere dayroom they sat on hard chairs and sipped tea.

—Nothing decent or drinkable here, sir, except a half-bottle of Sandeman's port.

—No thank you, guard. No port. The tea will suffice.

—Those are gallant shoes, sir, if you'll excuse me being so pass-remarkable. Hand-made jobs.

—Yes, hand-made.

—Costly, I'd say. But then they'd last for ever.

—Quite true, guard.

—He's coffined by now. The heat, you know.

—Don't remind me.

—Sorry, sir. But the facts of life are the facts of life. Making love one minute. In a coffin the next.

—The facts of death, guard. Alone withouten any company.

—True as you say, sir. He was a droll divil, poor Byrne, and he died droll.

—Among the roses, guard.

—It could happen to anyone, God help us. Neither the day nor the hour do we know. The oddest thing, now, happened once to the sergeant's brother that's a journalist in Dublin. This particular day he's due to travel to Limerick City to report on a flower show. But he misses the train. So he sends a telegram to ask a reporter from another newspaper to keep him a carbon. Then he adjourns to pass the day in the upstairs lounge bar of the Ulster House. Along comes the Holy Hour as they call it for jokes, when the pubs of Dublin close for a while in the early afternoon. To break up the morning boozing parties, you understand. There's nobody in the lounge except the sergeant's brother and a strange man. So the manager locks them in there to drink in peace and goes off to his lunch. And exactly halfways through the Holy Hour the stranger drops down dead. Angina. And there's me man that should be at a flower show in Limerick locked in on a licensed premises, the Ulster House, during an off or illegal hour, with a dead man that he doesn't know from Adam.

—An interesting legal situation, guard.

—Oh it was squared, of course. The full truth about that couldn't be allowed out. It would be a black mark on the licence. The manager might lose his job.

—People might even criticise the quality of the drink.

—They might, sir. Some people can't be satisfied. Not that there was ever a bad drop sold in the Ulster House. Another cup, Mr. Macmahon, sir.

—Thank you, guard.

—She'll come back, Mr. Macmahon. Blood they say is thicker than water.

—They do say that, do they? Yet somehow, in spite of what they say, I don't think she'll be back.

On she went, leaping, flying, describing jaunty parabolas. He would, of course, have to send her money. She was entitled to something legally and he could well afford to be generous beyond what the law demanded.

—So the long-nosed lover died, guard, looking at the roses.

—In a manner of speaking, sir.

—Possibly the only man, guard, who ever had the privilege. Look thy last on all things lovely.

But the guard was not aware of De La Mare.

—That's what we'll say, sir. It would be best for all. His wife and all. And no scandal.

—Days of wine and roses, guard.

—Yes, sir. Alas, that we have nothing here but that half-bottle of Sandeman's port. She was a great lady to grow roses, sir. That's how they met in the beginning, she told me. Over roses.

WILD ROVER NO MORE

The day my sister turned Hannah the Saint from the door because she couldn't find a copper in the house to give her there was, as my mother herself would have said, a row that ten could fight in. It was a Saturday, and Saturdays my mother helped out in the dining-room of the White Hart, the town's best hotel, and also helped out with the family budget; and Friday was normally Hannah's begging day so that my sister and myself, housekeeping and eating fried potatoes off the same pan, were caught copperless and unawares. Fried potatoes never tasted so good eaten off smooth soulless plates as they did taken hot and succulent from the metal, and eating from the pan was more than eating. It was a tiptoe, breathless conflict over property, and territory: your pile, my pile, and keep your potatoes in your own part of the pan.

The door closed and Hannah was gone. The sister sat down opposite me, peeked sharply through wisps of dark hair that were for ever blinding her and coming between her and her food. She said: You robbed when my back was turned.

There was no use in lying to her. So I confessed: Four. Only four tiny ones.

She compensated herself, and with interest, by an expert flick of the fork. She said: Nothing smaller in the house than a florin and it's the only coin in the Catskill jug. I couldn't give Hannah the only florin we have. There'd be murder.

An American aunt home on holiday had left us the jug cut from the wood of a tree that had grown in Rip Van Winkle's mountains, and faithfully on the kitchen mantelpiece it housed the petty cash.

—Hannah's mad anyway, I said and thought that a florin would be sadly wasted on a poor woman, the wrinkles of her face lined with dirt, who hadn't the right use of her wits.

—She shouts out her prayers at the altar rails. She thinks she's the Blessed Virgin.

—Funny thing, my sister said, when I told her I had nothing to give her. She wrapped the dirty old brown shawl around her, as haughty and high and mighty as if she was queen of England. And do you know what she said?

—How would I know?

—How indeed and you busy robbing my fried potatoes? She said: Sara Alice, I see some people forget old times. Sara Alice, she said. She called me by mother's name. Isn't that odd? But I couldn't give her the only florin in the house. There'd sure as God be murder.

The sister was fourteen and old enough to take in at the pores a feeling of guilt from the encircling air even if she had no formed idea as to what she was feeling guilty about. We finished the fried potatoes in a gloomy foreboding silence and lived to learn there was reason for foreboding because, florin saved or florin given in charity, there was murder anyway.

Buttoned boots with shiny patent toes you could see your face in were then still the fashion for women over forty and my mother, casting an armful of parcels on the kitchen table, collapsed in her old rocking chair while the sister knelt and unbuttoned her boots and pushed her a wooden footstool on which she rested her heels and waggled her toes. On a market day the White Hart dining-room was no paradise for weakly insteps. She said: Gulders of rich farmers from as far away as Strabane shouting for steak and porter as if they were never fed at home.

Her spectacles had misted over with her breathlessness and the effort of carting all those parcels up the Courthouse Hill; and with her hair escaped from hat and hairpins and half-veiling her peeping eyes she waited and listened while my sister told her about Hannah, and wiped the lenses. She was so short-sighted that if she put the spectacles down on the table she couldn't find them again except by groping and the sense of touch. Rocking, she listened, and seemed to continue listening long after my sister's narrative ended, and in a silence that had grown ominously chill. Then suddenly she groped for the glasses as if by seeing she could hear and understand better. The rocking ceased. She rested her tired feet flat on the floor. She said with a calmness that was worse than a shout or the blow of a stick: God in his heaven, don't tell me you turned Hannah from the door without a copper ha'penny.

My sister was frightened and already almost on the edge of tears. She said pathetically: Only one florin in the Catskill jug.

—You should have given it to her. You should have given her the jug. You should have given her the house. Given her something. Eggs. Bread. A pot of marmalade. A cup of tea. But not to turn her from the door with one hand as empty as the other. Pray heaven, the roof doesn't fall on us this blessed night.

The sister was sobbing. My startled imagination saw Hannah like a mad witch of a Meg Merrilees kneeling down to pray prayers of doom on us and our ill-fated house collapsing like so much sand.

—Repeat after me the two of you, she said, God's poor must never be turned away empty.

We repeated the words, my sister in gulps and sobs, my voice shaking.

—Hannah's not only God's poor, my mother said. She's my poor.

We had no notion what she meant. Then my mother cried and cried and that was the most frightening thing of all.

We couldn't understand why she made such a fuss about Hannah except it was that Hannah was religious, and daft enough to think she was the mother of God. The brown wooden angels on the rafters high above the nave of the Sacred Heart Church always, I thought, looked down on the altar rail antics of Hannah with a special sort of disapproving interest. How anyone could so disrupt the holy silence and get away with it, none of us, the young, could ever comprehend. Yet neither angel nor parish priest nor pious parishioner ever protested. Hannah and Joe the Musician, who wasn't quite as outspoken, had the freedom of God's house.

Joe the Musician was stout, short, bald, wore winter and summer an abrased leather motoring coat, played the fiddle for relaxation, owned a small confectionery shop in River Lane, and when the Church was empty and often even during service and ceremony had a sort of roving commission on the epistle side of the nave. He was to be found anywhere between the marble rails and the dark alcove by the door where the baptismal font was. Usually he prayed in a sibilant but unintelligible whisper but in moments of special fervour his voice took sound and shape and the angels above could hear him demanding prosperity and customers in plenty for his wee shop.

—Isn't God good enough to him, we used to say, that he has a wee shop to pray for.

The Lord may have heard him or perhaps he was merely a subtle advertiser. The shop certainly prospered.

But Hannah in a corner of the altar rails half hidden on the gospel side, a close neighbour to the two pews full of black-robed brothers of the Christian Schools, was a fixed star. She had her own place and no one who knew would have knelt there, even when she was wandering the town or absent with her simple daughter in a cottage a mile away where she was less at home, I'd say, that when she was before the altar. She had picked that place possibly because the sunlight when it was good brought the gaudy Munich blues down to it with the intensity of a spotlight from the Lady's mantle spread wide on the window above the tabernacle. Hannah, unlike Joe, had no mundane interests, no appeals to make for prosperity. Her rosary beads two feet long and each bead as big as a horse-chestnut, rattled like stones against the altar rails. She waved her arms then, with the composure of a pompadour, resettled her shawl on her shoulders. Her prayers, breathless and loud, came out in fragments that meant nothing to nobody except herself and the person to whom they were addressed. But we could make out that she spoke of herself as Mary and talked again and again of a heart wounded and pierced. She prayed as she walked too, on the Courthouse Hill, on the High Street or on the mile of road to her cottage, and my sister, who was inclined to fancy, said the blue light from the window followed her.

Once she splattered a handful of holy water from the font at the church door over one of the town's richest and most respected citizens and told him he needed a blessing more than any soldier from the barracks to Calcutta. But apart from that one incident she walked unmolesting and unmolested. No running children mocked her or called her names. We feared her as we did not fear the dirty old giant of a tramp, Mickey Alone, whose true name might have been Malone. One day he gave me twopence to light his stub of a clay pipe but his head was shaking so much with bad drink that I singed the wiry hairs off the tip of his nose and he chased me with his stick and, with pride, I have been telling the story ever since. Or as we did not fear Andy Orr who lived with his mother Tilda in one of the white cottages in the Back Alley and who was the image of Charlie Chaplin enduring a dog's life, and whom I once saw, roaring with Finest Old Red Wine at a shilling a bottle, being frogmarched to the lockup by two sombre embarrassed constables. Or as we did not fear the street-singer, Hit-Him-in-the-Kisser-with-a-Navvy's-Boot-in-our-Backyard-last-night, who had earned the name because he sang for coppers a song with that curious refrain. He sang also a song about the gallant Forty-Twa and every loyal regiment under the King's command and the South Down militia who were the terror of the land. When he sang that song he paced up and down like a sentry and to simulate a rifle carried a broomstick at the present, and danced, too, at the end of each verse.

To call names to that trinity and be chased in return was fair game, spice for their lives as for ours. But Hannah in her blue light walked alone under the Lady's mantle, and my sister was so worried after the unfortunate affair of the florin that, for Hannah's intentions, she made the thirty days prayer to the Blessed Virgin, and met Hannah on the street one day and gave her two shillings she had saved. Hannah thanked her, using my mother's name again. That was still a mystery to us because my mother never talked about Hannah and on Fridays sent my sister or myself to the door with the weekly contribution.

In the house we lived in, a twisted stairway went up from the kitchen, and underneath the stairway was the dark cave, called in Scotland and Northern Ireland the logey-hole, a storehouse for brushes and polishing cloths and a den for children. Our next-door neighbour, a tailor and a fat one, obeying some impulse a few hundred thousand years older than himself or tailoring, sought refuge always in his logey hole in thunderstorms.

A year or so after the day of the florin, that secluded corner became of a sad morbid importance to my sister and myself. Our father had died suddenly. The funeral over, our three brothers and three sisters, all older than us, had gone back to their jobs in Belfast, Dublin, Liverpool, London, one brother, our hero, to the Inniskillings at Aldershot. After their going, the house on Saturdays was a painful place where every object from the Catskill jug to my father's wooden shaving bowl had a voice to remind us of the pain of loss. The darkness under the stairs had mercy in it. It seemed easier there to face up to the bewilderment of death, to accept that a hole in the ground in the graveyard on a green hill above the Drumragh River could be the brown gateway to a heaven in the clouds, and that when somebody you knew even so well as your father had gone to heaven you would see or hear him no more until you too had passed through that gateway.

Then one Saturday my sister went rope-skipping, apple, jelly, jam-tart, tell me the name of your sweetheart, with her girl friends, leaving me alone to mind the house, and in the cosy darkness I fell asleep and in my dream saw Hannah's cottage. It was a mile away on the western road from the town at a place we called the Flush. It stood on a low rocky hill fifty yards back from the road. It had one storey, one door, two tiny peeping windows, a roof of corrugated iron once painted red but long rains had streaked and stripped the paint. The place was called the Flush because a small stream came there out of meadowland, crossed the road boldly, not hiding under any bridge and curved off somewhere round Hannah's hill. In my dream the stream was in flood swelling into a torrent until it seemed as if it would swamp Hannah's house, and I could hear her voice complaining. Then I awoke and thought I was still dreaming because to my amazement she was out there in the kitchen talking to my mother.

—On Drumard Wood they crowned me Queen, she was saying. Do you recall those days, Sara Alice?

She sounded sane, yet talk of her being crowned as a queen fitted in as part of her altar-rail ravings, especially when she went on to sing in a cracked quavering voice: Oh Mary, we crown thee with blossoms today, queen of the angels and queen of the May.

—Three spoons, Hannah?

—Three spoons, Sara Alice. How well you remember I always had the sweet tooth.

—I'll never forget those days, my mother said.

Sipping tea, spoons tinkling, they were silent for a while.

—I came to sit with you, Sara Alice, in your sorrow.

—That was thoughtful of you, Hannah. Old friendship is old friendship.

Then Hannah spoke poetry as clearly and sensibly as the schoolmaster. She said: Make new friends but keep the old, those are silver, these are gold.

—But it wasn't May and it wasn't blossoms made the crown, my mother said. It was the last Sunday in July, or the first in August. The beginning of harvest and the first new potatoes. It was Garland Sunday. The young ones now never heard of it, Hannah. That pair of canaries of mine, supposed to be housekeeping. Absent without leave. Vanished without trace. Like the birds of the air. More tea, Hannah? Is it sweet enough?

—Sweet and strong the way you know I always liked it. Boys and girls together from three parishes and one small town up Drumard Hill to the hazel-wood and the open moor, all together dancing and singing.

She must have put her cup down and gone, holding out her shawl, in a twirl around the kitchen because my mother was laughing and saying Hannah should be on the stage and that she was as light on her feet as a lassie of sixteen.

—All together up the hill hand in hand, Sara Alice. Picking the bilberries from the little bushes hiding in the heather. Then every boy with thread to make a necklace of bilberries for his girl and the leading girl to be crowned queen with the heather, purple and white.

—White for true hearts, Hannah. Purple for passion.

We were all mad jealous the day Tommy came there a stranger and crowned you before all others. He was the finest man we ever saw. We all envied you. I was with him the first day you met him, Sara Alice. Very fine he looked in his good brown suit.

—You have the memory. You're not rambling now, Hannah.

Hannah was singing again. She sang: Ramble away, ramble away, are you the young man they call Ramble Away.

She said: That was a song the girls made about a sailor.

—It was a Holy Thursday, Hannah, and your mother, no better

woman ever to those that worked for her, was off to her devotions and I
was behind the hotel bar when in he stepped, dying on his feet with the
drink and looking for a cure of brandy and burgundy mixed. It was the
fashion then.

—He travelled with a crowd of wild men, Sara Alice.

—He was a wild man himself, said my mother.

—At that time he was, she added. A wild rover.

—It's all as clear as if it was yesterday, Hannah said. Tommy's death
when they told me and I saw the funeral going down the High Street
brought everything back to me, good and bad, grave and gay.

She was crying.

—Drink your tea, Hannah. There's sweet cake here I always get on
Saturday for the two canaries and since they're not here we'll demolish
it ourselves.

She spoke as a conspirator. Hannah, I felt, was wiping her eyes and
smiling. There went our sweet cake while I was hiding and my sister
skipping tell me the name of her sweetheart.

—Whiles, Sara Alice, sitting out there listening to the Flush and the
wind in the bushes and looking at my poor child I keep thinking long,
the afflicted pierced heart, remembering everything. Running out to the
hotel yard, all white-washed walls, and the tarred doors of the stables,
to see the sun on Easter Sunday dancing as he came over the trees
beyond the Fairywater.

—Master Reid, Hannah, that gave me the book of Robert Burns with
the poems marked in it I wasn't to look at used to say: Those who do
not care to face the bright orb with the naked eye may be content to
look at its image in a tub of clean water.

—Your eyes were always weak, Sara Alice.

—I gave him the brandy and burgundy, my mother said, and watched
the shake in his hand and the glass rattling off his teeth. A fine young
man, I said, are you not ashamed? Have you no religion on a holy
Thursday? No home, no parents?

—You were sharp, Sara Alice.

—Somebody had to be sharp. He cried there at the bar like a child.

—Drink and loneliness, Hannah said.

The sunny village street outside like a picture. Not saint or sinner to
be seen. They were all at the devotions.

—Drink and loneliness, Hannah repeated. But my, when he steadied
up we heard the stories. The tales of a wild rover. The black girls of the
Barbadoes. Nova Scotia and Newfoundland, and how he and Pat
O'Leary from Cork had planned to break out of the army and head for

the Klondyke, and how a patrol of the Dublin Fusiliers on the plains of Africa had fired all night at a waving bush.

My mother was laughing: The Dublins weren't used to country places and bushes, he said. There was never anybody like him to tell stories, true or false. You know, Hannah, he was thirty-five the day he wept over the brandy and burgundy and he hadn't seen home or father or mother since he was eighteen. I brought him back to them for a visit when we were married, not that his mother, the old battleaxe, ever gave me much thanks. The father wasn't too bad but he was as stiff as a ramrod and could never forgive the eighteen-year-old who had betrayed his trust as he called it, as if he owned the Bank of England and his son had mislaid the safe. Sending a boy from the Donegal Mountains to Dublin for the first time with a wallet of money to do a man's business. He saw Capetown before he ever saw Dublin and woke up drunk in the Royal Oak at Parkgate on the outskirts of the city with the money gone and the King's shilling in his fist and the uniform as good as on his shoulders. That was the way they joined the army in those days.

—Wild boys, wild men, said Hannah. Wild rovers. Fine men, but all unsettled by war and foreign places. Even the tinker men from Mayo fell short of them the night of the Lammas hiring fair. Ash plants against belt buckles and the buckles won.

—Discipline he used to say, Hannah, and overall stategy.

—Wandering Ireland, a bunch of old comrades, measuring it with chains to make a map for the King of England as if a map of his own country shouldn't satisfy him. The survey they called themselves, but we called them the sappers. They'd hunt you a mile for calling them sappers. There was great life at the dances when they came and the song they all sang together about the boy that listed in the army at the Curragh Camp because of a broken heart.

My mother spoke slowly then, touching each word as if it were a separate lovely thought: Straight will I repair to the Curragh of Kildare since my true love is absent from me.

—The great dances that we had, Sara Alice, in Langfield Hall. The big farmers' daughters who'd rub a tiny smear of cow dung on a new print frock so that the world would know their father grazed cattle. The dances in Brown's house.

—I preferred the dances in Brown's house, my mother said. They were more friendly and no strangers from the town. I remember one night the procession of ponies and traps in the moonlight along Brown's boreen, the two Clara lakes down in the flat bog, shining like the eyes of a giant. All along the boreen above Conn's Brae we went, and the hazel-woods where John Hart, the tea traveller, lost a wheel of his cart and had to chase it down a mile of woods and across the street before Big Mick Gormley's farmhouse to catch up with it in Big Mick's midden. John said the devil or the fairies were in that wheel. That night in the moonlight the whole convoy sang the song of the wild rover until the woods and hills rang.

Once again she spoke with that low wounded lingering on each word: I went into an alehouse, my money was done, and I asked the landlady to credit me some. She came trippingly to me and sweetly did say she could have as good customers as me any day. But now I've money plenty, money plenty in store, and I'll be the good boy and I'll play the wild rover no more.

—He stopped roving then, Sara Alice. He was a good man and dying about you.

—He'll rove no more ever, Hannah. Death ends all roving.

Then to my fear and horror my mother cried out in a voice I had never heard before, calling and listening for a while as if she expected an answer, and then calling again.

—Tommy, Tommy, Tommy, she cried three times.

All the long day of the funeral she had kept talking, and serving food and drink to all, and the bishop's bottle to the parish priest. She hadn't cried a tear.

—Hush, Sara Alice, hush, don't worry the dead. You were happy with him and he's happy now with God and his blessed mother. How lucky you were and all the parts of the world he might have wandered, to find him, even if he needed brandy and burgundy and a talking to about his holy religion. I was the spoilt child that my mother thought would wed the Prince of Wales and my lot was a rascal of a fancy man with talk for a dozen, and promising me the world, to leave me in beggary on the streets of Glasgow carrying a child that was never right with the fit of temperament I had when she was born.

—True, Hannah, you had it sad, said my mother.

Then as if her first wild cries had been answered she repeated softly: Tommy, Tommy.

After that they may have talked for an hour. In fear and agony I sat feeling guiltily that, with no right in the world, I had seen something naked and bleeding. In the darkness I cried silently for a sunny Thursday and a singing moonlit night I had never seen. My ears I held shut, and flapped my hands up and down over them, so that I'd hear not voices but the happy quacking of ducks, and I could see the ducks. When I quit that fantasy Hannah was gone and my sister was back breathless from trying to learn by leaping over a rope, apple, jelly, jam-tart, what would be the initials of her sweetheart. She said: Don't cry, mother. Are you crying for da?

—I miss him, Kathleen. But I'm not crying for him. He's happy in heaven. I'm crying for them that were happy once and are now neither in heaven nor on earth.

Sitting crying, she may have seen but paid no attention to my creeping forth from the cave.

Or under the earth, I thought, and recalled from the school catechism a satisfying piece of resonance about how every knee in heaven, on earth or under the earth, should bend to honour the Lord's name.

Hannah the Saint is now long with those who are under the earth and bend no knee. One day she walked home in the blue spotlight that followed her from far beyond Munich and found that the simple daughter had cut the heads off all her hens and chickens and was screaming about the place. So they took her away beyond the river which was our euphemism for the mental hospital on the far bank of the Drumragh, across the water from the dead who were happy in heaven on their green hill. Hannah when her time came died also beyond the river. The cottage by the Flush is gone, too, eaten up by a boa constrictor of a new motor-road that swept away bad corners and made straight the way for a faster world. The Flush itself, that once sparkled across the roadway and dared the traffic and was a boon to thirsty horses, rumbles somewhere through the darkness in the entrails of that monster.

A BOTTLE OF BROWN SHERRY

Mr. Edward came home from hospital on the second day of the second summer holidays we spent at Delaps of Monellen.

That was the year old John Considine, the stone mason, laid the black basalt flagged floor in the hallway of the hotel. While the work was going on the guests used a side-door so that old John, the craftsman, we, the four children, the only children allowed to holiday in that sedate house, and the stuffed brown bear, the ornamental organ that wasn't meant to play, and the framed photograph of the big bearded man leaning on a long rifle and with a dead antlered stag on his shoulders, had the hall all to ourselves. The big man in the picture had also, John told us, shot the bear. John, as he worked, told us an awful lot.

—There's nothing, he would say, like having a trade. Even if it's only cutting thistles.

He did not intend to belittle his own craft and, indeed, his old back arched with pride at his ability to lay the stones smoothly, gently as a mother would lay a child in a cot, on their bed of resilient red sand. Sand and stones came from the coast visible across parkland and over high trees from the top windows of Monellen; and so close that the dazzle of surf and sunshine could brighten the shade of the surrounding greenery, and on a morning after a night of gale, salt and sand blurred the window-panes.

John wore an old bowler hat that he doffed for nothing or nobody, not even for the queenly grandeur of Miss Grania Delap herself, and although his work had him bending and straightening, kneeling and rising again, the hat held its place like a confident cormorant riding one familiar wave. The local louts had nicknamed him Apey Appey for he was hairless from birth as a ha'penny apple, and he had turned his back on all organised religion because he felt embarrassed about taking his hat off in church.

But his round purple cheeks showed that he worshipped frequently and publicly in the seaside taverns. As he bent and worked he puffed the cheeks out comically and talked in spurts, not to himself, but to the stuffed bear, to the tall hunter in the picture, to the flagstones and—

although they were outside the house and too far away to hear him—to the three aproned servant-maids who, in sunny moments of leisure, took their sport on a swing under an oak tree in the centre of the lawn.

Once when he knelt at work a robin hopped, picking, in from the lawn and perched on his left heel, and he chatted to the robin, apologising in the end for the cramp that compelled him to move and unsettle his guest.

Of my twin brother and myself and our two sisters, also twins, he never seemed much aware, yet he never made us feel unwelcome. So we stayed with him and carried tools for him and tried to make out who and what he was talking to.

—Aren't you smooth now as a bottle of the best, and shiny black like a well-fed crow in a good harvest? Won't the visitors be coming in droves to see you?

That was his praise for one of the flagstones.

—Don't I smell the sea when I touch you, and see the cliffs you were quarried from? If it wasn't for you and your likes the ocean would be flowing over us, and nothing but fish in Monellen, instead of priests and doctors eating lobsters. Master Gerald there, with the stag on his back like a sack of meal, was the man for the cliffs, hail or shine, gale or calm. Up there, he said, he could expand his lungs like the Lord God. There'll be rich feet and fancy shoes stepping now on you that kept the ocean from flowing over us for so long. And the silver woman looking down on the miracle.

The silver woman was a decorative bare-breasted Juno who stood with her peacock on the top of the highest dead pipe of the mute ornamental organ.

—'Tis you has the youth in you. 'Tis you're soople.

Slowly, caressingly, he rubbed a stone with the palm of his hand, and could have been talking to the stone or to the bouncing blonde maid who led the others in her frolics on the swing.

The hind-legs of the dead stag were under the armpits of the hunter and pointing up. The fore-legs were over his shoulders and pointing down, and laced to the hind-legs. The antlered head leaned sadly backwards. In a strong thick-nibbed hand an inscription was written under the photograph. It read like this: Carrying a deer a few miles on one's back stimulates a glorious dinner appetite. Love from Brother Gerald and the Maple Leaf.

—Any man, John said, who would walk with that burden to work up an appetite would be liable to get married, no matter how much the family was set against it. Master Gerald, my man, you took all the strength with you the day Edward and yourself saw the light. 'Tisn't you they'd have to send like poor Edward to the doctors of Dublin to have things unknown injected into you.

Straightening up, stamping on a flag to test its steadiness, fixing with both hands the bowler more firmly on his head, he looked out at the bright lawn, the windy woods beyond, and said in a singsong to suit the rhythm of his feet: Swing, Nora Crowley, swing, you that never knew a father, with your hair as bright as the silver woman, and your mother before you that could swing like a branch in the wind.

The Misses Delap tolerated my father and mother bringing four children with them into that haven for elderly ladies, golfing clergymen and doctors, because the Misses Delap were also twins, and Mr. Edward and the absent hunter, Mr. Gerald, as well. The coincidence intrigued Miss Grania—as so well it might.

Miss Deirdre painted beautifully, we thought, and did an ivy spray on the dining-room overmantel so real that you would have thought it was growing there. She gave us large round sweets as big as billiard balls— they were called, and were, gob-stoppers—and allowed us to stand, as round-jawed as John Considine, but mute and sucking, in her attic studio while she copied old masters out of an art book. She was a gamey old dame in the attic and she taught my brother and myself how to wink, but anywhere lower down in the house she was only a silvery silent wraith. For while she might paint and wink it was Miss Grania bought the lobsters and was boss over all and, although they were twins, Grania seemed and behaved like the elder of the two.

Deirdre's hair was a pale natural silver but Grania, to emphasise her empery, had tinted her hair an assertive colour you might call red, anywhere except in the presence of cooked lobsters. Those morose, doomed-to-be-boiled-alive crustaceans weren't red, of course, when Donnelly from the harbour would tumble five or six of them out of a sack on to the floor of the big basement kitchen. They still wore the secretive colours of the sea and the rock clefts that had sheltered them in a former life, and no lost soul precipitated into eternity could have been more bewildered than they looked as they clacked helplessly on the floor and stared from outshot eyes at the advance of Grania. If they saw little else in their hell or their heaven they certainly saw her. For she brought with her the power of life and death, and she was, at any time, and particularly before her morning toilet, a sight to catch the eye—even of a lobster. She was a tall woman, taller than her twin or than Mr. Edward. Her tinted hair was stiff with metal curlers that, as old John once muttered, were like hedgehogs roasted in a burning bush.

Her face, black and yellow with wrinkles, was alarmingly different from the creamy mask it presented later in the day.

Touching a lobster smartly with her right foot, she would say: How now brown cow.

The high-heeled, golden-coloured shoes she wore for that ritual were never seen at any other time of the day, and it did seem to us that they were special shoes for touching and choosing lobsters.

—How now brown cow number two and three and four. Put the others back in the tanks, Donnelly, and give them a chance to repent.

To find themselves keeping guests for money was a comedown in the world for the Delaps. Miss Grania, not so much by direct words as by continuous tyranny, never allowed the guests to forget it. She talked often and with solemn authority about low prices for farm produce and the crushing burden of rates on the owners of landed property. The implication was that only for those two reasons no paying guest would ever have crossed the threshold of Monellen.

After high rates and low prices, the next worst thing in the degenerating world seemed to be afternoon tea.

—Quite the thing, she would say, for salesmen and their wives in commercial hotels, I'm told, but it was never the custom at Monellen.

So it was sherry or port and biscuits, or nothing at all, in the dreamy, tree-surrounded afternoons. My mother, though, seemed to be a privileged person, for when the maids were having their afternoon meal it was permitted for one of them to bring her tea in her bedroom. Perhaps that was because she was that year in an ailing and expectant condition, and Miss Grania may have hoped to coax by kindness another set of twins into the world. As it turned out, she didn't.

But old widowed Mrs. Nulty, who was eighty-five if she was a day, and whose brother was a bishop, had no such expectations and no such privileges. When at one ill-guided, dyspeptic lunch-time, she turned up her nose at a bread pudding made, with currants, by Miss Deirdre, the retribution descended on her—soft-spoken but relentless.

—So they tell me, Mrs. Nulty, you didn't like Miss Deirdre's bread pudding. Perhaps it would suit us mutually if next year we severed connections. There are, I'm told, many more up-to-date establishments in the village and on the sea-front.

The brother, the bishop himself, had to exert his ghostly influence to save Mrs. Nulty from banishment to Sea View or Ocean Lodge. His Christian name was Alexander and, if he ever had occasion to warm his hands at the drawing-room fire, he did so, standing at the side of the fireplace, and reaching out his fingertips, to the point almost of overbalancing, towards the flames. He wouldn't stand on the hearth-rug because he thought it was made of cat-skin and, like Lord Roberts of Pretoria and many a lesser man, he couldn't stand cats.

—But how little he knew, John Considine said, and all his learning. I snared the rabbits myself.

As you may see, Monellen was a place with its own character, and Grania Delap an undoubted unchallenged queen. Deirdre, in her arty attic, dabbled in oils and water-colours, but the image of Grania could only have been cast in bronze, one conquering foot on a lobster large as a turtle. One of my sisters—greatly daring—once put her foot on the pet tortoise in the garden and hoarsened her voice to say: How now brown cow. But the effect wasn't even funny, and the four of us afterwards glanced around nervously in fear of detection and banishment.

For Monellen was a happy enough place for a holiday—with good food, freedom, open parkland, a toy lake, miles of magic wood, and the stream beyond; and one of the most exciting things about it was that other dominant image, not bronze, but muscled, living oak and iron, that the mediumistic mutterings of John Considine brought forth from the picture of the hunter in the hallway. Here was a giant of a man who shot bears and stags and who once from his foreign travels had brought back with him a dangerous stockwhip with which he demonstrated, beheading daisies on the lawn at thirty paces, and making cracks that set the grazing horses on the far side of the lake galloping wild in terror.

When a boy he had, for a dare and by moonlight, gone climbing for rooks' eggs up one of the highest trees in the woods, only to find when he got to the top that the birds, more matured than he had imagined, began to caw, and some of them even flew away.

—He was so vexed, John said, it was a God's wonder he didn't sprout wings and take after them.

For another dare he went when he was fourteen through the night woods to a pub at the harbour where the trawlers tied up, and drank whiskey, John said, until it came out of his ears; and walked home sober. It seemed likely, indeed, that from an early age he had carried, if not stags, horned goats, at least, on his shoulders.

Insignificant in the shadow of that great image, Mr. Edward, back from hospital, shuffled about the house. John Considine told our father about the day in the winter when the two doctors, grey grave men, had stood over Edward and decided he needed hospital treatment.

—There they stood like two curers over a side of bacon. Smoke a bit here. Slice a bit there. Streaky in one place. Fat in another. They say in the Harbour Bar that Miss Grania sent him off to fit him for marrying to continue the line of the Delaps here in Monellen. Not that she was so pleased when the man in the picture there dirtied his bib out and out by marrying a foreign woman, as dark as these flagstones, and rearing the family in the heat of Africa; and he left the place to her and never faced home again. The Delaps when they kept at home were never much the marrying kind.

Our father's comment was: That reminds me of the woman who said that to have no children was hereditary in her family.

—But not all the doses or doctors in Dublin, John said.

He addressed himself again to his auditors, the stones, who never answered back or interpolated.

—Not all the doses or doctors in Dublin could make the poor sprissawn the man his brother was. A hunched little mouse of a man, creeping about in carpet slippers and apologising to the fresh air for taking liberties with it when he breathes. There does be an unholy difference in the natures of twins.

As if he was reading the future, he looked at the two of us morosely. Our sisters were upstairs having tea with our mother.

Then we all looked far away across the lawn where poor Edward, walking on a stick, mufflered and overcoated even in the sunshine, was going timid as a mole across the grass; and Nora Crowley, propelled by the pushes of the other laughing maids relaxing after their midday meal, was swinging, skirts fluttering, in a flying curve between grass and sky, her blonde hair bright against the dark green of the woods.

The day our sisters gave us the dare and we took it, the four of us were sitting concealed on the carpet of brown needles under a big Lebanon cedar on the fringe of the woods just beyond the swing. The tree made a tent around us. It was a windy sunny day. The maids had gone back to work. From our shelter we had peeped out at Edward on a garden seat, watching them at play, an open book fallen unheeded to the ground before him. Even when they had gone running and laughing away, he didn't bother to pick up the book. Then our father joined him and they talked. While our father had a sonorous rumble of a voice that, behind his red whiskers, rolled all words into one pleasant but meaningless sound, Mr. Edward had a cutting whining beep-beep that would carry each word distinctly to the moon. We only half listened to him because in taunting whispers under the cedar, the sisters were giving us the dare that implied that, even if we were in lands where they were to be found, we would never carry stags nor kill brown bears.

Mr. Edward said: Our lamented father often took the two of us, Gerald and myself, with him when he went to thin young plantations. It was an exhausting and exacting task under his leadership and surveillance. He expected us to be as good almost as he was himself. Gerald often was.

—Not even whiskey then, said Nora. Just a weeshy bottle of mangy abominable sherry.

She had tasted sherry once and simultaneously discovered the word abominable.

James had reasonably pointed out that we were too young, in these puny times, to be served with whiskey in the Harbour Bar. Things had been different in Mr. Gerald's days—or nights.

—Pale or brown, I said, just to be difficult.

—Mr. Gerald was different, said Nora just to be nasty.

—Wet or dry, mocked Kathleen. The two of you would be feared to go through the woods by night.

—We never used big axes, Mr. Edward said, only light hand implements made by Douglas McDonnell, the land steward.

—Why don't ye go yourselves?

—We're ladies.

—We know. Young ladies don't go out at night. They might wet their bloomers in the dew.

But when we had to descend to offensiveness we knew they had us beaten.

—Douglas McDonnell's wife did housekeeper and baked yeast bread, getting the yeast from a friend of hers who had a small brewery in Altnamona. When she heard her friend was dead her only comment was that now she would be ill-fixed for barm.

—We'll make it easy for ye, Nora said. You don't have to drink the sherry in the Harbour Bar. Bring the bottle back with ye to show ye were there.

—We'll help to drink it, Kathleen said.

But Nora said not her, because sherry was abominable.

Except in their differing about the desirability of sherry our two red-headed sisters were enzygotics or identical twins. We never tested their fingerprints, as we did our own, to find—insofar as, not being Scotland Yard men, we could read them—that the books could be right in saying that the coincident sequence of papillary ridge characteristics had never been found to agree even in uniovular twins.

They both married. They were certainly identical in their love of hellery. They worked as one woman in taunting us and egging us on.

We pretended to be boys from Ocean View sent down for the bottle of brown sherry for our father who was sick in bed with a cramp.

—A sufferer, said one man at the counter of the Harbour Bar, from the Ocean View six-day joint, old cow to cottage pie in six painful moves.

My brother was quick tongued. He said: No. It was last Friday's caviar gave him the heartburn.

Thanks to his wit, our exit from the pub, clutching the bottle, was on a flowing tide of appreciative kindly laughter, and not as shamefaced as it might have been. Yet it was not the exit of a young hero who had drunk whiskey until it came out of his ears and was still sailing on a steady keel.

In that windy August of sudden squalls the dinghies moored in the harbour jumped and tossed their heels on the full turbulent tide, like hairy Connemara ponies restless at a fair. The moon leaped to drown into racing clouds, then surfaced again with a bound and a brightness that made us feel the whole world was watching ourselves and our sinful bottle. So, to hide from its silver revelations, and for the general mystery of the thing, we made the first stages of the return journey by what we called the Secret Passage. There was nothing very secret about it. It was merely a narrow sunken roadway that went inland from east to west across Monellen land to the village of Altnamona, following a right of way that the village people had used, since God knew when, as a short-cut to the shore for shellfish or seaweed for manure, or to dig the succulent sand-eels from the wide white strand when the spring tides had ebbed and the moon was full. Three stone bridges carried over it the private roads generations of Delaps had driven on. We walked steadily in silence and shadow, and were, to be honest, more than a little out of breath with fear. I carried the bottle. Like a stick in the fist it was comfort and company.

—I don't mind the nights, said James, if it's windy.

For he felt and I with him, that no evil thing could be abroad on a night when the wind bellowed so heartily and the moon and clouds played chasing games; and the sound of the orchestra of wind and swaying branches blotted out those subtle, unnerving, unidentifiable sounds that woods and the creatures in them make on calm nights. When we climbed up by the winding steps of an old belvedere to the main avenue, and saw the house, white in moonlight and distance, a curious exhilaration had conquered our fear. Afterwards, on long talk and reflection, we realised we had been possessed. Tall pines and cypresses lined the avenue, gracefully holding back two hunch-backed hordes of red oaks. One of the pines, leaning and sailing with the wind, must have been the highest tree in the world. We looked up, and the tip of it touched and pierced the moon, and at the moment of contact James said: To hell with those girls. We'll kill the sherry.

We were thirteen years apiece and not exactly novices. We had sampled on the sly everything we found at home in sideboard or undrained glass. As altar boys in the parish church we had nipped at the altar wine. Once, too, after a hasty gulp of whiskey James claimed that he had had in the bathroom the most comical double vision.

At my second gulp of the grocer's sherry I made a measured statement about the superiority of altar wine.

James was barking like a dog at the still impaled moon.

—Sure as God, he said, that was the tree he went up for the rooks' eggs.

—It tastes bloody, I said, but at least it's warm, and what better could you hope for from the Harbour Bar?

—Show me a bear and I'll shoot it and stuff it, he shouted. Show me a stag and I'll carry it to Miss Grania. How now brown cow?

He stamped his feet like a dancing Indian and howled into the blustery warm wind. We wrestled for the last drop of the brown sherry, and he had it and drank it, and tossed the bottle off spinning to some place where it fell in silence. We ran round and round in circles shouting about bears and lobsters, brown cows and stags. Then, James leading, we climbed the tree.

We went up easily into the light, regularly spaced branches as convenient as the rungs of a ladder. It was a comfortable tree to climb and for a while the swaying motion had a most comfortable effect on bellies warm with the cheap rough wine. Patterns of light and shadow, of pasture, tilled fields, woods, laid themselves out below us; and the lake was a glittering circle. Heads in the wild clouds, we turned dazzled eyes from the moon, and rested at the top of the tree, looked down at the lake and saw the moon again, and saw the sight, and thought at first that we were mad in the head with drink.

In days before the Delaps had made money in milling and bought the land, some eighteenth-century lord had brought from London a wandering Italian to plan that lake and the gazebo beside it. In classical afternoons, the lord and his ladies and friends would have been at their ease on the flat, tiled, octagonal roof. There now, in their space, on a stone seat was Mr. Edward, as many overcoats on him as an onion, his head bent, his mouth to the nipple of a living enlarged Juno who had stepped down, leaving her peacock behind her, from the organ in the hallway: of Nora Crowley, before God, that never knew a father, and her mother before her that could swing like a branch in the wind, and not a coat in the world on her, or a rag at all higher than her belly button.

She was laughing and tossing her blonde hair back, and pretending to push him away. Hunched with the weight of his coats he was trotting after her round and round the octagon. They were back again at the stone seat. He was kneeling before her and cutting all sorts of capers. They were circling the roof again. We could hear nothing except the wind but we could see that she was still laughing. We laughed a little ourselves, but in sadness and mystery, because we felt sorry for Edward who had never frightened horses with a stockwhip. Yet we would have gone on watching, held by the night of wind and moon and by those antics that seemed to be part of it, if our father's voice hadn't bellowed up at us from the avenue: Come down, you misbegotten monkeys. Come down, you niggering night-owls. What games are you playing up there?

Juno, startled by mistake, vanished with a whisk, like a fish frightened from a clear pool into the shelter of reeds and rocks. Poor many-coated slow-moving Edward was left alone on the eighteenth-century octagon. We looked down into gloom and shadow, and the sherry settled, and our stomachs turned over at the prospect of descending, feet feeling for dark branches, to explain to our father where we had been and what we had been doing on the top of the tree.

—Bird-nesting, said James. Remember we were bird-nesting. For owls' eggs.

I repeated queasily: Bird-nesting.

The thought of soft eggs made me feel ill.

—Go carefully, my father bawled. Don't break your necks.

No cautionary words were needed. We were sick and shivering, and most anxious about our necks. The tree below us was the pit of darkness. When we stepped painfully from the lowest branches, and I opened my mouth to talk about bird-nesting for owl's eggs, release of tension struck me like a kick in the ribs and out came the sherry, not, alas, through my ears and a little the worse for wear. It spattered the grass and pine needles at my father's feet.

—Arboreal activities by moonlight, he was beginning to say.

The woods stank of sour wine.

—Lord God what a reek, he said. Come home quick and wash your teeth before you put me off the drink for life.

The idea seemed to amuse him. So James, always an opportunist, snatched the chance of the moment to rattle out a doctored description of the sight we had seen while bird-nesting.

—He was sitting with Nora Crowley on the bench on the gazebo.

—By God and was he? By the bright silvery light of the moon. And what would he be at there?

—He had his arm round her and he was kissing her.

—Oh, sound man. Begod modern medicine can work the wonders.

He laughed a little, just as we had, and then stopped laughing. He said, half to himself: Get married or something quickly the four of you, and don't end up lost like poor Edward.

Absent-mindedly, and with a friendly thump apiece on the shoulder-blades he left us at the foot of the back-stairs and we knew that he had, in private, to tell our mother all about it, and that there wouldn't be much more said about where the sherry that had bespattered the pine needles had come from.

Our sisters thought it the joke of the world when we told them precisely what Mr. Edward had been kissing.

—Like a baby, they said.

And there were no secrets, not even the moon's secrets, to be kept from bald John Considine. On his knees, smoothing the listening flagstones, he would go off into fits of shrill giggles and mutters which we, most efficient receiving sets, caught and elucidated: A bottle of brown sherry for two bad boys and a doll to play with for the third. They'll have to send him to the Dublin doctors again to have something else done to him to keep him in the house at night. Anyway, 'twas like the casting of a spell, 'twas the magic of having too many twins about the one house. 'Twas enough to bring Mr. Gerald back over the seas to take possession of the place he owned. Wasn't there a man in Altnamona who talked like a Russian although he was never outside the parish?

So the hunter, we heard, had come back from Africa, or wherever he was, or stepped, stag on shoulders, out of the picture in the hallway, to walk in the stormy moonlit woods. We had more fellow feeling than ever for Edward because we knew that he wasn't the only man, on that night of gale and running moon, to be possessed by his brother's spirit. It was more than sherry had sent us climbing, and it was something more than our own efforts that had brought us safely down into darkness from the remote top of that tree.

When, at art in the attic, we asked Miss Deirdre about Mr. Gerald, she wept a little tear and told us she often tried to get in touch with him by clairvoyance or telekinesis. She explained to us about clairvoyance and telekinesis. She said: You may think it impossible with your harsh practical young minds. But I assure you children that I have in my time seen some very remarkable things. When we were at Dover once there was a lady who had a crystal. This colonel asked her about his son who was somewhere at sea, out China way. The lady described him as having or not having a moustache, whichever was wrong, and said he was cleaning a bicycle. They thought this was a poor show. But shortly afterwards the colonel got a letter with a photograph showing his son either with or without a moustache, whichever the lady had said, and saying that as they were near port, and as he had heard the roads were good in China, he hoped to get a run on his bicycle. Then another lady whose husband was in South Africa was told by the lady with the crystal that her husband was on a pile of boxes in a lake. This, of course, sounded most unlikely, but the lady heard by the next post that there had been a cloudburst, and the only dry place he could get to sit on was a pile of empty ammunition cases . . .

She talked on for a long time.

Grania of the Lobsters, though, was a sceptic, and next year, summarily dismissed, swinging Nora Crowley was gone forever from Monellen.

GOD'S OWN COUNTRY

The plump girl from Cork City who was the editor's secretary came into the newsroom where the four of us huddled together, and said, so rapidly that we had to ask her to say it all over again: Goodness gracious, Mr. Slattery, you are, you really are, smouldering.

She was plump and very pretty and enticingly perfumed and every one of the four of us, that is everyone of us except Jeremiah, would have been overjoyed to make advances to her except that, being from Cork City, she talked so rapidly that we never had time to get a word in edgeways. She said: Goodness gracious, Mr. Slattery, you are, you really are, smouldering.

Now that our attention had been drawn to it, he really was smouldering. He sat, crouched as close as he could get to the paltry coal fire: the old ramshackle building, all rooms of no definable geometrical shape, would have collapsed with Merulius Lacrymans, the most noxious form of dry rot, the tertiary syphilis of ageing buildings, if central heating had ever been installed. Jeremiah nursed the fire between his bony knees. He toasted, or tried to toast, his chapped chilblained hands above the pitiful glow. The management of that small weekly newspaper were too mean to spend much money on fuel; and in that bitter spring Jeremiah was the coldest man in the city. He tried, it seemed, to suck what little heat there was into his bloodless body. He certainly allowed none of it to pass him by so as to mollify the three of us who sat, while he crouched, working doggedly with our overcoats and woollen scarves on. The big poet who wrote the cinema reviews, and who hadn't been inside a cinema since he left for a drink at the intermission in *Gone With The Wind* and never went back, was typing, with woollen gloves on, with one finger; and for panache more than for actual necessity he wore a motor-cycling helmet with fleece-lined flaps over his ears. The big poet had already told Jeremiah that Jeremiah was a raven, a scrawny starved raven, quothing and croaking nevermore, crumpled up there in his black greatcoat over a fire that wouldn't boil an egg. Jeremiah only crouched closer to the fire and, since we knew how cold he always was, we left him be and forgot all about him, and he might well have gone on fire, nobody, not even himself, noticing, if the plump pretty secretary, a golden perfumed ball hopping from the parlour into the hall, hadn't bounced, warming the world, being the true honey of delight, into the room.

It was the turned-up fold of the right leg of his shiny black trousers. He extinguished himself wearily, putting on, to protect the fingers of his right hand, a leather motoring-gauntlet. He had lost, or had never possessed, the left-hand gauntlet. He moved a little back from the fire, he even tried to sit up straight. She picked up the telephone on the table before me. Her rounded left haunch, packed tightly in a sort of golden cloth, was within eating distance, if I'd had a knife and fork. She said to the switch that she would take that call now from where she was in the newsroom. She was silent for a while. The golden haunch moved ever so slightly, rose and fell, in fact, as if it breathed. She said: Certainly, your Grace.

—No, your Grace.

—To the island, your Grace.

—A reporter, your Grace.

—Of course, your Grace.

—And photographer, your Grace.

—An American bishop, your Grace.

—How interesting, your Grace.

—Confirmation, your Grace.

—All the way from Georgia, your Grace.

—Goodness gracious, your Grace.

—Lifeboat, your Grace.

—Yes, your Grace.

—No, your Grace.

—Next Thursday, your Grace.

—I'll make a note of it, your Grace.

—And tell the editor when he comes in from the nunciature, your Grace.

The nunciature was the place where the editor, promoting the Pope's wishes by promoting the Catholic press, did most of his drinking. He had a great tongue for the Italian wine.

—Lifeboat, your Grace.

—Absolutely, your Grace.

—Goodbye, your Grace.

The big poet said: That wouldn't have been His Grace you were talking to?

—That man, she said, thinks he's three rungs of the ladder above the Pope of Rome and with right of succession to the Lord himself.

She made for the door. The gold blinded me. She turned at the door, said to us all, or to three of us: Watch him. Don't let him make a holocaust of himself. Clean him up and feed him. He's for the Islands of the West, Hy-Breasil, the Isle of the Blest, next Thursday with the Greatest Grace of all the Graces, and a Yankee bishop who thinks it would do something for him to bestow the holy sacrament of confirmation on the young savages out there. Not that it will do much for them. It would take more than two bishops and the Holy Ghost. . .

She was still talking as she vanished. The door crashed shut behind her and the room was dark again, and colder than ever. Jeremiah was visibly shuddering, audibly chattering, because to his bloodlessness and to the chill of the room and of the harsh day of east wind, had been added the worst cold of all: terror.

—Take him out, the big poet said, before he freezes us to death. Buy him a hot whiskey. You can buy me one when I finish my column.

As he tapped with one gloved finger and, with a free and open mind and no prejudice, critically evaluated what he had not seen, he also lifted up his voice and sang: When the roses bloom again down by yon river, and the robin redbreast sings his sweet refrain, in the days of auld lang syne, I'll be with you sweetheart mine, I'll be with you when the roses bloom again.

In Mulligan's in Poolbeg Street, established 1782, the year of the great Convention of the heroic patriotic Volunteers at Dungannon when the leaders of the nation, sort of, were inspired by the example of American Independence, I said to Jeremiah: Be a blood. Come alive. Break out. Face them. Show them. Fuck the begrudgers. Die, if die you must, on your feet and fighting.

He said: It's very well for you to talk. You can eat.

—Everybody, for God's sake, can eat.

—I can't eat. I can only nibble.

—You can drink, though. You have no trouble at all with the drink.

His first hot whiskey was gone, but hadn't done him any good that you'd notice.

—Only whiskey, he said, and sometimes on good days, stout. But even milk makes me ill, unless it's hot and with pepper sprinkled on it.

I pretended to laugh at him, to jolly him out of it, yet he really had me worried. For he was a good helpless intelligent chap, and his nerves had gone to hell in the seminary that he had had to leave, and the oddest rumours about his eating or non-eating habits were going around the town. That, for instance, he had been seen in a certain hotel, nibbling at biscuits left behind by another customer, and when the waiter, who was a friend of mine, asked him in all kindness did he need lunch, he had slunk away, the waiter said, like a shadow that had neither substance nor sunshine to account for its being there in the first place. He was no man, I had to agree, to face on an empty stomach a spring gale, or even a half or a hatful of a gale, on the wild western Atlantic coast.

—And the thought of that bishop, he said, puts the heart across me. He's a boor and a bully of the most violent description. He's a hierarchical Genghis Khan.

—Not half as bad as he's painted.

—Half's bad enough.

So I told some story, once told to me by a Belfast man, about some charitable act performed by the same bishop. It didn't sound at all convincing. Nor was Jeremiah convinced.

—If he ever was charitable, he said, be sure that it wasn't his own money he gave away.

—You won't have to see much of him, Jeremiah. Keep out of his path. Don't encounter him.

—But I'll encounter the uncandid cameraman who'll be my constant companion. With his good tweeds and his cameras that all the gold in the mint wouldn't buy. How do the mean crowd that run that paper ever manage to pay him enough to satisfy him? He invited me to his home to dinner. Once. To patronise me. To show me what he had and I hadn't. He ran out six times during dinner to ring the doorbell, and we had to stop eating and listen to the chimes. A different chime in every room. Like living in the bloody belfry. Searchlights he has on the lawn to illuminate the house on feast-days. Like they do in America, I'm told. Letting his light shine in the uncomprehending darkness. Some men in this town can't pay the electricity bill, but he suffers from a surplus. And this bishop is a friend of his. Stops with him when he comes to town. His wife's uncle is a monsignor in His Grace's diocese. Practically inlaws. They call each other by their Christian names. I was permitted and privileged to see the room the bishop sleeps in, with its own special bathroom, toilet seat reserved for the episcopal arse, a layman would have to have his arse specially anointed to sit on it. Let me tell you that it filled me with awe. When they have clerical visitors, he told me, they couldn't have them shaving in the ordinary bathroom. I hadn't the courage to ask him was there anything forbidding that in Canon Law, Pastoral Theology or the Maynooth Statutes. God look down on me between the two of them, and an American bishop thrown in for good luck. They say that in the United States the bishops are just bigger and more brutal.

—Jeremiah, I said severely, you're lucky to be out with that cameraman. He'll teach you to be a newsman. Just study how he works. He can smell news like, like . . .

The struggle for words went on until he helped me out. He was quick-witted; and even on him the third hot whiskey was bound to have some effect: to send what blood there was in his veins toe-dancing merrily to his brain.

—Like a buzzard smells dead meat, he said.

Then the poet joined us. Having an inherited gift for cobbling he had recently cobbled for himself a pair of shoes but, since measurement was not his might, they turned out to be too big even for him, thus, for any mortal man. But he had not given up hope of encountering in a public bar some Cyclopean for whose benefit he had, in his subconscious, been working, and of finding him able and willing to purchase those shoes. He carried them, unwrapped, under his arm. They always excited comment; and many were the men who tried and failed to fill them. That night we toured the town with them, adding to our company, en route, an Irish professor from Rathfarnham, a French professor from Marseilles, a lady novelist, a uniformed American soldier with an Irish name, who came from Boston and General Patch's army which had passed by Marseilles and wrecked it in the process. Outside Saint Vincent's hospital in Saint Stephen's Green a total stranger, walking past us, collapsed. He was a very big man, with enormous feet. But when the men from Boston and Marseilles, and the poet and myself, carried him into the hospital he was dead.

All that, as you are about to observe, is another story.

We failed, as it so happened, to sell the shoes.

On that corner of the western coast of Ireland the difference between a gale and a half-gale is that in a half-gale you take a chance and go out, in a gale you stay ashore.

The night before the voyage they rested in a hotel in Galway City. The wind rattled the casements and now and again blew open the door of the bar in which Jeremiah sat alone, until well after midnight, over one miserable whiskey. Nobody bothered to talk to him, not even in Galway where the very lobsters will welcome the stranger. The bar was draughty. He wore his black greatcoat, a relic of his clerical ambitions. It enlarged his body to the point of monstrosity, and minimised his head. Dripping customers came and drank and steamed and went again. When the door blew open he could see the downpours of rain hopping like hailstones on the street. The spluttering radio talked of floods, and trees blown down, and crops destroyed, and an oil-tanker in peril off the

Tuskar Rock. The cameraman had eaten a horse of a dinner, washed it down with the best wine, said his prayers and gone to bed, to be, he said, fresh and fit for the morning. Jeremiah was hungry, but less than ever could he eat: with fear of the storm and of the western sea as yet unseen and of the bull of a bishop and, perhaps too, he thought, that visiting American would be no better. At midnight he drained his glass dry and afterwards tilted it several times to his lips, drinking, or inhaling, only wind. He would have ordered another whiskey but the bar was crowded by that time, and the barman was surrounded by his privileged friends who were drinking after hours. The wind no longer blew the door open for the door was double-bolted against the night. But the booming, buffeting and rattling of the storm could still be heard, at times bellowing like a brazen bishop, threatening Jeremiah. The customers kept coming and crowding through a dark passage that joined the bar and the kitchen. They acted as if they had spent all day in the kitchen and had every intention of spending all night in the bar. Each one of them favoured Jeremiah with a startled look where he sat, black, deformed by that greatcoat, hunched-up in his black cold corner. Nobody joined him. He went to bed, to a narrow, hard, excessively-white bed with a ridge up the middle and a downward slope on each side. The rubber hot-water bottle had already gone cold. The rain threatened to smash the window-panes. He spread his greatcoat over his feet, wearing his socks in bed, and, cursing the day he was born, fell asleep from sheer misery.

Early next morning he had his baptism of salt water, not sea-spray but rain blown sideways and so salty that it made a crust around the lips.

—That out there, said the cameraman in the security of his car, is what they call the poteen cross.

The seats in the car were covered with a red plush, in its turn covered by a protective and easily-washable, transparent plastic that Jeremiah knew had been put there to prevent himself or his greatcoat or his greasy, shiny pants from making direct contact with the red plush.

—Did you never hear of the poteen cross?

—No, said Jeremiah.

They had stopped in a pelting village on the westward road. The doors were shut, the windows still blinded. It was no morning for early rising. The sea was audible, but not visible. The rain came bellying inshore on gusts of wind. On a gravelled space down a slope towards the sound of the sea stood a huge bare black cross: well, not completely bare for it carried, criss-crossed, the spear that pierced, that other spear that bore aloft the sponge soaked in vinegar; and it was topped by a gigantic crown of thorns. The cameraman said: When the Redemptorist Fathers preached hellfire against the men who made the poteen, they ordered the moonshiners, under pain of mortal sin, to come here and leave their stills at the foot of the cross. The last sinner to hold out against them came in the end with his still but, there before him, he saw a better model that somebody else had left, so he took it away with him. There's a London magazine wants a picture of that cross.

—It wouldn't, said Jeremiah, make much of a picture.

—With somebody beside it pointing up at it, it wouldn't be so bad. The light's not good. But I think we could manage.

—We, said Jeremiah.

—You wouldn't like me, he said, to get up on the cross? Have you brought the nails?

He posed, nevertheless, and pointed up at the cross. What else could he do? We saw the picture afterwards in that London magazine. Jeremiah looked like a sable bloated demon trying to prove to benighted sinners that Christ was gone and dead and never would rise again. But it was undeniably an effective picture. Jeremiah posed and pointed. He was salted and sodden while the cameraman, secure in yellow oilskins and sou'wester, darted out, took three shots, darted in again, doffed the oilskins, and was as dry as snuff. They drove on westwards.

—That coat of yours, said the cameraman. You should have fitted yourself out with oilskins. That coat of yours will soak up all the water from here to Long Island.

—Stinks a bit too, he said on reflection. The Beeoh is flying.

That was meant to be some sort of a joke and, for the sake of civility, Jeremiah tried to laugh. They crossed a stone bridge over a brown-and-white, foaming, flooded river, turned left down a byroad, followed the course of the river, sometimes so close to it that the floodwater lapped the edge of the road, sometimes swinging a little away from it through a misted landscape of small fields, thatched cabins dour and withdrawn in the storm, shapeless expanses of rock and heather, until they came to where the brown-and-white water tumbled into the peace of a little land-locked harbour. The lifeboat that, by special arrangement, was to carry the party to the island was there, but no lifeboatmen, no party. A few small craft lay on a sandy slope in the shelter of a breakwater. Jeremiah and the cameraman could have been the only people alive in a swamped world. They waited: the cameraman in the car with the heat on; Jeremiah, to get away from him for a while, prowling around empty cold sheds that were, at least, dry, but that stank of dead fish and were floored with peat-mould terrazzoed, it would seem, by fragments broken from many previous generations of lobsters. Beyond the breakwater and a rocky headland the sea boomed, but the water in the sheltered harbour was smooth and black as ink. He was hungry again but knew that if he had food, any food other than dry biscuits, he wouldn't be able to eat it. All food now would smell of stale fish. He was cold, as always. When he was out of sight of the cameraman he pranced, to warm himself, on peat-mould and lobsters. He was only moderately successful. But his greatcoat, at least, steamed.

The rain eased off, the sky brightened, but the wind seemed to grow in fury, surf and spray went up straight and shining into the air beyond the breakwater, leaped it and came down with a flat slap on the sandy slope and the sleeping small craft. Then, like Apache on an Arizona skyline, the people began to appear: a group of three, suddenly, from behind a standing rock; a group of seven or eight rising sharply into sight on a hilltop on the switchback riverside road, dropping out of sight into a hollow, surfacing again, followed by other groups that appeared and disappeared in the same disconcerting manner. As the sky cleared, the uniform darkness breaking up into bullocks of black wind-goaded clouds, the landscape of rock and heather, patchwork fields divided by grey, high, drystone walls, came out into the light; and from every small farmhouse thus revealed, people came, following footpaths, crossing stiles, calling to each other across patches of light green oats and dark-green potatoes. It was a sudden miracle of growth, of human life appearing where there had been nothing but wind and rain and mist. Within three-quarters of an hour there were a hundred or more people around the harbour, lean hard-faced fishermen and small farmers, dark-haired laughing girls, old women in coloured shawls, talking Irish, talking English, posing in groups for the cameraman who in his yellow oilskins moved among them like a gigantic canary. They waved and called to Jeremiah where he stood, withdrawn and on the defensive, in the sheltered doorway of a fish-stinking shed.

A black Volkswagen came down the road followed by a red Volkswagen. From the black car a stout priest stepped forth, surveyed the crowd like a general estimating the strength of his mustered troops, shook hands with the cameraman as if he were meeting an old friend. From the red car a young man stepped out, then held the door for a gaunt middle-aged lady who emerged with an effort, head first: the local school-teachers, by the cut of them. They picked out from the crowd a group of twelve to twenty, lined them up, backs to the wall, in the shelter of the breakwater. The tall lady waved her arms and the group began to sing.

—Ecce sacerdos magnus, they sang.

A black limousine, with the traction power of two thousand Jerusalem asses on the first Holy Thursday, came, appearing and disappearing, down the switchback road. This was it, Jeremiah knew, and shuddered. On the back of an open truck behind the limousine came the lifeboatmen, all like the cameraman, in bright yellow oilskins.

—This is God's own country, said the American bishop, and ye are God's own people.

Jeremiah was still at a safe distance, yet near enough to hear the booming clerical-American voice. The sea boomed beyond the wall. The spray soared, then slapped down on the sand, sparing the sheltered singers.

—Faith of our fathers, they sang, living still, in spite of dungeon, fire and sword.

Circling the crowd the great canary, camera now at ease, approached Jeremiah.

—Get with it, Dracula, he said.

He didn't much bother to lower his voice.

—Come out of your corner fighting. Get in and get a story. That Yank is news. He was run out of Rumania by the Communists.

—He also comes, said Jeremiah, from Savannah, Georgia.

—So what?

—He doesn't exactly qualify as a Yankee.

—Oh Jesus, geography, said the cameraman. We'll give you full marks for geography. They'll look lovely in the paper where your story should be. If he came from bloody Patagonia, he's here now. Go get him.

Then he was gone, waving his camera. The American bishop, a tall and stately man, was advancing, blessing as he went, to the stone steps that went down the harbour wall to the moored lifeboat. He was in God's own country and God's own people, well-marshalled by the stout parish priest, were all around him. The Irish bishop, a tall and stately man, stood still, thoughtfully watching the approaching cameraman and Jeremiah most reluctantly plodding in the rear, his progress, to his relief, made more difficult by the mush of wet peat-mould underfoot, growing deeper and deeper as he approached the wall where sailing hookers were loaded with fuel for the peatless island. Yet, slowly as he moved, he was still close enough to see clearly what happened and to hear clearly what was said.

The bishop, tall and stately and monarch even over the parish priest, looked with a cold eye at the advancing cameraman. There was no ring kissing. The bishop did not reach out his hand to have his ring saluted. That was odd, to begin with. Then he said loudly: What do you want?

—Your Grace, said the great canary.

He made a sort of a curtsey, clumsily, because he was hobbled in creaking oilskins.

—Your Grace, he said, out on the island there's a nonagenarian, the oldest inhabitant, and when we get there I'd like to get a picture of you giving him your blessing.

His Grace said nothing. His Grace turned very red in the face. In increased terror, Jeremiah remembered that inlaws could have their tiffs and that clerical inlaws were well known to be hell incarnate. His Grace right-about-wheeled, showed to the mainland and all on it a black broad back, right-quick-marched towards the lifeboat, sinking to the ankles as he thundered on in the soft wet mould, but by no means abating his speed which could have been a fair five miles an hour. His long coat-tails flapped in the wind. The wet mould fountained up like snow from a snow-plough. The sea boomed. The spray splattered. The great canary had shrunk as if plucked. Jeremiah's coat steamed worse than ever in the frenzy of his fear. If he treats his own like that, he thought, what in God's holy name will he do to me? Yet he couldn't resist saying: That man could pose like Nelson on his pillar watching his world collapse.

The canary cameraman hadn't a word to say.

Once aboard the lugger the bishops had swathed themselves in oilskins provided by the lifeboat's captain, and the cameraman mustered enough of his ancient gall to mutter to Jeremiah that that was the first time that he or anybody else had seen canary-coloured bishops.

—Snap them, said Jeremiah. You could sell it to the magazines in Bucharest. Episcopal American agent turns yellow.

But the cameraman was still too crestfallen, and made no move, and clearly looked relieved when the Irish bishop, tall and stately even if a little grotesque in oilskins, descended carefully into the for'ard foxhole, sat close into the corner, took out his rosary beads and began to pray silently: he knew the tricks of his western sea. Lulled by the security of the land-locked sheltered harbour, the American bishop, tall and stately even if a little grotesque in oilskins, stood like Nelson on the foredeck. He surveyed the shore of rock, small fields, drystone walls, small thatched farmhouses, oats, potatoes, grazing black cattle, all misting over for more rain. Then he turned his back on the mainland and looked at the people, now marshalled all together by the parish priest and the two teachers in the lee of the harbour wall. The choir sang: Holy God, we praise thy name. Lord of all, we bow before thee.

An outrider of the squall of rain that the wind was driving inshore cornered cunningly around harbour wall and headland, and disrespectfully spattered the American bishop. Secure in oilskins and the Grace of state he ignored it. The cameraman dived into the stern foxhole. Jeremiah by now was so sodden that the squall had no effect on him. An uncle of his, a farmer in the County Longford, had worn the same heavy woollen underwear winter and summer and argued eloquently that what kept the heat in kept it out. That soaking salty steaming greatcoat could, likewise, stand upright on its own against the fury of the Bay of Biscay. It was a fortress for Jeremiah; and with his right hand, reaching out through the loophole of the sleeve, he touched the tough stubby oaken mast, a talismanic touch, a prayer to the rooted essence of the earth to protect him from the capricious fury of the sea. Then with the bishop, a yellow figurehead, at the prow, and Jeremiah, a sable figurehead, at the stern, they moved smoothly towards the open ocean; and, having withdrawn a little from the land, the bishop raised his hand, as Lord Nelson would not have done, and said: This is God's own country. Ye are God's own people.

The choir sang: Hail Glorious Saint Patrick, dear Saint of our isle.

From the conscripted and marshalled people came a cheer loud enough to drown the hymn; and then the sea, with as little regard for the cloth as had the Rumanian Reds, struck like an angry bull and the boat, Jeremiah says, stood on its nose, and only a miracle of the highest order kept the American bishop out of the drink. Jeremiah could see him, down, far down at the bottom of a dizzy slope, then up, far up, shining like the sun between sea and sky, as the boat reared back on its haunches and Jeremiah felt on the back of his head the blow of a gigantic fist. It was simply salt seawater in a solid block, striking and bursting like a bomb. By the time he had wiped his eyes and the boat was again, for a few brief moments, on an even keel, there were two bishops sheltering in the for'ard foxhole: the two most quiet and prayerful men he had ever seen.

—On the ocean that hollows the rocks where ye dwell, Jeremiah recited out as loudly as he could because no ears could hear even a bull bellowing above the roar and movement and torment of the sea.

—A shadowy land, he went on, has appeared as they tell. Men thought it a region of sunshine and rest, and they called it Hy-Breasil the Isle of the Blest.

To make matters easier, if not tolerable, he composed his mind and said to himself: Lifeboats can't sink.

On this harshly-ocean-bitten coast there was the poetic legend of the visionary who sailed west, ever west, to find the island where the souls of the blest are forever happy.

—Rash dreamer return, Jeremiah shouted, oh ye winds of the main, bear him back to his own native Ara again.

For his defiance the sea repaid him in three thundering salty buffets and a sudden angled attack that sent the boat hissing along on its side and placed Jeremiah with both arms around the mast. In the brief following lull he said more quietly, pacifying the sea, acknowledging its power: Night fell on the deep amid tempest and spray, and he died on the ocean, away far away.

He was far too frightened to be seasick, which was just as well, considering the windy vacuum he had for a stomach. The boat pranced and rolled. He held on to the mast, but now almost nonchalantly and only with one arm. The sea buffeted him into dreams of that luckless searcher for Hy-Breasil, or dreams of Brendan the Navigator, long before Columbus, sailing bravely on and on and making landfall on Miami Beach. Secure in those dreams he found to his amazement that he could contemn the snubbed cameraman and the praying bishops hiding in their foxholes. He, Jeremiah, belonged with the nonchalant lifeboatmen studying the sea as a man through the smoke of a good pipe might look at the face of a friend. One of them, indeed, was so nonchalant that he sat on the hatch-roof above the bishops, his feet on the gunwale chain so that, when the boat dipped his way, his feet a few times went well out of sight in the water. Those lifeboatmen were less men than great yellow seabirds and Jeremiah, although a landlubber and as black as a raven, willed to be with them as far as he could, for the moment, go. He studied on the crazy pattern of tossing waters the ironic glint of sunshine on steel-blue hills racing to collide and crash and burst into blinding silver. He recalled sunshine on quiet, stable, green fields that he was half-reconciled never to see again. He was on the way to the Isle of the Blest.

Yet it was no island that first appeared to remind him, after two hours of trance, that men, other than the lifeboat's crew and cargo, did exist: no island, but the high bird-flight of a dozen black currachs, appearing and disappearing, forming into single file, six to either side of the lifeboat, forming a guard of honour as if they had been cavalry on display in a London park, to escort the sacerdotes magni safely into the island harbour. Afterwards Jeremiah was to learn that lifeboats could sink and had done so, yet he says that even had he known through the wildest heart of that voyage it would have made no difference. Stunned, but salted, by the sea he arose a new man.

The parish church was a plain granite cross high on a windy, shelterless hilltop. It grew up from the rock it was cut from. No gale nor half-gale, nor the gates of hell, could prevail against it.

To west and south-west the land sank, then swept up dizzily again to a high bare horizon and, beyond that there could be nothing but monstrous seacliffs and the ocean. To east and north-east small patchwork fields, bright green, dark green, golden, netted by greystone walls, dotted by white and golden cabins all newly limewashed and thatched for the coming of the great priests, sloped down to a sea in the lee of the island and incredibly calm. The half-gale was still strong. But the island was steady underfoot. Far away the mainland, now a bit here, now a bit there, showed itself, glistening, out of the wandering squalls.

—Rock of ages cleft for me, he hummed with a reckless merriment that would have frightened him if he had stopped to reason about it, let me hide myself in thee. He was safe in the arms of Jesus, he was deep in the heart of Texas. The granite cruciform church was his shelter from the gale, providing him, by the protection of its apse and right arm, with a sunny corner to hide in and smoke in. He was still giddy from the swing of the sea. He was also, being, alas, human and subject to frailty, tempted to rejoice at the downfall and humiliation of another. He hath put down the mighty, he began to chant but stopped to consider that as yet there was little sign of the lowly being exalted.

This corner of the cross was quiet. One narrow yellow grained door was securely shut. All the bustle, all the traffic was out around the front porch: white-jacketed white-jerseyed islanders sitting on stone walls, women in coloured shawls crowding and pushing, children hymn-singing in English, Irish and Latin, real Tower of Babel stuff, the cameraman photographing groups of people, and photographing the bishops from a safe distance, and the church from every angle short of the one the angels saw it from. He was no longer a great clumsy canary. He was splendid in his most expensive tweeds. He was, nevertheless, a cowed and broken man.

For back at the harbour, at the moment of disembarkation, it had happened again.

The two bishops, divested of oilskins, tall and black but not stately, are clambering up a ladder on to the high slippy quayside, and they are anything but acrobatic. Jeremiah, a few yards away, is struggling to tear from his body his sodden greatcoat, to hang it to dry under the direction of an islandman, in the lee of a boathouse where nets are laid to dry.

The cameraman has jocosely snapped him. Then he directs the camera on the clambering bishops only to be vetoed by a voice, iron and Irish and clanging.

—Put away that camera, the Irish voice says, until the opportune time.

—Why Peter, says the American voice, that would make a fun picture.

—In Ireland we don't want or need fun pictures of the hierarchy. We're not clowns.

It is arguable, Jeremiah thinks. He recalls that archbishops, on their own territory and when in full regimentals, are entitled to wear red boots. But he keeps his back turned on the passing parade in sudden terror that his eyes might reveal his thoughts. He hears the cameraman say: Your Grace, there is on the island the oldest inhabitant, a nonagenarian. I'd like to . . .

But there is no response. The procession has passed on. Fickle, Jeremiah knows, is the favour of princes, particularly when, like the Grand Turk, they are related to you. But what, ever or how grievous the cause of offence had been that led to these repeated snubs, Jeremiah feels for the first time, burning through empty belly and meagre body, the corps-spirit of the pressman. Who in hell, anyway, is a bishop that he won't stand and pose like any other mortal man? All men are subject to the camera. Face up to it, grin, watch the little birdie. Only murderers are allowed to creep past, faces covered. If he won't be photographed, then to hell with him. He will be scantily written about, even if he is Twenty Times His Grace. And to hell also with all American bishops and Rumanian Reds, and with all colour stories of confirmations and of simple island people who, more than likely, spend the long winter nights making love to their own domestic animals which, as far as Jeremiah is concerned, they have a perfect right to do.

So here in the corner of the granite cross he had found peace. He didn't need to see the nonsense going on out there. When the time came to type, as no doubt it would, the Holy Ghost would guide his fingertips. The moment on the quayside mingled with the moment in the shelter of the church and he realised, for the first time since anger had possessed him, that he had left his greatcoat still drying with the nets. He had been distracted by a call to coffee and sandwiches intended to keep them from collapsing until the show was over. But to hell, too, he decided with all greatcoats; a man could stand on his own legs. He smoked, and was content, and heard far away the voices of children, angels singing. Then the narrow, yellow, grained door opened, a great venerable head, a portion of surpliced body, appeared, a voice louder than the choirs of angels said: Come here, pressman.

Jeremiah went there.

—On the alert I'm glad to see, His Grace said. Waiting to see me. What can I do for you?

Jeremiah, to begin with, bent one knee and kissed his ring. That little bit of ballet enabled him to avoid saying whether he had or had not been on the alert, waiting for an interview.

—You must be starved, His Grace said. That was a rough journey.

They were in the outer room of the sacristy. The walls were mostly presses all painted the same pale yellow, with graining, as the narrow door. In an inner room the American bishop, head bowed, was talking to two tiny nuns. From one of the presses His Grace took a bottle and a half-pint tumbler and half-filled the tumbler with Jameson neat.

—Throw that back, he ordered. 'Twill keep the wind out of your stomach.

He watched benevolently while Jeremiah gasped and drank. The whiskey struck like a hammer. How was His Grace to know that Jeremiah's stomach had in it nothing at all, but wind? Jeremiah's head spun. This, he now knew, was what people meant when they talked about the bishop's bottle. His Grace restored bottle and glass to the press.

—We mustn't, he said, shock the good sisters.

He handed Jeremiah a sheaf of typescript. He said: It's all there. Names. History. Local lore. All the blah-blah, as you fellows say. Here, have a cigar. It belongs to our American Mightyship. They never travel without them. God bless you now. Is there anything else I can do for you?

Jeremiah's head had ceased to spin. His eyes had misted for a while with the warmth of the malt on an empty stomach, but now the mist cleared and he could see, he felt, to a great distance. The malt, too, had set the island rocking but with a gentle soothing motion.

—There's a man here, he said, the oldest inhabitant, a nonagenarian. The cameraman who's with me would like a picture.

—No sooner said than done, oh gentleman of the press. That should make a most edifying picture. I'll call himself away from the nuns. We'll just have time before the ceremony.

But, for reasons never known to me or Jeremiah, he laughed all the time as he led the way around the right arm of the cross to the front of the church; and brought with him another cigar for the cameraman, and shook hands with him, and offered him his ring to be kissed.

Apart from Jeremiah and the cameraman and the island doctor it was a clerical dinner, the island parish priest as host, a dozen well-conditioned men sitting down to good food, and wines that had crossed from Spain on the trawlers without paying a penny to the revenue.

—One of the best men in the business, said His Grace, although he'd sell us all body and soul to the *News of the World.*

He was talking about the cameraman, and at table, and in his presence. But he was laughing, and inciting the gathering to laughter. Whatever cloud there had been between the relatives had blown away with the storm, or with Jeremiah's diplomacy. So Jeremiah felt like Talleyrand. He was more than a little drunk. He was confirmed and made strong by the sea and the bishop's whiskey. He was hungry as hell.

—And Spanish ale, he muttered, shall give you hope, my dark Rosaleen.

His mutter was overheard, relayed around the table, and accepted as unquestionable wit. He was triumphant. He ate. He fell to, like a savage. He drank, he said afterwards—although we suspected that he had conned the names from a wine merchant's list, red and white Poblet, and red Rioja, and red Valdapenas, and another wine that came from the plain to the west of Tarragona where the Cistercians had a monastery: the lot washed down with Fundadór brandy which the American bishop told him had been the brandy specially set aside for the Conclave of Pope John the Twenty-third.

—Thou art Peter, said Jeremiah, and upon this rock.

Once again the remark was relayed around the table. Awash on the smuggled products of Spain, Jeremiah was in grave danger of becoming the life and soul of the party.

A boy-child had that day been born on the island. The American bishop had asked the parents could he baptise the child and name it after himself.

—Episcopus Americanus O'Flaherty, said Jeremiah.

Pope John's Fundadór circled the board. The merriment knew no bounds. His Grace told how the great traveller, O'Donovan, had dwelt among the Turkomans of ancient Merv, whom he finally grew to detest because they wouldn't let him go home, but who liked him so much they called all their male children after him: O'Donovan Beg, O'Donovan Khan, O'Donovan Bahadur, and so on.

—It was the custom in ancient Merv, said His Grace, to call the newborn babes after any distinguished visitor who happened to be in the oasis at the time.

—It was not the custom in Rumania, said Jeremiah.

Renewed merriment. When the uproar died down, the American bishop, with tears in his eyes, said: But this is God's Own Country. Ye are God's Own People.

Jeremiah got drunk, but nobody minded. Later, outside a bar close by the harbour, he was photographed feeding whiskey out of a basin to a horse. The horse was delighted. The picture appeared in a London magazine, side-by-side with a picture of the nonagenarian flanked by bishops.

—You got him to pose, said the cameraman, when he rusted on me.

He meant, not the horse, but the bishop.

—Jer, he said, you'll make a newsman yet.

So, as Jer, a new man, eater of meat and vegetables, acknowledged gentleman of the press, he came back from the Isle of the Blest, sitting on the hatch above the bishops, feet on the gunwale chain. He was not beyond hoping that the swing of the sea and the tilt of the boat might salt his feet. It didn't. The easy evening sway would have lulled a child in the cradle.

—Episcopus Americanus O'Flaherty, he said to the lifeboatman who sat beside him and who had enough Latin to clerk Mass.

—True for you, said the lifeboatman. Small good that christening will do the poor boy. As long as he lives on that Island he'll never be known as anything but An Teasbog Beag—the Little Bishop. If he goes to the States itself, the name could follow him there. His sons and even his daughters will be known as the Little Bishops. Or his eldest son may be called Mac an Easboig, the Son of the Bishop. They'll lose O'Flaherty and be called Macanespie. That's how names were invented since the time of King Brian Boru who bate the Danes.

Behind them the island stepped away into the mist: the wanderer, crazed for Hy-Breasil, would never find it. The rain would slant for ever on rocks and small fields, on ancient forts and cliffs with seabirds crying around them, on currachs riding the waves as the gulls do. Visitors would be enthralled by ancient ways, and basking sharks captured. But as long as winds rage and tides run, that male child, growing up to be a lean tanned young man in white jacket and soft pampooties, leaning into the wind as he walks as his forebears have always done, courteous as a prince but also ready to fight at the drop of a half-glass of whiskey, sailing with the trawlers as far away as the Faroes, will continue, because of this day, to be known as the Little Bishop.

In the foxhole underneath Jeremiah, the American bishop was telling the Irish bishop and the cameraman that in the neighbourhood of the Okeefenokee Swamp, out of which the Suwannee River drags its corpse, and generally in the state of Georgia, there were many Southern Baptists with Irish Catholic names.

The water in the land-locked harbour was deadly still, and deep purple in the dusk. Sleepy gulls foraged on the edge of the tide, or called from inland over the small fields. Jer's greatcoat was still on the island, dry by now, and stiff with salt. He never wanted to see it again.

Shadowy people gathered on the harbour wall. The choir sang: Sweet Sacrament Divine, dear home of every heart.

—Ye are God's own people, said the American bishop. This is God's own country.

—Fuck, said the cameraman and in a painfully audible voice.

He had sunk over the ankles in soggy peat-mould, losing one shoe. But while he stood on one leg and Jer groped for the missing shoe, the bishops and the people and the parish priest and the choir, and the cameraman himself, all joked and laughed. When the shoe was retrieved they went on their way rejoicing.

In Galway City Jer ate a dinner of parsnips and rare roast meat and sauté potatoes that would have stunned an ox; and washed it down with red wine.

Far away the island gulls nested on his discarded greatcoat.

AN OLD FRIEND

Quincey in his long brown overall work-coat leans on the red, corrugated-iron barrier and sings to the river and the tall trees beyond, and to the heron fishing in the shallows, that we're both together dancing cheek to cheek. I'm in heaven, I'm in heaven, and my heart beats so that I can hardly speak.

It is the year of the abdication and Quincey has that morning put his arm around the considerable waist of Miss Annie Mullan.

—Aughaleague, Aughaleague, he says, Aughaleague onward.

He is at that moment standing beside Miss Mullan and facing the local delivery rack in the sorting office. The American letter that he holds in his right hand is not meant for the townland of Aughaleague but for the townland of Lissaneden which is much farther down the alphabet, so that the pigeon-hole for Lissaneden is on the far side of Miss Mullan who is standing to Quincey's right hand and is, at that very moment, slowly, thoughtfully, inserting a letter in the pigeon-hole whose contents will be delivered in the townland of Bomacatall. Quincey is much too much of a gentleman to reach across in front of the lady. To do so would also mean a conflict between the affairs of Lissaneden and Bomacatall. So he reaches around behind her, accurately flicks the letter on its way to Lissaneden, and receives a sharp clean smack on the left ear. That ear clangs and buzzes. His face reddens. Reading out the place names in their alphabetical order he says: Aghee, Altamuskin, Arvalee, Aughaleague, Augher, Ballynahatty, Beragh, Bomacatall, Brackey, Cavanacaw, Clanabogan, Claraghmore, Clogher, Clohogue and Creevan.

As he says afterwards to Bernard: Damn the thing else could I find to say. To think that that aged faggot who sings hymns on the street every Sunday morning and Saturday night could possibly think that me, or any man aged nineteen and with all the world to pick from, would put his arm around her waist. Lord, catch my flea, catch my flea, catch my fleeting soul. Send down sal, send down sal, send down salvation from the lord.

He chants as Annie Mullan and her faithful few chant outside the Y.M.C.A. on a Saturday night.

It is the year of the abdication. Quincey and Bernard walk from the back of the post office, through the yard where his abdicated majesty's red mail-cars are parked, then down a steep gravelly path and a flight of fourteen concrete steps to a square of matted uncared-for grass on a sort of platform thirty feet or so above the river. On that platform Quincey and Bernard spend as much time as they can steal, leaning on the red corrugated-iron barrier or bulwark, smoking, spitting into the river, talking about girls and telling dirty stories.

It is the year of the abdication and his majesty, while his two servants idle, is in perilous condition.

There is nothing in his majesty's regulations at that time, or before or since, to say that a rural postman shall not shave nor do his morning ablutions in the open air in the townland of Arvalee. The king and the men who make his regulations for him may, at that moment, be too preoccupied to think of that one; and there is a postman who takes advantage of their preoccupation. But only on summer mornings when the air is mild and the bloom on the heather and the lark singing. His eccentricity is celebrated in poetry. A fellow postman who has emigrated to Canada writes all his letters home in verse and one day the head postman reads these lines out of one of the letters:

> On mornings in summer when there is no fog,
> Does Johnny still lather in Arvalee bog?

Across the river which is wide at that place, fast running and shallow but speckled with still pools, and where, on a lucky day, the two brown-coated loafers can be entertained by one of the town's dryfly experts wading and casting, there is a greystone schoolhouse circled by horse-chestnut trees. At playtime the cries of the racing scuffling children come across sharply to them, a painful reminder to Bernard that childhood and youth are gone forever. They are working men now in a working world, sorting clerks and telegraphists in the employment of his majesty who has just abdicated. Quincey doesn't think that way. His father is a country schoolmaster.

—School. It gave me the creeps. A famous jockey said that all he ever knew about school was that you had to go there.

—It isn't necessary for a famous jockey to be a scholar. He has other ways of earning his living.

—Miss Annie Mullan, Quincey says, will never forgive King Edward. She's sure as God jealous.

—She's loyal to the crown.

—She never lets up about chambering and impurities.

Quincey sings: I'm in heaven, I'm in heaven.

—If it was only Bubbles, he says, that I'd gotten my arm around by accident. When we're both together dancing cheek to cheek.

Bernard says: Bomacatall, Bomacatall, Bomacatall backwards.

Quincey sings: And my heart beats so that I can hardly speak.

As he walks along the sea-front Bernard thinks that in the year of the abdication that must have been the favourite song of millions of people. The gospel-group on the concrete steps above the big swimming-pool are singing: *Everybody ought to love him, everybody everywhere.* He has watched and listened for a while to the four middle-aged ladies with black bonnets and sallow faces, the three middle-aged to elderly men, one with a huge grey moustache, one with bandy legs, none of them as tall as the ladies. *Lord, catch my flea.* The preacher is a pale-faced young man in a dark suit and he has two companions of his own age flanking him: to his right a big red-faced fellow in sandy tweeds whose hands, clasped before him, are huge; to his left a slight pretty brunette in a navy costume but with black stockings and flat spiritless heels. Her face isn't unlike what he thinks the face of Bubbles was thirty-four years ago, turned-up impertinent nose, one eye with the slightest, most attractive, not squint, but a sideways enticing look. But then since he made up his mind to the repentance of this visit he has been seeing the face of Bubbles everywhere, on the street, in restaurants, on trains and buses, in airports, in advertisements on television. The gospel group sings: *Jesus died for every nation, everybody, everywhere.* Below them, in the pool, naked unrepentant limbs flash like silver fish. There are shouts and screams of laughter and then half a dozen voices singing in parody: *On the cross, on the cross where the soldier lost his hoss.* Annie Mullan is long dead and gone to Jesus. *Aughaleague, Aughaleague, Aughaleague onward.*

There is no strand here, just granite rocks below the promenade to his left and the sunny sea churning around them. On one far-out rock five or six black seabirds sit, motionless as buzzards. To the right the shops and boarding houses are brightly painted for the season that's about to open, each man fancying his own colour, and one place glitters with a thousand colours because its owner has imbedded in the pebble-dashing a thousand fragments of coloured glass. High on the headland above him the big hotel dominates the place, nineteenth-century Gothic, the castle of a robber baron raised high above the common people.

—Walk right around under the cliffs this hotel stands on, the hall porter says to him, until you come to the harbour where the fishing-boats are.

The cliff is high above now, black and brown and dripping here and there with rusty water, and he can no longer see the hotel. Nor can he hear the singing from the steps above the pool. The wind is blowing it the other way to disperse the pious words over the distant strand and the bent grass whistling in the dunes. The black birds, cormorants, are still motionless on the rock.

A turn to the left and he is leaning on a low wall looking down on the harbour. The tide is ebbed and five trawlers are settled down, as if never to rise again, on black, salt-stinking mud.

—When we get the government grant, the porter says, we'll deepen the harbour. You can sniff the hogo from here at low tide. But they say it's a healthy smell. Mr. Sloan's house, God pity him, is to your left when you stand at the wall above the harbour. You can't miss it. Only two houses there and the other one's a pub. A long well-kept garden in front of it. Mr. Sloan was a great gardener when he had the health. A fine house in a sheltered corner and everything about it as it should be. To have everything and a fine wife as well, and then to be struck down like that, they say she has to feed him off a spoon. The irony of fate, sir, that's what I call it, I often say we're never half thankful enough.

Quarrelling over something that one of them holds in its beak, a flock of gulls go screaming, fighting, diving, soaring out over the harbour. The sea is lively out there and three homing trawlers wait for high water. The flow may be just beginning, because a long thin tongue of water corners around the head of the mole, darts suddenly up the black mud and is as suddenly withdrawn. A sea-serpent's tongue. An aproned red-headed girl stands at the door of the pub which is down the slope to the right. She shades her eyes with her hands and looks out at the waiting trawlers.

The hand of a gardener quite out of the ordinary has left its mark on this place. He has never known that Quincey gardened. Here are roses and rhododendrons and a long rockery brilliant with blinding white iberis. *You're nearer God's heart in a garden than anywhere else on earth. Oh, laburnum yellow, lilac and the rose, chestnut blossoms mellow in my garden close, and summer coming in. I'm in heaven, I'm in heaven.* But that was thirty-four years ago and the interest in gardening could have begun and developed after he married Bubbles. Here is yellow red-hearted broom, and those fuchsia bushes will soon be in blossom, red flowers with royal purple hearts, deora Dé, the tears of

God. *The kiss of the sun for pardon, the song of the bird for mirth, and my heart beats so that I can hardly speak.*

The hunted gull, still struggling to preserve whatever it is that it carries in its beak, has swung back in over the harbour. Three great grey gulls assault simultaneously. The morsel drops dead down to the black mud and the whole screaming family go after it. Dear God, it must be something most delectable. The robbed gull, disconsolate, flies away alone to perch on the rock wall behind the house. The garden would seem to go all the way round to that rock wall. He stands at the front door, under the shade of a candled horse-chestnut, and presses the bell. It is one of those chiming bells. There is a long delay, and he is about to ring again when the door opens so suddenly that he's startled. He has heard no footsteps. For a few seconds it seems as if she doesn't recognise him, or that she does recognise him because he has written to say he's coming, but that she is holding her breath for a moment, trying to add up and subtract what more than thirty years have made of him. She is bare footed and wearing tight red jeans. She has not put on weight. Indeed she is slimmer than he remembers her and her cheeks that were plump with youth and unplanned eating are longer now, somewhat hollowed, but there are no wrinkles showing on the forehead.

—Weight, she says, weight. You put on weight all over.

The awkward preliminary paces before the water-jump have been taken. They laugh and he steps inside and holds her hands and kisses her left cheek, a skin that always tanned well.

—We got your letter, Bernard. It was wonderful of you to remember us after all these years.

—It would have been wonderful if I had forgotten.

Does she blush? It is hard to say with that olive skin. He holds her to him and kisses her cheek again. After all it has been a long time, and beyond a certain age it may be that remembering and returning and repeating are much more satisfying, certainly less bothersome, than beginning anything new. Autumn is no time for ploughing. But her chest, under a white crepe-de-chine blouse, with black spots like a Dalmatian, is flat as a board, as it had not been that evening in the telegraphy room. The land shrivels. The hills are laid low. In the creaking swivelling chair she sat before the teleprinter to show him how the thing worked and he leaned over her and slipped both hands down her loose woollen blouse. No protest, to his honest surprise, a very *toilteanach* girl, a lovely Irish word, and good-humoured about it, a pleasurable ductility about her, as the man said, which spread a calmness over his spirits. The world needed more young women like her, and the devil take the teleprinter. He spun her round and round slowly, still stepping behind her, cupped hands still holding on. Dot, dot, dash, dot.

From the drawing-room to the right a clock chimes. They break, as in boxing. She brushes back a wisp of hair, tinted to keep its original brown, that has come down over her eyes. Her nose is regular, even sharp, and not at all like the nose of the pale flat-heeled girl who sang beside the preacher above the swimming-pool. Her eyes are as he remembers them: brown, short-sighted, in the office she wore spectacles, the left with just the hint of a sideways coy glance, not a cast by no means.

—Have you eaten?

He has, very well, and wined, with merry talkative travelling companions.

—Drink?

—A lovely idea.

He needs more drink because of what he has to say to her.

At a Sheraton sideboard in the dining-room she pours him a rich half tumbler, fine Waterford glass, of black Bushmills and shows him the siphon.

—Drink it all, Bernard. You may be disconcerted at first. He's not what he was.

She sips a pale sherry slowly while he drinks, then refills his glass: I prepared him for your visit. He can hear most of the time, we think. He said he would be glad to see you.

—He said?

—He can write, scribble, make marks, sort of. He's out under the rock now, getting the last of the sun. He loves to see the flowers. But he won't sit in the front where the people can see him. He doesn't mind the local people. He was very popular here. He's one of them. But strangers come down to the harbour. It's very beautiful when the tide's full. You should really see it on a stormy day.

He realises foolishly that he has expected to find Quincey in a long brown working-coat: *I'm in heaven, I'm in heaven, and my heart beats so that I can hardly speak.* The brilliant white iberis climbs up the rock wall behind him, varied with the pink and purple of aubretia, a stubborn plant that grows in crannies, flower in the crannied wall I pluck you out of the cranny. A border of wallflowers runs along the foot of the wall. Invisible somewhere above, the deprived gull croaks with melancholy at the brutally rapacious ways of his fellows. Blessed mother of God this is nobody he has ever known, this is an oriental image in a gaudy shrine, a withered guru in a Himalayan cave. But the wine in the hotel, the brandy after dinner, the Bushmills on top of that, stand to him like three stout musketeers. He puts out his hand and grasps for a moment the right hand resting on the arm of the wheelchair. It is surprisingly plump and warm. There is a small table, a collapsible leaf, attached to the arm of the chair, and a white pad on it and a blue biro.

—He scribbles on that off and on, Bernard. Not great orthography. But he scribbles.

They sit down on two chairs facing each other, facing the image in the shrine. Should they have knelt? Or said: Master, we have come seeking wisdom.

Like the dead he must know it all by now. Or half of it.

Because Bernard has not yet got to the point where he can look his old friend straight in the face, or the grey distorted mask that he now wears over his face, he finds himself, eyes cast down like a novice monk, contemplating her crimson crotch eloquent in tight jeans, and feeling with his left hand the cold iron of a five-barred gate, and smelling in the darkness the meadow-sweet along a lover's lane in the townland of Arvalee where the postman shaved by the bog pool.

—Orthography, he says.

He finds it impossible to call her Bubbles. Long ago, french-kissing in the long grass of Arvalee, it sounded like a joke: I'm forever blowing bubbles. But it was no name for a woman of fifty with a husband shrunken and helpless in a chair: Bubbles, Blossom, Baby, Trixy, all those names that drooling fathers, melted by tiny hands and dimples and creases in pudgy fat, pass on as sardonic curses to the next generation.

—Orthography, he says. Maxwell, the overseer, you remember him? He used to foam at the mouth if he saw one of us writing backhand. Once upon a time in the post office, he'd say, penmanship was all important.

She remembers Maxwell, a bald, impulsive, long-nosed man who got drunk every Christmas eve when the rush was over, and only then.

—He didn't like younger men to sit down, Bernard says. You could do nothing and get away with it all day long if you did it standing on your feet. One day when I quoted Churchill to him he nearly burst.

—What had Churchill to do with it?

—He said, like the common soldier, never stand when you can sit, never sit when you can lie down.

They have brought their glasses out with them, and a third one, Bushmills, for the guru in the chair. She puts that glass down beside the pad and the pencil. She spoons a little of the liquid into the mouth of the image. She bends down and kisses it lightly on the forehead, dancing cheek to cheek. She says: Poor Quincey has a lot of sitting to do these days.

She sits down again. Sooner or later he knows he will have to look his old friend in the eyes. Those eyes are not dead and can see and may even now be looking at him. Would it not be better if he departed politely and said nothing about what he had intended to say: penance was a macabre, masochistic idea, and whose good was he serving, Quincey's or hers or his own? Thinking desperately, he empties his Bushmills and she goes, laughing, back to the house for the bottle, leaving him alone with the man or the thing or the old friend in the chair, and wine and brandy and Bushmills booming in his ears, and the disconsolate gull croaking on the rock above them, and the air sleepy with the scent of flowers.

That rock wall even in winter would hold off the most inhospitable north-easter. Now it stands as a suntrap for the long evening, a blessed place for a garden and for a paralytic who's a sort of flower. Or shrub, or cabbage, nearer God's heart in a garden? The crimson crotch is no longer there to look at nor the woman to talk to. He can't go on staring at the grass or the chair she sat on, so he looks up and around at his old friend and says: Well, Quincey, it's been a long time.

The face is all sideways. The mask it wears is the silk stocking or the plastic thing that up-to-date bandits pull over their faces to distort without actually concealing. As he watches and smiles the tongue protrudes, tip bent inwards, lips spluttering. The hair incredibly is as blond as it was when they leaned on the red bulwark and Quincey sang across the river. Does she dye it so as to preserve something? The tongue withdraws. The face under the mask twitches. That could be a smile. The right hand creeps around on the little collapsible table and falls on the blue biro. He thinks as he sees, and thanks God, that she is coming back with the Bushmills and the siphon, that she had so often said that she would never marry a blond, that she had said about Quincey that she liked him but that he was a blond.

—Quincey, she says, always wanted a house like this. That is, a house with a garden and a stream at the bottom of it. Now he has the house and the garden and the whole ocean.

It is so plainly something that she says to everybody that no reply is necessary. She refills his glass and leaves the siphon on the grass beside him, and feeds another spoonful to the man in the chair, and rests her hand gently on the blond head. Brendan says: Repetatur haustus.

—I beg your pardon.

—It would be Latin, I suppose, for let the draught be repeated. Or the same again.

—Do you tell me so, professor? Do you still read as much as ever? But I suppose you have to.

He wishes that she would sit down and be still so that he could continue looking at her and, without impoliteness, take his attention away from Quincey, if you can be impolite to the flower in the crannied wall. Yet since Quincey can write or scrawl, or whatever it is, he must be able to hear; and he can certainly see, for his grey eyes flicker at the sudden departure of the despoliated gull. If a man or a flower or a cabbage can hear and see, then he, or it, or they, can feel impoliteness. The gulls, all reunited, are singing a hymn over the harbour. The sunlight is dying. Bernard is afraid that he's getting drunk. When she does sit down she says: Maxwell got drunk only once a year. On a Christmas eve when the worst of the rush was over.

—I remember. The one and only Christmas eve I was there he said to Quincey and myself that you young fellows shouldn't be working so hard. Pulling all the time at his beak of a nose. Go out, he says, and buy yourself a good fish supper in Yanarelli's. He gave us a pound. We were flabbergasted. But when we came back we saw the point. Maxwell and a postman drinking whiskey in the overseer's office, and singing. On His Majesty's premises. And not even a Christmas carol.

They laugh. The man in the chair seems to move but Bernard doesn't dare to look around to check. He stares into a crimson world. She says: And one highly-respected official slept all night in the room where the mailbags were kept because he was too drunk to go home to his wife. And Bernard, do you remember Dick Milligan who used to read all the mail-order catalogues?

—The only books he ever read.

—And buy the oddest things.

—And try to resell them in the office.

—Pen-knives and bedside lamps and, once, a baby's bottle.

—And a first-aid kit. You see he came from South Armagh where all the crooked horse-dealers used to come from and he couldn't resist a bargain. Or just the joy of bargaining. It was in his blood.

—And Peter Magee who was chairman of the local British Legion and who always wore a tweed jacket and whipcord breeches and riding-boots in the office.

—And who threw a fit when Mr. Somerville, the cynic, said that when Lady Haig visited the town she walked up the High Street with a ladder in her stocking.

—Magee roared: Lady Haig's the greatest lady in the empire. She couldn't have a ladder in her stocking.

He hasn't noticed it until now but she also is drinking Bushmills. Neat.

He says: They were an odd crowd.

As he stoops for the siphon he notices that the hand has grasped the blue biro, awkwardly, between the second and third fingers, steadying it in the hollow of the thumb, and is moving it slowly over the paper. It is a fascinating sight. But he says nothing about it and retreats guiltily to his crimson memories.

—But we were happy, she says. And do you remember Annie Mullan, the queen of the sorting-office?

—The goddess, you mean. The prophetess. The holy woman, Deborah, who with Barak preserved the people of the lord outside the Y.M.C.A. She was in my mind when I listened to the hymn-singers above the swimming-pool. I was thinking of the day Quincey put his arm around her by accident.

It was on the evening of that day that Bubbles and himself got to know each other over the teleprinter, a most romantic place, but it is unlikely that she'll remember that. She puts her glass down on the ground. She says: What is it, Quincey?

There is a sort of gurgling spluttering noise to his right. He knows that the tongue is protruding again but he refuses to look around and thinks the fool he was, for repentance or any other reason, ever to come near this place. The crimson memories are gone and he is looking at cold grass. The shadow of the house is moving sideways towards them.

—Bernard, Quincey has just said something.

She stands over him and holds the white pad before his eyes, then snatches it away in case Quincey will see that he can't make a damn thing out of the blue squiggles and scrawls. She says: What it says is catch my flea.

She reads very slowly: Catch my flea.

—That's all it says. Quincey, what on earth does it mean?
Bernard explains.

Then she is laughing and crying at the same time, and saying: Poor Annie Mullan, poor Annie Mullan, if she only knew.

When the woman comes who helps her to look after her husband they wheel him back slowly into the house. This woman has been a nurse but she married and retired and is a good neighbour and a godsend, and Bubbles says she doesn't know how she could cope without her.

The sunlight has gone. The calls of the seabirds are far away and faintly saying farewell. He holds the warm plump hand once again. She takes from a hallstand a heavy blue cardigan and drapes it around her shoulders. She pats the blond head and kisses the mask or the twisted cheek beneath it.

—I'll drive you back to the hotel, Bernard. Quincey won't mind if I leave him for a while. Will you Quincey? It isn't that often that an old friend calls. Catch my flea, indeed.

As they drive around under the seeping cliff to the sea-front he says to her that they picked a lovely place to live in, and has no sooner come out with that banality than he remembers that only one of them is, in fact, living. She says nothing. But when they come to the place where the avenue goes cork-screwing back towards the hotel she drives straight on instead of turning left, then swings right on a narrow dust-road.

—Kidnapper, he says.

Her laugh is a real one: Bubbles laughing long ago in the deep grass of Arvalee. There was one smooth magic place, circled by walls of whins and heather and under a crooked whitethorn.

—I want to show you something. How lovely this place can be.

She is still barefooted. The road twists, goes up more steeply, the last houses drop swiftly back into the shadows. She says: Don't look behind until I tell you. Quincey used to say that from this place you could see five Kingdoms. The Kingdom of Mourne. We're in that. Where the mountains of Mourne sweep down to the sea. Then across the water on a clear day you can see Galloway in the Kingdom of Scotland, and Scaw-fell in the Kingdom of England, and quite close at hand the Kingdom of Man. Not to mention Snowdon in the principality of Wales.

—That's four kingdoms.

—But look up, he used to say, and you see the kingdom of heaven.

—Fanciful.

He is sick with pain at the thought of the thing in the chair: once a man, playing like a happy child with that fantasy of five Kingdoms, staring across the water to catch in a lucky light a glimpse of Scawfell. He says: There's something I must tell you.

—Bubbles, he adds.

She doesn't seem to hear him, or hears only that mention of her name. She presses his right knee, and swings the car right, and parks. The ascending road has met at right angles another road. Wheels can go no higher. Above and beyond the new road there's nothing but the mountain. She leans against him and kisses his cheek. She says: It's too dark now to see the five Kingdoms. But come out and look. He used to love this place. He used to say that it would impress Bernard if he ever came this way. You see he never forgot you.

Chains clank around him and weigh down his limbs as he steps out of the car. They lean against a drystone wall and he puts his right arm around her shoulders, protectively, against the light wind growing colder in the darkness, against the agony of watching day after day, the twisted shrunken image in the chair. The land falling away from them is black as tar, even to the fingers of headlands, but the sea is shining with the last light and the trawlers that had earlier been prone in the black mud of the harbour are fanning out to sea. Spots of light wink from the sea-front. The hotel high on the rock is like an anchored liner with a party going on for the last night on board, but they hear no sound other than the indefinable noises of night on the mountain.

—Now, she says, look up. Slowly, slowly. This is the real view, the vision.

The mountain is black above them, but rimmed and sharply outlined by light.

—My god, he cries, it's a giant bird, it's an eagle.

The jagged peak in silhouette is the scrawny featherless neck and beaked head. The spurs to right and left are spreading wings, covering them, protecting them. The rocky barren land is alive above them. He might never have said what he had come to say if it hadn't been that the shadow of the eagle seemed to cut them off so completely from the rest of the world. No other kingdoms are visible across the water. He says: The last time I saw Quincey and yourself, you mightn't remember it, I had been away from the town for three years.

—You went to higher things, professor.

—And came back on a holiday. The first persons I met on the High Street were Quincey and yourself.

—You couldn't have met better.

He has rehearsed this speech again and again over the years. Her levity unsettles him.

—Man and wife.

—Well we had got married. All proper like. In a church.

—I felt about the size of a threepenny bit.

—Whatever for? And why?

It is so dark now that her face is only a blob in the shadow of the eagle crouching above them. The only light left in the world is in the hotel and on the sea-front, faint phosphorescence far out over the water. The trawlers have vanished. His arm is still around her shoulders. But the darkness of Arvalee, perfumed by meadow-sweet, is a long time ago.

—Because of something I'd said to Quincey, three years before that, when I left the town. To the effect that, well the exact words were: I leave you Bubbles, she fornicates.

There is a considerable silence.

—A threepenny bit, Bubbles. And a worn one at that. Believe me I've regretted those words to this day, or night. That day on the High Street I felt so small and lousy that I promised myself to guard my tongue for ever more, amen.

—You've done that, I'm sure.

—I knew I'd never be content until I'd apologised to both of you.

—Did you have to be content? Who in the whole world is content?

—Then when I heard he was ill I knew I had to.

—An apology would hardly set him walking again. But I know he was glad to see you.

Her shoulders are shaking under his arm and he is terrified for the moment that the reason may be anger or grief. Then to his amazement, and mild annoyance, he realises that she is laughing.

—Oh, Bernard, she says, you ageing professorial fool. What does it matter now what was said or done when we were young?

He knows in humiliation that he has been cherishing not repentance but happy daring memories.

—Anyway we did, Bernard, didn't we?

—Did what?

—Fornicate. And great fun it was. But that word. You would use a word like that. Even then. It makes it all so solemn.

She is holding on to him, breathless with laughter.

—You must have learned it from Annie Mullan and the bible and the poor king and the things she used to say about him. Quincey always said that she never forgave King Edward.

—Do you forgive me?

—Bless the boy, what is there to forgive? She kisses him lightly.

—Why if you hadn't said that to Quincey, he was very shy, he might never, being a blond and knowing how I felt about blonds, might never have had the courage or the curiosity to approach me, or marry me. We have been very happy. We still are. I can protect him. He knows I'm there.

The last light is vanishing from the sea. Somebody is methodically rubbing it out. When they turn again to look up at the eagle it has vanished into the darkness. There will be no moon.

—He never told me, Bernard, he never said a word about that. I suppose he couldn't say it to me. I mean use that word.

—He was always too gentle.

—He used shorter words. Poor Annie Mullan. I hope she found Jesus wherever she went to. That he didn't let her down the way the king did.

They listen for a while but no sound comes up from the sea-front nor the hotel. *Everybody ought to love him, everybody everywhere.*

—I'm not reproaching you, Bernard. I'm so glad you came to see us. I think I can understand why you came. After he had the stroke I nearly took religion, like old Annie or the crowd at the swimming-pool. Only I thought it wouldn't be fair to him to give him nothing to look at but a gloomy face. So we have parties often in the house, and people, and he seems to enjoy them, he seems to be happy. He writes down happy things. I keep everything he writes. I'll show them all to you some day. Tomorrow, before you go. We have good friends.

In a private sitting-room in the hotel his own four good friends are showing no sign of pain. Every man has his own bottle and glass. There is nothing niggardly about the way they take refreshment.

Dominic with the banjo is quietly sipping lager and now and again touching the strings. Peter, back from Boston, has divested himself of a coloured necktie as broad as the fifteen acres and, with shirt-front open for coolness and lung-play and with a glass of Jameson in his hand, is chanting a song about some historic outing from Cork city to the town of Macroom:

'On the journey back home sure we came to some blows,
Tim Buckley thanks God that he still has his nose,
For 'twas struck by an elbow with the devil's own thud ...'

The stout semanticist with the moustache is drinking vodka and soda, because tonic is fattening, and arguing ecumenism with the grave, wide-browed, senior civil servant who is drinking Paddy Flaherty.

They greet him and the strange woman with loud cries of joy. They say that wherever he goes, even though he's a squat blackavised monster of learning and no matinee idol, he has a handsome woman waiting on him. He notices, as time passes, that she has a particular fancy for the reassuring gravity of Ahearne, the civil servant, and he is momentarily jealous. But what does it matter now? Arvalee is as far away as Eden. She has found a new friend. Under the flowering rock wall Quincey will sit for ever, motionless, wordless, except for the scrawling now and again of happy things on a white pad. Man wants but little here below and my heart bleeds so that I can hardly speak.

When they ask him to do his party piece he is tempted wickedly to sing that song of the year of the abdication. Instead, making in mockery wild gestures in the fashion (he has read) of Burke and Grattan in the golden age of oratory, he begins to recite: Aughaleague, Aughaleague, Aughaleague onwards.

He is already well down into his bottle which is black Bushmills and from which he has helped her. Pouring more of the golden past into her glass, he goes on: Bomacatall, Bomacatall, Bomacatall backwards.

For Dominic and Peter and the stout semanticist some brief explanation is necessary. Ahearne, smiling more or less to himself, seems to understand.

With the nasal whine of an ill-trained and untalented choirmonk Bernard intones: Lord catch my flea, catch my flea, catch my fleeting soul. Send down sal, send down sal, send down salvation from the Lord.

That is the antiphon. Then making the music as he goes along he gives them the hymn:

> Lettery, Lissaneden, Tummery and Knocknahorn,
> Glengeen, Shanaragh, and Cumber in the summer morn,
> Mullaghmore, Tullybleety, Tannagh and old Shanmoy,
> Messmore and Mullycarnan where I roamed a happy boy.
> Streefe Glebe, Tirooney, Tonegan and old Tremogue,
> Drumduff, Gleeneeny, Eskeryboy and Tullahogue.

Dominic has got the idea and is carefully picking out the notes on the banjo. It could be called the song of the sorting-office. There are enough townland names in Ireland to keep a man singing for ever.

THE GREEN LANES

Every evening for several consecutive months, Saturdays and Sundays excepted, he waited for me outside the office of this religious magazine. It was a missionary magazine, quite bright as missionary magazines go, with pictures of Africans in white shirts standing in arranged groups, or of nuns at work in hospitals, or priests on horseback: Father Pat Garrigan from Cavan finds that the way with horses that he learned on his father's farm, near Arva, stands him in good stead on a Nigerian journey.

One elderly priest and myself made up the editorial staff. Myself and one bald hunchbacked man who was well into his sixties made up the despatch and circulation staff. We parcelled up the magazines in that black thick paper used for simulating rock walls in Christmas cribs and posted them to convents here and confraternities there and to private citizens all over the place. We had a thanksgiving column for divine favours received, and articles, edifying, by clerics and lay people, male and female, and short stories and serials, edifying and sentimental, by authors and authoresses, and a bigger circulation by the month than a lot of respectable newspapers had by the day. So that the parcelling was the biggest part of the work, and very dusty thirsty tiring work.

To escape from the dust and the grunting hunchback, from the clerical editor who never talked of anything except the skill and products of ancient Irish metal-workers, was really something. To escape to the company of Marcus and the delights of the Long Hall was to move into another world.

—This, the editor had been saying, is a photograph of the De Burgo— O'Malley chalice. I got the postcard for nothing in the national museum.

The hunchback had the biggest brownest eyes I've ever seen in a human being, but they could look wicked looks, something unusual in brown eyes, and they could talk as well as any tongue. What they said to me as they looked at me over the rim of a black parcel was: If he hadn't got it for nothing he wouldn't have it.

—The De Burgos, the Burkes, you understand, the Normans. The

O'Malleys, the wild Irish. The chalice is made of silver gilt and weighs thirteen ounces and fifteen pennyweights. It is eight inches in height. The inscription reads: *Thomas de Burgo et Graunia Ni Maile me fieri fecerunt*. As if to say, brought me into existence. The chalice, so to speak, speaks. In the year of the lord, 1696. That's a while ago.

—Grania of the Ships, said the hunchback who was a bit of an historian.

He grovelled and grunted, bald head perspiring, amid piled blocks and pyramids of rock-dark parcels.

—She became a sort of national heroine, said his reverence. But we are told in sober truth that she was a pirate and an immoral woman.

The hunchback staightened up as much as he could: 'Twas the lying Tudors said that. She shamed the lord of Howth into hospitality. She had more style than the King of Spain and the Queen of England.

His warmth surprised me because, like myself he generally listened, or pretended to, and said nothing. The reverend editor ignored him, sniffed so that the tip of his thin nose twitched, took back the photograph which he had just tendered to me, replaced it in its envelope and went his way, his black gown swishing around his square-toed shoes. He had the thickest rubber heels I've ever seen.

From the canyons and corridors between the black parcels my circulation assistant, my brown-eyed Caliban, said: A lot he knows about Grace O'Malley of the Ships, or sanctifying grace, or actual grace. Or hospitality. Two pounds eighteen shillings and sixpence a week and your stamps. No money for a married man.

—I never knew you were.

—You thought nobody would take me. Is that it? Anyway nobody did. It's still no wage for a married man.

His red face and high forehead shone like a creased and spotted moon from behind a black mountain of parcelled piety, and news flashes from the mission fields where, like in our dusty office, the labourers, as the lord said, were few.

Outside it was mild and late April, dusk thick in the narrow street between the high houses, the street lamps coming to life one by one. Marcus stood with his back to the high spiked railings that fronted the gaunt Georgian houses, and he himself was as straight as the railings. He had marched with the Dublin Fusiliers, and the British army had a name for being able to straighten a man. He stood, as if hiding, just out of the circle of light from a street lamp. He said: I'm watching that window across the street. Take a dekko.

The window was on the third floor of a five-storey house, counting the basement as the first floor. The house was five windows wide and built of Ballyknockan granite, a grey king amid the princely brick Georgian houses; and I regarded it, every time I passed, with a certain reverence.

—Marcus, do you know who lives there?

—Of course I know.

He mentioned the name of a renowned politician, so renowned and for so long that he had become as venerable as any politician ever could become.

—Of course I know. But it's not him I'm looking at. He's to be seen at any time. Watch that window.

The windows on the first floor were lighted and red-curtained, and light rayed upward from the windows in the basement area. Above that the house was dark.

—The flash of white, he said, watch for the flash of white. The belly of a salmon turning in a pool up the Liffey at Sallins. That's the time to hook them.

We watched the dark window. The evening traffic was lessening in the street. We watched the dark window and were rewarded after a few moments with a definite flash of white. It flashed, vanished, flashed again, then stayed steady behind the darkened glass.

—What do you think it is? he said.

—Not a notion.

—Use the brains God gave you, if they're not addled up in that place you work in, helping to pollute the free peoples of Africa.

But I couldn't guess what the white blob was. It was still steady at the window.

—God aid your eyesight. It's a maid's white apron. You don't see the rest of her because her dress is black.

—Is her face black too?

—It might be. Though that's not too likely. It's probably just not as white as her apron. Not boiled and starched.

—What's so wonderful about a maid's apron?

—She's looking out. She's looking at us.

—You mean she's looking at you.

—Well, I was here before you. She'd be lonely in that big house.

—They must have twenty servants in the basement.

—Then why isn't she down there? What's she doing alone at a window, looking out? She's homesick. Or yearning.

He took his wide-brimmed grey hat in his hand and waved it at the window. The blob moved, became a flash again, vanished.

—She's shy, he said. I've frightened her.

—You've frightened her apron.

We set off walking towards the warmth and glitter and glisten of the Long Hall, our pub, in George's Street.

—When the long bright evenings come, he said, we'll see more than her apron.

On Sundays, in all seasons and weathers we'd go walking in the hills to the south of the city, up over the Featherbed mountain where the stream overflows, wrestling with oval boulders, from the black tarn— it's the only word—of Lough Bray; higher still and over the ridge to the clear sources of the Liffey in Calary bog. He was a man for the open air, a fisherman and a good man to walk with, for he could, without saying he was doing it, train you to walk the way the army trained him: like a machine, with a measured easy tread that, without strain, covered the ground and could go on for ever.

We talked as we walked, sometimes but not often about the war. Or, on that topic, he talked and I listened, for he was a man in his forties and had been there, and I was all of eighteen and hadn't been anywhere. When he enlisted, he said, he did the right thing for the wrong motive, to get away from the mother for a while, just for a change like. There was something nasty that had happened to Turkish prisoners at the Dardanelles, and several times he started to tell me that one but stopped before he got to the details. Once in a while he would burst into song:

> Long may the colonel with us bide,
> His shadow ne'er grow thinner.
> It would, though, if he ever tried
> Some army stew for dinner.

But mostly, and especially when we walked in the green lanes on days when we hadn't time to go as far as the hills, he talked about girls. The green lanes stirred his memory and he had much to remember, and I was ready to listen and learn, although now and again I did think that girls and the war served the same purpose for him: to get him away from the mother for a while, just for a change like.

The green lanes are no longer green, no longer lanes, no longer even on the map. The city has eaten them up, and small semi-detached houses and suburban gardens are all over that gentle slope above the sea where generations of lovers had flattened grass under hawthorn hedges and made love in the open air, not in caves mortgaged to building societies. When, as we tramped through the maze of narrow paths we came on a loving couple, they carried on regardless and undisturbed. By ancient convention they had the freedom of the place and we were the intruders and should be ashamed to be there.

—But, he'd say, I've my rights here for long and faithful service. I've my citizenship papers.

Here in a hollow under a boortree bush he had had the most thundering experience of his whole career, apart from once in wartime France when the play had surpassed all description. Remembering, he touched gently the bark of the bush: She was a Dublin girl, too. Normally in those days the country girls were the liveliest. They were better fed. You picked them up in the Fun Palace on the quays, the place with the mirrors that show you up in all shapes and sizes. That never ceased to amuse the country girls, they were that simple.

He walked ahead of me, grey hat, brown overcoat, well-polished brown shoes, feet stepping like clockwork. The lanes were narrow. A five-barred iron gate opened a view through high dropping hawthorns, white with blossom, into a field. Down the slope was the sea and the high stacks of dockland. The green slope of that field below the four horse-chestnut trees had been, he told me, more comfortable than a plush circular bed in a rich man's house. There had been wild flowers down there and the white candles of the chestnuts to make posies for a queen.

—There's no harm, you see, in being romantic once in a while. It was unlucky to cut the hawthorn blossoms.

We always entered the green lanes from the road that went by the sea northward from the city. Once in the maze you were steeped in a green silence if you didn't know, that is, that life and whispering were going on all around you. To look down on the maze from a low-flying aeroplane would really be something. But then, he'd say, whip the roofs off all houses and think what God would see.

We always left the green lanes by bending low through a tangled shrubbery and climbing over a pile of stones and rubble where a six-foot stretch of the wall of an old estate had collapsed. The last owner of the estate had sold out to the city for housing development. But since the development had not yet begun, the place was a wilderness bisected by the straight main avenue that went for half a mile between pines and cedars to the burnt-out shell of an eighteenth-century mansion. Children played on the wide grassy margins of the avenue. On one corner of the gravel before the house there was a sort of perpetual card school. The players, interrupted only by nightfall or rough weather stood and swore and shouted and planked their cards with deadly accuracy on the ground. In the most intense moments they squatted like tailors, or Amazon Indians by a jungle fire, and were silent.

Fifty yards behind the house we'd duck through a barbed wire fence, and there was another road and green city buses and a village pub that kept a good pint but had none of the grandeur of the Long Hall.

Half way through May the girl in the darkened room switched on the light. He took that as a challenge: She wants to see us better. She wants us to know that she sees us: She wants us to see her.

Caught dazzled in brightness that came down like the beam of a lighthouse from the window to the spot where we skulked in the shadows, I tried to work out his meaning. We were later than usual that evening because his reverence had delayed me to tell me all, or all that he knew, about the collar of gold, a hollow necklet, found at Broighter in County Derry and dating from the first century after Christ. The home-going traffic had gone from the street, which was only a narrow side street anyway and the bright noisy flow of life honking like crowded wild geese, and the road to the Long Hall, was fifty yards to our left.

—She probably wants the police or her employer to see us.

—There's no other light in the house.

—They could be hiding behind the dark windows.

—Loitering with intent we are, he said, to see a virgin.

—Hope springs eternal, I said.

—She's from the country by the look of her, Marcus said.

—All maids are from the country.

—There was one that I courted in the conservatory of the burnt-out house at the green lanes. She had thick red hair and a laugh like a horse.

—But soft what light, I said.

We could see her pretty well where she stood spotlighted in the window. She had bronze hair that shone and her face was pale but, at the distance, we could make nothing out of the nature of her eyes. She was plump rather than slender. The black dress, the white apron were plain enough. Her hands were clasped before her breasts and holding some small white object which, with his expert knowledge, he was able to tell me was the hairband that maids would wear in a house of those dimensions.

—A hell of a house to be billeted in, he said. A hibernian harem.

He stood out into the light of the street lamp, took off his hat, bowed with great style and restored the hat quickly to its place. He was sensitive about the bald patch that marred his plentiful crown of dark curly hair. The girl waved back, the white object in her hand fluttered. Then, no mistake about it, she blew him a kiss and vanished.

—That's a beginning, he said as we walked on to the Long Hall. Who can despise the day of small beginnings? I read that once in a book called *Milestones of Progress*.

—Looking out through windows and in through windows is a wonderful thing, he said. Windows are wonderful.

—Like widows.

—I could tell you stories about widows. Beginning with my mother. And windows, too.

Late at night, walking home through narrow streets where the houses abutted on the pavement with no protective patches of garden, he had developed a habit of peeping through curtains or under window-blinds. It wasn't, I really think, that he was a voyeur in the limited, sad or nasty, sense of the word. He was just curious about other people's lives.

—You see the oddest things in other people's houses. Most houses should be on the stage.

Carefree in the glitter of the Long Hall, our pints before us, we had fun classifying homes we knew into groups to suit the city's theatres. Irish peasant to English light opera, solemn Norwegian to bare-legged burlesque, there was a stage for every home. Always in the Long Hall, a place of many mirrors, there was a shabby, silent little man who drank ale and port wine at the same time but out of separate glasses, an odd ritual; and it amused us, as men of the world, that because of where he sat and we sat, we could see him five times, the man himself and four reflections, five little men, ten little glasses.

Looking at himself, side by side in a mirror with one of the five men, Marcus pulled and pushed at his chin and mouth as if he were shaping plasticine. He was worried at the way the wrinkles were deepening, dry furrows on a dark land, downward from the corners of his mouth.

—Only fatherless girls, you know, go for old men, and they're in the minority. My own mother's house would make a man old before his time. It's so quiet it wouldn't be accepted on any stage. It's so shiny you'd be afraid to sit down.

—But who shines it?

—Oh, I do. But if I didn't the mother would never give me a moment's peace: You'll polish it all right for the woman who comes after me.

The lifelessness of his own home may have set him peeping through curtains and under blinds. As a french-polisher, shining was his business. He affected to dislike it, saying that the man who invented such work or any work, should have kept it to himself. But he was proud of being an exclusive sort of craftsman who could work where and when he pleased. French-polishers were few. The precision, the perfection of the method gratified something of the disciplinarian that the army had found and developed in him. But polishing costly sideboards and tables in big houses, and leaving them behind you at the end of the day for somebody else to study their faces in, was a different thing from polishing in a tiny house at the behest of a nagging widowed mother, always saying her son should get married, always scared to hell that he might.

Once only was I in the house and then only because he couldn't leave me waiting for him outside in the rain. The shine of the tables hurt the eyes. The old mother's thin white face also shone. She was polite and no more. There were no cushions to dim the shine of the chairs, which were hard and slippery under the buttocks. The stage to accommodate such a house had not yet been invented.

The love story of Marcus and the girl at the window was well on the way when I came back from Donegal, where I went once a year for the fluency of my Irish—to the rocks of the Rosses, the stone-wall patchwork of small fields, the white cottages, the turbulent sea, the fuchsia hedges. As in the previous two years the tiny silver-haired sister of Hudie who was seventy, the son of Cormac, who was ninety, McGarvey gave me the parcel of thick home-knitted socks for the reverend editor. She had cherry-blossom cheeks and talked like a bird chirping.

As in the previous two years the hunchback said when he saw the socks, which were grey-white and lumpy and as thick as chain mail: There surely to God must be something wrong with his feet or he wouldn't dare to wear those.

His reverence accepted the socks and went his way, having first told us about the shrine of the Cathach which was made between 1062 and 1098 both years of the lord, to contain a vellum psalter which dated to the year 550. When the O'Donnells of Donegal went into battle they carried the psalter with them as a guarantee of victory, which was why it was called the Cathach or the Battler.

The door closed behind his flat heels and his flapping gown.

—He's a battler himself, said the hunchback, God help us. He hasn't the blood of a louse. The pale thin face of him and the twitchy nose. I should give him some blood.

The parcelling for the month had not yet commenced. My assistant sat on a high stool at the sort of old-fashioned desk that hadn't been much in use since the boyhood of Dickens and made entries in a ledger with a plain pen that scraped and spluttered. On my holiday in Donegal I had decided to look for a better job, something in the world of bright girls and type-writers.

—Give him blood?

—Didn't you know?

He climbed down from the stool.

—But how would you since I never told you? Did you ever see the like of that?

It was a sort of certificate to show that he had been for a vast number of times a blood donor. For a long time I studied it, to show my interest and to hide my surprise. Then he took it back to his wallet and his inner breast-pocket. That day he was wearing an elegant dark-grey suit with a pin stripe, a starched white shirt, and he was so unusually clean-shaven that his strong, tanned, square-chinned handsome face was more than usually noticeable. Although he was an older man than Marcus he hadn't a wrinkle: a bad back, perhaps, but a better stomach.

—Was up there today, he said. That's why the glad rags. A man has to look his best before the nurses. There'd be a lot of people that, if they saw me, wouldn't want my blood. Did you ever know that my mother was an O'Donnell?

We always left by different doors, for he stayed behind me to lock up and to say some prayers for something or somebody in the chapel of the religious house to the rear of the office.

—Everything's going like a house on fire, Marcus said. We'll walk in the green lanes when you've had a bite to eat.

The overcoat had been cast aside. He wore a flannel jacket with a broad check, sharply creased grey pants, a cream shirt and a sporty tie with drawings on it, new suede shoes and, because of the bald patch, a green cloth cap.

—Everything what?

—Everything across the street, man. It's long gone beyond waving at the window.

His face shone with health, and the wrinkles seemed no longer so noticeable. Was it just that the salt air of the Rosses had cleaned and freshened my own eyes, making me see other men as younger and more handsome than they were? That day Marcus smiled more than he usually did. When he smiled he flashed the tips of two shiny teeth, a trick that commonly made him appear cunning but now seemed comic and catching.

—There's nothing better for a man, he said, as he gets older than to start something new and young. There's a chemist in the Coombe has pills would raise the dead.

—What's her name?

—Do you know I've never asked her. So far I've just called her miss.

—Very respectful.

—Or darling. Oh, we're very matey and all. I told her my name was Albert Heaney. But she didn't seem to bother about names. She's sweet and simple.

—You told her a lie.

—Force of habit, I suppose. My poor mother's about the only woman that ever knew my real name.

—Did you walk her in the green lanes yet?

So far, he told me, he hadn't. She didn't have much off-time. Yet that had not impeded the progress of love. By the door in the basement area he slipped in to see her. For the big granite house was by no means as crowded as we had supposed. The venerable politician, no longer active, and his wife spent most of the year either in the sun in the south of France or in a cottage by the Kenmare River. There were so many empty rooms in the place that you could run a disorderly house there without offending anybody. In the absence of the owners the establishment was managed by a few maids and an old housekeeper who was doddering and deaf as a post, and whose sitting-room was on the top-most floor because she liked to look over the roofs of the city towards the blue hills of Wicklow. While she sat at her high window, lifting her heart and her eyes to the hills, the maids in rotation made merry in the basement. For the visiting beaux food and drink were laid on at the expense of the absent politician who had never before in his career been of such benefit to the Irish people. It was cheaper by far than walking a girl out and, believe it or not, a broad kitchen table in a dry basement could be as cosy as a green bank or a bed of roses.

—Beds of asphodel, I said.

—Never heard of him. There are so many empty rooms that she thinks the house is haunted. She's more rural than you'd believe possible. From the County Clare.

—From the black stones of the Burren.

—From the stone age if you ask me. You wouldn't credit the extent of her ancient Irish superstition. Salt over the shoulder all the time. She'd sooner walk naked down Grafton Street than put her left shoe on before her right or walk under a ladder. She wears most of her underclothes inside out for good luck, she says, and turns her apron twenty times an hour, when she's wearing it. She's like a chiming chandelier with miraculous medals. But she's gentle and soft as a silk cushion.

His voice, which was normally sharp and clear, softened and shook a little. It startled me. I was listening to love.

—And trusting. She says to me again and again: You won't do me any harm. As if she was expecting nothing out of life but harm. Isn't that an odd one? But down in that basement, man, we could be on our own desert island. The only thing that disturbs or comes between us is the old housekeeper's bell that she rings when she wants somebody to do something for her. She doesn't ring it often though. She's a most undemanding old lady.

With a most aggravating complacence he said: It's the young ones makes the demands. The old ones keep their eyes on heaven or the far-away hills.

But three months later it became obvious that harm had been done and the idyll in the kitchen had ended. The old housekeeper may have been deaf and doddering but she wasn't blind, and the bitter irony was, Marcus told me, that if it hadn't been for her damned bell catching him off his guard on one sleepy Sunday afternoon, the disaster might never have happened.

—You might say, he said, that she's to blame, indirectly.

—Very indirectly. She took her thoughts away from heaven and the hills.

He was not amused and he told me so. A long and carefree life he had had, he said, and never a mishap like this until he made love on a kitchen table in another man's house. Let that be a lesson to all, respect for the domestic hearth and for the homes of our illustrious leaders. That such a thing should come to pass on a patriot's kitchen table. Damn that bell and the hag who rang it for she had also banished the girl in tears and disgrace to wait out the fullness of time with her aunt in a cottage in the green lanes.

—I never knew there was a cottage in the green lanes.

—There are several but nobody ever notices them.

—You could marry her, Marcus.

—And have another woman's face reflected in my mother's polished tables. The way of it is, you see, that I love the girl and I couldn't subject her to tyranny.

The two white tips of teeth did not flash. The lines downward from the corners of his mouth were deeper and darker than ever. It occurred to me to make a joke about the potency of the pills he got from the chemists in the Coombe but I decided against it. He was serious about his love. But it never did enter his mind that he or she could live anywhere else except in the box of a house in Ballybough that he had so brilliantly and grudgingly polished to please his mother.

Summer or winter, our reverend editor was always cold and shivering, perhaps because he really was bloodless, perhaps because he had spent four years in the missions in Africa and had grown to like the heat. Again and again the hunchback would say to me that the editor was a cowled monk, and each time he would laugh happily at his deplorable pun.

—The shrines of the early saints, our editor told us, took interesting, even bizarre, forms. A bronze reliquary shaped like an arm was made in the twelfth century to enshrine the arm of St. Lachtin of Freshford in the County Kilkenny. About 780 the Moylough Belt was made of tinned bronze ornamented with enamel, millefiori and silver panels, to enshrine the belt of a saint. We don't, alas, know which saint or anything about him.

—Except, said the hunchback, that he wore a belt and not braces.

He had been in a strange exalted humour that day and if I hadn't known that he was or said he was, a temperate man, I'd have sworn he was boozed. When his reverence had flat-heeled and flapped it out the door, he said: We'll make a reliquary of asbestos, shaped like two flat feet to enshrine his socks.

He was also wearing his blood-bank clothes with a coloured silk handkerchief, for extra panache in the breast-pocket. But when I asked him had he been donating blood and dazzling the nurses, he looked at me for a long time as if he were testing me for something. His brown eyes could be as still and lightless as deep pools under high banks. He said no, that he had the glad rags on today because the boy was twenty-one. He took his black leather wallet slowly from his inner breast-pocket, unzipped the back compartment in which men normally keep the letters they don't want the wife to find, took out something wrapped in tissue paper, unwrapped it and handed it to me. It was a coloured snapshot of a boy of about seven dressed in a sailor suit and holding, but not playing with, a humming top. He could have been interrupted in his play and made to pose for his picture. He was a very handsome little boy with long golden curls.

—The boy, he said.

—But he's not twenty-one.

—That was taken on his seventh birthday. I took it myself.

—Who is he?

—My son.

—But you told me you weren't married.

—When you're longer in the city you'll find out you can have sons without being married.

—I heard the rumour. Even in the country.

We laughed, and just then the eyes of the boy in the snapshot caught mine. They were the eyes of the father looking up over turrets and battlements of black parcels of piety and letters of thanksgiving and

news from darkest Africa. No doubt about it, the eyes stamped them
father and son.

—He has eyes like yours.

It was an awkward thing to say. Roughly, effectively, he disposed of
my awkwardness.

—But as straight as a ramrod, he said. No worry there, God be praised.

As straight as Marcus the soldier and the railings outside the
Georgian houses.

—The golden hair was after his mother. Her name was Julia, but I
called her Grania for her hair like a queen in history. Grania of the
Ships because her husband worked on the Liverpool boat and was away
from home six nights out of the seven.

—Does the boy's father know?

—I'm his father. Poor Jimmy, you mean. He'd never guess. He's
straight and honest but simple.

—Does the boy know?

—He'll never know. They won't mock at him. It makes me laugh
when I give blood.

He rewrapped the snapshot, put it back in his wallet and the wallet
back in his pocket. He said: I go to the house often. I'm going there now.
Jimmy and myself were always great friends. The boy will have what I
have to leave when I die. Mean and all as his reverence is, I managed to
hoard a bit.

He followed me to the door, the keys rattling in his hand.

—Wish him a happy birthday from me, I said.

—She's long dead and in Glasnevin, Grania of the Ships. Jimmy never
married again. After her, no man would need another woman.

The green lanes, Marcus was able to tell me, looked very different in the
early mornings, the times he slipped out to see the girl, because the
aunt, who kept a tight eye on her, worked mornings in the city as a
cleaner in a block of offices.

Mornings, the green lanes were as quiet as the garden of Eden before
the serpent whispered, or after our first parents were driven out.
Mornings, the green lanes could actually have been the garden of Eden,
for the place must be somewhere, empty for all eternity.

The sound of the city, never at its worst in the mornings, was then
very far away. Refreshed by dew the circles of grass, crushed by lovers
the previous evening, were springing up again. It was unspoiled virgin
earth except where, here and there some couple, more careful of their
clothes or more timorous of the damp, had made for themselves
mattresses of newspapers. Yesterday evening's headlines, helpless and

irrelevant on the ground, showed you how little, anyway, the news of the world outside Eden mattered.

This was rural peace and you could wander for ever through the hedgy maze with only a view, now and again, over a five-barred gate, of Howth Head asleep along the sea or, far to the south, the blue cone of the Sugarloaf Mountain, to remind you that you were in the world at all. The cottages were there and to be seen, yet they sank inoffensively back into the greenery. Until those mornings in the green lanes he had never seen the girl dressed in anything except her house uniform. Out there in Eden she wore a smart green coat so that if it hadn't been for her bronze hair and her healthy country face it would have been hard, at a distance, to pick her out against the background. Green, though, suited her colouring, and love prospered on quiet dewy mornings.

Until the day he looked ahead of him along a green tunnel of a lane and saw her in the company of an older woman. The mother had always told him that green was an unlucky colour. He, as an old soldier, should have been on his guard because at their previous encounter she had asked him to come on parade, next time, two hours later than usual. The children were already playing on the green margins of the avenue. For a change he had entered the place by way of the burnt-out house. The card school was already assembled on its corner of the grass-grown gravel before the house. Because he had time to kill he stood with them for a while, then sat with his back against a fire-scarred Doric pillar and rose a mild winner. He was always lucky at cards.

Advancing as he was then, from the house and not from the seaside, the backs of the girl and the woman were turned to him. The sky was dark with thunder to come. He had worn his overcoat so that he could lay it under them on the grass, and his face was oily with sultry sweat. So he hopped over a five-barred gate into a meadow and found a place where he could peep through the hedge. Who'd ever have thought that a girl so country, so soft and trusting, could have traitorously sold the pass? He saw them clearly enough as they paced back and forward like sentries. The woman's face was dark like the skies and ready for thunder. The hedge he peeped through was of a triple thickness, yet it seemed from what he could see of the girl's face that she was, or had been, weeping. He might have gone out to meet them if it hadn't been that the furious-faced aunt showed the shadow of a dark moustache. The future menaced him, and a polished world in which everything, good and bad, was seen twice. Aunt and niece walked up and down for the best part of an hour. The day by then was as black as night, and the first thunder had rolled, and flickering sheet-lightning brightened the green of meadow and hedges. Once when the pair were long in coming back he judged they had given him up and gone home, and he hopped over the gate and turned towards the sea road, and there they were twenty yards away, coming towards him. In a hoarse voice the woman shouted: Is that the man?

He ran back towards the avenue and the house. She called him sadly by the false name he had given her. He ran from her voice, from the future, from the aunt's shadow of a moustache. The rain came as he ran tangling and twisting through the maze of the green lanes. There wouldn't be a track of him left that even a desert Indian could find. At the meeting of four lanes he ran past the white-washed cottage in which the aunt lived. Rain danced with the sound of kettledrums on the corrugated iron roof. In bedraggled groups the playing children had huddled under the cedars. They cheered after him as he ran sloshing past. The card school had withdrawn into the scorched belly of the building. For a moment he thought he might join them. But on second thoughts he turned his winnings over in his pocket and went on his sodden way. Her good green coat would have been destroyed in the rain.

The shabby, silent little man, who drank ale and port wine, sat and spoke to nobody and didn't seem to know that we could see him drinking ale and port wine in four different mirrors.

—He gets more value for his money than any man in the Long Hall, Marcus said, and laughed at his own joke.

But it was a faltering class of a laugh. He was pale and unshaven, and ashamed before me.

—That very day, do you know, I was going to make a clean breast of it to the old mother. For I loved that girl and would have stood by her if she hadn't betrayed me to the aunt.

—Oh chandeliers and glistening glass, I said, and pints of bass and bottles of port wine. And Johnnie Walker for ever, with his tall hat and red-tailed coat and cream breeches and black knee-boots . . .

—Are you out of your mind?

—That's the song of the Long Hall. I'm writing a prose poem.

—You can trust nobody nowadays. My last and dearest love and she betrayed me.

—Oh silver tankards hanging by the handles and bellying bottles of Bisquit brandy and, on a high rail, ornamental plates with pictures of deep-bosomed ladies and birds in flight and knights in armour. And earthenware kegs of Jamaican rum with pictures of antlered stags. Do you know, Marcus, that the brains of man, like the antlers of a stag, are going to grow too heavy for his head?

—Some people won't have to worry, he said. You're a lot of talk.

We walked in silence through cold wet streets to our usual place of parting. He never waited for me any more in the evenings. He was running from the place where he used to stand up as straight as the railings. She might come to find him there. He never saw her again, nor did she ever find him, if she ever went looking for him. He abandoned the green lanes and, possibly, all the memories that went with them. The green lanes are no longer on the map, and green lanes anywhere into which a man can vanish and be no more are becoming very rare. Bank robbers are photographed, without as much as asking their leave, while they work. A father and mother can sit at home and see their son blown up in the jungle. If a man takes part in serious television discussions he should also remember not to use a false name when booking into hotels with young women who are not his wife.

That was the last summer I ferried socks from the Rosses of Donegal. That better job with girls and typewriters came my way and, anyway, the reverend editor died of cancer and went to where whatever was contrailte with his feet would trouble him no longer.

The hunchback I saw one day, crossing the street, being helped by a handsome young man. They were talking and laughing and he didn't see me.

Marcus fell at the french-polishing and was three months in bed before he died. His face was thin and old the last time I saw him and his sharp voice was failed to a feeble sort of a whisper. He has aged all of a sudden, I thought, but then I remembered that I was, at that moment, the age he was when I first met him. That's the way it is in being friendly for a long time with people older than yourself.

A BALL OF MALT
AND MADAME BUTTERFLY

On a warm but not sunny June afternoon on a crowded Dublin street, by no means one of the city's most elegant streets, a small hotel, a sort of bed-and-breakfast place, went on fire. There was pandemonium at first, more panic than curiosity in the crowd. It was a street of decayed Georgian houses, high and narrow, with steep wooden staircases, and cluttered small shops on the ground floors: all great nourishment for flames. The fire, though, didn't turn out to be serious. The brigade easily contained and controlled it. The panic passed, gave way to curiosity, then to indignation and finally, alas, to laughter about the odd thing that had happened when the alarm was at its worst.

This was it.

From a window on the top-most floor a woman, scantily-clad, puts her head out and waves a patchwork bed coverlet, and screams for help. The stairway, she cries, is thick with smoke, herself and her husband are afraid to face it. On what would seem to be prompting from inside the room, she calls down that they are a honeymoon couple up from the country. That would account fairly enough for their still being abed on a warm June afternoon.

The customary ullagone and ullalu goes up from the crowd. The fire-engine ladder is aimed up to the window. A fireman begins to run up the ladder. Then suddenly the groom appears in shirt and trousers, and barefooted. For, to the horror of the beholders, he makes his bare feet visible by pushing the bride back into the room, clambering first out of the window, down the ladder like a monkey although he is a fairly corpulent man; with monkey-like agility dodging round the ascending fireman, then disappearing through the crowd. The people, indignant enough to trounce him, are still too concerned with the plight of the bride, and too astounded to seize him. The fireman ascends to the nuptial casement, helps the lady through the window and down the ladder, gallantly offering his jacket which covers some of her. Then when they are halfways down, the fireman, to the amazement of all, is

352 · A BALL OF MALT AND MADAME BUTTERFLY

seen to be laughing right merrily, the bride vituperating. But before they reach the ground she also is laughing. She is brunette, tall, but almost Japanese in appearance, and very handsome. A voice says: If she's a bride I can see no confetti in her hair.

She has fine legs which the fireman's jacket does nothing to conceal and which she takes pride, clearly, in displaying. She is a young woman of questionable virginity and well known to the firemen. She is the toast of a certain section of the town to whom she is affectionately known as Madame Butterfly, although unlike her more famous namesake she has never been married, nor cursed by an uncle bonze for violating the laws of the gods of her ancestors. She has another, registered, name: her mother's name. What she is her mother was before her, and proud of it.

The bare-footed fugitive was not, of course, a bridegroom, but a long-established married man with his wife and family and a prosperous business in Longford, the meanest town in Ireland. For the fun of it the firemen made certain that the news of his escapade in the June afternoon got back to Longford. They were fond of, even proud of, Butterfly as were many other men who had nothing at all to do with the quenching of fire.

But one man loved the pilgrim soul in her and his name was Pike Hunter.

Like Borgnefesse, the buccaneer of St. Malo on the Rance, who had a buttock shot or sliced off in action on the Spanish Main, Pike Hunter had a lopsided appearance when sitting down. Standing up he was as straight and well-balanced as a man could be: a higher civil servant approaching the age of forty, a shy bachelor, reared, nourished and guarded all his life by a trinity of upper-middle-class aunts. He was pink-faced, with a little fair hair left to emphasise early baldness, mild in his ways, with a slight stutter, somewhat afraid of women. He wore always dark-brown suits with a faint red stripe, dark-brown hats, rimless spectacles, shiny square-toed brown hand-made shoes with a wide welt. In summer, even on the hottest day, he carried a raincoat folded over his arm, and a rolled umbrella. When it rained he unfolded and wore the raincoat and opened and raised the umbrella. He suffered mildly from hay fever. In winter he belted himself into a heavy brown overcoat and wore galoshes. Nobody ever had such stiff white shirts. He favoured brown neckties distinguished with a pearl-headed pin. Why he sagged to one side, just a little to the left, when he sat down, I never knew. He had never been sliced or shot on the Spanish Main.

But the chance of a sunny still Sunday afternoon in Stephen's Green and Grafton Street, the select heart or soul of the city's south side, made a changed man out of him.

He had walked at his ease through the Green, taking the sun gratefully, blushing when he walked between the rows of young ladies lying back in deck-chairs. He blushed for two reasons: they were reclining, he was walking; they were as gracefully at rest as the swans on the lake, he was awkwardly in motion, conscious that his knees rose too high, that his sparse hair—because of the warmth he had his hat in his hand—danced long and ludicrously in the little wind, that his shoes squeaked. He was fearful that his right toe might kick his left heel, or vice versa, and that he would fall down and be laughed at in laughter like the sound of silver bells. He was also alarmingly aware of the bronze knees, and more than knees, that the young ladies exposed as they leaned back and relaxed in their light summer frocks. He would honestly have liked to stop and enumerate those knees, make an inventory—he was in the Department of Statistics; perhaps pat a few here and there. But the fearful regimen of that trinity of aunts forbade him even to glance sideways, and he stumbled on like a winkered horse, demented by the flashing to right and to left of bursting globes of bronze light.

Then on the park pathway before him, walking towards the main gate and the top of Grafton Street, he saw the poet. He had seen him before, but only in the Abbey Theatre and never on the street. Indeed it seemed hardly credible to Pike Hunter that such a man would walk on the common street where all ordinary or lesser men were free to place their feet. In the Abbey Theatre the poet had all the strut and style of a man who could walk with the gods, the Greek gods that is, not the gods in the theatre's cheapest seats. His custom was to enter by a small stairway, at the front of the house and in full view of the audience, a few moments before the lights dimmed and the famous gong sounded and the curtain rose. He walked slowly, hands clasped behind his back, definitely balancing the prone brow oppressive with its mind, the eagle head aloft and crested with foaming white hair. He would stand, his back to the curtain and facing the house. The chatter would cease, the fiddlers in the orchestra would saw with diminished fury. Some of the city wits said that what the poet really did at those times was to count the empty seats in the house and make a rapid reckoning of the night's takings. But their gibe could not diminish the majesty of those entrances, the majesty of the stance of the man. And there he was now, hands behind back, noble head high, pacing slowly, beginning the course of Grafton Street. Pike Hunter walked behind him, suiting his pace to the poet's, to the easy deliberate rhythms of the early love poetry: I would that we were, my beloved, white birds on the foam of the sea. There is a queen in China or, maybe, it's in Spain.

They walked between the opulent windows of elegant glittering shops, doors closed for Sunday. The sunshine had drawn the people from the streets: to the park, to the lush green country, to the seaside. Of the few people they did meet, not all of them seemed to know who the poet was, but those who did know saluted quietly, with a modest and unaffected reverence, and one young man with a pretty girl on his arm stepped off the pavement, looked after the poet and clearly whispered to the maiden who it was that had just passed by the way. Stepping behind him at a respectful distance Pike felt like an acolyte behind a celebrant and regretted that there was no cope or cloak of cloth of gold of which he could humbly carry the train.

So they sailed north towards the Liffey, leaving Trinity College, with Burke standing haughty-headed and Goldsmith sipping at his honeypot of a book, to the right, and the Bank and Grattan orating Esto Perpetua, to the left, and Thomas Moore of the Melodies, brown, stooped and shabby, to the right; and came into Westmoreland Street where the wonder happened. For there approaching them came the woman Homer sung: old and grey and, perhaps, full of sleep, a face much and deeply lined and haggard, eyes sunken, yet still the face of the queen she had been when she and the poet were young and they had stood on the cliffs on Howth Head, high above the promontory that bears the Bailey Lighthouse as a warning torch and looks like the end of the world; and they had watched the soaring of the gulls and he had wished that he and she were only white birds, my beloved, buoyed out on the foam of the sea. She was very tall. She was not white, but all black in widow's weeds for the man she had married when she wouldn't marry the poet. Her black hat had a wide brim and, from the brim, an old-fashioned veil hung down before her face. The pilgrim soul in you, and loved the sorrows of your changing face.

Pike stood still, fearing that in a dream he had intruded on some holy place. The poet and the woman moved dreamlike towards each other, then stood still, not speaking, not saluting, at opposite street corners where Fleet Street comes narrowly from the East to join Westmoreland Street. Then still not speaking, not saluting, they turned into Fleet Street. When Pike tiptoed to the corner and peered around he saw that they had walked on opposite sides of the street for, perhaps, thirty paces, then turned at right angles, moved towards each other, stopped to talk in the middle of the street where a shaft of sunlight had defied the tall overshadowing buildings. Apart from themselves and Pike that portion of the town seemed to be awesomely empty; and there Pike left

them and walked in a daze by the side of the Liffey to a pub called The
Dark Cow. Something odd had happened to him: poetry, a vision of
love?

It so happened that on that day Butterfly was in the Dark Cow, as,
indeed, she often was: just Butterfly and Pike, and Jody with the red
carbuncled face who owned the place and was genuinely kind to the
girls of the town, and a few honest dockers who didn't count because
they had money only for their own porter and were moral men, loyal to
wives or sweethearts. It wasn't the sort of place Pike frequented. He had
never seen Butterfly before: those odd slanting eyes, the glistening high-
piled black hair, the well-defined bud of a mouth, the crossed legs, the
knees that outclassed to the point of mockery all the bronze globes in
Stephen's Green. Coming on top of his vision of the poet and the
woman, all this was too much for him, driving him to a reckless
courage that would have flabbergasted the three aunts. He leaned on the
counter. She sat in an alcove that was a sort of throne for her, where on
busier days she sat surrounded by her sorority. So he says to Jody whom
he did not yet know as Jody: May I have the favour of buying the lady in
the corner a drink?
—That you may, and more besides.
—Please ask her permission. We must do these things properly.
—Oh there's a proper way of doing everything, even screwing a goose.
But Jody, messenger of love, walks to the alcove and formally asks the
lady would she drink if the gentleman at the counter sends it over. She
will. She will also allow him to join her. She whispers: Has he any
money?
—Loaded, says Jody.
—Send him over so. Sunday's a dull day.
Pike sits down stiffly, leaning a little away from her, which seems to
her quite right for him as she has already decided that he's a shy sort of
man, upper class, but shy, not like some. He excuses himself from
intruding. She says: You're not inthrudin'.
He says he hasn't the privilege of knowing her name.
Talks like a book, she decides, or a play in the Gaiety.
—Buttherfly, she says.
—Butterfly, he says, is a lovely name.
—Me mother's name was Trixie, she volunteers.
—Was she dark like you?
—Oh, a natural blonde and very busty, well developed, you know. She
danced in the old Tivoli where the newspaper office is now. I'm neat,
not busty.

To his confusion she indicates, with hands moving in small curves, the parts of her that she considers are neat. But he notices that she has shapely long-fingered hands and he remembers that the poet had admitted that the small hands of his beloved were not, in fact, beautiful. He is very perturbed.

—Neat, she says, and well-made. Austin McDonnell, the fire-brigade chief, says that he read in a book that the best sizes and shapes would fit into champagne glasses.

He did wonder a little that a fire-brigade chief should be a quotable authority on female sizes and shapes, and on champagne glasses. But then and there he decided to buy her champagne, the only drink fit for such a queen who seemed as if she came, if not from China, at any rate from Japan.

—Champagne, he said.

—Bubbly, she said. I love bubbly.

Jody dusted the shoulders of the bottle that on his shelves had waited a long time for a customer. He unwired the cork. The cork and the fizz shot up to the ceiling.

—This, she said, is my lucky day.

—The divine Bernhardt, said Pike, had a bath in champagne presented to her by a group of gentlemen who admired her.

—Water, she said, is better for washing.

But she told him that her mother who knew everything about actresses had told her that story, and told her that when, afterwards, the gentlemen bottled the contents of the bath and drank it, they had one bottleful too many. He was too far gone in fizz and love's frenzy to feel embarrassed. She was his discovery, his oriental queen.

He said: You're very oriental in appearance. You could be from Japan.

She said: My father was, they say. A sailor. Sailors come and go.

She giggled. She said: That's a joke. Come and go. Do you see it?

Pike saw it. He giggled with her. He was a doomed man.

She said: Austin McDonnell says that if I was in Japan I could be a geisha girl if I wasn't so tall. That's why they call me Buttherfly. It's the saddest story. Poor Madame Buttherfly died that her child could be happy across the sea. She married a sailor, too, an American lieutenant. They come and go. The priest, her uncle, cursed her for marrying a Yank.

—The priests are good at that, said Pike who, because of his reading allowed himself, outside office hours, a soupçon of anticlericalism.

Touched by Puccini they were silent for a while, sipping champagne. With every sip Pike realised more clearly that he had found what the poet, another poet, an English one, had called the long-awaited long-expected spring, he knew his heart had found a time to sing, the strength to soar was in his spirit's wing, that life was full of a triumphant sound and death could only be a little thing. She was good on the nose, too. She was wise in the ways of perfume. The skin of her neck had a pearly glow. The three guardian aunts were as far away as the moon. Then one of the pub's two doors—it was a corner house—opened with a crash and a big man came in, well drunk, very jovial. He wore a wide-brimmed grey hat. He walked to the counter. He said: Jody, old bootlegger, old friend of mine, old friend of Al Capone, serve me a drink to sober me up.

—Austin, said Jody, what will it be?

—A ball of malt, the big man said, and Madame Butterfly.

—That's my friend, Austin, she said, he always says that for a joke.

Pike whose face, with love or champagne or indignation, was taut and hot all over, said that he didn't think it was much of a joke.

—Oh, for Janey's sake, Pike, be your age.

She used his first name for the first time. His eyes were moist.

—For Janey's sake, it's a joke. He's a father to me. He knew my mother.

—He's not Japanese.

—Mind your manners. He's a fireman.

—Austin, she called. Champagne. Pike Hunter's buying champagne.

Pike bought another bottle, while Austin towered above them, swept the wide-brimmed hat from his head in a cavalier half-circle, dropped it on the head of Jody whose red carbuncled face was thus half-extinguished. Butterfly giggled. She said: Austin, you're a scream. He knew Trixie, Pike. He knew Trixie when she was the queen of the boards in the old Tivoli.

Sitting down, the big man sang in a ringing tenor: For I knew Trixie when Trixie was a child.

He sipped at his ball of malt. He sipped at a glass of Pike's champagne. He said: It's a great day for the Irish. It's a great day to break a fiver. Butterfly, dear girl, we fixed the Longford lout. He'll never leave Longford again. The wife has him tethered and spancelled in the haggard. We wrote poison-pen letters to half the town, including the parish priest.

—I never doubted ye, she said. Leave it to the firemen, I said.

—The Dublin Fire Brigade, Austin said, has as long an arm as the Irish Republican Army.

—Austin, she told Pike, died for Ireland.

He sipped champagne. He sipped whiskey. He said: Not once, but several times. When it was neither popular nor profitable. By the living

God, we was there when we was wanted. Volunteer McDonnell, at your service.

His bald head shone and showed freckles. His startlingly blue eyes were brightened and dilated by booze. He said: Did I know Trixie, light on her feet as the foam on the fountain? Come in and see the horses. That's what we used to say to the girls when I was a young fireman. Genuine horsepower the fire-engines ran on then, and the harness hung on hooks ready to drop on the horses as the firemen descended the greasy pole. And where the horses were, the hay and the straw were plentiful enough to make couches for Cleopatra. That was why we asked the girls in to see the horses. The sailors from the ships, homeless men all, had no such comforts and conveniences. They used to envy us. Butterfly, my geisha girl, you should have been alive then. We'd have shown you the jumps.

Pike was affronted. He was almost prepared to say so and take the consequences. But Butterfly stole his thunder. She stood up, kissed the jovial big man smack on the bald head and then, as light on her feet as her mother ever could have been, danced up and down the floor, tight hips bouncing, fingers clicking, singing: I'm the smartest little geisha in Japan, in Japan. And the people call me Rolee Polee Nan, Polee Nan.

Drowning in desire, Pike forgot his indignation and found that he was liking the man who could provoke such an exhibition. Breathless, she sat down again, suddenly kissed Pike on the cheek, said: I love you too. I love champagne. Let's have another bottle.

They had.

—Rolee Polee Nan, she sang as the cork and the fizz ascended.

—A great writer, a Russian, Pike said, wrote that his ideal was to be idle and to make love to a plump girl.

—The cheek of him. I'm not plump. Turkeys are plump. I love being tall, with long legs.

Displaying the agility of a trained high-kicker with hinges in her hips she, still sitting, raised her shapely right leg, up and up as if her toes would touch the ceiling, up and up until stocking-top, suspender, bare thigh and a frill of pink panties, showed. Something happened to Pike that had nothing at all to do with poetry or Jody's champagne. He held Butterfly's hand. She made a cat's cradle with their fingers and swung the locked hands pendulum-wise. She sang: Janey Mac, the child's a black, what will we do on Sunday? Put him to bed and cover his head and don't let him up until Monday.

Austin had momentarily absented himself for gentlemanly reasons. From the basement jakes his voice singing rose above the soft inland murmur of falling water: Oh my boat can lightly float in the heel of wind and weather, and outrace the smartest hooker between Galway and Kinsale.

The dockers methodically drank their pints of black porter and paid no attention. Jody said: Time's money. Why don't the two of you slip upstairs. Your heads would make a lovely pair on a pillow.

Austin was singing: Oh she's neat, oh she's sweet, she's a beauty every line, the Queen of Connemara is that bounding barque of mine.

He was so shy, Butterfly said afterwards, that he might have been a Christian Brother and a young one at that, although where or how she ever got the experience to enable her to make the comparison, or why she should think an old Christian Brother less cuthallacht than a young one, she didn't say. He told her all about the aunts and the odd way he had been reared and she, naturally, told Austin and Jody and all her sorority. But they were a kind people and no mockers, and Pike never knew, Austin told me, that Jody's clientele listened with such absorbed interest to the story of his life, and of his heart and his love-making. He was something new in their experience, and Jody's stable of girls had experienced a lot, and Austin a lot more, and Jody more than the whole shebang, and all the fire-brigade, put together.

For Jody, Austin told me, had made the price of the Dark Cow in a basement in Chicago. During the prohibition, as they called it, although what they prohibited it would be hard to say. He was one of five brothers from the bogs of Manulla in the middle of nowhere in the County of Mayo. The five of them emigrated to Chicago. When Al Capone and his merry men discovered that Jody and his brothers had the real true secret about how to make booze, and to make it good, down they went into the cellar and didn't see daylight nor breathe fresh air, except to surface to go to Mass on Sundays, until they left the U.S.A. They made a fair fortune. At least four of them did. The fifth was murdered.

Jody was a bachelor man and he was good to the girls. He took his pleasures with them as a gentleman might, with the natural result that he was poxed to the eyebrows. But he was worth more to them than the money he quite generously paid after every turn or trick on the rumpled, always unmade bed in the two-storeyed apartment above the pub. He was a kind uncle to them. He gave them a friendly welcome, a place to sit down, free drink and smokes and loans, or advances for services yet to be rendered, when they were down on their luck. He had the ear of the civic guards and could help a girl when she was in trouble. He paid fines when they were unavoidable, and bills when they could no longer be postponed, and had an aunt who was reverend mother in a home for unmarried mothers and who was, like her nephew, a kindly person. Now and again, like the Madame made immortal by Maupassant, he took a bevy or flock of the girls for a day at the seaside or in the country. A friend of mine and myself, travelling into the granite mountains south of the city, to the old stone-cutters' villages of Lackan and Ballyknockan where there were aged people who had never seen Dublin, thirty miles away, and never wanted to, came upon a most delightful scene in the old country pub in Lackan. All around the bench around the walls sat the mountainy men, the stone-cutters, drinking their pints. But the floor was in the possession of a score of wild girls, all dancing together, resting off and on for more drink, laughing, happy, their gaiety inspired and directed by one man in the middle of the floor: red-faced, carbuncled, oily black hair sleeked down and parted up the middle in the style of Dixie Dean, the famous soccer centre-forward, whom Jody so much admired. All the drinks were on generous Jody.

So in Jody's friendly house Pike had, as he came close to forty years, what he never had in the cold abode of the three aunts: a home with a father, Austin, and a brother, Jody, and any God's amount of sisters; and Butterfly who, to judge by the tales she told afterwards, was a motherly sort of lover to him and, for a while, a sympathetic listener. For a while, only: because nothing in her birth, background, rearing or education, had equipped her to listen to so much poetry and talk about poetry.

—Poor Pike, she'd say, he'd puke you with poethry. Poethry's all very well, but.

She had never worked out what came after that qualifying: But.

—Give us a bar of a song, Austin. There's some sense to singing. But poethry. My heart leaps up when I behold a rainbow in the sky. On Linden when the sun was low. The lady of Shalott left the room to go to the pot. Janey preserve us from poethry.

He has eyes, Jody told Austin and myself, for no girl except Butterfly. Reckon, in one way, we can't blame him for that. She sure is the smartest filly showing in this paddock. But there must be moderation in all things. Big Anne, now, isn't bad, nor her sister, both well-built Sligo girls and very co-operative, nor Joany Maher from Waterford, nor Patty Daley from Castleisland in the County Kerry who married the Limey in Brum but left him when she found he was as queer as a three-dollar bill. And what about little Red Annie Byrne from Kilkenny City, very attractive if it just wasn't for the teeth she lost when the cattleman that claimed he caught gonorrhoea from her gave her an unmerciful hammering in Cumberland Street. We got him before he left town. We cured more than his gonorrhoea.

—But, Austin said, when following your advice, Jody, and against my own better judgment, I tried to explain all that to Pike, what does he do but quote to me what the playboy of the Abbey Theatre, John M. Synge, wrote in a love poem about counting queens in Glenmacnass in the Wicklow mountains.

—In the Wicklow mountains, said Jody. Queens? With the smell of the bog and the peat smoke off them.

Austin, a great man, ever, to sing at the top of his tenor voice about Dark Rosaleen and the Queen of Connemara and the County of Mayo, was a literary class of a fireman. That was one reason why Pike and himself got on so well together, in spite of that initial momentary misunderstanding about the ball of malt and Madame Butterfly.

—Seven dog days, Austin said, the playboy said he let pass, he and his girl, counting queens in Glenmacnass. The queens he mentions, Jody, you never saw, even in Chicago.

—Never saw daylight in Chicago.

—The Queen of Sheba, Austin said, and Helen, and Maeve the warrior queen of Connacht, and Deirdre of the Sorrows and Gloriana that was the great Elizabeth of England and Judith out of the Bible that chopped the block of Holofernes.

—All, said Jody, in a wet glen in Wicklow. A likely bloody story.

—There was one queen in the poem that had an amber belly.

—Jaundice, said Jody. Or Butterfly herself that's as sallow as any Jap. Austin, you're a worse lunatic than Pike.

—But in the end, Jody, his own girl was the queen of all queens. They were dead and rotten. She was alive.

—Not much of a compliment to her, Jody said, to prefer her to a cartload of corpses.

—Love's love, Jody. Even the girls admit that. They've no grudge against him for seeing nobody but Butterfly.

—They give him a fool's pardon. But no doll in the hustling game, Austin, can afford to spend all her time listening to poetry. Besides, girls like a variety of pricks. Butterfly's no better or worse than the next. When Pike finds that out he'll go crazy. If he isn't crazy already.

That was the day, as I recall, that Butterfly came in wearing the fancy fur coat—just a little out of season. Jody had, for some reason or other, given her a five-pound note. Pike knew nothing about that. And Jody told her to venture the five pounds on a horse that was running at the Curragh of Kildare, that a man in Kilcullen on the edge of the Curragh had told him that the jockey's wife had already bought her ball dress for the victory celebration. The Kilcullen man knew his onions, and his jockeys, and shared his wisdom only with a select few so as to keep the odds at a good twenty to one.

—She's gone out to the bookie's, said Jody, to pick up her winnings. We'll have a party tonight.

Jody had a tenner on the beast.

—She could invest it, said Austin, if she was wise. The day will come when her looks will go.

—Pike might propose to her, said Jody. He's mad enough for anything.

—The aunts would devour him. And her.

—Here she comes, Jody said. She invested her winnings on her fancy back.

She had too, and well she carried them in the shape of pale or silver musquash, and three of her sorority walked behind her like ladies-in-waiting behind the Queen of England. There was a party in which even the dockers joined, but not Pike, for that evening and night one of his aunts was at death's door in a nursing home, and Pike and the other two aunts were by her side. He wasn't to see the musquash until he took Butterfly on an outing to the romantic hill of Howth where the poet and the woman had seen the white birds. That was the last day Pike ever took Butterfly anywhere. The aunt recovered. They were a thrawn hardy trio.

Pike had become a devotee. Every day except Sunday he lunched in Jody's, on a sandwich of stale bread and leathery ham and a glass of beer, just on the off-chance that Butterfly might be out of the doss and abroad, and in Jody's, at that, to her, unseasonable hour of the day. She seldom was, except when she was deplorably short of money. In the better eating places on Grafton Street and Stephen's Green, his colleagues absorbed the meals that enabled higher civil servants to face up to the afternoon and the responsibilities of State: statistics, land commission, local government, posts and telegraphs, internal revenue. He had never, among his own kind, been much of a mixer: so that few of his peers even noticed the speed with which, when at five in the evening the official day was done, he took himself, and his hat and coat and umbrella, and legged it off to Jody's: in the hope that Butterfly might be there, bathed and perfumed and ready for wine and love. Sometimes she was. Sometimes she wasn't. She liked Pike. She didn't deny it. She was always an honest girl, as her mother, Trixie, had been before her—so Austin said when he remembered Trixie who had died in a hurry, of peritonitis. But, Janey Mac, Butterfly couldn't have Pike Hunter for breakfast, dinner, tea and supper, and nibblers as well, all the livelong day and night. She still, as Jody said, had her first million to make, and Pike's inordinate attachment was coming between her and the real big business, as when, say, the country cattle men were in town for the market. They were the men who knew how to get rid of the money.

—There is this big cattle man, she tells Austin once, big he is in every way, who never knows or cares what he's spending. He's a gift and a godsend to the girls. He gets so drunk that all you have to do to humour him is play with him a little in the taxi going from pub to pub and see that he gets safely to his hotel. The taximen are on to the game and get their divy out of the loot.

One wet and windy night, it seems, Butterfly and this philanthropist are flying high together, he on brandy, she on champagne, for which that first encounter with Pike has given her a ferocious drouth. In the back of the taxi touring from pub to pub, the five pound notes are flowing out of your man like water out of a pressed sponge. Butterfly is picking them up and stuffing them into her handbag, but not all of them. For this is too good and too big for any taximan on a fair percentage basis. So for every one note she puts into her handbag she stuffs two or three down into the calf-length boots she is wearing against the wet weather. She knows, you see, that she is too far gone in bubbly to walk up the stairs to her own room, that the taximan, decent fellow, will help her up and then, fair enough, go through her bag and take his cut. Which, indeed, in due time he does. When she wakes up, fully clothed, in the morning on her own bed, and pulls off her boots, her ankles, what with the rain that had dribbled down into her boots, are poulticed and plastered with notes of the banks of Ireland and of England, and one moreover of the Bank of Bonnie Scotland.

—Rings on my fingers, she says, and bells on my toes.

That was the gallant life that Pike's constant attendance was cutting her off from. She also hated being owned. She hated other people thinking that she was owned. She hated like hell when Pike would enter the Dark Cow and one of the other girls or, worse still, another man, a bit of variety, would move away from her side to let Pike take the throne. They weren't married, for Janey's sake. She could have hated Pike, except that she was as tender-hearted as Trixie had been, and she liked champagne. She certainly felt at liberty to hate the three aunts who made a mollycoddle out of him. She also hated, with a hatred that grew and grew, the way that Pike puked her with poethry. And all this time poor Pike walked in a dream that he never defined for us, perhaps not even for himself, but that certainly must have looked higher than the occasional trick on Jody's rumpled bed. So dreaming, sleep-walking, he persuaded Butterfly to go to Howth Head with him one dull hot day when the town was empty and she had nothing better to do. No place could have been more fatally poetic than Howth. She wore her musquash. Not even the heat could part her from it.

—He never let up, she said, not once from the moment we boarded the bus on the quays. Poethry. I had my bellyful.

—Sure thing, said Jody.

—Any man, she said, that won't pay every time he performs is a man to keep a cautious eye on. Not that he's not generous. But at the wrong times. Money down or no play's my motto.

—Well I know that, Jody said.

—But Pike Hunter says that would make our love mercenary, whatever that is.

—You're a great girl, said Austin, to be able to pronounce it.

—Your middle name, said Jody, is mercenary.

—My middle name, thank you, is Imelda. And the cheek of Pike Hunter suggesting to me to go to a doctor because he noticed something wrong with himself, a kidney disorder, he said. He must wet the bed.

—Butterfly, said Austin, he might have been giving you good advice.

—Nevertheless. It's not for him to say.

When they saw from the bus the Bull Wall holding the northern sand back from clogging up the harbour, and the Bull Island, three miles long, with dunes, bent grass, golfers, bathers and skylarks, Pike told her about some fellow called Joyce—there was a Joyce in the Civic Guards, a Galwayman who played county football, but no relation—who had gone walking on the Island one fine day and laid eyes on a young one, wading in a pool, with her skirts well pulled up; and let a roar out of him. By all accounts this Joyce was no addition to the family for, as Pike told the story, Butterfly worked out that the young one was well under age.

Pike and Butterfly had lunch by the edge of the sea, in the Claremont Hotel, and that was all right. Then they walked in the grounds of Howth Castle, Pike had a special pass and the flowers and shrubs were a sight to see if only Pike had kept his mouth shut about some limey by the name of Spenser who landed there in the year of God, and wrote a poem as long as from here to Killarney about a fairy queen and a gentle knight who was pricking on the plain like the members of the Harp Cycling Club, Junior Branch, up above there in the Phoenix Park. He didn't get time to finish the poem, the poet that is, not Pike, for the Cork people burned him out of house and home and, as far as Butterfly was concerned, that was the only good deed she ever heard attributed to the Cork people.

The Phoenix Park and the Harp Club reminded her that one day Jody had said, meaning no harm, about the way Pike moped around the Dark

Cow when Butterfly wasn't there, that Pike was the victim of a semi-horn and should go up to the Fifteen Acres and put it in the grass for a while and run around it. But when, for fun, she told this to Pike he got so huffed he didn't speak for half an hour, and they walked Howth Head until her feet were blistered and the heel of her right shoe broke, and the sweat, with the weight of the musquash and the heat of the day, was running between her shoulder-blades like a cloudburst down the gutter. Then the row and the ructions, as the song says, soon began. He said she should have worn flat-heeled shoes. She said that if she had known that he was conscripting her for a forced march over a mountain she'd have borrowed a pair of boots from the last soldier she gave it to at cut-price, for the soldiers, God help them, didn't have much money but they were more open-handed with what they had than some people who had plenty, and soldiers didn't waste time and breath on poetry: Be you fat or be you lean there is no soap like Preservene.

So she sat on the summit of Howth and looked at the lighthouse and the seagulls, while Pike walked back to the village to have the broken heel mended, and the sweat dried cold on her, and she was perished. Then when he came back, off he was again about how that white-headed old character that you'd see across the river there at the Abbey Theatre, and Madame Gone Mad McBride that was the age of ninety and looked it, and known to all as a roaring rebel, worse than Austin, had stood there on that very spot, and how the poet wrote a poem wishing for himself and herself to be turned into seagulls, the big dirty brutes that you'd see along the docks robbing the pigeons of their food. Butterfly would have laughed at him, except that her teeth by this time were tap-dancing with the cold like the twinkling feet of Fred Astaire. So she pulled her coat around her and said: Pike, I'm no seagull. For Janey's sake take me back to civilisation and Jody's where I know someone.

But, God sees, you never knew nobody, for at that moment the caveman came out in Pike Hunter, he that was always so backward on Jody's bed and, there and then, he tried to flatten her in the heather in full view of all Dublin and the coast of Ireland as far south as Wicklow Head and as far north as where the Mountains of Mourne sweep down to the sea.

—Oh none of that, Pike Hunter, she says, my good musquash will be crucified. There's a time and a place and a price for everything.

You and your musquash, he tells her.

They were wrestling like Man Mountain Dean and Jack Doyle, the Gorgeous Gael.

—You've neither sense nor taste, says he, to be wearing a fur coat on a day like this.

—Bloody well for you to talk, says she, with your rolled umbrella and your woollen combinations and your wobbly ass that won't keep you straight in the chair, and your three witches of maiden aunts never touched, tasted or handled by mortal man, and plenty of money and everything your own way. This is my only coat that's decent, in case you haven't noticed, and I earned it hard and honest with Jody, a generous man but a monster on the bed, I bled after him.

That put a stop to the wrestling. He brought her back to the Dark Cow and left her at the door and went his way.

He never came back to the Dark Cow but once, and Butterfly wasn't on her throne that night. It was the night before the cattle-market. He was so lugubrious and woebegone that Jody and Austin and a few merry newspaper men, including myself, tried to jolly him up, take him out of himself, by making jokes at his expense that would force him to come alive and answer back. Our efforts failed. He looked at us sadly and said: Boys, Beethoven, when he was dying, said: Clap now, good friends, the comedy is done.

He was more than a little drunk and, for the first time, seemed lopsided when standing up; and untidy.

—Clap now indeed, said Jody.

Pike departed and never returned. He took to steady drinking in places like the Shelbourne Hotel or the Buttery in the Hibernian where it was most unlikely, even with Dublin being the democratic sort of town that it is, that he would ever encounter Madame Butterfly. He became a great problem for his colleagues and his superior officers in the civil service, and for his three aunts. After careful consultation they, all together, persuaded him to rest up in Saint Patrick's Hospital where, as you all may remember, Dean Swift died roaring. Which was, I feel sure, why Pike wasn't there to pay the last respects to the dead when Jody dropped from a heart attack and was waked in the bedroom above the Dark Cow. The girls were there in force to say an eternal farewell to a good friend. Since the drink was plentiful and the fun and the mourning intense, somebody, not even Austin knew who, suggested that the part of the corpse that the girls knew best should be tastefully decorated with black crepe ribbon. The honour of tying on the ribbon naturally went to Madame Butterfly but it was Big Anne who burst into tears and cried out: Jody's dead and gone forever.

Austin met her, Butterfly not Big Anne, a few days afterwards at the foot of the Nelson Pillar. Jody's successor had routed the girls from the

Dark Cow. Austin told her about Pike and where he was. She brooded a bit. She said it was a pity, but nobody could do nothing for him, that those three aunts had spoiled him for ever and, anyway, didn't Austin think that he was a bit astray in the head.

—Who knows, Butterfly? Who's sound or who's silly? Consider yourself for a moment.

—What about me, Austin?

—A lovely girl like you, a vision from the romantic east, and think of the life you lead. It can have no good ending. Let me tell you a story, Butterfly. There was a girl once in London, a slavey, a poor domestic servant. I knew a redcoat here in the old British days who said he preferred slaveys to anything else because they were clean, free and flattering.

—Austin, I was never a slavey.

—No Butterfly, you have your proper pride. But listen: this slavey is out one morning scrubbing the stone steps in front of the big house she works in, bucket and brush, carbolic soap and all that, in one of the great squares in one of the more classy parts of London Town. There she is on her bended knees when a gentleman walks past, a British army major in the Coldstream Guards or the Black Watch or something.

—I've heard of them, Austin.

—So this British major looks at her, and he sees the naked backs of her legs, thighs you know, and taps her on the shoulder or somewhere and he says: Oh, rise up, lovely maiden and come along with me, there's a better life in store for you somewhere else. She left the bucket and the brush, and the stone steps half-scrubbed, and walked off with him and became his girl. But there were even greater things in store for her. For, Butterfly, that slavey became Lady Emma Hamilton, the beloved of Lord Nelson, the greatest British sailor that ever sailed, and the victor of the renowned battle of Trafalgar. There he is up on the top of the Pillar.

—You wouldn't think to look at him, Austin, that he had much love in him.

—But, Butterfly, meditate on that story, and rise up and get yourself out of the gutter. You're handsome enough to be the second Lady Hamilton.

After that remark, Austin brought her into Lloyd's, a famous house of worship in North Earl Street under the shadow of Lord Nelson and his pillar. In Lloyd's he bought her a drink and out of the kindness of his great singing heart, gave her some money. She shook his hand and said: Austin, you're the nicest man I ever met.

Austin had, we may suppose, given her an image, an ideal. She may have been wearied by Pike and his sad attachment to poetry, but she rose to the glimmering vision of herself as a great lady beloved by a great and valiant lord. A year later she married a docker, a decent quiet hard-working fellow who had slowly sipped his pints of black porter and watched and waited all the time.

Oddly enough, Austin told me when the dignity of old age had gathered around him like the glow of corn-stubble in the afterwards of harvest.

He could still sing. His voice never grew old.

—Oddly enough, I never had anything to do with her. That way, I mean. Well you know me. Fine wife, splendid sons, nobody like them in the world. Fine daughters, too. But a cousin of mine, a ship's wireless operator who had been all round the world from Yokohama to the Belgian Congo and back again, and had had a ship burned under him in Bermuda and, for good value, another ship burned under him in Belfast, said she was the meanest whore he ever met. When he had paid her the stated price, there were some coppers left in his hand and she grabbed them and said: give us these for the gas-meter.

But he said, also, that at the high moments she had a curious and diverting way of raising and bending and extending her left leg—not her right leg which she kept as flat as a plumb-level. He had never encountered the like before, in any colour or in any country.

THE WEAVERS AT THE MILL

Baxbakualanuxsiwae, she said to herself as she walked by the sea, was one of the odd gods of the Kwakiutl Indians, and had the privilege of eating human flesh. That pale-faced woman with the strained polite accent would devour me if her teeth were sharp enough. She even calls me, intending it as an insult, Miss Vancouver, although she knows damned well in her heart and mind, if she has a heart, that I don't come from Vancouver.

She loved the vast flat strand, the distant sea, the wraithlike outline of rocky islands that looked as if they were sailing in the sky, the abruptness with which a brook cradled by flat green fields became a wide glassy sheet of water spreading out over the sand.

A thatched cottage, gable end to the inshore gales, was palisaded against the sea by trunks of trees driven deep into the sand. On the sea-front road that curved around the shanty village, wind and water had tossed seaweed over the wall so regularly that it looked like nets spread out to dry. All the young men she met on the road wore beards they had grown for the night's pageant: not the melancholy, wishy-washy, desiccated-coconut pennants of artistic integrity but solid square-cut beards or shaggy beards that birds could nest in. To walk among them was a bit like stepping back into some old picture of the time of Charles Stewart Parnell: stern men marching home to beleagured cabins from a meeting of the Land League.

That woman would say: They are all so handsome.

She was long-faced, pale and languid, the sort of woman who would swoon with craven delight at the rub of a beard. Yet she could never persuade the old man to abandon his daily careful ritual with cut-throat razor, wooden soap bowl, the strop worn to a waist in the middle, the fragments of newspaper splattered with blobs of spent lather and grey stubble.

—Eamonn, she would say to her husband, if you'd only grow a beard you'd look like Garibaldi with his goats on the island of Caprera.

—I have no knowledge of goats. I'm not on my own island any more.

To the girl she would say: If your bags are packed I'll run you at any time to the station.

—My bags are always packed. There's only one of them. A duffle-bag, she'd answer. But if it doesn't inconvenience you too much I'd like to stay another day. There are a few details I want to fill in.

It needed nerve to talk to a woman like that in her own house. But what could the girl do when the old man was plaintively urging her not to go, not to go, pay no heed to her, stay another day.

They had breakfast in bed every day and lunch in their own rooms, and all the time until four in the afternoon free. It was in some ways the most relaxed life the girl had ever known. She had been there for a week since she had come from London across England, Wales, the Irish Sea and a part of Ireland, to write one more article in the magazine series that kept her eating. It was a series about little-known heroes of our time.

The woman had met her at the train. She drove a station-wagon piled high in the back with hanks of coloured wool. They drove round the village, foam glimmering in the dusk to their right hand, then across a humped five-arched stone bridge and up a narrow, sunken, winding roadway to the old Mill House in the middle of gaunt, grey, eyeless ruins where—above the river foaming down a narrow valley—two hundred men had worked in days of a simple local economy. Four grass-grown waterwheels rusted and rested for ever.

—Only my weavers work here now, she said. That's what the wool's for. Aran sweaters and belts—criosanna, they call them here—and scarves and cardigans. We sell them in the States where you come from.

She sounded as friendly as her over-refined, Henley-on-Thames voice could allow her to sound.

—Canada, the girl said. British Columbia. My father worked among the Kwakiutl Indians.

—Can't say I ever heard of them. What do they do?

—They were cannibals once. For religious reasons. But not any longer. They catch salmon. They sing songs. They carve totem poles. They weave good woollens, too. With simplified totem designs.

—How interesting.

The car went under a stone archway topped by a shapeless mass that she was to discover had once represented a re-arising phoenix—until rain and salt gales had disfigured it to a death deeper than ashes. They were in a cobbled courtyard and then in a garage that had once been part of a stables.

—You want to write about my husband's lifeboat exploits when he was an islandman.

—The famous one. I was asked to write about it. Or ordered. I read it up in the newspaper files. It was heroic.

She slung the duffle-bag over her shoulder and they walked towards the seven-windowed face of the old stone house. From the loft above the garage the clacking of looms kept mocking time to their steps. The woman said: Do you always dress so informally?

—I travel a lot and light. Leather jacket and corduroy slacks. You need them in my business. A protection against pinchers and pawsey men.

—You're safe here, said the woman. The men are quiet. All the young ones have just grown lovely beards for a parish masque or a pageant or something. You mustn't tire him too much. Sometimes he can get unbearably excited when he remembers his youth.

His youth, the girl reckoned, was a long time ago.

She spread out her few belongings between the old creaking mahogany wardrobe and the marble-topped dressing-table, and tidied herself for dinner, and remembered that she had left her typewriter, smothered in wool, in the station-wagon. The newspaper that had told her about the rescue had been fifty years old; and Eamonn, the brave coxswain and the leader of the heroic crew, had been then a well-developed man of thirty. The newsprint picture had faded, but not so badly that she couldn't see the big man, a head taller than any of his companions, laughing under his sou'wester with all the easy mirth of a man who had never yet been afraid.

From her bedroom window she could look down into the courtyard and see girls in blue overalls carrying armfuls of wool from the wagon up an outside wooden stairway to the weaving shed. The thatched roofs of the village were, from her height, like a flock of yellow birds nestling by the edge of the sea and, far across the water, the outlines of the islands of Eamonn's origin faded into the darkness, as distant and lost for ever as his daring youth and manhood. Yet she knew so little, or had reflected so little, on the transfiguring power of time that she was ill-prepared for the gaunt, impressive wreck of a man who came slowly into a dining-room that was elaborately made up to look like a Glocamorra farmhouse kitchen. He sat down on a low chair by the open hearth and silently accepted a bowl of lentil soup with fragments of bread softening in it. He didn't even glance at the low unstained oak table where the girl sat most painfully, on a traditional three-legged wooden chair. Dressed in black, her black hair piled on her head, her oblong face, by lamplight, longer and whiter than ever, the woman sat aloof at the head of the table. Two girls, daytime weavers magically transformed by the touch of the creeping dusk into night-time waitresses, blue overalls exchanged for dark dresses, white aprons, white collars, served the table; and a third stood like a nurse behind the old man's chair. He slopped with a spoon, irritably rejecting the handmaiden's effort to aid him. He recited to himself what was to the girl an unintelligible sing-song.

—Merely counting, the woman said. In Gaelic. One, two, three, and so on. He says it soothes him and helps his memory. I told him what you want. He'll talk when he's ready.

Suddenly he said: She cracked right across the middle, that merchant vessel, and she stuffed as full as a fat pig with the costliest bales of goods and furniture and God knows what. I can tell you there are houses on this coast but not out on the islands where the people are honest and no wreckers, and those houses are furnished well to this day on account of what the waves brought in that night.

The voice came out like a bell, defying and belying time, loud and melodious as when he must have roared over the billows to his comrades the time the ship cracked. Then he handed the empty soup bowl to the nervous weaver-handmaiden, sat up high in his chair, bade the girl welcome in Gaelic, and said to the woman: She's not one of the French people from the hotel.

—From London, said the woman.

—There's a fear on the people in the village below that there won't be a duck or a hen or any class of a domestic fowl left alive to them with the shooting of these French people. The very sparrows in the hedges and God's red robins have no guarantee of life while they're about. They came over in the beginning for the sea-angling and, when they saw all the birds we have, nothing would satisfy them but to go home to France for their guns. They say they have all the birds in France shot. And the women with them are worse than the men.

—Les femmes de la chasse, said the woman.

—Patsy Glynn the postman tells me there's one six feet high with hair like brass and legs on her like Diana and wading boots up to her crotch. God, Pats said to me, and I agreed, the pity Eamonn, you're not seventy again, or that the Capall himself is dead and in the grave. He'd manipulate her, long legs and boots and all.

—Our visitor, said the woman, is not here to write about the Capall.

—Then, girl from London, 'tis little knowledge you have of writing. For there have been books written about men that weren't a patch on the Capall's breeches. A horse of a man and a stallion outright for the women. That was why we called him the Capall.

With a raised right hand and cracking fingers the woman had dismissed the three girls. This was no talk for servants to hear.

—That John's Eve on the island, the night of the bonfires and midsummer, and every man's blood warm with poteen and porter in Dinny O'Brien's pub. Dinny, the old miser that he was, serving short measure and gloating over the ha'pennies. But, by God, the joke was on him and didn't we know it. For wasn't the Capall in the barn-loft at the back of the house with Dinny's young wife that married him for money, for that was all Dinny had to offer. She had to lie down for two days in bed, drinking nothing but milk, after the capers of the Capall and herself in the loft. He walked in the back door of the bar, his shirt open to the navel, no coat on him and the sweat on him like oil. Two pints he drank and saw for the first time the new barmaid, a niece of Dinny, that had come all the way from Cork City, and the fat dancing on her and her dress thin. So he lifted the third pint and said: Dhia! Is trua nach bhfuil dara bud ag duine.

Feeling that she did understand, and close to coarse laughter, the girl said that she didn't understand. Coldly and precisely the woman said: To put it politely he regretted that he was merely one man, not two.

—But he saved my life did the Capall. For the gale swept us, and the eight men we took off the broken vessel, eastwards before it to a port in Wales. There was no turning back in the teeth of it. There we were trying to moor the boat by the mole in another country when, with weariness and the tossing of the water, didn't I slip and go down between the wall and the boat, to be crushed, sure as God, if the Capall hadn't hooked his elbow in mine and thrown me back into the boat the way a prize wrestler would. Remember that bit, girl, when you write the story, and thank God you never met the Capall on a lonely road. He came from a place called the Field of the Strangers that was the wildest place on the whole island. From the hill above it you could see the wide ocean all the way to Africa, and the spray came spitting in over the roofs of the little houses, and the salt burned the grass in the fields. There was no strand in it, no breakwater, no harbour or slip for boats. Nothing man ever built could stand against that ocean. You held the currach steady and leaped into it from a flat rock as you shot out to sea. But there were men of strength and valour reared there who could conquer valleys before them and throw sledge-hammers over high houses. Dried sea bream we ate, boiled or roasted over hot sods, the strongest sweetest food in the world. And rock birds taken in nets where they'd nest in the clefts of the cliffs. Bread and tea for a treat, and potatoes boiled or brusselled in the griosach.

The woman explained: Roasted in the hot peat ashes.

—Then a cow might break a leg in a split in the rocks and have to be destroyed. A black disaster in one way. But in another way a feast of fresh meat and liver with the blood running out of it, food for men. All out of tins nowadays, and nobody has his own teeth.

The woman said: You were, Eamonn, talking about the lifeboat.

—Good for its own purpose the lifeboat, he said. But you couldn't feel the heart of the sea beating in it as you could in the canvas currach. We had one fellow with us that night who always had ill luck with currachs. Three of them he lost, and once he nearly lost his life. So we put him in the crew of the lifeboat to break his ill-fortune, and the trick worked. It could be that the sea didn't recognise him in his new yellow oilskins. Three days in that Welsh town we sweated in kneeboots and oilskins, having nothing else to wear, and the gales blowing in against us all the time. But the welcome we got. Didn't a deputation of ladies come to us with a white sheet of cloth to draw our names on, so that they could embroider our names for ever on the flag of the town's football team. Didn't the Capall write himself down as Martin McIntyre the Horse. There was the laughing, I can tell you, when the ladies wanted us to tell them why we put the title of the horse on Martin. They made heroes out of us. It was a sea-going town and there wasn't a woman in it hadn't a son or a husband or a lover on the salt water.

The attendant girls had come back silently. His great head, shaggy with uncombed white hair, sank down. With a napkin one of the girls mopped a splatter of soup from the green leather zipper jacket and, startlingly, with the yeeow of a shout a young fellow would give at a country dance, he came awake and slapped her buttocks before she could leap, laughing and blushing, and seemingly well used to the horseplay, out of his reach. The woman looked at the servant and then at her food. She said: Don't tire yourself.

—Never saw the tired day, he said, that the smell of a young girl wouldn't put life into me.

—Tell me more, said the girl, about the sea.

—What would you want to know about the sea and you from the smoky heart of London?

—I'm not from London.

—From Canada, said the woman. Her girlhood companions were cannibalistic Indians.

—On an island, the girl said.

He was wide awake, and interested, and upright. How tall he was when he sat up straight.

—Tell me, he said, about your wild Indians and your island.

Because he had hard blue eyes with a compelling icy light in them, and because for her benefit he had so carefully dredged his memory, she wanted to tell him. She wanted to tell him even more because as soon as he showed interest she had sensed the first stirrings of antagonism in the woman.

—Eamonn, the woman said, our guest may be tired.

—Tell me a little, he said. It's lucky to begin a story by lamplight.

—Nothing much to tell, she said. Don't think of me as sitting in the middle of a pack of noble savages, chewing on a hunk of Tyee salmon while they ate long pig. I didn't grow up with drums and war chants throbbing around me. I was some miles distant, on the other side of the hill. Of course I had plenty of contact with the confused no-man's-land Indian that the white man has made. Studied their history and sociology at college. But when I was a little girl the closest I got to them was to run to the top of the hill and peep down through cedar branches at the noble Indians pulling the guts out of salmon. Sounds bitter I know. But beauty and nobility had left them for a long while. And in our village the groups were so divided that not even the minds of the children could meet. When I was a girl I remember trying to get a little Indian girl to tell me some of her words. She stayed sullen and very silent. Then finally she and her little friend giggled and spat out one word. Matsooie—that was what it sounded like. I found out later that she had simply been saying: what's the matter with you? It was a rebuff.

—It's sad, he said, when people don't understand you, no matter what you do or try to do. We'll talk more tomorrow, girl, when you've rested after your journey.

—I've talked too much, she said. I came to listen to you.

He rose alertly when she passed him and shook her hand in a solemn old-fashioned way. He belonged to a time when men shook hands elaborately at every meeting and parting.

Later—very much later—she thought drowsily that she heard his slow tread on the old creaking stairs, his coughing in the next room as he lay down on his bed; and far away the faint sound of the sea along the shore and around the islands.

She carried two notebooks always in the right-hand pocket of her leather jacket.

All women, said the hopeful man she had met on the Irish Mail, are lascivious.

One of the notebooks was paper-backed, spined with spiral wire, and with tear-out leaves. It was for ephemera and temporalities—in other words, her work. The other book was stiff-backed, with stable, ruled leaves for the recording of the experiences she would use when the day would come and she'd sit down really to write. The stiff-backed book had another quality: it kept the weaker member straight in her jacket pocket, for she found nothing more maddening than note-taking on a page that was bent like a crescent.

The people she met she divided into two classes: tear-outs or stiff-backs.

This wonderful old man, an aged hero recalling islands, immured here by a female dragon, was as notable a stiff-back as she had ever encountered.

When the clacking of looms awoke her in the morning, she sat up in bed and reached for ball-point and stiff-back where she had left them in readiness on the bedside table. Or was it the looms had awakened her, or the purring of the motor-car engine in the cobbled yard, or the morning coughing of the old giant in the next room? For an ancient stone house, she thought, the walls were thin. But then she studied the slant of the ceiling, and realised that her room was only half a room and that the sound of coughing came to her, not through old stone, but through a wooden partition. She went to the window and looked out at three of the blue weaving girls walking in single file from the station-wagon to the weaving-shed and carrying hanks of coloured wool: obedient African kraal girls with burdens on their heads and disciplined by some wrinkled Zulu queen. Then the woman drove away under the faceless phoenix. When the girl was settled back in bed again, he spoke to her through the wall: I can hear you're awake. Has she driven off to do the shopping?

—Good morning, she said. She's driven off somewhere.

—Good morning to you, girl. Did you sleep well?

Her answer was lost in a fit of his coughing, and when his throat had cleared again, he said: No more rising with the lark for me. Nor the seagull itself. I'm old and lazy now. But I mind my father, the oldest day he was, walking barefoot in the dawn, the old greasy sailor's cap on his head, to the flagstone at the corner of the house, to look at the sea and the surf on the white strand, to sniff the wind and to tell the weather for the day to come. He had his own teeth to the age of ninety. If he was inland and far from the sea, he could tell by the smell of the wind whether the tide was ebbing or flowing. But it wasn't often he went inland, and he was never happy in an offshore wind.

This was the most wonderful way in the world to conduct an interview. The metallic voice came muted, but clear, through the timber. The looms, the sea, and the river made their noises. The wind muttered around grey stone. She could sit snug in bed, both notebooks open, and make notes at her ease without embarrassing her subject.

—Tell me more, she said.

He said: Tell me about your wild Indians.

So to entice him to talk, she talked about Quathiaski Cove at the mouth of the river, and about the wits among the Scots and Irish settlers who nicknamed it Quart of Whiskey Cove, about the great argonauts of salmon homing up the Campbell River, about people of many nations, Scots, Swedes, Irish, Indians, Chinese, Japanese, living in one way or another on the rich red body of the salmon.

—The very air in that place smells of salmon. When my mother first took me to visit Vancouver I thought there was something wrong with the place, something missing. Finally she told me I felt that way because I could no longer smell the salmon.

—Like myself, he said, when I came here with her. This far inland you can't sniff the salt properly.

—And tell me about their songs, he said. In my days on the island there were sweet singers and old men who could tell stories to last the night.

So, for his sake, she remembered that when she had been a little girl she had sneaked out one night to listen to the singing of the Indians. One song particularly stayed in her memory. Years afterwards, when she and her people had long left the place, she went north by boat with her father to revisit the haunts of her childhood. To one old noble chieftain she spoke of the songs—and of that special song. He answered her about all the forms of songs: morning songs, harvest songs, giving songs to be chanted at the potlatch when a man gave all he had to his neighbours, gambling songs, lullabies. And song after song he sang until she stopped him and said: That's it. That's the song I loved when I was a little girl.

Then, with tears in his eyes, the old chieftain said: That's my gambling song, written for me by my own songwriter.

Her story faded into coughing that rattled the partition between them. Later he said in a hoarse carrying whisper: Don't go away soon, girl. Stay as long as you can whether she wants you to or not.

It wasn't easy to think of any response.

—She doesn't like strangers about the place. She's cold, God help her, and has no failte in her. Even when I was married to my first wife, and herself only a stranger visiting the islands, she was always jealous to find me in the middle of a crowd.

—You were married before?

—To a woman of my own people. And year after year herself came as a tourist until my wife died. Then I went away with her and we were married in London. A watery class of a wedding they give you in cities. It wasn't love, as they call it. She was too grand for that. But she was there always—and willing. The islands do something to visiting women. And with creams and perfumes and the best clothes out of the London shops she was different from any woman I'd ever smelled or seen. You know how it is with a strong imaginative young fellow, and he only a few months married.

—I can guess, she said. Some minor poet said something about white arms beckoning all around him.

—Minor or major he was poet enough to know what he was talking about. We haven't slept heads on one pillow for twenty years now, but in secret corners in those old days we'd play hide and seek in our pelt on the bare rocks—when it was a sin moreover. And look at me now, here, wrapped in coloured wool, and broken in health, and surrounded by stupid women, weaving.

Propped by pillows, and taking notes, she squatted like a tailor, and made up her mind. She would stay a week if she could, just to please the old man and—her blood warming to the conflict—to spite that cold dried fish of a woman. In his youth, to judge by his talk, the old man had eaten better.

When he heard the station-wagon returning he said: I'll doze for a while now. She wouldn't like to hear us talking through the wall. She was hinting last night she'd run you to the station for the late train. But don't go, don't go, stay as long as you can.

They had a week of mornings together talking through the wall. Reading her notes afterwards she found that morning mingled with morning. One morning, though, was distinct because it had been a morning of gale and rain. The coy red-and-purple blossoms were being whipped off the tormented fuchsia bushes, and when she stepped out for her daily walk—the sea was too tossed for a swim—the sand and salt were in her eyebrows and gritting between her teeth. Bloated by a night of rain the brown mad river bellowed around the dead millwheels and, for once, the clack, the mocking one-two-three of the looms couldn't be heard.

Through the wall and the frequent fits of coughing he had said to her: I've grown younger since you came. A gift to me from the god of the sea himself, a beautiful young girl from a far island.

As a clergyman's daughter, the object of as many jokes as an Aberdonian, she was calmly aware of her looks: neither better nor worse than they were. She laughed. She said: I've a nose like a pack saddle, and a square face and freckles, although they tell me I've honest eyes.

—But you're young, he said.

After a silence she heard his dry choking laughter: There's a lump on my own nose still where I had it broken and I no more than a boy. The way it happened is a story will tickle you. There was this free and easy girl, a rare thing on the islands I can tell you—with the close way we lived. She wasn't an island girl, whatever. She came from the mainland in the tourist season and, as the song says, her stockings were white and you'd love to be tickling her garter, even if she was no better than a servant-maid in a lodging-house. This evening weren't we lined up to see her, like penitents going to confession, at the bottom of the orchard behind the house she worked in, and when Pat's Jameseen stepped out of his fair place in the line to go ahead of me, I fought him and, although he cracked my nose, hammered him back.

The dry laughter went on, choking now not with phlegm but with remembered devilment.

—That was the way with me when I was young. A chieftain among my own people, like your fine Indian, and respected by all. Then when my first woman died I never wanted to see the islands again. The English woman had it easy to carry me to the smoke of London, where, as God is my judge, I came near to choking. The islands pulled at me again, even though I got only this far and no farther. Old as I am, I think at times I'll take a boat and return. But they don't want me any more since I married a stranger, and grew grand, and left.

—It would be fun, said the girl, if we could go to an island I know in Spain. Life is simple and gentle there, and the food good, cooked over an open fire. Some rough wine, wild and coarse, but with a kind flavour. A little music and reading and story-telling by lamplight, and water all around.

—That would be a holiday to remember, he said.

With the gale that morning they didn't hear the station-wagon returning, and it was the woman opening the door of the old man's room that interrupted them. Afterwards, while the old man slept, she said, over black coffee, to the girl: Any time you're ready I'll run you to the station.

A conflict like this was, in some ways, worse than blows or eye-scratching. As steadily as she could the girl said: If it doesn't upset your arrangements too much I'd love to see the pageant. It would add colour to the story.

—Colour, the woman said. Well, the beards, yes. Please yourself. But don't talk to the girls so much. It holds them up at their work. They lose. I lose. They're paid by piece-work.

Walking out into the gale the girl, for the sake of peace and the old man, avoided the weaving-shed where, she had been glad to think, the sullen faces of the underpaid weavers brightened when she entered. She loved the soft coloured wool, the intricacies of warping mills and heddles, the careful spacing of the threads. When you looked at the process you were as much part of it as the woolwinder and the sound of the looms was comforting, not mocking.

In the hotel bar the French hunters, driven in by the tempest that had also driven the birds to shelter, clustered around Diana who wore tight red pants and sneakers. Through a red beard like a burning bush the barman told her how five years ago the old man had run amok: Terrified the bloody country for a week. Wandering around with a loaded shotgun. Shooting and spearing salmon in the pool below the old mill. Then pleurisy laid him low and he was never the same again. Out on the islands they're savages. Half-crazy with inbreeding.

The raised wind-driven sea was sucking around the tree trunks that palisaded the white cottage. She walked, fighting the gale, along the thin line of sand the water had not devoured.

Baxbakualanuxsiwae, she recalled, shared his house with his wife, Qominoqa, a frightful female who cooked his ghoulish meals. A female slave, Kinqalalala, rounded up victims and collected corpses, well-hung meat in the house of the gods.

The thunder of the waves made her want to run and shout. One Sunday morning the small, deep-toned drums of the potlatch had set the whole village vibrating, until her father was forced to abandon his pulpit and say with a good humour more than Christian: Let us marvel at the force of tradition which is also one of the works of the Lord.

Once, in one of the books in her father's library, she had read that the Dinka people of the southern Sudan had a special sort of priest known as Masters of the Fishing Spear. These men, if they had great names as heroes, could be honourably killed when old and failing, by being buried alive at their own request and before all their assembled kin.

The islands, lost in spume and low-running clouds, were not to be seen.

In the dusk the bearded young men came in twos and threes under the featureless phoenix, across the courtyard, out by another gateway at the back of the weaving-shed, and up the hill to the mounded rath that was to be the open-air, torch-lit stage for their pageant. They wore white shirts and saffron kilts, cowskin pampooties made on the islands and dyed all colours, and thick woollen stockings cross-gartered to the knees. Most of them carried long wooden spears with silvered cardboard heads, and cardboard shields bright with brassy tacks. Some of them carried and some of them even played the bagpipes.

The blue weaving girls gathered on the landing outside the door of the shed, and cat-called, and addressed the bearded heroes by their ordinary everyday names and nicknames. They asked with irony if the men were going to the wars or to stick flounder on the flat sands with the flowing tide. When one bandy-legged, hairy-kneed veteran tottered past carrying a huge harp, and preceded by the curate who was directing the pageant, the blue girls held each other up, embracing in paroxysms and pantomimes of suppressed mirth.

—Never yet, the old man said, did I hear tell of one of these pageants that wasn't a holy laugh in the end. The Orangemen in the North, they say, had a pageant about the landing of King Billy in Carrickfergus harbour. But the sea was choppy that day and the boat tilted and didn't his majesty land on his arse in the water. And in Straide in Mayo they had a pageant about the eviction of the family of Michael Davitt who founded the Land League. But they built the mock cabin so strong that all the guns of Germany, let alone the battering rams of the boys who were pretending to be the bailiff's men, couldn't knock it down. Still and all, for the laugh, we'll go up to the rath and drink porter and eat pork sausages with the rest. It'll be a fine night with a full moon.

—At your age, Eamonn, that's the worst thing you could do.

—At my age?

He tossed aside the blackthorn he leaned on and, on the flat flag at the door of the house, hopped, but stiffly, from one foot to the other.

—These days I'm a two-year-old. The Indian maiden here will lead me up the slope. Minnehaha.

The woman's eyelids came down—it seemed one after the other, and very deliberately—to hide her eyes.

—Please yourself, then. Those girls have wasted enough time. I'll go up later with coffee and sandwiches.

His arm was around the girl's shoulders as they walked up a twisting boreen towards bonfires reddening in the dusk.

—Kings lived on this high hill, he said. All gone now, and dead and buried, generations of ancient kings, but the mounds and the ramparts are as solid as the day they were raised.

For one night, she thought, the kings had returned. She sat beside him on a rug on the mound. They were sheltered by a blossoming whitethorn from the light seawind. She held his hand. A huge round moon was motionless in a cloudless sky. Under its influence, and in the glow of a dozen bonfires, the bearded, cross-gartered country boys, the one decrepit harper, were no longer comic.

It was a masque, not a pageant. In a hut in a forest a dozen old broken men, remnants of a beaten clan, waited sadly and with little hope for the fulfillment of a prophecy that told of the coming of a young hero to lead them back to victory.

—This, said the oldest of them, is the last day of the year of our foretold salvation, and the last hour of the last day, yet the prophecy still stands even if it was made by one of the faery women who make game of men.

Her own old man moved closer to her on the rug.

The blue girls were just ending the long day's weaving. The coffee and sandwiches, and the woman with them, were still a good hour away; and also the thought that her duffle-bag and typewriter had been stored, for simpler departure, in the hotel with the red-bearded barman. She felt a brute, but she had a job to do—such as it was—and an old man's dream couldn't go on for ever, nor could she any longer defy a woman who didn't want her about the place.

When he pressed her hand she returned the pressure. She felt the great bones from which the flesh had melted away. She could have wept.

—The pity, he said, I didn't meet you when I was a young blade.

—I wasn't born then.

—We'd have found our own island and lived on it.

—There was a Japanese poet, she said, who was born in 1911, the year after Halley's Comet. He reckoned with a sad heart that he'd never see the comet since it wouldn't come again until 1986. That it was the same case with human encounters. His true friend would appear after his death. His sweetheart had died before he was born.

—A fine young man there, he said.

For who should arrive at that moment but the red barman himself, striding from darkness into the glare of the fires. Spear on shoulder. With the firelight glinting in his bush of a beard he could only be the hero who was promised. The crowds, seated on the slopes of the rath, cheered him. He was a popular man. For the broken old men he brought venison from the forest, cakes impaled on spears, and rolling barrels of ale from an enemy fortress he had that day captured single-handed. Also a sackful of golden goblets, made out of cardboard, and all the tokens, including a severed head in a sack, to prove he was the man of destiny. The exigencies of the drama did not, mercifully, call for the production of the severed head.

Then the harper harped on his harp and, far away in the shadows, the pipers played, slowly advancing towards the circle of fires to show that they were an army of young men following their unique leader. The watching crowds broke up into groups to eat sausages and pigs' feet and to drink porter. The dancing began on the rough dry grass. Led by two of the pipers, the dancers moved to find a better surface between the weaving-shed and the millhouse. Then the woman was there, and the curate with her helping her to carry cups and sandwiches and the coffee pot.

—Not pigs' feet, Eamonn. Not all that greasy fat.

—'Tisn't often now I have a night out under the moon.

—A midsummer night, she said. Madness.

—I could leap through bonfires, woman. I feel like twenty. Pour milk on the ground for the good people who lived here before kings were heard tell of. It's not lucky to let them go hungry.

—What silly waste, the woman said.

Slowly the girl tilted her cup and let the coffee drain down to the grass. She said: They might fancy coffee.

His great hand was in the bowl of brown sugar and the fistful he took he tossed into the air, scattering it over the crowd. Faces, some laughing, some curious, turned towards them in the firelight.

—The world knows, he said, that the good people have a sweet tooth. Halley's Comet, Minnehaha, will come again.

They laughed loudly together. She noticed that they were again hand in hand. The curate, pretending to answer a call from one of the bearded men, moved away. The woman poured more coffee. By the farthest fire the girl saw the red man standing and beckoning. He probably had notions above his state in life, but he could give her a lift to the nearest town, and her leather jacket was stout enough to resist even the paws and the pinches of a man mentioned in prophecy. When the barman moved off down the slope towards the millhouse, she excused herself.

—Come back soon Minnehaha, the old man called after her. Don't delay. It's a fine night for seeing comets.

—Eamonn, isn't it time you went in out of the night air?

Like in movies about Italy, the girl thought, everything ends with a carnival. She walked down the slope, taking his second youth with her, towing the sailing islands behind her. She was the sea receding for ever from a stranded master of the sea.

By torchlight in the cobbled courtyard blue weaving girls danced with bearded warriors who had cast aside their spears.

She walked on under the stone phoenix that could never arise again because it had merely decayed, never been purified by fire and burned to ashes.

With car, duffle-bag and typewriter, the red barman was waiting. She sat beside him and was driven off to find her next little-known hero.

DOWN THEN BY DERRY

The first time Tom Cunningham ever saw Sadie Law's brother, Francie, that brother was airborne between the saddle of a racing bicycle and a stockade filled with female lunatics. Francie is not the chief part of this story, nor is his sister, but since he has been mentioned, it might be fair to his fame and memory to say who he was and what he was doing in the air in that odd place.

A resident medical officer in the district's mental hospital had, years before, been a believer in athletics as curative therapy for the crazy: running and jumping and the lord knows what. So he set those who were out of cells and strait-jackets, and otherwise capable, at the running and jumping, barring, for good reasons the throwing of the hammer or the discus, or the tossing of the caber—which can be dangerous occupations even for the sane. Then the medical officer, to introduce a sanative, competitive spirit, organised an annual sports meeting, with cups, shields and lesser prizes. The thing grew and grew. That medical officer died and went to Valhalla. The annual meeting continued to grow until it was one of the most notable sporting events in that part of the country. Professionals competed. The crazy men and women, those of them who could be out and about, were now only two small corralled sections among the spectators. They had been pushed back into the shouting or gibbering shadows where everybody, except the man in Valhalla, thought they belonged.

Francie Law was a famous track cyclist. That was how he came to be there in the air. There was one bad corner on the packed cinder track. This day there was a pile-up and Francie was catapulted clean, to land among the lunatic ladies. He survived. It was as a hero-worshipper bearing grapes to Francie's hospital bedside—Francie, wherever he was, always smelled of embrocation—that Tom Cunningham first met Francie's sister, Sadie, who was almost as famous as her brother, but not for track-cycling.

—She's Number One, according to all the talk, Tom said to his favourite friend who was five years younger than him.

Tom was nineteen.

—And she liked me, Tom said. We have a date. She wore a black leather coat with a belt. There was a good warm smell off it. Like the smell of the plush seats at the back of the cinema where all the feeling goes on. Hot stuff, boy. Also the smell of embrocation. Rub it up good. Frank Mullan told me she was okay and easy to get, if you once got to know her. And the May devotions are on the way. Long evenings. Warm grass. And Frank Mullan should know. He knows them all.

Of course it goes without saying that the devotions on May evenings in the parish church, with the high, limping, Gothic spires, went away back to something far before the worship of holy purity and the blessed virgin, to some pagan festival of the rites of spring. This he found out afterwards by reading, and by much dull talk, in more sophisticated places, heaven help us, than his own native town. But in the spring of that year he neither knew nor worried about such things, as he knelt beside Tom Cunningham in the side aisle to the left hand of the high altar.

Oh, those brown angels cut in wood of a slightly lighter colour than the wood of the beams to which they provided a figurehead finish. They swooped out towards each other over the nave and eyed the praying people. Once he had tried to write a poem about them:

> In church the angels cut in wood,
> In row on row arranged,
> Stand always as before they stood,
> And only I am changed.

But it wouldn't work. The angels weren't standing, for God's sake, they had no legs or feet to stand on, or, if they had, those legs were buried in the wood of the beams from which winged torsos and long-haired oaken heads seemed to have instantaneously, ecstatically, emerged. Times, he still saw those angels in his dreams, soaring, in a sort of a way, over altar, incense, monstrance, praying priest, responding mumbling people, over Tom Cunningham in the side aisle making cute sideways eyes and secret signs at Sadie Law who knelt with her favourite friend directly under the angels in the nave. Whatever about bullshit talk and the rites of spring, the devotions on May evenings was where you met people for good or evil; and all around the church, high on a hill with its hopalong spires, the rolling country was rich in deep grass and the birds were making mocking calls along hidden lovers' lanes. The high grassy embankments along the railways that went out of the town to the Donegal sea at Bundoran, or to Dublin or Belfast, or down then by Derry to the northern sea, were a sort of secret world where only lovers went in the long evenings. No respectable girl would be seen walking along the railway. The art was in not being seen.

His daughter, who was eighteen years of age, said to his mother who admitted to being eighty-five: Dad must have been happy here in this town in his schooldays. He's always singing a song. Well, not singing exactly. It has no particular tune. No beat. Dad's a bit of a square. It goes more like an African chant.

—Wallawalla boom boom, said his son who was fourteen.

—John, said the daughter, mind your manners. Granny doesn't dig Swahili. No granny. The song begins like this. Thrice happy and blessed were the days of my childhood and happy the hours I wandered from school, by green Mountjoy's forest, our dear native wildwood, and the green flowery banks of the serpentine Strule.

—Mountjoy forest, he said, was part of the estate of Lord and Lady Blessington. Back in the days of the great Napoleon. That was an old song.

—He was a good scholar, his mother said. He was very fond of reading poetry out loud. In the mornings after breakfast. Before he went to school.

As if he wasn't there at all. His daughter giggled.

He was accustomed to his mother rhapsodising in this way, talking about him to other people in his presence. Once she had said to a friend of his: He would be the best man in Ireland if it wasn't for the little weakness.

Afterwards his friend had said with great good humour: with you standing there I couldn't very well ask her which weakness she meant.

Another time and under similar circumstances she had said to the same friend: His father, God rest him, put on some weight when he passed forty, but he never swelled like that.

Pointing to him. As if, by God, the son, had had a dropsical condition.

To her grand-daughter and grandson she said: He read Shelley. If Winter comes can Spring be far behind. I liked that. Shelley was a good poet. Although my own mother could never understand about Tennyson and the brook. She used to say: Poor fellow, could nobody stop him. I think she thought it was about some unfortunate man that had something astray with his bowels. Then there was one poet that droned on and on about Adam and Eve and the fall of Satan.

She spat mildly and politely towards the fireplace where, winter or summer, there was always a fire. She preserved many old country customs. One was to spit when, by inadvertence or necessity, one mentioned a name of the devil—and his names were legion.

Twenty-eight years later he was still a little ashamed that he had inflicted on his mother's patient ears the monotony of Milton, even to the utter extremity of the Latin verses.

—Milton, he said, a bit of a bore.

But nobody paid the least attention to him. So he closed his eyes and his mind to the lot of them: the mother, old, wrinkled, wearing a battered old felt hat that looked like a German helmet, but with an eye as bright and inquisitive as it must have been when she was a lively singing country girl, and the man she was to marry was walking round and round the South African veldt; and he himself wasn't even a fragment of an imagination, or a gleam or a glint in his father's eye; the daughter, pert, small, lively, endlessly talkative; the son, tall, easy-going, slouching when he walked—as his grandfather had done. It was uncanny to observe such resemblances.

Since not one of the three of them paid any attention to him he shut his eyes and his mind to them and went on his own through the town, and back to the past that had made the town and him.

The two tall limping Gothic spires rose high above the hilly narrow streets. Those two spires and the simple plain spire of the Protestant church—that would be Church of Ireland, for the Methodists and Presbyterians did not rise to spires—could be seen for a distance of ten miles. They soared, they were prayers of a sort, over the riverine countryside.

The taller spire was all of two hundred and thirty feet high, thirty of that being for the surmounting cross. To climb up the inside of that spire you went first by a winding stone stairway to the organ loft, then by a steep straight wooden stairway to the shaky creaky platform where the sexton stood when he pulled the bell-rope, then up a series of perpendicular ladders to the place where the two bells were hung, sullen and heavy, but ready at the twitch of a rope to do their duty. From that eminence, one hundred and fifty feet up, you could look down on everything. The town was almost flat, no longer all humps and hills and high ridged roofs and steep narrow streets. Down there was the meeting place of two rivers, the Camowen and the Drumragh: a sparkling trout-water, a sullen pike-water. Who could comprehend the differences there were between rivers, not to speak now of the Amazon and the Seine and the Volga and the Whang-ho and the Ohio, but even between neighbouring rivers destined to marry and to melt into one? United, the waters of Drumragh and Camowen went on under the name of the Strule, sweeping in a great horseshoe around the wide holm below the military barracks, tramping and tossing northwards to meet yet another river, the Fairywater, then to vanish glistening into a green-and-blue infinity.

Except you were the sexton, or some lesser person authorised by him, you were not, by no means, supposed to be up there at all. Dusty boards, with crazy, dizzy gaps between them, swayed and bent under your feet. Vicious jackdaws screeched. The blue-and-green infinity into which the sparkling water vanished was the place where Blessington's Rangers had once walked, speaking Gaelic, great axes on shoulders. They cut down the trees to make timber for war against Bonaparte, and money to keep Lord and Lady Blessington, their daughter, and the ineffable Count D'Orsay gallivanting.

One day coming home from school alone—that was a time of the day when it wasn't easy to be alone but, with cunning, it could be managed—he had found the door at the foot of the stone stairway open and had taken the chance that it was open by accident. It was. He made the climb. He saw the world. He was alone with the jackdaws and the moan of the wind. Then on the way down the perpendicular ladders he had missed a rung, slipped, screamed with the jackdaws, grabbed desperately and held on. Just about where the sexton would stand to pull the bell-rope he had vomited a sort of striped vomit that he had never seen before. Even in boyhood there was the fear of death.

Nobody, thank God, had ever found out who had thus paid tribute, made offertory, in the holy place. For weeks afterwards he had felt dizzy even when climbing the stairs to his bedroom.

When the war was over and Boney beaten, the gallivanting lords and ladies had no more use for the woodsmen of Mountjoy. For the last time they walked down there below in the old Flax Market that hadn't changed much since 1820: in their rough boots and frieze coats, axes on shoulders, speaking a guttural language that was doomed almost to die, singing, drinking, fighting among each other, but standing shoulder to shoulder or axe to axe against the world. The paltry townsmen and shopkeepers must have breathed easily when the woodsmen went north to Derry to board the American boat.

As a boy he had known of them and walked among their shadows in the Old Market: No more will we see the gay silver trouts playing, or the herd of wild deer through its forest be straying, or the nymph and gay swain on its flowery bank straying, or hear the loud guns of the sportsmen of Strule.

On those May evenings the steeplejacks were swinging on the spires, tiny black dwarfs sitting in wooden chairs at the ends of ropes. They were pointing the stones, which meant that they smeared in fresh cement, netted the soaring prayers in nets of new white. Snug and

secure in deep warm grass on a railway embankment from which there
was a view both of the tips of the roofs of the town and of one deep
curve of the slow pike-infested Drumragh River, Tom and Sadie, Tom's
friend and Sadie's friend, lay on their backs and watched the dwarfs on
the steeples.

—Why, Angela said, did they not build one steeple as long as the
other?

—As high, he said, you mean.

—High or long, she said, what's the difference?

She had a wide humorous mouth that, some evening, with the help of
God, he would get around to kissing.

—It all depends, Tom said, on which way you're going. Like up or
down or sideways.

—Why, she repeated.

She was a stubborn girl. He held her hand.

—In this life, Tom said, there is nothing perfect.

—No, he said.

Because he knew.

—Two men were killed on the smaller steeple. So they stopped.

—Brian, said Tom, always has a better story. Say us a poem, Brian.

—That's no story. It's gospel truth.

Tom and Sadie were kissing, gurgling. Angela tickled his palm.

—That's a job, he said, I wouldn't have for all the tea in China.

He meant being a steeplejack.

Tom surfaced. He said: I'm not so sure. I wouldn't mind being able to
get up as high as that.

Sadie said: You could always try.

With her left hand she gently massaged Tom's grey-flannelled crotch.

He watched Sadie's small moving hand. He wondered how many
people within a ten-mile radius, in the town, in villages, from
farmhouse doorways, walking along laneways, or fishing, or lying on
grass, were watching the steeplejacks on the spires.

For no reason that he could explain he thought it would be exciting to
see that face again, the wide humorous mouth, the brown hair that
curled like two little brown horns over her temples, the plump fresh
cheeks. The hair, though, wouldn't be brown any more. Don't forget
that. Look for something older. Three years older than yourself: a
reasonable gap of years, once upon a time, for a girl who could teach and
a boy who was willing, even afraid, to learn.

—That woman, his daughter said, who writes you those letters from

Indiana. What part of this town did she live in? When she was a girl, I mean.

The three of them were walking down the steep High Street. Behind and above them, where two narrower streets met to form the High Street, was the eighteenth-century courthouse, high steps before it and Doric columns, dominating the long undulations of High Street and Campsie Avenue until the houses ended and the point of vision was buried in deep trees.

He told them that there had once been in the town a policeman so lazy that he hated to walk. So he sat all day, when the day was sunny, on the courthouse steps. When his superior officers asked him what he thought he was at, he defended himself by saying that he had the whole town under observation.

This grey day, the last sad day but one of the old year, would have been no day for sitting on the steps.

They laughed at the memory of the lazy policeman, and descended the steep street. The daughter said: You never met her, all the times you were in the States?

—I never even met her, I only saw her, when we were young together here in this town. She's a shadow, a memory.

—Shadows, she said precisely, don't write letters. Memories might.

—One time last year, he said, I had hoped to meet her. I was, so to speak, passing that way. That is, within a few hundred miles or so of where she lives. That's not far, out there.

—Just next door, his son said.

—It was in March, he said, and I was on the way north to give a lecture in Minnesota. I crossed Indiana.

—See any Injuns dad, said the son.

—No, what I mostly remember about Indiana is big barns and ducks, the big ducks that we call Muscovy ducks. Never saw so many Muscovy ducks, anywhere else in the world.

—But then dad, his daughter said, you never were in Muscovy.

—Or if he was, said the son, he never told us.

In March in Indiana the endless flat brown land still shivered. The harness-racing tracks by the roadside were soggy and empty. The last of the snow lay here and there in sordid mounds. Cattle, with a certain guilty look about them, foraged among the tall battered corn-stalks of last year's harvest. There was ice at the fringes of creeks and rivers that looked far too small to negotiate such interminable expanses of flat land. Great round-roofed barns stood aloof from, yet still dwarfed, the neat houses. Flat and sombre the land went every way to a far horizon . . .

—A small American penny, his daughter said, for your wandering thoughts.

He told her that in one small field near the city of Lafayette he had seen a flock of more than two hundred Muscovy ducks. The field had been between a railway and a line of power pylons.

—Nothing, he explained, more emphasises distance in flat land than a line of pylons striding on and on for ever, giants marching, carrying cables on their shoulders, until they vanish east or west.

—Or north or south, his son said.

—Now, she said sweetly, we know all about electricity. Dad, you're such a dear old bore. We couldn't care less about ducks or pylons. We want to know about the woman who writes you those marvellous letters from Indiana.

—She was an orphan, he said. In an orphanage. In Derry City.

—So far so good, his son said.

—She was taken out of the orphanage by this woman and reared in this town. She suffered a lot from illness. She wore a leg-splint when she was a child. She grew up. She read books. My father used to talk a lot about her. He used to say: You should meet that young woman. She's a wonder.

—But I was in college in Dublin, by that time, coming and going and somehow or other I never did get the opportunity of speaking to her. My memory is of a rather long beautiful face, sort of madonna, and fair hair. Framed like an old picture in glass and wood, against a background of coloured magazines and paperbacked books. Because my last recollection of her is that she was working in the bookstall in the railway station. During the war she went off to London, married an American. Then seven or eight years ago she read something I'd written and wrote to me. That's the whole story.

She had written: You may have a vague recollection of who I am when you read my name. Then again you may not. It's been a long time. About thirty years. But I remember you very well, indeed: on your way to school, to church, walking the roads around our town, always, it seemed to me, alone.

That would be a romantic young girl confusing an average sullen lout of a fellow with her private image of Lord Byron.

—We rarely said more than hello. We lived in the same town all our growing years. We walked the same roads, knew the same people, and didn't meet at all. We might have shared a common interest. I loved books, poetry, music, but had little opportunity to enjoy any of them. I did manage to read quite a lot, and to remember poetry, and get a little music on an old radio. I walked, and thought of the books I'd read, and repeated the poetry to myself, and could hear the music again along the quiet roads. Thus I survived the town I was born in. Though mostly I remember it with love, because of Margaret, the woman who reared me. She was gentle, poor, uneducated, but with a lively mind and kind to all things living—especially to me when she took me from the nightmare of the orphanage in Derry, haunting me even now with its coldness, the crooked hilly streets of Derry, the jail, the Diamond, the wide Foyle which is really our own Strule, and the ships.

—Another penny for your thoughts, his daughter said. Or a measly nickel.

They turned right from the Market Street along the Dublin Road, past a filling station and a Presbyterian church, a toy-like gasworks, the old white houses of Irishtown. Beyond Irishtown, he told them, was the Drumragh River and the old humped King's Bridge where James Stuart, falling back from the walls of Derry, had watched the town burn behind him.

Then they were ascending through a pleasant affluent suburb.

—No, he said, this wasn't the part of the town she lived in. We're not going that way just at the moment.

They were, in fact, walking to say a prayer at his father's grave. Everywhere he went he carried with him for luck a white stone from the grave. A white stone from the grave of a kind man would have to be lucky, wouldn't it, if there was the least pick of reason in the universe? But in a drunken moment in Dubin City he had loaned the stone to a man who ran greyhounds, and this particular greyhound had won, and the man begged to be allowed to keep the stone. Today he would say his prayer and take away with him another white stone.

The Protestants lay to the left of the cemetery's main avenue, the Catholics to the right, and between them, on a slight rise, the stone oratory, cold and draughty, where on harsh days the last prayers were said over the coffins. He never remembered the wind around the corners of that oratory as being, even in summer, anything but bitterly cold. This last dead day, but one, of the year it was unbearable. Bravely the boy and girl knelt on the damp earth and prayed. He knelt with them, not praying, talking without words to the man under the clay, or somewhere in the air around him, and around him wherever in the world he went: the dead hover for ever over the living.

Low dark clouds travelling, or being forced to travel, fast, bulged with rain. To the lee of the empty oratory the three of them stood and looked over the forest of obelisks and Celtic crosses, Sacred Hearts and sorrowing mothers, at the distant sweep of the flooded Drumragh, at where the railway line used to cross it by a red metal bridge. The bridge was gone and the railway too—sold for scrap. But three hundred yards to the east of the river, there was still the stone bridge under the embankment—it looked like a gateway into an old walled city—and the lovers' lane that led into the fields, and across the fields to the wooded brambly slope above one of the deepest, most brooding of the river's pike-pools.

Would it be sin or the beginning of living to touch the hidden flesh of Angela? His dream of fair women was all about the creeping hand, the hair, the warmth. That was all that Tom and the other boys talked about.

She lay on her back in the brambly wood—the pike hovering in the pool below them—and he fumbled fearfully, and tickled her, his hand timidly outside her dress. But when she reached for him he rolled away. She laughed for a longer time than seemed necessary. From the far side of a clump of bushes he heard Tom say to Sadie: There must be nothing in Brown's house that doesn't smell of embrocation.

—The grave was very weedy, the daughter said.

—So I noticed. Your grandmother pays good money to have it kept clean and covered with white stones. On the way out I'll call to the caretaker's house and talk to him.

The clay in the centre of the grave had sunk. He was glad that neither son nor daughter had noticed that. It would be so painful to have to explain to young people, or even to oneself, that clay sank so when the coffin underneath had collapsed.

The hotel they stopped in was a mile outside the town, a domed mid-nineteenth-century house, miscalled a castle, on a hill top with a view of the heathery uplands the Camowen came from, and quite close to a park called the Lovers' Retreat, but known to the soldiers in the barracks as Buggers' Den.

The aged mother was safely at home in bed, in her small house across the narrow street from those gigantic limping spires. She liked to be close to the quietness of the church, the glowing red circle around the sanctuary lamp where she remembered and prayed for and to the dead man.

Leaving her in peace they had walked through the lighted crowded town, along a quiet dim suburban road, over a bridge that crossed the invisible talkative Camowen—there was a good gravelly trout pool just below that bridge. They dined late in a deserted dining-room. Along a corridor there was the noise of merriment from the bar. His son asked him which room had been the haunted room in the days when the hotel had been a castle.

—For the sake of the ghost, the daughter said, let's hope it wasn't where the bar is now.

—Ghosts, he told her, might like company.

—Not mine I pray, she said.

—Fraidy cat, the son said. A ghost couldn't hurt you.

—That ghost, he told them, couldn't hurt anyone. The story was that the people who lived here called in the priest and he blessed the room and put the ghost in a bottle.

—Poor ghost, she said.

—But where, she wondered, did the priest put the bottle.

—On the river, the son said. And it floated over the sea, to England, and somebody found it and opened it, and got a ghost instead of a message.

He saw them to their rooms. No ghost could survive in such up-to-date comfort. No ghost could rest in peace in any of the coloured bottles in the bar. The noisy local drinkers had gone home, taking their din with them. A few commercial men, talking of odds and ends, drinking slowly but with style, sat in an alcove. He joined them.

—Did you like it out there, they asked him.

—You were a friend of Tom Cunningham, they said.

—It's good out there. Fine people. Hospitable. The sort of people I meet.

—Tom went into the Palestine police after the war, they said. Then he went farther east. Never heard of since.

—Chasing the women in China, they said.

—But the crime in America, they said. Did you ever come up against that?

—It's there. But I never came up against it. Except in the newspapers.

—By God, they said, they have picturesque murders out there. We never have anything here except an odd friendly class of a murder. But out there. That fellow in Chicago and the nurses. And the young fellow that made the women in the beauty parlour lie down like the spokes of a wheel and then shot the living daylights out of them.

—The one that sticks most in my mind . . .

They were all attention.

. . . was the girl in the sump. This sump is an overflow pond at the back of a dry-cleaning plant. One morning a man walking by sees a girl's leg standing up out of the water.

—Clothed in white samite, they said. Mystic, wonderful.

—Seems she had been by day a teller in a bank and by night a go-go dancer in a discotheque. One day she walks out of the bank with a bagful of thousands of dollars. She is next encountered in the sump, one leg surfacing, her hands tied behind her back, her throat cut, the bag and the dollars gone. A barman from the discotheque is also missing.

—All for love, they said.

The long cold day, the search for the past, the drink, the warm company, had made him maudlin.

—When I read the newspapers today there are times I think I was reared in the Garden of Eden.

—Weren't we all, they said.

But it hadn't been the Garden of Eden for one waif of a girl, now a woman in far-away Indiana. From Atlanta, Georgia, where he had been for two years he had remailed to her the local newspapers that had come to him from this town.

She had written: That photograph of the demolition of the old stone railway bridge at Brook Corner saddened me. I recall that bridge with affection. When I'd spent about fourteen months flat on my back in the County Hospital, and was at last permitted up on crutches, I headed, somewhat shakily, under that bridge to begin the first of many walks. I still remember the bridge framing the road beyond like a picture, and the incredible green of the fields, the flowering hedges, the smell of hawthorn. The bridge became for me a gateway: to happy solitude. When I had trachoma and thought I might go blind my bitterest thought was that I might never again see the world through that bridge. Margaret's brother, Fred, was my companion and consolation in those dark days. He had been hired out at the age of six to work with a farmer and Margaret remembered seeing the golden-curly-haired child going off in the farmer's trap.

—Perhaps that was why Fred never cared to work. He hadn't, for about twenty-five years before he died, not because he couldn't but simply because he didn't want to. Oh, on a number of occasions he worked, briefly, for farmers at harvest time, was rarely paid in cash but in kind; and only on condition that his dog, Major, could accompany him. Major barked all day, every day, as though indignant at his master's labours, and much to the chagrin of the other workers and the farmer. But since, when he wanted to, Fred could work as well as the others, his services were always desired and he was permitted to stay, dog and all.

—He was a strange silent man who sat by the fire all day with a far-off look in his eyes. He had very blue eyes. He rarely spoke to anybody outside the house. He was my sole companion during many long hours when I was confined to bed. I would read to him and ask him to spell and he would deliberately mis-spell and would be delighted when I would sharply correct him. I never knew how much I loved him until he died.

—Margaret housekept for Morris, the lawyer, who lived in the Georgian house beside the church with the high spires, and that left Fred and me a lot alone, and Fred would cook for me. Once, after I had been with Margaret several months, some sadistic neighbour woman told me that I was being sent back to the orphanage. So terrified was I that I hobbled up to the church and stood for hours across the street from the lawyer's house, waiting, the wind moaning away up in the spires in the darkness, until Margaret came and comforted me, led me home by the hand to Fred and Major and numerous cats, and a one-legged hen who had a nest in the corner and who was infuriated if another hen ever came to the back door in search of scraps.

His room was haunted, sure enough. He had sat too late, drunk too much, perhaps released the ghosts from the bottles. Oaken angels sang from the ceiling. A tearful crippled girl waited in the darkness at the foot of spires lost also in the windy darkness, no longer magic towers from which one could see the world. The leg of a girl who had stolen for love stood up like a stump of wood out of stagnant water.

Very cautiously he had asked his mother: Do you remember a family called Law? Are they still in the town? One of them, I think, was a famous racing cyclist.

Cautiously: because in her eyes there were times when he was still fourteen or less and there were people that he wasn't supposed to know.

—Oh, I remember the Laws. They were famous, indeed.

Around the house she had a fancy for dressing as if she were a pirate chief. Or perhaps it was a gipsy queen. Sometimes instead of the helmet-shaped hat she wore a white gipsy head-handkerchief; and a long red dressing-gown and a Galway shawl with the corners tucked back under her oxters and pinned behind.

—One of them called in to see me one morning after Sunday mass. A Law or a half-Law or a quarter-Law or a by-Law. You wouldn't have much time for the like of them. Not condemning anyone for the weakness, but there were more distant cousins in that clan than was natural. Or godly.

That seemed to be that.

—You wouldn't have expected much of the Laws, she said. But it's heartrending to see the fate of some families that had every chance that God and man could give them.

—Like who, for instance?

—Like many I've seen. Like the Glenshrule family, for one.

The red bull of Glenshrule roared through his haunted dreams.

—Glenshrule's sold, she said, and in the hands of strangers.

The bull, he supposed, had been sold to make bovril.

Two private roadways led into the old house at Glenshrule, one from the steep by-road along which the crippled girl had hobbled to find peace, one from the road that led west to the Donegal sea. To either hand on either road it was all Glenshrule land, green, bountiful, a little unkempt, cattle country, little tillage. The three bachelor brothers of Glenshrule were gentlemen farmers: which meant whipcord breeches and booze and hunting horses. But they were frank, reckless, generous, easy in their money and good breeding, and made no objection to the townspeople using their private roads for circular walks on Sunday afternoons. Roving boys used those roads all the time, and the fields around them, and the only prohibiting notice to be seen told you to beware of the red bull.

—Christ, look at the size of him, Tom cried with an artist's enthusiasm. Boy, if you were built like that you'd be welcome anywhere.

They sat on a five-barred iron gate. Between them and the bull's private meadow was the additional fortification of a strong wooden gate. He was an unruly bull. His red coat shone. He had a head near as big as the head of the mouldy bison they had seen in the Old Market in Bostock and Wombell's travelling menagerie. He rooted at the ground with one fore-foot. The great head rose and fell. He didn't roar. He rumbled all the time like a train, far away, going into a tunnel.

—There's a lot to be said, Tom said, for being a bull.

—Everybody puts up with your tantrums.

—There's more to it than that.

Then the lady of Glenshrule, the one single sister of the three bachelor brothers, rode by on a bay mare. To acknowledge that they existed she raised her riding-crop, she smiled and said: Don't tempt him. Don't enter the meadow. Bulls eat boys.

—Boys, Tom muttered.

He was very bitter.

—There's also a lot to be said, he said, for being a bay mare.

She was bareheaded. She was blonde. She was twenty-five. She was blonde, she was blonde, she was blonde and calm-faced, and all the officers in the barracks pursued her. Years afterwards—altering the truth, as memory always does—he thought that he had then thought about queen and huntress, chaste and fair. But he hadn't. He had been too breathless to think of anything except, perhaps, that Sadie and Angela, lively and provoking as they could be, were still only in the servant-maid class.

She rode on towards the Donegal road. The sound of the hooves died away. The red bull, calmed, had lain down on the grass.

—One Sunday evening I sat beside her in the church, Tom said. My right leg against her left. It burned me. I can feel it still.

He rubbed his right thigh slowly, then sniffed his hand.

—I swear to God, he said, she pressed her thigh against mine. It made short work of the holy hour.

That was the year Tom and himself had been barred from the town's one cinema because Tom, ever an eager and enquiring mind, had discovered the anti-social use of hydrogen sulphide. A few sizzling test-tubes planted here and there in the darkness could have tumultuous effects on the audience. Old Mr. Pritchard—he was so old that it was suspected he had fought in the Zulu war—was heard to say in a barracks-square voice that some bloke here needed a purge of broken bottles. But three burly ushers simply purged Tom and his companion from the audience, two of them to hold Tom, the other to herd the companion before him.

Such a splendid deed and its consequences gave the two of them the glory of outlaws among their contemporaries. And to be barred from the delights of Eddy Cantor's Rome, or of Broadway with its gold-diggers, or of Wallace Beery's Big House, meant more nights in the Old Flax Market. That was fair enough, because the Old Flax Market was the place for outlaws. Black-uniformed constables patrolled the streets but, unless there was very audible drunken disorder, they left the Old Flax Market alone. No flax was ever sold there any more.

—The ghosts of the woodsmen are still here, he told Tom. This was their place when they came to town.

—You and those bloody woodsmen. You're a haunted man.

The unpaved three acres of the Old Market were sodden and puddled. A sharply-defined half-moon cut like a cleaver through wispy running clouds. He shouted at the moon: No more will the fair one of each shady bower hail her dear boy of that once happy hour, or present him again with a garland of flowers that they oft times selected and wove by the Strule.

—And poetry, boy, will be your ruination. Poetry will get you nowhere with Angela. Move in man. Angela demands action.

The moon, even if it was only half a moon, was useful to outlaws in a land of outlaws. For there were only three gas-lamps in the whole of the Old Flax Market and gas-lamps were little use on windy nights or when somebody, for fun or hellery, wished to quench them. One lamp was on a wall-bracket at the corner of a rowdy dance hall. It lighted, when it was allowed to, the wooden stairway to the door of the dance hall, and the people ascending or descending or standing in groups making noise. One lamp lighted the covered cobbled entry-way from the High Street. The third lighted the muddy uncovered exit to a dark riverside walk from which an irate lover had, about that time, heaved his fancy into the river.

—Let's have a look, Tom said, at the Jennet's corner. You'd see things there you never saw at the pictures.

—But look, he said, there goes the Bluebottle, her legs like elevenpence marked on a new bucket.

The drum boomed, the horn blared from the dance hall. The half-moon coldly shone on the Strule waters that flowed by one side of the Old Market.

—If your woodsmen ever walked here you can bloody well guess what they were after.

A tall thin girl in a blue coat was being eased into the shadows by a drunken man.

—Would you believe it, Tom said, she fought like a cat here one night with one of the Fighting McDermotts. The one with the dinge in his temple where some decent man brained him with a bottle of port-wine. When she wouldn't go with him he shouted he'd tell her father that sent her out for money, and her uncle that broke her in. She tore the red face off him.

—He rings the bell, her uncle.

—They say he rang the bell for her when she was thirteen.

There then was the terror of the dark walk by the river. The uncle who rang the bell as one of the last town-criers was a figure out of a German fairy-tale, a pied piper, tall hard hat, tailed coat, long grey moustache, a small man with a voice of thunder, swinging his handbell, shouting out fragments of news: that a group of strolling players would perform in the town hall, that the water supply would be turned off—for repairs to pipes in this or that part of the town, that such and such a house property would be auctioned. Was it credible that a comic fairy-tale figure should also be a part of some sniggering story? The Bluebottle vanished ahead of them into some riverside bushes. Where the river made an elbow bend a group of smoking muttering men waited at the Jennet's corner. Her shady bower was a wooden shelter put there by the town council to protect Sunday walkers from sudden showers. The council had not intended to cater for the comfort of the Jennet and her customers. She was a raw-boned red headed country girl whose husband was in the mental hospital.

—Good natured and charges very little, Tom said.

Some of the shadowy courtiers called after them.

—But, boy, a little bit too open to the general public for men of taste like ourselves. Take me back to sweet sinful Sadie. Or the lady of Glenshrule on her bay mare.

She rode on to the Donegal road, the hooves dancing clippety-clop, and the bull lay down in the meadow.

—What went wrong there, he said to his mother. They had everything.

—What would go wrong but debt and drink and the want of wit. The three brothers fled to Canada.

—They followed the woodsmen.

His mother didn't hear him.

—And my, she said, she looked lovely when she rode out astraddle on that bay mare.

—Tom Cunningham would have agreed with you.

—Oh, Tom Cunningham was a rare one. Very freckled when he was a little boy. And curly-haired. I'm amazed you remember him. He went to the war and never came back when it was over. But then you always had a good memory.

—I always had.

—She lived alone after the brothers left, and she never married, and went on drinking. There was a bit of scandal, too. But I never paid much attention to that sort of talk. She died in the ambulance on the way to hospital. But not, thank God, without the priest. For one of the curates was driving past just at that moment.

On the road she had ridden over on the bay mare.

—The Lord, his mother said, has everything mixed with mercy.

—He must have a lot of mercy for orphans, he said.

—Tell granny that story, dad, about the girl in the rain. The woman who writes to you. When she was a child, I mean.

She could still be outside there, the ghost of a frightened child, standing in the darkness at the foot of the spires. But one day in the orphanage playground she had broken out in rebellion.

—A sudden storm came up. The nuns called us in. We were to shelter, cold and miserable, in a sort of arcade or cloister. I started in with the rest, but suddenly I stopped and ran back to the playground. It was pouring. I was alone. The nuns called me. I wouldn't come. I danced around that playground in my bare feet, hair and dress soaking wet. Repeated calls failed to move me. Two nuns came after me. I ran and danced from one side to the other, dodging the hands that tried to clutch me. I laughed and danced in the wind and rain. I'd wait until they got close and then I'd run like the wind. Their long robes were heavy with water. They were exhausted. But I was exhilarated. Until suddenly I collapsed and was dragged inside. Mute and terrified and expecting to be lashed. I don't know why, but my defiance was forgiven.

—It was a ballet, his daughter said. The truant in the rain.

—Nuns on the run, said the son.

The German poet, long ago, went walking in the botanical gardens, saw plants, that elsewhere he had seen only in pots or under glass, growing cheerfully under the open sky. Might he not discover among them, the original plant from which all others are derived? After all, the poet thought, it must exist, the innermost nucleus.

A crazy idea. A wise old woman dressed like a gipsy or a pirate chief. A pert young girl curious about the American woman who had once been an orphan child in this town. Sadie Law with her leather coat and the smell of embrocation. A blonde horse-riding queen and huntress dying of drink in the back of an ambulance. Two sad creatures, nicknamed, one for the colour of her only coat and the hard meagre shape of her body, the other because it was said, with sniggers, that she was hopeless of progeny and disreputable in her ancestry. Angela running hand in hand with him on a wet Saturday afternoon through the Old Flax Market.

The place was empty that day. Not even the ghosts of the woodsmen walked in the grey light and the rain. He couldn't remember where Sadie and Tom had been at that time. The Jennet's corner was also empty. In the wooden shelter, hacked with names and odd obscenities and coy references to local love affairs, they sat on a creaky seat and kissed and fumbled. Then around a corner of the shelter came the Jennet herself, leading a staggering cattle-drover, his ash-plant in his hand.

—Wee fellow, he said with great camaraderie, I suppose you're at the same game as myself.

—He's too bashful, Angela said.

—He'll live to learn, the Jennet said. They all do.

The rain ran down her bony face. Wet yellow hair stuck out from under a red tam o'shanter. Her eyes were of such a bright blue as to make her seem blind.

—The good book, the drover said, says that the wise man falls seven times. And, as sure as my name is Solomon, I'm going to fall now.

So the wee fellow retreated from the shelter, dragging Angela with him for a little way until she dug her heels into the muddy ground. The river was a brown fresh, taking with it broken branches and hay from flooded meadows, sweeping on, down then by Derry our dear boys are sailing. Now he remembered that that day Angela had been wearing a sou'wester and Sadie's black coat, a little big for her but a stronghold against the rain.

—What do we need to run for? You might learn something.

He said nothing.

—Wee boy, she said. I'm going back for a peep.

He stood alone looking at the turbulent river, looking across the river at the limping spires, one proud and complete, one for ever unfinished, a memory of defeat and death. What would a wild woodsman have done? Down along the river valley it was said that there were trees on which the woodsmen, just before they left, had carved their names so strongly that the letters could still be read. But that must be a fable, a memory out of the old song: Their names on the trees of the rising plantation, their memories we'll cherish, and affection ne'er cool. For where are the heroes of high or low station that could be compared with the brave boys of Strule?

—That was as good as a circus, Angela said. You've no idea in the world what you missed.

At breakfast in the hotel in the morning the chatty little waitress shook his belief in himself by saying to him and his children that she had never heard of anybody of his name coming from this town.

—The great unknown, his daughter said.

—Fooling us all the time, the son said. He came from Atlanta, Georgia.

But then it turned out that the waitress came from a smaller town twenty miles away and was only eighteen years of age.

—Off we go now, said the daughter, to see where granny came from.

—Bring no whiskey to Claramore, his mother said. There was always too much whiskey in Claramore. Returned Americans coming and going.

The son and the daughter wished her a happy new year.

—Drive down the town first, she said. I owe a bill I must pay.

—Won't it wait?

She was dressed in high style: widow's black coat, high hat and veil, high buttoned boots for walking in country places.

—Never begin the new year in debt was a good maxim. I'll stick to it while I have breath.

Her grand-daughter, sitting beside her in the back of the hired car, giggled. Sourly he accepted the comments, one unconscious, one conscious, of two other generations on his own finances.

He drove down the High Street. They waited for her outside a hardware shop. The sky was pale blue, cloudless, and last night's unexpected white frost lay on the roofs and spotted the pavements. His daughter said: Granny never heard of a credit card.

More sordidly the son said: Nor hire purchase. Nor a post-dated cheque.

—It was a different world, mes enfants. They paid their way or went without.

But he knew that he had never worked out where—in the world that he had grown into—that terrifying old-fashioned honesty had gone: no debt, no theft, no waste. Beggars were accepted, because Joseph and Mary and the Child Jesus had gone homeless into Egypt. But debt was a sort of sin.

—Eat black bread first, she would say. But let no man say you're in his debt.

He had never taken to black bread. He hadn't told her that in a briefcase in the boot he had two bottles of Jack Daniels as a gift for his cousin—and for himself. A decent man could not with empty hands enter a decent house, and two bottles of American whiskey would be a fit offering to a house that had sent so many sons and daughters to the States.

She was back in the car again, settling herself like a duchess, her small red-headed grand-daughter helping her to tuck a rug around her knees. She refused to believe that a moving vehicle could be heated like a house.

It was a twelve-mile drive, first down the Derry road, over the steep hill that, in spite of all the miracles of macadam, was called, as it had been called in the eighteenth century, Clabber Brae. Then west, over the Drumquin railway crossing. There was no longer any railway to cross. Once upon a time the crossing-keeper's daughter had been as famous as Sadie Law. Then by Gillygooley crossroads where, one June day, Tom and himself, coming tired from fishing perch in the Fairywater, had seen Angela climbing a gate into a ripe meadow just opened for the mower. Her companion was a stocky-shouldered black-avised soldier. That much they could see. A hundred yards ahead, Tom rested from his cycling and was silent for a long time. Then he said: Boy, I'd leave that one alone for the future.

—She's leaving me alone. Who's she with?

—The worst in the barracks. Fusilier Nixon. And he'll never rank higher.

—Why so?

—Four years ago when he came back from India he was all but drummed out for raping a slavey in the soldiers' holm.

—There's a great view of the holm from the tall spire.

—If you had been up there you could have seen the fun. His bacon was saved by a major whose life he saved, or something, in India. And God help the slaveys. The offspring of that bit of love at first sight is now toddling around Fountain Lane. I'll point him out to you some day. You'd have something in common.

They cycled on.

—I'll tell Sadie, Tom said, what we saw. Sadie has some sense. She wouldn't want to be seen in the company of Fusilier Nixon.

Their bicycles bumped over the railway crossing. The keeper's daughter waved, and called: Hello, Tom Cunningham.

—Cheer up, boy. You'll get another girl.

—I suppose I will.

—From here to China the world's full of them.

—I liked Angela.

He found it hard not to sob. Angela peeping around a corner at the animals in the circus. Angela in the clutches of a black-chinned brute. He had, too, really liked her. More than thirty years later he foolishly looked for her face on the streets of the old town and the face he looked for could not, in reason, ever be there. He would see, instead, a Madonna—whom, also, he had never known—against a background of the coloured covers of magazines.

Now as he drove on, he looked at the gate that Angela had climbed into the meadow. But one gate was very like another and, under white frost, all meadows were the same. Although this valley to him would always be summer holiday country. Every mile of it he had walked or cycled. A hay-shed by a prosperous farmhouse meant for him mostly the sultry July hush before the rain came, the smell of sheds and barns, heavy rain on tin roofs, or soda bread and strong tea by peat fires on open hospitable hearths.

There now across the stilled, white fields was the glint of water at the pool where Tom and himself would first strike the Fairywater. The road climbed here, up over the stony place of Clohogue, then switchbacked for miles in and out of hazel glens, over loud rough brooks, then on to a plateau, high, very high; and visible in such clear frosty air, and a good seventy miles away by the edge of the Atlantic, the pigback of Muckish Mountain, the white cone of Mount Errigal, the Cock of the North. Claramore was just below the plateau. It was a place of its own, in a new valley.

From the Barley Hill beyond the old long white farmhouse you could also see those two far-away mountains and, in the other direction and looking down the valley of the Fairywater, the tips and crosses of the two limping Gothic spires, but not the smaller plain spire of the Protestant church.

—On a calm evening, his cousin said, they seem so close that you'd imagine you could hear the bell ringing for the May devotions.

He asked his cousin: Do the young people still climb Drumard in autumn to pluck the blayberries?

—We've heard a lot about those same blayberries, his daughter said. To pluck and eat them, dad says, was a memory of some ancient pagan feast.

—The young people, his cousin said, have their own pagan feasts.

The four of them walked on the boreen that crossed the Barley Hill to the place where the men were building a house for his cousin's son and the bride he would bring home with him in three months' time. Hard frost had slowed up the building work. Among the men, half-loitering, working just enough to keep warm, keeping as close as possible to an open brazier, his cousin passed round one of the bottles of bourbon. They drank from cracked cups and tin mugs, toasted the health of the visitors, of the bride-to-be, wished luck for ever on the house they were building. High above a jet plane, westward-bound out of Prestwick, made its mark on the cold pale blue.

—They'll be in New York before you, his son said.

The drinking men, circling the brazier, saluted the travellers in the sky and raised a cheer. It was only a few hours to New York from the Barley Hill or the pagan blayberries of Drumard. Breath ascended in puffs as white as the jet's signature. On the far side of the hill from the long farmhouse the Fairywater, glittering black, looped through frosted bottom-land.

—Phil Loughran, that used to work for you, he said. He was about my age. Where did he go?

The Black Stepping Stones were at that bend of the Fairywater, the seventh bend visible from where they stood; and above the Black Stones the pool where the country boys went swimming. Willows drooped over it. The bottom was good yellow sand. The water had the brown of the peat and was nowhere more than four feet deep. It was an idyllic place, had been an idyllic place until the day he had that crazy fight with Phil Loughran.

—He went to Australia, his cousin said. We hear he's doing well. The family, what's left of them, are still living here on my land.

Even to this day, and in the frosty air, he blushed to think of the lies he had told to Phil Loughran down there by the Black Stones—blushed all the more because, country boys being so much more cunning than towny boys, Phil almost certainly hadn't believed a word he said. Phil as he listened would have secretly laughed.

—So her name is Angela, he said.

Phil was a squat sallow-faced young fellow, dressed in rough corduroys and heavy nailed boots, his brown hair short-cropped, his eyes dark brown and close together. There was always a vague smell of peat smoke, or stables or something, from those corduroys.

—Angela the walking angel, he said.

They were dressing after a swim. Three other boys splashed and shouted in the pool. A fourth hung naked from a trailing willow, swinging like a pendulum, striking the water with his feet.

—So you tell us, Phil, you had the little man out of sight.

He made a sideways grab, as Angela had done on the wooden brambly slope above the pike-pool on the Drumragh. He was laughing. He said: Little man, you've had a busy day.

Then the two of them were rolling on the grass, swiping at each other, Phil still laughing, he sobbing, with temper, with the humiliation of having his tall tales of conquest made mockery of. Four naked dripping boys danced and laughed and shouted around them. It was the last day but one that he had been at the Black Stones. He had come second best out of that fight but he had a mean miserable sort of vengeance on his very last visit to the place.

Phil in his best corduroys—since it was Sunday—is crossing the water, stepping carefully from stone to stone, in his right hand the halter with which he is leading a love-stricken Claramore cow to keep her date with a bull on the farm on the far side of the river. So he calls to Phil to mind his Sunday-go-to-meeting suit and Phil, turning round to answer, is off his guard when the restive beast bolts. It is, fair enough, his turn to laugh, sharp, clear and cruel, as Phil, bravely holding on to the halter is dragged through the shallow muddy water below the stones. There are seventeen in Phil's family, and he is the eldest, and those corduroys will not be easily replaced.

Over the hard frosted fields his own laughter came back to him.

—I'm glad to hear he did well in Australia.

—They were a thrifty family, his cousin said. A sister of his might visit us this evening, the youngest of the breed, a god-daughter of mine.

The trail of the jet was curdling in the cold sky. The men had gone back to work. For penance he told his cousin and son and daughter how he had laughed on the day the cow dragged Phil through the muddy water. They stood by a huge sycamore a little down the slopes from the unfinished house. Icicles hung from bare branches. He said, nothing about how James had mocked his boasting.

—Weren't you the beast, dad, his daughter said.

—But it was funny, the son said.

—The young, his cousin said, can be thoughtless. Present company excepted.

For the daughter, the face of a good mimic distorted with mock fury, was dancing towards the cousin to stab him with an icicle broken from the sycamore.

—No, but seriously, he said when they had played out their pantomime of fury and terror: a grey man over sixty with a restful singing sort of voice and a pert little girl of sixteen.

—Seriously. Look at the sycamore. It was planted here more than a hundred years ago by an uncle of mine who was a priest. He died young, not long after ordination. He planted this tree on the day he was ordained, and blessed the earth and the sapling. You may recall, when you were young yourselves, some of his books were still about the house. Mostly Latin. Theology. Some novels. I told you about one of them and you rushed to get it. The *Lass of the Barns*, you thought I said. But, man alive, were you down in the mouth when you discovered it was the *Last of the Barons*.

—Oh dad, his daughter said.

—But I know the age of this tree by checking on the date on the priest's tombstone in Langfield churchyard. And my son says to me: We'll cut it down. It'll spoil the view from the new house. So I said: The house may fall, but this tree will stand while I do. The old have a feeling for each other.

—Lucky tree, the daughter said, that has somebody to stand up for it.

They went, laughing, back down the Barley Hill towards the warmth of the great kitchen of the farmhouse. Under the pall of the white frost it seemed as if nothing here would ever change: not the sycamore, not his cousin, nor the ancient sleeping land. Nothing would change, no matter how many airliners swept westwards up there, leaving nothing behind them but a curdling dissolving mark on the sky. All the ships that had carried all those people westwards, even so many sons and daughters of this house, and the ocean was still unmarked and the land here as it had been. It was elsewhere in the world the changes happened.

—But this fatal ship to her cold bosom folds them. Wherever she goes our fond hearts shall adore them. Our prayers and good wishes will still be before them, that their names be remembered and sung by the Strule.

The pond at the corner of the avenue was frozen over. He had fallen into it once, climbing the fence above and beyond it to chase a

wandering bullock out of a field of young oats. The fence-post he had
been holding on to had broken. The water, he had always imagined, had
tasted of duck-dirt. But then how in hell would one be expected to
know what duck-dirt tasted like? The fence-post, he noticed, was now
made of iron, and that might be some indication, even here, of change.
But not much.

The ash-grove to the left before you came to the stables—in that
grove he had once criminally broken a young sapling to make a fishing
rod—was now a solid wall of grown strong trees, a windbreak on days of
south-westerly gales.

Would the horses in the stables be the same, with the same names, as
they had been thirty years ago? He was afraid to ask, to be laughed at, to
be told what he knew: that even here, even loved familiar farmhorses
didn't live for ever. The dogs seemed the same—collies, with more
sprawling pups underfoot than had ever seemed natural. The pattern of
farming though, had changed somewhat, he had been told: more barley,
more pigs fed on the barley, less oats, less root crops, more sucking
calves bred in season on the open pasture, taken early from their
mothers and sold to be fattened somewhere in confinement, and
slaughtered.

In the house ahead of them somebody was playing a melodeon, softly,
slowly, and that was something that hadn't changed, because in the
past in that house there had been great country dances to pipe, fiddle
and melodeon. That was before so many of his cousins, all much older
than himself, had gone to the States.

His mother had enjoyed herself. She was red in the face and moist-eyed
from sitting by the open hearth with its high golden pyramid of blazing
peat; from remembering, for the instruction of a younger generation,
the comic figaries of her dear departed dowager of a sister, Kate, who, as
a widow in her thirties, had ruled not only Claramore but half the
countryside; and from, let it be admitted, sipping at the bourbon. For
while she was a great one to lecture about the dangers of drink, she was
liable the next minute to take from her sideboard a bottle of brandy and
a bottle of whiskey, to ask what you were having, and to join you
herself, and she instinctively thought the worst of a man who neither
smoked, drank, swore, nor rode horses.

—The young people, she said, are growing up well, God bless them.
They haven't forgotten the old ways. That house was never without
music and dancing.

The Claramore people had stood around the car, under a frosty moon,
and sang Auld Lang Syne as their guests departed.

—That Loughran girl was a good hand at the melodeon. Did you all see her making up to the widow man, the returned American?

She poked him between the shoulder-blades as he drove slowly over the icy plateau.

—She sat on your knee, dad, the daughter said.

He could still feel the pressure of the underparts of the girl's thighs. She was conventionally slim and dark and handsome, with wide brown eyes; in appearance most unlike her eldest brother. She had sat on his knee in the dancing kitchen to tell him that Phil, in every letter he wrote from Australia, enquired about him. She stayed sitting there while his cousin sang: There was once a maid in a lonely garden when a well-dressed gentleman came passing by.

—Was that story true granny, the son asked. The one about the lone bush.

—Would I tell it if it wasn't.

They descended into the first hazel glen. Over the rushing of its brook they could hear the roaring of another jet, out of Prestwick, bound for New York.

—They're lining up to get into America, the son said.

—To get out of it too, son.

Six hours or so to the bedlam of Kennedy airport: But now our bold heroes are past all their dangers. On America's shores they won't be long strangers. They'll send back their love from famed Blessington's Rangers to comrades and friends and the fair maids of Strule.

People who travelled by jet left no shadows in old market-places. Generations would be born to whom the ache and loneliness in the old songs of exile would mean nothing.

—Jordan Taggart the cobbler, as I said, had his house on the road from Claramore to Carrickaness, and a small farm to boot. Against the advice of all, even against Father Gormley the priest that cured people, he cut down a whitethorn that grew alone in the middle of his meadow and, at nightfall, he dragged it home behind him for kindling. In the orchard before his house he saw two small children, dressed in white, and he spoke to them but they made no answer. So he told his wife and his three sons, who were also cobblers, that there were two shy children waiting, maybe for mended shoes in the orchard. But when two of the sons went out and searched they saw nothing. Then Jordan ate the supper of a healthy man and went to bed and died in his sleep.

—But he wasn't really dead, the son said.

—No, the white children took him. God between us and all harm.

In the darkness in the car she spat, but slightly and politely, and into her handkerchief.

The daughter said nothing.

They were back again in the meadow country where Angela had climbed the gate and, except for one last meeting, had climbed out of his life for ever. They bumped over the Drumquin crossing where there was no longer any railway to cross, no easy girl to call longingly after Tom Cunningham who was chasing girls in China and never wrote to enquire about anybody.

The daughter was alert again. She was giggling. She said: Dad, Granny wants to do something about the way you dress.

—I was only thinking about his own good, his mother said.

Although he was carefully driving the car over Clabber Brae, he knew by the way she talked that he was no longer there.

—But when I was by the seaside at Bundoran I saw these young fellows wearing loose coloured patterned shirts outside their trousers. I was told it was an American fashion, and I was sure that he would be wearing one of them when he came home.

He said: I'm no young fellow.

—What I thought was that it would cover his middle-aged spread.

As they descended by the military barracks into the town the daughter's giggles rocked the car.

—A maternity shirt, she said.

—For how could he expect anyone to look at him at his age and with a stomach like that.

Castle Street went up so steeply that it seemed as if it was trying to climb those dark grotesque spires.

—A young one, for instance, like that Loughran girl who sat on his knee because the chairs were scarce.

—That one, he said. All that I remember about the Loughrans is that her bare-footed elder brothers were always raiding Aunt Kate's cherry trees and blaming the depredation on the birds.

In the hotel bar only two of the commercial men were left. They said: What do you think now of your happy home town?

—How do you mean?

—Last night's tragic event, they said. Didn't you hear? Didn't you read the paper?

—I was in the country all day.

Back in the past where one didn't read the newspapers.

—A poor man murdered, they said. What your American friends would call a filling-station attendant.

—Robbed and shot, they said. Just when we were sitting here talking about murder.

The grandfather clock in the hallway chimed midnight.

—The New Year, he said. May it be quiet and happy.

In the ballroom in the far wing of the hotel the revellers were clasping hands and singing about old acquaintance.

—We should be there singing, he said.

—The second murder here this year, they said. The other was a queer case, two young men, a bit odd. Things like that usen't to happen. This town is getting to be as bad as Chicago.

—It isn't as big or as varied.

They laughed. They agreed that the town was still only in a small way of business. He asked them was the park called the Lovers' Retreat still where it had been.

—If that's the way you feel, it is.

More laughter.

—But it's gone to hell, they told him. It's not kept as it used to be. The young compulsory soldiers in national service wreck everything. They haven't the style of the old Indian army, when the empire was in its glory. Children's swings uprooted now. Benches broken. One of the two bridges over the millrace gone completely. The grass three feet long.

—Nothing improves, they said.

When they left him he sat on for a long time, drinking alone. Was it imagination, or could he really hear the sound of the Camowen waters falling over the salmon leap at the Lovers' Retreat? That place was one of the sights of the town when the salmon were running: the shining curving bodies rising from the water as if sprung from catapults— leaping and struggling upwards in white foam and froth. But one year the water was abnormally low, the salmon a sullen black mass in the pool below the falls—a temptation to a man with Tom Cunningham's enterprise. The water-bailiff and his two assistants and his three dogs came by night and caught Tom and his faithful companion with torch and gaff and one slaughtered salmon. But since the bailiff, a bandy-legged amiable man, was also the park-keeper he said not a word to the police on condition that the two criminals kept the grass in the park mowed for a period of six months.

—Hard labour, by God, boy. He has us by the hasp. The Big House with Wallace Beery. You be Mickey Rooney.

The bad news travelled and was comic to all except the two mowers. Then one day from the far side of the millrace that made one boundary to the park they heard the laughter of women, and saw Sadie and Angela, bending and pointing.

—Two men went to mow, they sang, went to mow the meadow.

—Grilled salmon for all, they called.

Tom crossed the millrace by leaping on to the trunk of a leaning tree that was rooted on the far bank. Sadie, laughing, screaming in mock terror, and Tom in pursuit, vanished into the bluebell woods. Tom's companion crossed the millrace prosaically by one of the wooden footbridges. Was it the one that the wild young resentful compulsory soldiers had destroyed? She didn't run. She wasn't laughing any more. Her brown hair no longer curled in little horns on her temples but was combed straight back. But the wide mouth, in spite of the black fusilier, was to him as inviting as ever. She said: You're a dab-hand at mowing. You've a future in cutting grass.

He said: I never see you any more.

—Little boys should take what's offered to them, when it's offered. Go back to your scythe.

—Go back to the fusilier, he said.

He went back to his scythe by climbing along the trunk of the leaning tree and leaping the millrace. The grass that fell before his scythe was crimson in colour and swathed in a sort of mist. The swing of the scythe moved with the rhythm of the falling water sweeping on to meet the Drumragh, to become the Strule, to absorb the Fairywater and the Derg and the Owenkillew, to become the Mourne, to absorb the Finn, to become the Foyle, to go down then by Derry to the ocean, taking with it the shadows of the woodsmen, the echoes of the brass and pipes and tramping feet of the army of a vanished empire, the stories of all who had ever lived in this valley.

He knew he was drunk when he heard the woman's voice speak respectfully to him and saw her through the crimson mist through which long ago he had seen the falling grass. She said: You wouldn't remember me, sir.

He didn't. She wore the black dress, white collar and cuffs of the hotel staff. She would be sixtyish. She said: We saw you on the teevee one night and I said to Francie who you were. But he said he didn't know you. He knew your elder brother better.

—My brother was well known.

—Francie's my brother. You might remember he used to ride racing bicycles. I saw you in the dining-room. I work in the kitchen. I knew it was you when I saw your son, and from the teevee.

—You're Sadie Law.

—I didn't like to intrude on you and the children.

He said there was no intrusion. They shook hands. He asked her how her brother was.

—He's in a chair all the time. He broke his back at the tom-fool cycling. But he does woodcarving, and I work here. We manage. I never married.

Her face did not remind him of Sadie Law, but then he found that he could not remember what Sadie Law's face had looked like.

—Nobody, he said, could replace Tom Cunningham.

She neither smiled nor looked sorrowful. Her face remained the same. She said: Oh, Tom was a card. He went away.

Some revellers from the ballroom came in, drunk, singing, wearing paper hats. She said: I must be off.

—I'll see you in the morning.

—I'm off duty then. Because of the late dance tonight. But we hope you'll come back often to see the old places.

—Do you ever remember, he asked, a Fusilier Nixon, a wild fellow.

She thought: No. But there were so many fusiliers. A lot of them we'll never see again.

—We'll look out for you on the teevee, she said.

They shook hands again.

They said goodbye to his mother and drove away. His daughter said: Dad, this isn't the Dublin road.

—There's a place I want to see before we leave.

It was the place that Tom and himself used to go to when they considered that the mental strain of school was too much for them. For it was an odd thing that in all the comings and goings of that railway station nobody ever thought of asking a pair of truants what they were doing there. Everybody thought that everybody else was waiting for somebody else, and there were always porters and postmen who knew what you were at, but who kept the knowledge to themselves, and would share talk and cigarettes with runaway convicts, let alone reluctant schoolboys. No police hunted for drifters or loiterers as in American bus stations: and the sights were superb and you met the best people. They had spent several hours one day with Chief Abidu from southern Nigeria and his Irish wife and honey-coloured brood. He danced on broken glass and swallowed fire in a wooden booth in the Old Market, and, beating on his breast, made the most wonderful throaty noises; and came, most likely, from Liverpool.

—I understand, she had written, that the railway station is closed now. Only the ghosts of those who passed through it abide there. Some were gentle, some were violent men, morose or gay, ordinary or extraordinary. I had time to watch them passing by. It is pain that they died so young, so long ago.

The tracks were gone, the grass and weeds had grown high through the ballast. The old stone buildings had been turned into warehouses. Two men in dusty dungarees kept coming and going, carrying sacks of meal, at the far end of the platform. But if they spoke to each other they were too far away for their voices to be heard, and the cold wind moved as stealthily in grass and weeds as if it were blowing over some forlorn midland hillside. Where the bookstall had been there was just a scar on the granite wall, where she had stood, framed against coloured books and magazines, and watched the soldiers coming and going.

—The young English poet you mention, I knew briefly. He came to buy books. At first he had little to say, simply polite, that's all. Then one day he and another young man began to talk. They included me. But mostly I listened. It was fascinating. After that, when he came he talked about books. He asked questions about Ireland. He was uneasy there, considered it beautiful but alien, felt, I think, that the very earth of Ireland was hostile to him, the landscape had a brooding quality as though it waited.

—He was five or six months garrisoned in our town. They told me he could be very much one of the boys, but he could also be remote. He treated me kindly, teased me gently. But he and a brilliant bitter Welshman gave me books and talked to me. Sometimes they talked about the war.

—It was only after he was reported missing in Africa that I learned he was a poet. But I think I knew anyway.

—I never heard if the Welshman survived. I had several long letters from him and that was all.

Ghosts everywhere in this old town.

—Now I have a son who may pass through a railway station or an airport on his way to war.

He said to his daughter: That's where the bookstall was.

—Will you go to see her, dad? In the States, I mean.

—In a way I've seen her.

He was grateful that she didn't ask him what on earth he was talking about.

—As the song says, I'll look for her if I'm ever back that way.

The ghost of his father stood just here, waving farewell to him every time he went back after holidays to college in Dublin.

They walked through the cold deserted hall, where the ticket offices had been, and down the steps, grass-grown, cracked, to the Station Square, once lined with taxis, now empty except for some playing children and the truck into which the dusty men were loading the sacks. From the high steeple the noonday angelus rang.

—How high up is the bell? his son asked.

He told him, and also told him the height of the spire and of the surmounting cross, and why one spire was higher than the other, and how he had once climbed up there, and of the view over the valley, and of how he had almost fallen to doom on the way down, and of the vertigo, the fear of death, that followed.

—And a curious thing. Once, on top of the Eiffel Tower, that vertigo returned. And once over the Mojave desert when I thought the plane was going to crash. But I didn't see Paris or the Mojave desert. I saw that long straight ladder.

The bell ceased. The spires were outlined very clearly in the cold air, looked as formidable as precipices. Around them floated black specks, the unbanishable jackdaws.

—Once I got a job from the parish priest because I was a dab hand with a twenty-two. The job was to shoot the jackdaws, they were pests, off the spires. It was going fine until the police stopped me for using a firearm too close to a public highway. The sexton at the time was a tall man in a black robe down to his feet, more stately than a bishop. One day, when he was watching me at work, a bird I shot struck one of those protruding corner-stones and came soaring, dead, in a wide parabola, straight for the sexton. He backed away, looking in horror at the falling bird. But he tripped on his robe, and the bird, blood, feathers, beak and all got him fair in the face. At that time I thought it was the funniest thing I had ever seen.

—Grisly, his daughter said.

—But once upon a time I laughed easily. It was easy to laugh here then.

High Street, Market Street, the Dublin Road. A stop at the grave where the caretaker's men had already done their job. The weeds were gone, the sad hollow filled, new white stones laid.

Then on to Dublin, crossing the Drumragh at Lissan Bridge where, it was said, Red Hugh O'Donnell had passed on his way back from prison in Dublin Castle to princedom in Donegal and war with Elizabeth of England. The wintry land brooded waiting, as it had always done, and would do for ever.

He sang at the wheel: There was once a maid in a lovely garden.

—Oh dad, his daughter said.

So he thought the rest of it: Oh, do you see yon high high building? And do you see yon castle fine? And do you see yon ship on the ocean? They'll all be thine if thou wilt be mine.

A Cow in the House

MAKE STRAIGHT FOR THE SHORE

Breakfast was perfunctory and the main meal of the day was taken at a place called the Continental Café or the Café Continental where we used to eat bangers and mash by the hundredweight and dance with the waitresses to a voice and a tune on the radio: There's a lovely lake in London where Rhododendrons grow.

It was a very popular tune at the time. I can't remember if that other song had then surfaced: At the Café Continental like a fool I fell in love.

Not one of the three of us did fall in love there. The waitresses were all as fat as fools: from snapping-up all day long unconsidered trifles of bangers and mash. Our ideal then was Ginger Rogers, the young Ginger Rogers, the Ginger Rogers of *Roxy Hart*: her dancing was different.

When there wasn't a lovely lake in London there were red sails in the sunset, way out on the sea. We picked up a lot of our current and popular music by hanging around bicycle shops: We'll build a nest way up in the west 'neath a sky of heavenly blue, a one-room flat and a two-pants suit and three square meals a day, I've told every little star just how sweet I think you are, with a carpet on the floor made of buttercups and clover. In more elevated moments we listened to John McCormack and Enrico Caruso and had strong controversy as to which of them was the greater. Caruso had, hadn't he, broken a wine-glass just by singing into it? But McCormack was one of our own.

Radio sets were scarce, so were the fourpences for the pit in the picture-house and scarcer still was the money to buy the records we coveted and not every household had a gramophone. So bicycle shops it had to be. We never even wondered: why bicycle shops? Why not confectioneries or groceries or newsagencies, where you might expect music to go with literature: or draperies or haberdasheries or hardware merchants?

Busto looked like this: I draw a circle supported by a larger circle supported by two stumpy rectangles. Lanko looked like this: I draw a small circle supported on two parallel lines. They were both Christian Brothers and both surnamed Burke, one from Dublin and the other from

Tipperary, and because of them the three of us were in Belfast City dancing with the waitresses, walking the town like men of the town, watching the dark clouds of starlings around the gigantic but dignified Victorian city hall and in our leisure moments doing an entrance examination for the British civil service. In the late spring the clouds of starlings are a sight to see.

This day Lanko came to me after Latin class and said: Because of that arithmetic paper you haven't a hope in this world or the next of getting King's scholarship.

He was, as you may have guessed, a tall man, so tall he looked thin which he really wasn't, and he had a handsome blackavised face, a gentle musical Munster accent, and all the matrons in the town and a lot of the maidens were mad about him—the inaccessible, almost, in those days. He had played hurling for Tipperary, and the long black Christian Brothers' habit, especially long in his case, went very well with the easy athletic way he walked.

—No the arithmetic paper, he said, would be your Waterloo.

It was my final year in secondary school in an Ulster provincial town and, at that time and in those parts, the only future for the average secondary student was to go to training college for two years and resurface as a primary-school teacher so as to teach primary students to become secondary students. You could, if you were lucky, become an artisan, or dig holes in the street for the town council and nobody would ever see anything of you except the top of your head. As in greater towns like New York somebody was always digging holes in the street: constant employment. You could, of course, become a priest or a nun or, if your parents had the means, you could go to the university and follow one of the professions, or become a secondary teacher and teach other secondary students to become primary teachers, and so on. The United States produces every year, somebody told me, 30,000 doctors of philosophy and there can't be that many philosophers in the whole world: take a look at it, for God's sake.

But in 1936 about 50 per cent of my class were doomed to sit for this examination called King's scholarship and to go, if they were successful, to a place in Twickenham, near London, called Strawberry Hill, sacred to the memory of Horace Walpole who had lived there and of Seán Ó Faoláin who had taught there, and to become primary-school teachers. The big hurdle in that examination was an arithmetic paper of four diabolical problems, and the way to take it was: if question one didn't provide an answer, to take a run at two and three and four so that, with the law of averages and good luck and one of them out of the way, there were fewer to bewilder you and your confidence was quadrupled. Or is quadrupled, I wonder, exactly what I mean?

A good friend of mine wouldn't or couldn't work that way: he'd stick with question one until the bell rang, with the result that he never became a primary-school teacher. Instead he became a wealthy businessman and still is one, and a credit to the country and a great benefit, I'm told, to the poor in the town he lives in.

As for myself, I never even attempted or was allowed to attempt King's scholarship. The thought of that arithmetic paper turned me off, and subtraction was the only sort of arithmetic I was ever any good at, and Lanko said gently: No, dear boy, you'd never take that hurdle. But there is this exam for the British civil service if you don't mind serving the king, and it's becoming very popular nowadays, good conditions, good pay, you can rise to the top, no sectarianism across the water, and you could see a bit of the world into the bargain, beginning with Belfast where the exam is held.

Busto didn't put it so gently: Busto had a kind heart but blunter ways, picked up, perhaps, in the scrum when in his youth he had played rugby football for Blackrock; and about the kind heart I didn't find out until years later I met him in Dublin when he was ailing in health and wasn't even Busto any more, and his cheeks were hollow and his feet flat and his clothes had grown too big for him. But Busto he still assuredly was when he stopped me one day in the corridor outside the chemistry lab. and told me of my prospects in the service of the King of England. He (Busto) had a deft way of lifting youths by their incipient sidelocks and occasionally booting them in the buttocks in a friendly but efficient fashion. For Blackrock, it was said, he had been the supremo among place-kickers.

He was the Brother Superior and students were sent to him for punishment, and they got it. One poor sniveller came in from a history class to meet his deserts and his whipping. So Busto says: What are you here for?

—Please sir, I forgot how a man died.

—Why, says Busto, didn't you say he forgot to draw his breath.

And lifted the non-historian with one well-placed boot.

But at the door of the stinks lab, he merely tweaked my nose and said jovially: You can't put two and two together. You'll never get King's scholarship. You'll never be able to put two and two together. But there's the British civil service. To judge by the stupid things they do in Whitehall they'll never notice you in the crowd. Proceed and prosper and God save the king.

Unkicked, I proceeded.

And there we were, the chosen three, living on bangers and mash and dancing with fat waitresses to the tunes of a lovely lake in London and swift wings we must borrow, make straight for the shore, and more besides. As I said, we knew the tunes already from our regular scholarly attendance at a bicycle shop, one very special bicycle shop: and for the moment we were gentlemen on the town, three fine free right feet and fellows for them, truly at large and out of the reservation for the first time in our lives, living in an hotel at the back of the city hall and studying the black driving clouds of shrieking starlings. Have the bombs, I wonder, dispersed the starlings?

For the last time I was in that hotel the screaming birds were still blackening the sky but the bombs were just beginning. Thick as night or locusts the starlings were around the city hall and in the hotel there was no water in the taps. The hotel has changed its name now, or it may not, because of the bombs, be there any more; one new and neighbouring hotel was bombed nineteen times, room service how are you. But eight years ago it was still there and had then changed its name, and I sat sipping in the lounge, looking at a pop-group called the Necromancers and remembering the bright blonde hair of Trudi. Looking at, not listening to, I'm overjoyed to say, for the Necromancers were merely relaxing after their labours of the night before. A few of them were asleep or half asleep. There was little talk between them. They were possibly saving their breath for the night to come. An interestingly-mixed group: West Indian, Afro-American, European, which I could see for myself, Irish and English and German which I had been told. Two of them who were not slumbering ordered drinks, real drinks, which surprised me: who had always assumed that pop-groups and show-bands lived on cow's milk and pills. A slim young blonde girl from the hotel staff brought them a telegram. O the blonde head of my Trudi long ago when Rhododendrons grew around the lovely lake in London. As she bent to deliver the telegram the girl blushed to the backs of her mini-skirtless thighs at having been chosen for the honour of carrying a message that came through the air, to the corner where the gods reposed: no harpers those to learn their songs and melodies in bicycle shops, red sails in the sunset I'm trusting in you.

Later as I sat at dinner with a BBC ballad-singer and a Dublin political, both convivial men, we heard a great sound. At first we thought that a large part of Belfast had been blown up. But later still it was reported that a meteorite had splashed down, hitting nobody as far as was known—the heavens were harmless—in a peat-bog in County Down.

The ballad-singer said: At all times of crisis and calamity there are signs in the sky.

The political said: Rockets from Russia.

The hotel was full of pressmen. Rumour, painted all over with tongues, was running wild to tell us that, for instance, the papishes were to march on Sandy Row at ten o'clock when the pubs closed.

To prove what?

Why, to prove to the Protestant Sandy Rowers that the IRA did not blow up the aqueduct near the big reservoir in the Silent Valley in the Mountains of Mourne: which was why there was no water in the taps in the hotel nor in the hospitals nor anywhere else, almost, in Belfast.

That demonstration would have made a lot of sense: just as much as when the Holy Rollers of Dayton, Tennessee, proved to their own satisfaction, by rolling all together on the ground, that man was not descended from the monkey.

Trudi I could see quite plainly, although the dining-room, which we three students long ago hadn't much frequented, had been altered and redecorated and, anyway, her sort of hotel-work didn't bring her into the dining-room.

Later still we heard that the rumour was false and that the demonstration was not to take place. But the pressmen who, because of the unhappy nature of their calling, are obliged to give at least a friendly nod to every rumour, were already on the way to Sandy Row, just to see.

We had an excellent dinner and much wine. Later still we heard that the meteorite had splashed down not in County Down but in County Derry: and jocose speculation continued about the nature of the great sound.

The Holy Ghost descending at long last on the collapsing parliament in Stormont Castle.

Dr Ian Paisley ascending from the Crumlin Road Jail in a flaming flying saucer and all the trumpets sounding for him from the other side as they did for Mr Standfast. For Dr Paisley was that night in Pauline chains for disturbing the peace outside the Presbyterian assembly building five minutes walk away in Fisherwick Place: in which pinnacled, dark-stone, ice-cold building Bill and Fuzzy-Wuzzy and myself had long before sat, more or less, for that civil service examination.

The evening papers had reported that Dr Paisley's aide-de-camp, the Rev. Mr Foster, who had just been released, said that Dr Paisley was the happiest man in the prison, happier even than the governor, because Dr Paisley was with God.

The ballad-singer wondered if governors of prisons were necessarily happy.

The political wondered if governors of prisons were of necessity not with God.

We sipped our brandy and I remembered Trudi.

Later still I tried to tell the manager, a brusque, busy fellow, how a female member of the staff of that hotel had, away before his time, kept me out of the second world war and thus may, by several years, have postponed the German defeat. But he seemed in too much of a hurry to try or to bother to understand.

There she was on the very first morning the three of us woke up in that hotel. We had a room each, small rooms and not over-elegant but independent and our own. Belfast we had often visited, on the lead with parents or led by teachers, to rugby games in Ravenhill, but this was different. What could a man have done or said to Trudi if he had been sandwiched between parents or crocodiled on the sporting road to Ravenhill? O, the long bright blonde hair of Trudi, an Easter sun dancing over a new-arisen world. In the hometown I knew two sisters, one called Deborah, the other Rachel, Presbyterians, naturally, with names like that, but never a girl called Trudi and never a girl so blonde.

—Trudi, I said, is your name really and truly Trudi.

—That's what my father and mother call me, and my brothers and sisters all seven of them, and the neighbours, who speak to me. Where I come from everybody doesn't speak to everybody.

She was a wit. She had to be, she was so beautiful.

—Do you come from Germany? Or Switzerland?

Switzerland was all hotels and mountains.

Her accent should have told me but I hadn't travelled much at the time and all beautiful women spoke with the same accent. She was, at that moment, stripping my bed preparatory to re-making it: the lass that made the bed to me, I knew my Burns, it was the closest that poetry had brought us to such matters. She wore a grey dress and a white apron and a funny white little hat all lost and unbalanced and loveable and comic on the crown of that shining head: her hair was like the links o' gowd, her teeth were like the ivorie, her cheeks like lilies dipped in wine.

—Germany, she said. Switzerland, she said. I couldn't spell Switzerland if you paid me. Germany I can manage.

She did, haltingly, all seven letters, music to mine ears her voice was.

No, she was from Castledawson in County Derry, not too far from where, 33 years later, the meteorite was to splash down, and her family name was Beatty and Trudi came out of a magazine called *Peg's Paper* that her mother read. Her father kept an unlicensed bull that was worth a fortune, he worked so hard, even at half the legal price, but it was cash down for if it wasn't some of them wouldn't pay you at all, you had no legal way of getting at them, and that was about the meanest thing she ever heard of. Cash and carry, her father, who was a joker, said. That was the name of one of those new-fangled supermarkets. On the first morning she told me about Castledawson and Beatty and *Peg's Paper* but it was the third morning, we were rapidly growing closer, before she told me about the unlicensed bull, and laughed like a music box when she told me: You should see him, the solemn face of him.

She was lovelier than the lovely lake in London, lovelier than red sails in the sunset although Fuzzy-Wuzzy would never agree with that and disapproved of Trudi: jealous, I thought at first, but no, I knew after a while that he was just shy of women. It was the red sails in the song that enchanted him, not the loved one that the red sails were to carry home safely to the singer. Bill, a big affable man whose longest speech about anything was a grunt of good-natured assent, was neutral although he did whisper to Fuzzy-Wuzzy to whisper to me that there'd be hell to pay when Busto found out, as find out he sure as hell would, that time was spent helping the lass that made the bed to me that should have been spent in the Presbyterian assembly building in Fisherwick Place outside which, 33 years later, Dr Paisley was picked up for disturbing the peace.

As for Fuzzy-Wuzzy, everywhere he went he must have seen red sails in the sunset. He hummed the tune of it all the time, or something not unlike the tune. He never could make any fist of the words although, God knows, he tried very hard. He was six feet two inches when he was seventeen and he walked on his toes, bouncing a bit, and always leaned forward a little as if he were eager to fly or take off like a rocket for the moon. His real name was Patrick Ignatius O'Kane and his people were far-out relations of my mother, and he wore grey tweed trousers and a serge navy-blue jacket, the jacket always too big for him and the trousers always too small. In the village he came from, we reckoned, there must be a very special tailor, either that or his father had a very large family of boys all older than Fuzzy-Wuzzy. Some in navy-blue serge, others in grey tweed.

Most of our last year at school he spent in Peter Sloper McAleer's bicycle shop trying to learn the words and music of Red Sails in the Sunset. He could, as I've said, make a stab at the music but never, no, no never, he could never get the words right. He cycled into the town to school from his village twelve miles away, so that he had a legitimate reason for being in Peter Sloper's where he parked his bike: and Peter Sloper with his tan shopcoat all marked with streaks of oil, and his small, exactly-oval gold-rimmed spectacles, and his wrinkled monkey-face and his five ribs of grey hair plastered straight across his bald crown, was a man to reckon with. He walked out young nurses from the county hospital until he was the age of 80, nurses, only nurses: the nurses, he used to say with great solemnity, the nurses are the worst, they know it all. My cousin Brigid who was a great deal older than me and who was hospital matron for a time said that it was on the records that Peter Sloper had started walking out nurses when he was eighteen, that was 62 years of young nurses, and never proposed matrimony to one of them which was why he was called Sloper. He was mean, too, or at least tight or careful about money, and never had it been heard of that he bought a drink for anybody except once when a telegram came to him that he had won £50,000 in the Irish Hospitals Sweepstake, and he went crazy and toured the town and bought drinks for one and all and everybody in every pub, to find out too late that the telegram had come from his best friend, a greengrocer, who was noted for practical jokes. It was the same greengrocer who, when Peter Sloper died, suggested that on his tombstone the words should be cut: The nurses were the worst. But the parish priest put a stop to that.

Well anyway, there in the middle of a maze and a pop-art swirl of bicycles was a gramophone with a high green horn playing music that could be heard two blocks away and Fuzzy-Wuzzy, his head half up the horn, trying in vain to learn the words of Red Sails in the Sunset, way out on the sea, oh carry my swift wings straight home to the shore. Never, oh never could he get the words right: and he was called Fuzzy-Wuzzy because his hair was black as coal-tar and bristly and closely clipped.

Bulky affable Bill with a voice like a bugle was such a genius at Latin composition that his themes or exercises were in constant demand for what we called cogging and American students rather grandly called plagiarization. Shakespeare and Eliot plagiarized. We grimly cogged in the early morning-oh—so that, by popular request, Bill had to be up early and into the classroom before our teachers were astir to trouble the air. One morning the demand for pure Ciceronian Latin was so brisk that a fight began and the golden book of Bill's themes was torn to shreds. A day of sharp questioning, discoveries and retribution followed.

—*Festina lente*, Bill said on the third morning in Belfast.

He blushed and looked the other way when he said that. It was the only attempt he made to reproach me. No, warn me, guide me, save me, counsel me. He couldn't have reproached anybody: but dancing with fat waitresses was one thing, dallying in bedrooms and dereliction of duty that might land the three of us in the stockade, another. My companions were rattled. Fuzzy-Wuzzy repeated: *Festina lente.*

But with a sort of shy, awkward half-laugh. And I marvelled that he was able to get the two words in their right order.

For myself and the blonde belle of Castledawson were into the straight and ahead of the field, and little was I seeing of the cold, stone, high-windowed hall where on solemn occasions pious Presbyterians assembled. At one history paper to which I went because I liked history, and knew how men died and even when, and Trudi was not that morning available, the man at the next desk to mine had an epileptic fit and desks and papers and inkwells went flying. That can't much have affected me: my history marks turned out to be the best I had when I had any at all.

She taught me to make beds. She taught me to mitre sheets as neatly as any young nurse ever did in any hospital. She taught me as the woman lovely in her bones taught the poet: Turn and Counter-turn and Touch and Stand. The outlaw bull, benevolent, beneficent in his secret Castledawson meadow, bellowed his blessing: and I taught her a lot about King Charles and Robert Burns. Not the Charles who lost his head, I assured her, but the Charles who held on to his head and had all the women he could count. Like Rudolf Valentino.

—The blackguard.

—Who?

—Both of them. Easy for him and he a king.

—Valentino wasn't a king.

—He was a film-star.

—He died from sleeping with women.

That was a gentlemanly way of putting what we then happily and enviously believed.

—He should have slept on his own, so.

But it wasn't often that we argued seriously. King Charles on the run from the Roundheads and the lass, who, according to the legend and the poem that Robert Burns based on the legend, made the bed for the fugitive king were better company for us than Valentino who had it all too easy: I bow'd fu' low unto this maid, And thank'd her for her courtesie; I bow'd fu' low unto this maid, And bade her mak a bed to me . . .

Loftily, and with the style of a man who was a scholar when he hadn't better things to occupy his mind, I told her; Some people say that it wasn't about King Charles at all but Robbie Burns writing about himself and remembering some girl he met in some inn. He met a lot of girls and wrote a lot of poems about them.

—He was a bit of a playboy, she said. My uncle who's a teacher near Limavady knows a lot about Burns. He was standing in a gateway with a girl, Burns was . . .

She was turning the upper sheet, patting down pillows.

. . . and a wee fellow came by. Eating a bun. And stopped to look. And Robert there and then made a poem: Walk on my son and munch your bun. The works of nature maun be done.

In our places Burns was as much part of the folklore as he was in the land he was born in.

We laughed over the story. We tackled the bed in the next room. Once only had I to run and hide when a stout, supervising, old lady came along. Trudi, while I stood mute in a built-in wardrobe, sang, sweetly and with a Scot's accent as good as real, that her love was like a red red rose. In the darkness I thought: She took her mither's holland sheets, and made them a' in sarks to me. Blythe and merry may she be, the lass that made the bed to me.

Burns and the lass and the king, perhaps, were with us in whatever room we happened to be in. They didn't intrude. They encouraged us in happiness and folly. Long afterwards I read a translation from some Spanish (I think) poet, and knew then what we were up to and, because I couldn't put it better myself, memorised the words: My chosen part to be with a girl and alone with her secret and her gift.

Morning after morning the real true scholars marched off with pen, pencil, ruler, box of mathematical instruments and the accumulated wisdom of the ages to the grim assembly hall. Some of the times I went with them but my heart wasn't in it, my mind wasn't on it. Trudi, whether present or not, was a dream of my early morning and, as I've said, breakfast was perfunctory and the main meal of the day, a very late lunch, was eaten in the Café Continental or the Continental Café when the regulars were fed and back in their shops and offices, and the floor and the air clear for dancing and music. Our examination papers of the day were disposed of by that time and we were free to roam the town, men of the town, and one night even so reckless and led by the great lover who for love had given up learning, as to accost a woman of the town. Not an easy thing to do for the first time, as every gentleman knows. Fuzzy-Wuzzy loitered in the rear, dreaming of red sails, and was useless in the action. Bill, imperturbable, all good nature and prepared to be at least polite, came two paces behind me and I, in the van, pondered on the best, most telling words to begin with. All I could think of was: Miss, could you show us the way to the Great Northern station?

It was past ten o'clock and all the trains long gone.

She didn't even alter her stride. She said: Wee fella, could you show me the way to the Albert Clock.

And walked on. It wasn't a question, or a pretended question. The Albert Clock, high on the most prominent tower in Belfast and beaming like the moon, was 30 yards away from us.

One evening, after music and dancing and bangers and mash, we did the bookstalls and the curio shops in Smithfield market, a Persian bazaar sort of a place, and I bought Johnson's *Lives of the Poets* and Adam Smith's *The Wealth of Nations*. In one of my history text-books I had read that the younger Pitt had read *The Wealth of Nations* and anything the younger Pitt could do I could do better: it was not recorded in the text-book that he had ever tried to accost a girl under the most prominent tower in London, whichever it then was. The Tower, I suppose.

One evening we came out from Eddie Cantor's *Roman Scandals* and saw, in the queue waiting to get in—it was our last day but one in Belfast—Trudi and a young man arm-in-arm and smiling into each other's eyes. They didn't see us. Fuzzy-Wuzzy blushed and said nothing. Oh, carry my loved one home safely to me, we'll marry tomorrow and go sailing no more. Bill said sadly that women were women and it might be that I was her beau only in the early morning. Even for then, beau was a curiously Edwardian word to use. Next morning she told me that it was her cousin from Castledawson and surely to God it was no sin to go to the cinema with her cousin and that, moreover, I'd never asked her out in the evening. Which I had to admit was the bare truth. She had been so much a part of the morning that it had never occurred to me that she might be free in the evening and what, without me, would Bill and Fuzzy-Wuzzy have done, parading the town and lacking their natural leader? We made it up and made the beds and that was the last time but one I saw her.

The starlings may still be there but the old Persian markets are gone, destroyed by bombs. The black news never mentions the starlings.

Lanko was gentle about it when the results came out and Bill and Fuzzy were called and I was not. But he seemed a trifle puzzled, a trifle hurt. There were, after all, three quite inexplicable zeros. Busto huffed and puffed but to my amazement and relief made little comment, and not one place-kick, not one attack on my hair style. But I knew that he knew that something out of the ordinary had happened, that God had saved the king from my services: and he hoped that, for me, something else would turn up.

Those zeros? Well, not quite inexplicable. At least with audacity, *De l'audace, et encore de l'audace, et toujours l'audace*, as the man said who died by the guillotine, with audacity and the aid of friends they could be explained away.

Because three months previously, flogging a mountain stream for trout, in my brother's company and with a triple-hooked bait-tackle that was just about legal, I'd gone in ass first, fished all day in wet clothes and caught one trout, spent three weeks in bed, tossing and turning, my brain tormented, as the brain of man coming out of a bad attack of alcohol might be, by a turning and turning repetition: I would that we were, my beloved, white birds on the foam of the sea.

Over and over and over again. Turning, turning, turning, turning, turning.

Perhaps that had set me in the mood for Trudi, and Bill and Fuzzy-Wuzzy may not have been so far out when they lied like heroes about the flushed and feverish state I'd been in on three Belfast mornings. As heroes I gratefully remember them.

Busto said: Watch it. First in one exam. Twenty-first in the next. Up and down, up and down, watch it, boy.

He may have been a bit of a prophet. For the moment all were happy except my mother who worried about her delicate boy. For a while.

Twice I wrote to Trudi, once to Belfast and once to Castledawson and never had an answer. She couldn't spell Switzerland so that she mightn't have been so good at the writing. Better by far at the making of beds and the mitring of sheets: Her bosom was the drifted snaw, twa drifted heaps sae fair to see; her limbs the polish'd marble stane, the lass that made the bed to me.

And it came to pass that Bill was called to the civil service of the King of England to the city of Carlisle, and then to the army in 1939. After the war (that one) he went into the Palestine police and, after that, to somewhere farther east of Suez and never came home again. Fuzzy-Wuzzy, being called, went to London and its lovely lake and then to the royal navy and, in 1941, sank with a minesweeper in the Channel: oh carry my loved one home safely to me. He never could get the words right.

Flat on my back in a Dublin hospital I heard the news of his death and saw him with his head up the green horn in Peter Sloper's and wondered where I'd be at that moment if Trudi hadn't come between me and the assembly hall: and saw red sails in the sunset and the Rhododendrons round the lovely lake and, through misted eyes, two student nurses mitring my sheet at the corners of my bed: the nurses are the best.

An authority on such things—a man who wrote a book on John McCormack—tells me that the reason why we studied music in bicycle shops was this: the sale of push-bikes in Edwardian times was seasonal, you sold them in the summer. The sale of phonographs and, before them, of the primitive wax cylinders was also seasonal; you sold them in the winter. Bicycle sales, he tells me, thrived during the summer and slumped in winter. Phonographs sold well coming up to Christmas and hardly at all after the festive season. So that, if you were, like Peter Sloper, into both bicycles and phonographs you prospered all the year round and walked the student nurses in your leisure moments.

Where I came from, Edwardian days lasted until 1939.

THERE ARE MEADOWS IN LANARK

The schoolmaster in Bomacatall or McKattle's Hut was gloved and masked and at his beehives when his diminutive brother, the schoolmaster from Knockatatawn, came down the dusty road on his high bicycle. It was an Irish-made bicycle. The schoolmaster from Knockatatawn was a patriot. He could have bought the best English-made Raleigh for half the price, but instead he imported this edifice from the Twenty-six into the Six Counties and paid a mountain of duty on it. The bike, and more of its kind, was made in Wexford by a firm that made the sort of mowing-machine that it took two horses to pull. They built the bikes on the same solid principle. Willian Bulfin from the Argentine who long ago wrote a book about rambling in Erin had cycled round the island on one of them and died not long afterwards, almost certainly from over-exertion. There was a great view from the saddle. Hugh, who was the son of the schoolmaster from Bomacatall, once on the quiet borrowed the bike and rode into the side of a motor-car that was coming slowly out of a hedgy hidden boreen. He was tossed sideways into the hedgerow and had a lacework of scratches on his face. The enamel on the car was chipped and the driver's window broken. The bike was unperturbed.

The little man mounted the monster by holding the grips on the handlebars, placing his left foot on the extended spud or hub of the back wheel and then giving an electrified leap. This sunny evening he dismounted by stepping on to the top rail of the garden fence at Bomacatall. He sat there like a gigantic rook, the King Rook that you hear chanting base barreltone in the rookery chorus. He wore a pinstriped dark suit and a black wide-brimmed hat. He paid no attention to the buzzing and swarming of the bees. The herbaceous borders, the diamond-shaped beds at Bomacatall would blind you. There was a twisting trout stream a field away from the far end of the garden. To his brother who was six feet and more the little man said: I have a scheme in mind.

From behind the mask the big man said: Was there ever a day that God sent that you didn't have a scheme in mind?

—It would benefit the boy Hugh. *Cé an aois é anois?*

That meant: What age is he now?

—Nine, God bless him.

—Time he saw a bit of the world. Bracing breezes, silvery sands, booming breakers, lovely lands: Come to Bundoran.

That was an advertisement in the local newspaper.

—You could sing that if you had a tune to it, said the man behind the mask.

—The holiday would do him good, the King Rook said, and for three weeks there'd be one mouth less to feed.

That was a forceful argument. The master from Knockatatawn, or the Hill of the Conflagrations, was a bachelor. Hugh was midways in a household of seven, not counting the father and mother.

The bees settled. The bee-keeper doffed the mask and wiped the sweat off a broad humorous face. He said: James, like St Paul you're getting on. You want another to guide you and lead you where thou would'st not.

—John, said the man on the fence, in defiance of Shakespeare, I maintain that there are only three stages in a man's life: young, getting-on, and not so bad-considering. I've a sad feeling that I've got to the third.

The nine-year-old, as he told me a long time afterwards, was all for the idea of Bundoran except that, young as he was, he knew there was a hook attached. This was it. At home on the Hill of the Conflagrations there wasn't a soberer man than the wee schoolmaster, none more precise in his way of life and his teaching methods, more just and exact in the administering of punishments or rewards. But Bundoran was for him another world and he, when he was there, was another man. He met a lot of all sorts of people. He talked his head off, behaved as if he had never heard of algebra or a headline copy-book, and drank whisky as if he liked it and as if the world's stock of whisky was going to run dry on the following morning. Yet, always an exact man, he knew that his powers of navigation, when he was in the whisky, were failing, that—as Myles na Gopaleen said about a man coming home from a night at a boat-club dance in Islandbridge—he knew where he was coming from and going to, but he had no control over his lesser movements. He needed a pilot, he needed a tug, or both combined in one: his nephew. There was, also, this to be said for the wee man: he was never irascible or difficult in drink, he went where the pilot guided him and the tug tugged him. He was inclined to sing, but then he was musical and in the school in Knockatatawn he had a choir that was the terror of Féis Doire Cholmcille, the great musical festival held in Derry in memory of St

Colmcille. He even won prizes in Derry against the competition of the Derry choirs—and that was a real achievement.

So for one, two, three, four years the nephew-and-uncle navigational co-operation worked well. The nephew had his days on the sand and in the sea. He even faced up to it with the expert swimmers at Roguey Rocks and the Horse Pool. By night while he waited until his uncle was ready to be steered back to the doss he drank gallons of lemonade and the like, and saw a lot of life. With the natural result that by the time the fifth summer came around, that summer when the winds were so contrary and the sea so treacherous that the priest was drowned in the Horse Pool, the nephew was developing new interests: he was looking around for the girls. At any rate, Bundoran or no Bundoran, he was growing up. Now this was a special problem because the schoolmaster from Knockatatawn had little time for girls, for himself or anybody else and, least of all, for his nephew who, in the fifth summer, had just passed thirteen.

One of the wonders of the day on which they helped the schoolmaster from Knockatatawn to the hotel and happed him safely into bed by four o'clock in the afternoon was that Hugh saw a woman, one of the Scotchies, swimming at her ease in the pool where the priest had been drowned. She was a white and crimson tropical fish, more blinding than the handsomest perch in the lake at Corcreevy or the Branchy Wood: white for arms, shoulders, midriff and legs; crimson for cap and scanty costume. Women were not supposed to be in the Horse Pool on any account but so soon after the drowning, the usual people were shunning it, and that woman either didn't know or didn't care. The Scotchies who came to the seaside to Bundoran in the summer had a great name for being wild.

In the hotel bedroom the sun came in as muted slanted shafts through the cane blinds. The shafts were all dancing dust. Carpet-sweepers weren't much in use in that hotel. They helped the wee man out of his grey sober clothes and into a brutal pair of blue-and-white striped pyjamas. He was a fierce hairy wee fellow. Arms long like an ape and a famous fiddler when he was sober. The big purple-faced schoolmaster from Lurganboy said: Begod, you're like a striped earthenware jar of something good.

The little man waved his arms and tried to sing and once slipped off the edge of the bed and sat on the floor and recited word-perfect:

> A Chieftain to the Highlands bound
> Cries: Boatman, do not tarry,

And I'll give thee a silver crown
To row me o'er the ferry.

The lot of it, every verse, all about how the waters wild swept o'er his child and how Lord Ullin's daughter and her lover were drowned. The drowning of the priest must have put it into his mind. The purple-faced man from Lurganboy, rocking a little, listened with great gravity, his head to one side, his black bushy eyes glistening, his thick smiling lips bedewed with malt. He said: In the training college he was renowned for his photographic memory. And for the fiddle.

Hugh said nothing. He was sick with delight. His uncle was a blue-and-white earthenware jar of Scotch whisky, as full as it could hold. He always drank Scotch in Bundoran, out of courtesy, he said, to the hundreds of Scotchies who came there every year on their holidays and spent good money in the country. The music of hurdy-gurdies and hobby-horses and the like came drifting to them from the strand, over the houses on the far side of the town's long street. This blessed day the blue-and-white jar could hold no more. He would sleep until tomor-row's dawn and Hugh was a free man, almost fourteen, and the world before him.

—He'll rest now, said the red-faced master from Lurganboy.

They tiptoed out of the room and down the stairs.

—What'll you do now, boy?

—Go for a walk.

—Do that. It's healthy for the young.

He gave Hugh a pound, taken all crumpled out of a trouser pocket. Then nimbly, for such a heavy man, he sidestepped into a raucous bar and the swinging doors, glass, brass and mahogany, closed behind him. It was an abrupt farewell yet Hugh was all for him, and not only because of the crumpled pound, but because in him, man to man and glass for glass, the schoolmaster from the Hill of the Conflagrations had for once taken on more than his match. Several times as they helped the little man towards his bed the unshakeable savant from Lurganboy had said to Hugh: Young man, you are looking at one who in his cups and in his declining years can keep his steps, sir, like a grenadier guard.

He had the map of his day already worked out in his head. The Scotchy girl wouldn't be sitting on the high windowsill until seven o'clock. She was there most evenings about that time. She and God knew how many other Scotchies, male and female, lived in a three-storeyed yellow boarding-house at the east end of the town. There was a garden in front of it, a sloping lawn but no fence or hedge, and the two oval flower-beds were rimmed with great stones, smoothed and shaped by the sea, tossed up on the beach at Tullaghan to the west, gathered and painted and used as ornaments by the local people. This Scotchy girl was one that liked attention. The way she went after it was to clamber out of a bedroom window on the third floor and to sit there for an hour or more in the evening kicking her heels, singing, laughing, pretending to fall, blowing kisses, and shouting things in unintelligible Scottish at the people in the street below, throwing or dropping things, flowers, chocolates, little fluttering handkerchiefs and once, he had heard, a pair of knickers. He had only seen her once at those capers when one evening he navigated past, tug before steamship, with his uncle in tow. But a fella he knew slightly told him she was to be seen there at that time most evenings. She sure as God was there to be seen. It wouldn't have been half the fun if she'd worn a bathing-suit, but a skirt with nothing underneath was something to tell the fellas about when he got back to Bomacatall. Not that they'd believe him, but still.

Behind her in the room there must have been 30 girls. They squealed like a piggery. That was a hell of a house. A randyboo, the wee master called it. Bomacatall, Knockatatawn and Corcreevy all combined never heard the equal of the noise that came out of that house. On the ground floor the piano always going, and a gramophone often at the same time, and a melodeon and pipes, and boozy male voices singing Bonny Doon and Bonny Charlie's noo awa' and Over the sea to Skye and Loch Lomond and The Blue Bells of Scotland and Bonny Strathyre and Bonny Mary of Argyle and, all the time and in and out between everything else:

> For I'm no awa tae bide awa,
> For I'm no awa tae leave ye,
> For I'm no awa tae bide awa,
> I'll come back an' see ye.

—They work hard all year, the wee master said. In the big factories and shipyards of Glasgow. Then they play hard. They're entitled to it. The Scots are a sensitive generous people and very musical.

This was the map that was in Hugh's mind when the red- or purple-faced master from Lurganboy left him outside the swinging doors of the saloon bar. That Lurganboy man was a wonder to see at the drink. When he moved, Hugh thought, he should make a sound like the ocean surf itself with the weight of liquid inside him. He had also said something remarkable and given Hugh a phrase to remember. For as they'd steered the Knockatatawn man round a windy corner from the promenade to the main street, a crowd, ten or eleven, of Scotchy girls had overtaken them, singing and shouting, waving towels and skimpy bathing-suits, wearing slacks and sandals, bright blouses, short skirts, sweaters with sleeves knotted round their waists and hanging over rumps like britchens on horses.

—This town, said the master from Lurganboy, is hoaching with women.

That was the northern word you'd use to describe the way fingerlings wriggle over and around each other at the shallow fringes of pools on blinding June days.

—Hoaching. Hoaching with women, Hugh said to himself as he set out to follow the map he had drawn in his mind that would bring him back at seven o'clock to the place where the daft girl kicked her heels and more besides on the windowsill.

From the house of glass to the Nuns' Pool by way of the harbour where the fishing boats are. It isn't really a house of glass. This shopkeeper has a fanciful sort of mind and has pebbledashed the front wall of his place with fragments of broken glass. The shop faces east, catching the morning sun, the whole wall then lives and dances like little coloured tropical fish frisking, hoaching, in a giant aquarium. Hugh can look down on it from his window which is right on top of the hotel across the street. Some people say the wall is beautiful. Some people say the man is crazy. The seer from Knockatatawn says that's the way with people.

Westward the course towards the Nuns' Pool. Passing the place where the sea crashes right into the side of the street, no houses here, and only a high strong wall keeps it from splattering the traffic. Here in the mornings when the tide is ebbed and the water quiet a daft old lady in a long dress walks out along rocks and sand, out and out until she's up to her neck in the water, dress and all, and only her head and wide-brimmed straw hat to be seen. Then she comes calmly out again and walks home dripping. Nobody worries or bothers about her. The bay is her bath tub. She lives here winter and summer.

This day the harbour is empty, a few white sails far out on the bay, pleasure boats. He sits on the tip of the mole for a while and looks down into the deep translucent water. On the gravelly bottom there are a few dead discarded fish, a sodden cardboard box, and fragments of lobster claws turned white. If he could clamber around that sharp rock headland and around two or three more of the same he could peep into the Nuns' Pool and see what they're up to. Do they plunge in, clothes and all, like the mad woman in the morning? It's hard to imagine nuns stripping like the Scotchy in the pool where the priest was drowned. Surely the priests and the nuns should share the one pool and leave Roguey Rocks and the Horse Pool to the men and the wild Scotchies. The strand and the surf are for children and after five summers he knows he's no longer a child.

But he's also alone and he knows it. Tugging and steering his mighty atom of an uncle has taken up all his time and cut him off from his kind. On the clifftop path by the Nuns' Pool there are laughing girls by the dozen, and couples walking, his arm as tightly around her as if she had just fainted and he is holding her up. In corners behind sod fences there are couples asprawl on rugs or on the naked grass, grappled like wrestlers but motionless and in deep silence. Nobody pays the least attention to him. Fair enough, he seems to be the youngest person present. Anyone younger is on the sand or in the surf. Or going for rides on donkeys. He is discovering that, unless you're the tiniest bit kinky, love is not a satisfactory spectator sport.

Steep steps cut in rock go down to the Nuns' Pool. Was it called after one nun or gaggles of nuns, season after season? It must have been one horse. But what was a horse ever doing out there on rocks and seaweed and salt water? He sees as he walks a giant nun, a giant horse. The steep steps turn a corner and vanish behind a wall of rock as big as Ben Bulben mountain. Only God or a man in a helicopter could see what goes on in there. Do they swim in holy silence, praying perhaps, making aspirations to Mary the Star of the Sea? He listens for the sort of shouts and music and screaming laughs that come from the house where the girl sits on the window-sill. He hears nothing but the wash of the sea, the wind in the cliffside grass, the crying of the gulls. What would you expect? It is ten minutes to five o'clock.

He has time to walk on to the place where the Drowes river splits into two and goes to the sea over the ranked, sea-shaped stones of Tullaghan, to walk back to the hotel by the main road, feast on the customary cold ham and tomatoes and tea, bread and butter, wash his hands and face and sleek his hair with Brylcreem and part it up the middle, and still be on good time and in a good place for the seven o'clock show. He does all this. He is flat-footed from walking and a little dispirited. On the stony strand of Tullaghan there isn't even a girl to be seen. If there was he could draw her attention to the wonderful way the sea forms and places the stones, rank on rank, the biggest ones by the water line and matted with seaweed, the smallest and daintiest right up by the sand and the whistling bent-grass. They are variously coloured. The tide has ebbed. Far out the water growls over immovable stones.

He rests for a while by the two bridges over the Drowes river. If there was a girl there he could tell her how the river flows down from Lough Melvin, and how the trout in the lake and the trout in the river have the gizzards of chickens and how, to account for that oddity, there's a miracle story about an ancient Irish saint. There is no girl there. A passing car blinds him with dust. Has the evening become more chilly or is that just the effect of hunger? He accelerates. He knows that while a Scotchy girl might show some interest in stones shaped and coloured into mantelpiece or dressing-room ornaments, she would be unlikely to care much about trout or ancient miracles. In the hotel the master is sound asleep in blue-and-white bars, the bed-clothes on the floor. He doesn't snore. Hugh eats four helpings of ham and tomatoes, two for himself, two for the recumbent fiddler from the Hill of the Conflagrations.

The evening is still ahead of him and the fleshpots delectably steaming. There is no glitter from the house of glass. The hot tea and ham, the thought of the kicking girl on the high windowsill have done him a lot of good. In the evening most of the children will be gone from the strand, the Palais de Danse warming up, the hoaching at its best.

He wasn't the only one watching for the vision to appear, and right in the middle, like a gigantic rugby-football forward holding together a monumental scrum, was the purple-faced man from Lurganboy. The Assyrian, Hugh thought, came down like a wolf on the fold and his cohorts were gleaming in purple and gold. He wasn't his uncle's nephew for nothing, even if he wasn't quite sure what a cohort meant. As he told me long afterwards in the Branchy Wood, or Corcreevy, if his literary education had then advanced as far as *Romeo and Juliet* he would have been able, inevitably, to say: But soft what light through yonder window etc. The man with the face as purple as cohorts saw it differently. To the men that ringed him round he said: Lads, I declare to me Jasus, 'tis like Lourdes or Fatima waiting for the lady to appear. All we lack is hymns and candles.

—We have the hymns, one voice said, she has the candles.

—*Ave ave*, said another voice.

The laughter wasn't all that pleasant to listen to. They were a scruffy enough crowd, Hugh thought, to be in the company of a schoolmaster that had the benefit of education and the best of training; the master from Bomacatall, kind as he was, would have crossed the street if he'd seen them coming. Shiny pointy toes, wide grey flannels, tight jackets, oiled hair; the man from Lurganboy must, at last, like the stag at eve, have drunk his fill or he wouldn't, surely to God, be in the middle of them. Hugh dodged. There was a fine fat flowering bush, white blossoms, bursting with sparrows when the place was quiet, right in the middle of the sloping lawn. He put it between himself and the waiting watching crowd. His back was to the bush. He was very close to the high yellow house. The din was delightful, voices male and female, a gramophone playing a military march, somebody singing that there are meadows in Lanark and mountains in Skye—and he was thinking what a wonderful people the Scots were and what a hell and all of a house that must be to live in, when the high window went up with a bang and there she was, quick as a sparrow on a branch, but brighter, much brighter.

He had heard of a bird of paradise but never had he, nor has he up to the present moment, seen one. But if such a bird exists then its plumage would really have to be something to surpass in splendour what Hugh, in the dying western evening, saw roosting and swinging on the windowsill. Far and beyond Roguey Rocks the sun would be sinking in crimson. The light came over the roofs of the houses across the street, dazzled the windows, set the girl on fire. Long red hair, red dress, pink stockings, red shoes with wooden soles. She was so high up, the angle was so awkward, the late sunlight so dazzling, that he could find out little about her face except that it was laughing. The scrum around the Lurganboy man cheered and whistled. He knew she was laughing, too, because he could hear her. She was shouting down to the Lurganboy contingent, the *caballeros*, but because of the noise from the house and the street he couldn't pick out any words and, anyway, she would be talking Scottish. Nor could he be certain that he had been correctly informed as to what, if anything, she wore underneath the red dress although when he got home to his peers in McKattle's Hut or Bomacatall he sure as God wouldn't spoil a good story by unreasonable doubts.

All told it was an imperfect experience. She twisted and tacked so rapidly, agile as a monkey, that a man could see nothing except crimson. He couldn't even have known that her red shoes had wooden soles if it hadn't been that, with the dink of kicking, one of them came unstuck, and landed as surely as a cricket-ball in his cupped palms where he stood in hiding behind the bush. It was in the pocket of his jacket before he knew what he was doing. Cinderella lost her slipper. He was off through the crowd in a second and nobody but the girl saw him go. The eyes of Lurganboy and his men were on the vision. She screamed high and long. From the far end of the crowd he glanced back and saw her pointing towards him. But nobody bothered to look the way she was pointing. The map of his evening was as clear in his mind as the strand before him, as sure as the shoe in his pocket, and hunt-the-slipper was a game at which anything might happen.

The people in this place have, like the tides, their own peculiar movement. Evening, as he expected, draws most of the children away from the strand to a thousand boarding-house bedrooms. The promise of the moon draws the loving couples, the laughing and shouting groups away from the westward walk by the Nuns' Pool to dry sheltered nooks between strand and dunes, to the hollows in the grassy tops of the high cliffs above Roguey, to the place where later the drums will begin to feel their way in the Palais de Danse. Every night, including Sunday, in the palais there is not only a dance but a few brawls and a talent competition.

No moon yet. No drums yet. The last red rays are drowned in the ocean. The light is grey. The strand is pretty empty and a little chilly, the sea is far out. But as he runs, ankle deep in churned sand, down the slope from the now silent motionless hobby-horses and hurdy-gurdies, he sees a slow, silent procession of people coming towards him around the jagged black corner of Roguey Rocks. The sea washes up almost around their feet. They step cautiously across a shelf of rock, then more rapidly and boldly along the slapping wet sand by the water's edge. Four men in the lead are carrying something. He runs towards them, all girls forgotten. Whatever chance, anyway, he had of meeting a girl during the day he can only have less now in this half-desolate place. The red shoe will be his only souvenir, yet still something to show to the heathens in Bomacatall. Halfways across the strand a distraught woman in shirt and cardigan, hair blowing wild stops him. She says: Wee boy, see if it's a wee boy with fair hair. He's missing for an hour and I'm distracted. Jesus, Mary and Joseph protect him. I'm afraid to look myself.

But it isn't a wee boy with fair hair. It isn't even the crimson-and-white Scotchy girl who had been swimming in the Horse Pool and whom the sea might have punished for sacrilege, for surely a dead drowned priest must make some difference to the nature of the water.

What he sees is nothing that you could exactly put a name to. The four men carry it on a door taken off its hinges. It's very large and sodden. There's nothing in particular where the face should be—except that it's very black. A woman looks at it and gasps. Somebody says: Cover that up, for God's sake.

A tall red-headed man throws a plastic raincoat over the black nothing in particular. Hugh walks back to the woman in the skirt and cardigan. He tells her that it isn't a wee boy with fair hair. She thanks God.

—It's a big person that must have been a long time in the water.

But she has moved away and isn't listening. He falls in at the tail of the procession. People leave it and join it, join it and leave it. It's a class of a funeral. An ambulance comes screaming down the slope from the long town and parks beside the stabled silent hobby-horses. Two civic guards come running, a third on a bicycle. Behind on the strand one single man in a long black coat walks, fearing no ghosts, towards Roguey Rocks. No couples or laughing groups are to be seen, even on the grassy clifftops. He fingers the shoe in his pocket to remind him of girls. A drum booms, a horn blares from the Palais de Danse which is halfways up the slope towards the town. He gets in, and for free, simply by saying that he's singing in Irish in the talent competition.

The hall was already crowded because the evening had turned chilly and the threat of rain was in the air. He found a seat in a corner near the ladies where he could watch the procession coming and going. They came and went in scores and for all the attention any of them paid to him he might have been invisible. He was grateful for the anonymity. He was too weary to carry on with the hopeless chase and that grim vision on the beach had given him other things to think about. It was still fun to sit and watch the women, all shapes and sizes and colours, and moods. They went in demure and came out giggling. That was because most of them, he had heard, kept noggins of gin and vodka concealed in the cloakroom. It was a great world and all before him. The band was thunderous, the floor more and more crowded until somebody thumped a gong and everybody who could find a chair sat down: girls who couldn't sitting recklessly on the knees of strangers, nobody on his. So he stood up and gave his chair to a girl who didn't even say thanks. The band vanished. A woman sat at the piano, a man with a fiddle and a young fellow with a guitar stood beside her. This was the talent competition.

A grown man long afterwards in the Branchy Wood, or Corcreevy, he couldn't remember much of it. The time was after eleven, he had been on foot all day, his eyes were closing with sleep. A man with long brown hair and long—the longest—legs and big feet came out, sang in a high nervous tenor about the bard of Armagh, then tripped over the music stand and fell flat on his face. That act was much appreciated. A little girl in a white frock and with spangles or something shining in her hair, tiptoed out, curtsied, holding the hem of her skirt out wide in her hands, danced a jig to the fiddle, then sang a song in Irish that meant:

There are two little yellow goats at me, courage of the milk, courage of the milk. This is the tune that is at the piper, Hielan laddy, Hielan laddy. And more of the same. A fat bald man sang: While I'm jog jog jogging along the highway, a vagabond like me. Then there were tin whistles and concertinas, six sets of Scottish and two of Irish or Uillean pipes, piano accordions, melodeons, combs in tissue paper and clicking spoons, cornet, fiddle, big bass, drum, something, something and euphonium. As the song says.

He lost interest. His insteps ached. He would unnoticed have slipped away only a crowd and girls hoaching was always better than a lonely room. Surveying the crowd from China to Peru he saw in the far corner the man from Lurganboy, like the old priest Peter Gilligan, asleep within a chair, his legs out like logs, hands locked over splendid stomach and watch-chain and velvet waistcoat, chin on chest, black hat at a wild angle but bravely holding on to his head. No angels, as in the case of Peter Gilligan, hovered over him, none that Hugh could see. Five other adults sat in a row beside him, all awake except Lurganboy. Angels that around us hover, guard us till the close of day. Singing that, the Knockatatawn choir had once won a first prize in Derry city.

As Hugh watched, Lurganboy awoke, pulled in his legs, raised his head, gripped the arms of his chair and hoisted himself to sit erect. The ballroom was silent. Was it the oddness of the silence made the sleeper awake? No, not that, but something, Hugh felt, was going to happen. The drummer was back on the stage. He struck the drum a boom that went round the room, echoing, shivering slowly away. Then the compère said: Ladies and gentlemen.

He said it twice. He held up his right hand. He said again: Ladies and gentlemen, while the judges, including our old, true, tried and stalwart friend from Lurganboy are making up their minds, adding up points, assessing the vast array of talent, not to mention grace and beauty, we will meet again an old friend, a man who needs no introduction, a man who many a time and oft has starred on this stage and who, in days gone by but well remembered has worn more laurels for music than——

The cheers hit the roof, and out on the stage like a released jack-in-the-box stepped the wee master from Knockatatawn, sober as a judge, lively as a cricket, dapper as a prize greyhound, fiddle in one fist, bow in the other. When the cheering stopped he played for fifteen minutes and even the gigglers, resurfacing after gin and vodka, kept a respectful silence. Lord God Almighty, he could play the fiddle.

It could be that the way to get the women is to be a bachelor and play the fiddle, and drink all day and pay no attention to them. For I declare to God, the schoolmaster from Corcreevy said long afterwards, I never saw anything like it before or since, flies round the honeypot, rats round a carcase, never did I see hoaching like that hoaching, and in the middle of it and hopping about on the stage like a wound-up toy, a monkey on a stick, the red Scots girl from the windowsill, and her shoe in my pocket. Radar or something must have told her where it was. She saw me, isolated as I was, standing like a pillar-box in the middle of the floor, for the crowd was on the stage or fighting to get on the stage, and the drum was booming and the compère shouting and nobody listening. She came towards me slowly and I backed away and then ran for the beach, and then stopped. The moon was out between clouds. There was a mizzle of rain.

He stopped running and looked at the moon and the moonlight on the water. This was destiny and he had no real wish to run from it. The moon shines bright, on such a night as this. As he is now, a moonlit beach always reminds him of loneliness, a crowded beach of faceless death. She was a little monkey of a girl and she crouched her shoulders and stooped when she talked. Her red hair was down to her hips. She said: Wee laddie, will ye no gie me backma shoe?

He was learning the language.

—I'm as big as ye are, yersel.

—Will ye no gie me back ma shoe?

She wasn't pleading. She wasn't angry. He knew by her big eyes that it was all fun to her, all part of the holiday. She really wasn't any taller than himself and her foot fitted into his pocket.

—It's no here. It's in ma room.

—You'll bring it tae me.

—For sure. It's no awa tae bide away.

—Guid laddie. Do ye dance?

—Thon's my uncle wi' the fiddle.

—Ye're like him. Ye were quick away wi' ma shoe. I'll no tell him ye're here.

The red shoe was his ticket of admission to the wild happy house. Nothing much, naturally, came of that except a lot of singing and some kisses in the mornings from a sort of elder sister. He learned to talk and understood Scots and to this day, and in his cups, can sing that he's no awa tae bide awa with the best Glaswegian that e'er cam doon frae Gilmour hill. Like his uncle he enjoyed his double life. Not for years, though, not until he had been through college and had his own school, in Corcreevy or the Branchy Wood, did he tell the tale to the old man who by that time was retired and able to drink as he pleased. The old fellow, mellow at the time, laughed immoderately and said: Seemuldoon, I always hold, is a land of milk and honey if you keep your own bees and milk your own cow.

That was a favourite and frequently irrelevant saying of his. Seemuldoon, meaning the dwelling-place of the Muldoons, was, in all truth, the place he came from, and not Knockatatawn. Nor did the man from Lurganboy really come from Lurganboy: I used the name just because I like it, and when people ask me to go to Paris and places like that I say no, I'll go to Lurganboy. Because you don't *go* to Lurganboy, you find yourself there when you lose the road going somewhere else.

BLUEBELL MEADOW

When she came home in the evening from reading in the park that was a sort of an island the sergeant who had been trounced by the gipsies was waiting to ask her questions about the bullets. He had two of them in the cupped palm of his right hand, holding the hand low down, secretively. His left elbow was on the edge of the white-scrubbed kitchen table. The golden stripes on his blue-black sleeve, more black than blue, were as bright as the evening sunshine on the old town outside. He was polite, almost apologetic, at first. He said: I hate to bother yourself and your aunt and uncle. But it would be better for everybody's sake if you told me where you got these things. People aren't supposed to have them. Least of all girls in a convent school.

There had been six of them. The evening Lofty gave them to her she had looked at them for a whole hour, sitting at that table, half-reading a book. Her uncle and aunt were out at the cinema. She spread the bullets on the table and moved them about, making designs and shapes and patterns with them, joining them by imaginary lines, playing with them as if they were draughts or dominoes or precious stones. It just wasn't possible that such harmless mute pieces of metal could be used to kill people. Then she wearied of them, put them away in an old earthenware jug on the mantelpiece and after a while forgot all about them. They were the oddest gifts, God knew, for a boy to give to a girl. Not diamonds again, darling. Say it with bullets.

This is how the park happens to be a sort of an island. The river comes out of deep water, lined and overhung by tall beeches, and round a right-angled bend to burst over a waterfall and a salmon leap. On the right bank and above the fall a sluice-gate regulates the flow of a millrace. A hundred yards downstream the millrace is carried by aqueduct over a rough mountain stream or burn coming down to join the river. Between river and race and mountain stream is a triangular park, five or six acres, seats by the watersides, swings for children, her favourite seat under a tall conifer and close to the corner where the mountain stream meets the river. The place is called Bluebell Meadow. The bluebells grow in the woods on the far side of the millrace.

When the river is not in flood a peninsula of gravel and bright sand guides the mountain stream right out into the heart of the current. Children play on the sand, digging holes, building castles, sending flat pebbles skimming and dancing like wagtails upstream over the smooth water. One day Lofty is suddenly among the children just as if he had come out of the river which is exactly what he has done. His long black waders still drip water. The fishing-rod which he holds in his left hand, while he expertly skims pebbles with the right, dips and twiddles above him like an aerial. The canvas bag on his back is sodden and heavy and has grass, to keep the fish fresh, sticking out of the mouth of it. One of the children is doing rifle-drill with the shaft of his net. She has never spoken to him but she knows who he is.

When she tires of reading she can look at the river and dream, going sailing with the water. Or simply close her eyes. Or lean back and look up into the tall conifer, its branches always restless and making sounds, and going away from her like a complicated sort of spiral stairway. She has been told that it is the easiest tree in the world to climb but no tree is all that easy if you're wearing a leg-splint. She is looking up into the tree, and wondering, when Lofty sits beside her. His waders are now dry and rubbery to smell. The rod, the net and the bag are laid on the grass, the heads of two sad trout protruding, still life that was alive this morning. Her uncle who keeps greyhounds argues that fishing is much more cruel than coursing: somewhere in the happy river are trout that were hooked and got away, hooks now festering in their lovely speckled bodies. She thinks a lot about things like that.

Lofty sits for five minutes, almost, before he says: I asked Alec Quigley to tell you I was asking for you.

—He told me.

—What did you say?

—Did he not tell you?

—He said you said nothing but I didn't believe him.

—Why not?

—You had to say something.

—If I said anything Alec Quigley would tell the whole town.

—I daresay he would.

—He's the greatest clatter and clashbag from hell to Omagh.

—I didn't know.

—You could have picked a more discreet ambassador.

The words impress him. He says: It's a big name for Alec Quigley. I never thought of him as an ambassador.

—What then? A go-between? A match-maker? A gooseberry?

They are both laughing. Lofty is a blond tall freckled fellow with a pleasant laugh. He asks her would she like a trout.

—I'd love one. Will we cook it here and now?

—I can roll it in grass for you and get a bit of newspaper in McCaslan's shop up at the waterfall.

—Who will I tell my aunt and uncle gave me the trout?

—Tell them nothing. Tell them you whistled and a trout jumped out at you. Tell them a black man came out of the river and gave you a trout.

He left his bag and rod where they were and walked from the apex of the triangular park to the shop at the angle by the waterfall. He came back with a sheet of black parcelling paper and wrapped up the trout very gently. He had long delicate hands, so freckled that they were almost totally brown. The trout, bloody mouth gaping, looked sadly up at the two of them. Lofty said: I'd like to go out with you.

—I'm often out. Here.

So he laughed and handed her the trout and went on upstream towards the falls, casting from the bank at first, then wading knee-deep across a shallow bar of gravel and walking on across a green hill towards the deeps above the falls. She liked his long stride, and the rod dipping and twiddling above him, and the laden bag—even though she knew it was full of dead gaping trout. She knew he was a popular fellow in the town. Yet she didn't tell her aunt and uncle who exactly it was had made her a gift of the trout. She said it was an elderly man and she wasn't quite sure of his name, but she described him so that they'd guess he was a well-known fisherman, a jeweller by trade and highly respected in the town. Not that Lofty and his people were disrespectable.

The gipsies who trounced the sergeant hadn't been real romany gipsies but tinkers or travelling people from the west of Ireland, descendants, the theory was, of broken people who went on the roads during the hungry years of the 1840s and hadn't settled down since. Five of them, wild, ragged, rough-headed fellows came roaring drunk out of a pub in Bridge Lane. The pub was owned by a man called Yarrow and the joke among those literate enough to appreciate it was about Yarrow Visited and Yarrow Revisited. There was also an old English pishroge about girls putting Yarrow, the plant, between two plates and wishing on it and saying: Good morrow, good morrow, good yarrow, thrice good morrow to thee! I hope before this time tomorrow thou wilt show my true love to me.

One of the five fell with a clatter down the three steps from the door of the pub. In their tottering efforts to pick him up two of the others struck their heads together and began to fight. The remaining two joined in and so, when he was able to stand up, did the fellow who had fallen down the steps. The sergeant was walking past and was fool enough to try to stop them. In the west of Ireland the civic guards had more sense and stood as silent spectators until the tinkers had hammered the fight out of each other.

The five of them, united by foreign invasion, gave the sergeant an unmerciful pounding. He had just enough breath left to blow his whistle. More police came running. More tinkers came shouting, men, women and children, out of the pub, out of dark tunnels of entryways between houses, out of holes in the walls. The battle escalated. More police came. The tinkers made off on two flat carts. One old man was so drunk he fell helpless off a cart and was arrested. The police followed in a tender.

At their encampment of caravans a mile outside the town the tinkers abandoned the carts and took in the darkness to the fields and the hedgerows and even, it was said, to the tops of the trees. The police wisely did not follow, but set a heavy guard on the camp, caravans, carts, horses, scrap metal and everything the tinkers owned. Sober and sheepishly apologetic they reappeared in the morning and gave themselves up and half a dozen of them went to jail. But for a long time afterwards when the sergeant walked the town the wits at the street-corner would whistle: Oh, play to me gipsy, the moon's high above.

Thanks to Arthur Tracy, known as the Street Singer, it was a popular song at the time.

In spite of all that, the sergeant remained an amiable sort of man, stout, slow-moving, with a large brown moustache and a son who was a distinguished footballer.

Yarrow is a strong-scented herb related to the daisies. It has white or pink flowers in flat clusters.

One Sunday in the previous June in an excursion train to Bundoran by the western sea she had overheard Lofty's mother telling funny stories. As a rule Protestants didn't go west to Bundoran but north to Portrush. The sea was sectarian. What were the wild waves saying: At Portrush: Slewter, slaughter, holy water, harry the papishes every one, drive them under and bate them asunder, the Protestant boys will carry the drum. Or at Bundoran: On St Patrick's day, jolly and gay, we'll kick all the Protestants out of the way, and if that won't do we'll cut them in two and send them to hell with their red, white and blue.

Nursery rhymes.

She sat facing her aunt in the train and her uncle sat beside her. They were quiet, looking at all the long beauty of Lough Erne which has an island, wooded or pastoral, for every day in the year. Her aunt, a timid little woman, said now and again: Glory be to God for all his goodness.

Her uncle said just once: You should see Lake Superior. No end to it. As far as the human eye can see.

Then they were all quiet, overhearing Lofty's mother who had no prejudices about the religion of the ocean and who, with three other people, sat across the corridor from them, and who had a good-natured carrying voice and really was fun to listen to. She was saying: I'm a Protestant myself, missus dear, and I mean no disrespect to confession but you must have heard about the young fellow who went to the priest to tell him his sins and told him a story that had more women in it than King Solomon had in the Bible and the goings-on were terrible, and the priest says to him, Young man are you married?, and the young fellow says back to him, dead serious and all, Naw father but I was twice in Fintona.

The train dived through a tunnel of tall trees. The lake vanished. Sunlight flashing and flickering through leaves made her close her eyes. Everybody on the train, even her aunt, seemed to be laughing. A man was saying: Fintona always had a bit of a name. For wild women.

Lofty's mother said, I was born there myself but I never noticed that it was all that good, nobody ever told me.

She opens her eyes and the sunlight flickers down on her through the spiralling branches of the great conifer. There's a book in the public library that has everything, including pictures, about all the trees of Great Britain and Ireland. Lofty is on the very tip of the peninsula of sand and gravel, demonstrating fly-casting to half a dozen children who are tailor-squatting around his feet. She is aware that he's showing off to impress her and the thought makes her warm and pleased, ready to laugh at anything. But to pretend that she's unimpressed she leans back and looks up into the tree in which the sunlight is really alive, creeping round the great bole, spots of light leaping like birds from one branch to another. She thinks of the omú tree which grows on the pampas of South America. Its trunk can be anything up to 40 or 50 feet thick. The wood is so soft that when cut it rots like an over-ripe melon and is useless as firewood. The leaves are large, glossy and deep green like laurel leaves—and also poisonous. But they give shade from the bare sun to man and beast, and men mark their way on the endless plains by remembering this or that omú tree. She has read about omú trees. Her own tree is for sure not one of them. She sits up straight when her book is lifted from her lap. Lofty is sitting by her side. The children are pointing and laughing. He must have crept up on hands and knees pretending to be a wild animal, a wolf, a prowling tiger. He's very good at capers of that sort. His rod and net lie by the side of the burn.

It was April when he first sat beside her. It is now mid-June. Her school will close soon for the holidays and she will no longer be compelled to wear the uniform: black stockings, pleated skirt of navy-blue serge, blue gansey, blue necktie with saffron stripes, blue blazer with school crest in saffron on breast-pocket, blue beret, black flat-heeled shoes. Even Juliet, and she was very young, didn't have to wear a school uniform. If she had Romeo wouldn't have looked at her.

Not that they are star-crossed lovers or Lofty any Romeo. They haven't even crossed the millrace to walk in the bluebell woods as couples of all ages customarily do. She isn't shy of walking slowly because of the leg-splint but she knows that Lofty hasn't asked her because he thinks she might be: that makes her feel for him as she might feel, if she had one, for a witless younger brother who's awkward. And a bit wild: for a lot of Lofty's talk doesn't go with the world of school uniforms mostly blue for the mother of God. What the saffron is for, except variety of a sort, she can't guess. Lofty's rattling restless talk would lift Mother Teresa out of her frozen black rigidity.

Lofty with great good humour fingers the saffron stripes and says that, in spite of everything, she's a wee bit of an Orangewoman. They hold hands regularly. Lofty can read palms, a variant reading every time. They have kissed occasionally, when the children who are always there have been distracted by a water-hen or rat or leaping fish or a broken branch or an iceberg of froth from the falls.

—Don't look now, he says one day, but if you swivel round slowly you'll see my three sisters in action.

Beyond the millrace and against the fresh green of woods she can see the flash of coloured frocks, the glint of brass buttons and pipe-clayed belts. In those days it was only the wild ones who went with the soldiers: it wasn't money and security they were after.

—They're hell for soldiers, he says, between the three of them they'd take on the Germans.

Lofty himself reads a lot of military books, campaigns and generals, Napoleon and Ludendorf, all the way from Blenheim to the Dardanelles. When he doodles as he often does on the writing-pad she always carries with her—to make notes on her reading, to transcribe favourite poems—he doodles uniforms, every detail exact. Yet he listens to her when she reads poetry or the splendid prose of a volume of selected English essays, Caxton to Belloc.

—They're advancing on us, he says. They have us surrounded, enfiladed, debouched and circumnavigated.

—We'll tell Maryanne, the three sisters say, that you're with another.

Two of them, Mildred and Rosemary, are plump, laughing, blonde girls, and Mildred who is the youngest is as freckled as her brother. Gertie, the eldest, is olive-faced, with jet-black hair, wrinkles on the forehead and around the eyes like her mother. She is never to see the father of the family but the gossip of the town is to tell her that he's away a lot in Aldershot and India and that Lofty's mother, that merry woman, is friendly with more soldiers than the one she's married to.

The three British soldiers who are with the sisters are, one of them from Sligo, one from Wexford and one actually from Lancashire, England. They all talk and laugh a lot and she likes them. The Lancashire lad climbs right up to the top of the tree and pretends to see everything that's going on in the town and tells them about it: he has a lurid imagination. Then they go away towards the waterfall, still laughing, calling back about telling Maryanne. She asks him who Maryanne is. Lofty who clearly likes his sisters is not in the least embarrassed by the suggestion that he has another woman.

—Oh Maryanne's nobody or nobody much.

—She has a name. She must be somebody.

She's not really jealous, just curious.

—Maryanne's a girl I met one day on the road beyond McCaslan's shop.

—You met nobody on the road?

—She was wheeling a pram.

—She's married to Mr Nobody?

—It wasn't her pram. She's the nursemaid in Mooney's, the fancy-bread bakery. There was a lovely smell of fresh bread.

—Had you a good appetite, apple-jelly, jam-tart?

But since the rest of that rhyme to which children, Protestant and Catholic, rope-skip on the streets, is tell me the name of your sweetheart, she doesn't finish it and finds herself, to her annoyance, blushing. Lofty doesn't seem to notice.

—There were twins in the pram. I pushed it for her up the hill to the main road. Then she said I bet you wouldn't do that for me if it was in the town on the court-house hill where everybody could see you. I said why not and she said Christian Brothers' boys are very stuck-up, I've met some that would do anything they could or you'd let them if they had a girl in the woods or in the dark, but that wouldn't be seen talking to her on the street, maids aren't good enough for them. I didn't tell her I was a Presbyterian and went to the academy.

—Why not?

—She mightn't like a Presbyterian pushing her pram.

They laugh at that until the playing children turn and look and laugh with them. Cheerful voices call from beyond the millrace where soldiers and sisters are withdrawing to the woods.

—We have girls at the academy, on the house, what Harry Cassidy and Jerry Hurst and the boys don't have at the Brothers. Harry and the boys are mad envious when we tell them about the fun we have feeling Daisy Allen under the desk at school. All lies of course.

—I hope Daisy Allen doesn't hear that.

—Och Daisy, she's well handled anyway, she's going about with a bus-driver and he's a married man as well, he ruined a doctor's daughter in Dungannon. Harry and the Catholic boys think the Protestant girls are wilder because they don't have to tell it all in confession. That isn't true either.

One other funny story she had heard Lofty's mother telling that day as the train in the evening left Bundoran station and the great romantic flat-topped mountains diminished into the distance. This time the story-teller faced her aunt and sat beside her uncle who had been talking about jerry-building in a new housing estate. Lofty's mother agreed with him. She had a shopping-bag of sugar to smuggle back into the Six Counties where it cost more. The sugar was tastefully disguised under a top-dressing of dulse. With content and triumph Lofty's mother sang a parody popular at the time: South of the border down Bundoran way, that's where we get the Free State sugar to sweeten our tay.

She was great fun. She had bright blue eyes and a brown hat with a flaring feather, and a brown crinkly face. She said: Those houses are everything you say and worse. Fancy fronts and ready to fall. When you flush the lavatory in them the noise is heard all over the town. Only the other day the lady who lives in number three sent down to River Row for old Mr Hill, the chimney-sweep, and up he came and put the brush up the chimney and then went out, the way sweeps do, to see if the brush was showing out of the top of the chimney. No brush. In he went and screws on another length of handle on the brush and pushes for dear life, and out again to look, but no brush. In again and screws on the last bit of handle he has, and he's pushing away when the lady from number eleven knocks on the door. Have you the sweep in, missus dear, she says. I have, missus dear, says the lady from number three. Then please ask him to be careful, missus dear, she says, that's twice now he's upset our wee Rosy from the lavatory seat.

Because of her happy carrying voice passers-by in the corridor stop to join the fun. The smuggled sugar is safely across the border.

Remembering Lofty's laughing mother makes it easier still to like Lofty. The three sisters also look as if they'd be good for a lot of laughs.

Her uncle is a tall broad-shouldered man with a good grey suit, a wide-brimmed hat, two gold teeth and a drawl. Years ago he was in the building trade in the United States and knows a lot about jerry-building. He gets on very well with Lofty's mother.

It was well on towards the end of August when the black man sat on the bench beside her. She was looking sideways towards the bridge over the millrace, and laughing: because two big rough young fellows were running like hares before Mr McCaslan's boxer dog. Mr McCaslan who owned the shop was also water-bailiff and park-keeper. The rough fellows had been using, brutally, one of the swings meant for small children, so brutally that the iron stays that supported it were rising out of the ground. Mr McCaslan had mentioned the matter to them. They had been offensive, even threatening, to the old rheumatic man so he hobbled back to his shop and sent the boxer dog down as his deputy. The pair took off as if all hell were behind them. It was funny because the dog didn't bark or growl or show hostility, didn't even run fast, just loped along with a certain air of quiet determination and wouldn't (as far as she knew) savage anybody. But he was a big dog even for a boxer and the retreat of the miscreants was faster than the Keystone Cops. She laughed so much that the book fell on the grass. The black man picked it up and sat down beside her.

She thought of him as a black man not because he was a Negro but because her uncle had told her that he was a member of the black preceptory which was a special branch of the Orange Order. She had seen him walking last twelfth of July in the big parade in memory of the battle of the Boyne, which happened a long time ago, and in honour of King William of Orange who was a long time dead and had never been in this town. He had worn the black sash, with shining metallic esoteric insignia attached, as had the other men who marched beside him. The contingent that followed wore blue sashes and were supposed to be teetotallers but her uncle said that that was not always so. One of the blue men, a red-faced red-headed fellow was teetering and might have fallen if he hadn't been holding on to one of the poles that supported a banner.

The drums drummed, the banners bellied in the breeze, the pipes and fifes and brass and accordions played:

> It is old but it is beautiful
> And its colours they are fine,
> It was worn at Derry, Aughrim,
> Enniskillen and the Boyne.
> My father wore it in his youth,
> In bygone days of yore,
> And on the Twelfth I'll always wear
> The sash my father wore.

The name of the black man who sat beside her was Samuel McClintock and he was a butcher. It was said about him for laughs that if the market ran out of meat the town could live for a week on McClintock's apron: blue, with white stripes. That August day and in the public park he naturally wasn't wearing the apron. He had a black moustache, a heavy blue chin, a check cloth-cap, thick-soled boots, thick woollen stockings and whipcord knee-breeches. The Fomorians, the monsters from stormy seas had, each of them, one arm, one leg and three rows of teeth. He said: The dog gave those ruffians the run.

The way he said it took the fun out of it. She said: Yes, Mr McClintock.

She wished him elsewhere. She half-looked at her book. She was too well-reared to pick it up from her lap and ostentatiously go on reading. The river was in a brown fresh that day, the peninsula of sand and gravel not to be seen, nor Lofty, nor the children. The black man said: Plenty water in the river today.

She agreed with him. It was also a public park in a free-and-easy town and everyone had a right to sit where he pleased. Yet this was her own seat under the tall tree, almost exclusively hers, except when Lofty was there. The black man said: The Scotchies have a saying that the salmon's her ain when there's water but she's oors when it's oot.

He explained: That means that often they're easier to catch when the water's low.

He filled his pipe and lighted it. The smell of tobacco was welcome. It might have been her imagination but until he pulled and puffed and sent the tobacco smell out around them she had thought that the resinous air under the tree was polluted by the odours of the butcher's shop and apron. He said that the salmon were a sight to see leaping the falls when they went running upstream. She said that she had often watched them.

—I'm told you're very friendly with a well-known young fisherman of my persuasion.

—Who, for instance?

—You know well. That's what I want to talk to you about. It's a serious matter.

—Being friendly with a fisherman?

—Don't play the smarty with me, young lassie. Even if you do go to the convent secondary school. Young people now get more education than's good for them. Lofty at the academy and you at the convent have no call to be chumming it up before the whole town.

—Why not?

But it occurred to her that they hadn't been chumming-up or anything else before the whole town. What eyes could have spied on them in this enchanted island?

—His uncle's a tyler, that's why.

—I never knew he had an uncle.

—His mother's brother is a tyler and very strict.

—What's a tyler?

—I shouldn't repeat it, lassie. But I will, to impress on you how serious it is. A tyler he is and a strict one. Wasn't it him spoke up to have Lofty let into the B Specials?

—Don't ask me. I never knew he was a B Special.

But one day for a joke, she remembered, he had given her a handful of bullets.

—The nuns wouldn't tell you this at school but the B Specials were set up by Sir Basil Brooke to hold Ulster against the Pope and the Republic of Ireland.

The nuns, for sure, hadn't told her anything of the sort: Mother Teresa who was very strong on purity and being a lady and not sitting like a man with your legs crossed had never once mentioned the defensive heroisms of the B Specials who, out in country places, went about at night with guns and in black uniforms, holding up Catholic neighbours and asking them their names and addresses—which they knew very well to begin with. The Lofty she knew in daylight by this laughing river didn't seem to be cut out for such nocturnal capers.

—If his uncle knew that the two of you and you a Catholic girl were carrying-on there'd be hell upon earth.

—But we're not carrying-on.

—You were seen kissing here on this bench. What's that but carrying-on?

—What does he level?

—What does who level?

—The uncle who's a leveller or whatever you called him.

—Speak with respect, young lassie. A tyler, although I shouldn't tell you the secret, is a big man in the Order at detecting intruders. His obligation is this: I do solemnly declare that I will be faithful to the duties of my office and I will not admit any person into the lodge without having first found him to be in possession of the financial password or without the sanction of the Worshipful Master of the Lodge.

Then after a pause he said with gravity: And I'm the worshipful master.

He was the only one of the kind she had ever met or ever was to meet and she did her best, although it was all very strange there by the river and the rough stream and under the big tree, to appear impressed, yet all she could think of saying was: But I'm not interfering with his tyling.

Then she was angry and close to tears, although it was also funny: For all I care he can tile the roofs and floors and walls of every house in this town.

The big man hadn't moved much since he sat down, never raised his voice, but now he shouted; Lassie, I'll make you care. The B Specials are sworn to uphold Protestant liberty and beat down the Fenians and the IRA.

—I'm not a Fenian nor an IRA.

—You're a Roman Catholic, aren't you? And there isn't any other sort. Sir Basil Brooke says that Roman Catholics are 100 per cent disloyal and that he wouldn't have one of them about the house.

—Sir Who's It?

—No cheek, lassie. Didn't he sit up a tree at Colebrook all night long with a gun waiting for the IRA to attack his house? Didn't he found the B Specials to help the police to defend the throne and the Protestant religion?

What was it to her if Sir Somebody or Other spent all his life up a tree at Colebrook or anywhere else? The Lancashire soldier had climbed her tree and been as comic as a monkey up a stick. The black man calmed himself: Your own clergy are dead set against mixed marriages.

—We weren't thinking of marriage.

—What of then? Silliness and nonsense. The young have no wit. What would Mother Teresa say if she heard you were keeping company with a Protestant?

—Who would tell her?

—I might. For your own good and for Lofty.

He knocked the ash out of his pipe and put it away. The pleasant tobacco smell faded. She smelled blood and dirt and heard screams and knew, with a comical feeling of kindness, that she had been wrongly blaming him for bringing with him the stench of the shambles. There was a piggery at the far end of the field beyond the river and the wind was blowing from that direction.

—That's the piggery, she said. It's a disgrace.

—Time and again I've said that on the town council. You must have read what I said in the papers. It's a sin, shame and scandal to have a piggery beside a beauty spot. Not that I've anything against pigs, in my business, in their own place.

He stood up and patted her on the shoulder. He was really just a big rough friendly man: You don't want him put out of the Specials or the Lodge itself.

—Why should he be?

—These are deep matters. But they tell me you read a lot. You've the name for being one of the cleverest students in this town, Protestant or Catholic. So I'll talk to you, all for the best, as if you were a grown-up and one of my own. It is possible but very difficult for a convert to be accepted as a member of the Orange Order.

He was as good as standing to attention. He was looking over her head towards the waterfall.

—A convert would have to be of several years standing and his background would have to be carefully screened. His admission would have to be authorized by the Grand Lodge. They'd have to go that high, like Rome for the Catholics. No convert can get into the Black Preceptory if either of his parents is still living, in case the Roman Catholic Church might exert pressure on a parent.

He was reciting. Like the sing-song way in which in school the children learned the Catechism.

Q: What are the seven deadly sins?
A: Pride, covetousness, lust, gluttony, envy, anger and sloth.
Q: What are the four sins that cry to heaven for vengeance?
A: Wilful murder, sodomy, oppression of the poor and defrauding the labourer of his wages.

Dear Sacred Heart it was a cheery world.

—A convert who was even a Protestant clergyman was blacked-out because one of his parents was still living, and there is automatic expulsion for dishonouring the Institution by marrying a Roman Catholic.

The great tree creaked its branches above them. The brown water tumbled on towards the town.

—You see what I mean, lassie.

She supposed she saw. In a way she was grateful. He was trying to help. He shook her hand as if they were friends forever. He went off towards the waterfall so that, without turning around, she could not see him walking away and he could not, thank God, see her face laughing, laughing. For, sweet heart of Jesus fount of love and mercy to thee we come thy blessings to implore, but it was comic to think of him marching up the convent grounds (he should wear his black sash and have a fife and drum before him) holy white statues to left and right and a Lourdes grotto as high as Mount Errigal, to relate all about the love-life of Lofty and herself to Mother Teresa who had a mouth like a rat-trap—and a mind. A worshipful master and a most worshipful reverend mother and never, or seldom, the twain shall meet. She was an odd sort of a girl. She sat around a lot and had read too many books. It was funny, also, to think of his daughter, Gladys, a fine good-natured brunette with a swinging stride, a bosom like a Viking prow, and a dozen boy friends of all creeds and classes. Nothing sectarian about Gladys who was one of his own kind and the daughter of a worshipful master. Somebody should tell the tyler to keep an eye on her. But she was too clever to be caught, too fast on her feet, too fast on her feet.

Walking slowly past the Orange hall on the way home she thought that the next time she met him she would have a lot to tell to lazy, freckled, lovable Lofty. The Orange hall was a two-storeyed brownstone building at a crossroads on the edge of the town. High on its wall a medallion image of William of Orange on an impossibly white horse rode forever across the Boyne. The two old cannon-guns on the green outside had been captured from the Germans in the Kaiser war. In there, Lofty's lodge met and it was a popular joke that no man could become a member until he rode a buck goat backwards up the stairs. Sometimes in the evenings bands of music played thunderously in there, practising for the day in July when they marched out, banners flying. It was crazy to think that a man on a white horse, riding across a river 200 years ago could now ride between herself and Lofty. Or for that matter—although Mother Teresa would have a fit if she thought that a pupil of hers could think of such things—another man on a chair or something being carried shoulder-high in the city of Rome.

All this she meant to mention to Lofty the next time he came to the seat under the tree. But all she could get around to saying was: Lofty, what's a tyler?

He had no rod and net and was dressed, not for fishing, in a new navy-blue suit. The children called to him from the gravel but he paid no attention to them. At first he didn't pretend to hear her, so she asked him again. He said that a tyler was a man who laid tiles. That was the end of that. Then it was winter. One whole week the park was flooded. She couldn't exactly remember when it was that Lofty had given her the bullets.

It was also crazy to think that Lofty's laughing mother could have a brother who went about spying on people and nosing them out. What eyes had spied on Lofty and herself on the enchanted island? What nosy neighbour had told somebody who told somebody who told the sergeant that she had bullets in the earthenware jug?

—If you don't tell me, the sergeant says, it will be awkward for all concerned. What would Mother Teresa think if she thought you had live bullets in an earthenware jug?

It wasn't possible to control the giggles. What, in the holy name of God, would Mother Teresa think, if the sergeant and the worshipful master descended on her simultaneously, what would she say, how would she look? Keeping live bullets in a jug must be one of the few things that she had not warned her girls against.

—You'll have to come down to the barracks with me. I'll walk ahead and you follow just in case the people are passing remarks. They might think I'm arresting you.

—What are you doing?

—Och, I'd just like you to make a statement. It's not a crime to have bullets. Not for a young lady like you who wouldn't be likely to be using them. But we have a duty to find out where they came from. My son Reggie speaks highly of you, Reggie the footballer you know.

She knew. It was a town joke that the sergeant couldn't speak to anybody for ten minutes without mentioning Reggie who parted his hair up the middle, wore loud scarves and played football very well: it was clear that the sergeant thought that to be thought well of by Reggie was a special distinction.

Old low white houses line the hill that goes up from the brook and the co-operative creamery to the centre of the town. The sergeant plods on, twenty yards ahead of her. The town is very quiet. His black leather belt creaks and strains to hold him together. The butt of his pistol, his black baton case shine. She has never noticed before that Lofty has a stutter. Another sergeant sits behind a desk in the dayroom and makes notes. Two young constables are laughing in the background. The black man comes in and says: I warned the two of them.

Her own sergeant says: There wasn't much harm in it.

—Not for the girl, says the man behind the desk. But for him a breach of discipline.

Lofty has surely never stuttered when he talked to her by the meeting of the waters.

—Did you tell them I gave you the bullets?

—Dear God, it wasn't a crime to give me bullets.

—Did you tell them?

—I did not.

—They said you did.

—So.

Her own sergeant looks ashamed and rubs his moustache. The other sergeant says: Case closed.

Then her uncle walks in, and so hopping mad that he seems to have a mouthful of gold teeth. He talks for a long time and they listen respectfully because he's a famous man for keeping running dogs which he feeds on brandy and beef. He says over and over again: You make a helluva fuss about a few bullets.

—A breach of discipline, says the man behind the desk.

—My ass and yours, says her uncle. A helluva fuss.

And repeats it many times as they walk home together.

—But all the same they'll put him out of the Specials, he says. And I dare say he shouldn't have been assing around giving away government issue.

Over the supper table he remembers the time he had been a policeman in Detroit: Some Negro trouble then and this rookie policeman from Oklahoma was on patrol with a trained man. The rookie has no gun. So they're rushed by twenty black men and the first rock thrown clobbers the trained man unconscious. But the Oklahoma guy he stoops down, takes the pistol out of the other man's holster and shoots six times and kills six black men, one, two, three, four, five, six. He didn't waste a bullet.

—Sacred Heart have mercy, says her aunt.

—What did the other black men do, uncle?

—They took off for home and small blame to them. He was a cool one, that rookie, and a damned good shot. Here in this place they make a helluva fuss over a few bullets. I told them so.

Lofty came never again to the tall tree. They met a few times on the street and spoke a few words. She left the town after a while and went to work in London. Once, home on holidays, she met Lofty and he asked her to go to the pictures, and she meant to but never did. The Hitler war came on. She married an American and went to live in, of all places, Detroit. Her uncle and aunt and the sergeant and the worshipful master and the tyler and, I suppose, Lofty's mother and old McCaslan and his dog died.

Remembering her, I walked, the last time I was in the town to revisit Bluebell Meadow. The bridge over the millrace was broken down to one plank. Rank grass grew a foot high over most of the island. The rest of it was a wide track of sand and gravel where the river in fierce flood had taken everything before it. The children's swings and all the seats were gone, smashed some time before by reluctant young soldiers from the North English cities doing their national service. Repair work had been planned but then the bombings and murders began.

No laughing Lancashire boy in British uniform will ever again climb the tall tree. For one thing the tree is gone. For another the soldiers go about in bands, guns at the ready, in trucks and armoured cars. There are burned-out buildings in the main streets—although the great barracks is unscathed—and barricades and checkpoints at the ends of the town. As a woman said to me: Nowadays we have gates to the town. Still, other towns are worse. Strabane which was on the border and easy to bomb is a burned-out wreck. And Newry, where the people badly needed shops and factories, and not ruins. And Derry is like Dresden on the day after.

When I wrote to her about this she said, among other things, that she had never found out the name of that tall conifer.

A COW IN THE HOUSE

There was something different and a little disconcerting about Harry the Barber, possibly because he drank and had a red face and his hand shook and he kept a cow in the house. The only other man I had ever heard of who kept animals in his dwelling-place was a one-eyed, story-book giant who lived in a cave and came to a bad end. So I went cold all over the Friday morning my mother told me to trot down the town to Harry's and take four-pence with me and ask him to trim my hair. Up to that fatal moment, when manhood opened before me like an abyss, my mother herself had done what barbering I needed: combing, snipping and trimming while I, my eyes tightly closed against detached, descending hairs, and robed, like a pantomime Bedouin, in a bath towel, stood on a kitchen chair.

I pleaded: Couldn't you trim my hair yourself? You did it last Saturday.

—You're big enough now to need a real barber. You're like a rabbit hiding under a bush.

The giant had roared loudly enough to shatter the roof when the burning stake plunged into his only eye.

I said: Harry the Barber keeps a cow in the house.

—Isn't he the lucky man to have a cow?

—Wouldn't you like to go with your father, she said, and see the capital city and visit Sister Barbara in the Nazareth Home?

My mother was all flour. That's how I knew so well it was Friday morning for Friday morning was three things: our big weekly baking, particularly of treacle scones which my father loved; the busiest milk delivery day at the co-operative creamery up the road past our house; the day they shod cartwheels across the road and below our terrace on the space of waste ground before Hamilton's smithy. My mother, white as a snowman, stood baking at a table where she could look out of a kitchen window and see the farmers' carts, laden with jingling silvery cans, passing up and down the road; and see the smoke and steam rising as the red-hot metal hoops were fitted on to the wooden wheels and then cooled and contracted with cold water.

The three Hamiltons were giants of men: the white-headed father, the tall dark-visaged sons with deep creases in their faces to catch and hold the smoke and soot of the forge. They swung and stooped over the ancient process, setting alight the circle of peat around the iron hoop, blowing the flames with hand-bellows, dragging out with a huge tongs the sparking crimson circle, fitting it to the wood and skilfully applying the rhythmical hammers. But they had six kind eyes between them and they didn't keep cows in the smithy. They had a horse but they kept him decently, housed, bedded and cleaned out, in a stable in Tansey the carter's yard at the end of the town.

My mother laid the foundations for yet another scone. The carts shone and jingled up and down the road. Smoke of singed wood, and steam from the cooled iron arose like a mushroom.

So, for all those reasons, it was Friday morning, but for me the light had gone out of the sunshine. Inching towards the door I said: I'll go look at the Hamiltons.

—You'll go off to Harry the Barber's for a new hair-style. Don't you want to see the capital city of Ireland? Your father says it's time you saw a bit of the world.

—I saw it all in school. It's a shiny round ball. It spins when you touch it.

—You're too clever for your years.

But, in spite of the flour, I could see she was proud of my wit; and I was wise enough to know that going to the capital meant a long glorious journey by train and something to boast about for life. No boy in Primer, which was my grade at school, had ever been further in a train than the mere 40 miles to the sea at Bundoran. Between me and the delights of the long journey to Dublin stood the monster I must pass; the shaking red-faced barber and the cow that would startlingly step out of the hall-door. There was nothing for it but to close my eyes and fare forward. By ill-luck I didn't wear my cap.

A cow's floppy cloven hooves were never made for a hard pavement. Slithering clumsily, the red creature emerged and crossed the footwalk to the street. The shop-door closed behind her and the bell fixed at the top of it jangled. To my alarm she swung her head sideways and looked at me out of enormous eyes. She had a crumpled horn, like the cow that was milked by the maiden all forlorn, and wisps of hay which she was champing at, meditatively, stuck out of the corners of her mouth and wiggled like cats' whiskers. No maiden, forlorn or otherwise, drove the beast from the byre in the barber's backyard to the pasture at the edge of the town. But behind her walked one of the barber's children; a ragged boy with close-cropped head, and trousers that had once belonged to an elder brother and, cut down and all, were still too big for him. The inexpert re-tailoring made him look as if one of his buttocks was twice the size of the other. He made hup-hup noises. He poked with an ash-twig at the animal's flank. He grandly ignored me; and I was too absorbed by the mystery of the cow that used the shop-door to think twice about the significance of that little cropped head. Clutching my fourpence and facing up to fate, I pushed open the door. The same bell rang to herald my entrance that had rung to tell of the departure of the cow.

Harry the Barber was saying: It's kinda awkward at times. You'd be amazed how some people are affected when she walks in one door and out the other. But the only other exit is to make her swim the river at the bottom of the yard.

—You've no back entrance, said one of the two customers.

He had two gold teeth and talked through his nose.

—Nor exit, said Harry.

—The town, said the second customer, isn't much of a place for a cow or a collie dog.

He was a mountainy farmer with a spade-shaped beard.

—Still she's as good as gold, Harry said. Here in the shop she never once transgressed.

—House trained you might say, said the man with the gold teeth.

—Nothing amiss with dung in its own place, said the farmer.

Harry's professional coat had once, but a long time ago, been white. He was shaving the man with the gold teeth and trimming the farmer, and he moved between them like a man who couldn't make up his mind which was which. Now and again he paused before a spotty mirror, and pulled and pushed at the mottled skin of his face and studied his bloodshot eyes. His hand was shaking very badly.

—It's a godsend, he said, to have your own cow when you have a lot of children.

A battered radio, fixed to the wall above the mirror, allowed a human voice, punctuated by atmospheric explosions, to sing about Genevieve, sweet Genevieve.

—The old girl's still threshing, said the man with the gold teeth. Last heard her name mentioned in Boston.

He made himself comfortable in the chair while Harry absented himself for a moment to snip at the farmer. He crossed his long legs. He had huge feet and shiny patent-leather boots which he surveyed with interest.

—It riles me, he said. Young folk around here have no enterprise.

Market-day now, go-ahead young fellow could take a fortune out there on the High Street. As a shoeshine.

—He'd have to kneel down, said the farmer.

Quoting from a patriotic ballad I'd learned at school, in which a brave blacksmith refused to stoop to shoe the horse of a redcoat captain, Harry said: I kneel but to my God above, I ne'er will bow to you.

—People in this town, said the farmer, find it hard enough to kneel to the Creator that made them, let alone to clean another man's shoes. Towney pride.

—Pride never pockets dollars, said the man from Boston.

Inexplicably the volume of the radio rose like a tidal wave and the talk was drowned in one last despairing wail to Genevieve.

—Switch her off, said the Boston man. Get her outa here.

—More likely, said Harry as he evicted Genevieve, the mean mountainy farmers would spit on you or walk over you if you were misguided enough to kneel down to clean the cowdung off their boots.

—No harm in cowdung, said the farmer, in its proper place.

—Country's not organized, said Gold Teeth. No co-operation.

They went on like that while, unnoticed, I sat in trepidation and foreboding of the moment when the two would leave and I would be alone with, and at the mercy of, Harry.

The old farmer was the first to go. He stood up stiffly and Harry handed him a black bowler and a blackthorn stick. He wore nailed boots and leather leggings. When he took out a cloth purse to pay, as he put it, for the shearing, he turned his back on the company while he opened it and extracted the coins. But he gave me a penny as he passed and a pat on the head. The Boston man was better still. He mopped his face for a long time with a hot damp towel, and swayed like a feinting boxer before the mirror, and dried his face with another towel, and tossed a wide-brimmed straw hat in the air, and caught it on his head as it was descending, and shook hands with Harry and pretended to box him, and spun a half-crown at me, and shook my hand when I fielded it and was gone with a slam of the door that set the bell jangling for ages. Rich I was then beyond the dreams of avarice, but I needed it all as divine compensation for what was to follow.

—Kneel up on the chair, lad, said Harry, or my back will be broke stooping to you.

Brightly I began to recite: I kneel but to my God above . . .

—The cleverness of some people, said Harry. But kneel up all the same.

So up I knelt, my back to the mirror, my face to a wall papered with coloured illustrations of running horses, and Harry the High Priest robed me in a sacrificial cloth that like his coat of office had been white a long time ago. From faraway pastures the diminutive cowherd returned, ash twig in hand, and stood boldly staring at my misery; and only then, as I looked at the little round marble of a close-cropped head, and as the scissors began to snip around my ears, did I realize with sickening horror what was in store for me. Doomed I was to receive one of the first crew-cuts ever administered in our town—outside Harry's own family, that is, or the fever hospital where they cropped the heads of the scarlatina patients.

That negative hair-style has since then become for a while one of the fashionable things but, at that period and in that town, it was a disgrace and humiliation. To be balded was a rural disorder, to be an object of laughter like the country boys who came with their parents into the town for market-days and holidays of obligation. To be balded was an uncouth and backward way to be; and, to make things worse, once already in my life I had, through an excess of masculine vanity, brought that disgrace and humiliation on myself. The relentless scissors snipped. The hideous little herd eyed me. Swathed in off-white cerements I was powerless to escape. Behind tightly-shut eyelids I saw my aunt's long, thatched, white-washed farmhouse, ten miles from the town. Every summer I holidayed there. There was a great farmyard with barns, byres and stables, a deep orchard, and stepping-stones across the bog-red water of the burn that went down to join the Fairywater. There was a vile-tasting duck-pond that I once fell into, cherry trees that were regularly spoliated by the blackbirds and by barefooted boys passing the road to school; and my dowager of an Aunt Kate peering through spectacles on the tip of her nose at the eggs she polished for market.

There was also Cousin Patrick's enviable jungle of glossy, curling, black hair.

—Aunt Kate, my query would go, how can I make my hair curl like Patrick's?

She was a tall, aged, angular widow, clad in black bombazine with beads on the bosom; and buttoned boots; and skirts to her ankles. Polishing eggs and peering she would answer absently: Patrick was forever and always out in the rain. It was the rain made his hair curl.

So every shower, soft or heavy, that blew up that summer from the south-west, found me standing under it as patient as the stump of a bush. The wagtails, for whom the rain brought up the worms and the white grubs, picked and hopped around me like mechanical toys. I became their friend and familiar. The way to catch wagtails, I was told, was to put salt on their tails and then catch them, but that summer I felt that I could, without salt, have captured the full of an aviary. We were rain-worshippers together. But when, in the middle of a downpour that came to cool earth and air after thunder and lightning, I was found, soaked to the skin and standing under a sycamore to get the added hair-curling benefit of the drops from the sodden leaves, Aunt Kate altered her advice.

—Once, she said, Patrick had his hair cut very short and it was curly when it grew again.

She was too old and too gentle, and too interested in polishing eggs, to allow for the ruthless literalness and pure faith of childhood, or to foresee the self-shearing I was to do with her best scissors out behind the red-currant bushes in the most secluded corner of the orchard. The roars of laughter with which the servant-boys around the farm greeted me convinced me that a shorn head was a shameful thing, and that I had accepted too readily the casual words of a rambling old woman; and a balded head became forever the mark of a fool. But then it didn't matter so much in the country where bald-headed little boys were the fashion and where there was nobody of much importance to see you. By the time the holidays were over my luxuriant locks had almost grown again—as uncurled as ever.

But this was farandaway worse. The barber's baleful little son stared at me without speaking and then, unfeelingly, began to munch a crab-apple. Harry was a shaking, red-faced, savage Apache, and I knew I was being scalped. Between me and the shelter of home and my school-cap there were leagues of crowded streets where everybody knew me, and on the day after tomorrow, the fabulous city of Dublin where there was no such thing as a baldy boy, and where thousands of people would stop on the street to look and laugh at the wonder.

Like a terrified mouse I ran all the way home, taking no time even to buy sweets with my hoard of money. Only it would further have drawn attention to my nakedness I would have tried to hide my shaven crown with my hands. One corner-boy, perceiving my plight, called: Wee scaldy-bird, did you fall out of the nest?

The memory of featherless baby-birds, once seen in a nest, afflicted me with nausea.

—He cut you a bit close, my mother said placidly. But it'll grow again.

Putting on my school-cap firmly I went out to the garden at the back of the house and sat on a stone and just looked at the ground.

The journey was a glory. The world stayed there, swimming in sunshine, while I swept past like a king or an angel and inspected it from on high. It gave me my first vision of the Mountains of Pomeroy, as the song calls them, which aren't mountains at all but green, smooth, glacial hills; and the apple-orchards of Armagh; and the slow-flowing sullen River Bann; and the great valley around the town of Newry; and the Mountains of Mourne, which are real mountains, sweeping down to the sea as they do in another song; and the Irish Sea itself, asleep along the flat shores of Louth and Meath and North County Dublin, or creeping on hands and knees into estuaries and the harbours of little towns. I sucked hard sweets and kept my eyes to the window and didn't have to expose myself by taking off my head-covering. My father told me the name of everything, and once when a hapless fellow-townsman, who was travelling in the same carriage, made a fool of himself by mistaking the Mourne Mountains for the Hills of Donegal, my father silenced him with a genial glance and the words: Weak on topography, James.

—I never travelled like you, Tommy, the sad man said apologetically. I never saw Africa nor the Barbadoes.

Being at the age when a boy thinks his father knows everything—before he grows a little older and comes to think, with equal foolishness, that his father knows nothing—I was mightily pleased, and so was my father who prided himself on his knowledge of places.

So, two happy men, we came to the station at Dublin and stepped out on to the interminable platform, and I took three steps and knew I was doomed. It was bad enough to be a leper, but it was torture out-and-out to have to carry a bell to draw public attention to your misfortune. Those three steps on the hard platform told me that, as fatally as any leper, I bore with me my self-accusing bell. It went clink-clink-clink. It was the iron tip on the heel of my left shoe. For days it had been threatening to come loose and jingle and this, in the sorry malevolence of things, was the moment it would choose. Clink, clink, clink. To me it was as audible as the clanking chains of an ancestral ghost. The irritating sound came up distinctly over the puffing and shunting of engines, the shouting of porters, the rattling of their barrows. It went to hell altogether as I hobbled, trying to be inconspicuous, down the marble steps to the street, and was still audible above the sound of trams and buses, motor-cars and four-wheeled horse-drays. To the furthest limits of the city I heard it proclaim the arrival of that wonder of wonders, the Celebrated Bald Boy who was ashamed to take off his cap. All around me moved thousands of smooth-spoken, elegantly-dressed, hatless, capless, velvet-footed people with heads of hair to be proud of. No city person would be barbarous enough to have iron tips on the heels of his or her boots or shoes. They didn't seem to notice me as I passed, but I imputed that to their excessive politeness. Behind unsmiling masks of faces they were really paralytic with mocking laughter. To look back I didn't dare in case I'd see somebody staring in hilarious wonder after my clinking retreat.

—The zoo I promised you, my father said. The zoo you must have. We'll have the convent afterwards for a change. You're rattling like all the hammers in Hamilton's smithy.

That recall to the homely image of the three good giants and their workshop fortified me for the walk to the restaurant for lunch. Keeping my eyes steadfastly down, and priding myself on coming from a land where giant men could swing hammers as city people couldn't, I resolved to see only the feet of the passing people and, after a while, I found myself repeating to myself, as if the words had magic and amusement in them: Feet, feet, feet, big feet, little feet, clean feet, dirty feet, and so on. For there were all sorts of feet in the world and, lacking feet, walking was not possible, and thinking of feet took my mind away from heads. The restaurant posed no new trials. Undisturbed, my heel didn't rattle. It was the day of a big hurling match and the place was full of red-faced countrymen who ate with their caps on. Their example was good enough for me and, eating my food, I told myself with heavenly glee that within an hour I would, for the first time in my life, see elephants and monkeys, lions, tigers, cobras, kangaroos, all the wonders of swamp, savannah and jungle.

But, alas, even my time in the zoo was torn and agonized by changing, conflicting emotions. Most of the caged animals, like the red-faced countrymen with their caps on, seemed to be my allies. There was a lot of baldness among them, particularly on the most unexpected parts of the monkeys. The brown orang-outang, swinging round and round on a pole and apparently content to do just that for the whole long day, didn't appear to be in the least worried by his bald patches. But was the pitiful, pacing restlessness of the spotted hyena the result of some clumsy jungle barber stumping his tail—possibly with snapping teeth? The long grey-white hair of the lazy, peaceful llama; and hair like a crown on the top of the hump of the white Arabian dromedary; the legs of the polar bear that were so hairy they made him look as if he were wearing white pyjamas far too big for him; the mane of the king of beasts that no drunken barber would ever defile—all these convinced me that hair was immortal and resilient and would, except in the case of the crowns of old men, grow again. But then the hairless, slinking creatures filled me with horror: pythons, crocodiles, alligators, terrapins, turtles, monitor lizards with forked darting tongues, even the enormous hippo wallowing in muddy water and turning his unmannerly tail-end to all visitors. The sea-lion was redeemed by his antics and his whiskers.

The lovely little hairy toy-ponies from Shetland pulled charabancs crowded with laughing children and clinked their harness bells so as to drown the noise of my loose heel-tip. Every time they swept past, my father said: Care for a jaunt, boy?

To the point of tears I refused, for my heart was bursting to board one of those charabancs. But how could I explain that I was afraid and ashamed in case some boisterous city boy among the passengers might knock off my cap and expose me to mockery?

A great eagle, motionless and alone in pride on a tree in a high-wired enclosure, looked as if he was even proud of his bald head. But other birds, I thought, leave him solitary up there just because he is bald; and his grim, stern, isolated image haunted me all across the city to the gate of the convent, the Nazareth House, where my cousin, Sister Barbara, was a nun and where my greatest agony was to begin. Looking, with my cap on me, at captive animals, was one thing. Being looked at, when my cap was off, was another and nuns and orphans are awful people for looking at you.

—Call everybody sister, said my father, except the reverend mother and, when I find out which of them she is, I'll give you a dig in the ribs. And take your cap off, I'm sorry to say, said he. We have to act like gentlemen and nuns are ladies.

He pressed the convent bell. The gate slowly opened and we looked into a whole cosmos of giggling girls in blue dresses and white bows and pigtails and shiny shoes. Oh my misfortune and unholy luck that it should have been playtime for all the little female orphans in the convent just when I arrived among them looking more like an orphan than any one of them. They didn't, I suppose, see many boys, and a bald-headed boy, his face purple with blushing, his cap in his hand, his heel-tip rattling, was just too good to be true. Looking back at it now I can, perhaps, admit that those little atomies of womanhood giggled every day and all the time, at playtime. But, at that moment, when the door-portress, all swinging rosary beads and flapping black tails, led us across the playground I felt that every giggle was meant for me, and I cursed Harry the Barber to places Dante never heard of and hoped that overnight his red cow with the crumpled horn would change into a slinking, odorous, odious hyena; or into a pacing tiger that would devour his cowherd of a son; or that all his customers would change into reptiles condemned to wander sleek and hairless to the judgement seat of God and beyond.

A door closed behind us. The giggles were no longer heard. We followed the portress along a passage polished with such extravagance that it must have cost many a visitor, or hapless convent chaplain, a broken femur or radius. Into a parlour with a bare polished table in the centre of the floor, twelve stiff chairs around, and a portrait on the wall of a man that my father said was an archbishop. Nobody, you were sure, had ever lived or laughed in that room. The door closed behind the departing portress. The archbishop frowned down at us.

—Your heel in the passage, said my father, would outsound the convent bells.

With the shame burned into me by the giggles I hadn't for a while heard the heel. I had been the fox who lost his brush, the Chinese mandarin who lost his pigtail.

—Put your hoof on this chair here to see can I do anything about it.

He pulled and hammered, and stopped pulling because he said if the heeltip came the shoe would come with it and, possibly, the foot as well. He was still hammering, hoping for the best, when the door opened and six nuns entered, including the reverend mother; and, bringing up the tail of the procession, two lay-sisters bearing food for the two of us. What they saw was a perspiring middle-aged man beating with the black bone-handle of the big claspknife with which he cut his tobacco at the heel of the shoe of a bald little boy.

With what composure he could muster my father greeted them, introduced his heir, and the two of us sat down to eat and the five nuns and the reverend mother sat down in a semi-circle to look at us. That's the way you eat when you go to a convent. This was the zoo and my father and myself were the nut-cracking monkeys. There was talk, too, of course, and Sister Barbara gave us each an envelope full of holy medals and leaflets. But at no moment would I have been surprised if reverend mother had tossed me a nut and, obeying instinct, I had fielded, shelled and eaten it all in one sweeping gesture, as but lately I had seen the black baboon do.

When the eating was over the reverend mother said: Now your little boy, I feel sure, can sing.

She might also have said: Your little boy can, I feel sure, by the cut of him and the head of him, swing round a pole like the orang-outang.

The way it was I might as well have been singing as sitting there, so up I stood and breathed deeply and squared myself for action. If I had had hair on my head I wouldn't have lost my wits and would, like any Christian gentleman, have sung about Erin remembering the days of old ere her faithless sons betrayed her. As it was, with the strain and the shame, and with the naked soft top of my head exposed to the raging elements, I went mad and sang a song I had heard sung when the Hamiltons swung their mighty hammers above the burning iron.

—One Paddy Doyle, I told the nuns, lived in Killarney and he loved a maid named Betsy Toole.

It went on from bad to worse, but when my mortified parent made a move to stop me the reverend mother raised her hand and said: It was my father's favourite song—Doran's Ass.

—Now Paddy that day had taken liquor, I assured them, which made his spirits feel light and gay. Says he, the divil a bit use in walking quicker for I know she'll meet me on the way.

The shrill playing voices of the giggling girls were faraway as I related how drunken Paddy fell asleep in the ditch with Doran's jackass and embraced the animal in mistake for his true love. My voice was a bawdy bleat in the hollow, holy heart of eternity.

When the song had ended and I had modestly accepted the applause there was more talk and the lay-sisters brought in ice-cream. Then the reverend mother and Sister Barbara walked us across a playground now mercifully empty and bade farewell at the gate. The reverend mother put her hand into a slit in the side of her habit and went down and down until the better half of her arm vanished, then surfaced again with a box of chocolates in the hand. She gave it to me, and stooped and kissed the tonsured crown of my head.

—That song, she said, I haven't heard it in years.

—That I could easily believe, said my father as the gate closed behind us.

Then in awed tones he added: There's no doubt about it. Suffer the little children. Come on, son, and we'll see the laughing mirrors in the Fun Palace before we catch the rattler.

The box of chocolates shone like a sun.

—Haven't nuns, Da, I said, terrible deep trouser pockets?

So perturbed I was and yet, because of the chocolates, so overjoyed that I was in the tram on my way to the centre of the city before I realized I had left my cap in the convent parlour.

—Leave it be, said my father. They can have it as a relic of the man who told them about Paddy Doyle and Doran's ass. Their prayers and that kiss of peace will make your golden locks grow again as strong as corn stubble.

In the Fun Palace there were two girls in bathing-suits lying in cubes of ice to show they could do it, and a fat woman who weighed 40 stone and wore an outsize bathing-suit and who looked at me and slapped her thigh and laughed and said to my father: Ain't I a dainty little lass?

In this underground world the Celebrated Bald Boy could fade into his background and be a freak among freaks.

In a glass case a witch with a conical hat raised both hands when sixpence went into a slot and a printed slip telling your fortune came out of another slot. In another glass case a ghost, obligingly, and also for sixpence, entered a sombre panelled room and frightened a man in a four-poster bed so that he hid under the bedclothes. The ghost, having done his sixpennyworth of haunting, vanished backways through a crack in the panelling.

Ardent queues lined up to peer into a small lighted glass box to share the butler's keyhole vision.

—It wouldn't interest us, my father said.

He steered me past the devotees and we paid our money and stepped into the hall of mirrors which, at first sight, might have been the hall of maniacs, because the six or seven people within were looking at the walls and doubling up and roaring with laughter. So I turned and looked into the first mirror and saw my father, twelve feet long if he was an inch, and wriggling like the eel I once saw in semi-sunlight water under the arch of Donnelly's bridge on the Camowen river. Standing beside him, as I was, I was yet, in the most uncanny fashion, completely invisible; and in the second mirror my father was a little fat schoolboy and my bald head was a Shrove Tuesday pancake with currants for eyes; and in the third mirror my father was all head and no body and I was all legs topped by a head like a pine-cone. By the fourth mirror the tears of laughter were blinding me and, in blurred vision, I saw red-faced Harry shaking like an aspen leaf; and the man from Boston, all gold teeth, jumping and dancing and swinging from the farmer's beard; and the reverend mother with an arm a mile long pulling boxes of chocolates out of a bottomless pocket; and the red cow with floppy feet slithering and sitting down in Harry's shop and refusing to get up; and the giant Hamiltons, adopting all shapes and sizes, and confronted with hammers either so tiny as to be useless or too big and heavy to raise off the ground. The whole world I knew and the people in it were subject to comic mutation.

—Stop laughing, son, said my father at last, or we'll miss the train.

He wiped the tears from my eyes but he mightn't have bothered. They were as wet as ever before I got to the street. Every man and woman I looked at could have been cavorting before a comic, distorting mirror. There was something laughably odd about every one of them: big noses, red faces, legs too long or too short, behinds that waggled, clothes that didn't fit. Every one of them had a cow in the house. My bald head mattered no longer: it cut me off from no community. Let whoever liked laugh at me, I'd laugh back.

Tramping up the long platform I realized that a great silence had come around us. Engines snorted and shunted, trucks rattled, porters called each other names, newsboys sang their wares in sounds that weren't real words, fat women panicked and began to gallop in case the train might elude them. Yet, lacking one sound, it was all silence, and there was no clink-clink-clink, no warning note of my leper bell. Somewhere between the laughing mirrors and the station the iron tip had parted company with the heel and left me to walk as catfooted as an Aran islander or a wild Indian in pampooties, while it lay lost and neglected forever to be rolled over or walked on by the city's traffic. A part of me and of my town had died in exile and sorrow touched me for a while. Had I only detected the moment of our parting I could have preserved the heel-tip as a keepsake—warm in my trousers pocket.

But it was no evening for enduring sorrow. Before me lay the sights and thrills of the journey, and the reverend mother's chocolates, and the joys of telling and re-telling, and expanding for colour and poetry, my traveller's tales. In the school-room again when the shiny round ball that was the world was set spinning I knew I could follow it for more than 100 miles and tell my compeers that convents in the city were stuffed full of boxes of chocolates to reward brave boys who could sing; that, while China might be bursting with Chinamen, there were, in a house on the quays by the Liffey, mirrors that turned all men into objects of laughter; and that, while Harry the Barber might keep a cow in the house, it was little to what they kept closed in cages in the Phoenix Park in Dublin.

THE NIGHT WE RODE WITH SARSFIELD

That was the house where I put the gooseberries back on the bushes by sticking them on the thorns. It wasn't one house but two houses under one roof, a thatched roof. Before I remember being there, I was there.

We came from the small village of Dromore to the big town of Omagh, the county town of Tyrone, in the spring of 1920, bad times in Ireland (Violence upon the roads/Violence of horses) particularly bad times in the north-east corner of Ulster. There have been any God's amount of bad times in the north-east corner of Ulster. There were no houses going in the big town and the nearest my father could find to his work was three miles away in the townland of Drumragh and under the one roof with Willy and Jinny Norris, a Presbyterian couple, brother and sister. They were small farmers.

That was the place then where I put the gooseberries back on the bushes by impaling them on the thorns. But not just yet because I wasn't twelve months old, a good age for a man and one of the best he's ever liable afterwards to experience: more care is taken of him, especially by women. No, the impaling of the gooseberries took place seven to eight years later. For, although we were only there six or so months until my father got a place in the town—in the last house in a laneway overlooking the green flowery banks of the serpentine Strule— we went on visiting Willy and Jinny until they died, and my father walked at their funeral and entered their church and knelt with the congregation: a thing that Roman Catholics were not by no means then supposed to do. Not knelt exactly but rested the hips on the seat and inclined the head: Ulster Presbyterians don't kneel, not even to God above.

It was a good lasting friendship with Willy and Jinny. There's an Irish proverb: *Nil aitheantas go haontigheas.* Or: You don't know anybody until you've lived in the one house with them.

Not one house, though, in this case but two houses under one roof which may be the next best thing.

Willy and Jinny had the one funeral because one night the house burned down—by accident. Nowadays when you say that a house or a shop or a pub or a factory burned down, it seems necessary to add—by accident. Although the neighbours, living next door in our house, did their best to rescue them and to save the whole structure with buckets of water from the spring-well which was down there surrounded by gooseberry bushes, they died, Willy from suffocation, Jinny from shock, the shock of the whole happening, the shock of loneliness at knowing that Willy was dead and that the long quiet evenings were over. However sadly and roughly they left the world, they went, I know, to a heaven of carefully-kept harvest fields, and Orange lilies in bloom on the lawn before the farmhouse, and trees heavy with fruit, and those long evenings spent spelling-out, by the combined light of oil-lamp and hearth fire, the contents of *The Christian Herald*. My three sisters who were all older than me said that that was the only literature, apart from the Bible, they had ever seen in the house but, at that time, that didn't mean much to me.

The place they lived in must have been the quietest place in the world. This was the way to get there.

The Cannonhill road went up from the town in three steps but those steps could only be taken by Titans. Halfways up the second step or steep hill there was on the right-hand side a tarred timber barn behind which such of the young as fancied, and some as didn't, used to box. My elder brother, there, chopped one of the town's bullies, who was a head-fighter, on the soft section of the crown of his head as he came charging like a bull, and that cured him of head-fighting for a long time. Every boy has an elder brother who can box.

The barn belonged to a farmer who would leave a team of horses standing in the field and go follow a brass band for the length of a day. Since the town had two brass bands, one military, one civilian, his sowing was always dilatory and his harvests very close to Christmas. He owned a butcher shop in the town but he had the word, Butcher, painted out and replaced by the word, Flesher, which some joker had told him was more modern and polite but which a lot of people thought wasn't exactly decent.

If you looked back from Cannonhill the prospect was really something: the whole town, spires and all, you could even see clear down into some of the streets; the winding river or rivers, the red brick of the county hospital on a hill across the valley, and beyond all that the mountains, Glenhordial where the water came from, Gortin Gap and Mullagharn and the high Sperrins. Sometime in the past, nobody knew when, there must have been a gun-emplacement on Cannonhill so as to give the place its name. Some of the local learned men talked vaguely about Oliver Cromwell but he was never next or near the place. There were, though, guns there in 1941 when a visit from the Germans seemed imminent and, indeed, they came near enough to bomb Belfast and Pennyburn in Derry City and were heard in the darkness over our town, and the whole population of Gallowshill, where I came from, took off for refuge up the three titanic steps of the Cannonhill road. It was a lovely June night, though, and everybody enjoyed themselves.

If any of those merry refugees had raced on beyond the ridge of Cannonhill they would have found themselves, Germans or no Germans, in the heart of quietness. The road goes down in easy curves through good farmland to the Drumragh River and the old graveyard where the gateway was closed with concrete and stone long before my time, and the dead sealed off forever. There's a sort of stile made out of protruding stones in the high wall and within—desolation, a fragment of a church wall that might be medieval, waist-high stagnant grass, table tombstones made anonymous by moss and lichen, a sinister hollow like a huge shellhole in the centre of the place where the dead, also anonymous, of the great famine of the 1840s were thrown coffinless, one on top of the other. A man who went to school with me used to call that hollow the navel of nothing and to explain in gruesome detail why and how the earth that once had been mounded had sunk into a hollow.

That same man ran away from home in 1938 to join the British navy. He survived the sinking of three destroyers on which he was a crew member: once, off the Faroes; once, for a change of temperature, in the Red Sea; and a third time at the Battle of Crete. It may be possible that the crew of the fourth destroyer he joined looked at him with some misgiving. A fellow townsman who had the misfortune to be in Crete as a groundsman with the RAF when the Germans were coming in low and dropping all sorts of unpleasant things to the great danger of life and limb, found a hole in the ground where he could rest unseen, and doing no harm to anybody, until he caught the next boat to Alexandria.

When he crawled into the hole who should be there but the thrice-torpedoed sailor reading *The Ulster Herald*. He said hello and went on reading. He was a cool one, and what I remember most about him is the infinite patience with which he helped me when, impelled by a passion for history, I decided to clean all the table tombstones in old Drumragh and recall from namelessness and oblivion the decent people who were buried there. It was a big project. Not surprisingly it was never completed, never even properly commenced, but it brought us one discovery: that one of the four people, all priests, buried under a stone that was flat to the ground and circled by giant yews, was a MacCathmhaoil (you could English it as Campbell or McCarvill) who had in history been known as the Sagart Costarnocht because he went about without boots or socks, and who in the penal days of proscribed Catholicism had said Mass in the open air at the Mass rock on Corra Duine mountain.

For that discovery our own parish priest praised us from the pulpit. He was a stern Irish republican who had been to the Irish college in Rome, had met D'Annunzio and approved of him and who always spoke of the Six Counties of north-east Ulster as *Hibernia Irredenta*. He was also, as became his calling, a stern Roman Catholic, and an antiquarian, and in honour of the past and the shadow of the proscribed, barefooted priest, he had read the Mass one Sunday at the rock on Corra Duine and watched, in glory on the summit like the Lord himself, as the congregation trooped in over the mountain from the seven separate parishes.

This ground is littered with things, cluttered with memories and multiple associations. It turns out to be a long three miles from Gallowshill to the house of Willy and Jinny Norris. With my mother and my elder sisters I walked it so often, and later on with friends and long after Willy and Jinny were gone and the house a blackened ruin, the lawn a wilderness, the gooseberry bushes gone to seed, the Orange lilies extinguished—miniature suns that would never rise again in that place no more than life would ever come back to the empty mansion of Johnny Pet Wilson. That was just to the left before you turned into the Norris laneway, red-sanded, like a tunnel with high hawthorn hedges and sycamores and ash trees shining white and naked. My father had known Johnny Pet and afterwards had woven mythologies about him: a big Presbyterian farmer, the meanest and oddest man that had ever lived in those parts. When his hired men, mostly Gaelic speakers from West Donegal, once asked him for jam or treacle or syrup or, God help us, butter itself, to moisten their dry bread, he said: Do you say your prayers?

—Yes, boss.

They were puzzled.

—Do you say the Lord's prayer?

—Yes, boss.

—Well, in the Lord's prayer it says: Give us this day our daily bread. Damn the word about jam or treacle or syrup or butter.

When he bought provisions in a shop in the town he specified: So much of labouring man's bacon and so much of the good bacon.

For the hired men, the imported long-bottom American bacon. For himself, the Limerick ham.

He rose between four and five in the morning and expected his men to be already out and about. He went around with an old potato sack on his shoulders like a shawl, and followed always by a giant of a gentleman goat, stepping like a king's warhorse. The goat would attack you if you angered Johnny Pet, and when Johnny died the goat lay down and died on the same day. Their ghosts walked, it was well known, in the abandoned orchard where the apples had become half-crabs, through gaps in hedges and broken fences, and in the roofless rooms of the ruined house. Nobody had ever wanted to live there after the goat and Johnny Pet died. There were no relatives even to claim the hoarded fortune.

—If the goat had lived, my father said, he might have had the money and the place.

—The poor Donegals, my mother would say as she walked past Johnny Pet's ghost, and the ghost of the goat, on the way to see Willy and Jinny. Oh, the poor Donegals.

It was a phrase her mother had used when, from the doorstep of the farmhouse in which my mother was reared, the old lady would look west on a clear day and see the tip of the white cone of Mount Errigal, the Cock o' the North, 60 or more miles away, standing up and shining with shale over Gweedore and the Rosses of Donegal and by the edge of the open Atlantic. From that hard coast, a treeless place of diminutive fields fenced by drystone walls, of rocks, mountains, small lakes, empty moors and ocean winds the young Donegal people (both sexes) used to walk eastwards, sometimes barefoot, to hire out in the rich farms along the valley of the Strule, the Mourne and the Foyle—three fine names for different stages of the same river.

Or the young people, some of them hardly into their teens, might travel as far even as the potato fields of Fifeshire or Ayrshire. They'd stand in the streets at the hiring fairs to be eyed by the farmers, even by God to have their biceps tested to see what work was in them. The last of the hiring fairs I saw in Omagh in the early 1930s but by that time everybody was well dressed and wore boots and the institution, God be praised, was doomed. There was a big war on the way and the promise of work for all. But my mother, remembering the old days and thinking perhaps more of her own mother than of the plight of the migratory labourers, would say: The poor Donegals. Ah, the poor Donegals.

Then up the sheltered red-sanded boreen or laneway—the Gaelic word would never at that time have been used by Ulster Presbyterians—to the glory of the Orange lilies and the trim land and in the season, the trees heavy with fruit. Those gooseberries I particularly remember because one day when I raided the bushes more than somewhat, to the fearful extent of a black-paper fourteen-pound sugar-bag packed full, my sisters (elder) reproved me. In a fit of remorse I began to stick the berries back on the thorns. Later in life I found out that plucked fruit is plucked forever and that berries do not grow on thorns.

Then another day the three sisters, two of them home on holidays from Dublin, said: Sing a song for Jinny and Willy.

Some children suffer a lot when adults ask them to sing or recite. There's never really much asking about it. It's more a matter of get up and show your paces and how clever you are, like a dancing dog in a circus, or know the lash or the joys of going to bed supperless. Or sometimes it's bribery: Sing up and you'll get this or that.

Once I remember—can I ever forget it?—the reverend mother of a convent in Dublin gave me a box of chocolates because in the presence of my mother and my cousin, who was a nun, and half the community I brazenly sang:

> Paddy Doyle lived in Killarney
> And he loved a maid named Bessy Toole,
> Her tongue I know was tipped with blarney,
> But it seemed to him the golden rule.

But that was one of the exceptionally lucky days. I often wondered, too, where the reverend mother got the box of chocolates. You didn't expect to find boxes of chocolates lying around convents in those austere days. She dived the depth of her right arm for them into a sort of trousers-pocket in her habit, and the memory of them and of the way I won them ever after braced me in vigour (as the poet said) when asked to give a public performance.

—Up with you and sing, said the eldest sister.

Outside the sun shone. The lilies nodded and flashed like bronze. You could hear them. On a tailor's dummy, that Jinny had bought at an auction, Willy's bowler hat and sash were out airing for the Orange walk on the twelfth day in honour of King William and the battle of the Boyne. The sash was a lovely blue, a true blue, and the Orangemen who wore blue sashes were supposed to be teetotallers. Summer and all as it was the pyramid of peat was bright on the hearth and the kettle above it singing and swinging on the black crane, and Jinny's fresh scones were in three piles, one brown, one white, one spotted with currants and raisins, on the table and close to the coolness of the doorway.

—Sing up, said the second sister. Give us a bar.

—Nothing can stop him, said the third sister who was a cynic.

She was right. Or almost. Up I was and at it, with a song learned from another cousin, the nun's brother, who had been in 1920 in the IRA camp in the Sperrin mountains:

> We're off to Dublin in the green and the blue,
> Our helmets glitter in the sun,
> Our bayonets flash like lightning
> To the rattle of the Thompson gun.
> It's the dear old flag of Ireland, boys,
> That proudly waves on high,
> And the password of our order is:
> We'll conquer or we'll die.

The kettle sputtered and spat and boiled over. Jinny dived for it before the water could hit the ashes and raise a stink, or scald the backs of my legs where I stood shouting treason at Willy and the dummy in the bowler and the teetotaller's blue sash. It may have been a loyal Orange kettle. Willy was weeping with laughter and wiping the back of his left hand sideways across his eyes and his red moustache. In the confusion, the eldest sister, purple in the face with embarrassment, said: If you recited instead of singing. He's much better at reciting.

So I was—and proud of it. Off I went into a thundering galloping poem learned by heart from the *Our Boys*, a magazine that was nothing if not patriotic and was produced in Dublin by the Irish Christian Brothers.

> The night we rode with Sarsfield out from Limerick to meet
> The waggon-train that William hoped would help in our defeat
> How clearly I remember it though now my hair is white
> That clustered black and curly neath my trooper's cap that night.

This time there was no stopping me. Anyway Willy wouldn't let them. He was enjoying himself. With the effrontery of one of those diabolical little children who have freak memories, even when they don't know what the words mean, I let them have the whole works, eight verses of eight lines each, right up to the big bang at Ballyneety on a Munster hillside at the high rock that is still called Sarsfield's Rock.

It is after the siege of Derry and the battle of the Boyne and the Jacobite disaster at the slope of Aughrim on the Galway road. The victorious Williamite armies gather round the remnants of the Jacobites locked up behind the walls of Limerick. The ammunition train, guns, and wagons of ball and powder, that will end the siege rumble on across the country. Then Sarsfield with the pick of his hard-riding men, and led by the Rapparee, Galloping Hogan, who knows every track and hillock and hollow and marsh and bush on the mountains of Silver Mine and Keeper and Slieve Felim, rides north by night and along the western bank of the big river:

'Twas silently we left the town and silently we rode,
While o'er our heads the silent stars in silver beauty glowed.
And silently and stealthily well led by one who knew,
We crossed the shining Shannon at the ford of Killaloe.

On and on from one spur of the mountains to the next, then silently swooping down on the place where, within a day's drag from the city's battered walls, the well-guarded wagons rest for the night. For the joke of it the Williamite watchword is Sarsfield:

The sleepy sentry on his rounds perhaps was musing o'er
His happy days of childhood on the pleasant English shore,
Perhaps was thinking of his home and wishing he were there
When springtime makes the English land so wonderfully fair.
At last our horses' hoofbeats and our jingling arms he heard.
'Halt, who goes there?', the sentry cried. 'Advance and give the word.'
'The word is Sarsfield,' cried our chief, 'and stop us he who can,
'For Sarsfield is the word tonight and Sarsfield is the man.'

Willy had stopped laughing, not with hostility but with excitement. This was a good story, well told. The wild riders ride with the horses' shoes back to front so that if a hostile scouting party should come on their tracks, the pursuit will be led the wrong way. The camp is captured. Below the rock a great hole is dug in the ground, the gun-powder sunk in it, the guns piled on the powder, the torch applied:

We make a pile of captured guns and powder bags and stores,
Then skyward in one flaming blast the great explosion roars.

All this is long long ago—even for the narrator in the poem. The hair is now grey that once clustered black and curly beneath his trooper's cap. Sarsfield, gallant Earl of Lucan, great captain of horsemen, is long dead on the plain of Landen or Neerwinden. Willy is silent, mourning all the past. Jinny by the table waits patiently to pour the tea:

For I was one of Sarsfield's men though yet a boy in years
I rode as one of Sarsfield's men and men were my compeers.
They're dead the most of them, afar, yet they were Ireland's sons
Who saved the walls of Limerick from the might of William's guns.

No more than the sleepy sentry, my sisters never recovered from the shock. They still talk about it. As for myself, on my way home past the ghosts of Johnny Pet and the gentleman goat, I had a vague feeling that the reason why the poor girls were fussing so much was because the William that Sarsfield rode to defeat must have been Willy Norris himself. That was why the poem shouldn't be recited in his house, and fair play to him. But then why had Willy laughed so much? It was all very puzzling. Happy Ulster man that I then was I knew as little about politics and the ancient war of Orange and Green as I knew about the way gooseberries grew.

It wasn't until after my recital that they found out about the black-paper fourteen-pounder of a sugar-sack stuffed full of fruit. The manufacturers don't do sacks like that any more in this country. Not even paper like that any more. It was called crib-paper, because it was used, crumpled-up and worked-over and indented here and bulged out there to simulate the rock walls of the cave of Bethlehem in Christmas cribs.

For parcelling books I was looking for some of it in Dublin the other day, to be told that the only place I'd come up with it was some unlikely manufacturing town in Lancashire.

THE PLAYERS AND THE KINGS

The tall, mild, bald Catholic curate crossed his long legs, wiped his pince-nez, and assured us that the play we were rehearsing was full of biblical lore. That was a mediocre form of encouragement, or consolation; because not the presence of King Herod, Gaspar, Melchior, Balthasar, nor of Annas the high priest, nor of the lovely spectre of the long-dead Mariamne, could make up for the play's one dreadful defect: there was no part in it for Harry the Pawn.

By legitimate descent, and by talent inherited from his father before him, Harry the Pawn was the town's chief comic. A play without the laughter that Harry could not help provoking was no play at all. Biblical lore might be all very well for gentle clergymen, Sunday sermons and fanatics. But do you remember the play in which Harry had been a horse-coper with a yellow muffler around his neck, and a yellow straw that he was chewing in the side of his mouth, and he making love to a servant girl that was seven feet high in a scarlet dress, telling her that she was as lovely as the pillar of fire that walked before Moses?

Or the play in which he had been a rascal of a poacher with a ferret in a box, or the other one in which he had been a journeyman house-painter with a Dublin accent you could cut with a knife?

In all those plays and parts he had been, quite simply, himself: the son of his father who was the best man ever to sing the song about the old grey mare. As in the case of his father the laughter began a few seconds before he stepped on the stage. Instinct told the people he was coming. There'd be electricity in the air in the town-hall theatre. It was hard with the laughter to hear what he was saying. But every little hop, skip and jump he made, every face he pulled, particularly behind the elongated back of the servant maid, registered as uproarious.

If, for a week afterwards, you came on three people laughing together on the Courthouse Hill or the High Street or in the Diamond before the church, you might know they were moved by the delights of memory. Some of the older people might even recall, tears in their eyes, the antics of a father who, straddled on a phantom grey mare, had long since moved off into the shadows, leaving to his son an inheritance of quicksilver.

—If there's laughter in heaven as well as joy, said Peter Quinlan, the schoolteacher, then that reclaimed sinner, Old Henry, and his grey mare would be the cause of it. But even in heaven, I'd say, they'd draw the line at biblical lore and no part for Harry the Pawn.

—Oh answer me, said Charles Edward Gogan the insurance agent.

He was at rehearsals in the musty decaying tottering parish hall: three old houses knocked, very awkwardly, into one. There was a poker school in every one of its lesser, dirty, gas-heated, gas-lighted rooms. But the eighth and largest room was sacred to the arts.

—Oh answer me, he intoned. Like rose leaves that enrich the dark brown earth, thy tremulous whispers will bedew my heart.

He was Herod and proud of it, because he loved to hear himself talk and Herod had most of the play to himself, torrents of fine words and two long-drawn-out fainting fits. He was asking an answer from the ghost of his murdered queen, Mariamne, who, out of understandable pique, stayed mute.

—In golden stars and zones and galaxies, said Napper Patterson, the draper who had once travelled for a season with a professional company.

He was Gamaliel, and this business of the star that guided the men from the east had set him off on astrology, which was quite in order, except that Napper, through misunderstanding or mispronunciation, made Gamaliel talk not of galaxies but of gallases, or suspenders, which he sold in his trade to keep the pants of the town in their proper places.

That was the style of the play. As you can see, it was a long ways away from horse-copers, journeymen with Dublin accents, and long servant girls in scarlet dresses.

Charles Edward Gogan was vain about some things: his fine singing and speaking voice, his Napoleonic stature and profile, his pigskin gloves lined with lambs' wool. He was never seen to wear the two gloves at the same time, but always to wear one and to carry the other. Stroking his impressive forehead with his gloveless hand he would say: Pause a moment. You're impinging on my sphere of thought.

Or sometimes it was: You're interrupting my train of thought.

When he was in one of those moods of infinite abstraction Napper Patterson said to him that no ancient and historic town was completely civilized if it hadn't its own set of players.

—As essential, Charles Edward, as the gasworks, or the drapery business. The costumes readymade for it in Harry the Pawn's army-and-navy stores.

With medals won in Africa or on Flanders' fields, and disposed of by old soldiers in days of penury, with swords and antique guns, and stuffed uniforms like watching men in the shadows, that store was more of a museum than a pawnshop.

—My train of thought exactly, Charles Edward said. But first to win over the Church.

So, bravely in step, they went to see the parish priest, Napper occasionally leaping from sidewalk to street, sidestepping and lunging to show how his old pro., leader of the travelling troupe, had taught him how to fight stage duels.

They sat in the pastor's brown leathery parlour, walled as solid as a fortress with theological tomes, and told him that a small section of the more intelligent young men of the town hoped to start a dramatic society to occupy pleasantly the long winter evenings in educative rehearsals, to keep other young men off the streets, out of pubs and card schools and, it was implied, off dark roads where they might be the ruin of young women. They mentioned tentatively Pope Pius XI, the Pope of Catholic Action.

The parish priest, grey, austere, unsmiling—no gentle curate had he ever been—sniffed snuff and listened.

They would like his approval and one of the curates as spiritual director.

He sneezed.

They pointed out that the proceeds would, naturally, go to decrease the debt on the church and the parish schools.

With the affability of the spider to the fly he said: What play were you thinking of making a start with?

Charles Edward had been to the university in Dublin. He acted once with the college players and once, at a theatre bar, had stood drinking beside, although he hadn't actually spoken to, the city's most notable dramatic critic. To people who never went to Dublin for longer than a fortnight at a stretch that contact amounted almost to celebrity and, because of it, Charles Edward's opinions on theatre were respected. At the committee meeting that sent Napper and himself out as ambassadors, everybody had agreed with his suggestion—with the exception of a sad reactionary who had mentioned the Colleen Bawn and Con the Shaughran and Arrah Na Pogue.

—My train of thought, said Charles Edward, has crashed. Poor William Yeats. Poor John M. Synge. Poor Augusta Lady Gregory. The world has changed in 50 years. Boucicault is dead and gone.

But in the presbytery parlour he could command no such withering sarcasm: the Abbey Theatre had suddenly no more significance than a horse-box; the college players and the noted critic were distant gesticulating puppets.

With a quiver in his voice he said: *The Plough and the Stars*, Father. O'Casey you know, Father.

The four last words had something of the awesome significance of the four last things. Napper Patterson looked earnestly out of the window, down the slope, over the trees, to humpy old roofs and sideways chimneys with smoky autumn dusk thickening around them—as if he expected to see there something nobody had ever seen before. Charles Edward studied his gloves. The parish priest looked into infinity. He said: I know only too well. The dirty dog. If that man wrote the Stations of the Cross you couldn't say them.

Memories of the college players and the critic and first nights at the Abbey came bravely, yet as wounded companions on a lost field, back to Charles Edward. He began: As Patrick Henry Pearse said of John Millington Synge . . .

He always gave every man his full name and hoped that the world would deal likewise with him.

—Pearse, the priest said. Didn't that man say that the grave of Wolfe Tone, a Protestant who cut his throat in jail, was a holier spot than the grave where St Patrick lies in Downpatrick? Didn't Synge write about James Lynchechaun, the murderous playboy of the western world, and disgrace us throughout the length and breadth of the United States of America?

—Not Exactly, Father.

—Not exactly? Sure God look to your wit, Charles Edward, son, and you running to school the day before yesterday, and short pants on you. Go ahead and start your playactors, and the blessing of the Almighty on the work. But let the plays you pick be uplifting plays or plays with a bit of decent fun in them. Father Gough will look after you. Good-night, now.

So they selected plays that would entertain the people without offending the parish priest and, for obvious box-office reasons, they went for decent fun rather than uplift.

That was where the horse-coper came in, straw in the corner of his mouth, to caper fore and aft of the scarlet servant; and the poacher with the ferret in the box; and the Dublin journeyman, and several other manifestations of Harry the Pawn. The soul of Charles Edward was in hell but our town-hall audiences were the gainers. They didn't give a twopenny ticket for Yeats, Synge, O'Casey or Shaw. They wanted and they got Harry, as funny with his black jowl on the stage, as he was on the street on a market-day selling old clothes to cautious farmers. He wore a pin-stripe, and a bowler on the back of his head; and his voice was good for 60 yards: Ladies and Gentlemen, I didn't come here to make my fortune. I've enough to last my lifetime—that is, if I die tonight. Gentlemen, a pair of pants that saw six harvests on the meanest farm on the mountains. Ladies, an elegant skirt, never lifted except in fun and, until recently, the property of a titled lady . . .

Then in the second month of the third season Father Gough, coming in sections out of the Baby Austin he drove with a knee high on each side of the wheel, stopped Charles Edward and myself on the street and told us of the idea. As a schoolboy with talent—meaning a loud voice, an examination knowledge of Shakespeare, an ability to read and memorize—I was involved in the idea to the extent of doubling as Annas the high priest (acts one and two) and one of the magi, the black one (acts three and four).

Father Gough had a friend who wrote mellifluous verse plays with echoes of Shakespeare, Shelley, Byron, Tennyson, Francis Thompson, Stephen Phillips and six or seven others. In one of his higher moments he let loose the full deluge of his verse to sweep the magi into our town on the first Sunday after the feast of the Epiphany. Sick and tired of comic horse-copers Charles Edward was ready for anything. This wasn't Shaw or Ibsen or even Claudel. It most certainly wasn't O'Casey. But it was verse of an order made to match the surge and thunder of Charles Edward's undeniably fine voice. So he assumed the king. As ruthless as any Herod he herded us, intoning the blankest of verse, before him. To this day sometimes in my dreams I go north with the Nile, the black king following the improbable star, sailing—as the verse said—for many evenings when the stream, the flaming mirror of a flaming sky, seemed lifeless, and I came to think myself the one thing living in a land long dead, till, black against a sky of blood and gold, some bird flapped by on lazy leaden wings.

At rehearsals only the sternest self-control kept my arms from becoming wings and bearing me away.

The lesser breeds who could speak no verse were kept busy making oriental costumes and furnishings out of the most unlikely materials. Butter boxes upended and covered with coloured paper became cushioned seats around the throne. Bowler hats, with cardboard crests glued on and the whole works covered in tinfoil, became Roman helmets. Frenzy of preparation seized everybody so violently that the ghost of Mariamne, Kitty Feeny who was a schoolmistress and who had no lines to speak, brought me twice a week to one of the smaller rooms in the parish hall. In the daytime absence of the poker players, she coached me in verse-speaking and stage movement. She elocuted. I echoed. She pushed me here and there until I was dazed with buffeting, drugged and breathing her perfume; and, although I was both a Jewish high priest and a black wise man from the Upper Nile, just a little puzzled as to what she was about.

But Harry the Pawn sulked and stayed away from rehearsals.

Peter Quinlan said: We can't leave him out. He'd never forgive us. The people would tear down the hall.

—We can't put him in, Charles Edward said. They'll laugh as soon as they see him. Laughter, think of it, in the halls of Herod.

—Couldn't we change it a bit, Napper Patterson said. My old pro. was always chopping and changing. Even Shakespeare. Put in a song or something. A porter in Herod's palace. Knock. Knock. Knock. Enter Gamaliel in haste.

—Do you want us all and Father Gough, to end up in Derry Jail? Shakespeare's dead, said Charles Edward sadly. A living poet has his rights. We're not poets.

—No, Napper said. Still, Paddy Mack, the postman's not bad. You remember the one he wrote when Alexander McClintock, a stranger from Portadown, got the job in the new powerhouse over the head of Peter Brady who was born and reared in this town? Or the one about the postman on the rural walk who had his shave every morning by the edge of a bogpool on Arvalee moor?

Then the Holy Ghost descended on Father Gough. He said: God be praised. Put Harry in as the Roman envoy to the court of Herod. A short part, a few words. He'll be on and off before they get time to laugh. No one can say he didn't appear in the play.

So it was done. Rehearsals went on, with Harry as envoy from Caesar to Herod. Lines were learned and rehearsed to the grievous affliction of the non-acting members of any family that included one of the players. A schoolfellow of mine, who was a minor member of the cast, and myself came close to ignominious expulsion for fencing with two ancient cavalry sabres brought from Harry's shop to form portion of the accoutrement of the Nubian eunuchs. Christmas passed and a cold sleety New Year's Day. The dress rehearsal was held on the day after Epiphany. Brazen trumpets heralded the approach of Caesar's envoy. The trumpets were, in fact, Jamesy Lever of the town band blowing a French horn and walking up the rickety stairs behind the stage. The envoy, radiant in tinfoil, spoke his sparse lines, performed his scanty Roman civilities, delivered to Herod a schools-examination certificate rolled up to resemble an ancient scroll. While Herod unrolled the certificate the envoy went out backwards and bowing. Jamesy Lever, sitting on the stairs with Kitty Feeny, blew a valedictory blast, and only then did Peter Quinlan notice that the Roman envoy was in his bare feet.

Peter had made for the magi and the rest of the cast, slaves and eunuchs excepted, sandals of cheap yellow leather. The father of Peter had been a cobbler, but Peter had been educated, sent to London to Horace Walpole's Strawberry Hill to be trained as a teacher, torn up by the roots from hacked benches, smells of waxend and liquid blacking, from awl and hammer, idly-gossiping customers, and all the true skills of cobbling. So the sewing of the sandals wasn't everything it might have been. Yet they were well calculated to dazzle the eyes of our audience looking across footlights into the palace of an eastern king. Their yellow glory would by contrast make a bare-footed envoy look conspicuous—and funny. A provocation to the people. Time was short, the leather supply was finished, and Peter had left Harry out of his calculations.

Peter was the yellow king. He said: Harry, use my sandals on Sunday. I'll throw them across backstage when I make my first exit.

—Them things. I'd be a sight more comfortable in my bare ones.

—Merciful God, Harry. You're supposed to be an envoy from Augustus Caesar. Not a cotter's son going to school over the bog at the back of Dooish mountain. You're not a slave. You're not a eunuch.

—No, thank the Lord. And many a decent man's son went to school at the back of the mountain and learned as much as they learn in London.

Peter with patience passed over that one.

—Take my sandals, all the same. You'd make a horse's collar of the whole thing, going on in your bare feet. Do you think a man could go all the way unshod from Rome to Jerusalem?

—I've only to walk from the dressing-room to the stage. Barring a wood splinter, I don't see what could happen to me.

—Look, Harry. Myself and the other two kings make our exit to the left. Then the trumpet sounds. You're right, waiting. I slip off the sandals, throw them over to you. With the noise of the trumpet nobody will hear a sound. You slip them on and make your entrance, looking respectable.

—Amen, said Father Gough. Fit company for kings.

On the Sunday night the three kings, black, yellow and red, presented their credentials to Herod, listened politely to his long speeches and, meditating on golden stars and zones and galaxies, made their exit. In the left wing I helped Peter Quinlan to unbuckle his sandals. Down at the bottom of the stairs Jamesy Lever blew his first blast. It throbbed in the stage timbers, rustled the curtains, unsettled the ancient plaster yellowing on the walls. A French horn is a resounding instrument and Jamesy was a man of notable lungs.

Peter threw one sandal. I threw another. With the tumult of Jamesy Lever nobody heard the sound of their landing. Nobody, not even Harry, saw where they landed for the right wing was as dark as the black hole of Calcutta. On his bare knees Harry crawled in circles, accumulating splinters, cursing sibilantly, richly, methodically. His pasteboard and tinfoil lorica, his crested bowler hat glimmered in the darkness. In the darkest corner the tall mild bald curate sat in motionless silent discomfort, hiding in the shadows rather than join in the search and risk embarrassing Harry by thus admitting that he had overheard such market-day language.

Harry found the sandals and pulled them on. A strap of cheap leather snapped like sewing thread. Soldier of pagan Rome he invoked things nearer home than the shades of Hector or Hercules. The priest of Christian Rome sat further back into the shadows. Then Harry was on his feet and striding across the threshold of Herod's palace. Hopefully the people, weary with long speeches, applauded. Unhappy in his panoply of cardboard and tinfoil, and in the thought that he was doomed to disappoint his adorers, he glanced nervously over the footlights, stepped on the loose end of the broken strap, and arrived on hands and knees before the throne of Herod, above him a Nubian eunuch holding an ancient cavalry sabre.

Charles Edward did his best. He grasped the school certificate, raised his hand and the certificate in what he would have called a regal gesture. He gagged:

> Rise, Roman envoy, rise, nor have it said
> That Roman knee was hooked at Herod's throne.

But Harry the Pawn's people were on their feet, all the cloying, unintelligible blank verse forgotten in the ecstasy of the fun that only Harry could inspire. The merit—undeniable—of Charles Edward's impromptu composition, even the last roars of Jamesy Lever's horn were lost in the cheering, laughing, whistling, hand-clapping, foot-stamping appreciation.

One voice called: Who goes there?

Another voice answered: Harry from the pawnshop on his old grey mare.

At the back of the hall twenty boys from Stream Hill began to chant: Hear, hear, Harry's here.

The whole hall, apart from the swanky people in the front rows of seats, took up the chorus: What the hell do we care now?

Louder and louder, as the heavy moth-eaten curtain descended like the centuries cutting off Herod's Jerusalem from our town as Harry the Pawn had fashioned it.

Until order was, in a sort of a way, restored by the gentle pleading of Father Gough.

There were funnier things in the play but nobody noticed them. St Joseph in the last act forgot altogether about his white beard and when, too late, he realised his nakedness, he panicked and mispronounced every long word in the seventeen lines he had to say. A Nubian eunuch presenting, at Herod's command, a seat to Annas, turned up a coloured-paper-covered butter box so far that the naked wood and the legend printed on it—Shaneragh Creamery. Twenty-eight Pounds—were visible halfways down the hall.

But the decent men who played the parts of St Joseph and that Nubian eunuch weren't natural-born comics, and Harry the Pawn was; and Harry sat in the dressing-room with his head in his hands, ashamed, for the first time in his life, of the fun that followed him, saying again and again: They'll never take me seriously. Boys, I disgraced myself and I disgraced the players.

Every time he said that, Peter Quinlan answered him and said: My fault, Harry, and those sandals.

Until Harry shouted: Now listen to me, Peter. You wouldn't, would you, expect an envoy from Augustus Caesar to come from Rome to Jerusalem on his bare feet?

On the dark streets as I walked home groups of contented people were saying: That Harry's a good one. Like his father before him. He'd split the sides of a carthorse. Or the old grey mare, herself. He'd put life into anything.

I was the black king and I had forgotten to take the grease off my face. The Court-house clock struck midnight. My cheeks were tight and stiff and there was an oily taste in my mouth. Through the dark dying streets I sailed for many evenings when the stream, the flaming mirror of a flaming sky seemed lifeless, and I came to think myself the one thing living in a land long dead.

In the hallway of Kitty Feeny's lodgings, Kitty and Jamesy Lever were grappled like catch-as-catch-can wrestlers. The French horn, wearing a white coat, was on the ground beside them.

Some bird flapped by on lazy leaden wings.

The sound of kissing was distinct and succulent, and too late I knew the benefits of elocution and stage movement.

Like rose leaves that enrich the dark brown earth.
Thy tremulous whispers.
Oh, answer me.

THE FAIRY WOMEN OF LISBELLAW

If it hadn't been for an elderly blonde that I saw sitting in the sun in a bikini on a lawn in Atlanta, Georgia, I'd never have remembered him again. She was a good 40 paces away from me as I stepped out with two friends from the door of my yellow-brick apartment building. Her back was towards us. She was the only object that disturbed the green grass, and very green it was to grow up out of the red clay of the dry sunny south.

She swivelled her head, left to right, and looked around at us. Although I didn't know who she was and had never even seen her before or, at any rate, had never seen that much of her, I waved my right hand. For beyond her, although in reality there was nothing but the street called Ponce de Leon where it ceases to be suburbia and becomes a stretch of rooming-houses and heavy traffic, and black girls washing cars, and a good Greek restaurant on the far side of the traffic, I saw clearly the Atlantic rolling in on the cliffs of Donegal, and the dark rocks of Roguey under which only the most courageous ever venture to swim.

So Gene asked me who the blonde on the grass was and I said I didn't know.

—But you waved at her.

—Wouldn't you wave at any girl in a bikini?

—A girl, Dolores said.

—I waved at the past.

—You sure did, Gene said. She's 90. You crazy Irish.

—We're a friendly people, I said.

We walked away from the aged blonde towards the car-park at the back of the apartments.

I gave up trying to be a Jesuit in the second year of the novitiate, not because my vocation, as we called it, had weakened—I gravely doubt if I'd ever heard a voice calling me anywhere—but because I had a broken back. Well, it wasn't exactly broken the way you'd snap a twig. It was a spinal lesion, an injured spot on which the bacillus that lurks in all of us settled to make it difficult for me to bend if I was straight or to straighten up if I was bent, and to make me feel that some unseen demon stabbed now and again, slowly and carefully, with a thin red-hot knitting-needle about the region of the third lumbar lump. Eighteen months of Christian patience it took to exorcise that demon.

The Atlantic breakers, white and blue and green, and flashing a lot of colours I could put no name to, came trampling and tumbling up Bundoran strand. The surf was crowded with happy shouting bathers. Little children, grave with excitement, rode slowly on tiny brown hairy donkeys, and one enterprising entertainer had even introduced a baby elephant. The hurdy-gurdy at the hobby-horses and chairaplanes was squeezing the last drop of melody out of the tune that went to the words about the old rustic bridge by the mill:

'Twas oftimes, dear Maggie, when years passed away,
And we plighted lovers became . . .

The town was a long thin line along the coast behind me as I left the red strand and climbed the steep short-grassed slope to the top of the cliffs above Roguey Rocks. Golfers, like jerky clockwork toys, moved, bent with no pain, drove with the intensity of cyclones, on the windy links around Bundoran's grandest hotel. That wind was strong and salty. Behind the town the flat-topped mountains, all the way from Rossinver Braes to bare Ben Bulben, lay like sleeping purple animals. The straps that held my back-splint in place were cutting into my armpits and crotch. My shiny black jacket, that had fitted well enough when I went into the hospital eighteen months previously, had a hard job now to keep buttoned because of the back-splint and a slight stomach spread developed in hospital. In that place of rolling ocean and salt shouting wind, purple mountains, hurdy-gurdies and near-naked bathers, I was, and felt I was, a cheerless sombre figure.

This clifftop walk was my path of escape. It brought me away from the happy all-together crowds that seemed so nastily to emphasize my own isolated predicament. Beyond Roguey the cliffs—flung spray rising high above them, high as they were, and spattering the rocks—swung directly eastwards and so, unavoidably did the path. It brought me by the bowl-shaped fresh-water spring, clear as crystal against solid rock, that was one of the wonders of those cliffs. It brought me by an even more wonderful wonder, the Fairy Bridges, where the sea had moled its way through weaknesses in the dark rock and, far back from the dangerous slanting edge of the cliffs, you could look down into deep terrifying cauldrons of boiling froth. Tragedies were always happening there: daring young people clambering down the sides of the cauldrons, to what purpose God alone knew, and losing foothold or handhold, and falling down where not all the lifeguards in the world could be of the least assistance to them.

Beyond those fatal Fairy Bridges the holiday crowd had vanished. There was an odd courting couple, snug from the wind behind a fence of green sods or a drystone wall, grazing nimble goats who sometimes attacked people; and inland, protected from the cliffs by walls and fences, easy grazing cattle. The great flat mountains were still visible, but the eye and imagination were taken now by the long rising-and-falling range of highlands far across the bay.

Poems had been written about this place: that vision of highlands, strand and sea, and far away the estuary of the River Erne. The strand was perilous with quicksands and so generally deserted.

> From Dooran to the Fairy Bridge
> And down by Tullan Strand,
> Level and long and white with waves,
> Where gull and curlew stand . . .

The wooden shelter that I sat and read in was as near to being my own exclusive property as made no difference. It was roofed with red tiles, and had no sides, and a cruciform wooden partition held up the roof and divided the structure into four parts so that no matter from what airt the wind did blow, myself and my book always had shelter. There I sat reading, day-dreaming, I was nineteen, remembering. Remembering now and again the Jesuit novitiate where, inexplicably, I had been happy in a brief fit of religious frenzy that was to be my ration ever since. A classical rectangular house that had once belonged to a great lord and, with red carpet on the main avenue, given welcome to an English king, sheltered in deep pine woods in the sleepy Irish midlands. Bells divided the holy day. Black-gowned neophytes made their meditations, walked modestly, talked circumspectly. Wood pigeons cooed continuously, and there were more bluebells and daffodils and red squirrels in those woods than I have ever seen anywhere else in the world.

But, to be honest, I was never quite sure what I was doing there and, if I was happy, it was happiness in a sort of trance that I felt uneasily must have its end. My lumbar spine made up my mind for me, and eighteen months surrounded by fresh and pleasant young Irish nurses convinced me that there were certain things that Jesuits were not normally supposed to have. So that my memories in the cruciform shelter were less about the Ignatian spiritual exercises than about dreams of fair women in blue-and-white uniforms. They were all there, around the corner by Ben Bulben and off through Sligo on the high road to Dublin. To the rocks and the seawind I repeated the names of the seven or eight of them I had fallen in love with: Lane, Devlin, Brady, Love, Callaghan, Mullarkey, O'Shea, Rush and Moynihan. On a recount: nine.

Far away a black-sailed boat that seemed scarcely to be moving came down the sand-channel of the Erne estuary to the sea. In the privacy of the shelter I eased the crotch-straps of the back-splint. It was made of good leather stretched on a light steel frame, it travelled from the neck to the buttocks, it smelled of horse-harness.

—Head out to sea, I said, when on your lee the breakers you discern. Adieu to all the billowy coasts and the winding banks of Erne.

The tide, the bathers, the children, the donkeys, and even the baby elephant, had withdrawn for a while from the red half-moon of Bundoran Strand. Far out the frustrated breakers were less boisterous. The hurdy-gurdy was silent and the hobby-horses resting at their stalls, and in hotels and boarding-houses the evening meal was being demolished. In Miss Kerrigan's old-fashioned whitewashed Lios na Mara, or the Fort, God help us, by the sea, my mother looked up from her ham salad to say that I was late as usual.

—Sara Alice, leave him be, Miss Kerrigan said. He's thinking long. Waiting for the happy day when he gets back to his studies. Looking forward to his ordination, God bless him, the holy oil, the power to bind and loose.

Listening to her I kept my thoughts fixed on red squirrels flashing in bluebell woods, on the wasps' nest at the foot of the Spanish chestnut tree close to the croquet court, on the dark silent file of neophytes, eyes cast down, obeying the holy bell and walking to the chapel to morning oblation—along cold corridors and down a stairway up which unholy royalty had once staggered to bed. For I felt if my thoughts were on laughing young nurses, Lane, Devlin, Brady, Love, Callaghan, Mullar-key, O'Shea, Rush and Moynihan, my nine blue-and-white Muses, Miss Kerrigan's sharp brown eyes would discover those thoughts and betray the old Adam hiding behind the shiny black suit.

—Thinking long, she said again.

She was very fond of me and I wouldn't have hurt her for the world. Lios na Mara, too, was a place that caught the fancy as the average seaside boarding-house most certainly did not. It stood well back from the town's one interminable street, under a stone archway, secure and secluded in a grassy courtyard that overlooked the toy harbour where the fishing-boats and the seagulls were. It wasn't New York or Liverpool but it was the first harbour I ever saw and, as a child, I had actually thought that ships might sail from that harbour to anywhere or Antananarivo.

—This, said Miss Kerrigan, is Master McAtavey.

He had come into the room silently while, with my back to the door, I was fumbling with a napkin and sitting down to attack my ham. It was a surprise to find anyone except my mother and Miss Kerrigan who were girlhood friends, and myself, of course, by right of inheritance, in that small private parlour. The other guests ate elsewhere and did not presume.

—My only sister's son, said Miss Kerrigan.

—From the Glen of Glenties, said my mother who was hell all out for geography.

He was still standing, very tall and awkward, three paces away from the table.

—Sit down, Eunan dear, said my mother. Don't be shy.

She disliked shy people. She suspected them of dishonesty.

—He teaches school, said Miss Kerrigan.

—In the Vale of Dibbin, said my mother. A heavenly place. You know it, she said to me.

Then he blushed. Never before or since have I seen a blush like it. He had fair curly hair that was cropped too short and his eyes were a startlingly bright and childish blue. His navy-blue pinstripe was too short in the sleeves and, above strong square hands, the knobs on his wrists were as large as golfballs. He had taken two paces forward abruptly as if he were a sentry under command, towards his provender, so that the lower half of him was hidden by the table and I couldn't see whether the legs of his pants, like his sleeves, were too short. Not that I, with my shiny coat of clerical black straining to meet around my back-splint, was in any position to criticize. His blond skin—once it must have been blond—was so beaten by the heathery wind of the Glen of Glenties, and burned by the same sun that shines both on Glenties and Georgia, that even experts on the matter would have considered it quite impossible for him to blush.

But he did. The blush went upwards in little leaps or spurts, an inch or so at a time, from the tight white collar that squeezed his long neck, up and up, spreading, intensifying until his whole face shone, as the man said about the sunset, like a forge. He was a very shy master and let me say, to my credit, that I leaped up, offered him a chair, seated him at his ham salad, sat down again and talked non-stop for half an hour about the Vale of Dibbin and the Glen of Glenties. He choked over his ham, and played back to me the occasional yes or no, and I wasn't sure whether he was grateful or resentful. But I didn't care much, for I did know the places I talked about and to talk about them was a pleasure in itself.

The town of Glenties, I told them, was always bright with paint and so spotlessly clean that a scrap of paper or cigarette butt wasn't to be seen on the street, and a bluebottle fly, invading from some less-regulated town, wouldn't last for five minutes. A few miles away, the sands, under clear water where the Gweebarra River turned salt, shone like silver. In the Vale of Dibbin the neat white-washed farmhouses stood along the breast of the mountain and the clean fields sloped steeply down to a trout stream, all white cataracts and deep populated pools. On which river I had fished with my brother and a fat man called Joe Maguire who had fought at the Dardanelles and who wore a bowler hat even when he was fishing.

The life and times of Joe Maguire could have kept me going for half a day, but time was passing and I prized the private hours ahead when I would sit in my room and read and look down on the harbour and across the water at the happy company on the strand. They couldn't see me but I could see them and that, in some way or other, helped my morale. When I stopped to draw breath and chew ham I was glad to see that his blush had faded.

Miss Kerrigan listened, and watched me with loving brown eyes that were set deeply in a long wrinkled yellow face. She continuously rubbed her feet on the floor in a nervous way she had. That nervousness increased when she went to whist-drives and it was said that once, when she was running hard for first prize, she had rubbed a hole in the uncarpeted floor of the cardroom in a parish hall in a neighbouring town. She always dressed in black, in mourning for her father and mother who had died within the one week 30 years ago, and she was six feet two inches in height.

—What a memory, she said.

—A powerful man to tell stories, said my mother, like his father before him.

—A blessed gift, Miss Kerrigan said, and will stand to him well after ordination.

She must have meant something else, for no one could have suspected Miss Kerrigan of anti-clericalism.

—In the pulpit I mean, she said.

That didn't make it any better.

—I'll go for a walk now, said Eunan McAtavey.

Those were the first words I'd heard him say. They began as a whispering squeak and then spread out like a shout. They had clearly cost him premeditation and effort. He stood up. He didn't overturn his chair. He did drop his napkin. I picked it up for him.

—Bernard will go with you, Miss Kerrigan said.

—Bernard, my mother said, Eunan was never here before. He doesn't know his way around.

There went my private hours, but politeness compelled me and, at any rate, the ladies had me trapped.

Three lovely old ladies lived in that block of yellow-brick apartments. Taken all-together they were a sort of sign that something remained in a place where everything was rapidly changing.

They lived in a world of their own and had memories that had nothing whatsoever to do with the neighbours. Forty years ago, when they had come to live there, those apartments had been new and quite the thing. But suburbia in automobiles had swept far beyond them. The district decayed. The old ladies stayed on because they were too old, perhaps too poor, to move. Their neighbours now were myself, and the withered blonde whoever she was, and rowdy students who had lively parties and were occasionally evicted because the landlord would find six living in an apartment he had rented to two. To evict one such group his workmen had to take the door off the hinges. A few decent quiet linotype men lived there. The paper they had worked for in a more southern city had folded and they had come north to Atlanta to find work. A flock of go-go girls who were working down the street stayed for a while, brightened the lawn with bodies more naked than had ever startled Eunan McAtavey on Bundoran Strand, then flew off elsewhere. Their place was taken one evening by a fat oily bald man. From their windows the students made offensive noises. Two burglars who lived in another part of the city rented one of the yellow apartments to keep their loot in. The police came and were a whole afternoon carrying out and counting miscellaneous objects. My next-door neighbour was a girl from Nashville who was married at fifteen and whose husband dressed up as the tiger in the tank at a filling-station. He walked out every morning in his costume, his own head showing, the tiger's head grinning in his hand.

Gene drove down the slope. We passed the hotel where the black girl, coming to fill her fifth date for the night, had changed her mind and tried to steal the cash register instead, and had been shot dead by the night porter. We passed three liquor stores, an army induction centre, a Sears Roebuck, a waste-patch that had once been a ball-park and would, any day henceforth, sprout skyscrapers. The twenty black girls washing cars were, to keep cool, squirting water over each other. We passed a Yarab shrine, a Presbyterian centre, a motel, three churches, a pop place painted all purple, saloons, and shops, and one skyscraper hotel at the corner of Peachtree Street. Dolores was on the way to a suburban shopping centre to buy shoes.

That was the first of seven walks, dull enough, silence mostly between us, our chief activities just walking, or tossing driftwood back into the tide, or simply sitting and gazing out to sea. He couldn't swim and I because of my third lumbar lump and my back-splint, wasn't allowed to. Now and again, to break the silence, I played courier and pointed out the estuary, named the mountains and quoted the poetry. He showed no interest. He would walk stolidly beside me, and I had a crazy feeling that his arms swung together, both before him at the same time, both behind him at the same time, if you know what I mean. The pinstripe trousers were, indeed, too short, and the feet were considerable. When he put away the pinstripe—he said it was his Sunday-best and that the salt air faded dark cloth—and put on grey flannels with a dangerous crease, they also were too short. His oatmeal tweed jacket creaked from the shop and my back-splint answered. We were a fine pair to be seen on any gay promenade. He never nonchalantly put his hands in his pockets. When he stood up they hung by his side as if he had no control over them.

On the fifth walk I talked about the Jesuits and the novitiate and the weedy lake where boating and bathing were allowed, depending on the weather, on major Christian festivals. He responded by telling me, in broken spurts and mumbles, how he had spent two years of hell in a teachers' training college in Dublin, and that he might as well, for all the college ever taught him about life, have been incarcerated, he used that word, in Mountjoy Jail. That reference to life should have warned me.

On the sixth walk I mentioned the nurses and litanied the nine magic names and, growing reckless with wishful thinking, hinted at nights of love under dimmed lights. On the seventh walk he stopped in the sunshine, on a path through the dunes beyond Tullan Strand, and raised his stiff right arm to indicate the curves and hollows of the dry sand, the sleek comfort of the bent grass, and said hoarsely: This would be a bloody great place to have a woman.

—True enough, I said and felt guilty before his awkward innocent passion.

For by day in the shelter when the crotch straps were eased, by night in bed when my black garments were laid aside, I had skipped in fantasy up and down those same dunes, a satyr in pursuit of nine nymphs, or lurked in grassy corners to cut off unclad stragglers.

—The way you talk about the place I come from, he said, you'd think it was Blackpool or the Land of Youth.

It took me until the following day to appreciate that juxtaposition but, on reflection in the quietude of my room, it seemed reasonable. The poets don't tell us, but there must have been beaches and bathing beauties in the land to which Niamh led Oisin. Eunan, clearly, had given the matter long thought.

—It's lovely country, I said. A home for poets. The fishing's good.

—I don't fish. The only poetry I ever learned off by heart was this.

He stood up stiff as a guardsman, filled his lungs with seawind and let fly: Bracing breezes, silvery sands, booming breakers, lovely lands. Come to Bundoran.

It didn't occur to me, I remember, to be surprised at this display of eloquence. Being talkative myself, I must have assumed that there was as much talk in everyone, that it was welling up in him and that some day the dam would burst.

—I learned that out of an advertisement in the newspaper because it was my intention to come here to Bundoran for the women. I'd heard time and again that the place was hoaching with them during the Scottish holiday season.

Hoaching was a word we used to describe the way fingerling fish, in low water and warm weather, would swarm together at the mouths of pools. It was an evocative sultry word.

—What's holding you up? I said. They're everywhere to be seen.

Even in the lonely dunes that was true. Couples sprawled in sheltered corners. When they couldn't be seen they could be heard: muffled voices, and shrills of laughter quickly stifled, to remind the horseman passing by that love was all. The path we followed skirted the barbed wire of a military camp, went down a slope past an ancient churchyard to join the main road to Ballyshannon, Enniskillen, Omagh and Donegal town. Four green soldiers stood where the path joined the roadway and bantered and jackacted with six girls with bright flaring skirts and Glasgow accents.

—A surplus of two, he said. The soldiers have all the luck. You were lucky, too, with all those nurses. You struck it lucky. All good things. They say the nurses are the best. They know everything.

If I had not already come close to believing that my own imaginings were reality I might have had an attack of conscience for all the tall tales I had told him.

—My trouble, Bernard, is that I can't talk to women. Even your

mother and Miss Kerrigan frighten me. I never had the training. Where
would I get it? With mountainy women as wild as the mountain sheep?
Hands on them as hard as flagstones. I never got a bloody chance. Even
in Dublin. The priests in the college wouldn't let you see daylight. The
Vincentians.

—No, I said, I suppose the Vincentians wouldn't be so good at that. It
wouldn't be on the curriculum.

It worried me a little that he didn't laugh at the idea. He looked
straight in front of him. His mouth, and it was a small tight one for
such a large man, was tightly closed—now that his talking was over for
the moment. Muscle stood out on the point of his left jaw as if he had
his teeth clenched on his grievance. The hard sidewalk, crowded with
women, I suppose there must have been men there too, was hot under
our feet, the long town ahead. He had touchingly used my name for the
first time and so made me his ally, his sworn brother sweet, his voice
when it came to putting chat on the women.

He was so awkward on his feet that he came into the class of men who
can be described as getting in their own way. Walking beside him had
all sorts of problems. It wasn't so bad when he was silent, as he seldom
was after he had confessed to me his true reason for coming to
Bundoran. For when he was silent he could follow a straight course as
well as any man. But when he talked he moved, inch by inch as his
blush did, sideways in little spurts towards his listener, and to
emphasize his point he jabbed with his elbows. Or they did the jabbing
all on their own, for of all the men I've ever known, he had the least
control over his hands and elbows and feet. To make his feet more
noticeable he purchased and wore a pair of those rubber-and-corduroy
pampooties known to the civilized world as brothel creepers. They
didn't go with the iron crease of his grey flannels nor the creaking jacket
of honest oatmeal tweed. They were also too big for him, although that
seemed impossible, but the toes certainly flopped when he walked or
stumbled along sideways, elbowing, so that every 50 yards or so I had to
dodge to the other side of him to save myself from bruises and correct
our course. We were the rarest-looking pair of Romeos that ever walked
out to rummage and ruin the girls, Scottish or Irish, that hoached in
that summery pool.

—You're a man of the world, he said. You can talk to people.

Nobody had ever said that to me before. Nobody has ever said it
since, although two months later, as a student in Dublin walking home
by night, I picked up a little girl with a blue beret and a brown belted

coat and protruding teeth, and kissed her good-night at her garden gate. She breathed deeply. She said: Boy, you've got technique.

Afterwards the risks I took with more sophisticated college lasses, to establish my claim to a technique of which until then I had been quite innocent, must have earned me an odd sort of reputation. But breathing bracing breezes, walking silvery sands, listening to, because I was unable to plunge into, booming breakers, it was up to me, as a man of the world, to do something for my hapless mountainy man. It wasn't going to be easy.

—Not that one, Bernard. She's as bold as brass by the cut of her.

—Isn't that what we're after, Eunan?

—She would talk the ass out of a pot. And the laughs of her.

The plump girl in orange swimsuit and blue bathing-cap ran, leaping and laughing, into the surf. Her thin blonde companion, in red suit and no cap, trotted demurely behind her, squeaking a little now and again. Little did the plump girl know how close she had come to the arms of Eunan McAtavey. He looked after her for a long time. He fancied her but he was afraid of her laughter.

—Not that one, Bernard, You couldn't get near her for lipstick.

This was a tall redhead, long flying red hair, who went round and round riding sidesaddle and flashing thighs on the hobby-horses. Her crimson mouth was, indeed, a size larger than nature, but only a man who had more on hand than he could deal with, would have faulted her for that. For a man who had nothing at all, nor ever had, Eunan of the Glen was mighty choosey. He feared laughter. He feared lipstick. He didn't want to spend money.

—Not that one, Bernard. She's a chain-smoker. Look at the butts on the ground around her. A bank manager couldn't keep her in cigarettes.

The thin girl in dark slacks and dark woollen sweater sat on a bench outside the Hamilton Hotel and blew out smoke as if she meant to blind the passers-by. She was gone beyond her first bloom but there was something appealingly wistful, and promising, about her dark steady eyes, and cheeks that hollowed as she sucked smoke.

—Not that pair, Bernard. They remind me of the mountainy girls at home.

They were sisters, two country girls, bright red berets, damp tails of hair straggling out from under the berets, belted fawn raincoats. Like ourselves and a hundred others, they had raced for shelter from an Atlantic squall to play the machines in hurdy-gurdy country. They stamped with delight in the deep churned discoloured sand. For fun, they shouldered each other like county footballers while they both grabbed for the one arm of the one-armed bandit. They laughed so as to be heard above the noise of a crowd of people crushed suddenly into a small space, even above the steam-organ hurdy-gurdy noises. The hobby-horses, all mounted, circled, the redhead sidesaddle. The rising-and-falling mountain range beyond the bay was hidden by a pitch-black cloud that came down like a smothering curtain. Then the curtain was split by forked lightning and the thunder came before the flash had faded. Under the wooden roof of the place of hobby-horses and bandits it was then so dark that one of the showmen switched on the lights. More lightning, the thunder seemed to come closer. A woman screamed and more children than you could count or kill began to cry. The elder of the two laughing sisters turned round and looked at us, and began to laugh as if she had just learned the secret. No question or doubt about it, nor was there any point in mentioning the matter to Eunan—but she was laughing at us.

Dolores is a slender sensitive woman who paints well and exhibits and sells her paintings. Gene, in spite of an English surname, has Arab blood in him that makes him look like a non-aggressive, even affable, slightly smaller version of General Nasser. On Saturday afternoons Rich's in Lennox Square in Atlanta, Georgia, is as good a field as I've ever seen for the wholehearted bird-watcher. Gene and Dolores couldn't see him, but Eunan of the Glen, lost to me long ago by the Donegal sea, was beside me on the escalator on the way up to the shoe department. He was so real to me that day, for the first time in 27 years, that I was ready to speak to him out loud, ready to hear him say: No, Bernard, not that one. She couldn't be a modest girl. Look at the bare back of her. Be the holy, if the parish priest saw the like of that on a teacher's wife in the Glen of Glenties, there'd be a new teacher in the school before the end of the month if not sooner.

Yet Eunan—it must have been something he read—had desired, I think, silks and perfumes with the sins he imagined and feared: and the silks and perfumes were all here. It was the women of his own mountainy place and people that he feared most. He told me of a girl who grabbed his hand in the darkness of the schoolhouse at a travelling movie show: She had a palm, Bernard, as hard as a whinstone rock. It would frighten you. A woman shouldn't be like that. A woman should be gentle. And true. Terrible things, Bernard, can happen to country schoolmasters. A man I heard tell of got into trouble with the girls in the school, two of them, and one was jealous of the other, and she told. The country girls are deceitful. And if you married the wrong one your job's ruined.

Looking up the escalator at the bare-backed beauty ahead of us, I said that you could play the zither on the knuckles of her spine.

She was a tall olive Amazonian, with her right shoulder arrogantly bare, and white pants so tight that her bottom looked like an outsize meringue; and a crimson waistcoat all front and no back, that was a miracle of cantilever.

But it was Gene, not Eunan, that heard. Bundoran was 27 years away, and 4,000 miles.

—Hardly worth while, he said, for her escort to take her home. Nothing more left to see. Billy Graham says that it's okay for girls to wear miniskirts if there is no intention of provoking sensual desire.

Oh Eunan McAtavey where are you now?

Failure after failure, he wouldn't take the jump, so there was nothing for it now but the Palais de Danse. As a man I know says: If you want to get it you must go where it is.

Miss Kerrigan would say to me: You're more cheerful now, Bernard, since Eunan came. You're not thinking long any more. I'm so glad the two of you get along together. Good healthy walks, bracing breezes, silvery sands.

Everybody in the bloody place seemed to know that jingle off by heart.

—Booming breakers, lovely lands, rhymed my mother.

—That's real poetry, she said smugly and just to madden me for she knew that I kept hidden in my room above the harbour the steadily accumulating collected works: three developing epics, one on Barac, Deborah and King Sisera in the *Book of Judges*, one on the Easter Rising of 1916, one on the lighting by St Patrick, on the Hill of Slane, of Ireland's first-ever Pascal fire. Apart of course, from many shorter pieces of an intense lyricism, inspired by one or other or all of the chosen nine: Could I into that silent shrine advance, to where the sacred flame makes all things plain, what joy were mine to find engraven there my name.

—Good healthy walks, said Miss Kerrigan. But don't overdo it. Think of your back and all that lying down and standing up for ordination.

She was right: I mean about the thinking long. For I had now an interest in life outside myself, and was more anxious that Eunan should find his woman, and find engraven there his name, than he was himself. He had nothing: my hoard or pocket of nine nurses was in Dublin beyond the mountains, I could afford to be generous. For to be afflicted by desire for hoaching Scottish lasses, and yet not be able to say a blessed preliminary word to any one of them must have been pain beyond pain. Once in a while he would whisper, spluttering sideways into my ear, gripping my bicep hard enough to hurt, as if he were trying to hold himself back from leaping on the lady there and then: That one, Bernard. That's the ticket. God, it would be something to give her a run for it in the sandhills.

Nearly always the desired one was pale, golden-haired, prim, modestly dressed and an obvious member of the Children of Mary. This puzzled me for a while until I realized sadly that Eunan, perhaps subconsciously, was attracted to young women whose appearance would please the parish priest. When I managed to put chat on one of these votaresses Eunan was no help at all arms dangling, mouth like a vice, gaze at a tangent—towards the breakers, or the bulk of Truskmore concealing Ben Bulben, or the cliffs of Slieve League across the bay. So there was nothing for it but the Palais de Danse where not even a shy buck like Eunan would have a chance of escape, for far and wide the place was notorious for frenzied women. Even the boom-thump-boom-thump-boom of it, echoing night after night from the sea to the hills and back again was the cause of protests and letters to the local paper.

—See it, Eunan, you must. If you went back to Glenties and said you'd never seen the inside of the palais they'd laugh at you. They'd do worse. They'd worry about you.

The palais had also the name for being a rough class of a place. There was a long-nosed man I knew from my own town, who kept the entire works of Edgar Wallace in a tin trunk under his bed, and had got mildly drunk one night in the palais and had bones broken by the gorillas. Not a word of this did I tell to Eunan, he was nervous enough as it was, nor was I all that happy myself: shiny tight black suit and creaking back-splint smelling like horse-harness weren't exactly standard equipment for the palais. What would I say to the first girl who put her arm around me to convince her that I wasn't made of leather or wood, or about to perish with a petrifying disease?

We crossed the strand. A mist-swollen moon was coming up slowly from behind Truskmore. The surf shone, the cliff-shadows were jet-black on the sand, the small stream that dribbled across the strand was silver. The glaring lights, the boom-thump-boom of the palais were sacrilege. Restive Eunan at any moment might turn and bolt like a colt running from harness and, if he did, I'd have no power to halt him. For now that I was face-to-face with the palais I was damned near as nervous as he was, and not much more of a man of the world. Nearer and nearer. The entering crowd shuffled around a doorway guarded by the two gorillas who had beaten up the long-nosed devotee of Edgar Wallace. The lights were blinding, the noise deafening. Eunan was moving more slowly, had, indeed, almost come to a halt, when a woman's voice said clearly into my ear: Is it going to say Mass you are, your reverence? Or has somebody had a sudden heart-attack?

It was the laughing girl. She was still laughing. So was her sister. They were linked, and leaning against each other with unaffected gaiety.

—It's no place for a clerical student, the elder sister said.

—An ex-clerical student.

—A clerical error, then.

They laughed fit to fall at the ancient joke and I couldn't but laugh with them, while Eunan stood there as stiff as my back-splint.

—There was a fight in there already, she said.

The younger sister, as I recall, never spoke, but only laughed.

—Drunken animals. The civic guards took away two that you couldn't see for blood.

She took my arm: Let's go for a walk to Tullaghan. There's a lovely moon.

Tullaghan was two miles to the side of the town away from the Fairy Bridges and my four-cornered wooden shelter. A concrete pathway led along the tops of low cliffs, the sea to the right, quiet residential hotels to the left. Beyond the rock bathing-pool that was reserved for nuns the hotels ended and there was nothing but grass, grey-white under the moon, and the moon shining on the water.

—I'm Ellen, she said. That there behind is Madge, my sister. We'd be twins only she's two years younger.

Behind us in the salty moonlight Madge was laughing gently but continuously, Eunan wasn't making even a grunt, and it was a wonder to God to me that he had come walking at all: except to escape from the more certain horrors of the palais.

—She's very like you. Except that she laughs more.

—We both laugh a lot. But Madge laughs more because she's shy.

—She's in proper company this blessed night.

—He does look shy, too. Where's he from?

—The hills of Donegal.

—All night and day I'm dreaming, she sang, of the hills of Donegal.

Then she said: We're from the meadows of Fermanagh, from Lisbellaw.

Lisbellaw I knew, as I knew even then the half of Ireland: Lisbellaw, and the sleepy lake shore and grass meadows all around. The map shows a filigree pattern of blue, Upper Lough Erne, on a field of flat green: restful country, quiet towns, little harbours with long names where you could idle away ten life-times fishing spoon or spinning minnow for pike and perch and bream. It made me warm to her right away that she came from a countryside meant for laziness or, since I was literary then, lotus-eating. She swing easily on my arm, and sometimes went one, two, three and a one, two, three on the tips of her toes as if she were readying to dance the Walls of Limerick. So I slipped my arm around her waist and felt like the hell of an ex-cleric, and hoped I was giving good example to Eunan lumbering along behind us.

She was wearing a green sort of dress, not a raincoat as when she had first surfaced in the place of the one-armed bandits. She had a small golden-coloured harp as a clasp at the cleavage, no beret, her dark hair dry and shampoo-shiny, and held in place by a golden-coloured snood; nor did she smell of peat smoke as it was generally said that rural beauties did. Thus, we came to the old square tower that guards the eel-weir at Bundrowes, where the Drowes, which is a magic river, meets the sea, and all the wonder of Tullaghan Strand was before us: no ordinary level of sand where people went bathing, but rank upon rank of oval stones that the sea had shaped. They shone, between salt and moonshine, like gigantic jewels. All along the country roads out of Bundoran, into Donegal and Leitrim and Sligo, you could see Tullaghan stones painted all colours and making borders for beds in flower gardens.

Ellen and myself sat in the shadow of the tower and looked out on the flashing Drowes where the trout have the gizzards of chickens because of a miracle performed by a saint back there at Lough Melvin where the river comes from. She said that when she and Madge went back to Lisbellaw they'd take Tullaghan stones with them, and paint them striped, and keep them as souvenirs of this lovely night. That set us kissing and grappling merrily in the shadows. When we came up for air she asked: Where are they?

Oh, there they were, sure enough, not rolling on the grass or wrestling in the shadows but standing 50 yards from us on the bank of the Drowes, and five yards from each other: Eunan, a dark statue, arms by its side, that looked as if it had been there as long as the tower. They were too far away for us to hear if Madge were still laughing. Since there was nothing, short of roping them together that we could do about it, we kissed and grappled again and when we had surfaced again they were exactly as we had last seen them enchanted to stone by magic river and sea and moon. Ellen breathed a long breath and slowly let it loose again. She said: They'd never credit it in Lisbellaw.

—Ellen, I know a song about Lisbellaw.

—Sing it, for God's sake.

—It's in Irish.

—Sing it in Irish.

So I sang in Irish the verse that mentions Lisbellaw.

—What does it mean?

—Something like this: I met a fairy woman down at Lisbellaw and asked her would any key unlock the lock of love. In low and kind and gentle voice she answered me: When love locks the heart the lock will never be loosened.

—It would be grand, she said, but I doubt if it's true.

We kissed again, quietly and without grappling. She stood up and smoothed down the green dress and said we'd better walk home before Madge froze to death or leaped in the Drowes for lack of anything better to do.

The fighting was over for the night in the Palais de Danse. The long moonlit town, painted all colours for the holiday season, was asleep, it seemed, and silent, except that you could guess that here and there and everywhere it was still a holiday and the fun was going on. We left the sisters at the door of their boarding-house. Because of Eunan, or rather because of Madge, I forbore kissing Ellen good-night, but she understood, and gripped my hand hard, and dug her nails into my palm, and said we'd meet tomorrow night by the hobby-horses, and hoped that the moon would be out again.

Eunan and myself walked wordless home along the bright empty street. It wasn't until we were at Miss Kerrigan's door that he spoke: Bernard, she had a very hard hand.

I said nothing.

—That one, Bernard, was laughing at me all night.

—Not at you, Eunan. She was laughing because she's young and on her holidays.

After a while I added: And walking out with a young man by the bright silvery light of the moon.

—Bernard, ever since the first day I went to school country girls have been laughing at me.

Up in my silent room I couldn't even read myself to sleep, feeling sorrier then for lonely Eunan than out at Tullaghan I had felt for laughing Madge.

The morn was breaking fresh and fair and the lark sang in the sky, and it was as lovely a day as you would expect after such a night of moonlight. Eunan and myself walked like automatons across the strand. What, I asked myself, are the wild waves saying, for Eunan hadn't a word to throw to land or ocean, nor could I think of anything to say that wouldn't make the poor man more miserable than he obviously was already. In sad silence we came to the two high flights of wooden steps that went up from a moist cliff-shadowed corner of the strand to the top of Roguey. Eunan climbed up ahead of me—as blithely as a man climbing to the scaffold. He had his pinstripe on and his trousers, God help me, seemed to have shrunk. Up above us there was music and dancing and singing voices. The local branch of the Gaelic League kept an open-air dancing-floor at that point on the clifftop, and all day long, Maryanne, weather permitting, the young people were at it hammer and tongs: slip jig and hornpipe and fourteen-hand reel, the Walls of Limerick, the Waves of Tory, Saddle the Pony, the Mason's Apron and the Chaffpool Post. It was such a lively place and such a beautiful morning. Far out, wisps of mist drifted over dark-blue unbroken water. There was autumn in the air. The flat-topped mountains were still hidden. Because of the noise of the music and dancing the cries from the strand were inaudible, so that the silent movements of the people on the edge of the surf, and of the donkeys and the baby elephant, seemed completely senseless. White mist, too, drifted in bundles over the golf-links, and the clockwork figures stepping out of the mist, vanishing into it again were crazily comic.

It was part of the mood of the morning that I should at that moment see the blonde and purple woman, 50 yards away, higher up the slope on the path to the Fairy Bridges. She sat quite close to the cliff's edge. She waved and I waved in return.

—Who is that? says Eunan.

—What we're after, Eunan. Scottish and glamorous. Look at that purple dress, that blonde hair.

The blonde hair shone in the morning. She waved again.

—That there's no laughing country girl, Eunan. Perfume, I'd say, that would flatten a regiment. If there was a wind this morning we'd get the perfume already.

Side-by-side, keeping step, we advanced up the slope. Behind us the dancing and music went on as if we never had been. His big feet beside me were no longer flopping in brothel creepers but solid and determined in square-toed black shoes. The woman was reading a book, her head turned away from us. At 60 paces it was clear that I had been right about the perfume.

—Good-morning, I said.

It was an irreproachable and perfectly accurate remark.

She turned her head and looked at us and said: To whom have I the honour of speaking?

It wasn't that she was old: remembering her now I suppose she couldn't have been more than 60. She wore red shoes and purple stockings, and her short purple dress, tucked up to allow her to squat in comfort, showed fat knees with pads of surplus flesh to the insides of the kneecaps. It wasn't that she was ugly. It was the desperate effort to defeat ugliness that made me feel that life could be a losing battle. She wore a loose purple jacket about as long as the dress, and a striped blouse—I can't remember the colour of the stripes—and a foamy sort of syllabubbly chiffon scarf emerging from the neckline of the dress, which was cut like a schoolgirl's gym-frock. That now was what she wore, for she was the sort of woman that you looked first at the radiant clothes before you came face to face with her face. On her left hand she seemed to wear two wedding rings and an engagement ring and a keeper. She had fine plump hands. But the face was a mask, with long false lashes and, below the eyes, radiating black streaks that looked as if they had been done with a sharp knife dipped in cobbler's dye. The eyes, which were not unkind, moved almost audibly when they moved at all. It wasn't that we were disappointed in her, it was my awful feeling that she too had her dreams and that the pair of us did not fulfil them.

Her voice, I will confess, was a little shrill and she had, in so far as I could judge, a Lancashire way of speaking which is fine in its own way but you want to know English very well to keep up with it. To this day I can see her quite clearly, apart from the colours of the stripes in her blouse, and I remember her with interest and a great curiosity. I can even hear her talking—about her husband who was coming to Bundoran to join her. She was a fit rival for the mysterious Atlantic which was at that moment her background: oceans of woman, all waiting for daring young mariners.

But Eunan, like Bishop Berkeley, thought otherwise. He was already ten yards away and moving fast while I was preparing to squat beside her, even though squatting in a back-splint was a trick that took some rehearsing.

—My husband, she said, had a special sort of tandem bicycle built all to his own specifications. We frequently take trips on it.

At least that's what I thought she said. But what between the Lancashire accent and the state of confusion in which Eunan's retreat left me, I could have imagined the words: they didn't seem very likely. There he went, his arms stiff as logs, his trouser-bottoms halfways to his knees.

—What's wrong with your friend? she said. Was he short-taken?

She laughed fit to frighten the gulls and, since I couldn't think of anything to say and couldn't laugh with her, I fled. Her laughter followed me. My back-splint seemed to have slipped its moorings, but that also was imagination. Truskmore was pushing one jagged rocky shoulder out of the mist. Come and cover me, oh mist, hide me from that laughter, and hell run away with Eunan McAtavey who could at least have stood his ground until, with dignity, we retreated together. But when I came on him in the crowd by the dancing-floor he looked so hapless that I could find no word of reproach.

—An error of judgement, Eunan, I said, She looked all right from a distance.

—They all do.

The dancers were having the time of their lives. Nobody paid the least attention to us.

—That's the sort of woman, he said, that you're warned against in the catechism.

—You're from a different diocese, Eunan. The catechism where I came from never mentioned the likes of her.

—She was mentioned somewhere if it wasn't in the catechism.

We walked on by the freshwater spring and the Fairy Bridges and the four-cornered shelter in which, to my annoyance, there was a young couple holding hands and gazing out to sea: Head out to sea when on your lee the breakers you discern. Oh, adieu to all the billowy coasts.

We crossed Tullan Strand with its gulls and curlews, and crossed the sand-dunes and walked the long street to Lios na Mara and didn't swap a word all the way. Up in my room I opened my neglected books, took notebook and pencil and set to the reading: this was my business, I was a frost and a failure as a man of the world and, as a pimp, quite preposterous. He was so silent at lunch and again at high tea, ham salad, that I knew Miss Kerrigan and my mother thought we had had a row, but were too polite to say anything about it; and that night there was no moon and no Eunan.

The morning mist had dissolved into mizzling rain. He hadn't even told Miss Kerrigan that he was going. Without any feeling in her voice my mother said: I hope you weren't rude to him. He was so shy.

The lights around the hurdy-gurdies were bleary weeping eyes. The hobby-horses, riderless, went round a few times, then halted hopelessly, and their music stopped and there was no sound between the sea and the mountains but the boom-thump-boom of the palais. I wore a heavy black cloth coat and a black hat and looked, Ellen said, like a parish priest on the run. With a rain-coated girl on each arm I walked as far as the four-cornered shelter. The weather was telling us that the holidays were over and that everything came to an end.

—He ran away from us, Ellen said. He was afraid of the fairy women of Lisbellaw.

When I told them about the purple blonde on the clifftop they laughed for ten minutes, and went on laughing at the idea of Eunan, suitcase in hand, legging it back to the mountainy safety of the Vale of Dibbin. In the four-cornered shelter I profited by his absence and made gentle love to the two of them. Oh, it was all very harmless: running from one corner to another, grappling, kissing, with two girls who couldn't stop laughing; discovering that shy Madge was far and away the more ardent of the two. We walked back through rising wind that blew the clamour of the palais off towards Lough Melvin. The town was a long line of weeping lights. When we came as far as the hobby-horses, the music—although the animals were at rest—was playing about the old rustic bridge by the mill, and Ellen and Madge sang:

> But one day we parted in pain and regret,
> Our vows then we could not fulfill.

—Too true, Ellen said, We're off tomorrow.
—But you'll write, Madge said.
—And we'll meet again next year, Ellen said.
—Maybe, said Madge, you might come to see us in Lisbellaw.
Although I meant to write, I never did: Dublin and the nine, and other things, distracted me. The next year I wasn't in Bundoran; and although ten years later I passed briefly through Lisbellaw, there was another woman with me and I never even thought of Madge and Ellen. As I said, if it hadn't been for the ancient blonde on the green in Atlanta I'd never even have remembered Eunan.

A beautiful blonde girl sat in a chair and in the most queenly fashion allowed herself to be fitted with pink shoes. A serious youth, he couldn't have been more than eighteen, knelt at her feet and did the fitting. She was searching for a shoe of a colour that would match some detail in the dress she wore. Patiently the young fellow eased the dainty foot into shoe after shoe after shoe. We marvelled at his restraint.
—What, Gene said, is behind the American rape epidemic?
That had been a joke between us, not a very good one, ever since we had seen the question printed on the cover of a lurid magazine, and with it the picture of a man with billiard-ball eyes roping a buxom, and quite unconcerned, lady to a chair. We were still guessing at answers, and watching the young kneeling troubadour and the girl of the pink shoes, when Dolores returned. We drove back to my place. The aged blonde was gone from the green.

On that very day my mother was writing me a letter. That sort of coincidence is common. For instance, on a day in a college in Virginia when a student was asking me about a friend of mine, a singer, he, in Chicago, was mailing me his newest long-player.

My mother wrote:

Miss Kerrigan, whom you may recall, died recently and I went Bundoran to the funeral. May she rest in peace. She was a dear woman, albeit a little eccentric, and thought the world and all of you, and thought in her final doting days that you were a priest and wondered why you never came to see her. I always told her you were far away on the foreign missions and that the Jesuits were strict and didn't allow you home often. It wasn't much of a lie, and I feel that God and even the Jesuits would forgive me. She prayed for you every night. But who should be at the funeral only your companion of long ago, Eunan McAtavey, with his wife and nine children, a car-load of them. They seemed very happy. He was asking for you. He said he read everything you wrote, in newspapers and even in books.

On what dusty lovely Donegal roadway, walking home from school or Mass or market-day shopping, did he, or how did he, manage to tell a girl that he loved her?

They seemed very happy, she said. He was asking for me. He had read everything I had written. Ah well, his memory was better than mine. He couldn't very well explain to my mother and his wife why he ran, or thought he was running, from. What ever became, I wonder, of the fairy women of Lisbellaw?

ELM VALLEY VALERIE

One Saturday morning my Aunt Brigid said to me that she doubted if Valerie would ever marry that horrid Mr Craig from London. Twelve months previously my Uncle Owen, who lived up in the mountains and lilted, said that if Brigid came home from Philadelphia he would raise the roof. She had been 50 years almost in the United States. Owen meant that to celebrate her return he would add another storey to his long white farmhouse, a meeting-place for musicians in that part of the country. His own lilting or mouth music was part of the entertainment that went on there and it was told that, when he was a young fellow and going to the country dances, he had, because the fiddler fell ill, lilted all night at a dance to keep the dancers going.

My mother, who sang ballads, was very proud of that achievement of her brother's youth and told the story any time she had a chance. He was a tall man with a red moustache and a long bouncing stride. With a sharp knife and any old broken branch he could carve you nearly anything you'd mention from a primitive statue to a whistle that would play tunes. He did raise the roof, too, or he got two fiddlers and a melodeon player and a journeyman carpenter who played the flute and a plasterer who was a piper to help him to do it. Music, we are told, built the towers of Troy. Aunt Brigid did come home from Philadelphia. She was 68.

She taught a lot of us to play euchre which was her favourite card-game, as with Bret Harte's Heathen Chinee which I wish to remark and my language is plain. Her favourite delicacy was a sort of a grey soup frozen to semi-solidity and archipelagoed with slivers of dead and butchered chickens. When she had her own house in our town for a while every visitor calling to see her had to take a spoonful or two of the stuff which was supposed to do something for you. It made most people queasy. As for myself I grew to like it because I liked her and I'd do anything for a friend.

For her first three months in Ireland she lived with us. That's how I know that like the best generals on long-ago battlefields she owned a portable toilet which she delicately called a commode, an object of polished wood that I thought was a cabinet gramophone until, sneaking around one day when the house was empty, I opened it. When the news got around the neighbourhood, as it did, though not through me, its existence caused some comment, and neighbours visiting the house were always anxious, though they were too polite to say so, to sneak up and have a peep: when the owner was out, that is, and the object not in use. In our world in Ulster in those days nobody locked doors, or needed to.

—Valerie's aunt, she said to me, doesn't approve of the cinema.

My eyes were on *Allen's Latin Grammar, ante apud ad adversus circum circa citra cis.* My mind was in the murderous swamp with the *Master of Ballantrae* about whom I had been reading the night before until the fire crumbled and, with the rest of the house abed and with the creeps the story had given me, I'd been afraid to go out in the dark, to fill the scuttle. My heart was in the highlands ten miles from the town, chasing the wild deer and following the roe, and chatting up the American female cousin of a schoolfriend of mine who lived up there and cycled every day to school, twelve miles there and, of course, twelve miles back. The female cousin and her gold-toothed father were vacationing. It was the season for romance.

It was a sunny Saturday morning and three hours school were ahead of me, like a smoky hazardous tunnel. Aunt Brigid's voice came to me as it always did on Saturday mornings from the heart of some numinous cloud. But I had developed a knack of hearing and answering without really listening: what she said I more or less heard but it was always of something else I was thinking. She talked at speed and didn't much bother about responses. I said: That's a bit old-fashioned, isn't it, even for them?

—They're old-fashioned people. Of Huguenot origin, the father's people, weavers and Protestants who came to Ireland from France more than 200 years ago. Her mother was real French and very beautiful it was said. She met Valerie's father when she was a nurse at the western front and he was a young officer in the Irish Guards. They say that she had that grace and charm transmitted down the decades by women of her family softening the rather narrow-minded outlook which Valerie's father inherited from Puritan forebears.

Decades of the holy rosary I had heard about and, when the family knelt together for prayers, participated in. Decades of women was an idea that needed some grappling with. But what the hell and *ante apud ad adversus.* The colonel, Aunt Brigid, doesn't look to me as if anything ever had softened him.

Like a statue set in motion the retired colonel went through the town on his high green bicycle, three-speed gear on the cross-bar, salmon gear on his back. His knees went up and down like parts of machinery. He looked neither to right nor left. He seldom spoke. He nodded to the occasional person but made no distinctions in religion or social rank: he nodded just when he happened to notice somebody was there and he seldom noticed anybody. He looked much too old to be his daughter's father. She must then have been in her middle twenties and looked like all the world was lovely to men approaching or a little past the crisis of eighteen.

— She was reared in a château, Valerie's mother that is.

Château, *circum, circa, citra, cis,* didn't convey a lot to me, yet it was accepted that people who were reared in châteaux couldn't look or feel too easily at home in either of the town's two cinemas. One of them was a corrugated iron shed, painted red and called the Galaxy Kinema. To get into the other one you had to pass through the backyard of an hotel, the backyard being, in that transitional period of the world's history, half stableyard and half garage: so that above the music of the songs of the time, like Tiptoe through the Tulips and Sonny Boy, you heard the stamping of hooves and the thunderous backfiring of primitive engines. In the Galaxy Kinema the projector broke down every twenty minutes or so with such interesting regularity that a blank white screen was accepted as part of the programme and no longer even inspired obscenities in the wits who sat on hard wooden benches in what was aptly called the Pit. Once though, the machine clogged and the screen didn't go blank. Harry Carey, as the man with the badge, was left, gun in each hand, in the act of leaping from a two-storey hotel to crash, guns blazing, through the roof of a one-storey bank and so to interrupt a robbery. There he was like Mahomet's tomb for a good ten minutes or so before gravity resumed her reign, and some of the advice proffered to him from the Pit I can still remember.

In the picture-palace above the stable-garage breakdowns were less to be relied on and when they did happen a fat fiddler in a leather motoring-coat played music to while away the time. In the days of the silent film that same fat fiddler stood behind the screen and made noises that were called effects: like rattling thin sheets of tin to simulate the guns at the battle of Mons.

No!—châteaux on the splendid Loire or anywhere else had nothing to do with all that, and I had never seen Valerie in either of those places. But I saw her that Saturday morning, on my way to school and she smiled as she passed me by. She smiled much as her father nodded, as if vaguely aware that the world was out there somewhere. Except that, unlike her father, she was beautiful, a rather large woman, blonde hair down her back, eyes like lakes where regiments of guardsmen could drown, complexion all peaches and roses and cream, as God is my judge no other way to describe it. Like her father she went on a bicycle. Her bicycle always seemed to be too low for her and the thought of her thighs moving up and down under her navy pleated skirt used to send us all into frenzies of lust. A wickerwork basket on the handlebars overflowed with magazines. A wickerwork basket at the back of the saddle was all groceries and things. She smiled at all, perhaps she smiled all the time. A chemist in our town who had once won a prize for looking like Rudolf Valentino said she was the most beautiful woman in the world. An Irish setter trotted behind her, tongue out like the rest of us. The chemist said: She walks in beauty like the night.

Surely to Christ a man who looked like Rudolf Valentino should know what he was talking about. But not like the night, like the sun dancing on Easter Sunday morning. God, those secret thighs, that pleated skirt, those adorable flat-heeled yellow brogues. Up and down, up and down, oh to be a saddle of her bike. That morning, still shaken, I said to my pal Alec: Valerie smiled at me.

He said: Don't worry. There are funnier-looking men in the town than you.

That annoyed me so much that I never told him a word of all that Aunt Brigid had told me: among other things, that Valerie's mother had been a reputed beauty in the most aristocratic circles in Paris and that, like many French women, she made her own clothes. That pleated skirt. That sky-blue jacket. Oh to be her Irish setter scenting forever her fragrance down the wind: a big girl but beautiful.

We are by no means a mercenary people. Aunt Brigid, a small dainty woman with glass beads on the ruched bosom of her dark modest dress, had a lot of dollars with her when she came home from the States. She was, as I said, 68. We hoped she would be with us for years, moving restlessly as she did from one relative's house to that of another, lodging with people who were no relations, retiring for a while into a home for old ladies—they were all too old or ill or tiresome for her – finally setting up house on her own in the village of Drumgoole, about ten miles from the town. She had been for so long among strangers in a faraway land that she found it difficult to settle. We understood this and wished her joy and, I repeat, hoped that she would be with us for years to come. Yet if the Almighty in his infinite goodness deigned to call her to himself, saying well done thou good and faithful servant, well then the dollars were always there and wouldn't go to waste.

The Almighty deigned to do nothing of the sort. She lived to see 90 plus and to dispose elegantly of 99 per cent of her own dollars. One frosty Christmas morning when she was over 80 she broke both legs on the ice when walking to Mass. The bones knit again as if she had been eighteen. To her last hour she could sip and enjoy a glass of whiskey as large as herself for (as happens) she became smaller with age: and devil the effect the whiskey ever had on her except to give her eyes a sparkle and to set spots of girlish blushes on her cheeks. She was a great lovable lady and with great last in her and one Saturday morning she said rather sharply: Oh Mr Craig I hate you. Of course I can see that you have your disappointments and scruples. You're deeply in love with a young woman who has grown very dear to you. You see perfectly well that she doesn't care for you. She likes you just the way she should like a distant cousin, which you are.

—But marriage is a different matter. Then there's the house and the land, so much more spacious than what you're used to in London.

There was nobody to be seen in the room except Aunt Brigid and myself. Out in the scullery my mother was singing and rattling, taps flowing. Perhaps Craig was, like James Durie the Master of Ballantrae, here when he was there, dead and alive at the same time. If he had suddenly materialized, then slowly faded until nothing was left but his smile or scowl or look of perplexity or agonized love, then at least I'd have known what he looked like. By sight I knew the colonel's nod and Valerie's smile: but nothing at all about Craig, although his living most of the time in London, and the rest of the time in the large, remote, park-surrounded house that, shell for the pearl, contained the perfections, clothed and, ah God, unclothed, of Valerie, would rationally account for that.

At the far end of the town from the place where we lived you came to the crossroads called the Gusset. Why the Gusset, God knew: the place had nothing to do with tailoring or dressmaking, and I remember it only for two things. Once there by the light of a street lamp I saw a tiny bewildered lizard, the sort we called man-eaters and that were found only in bogs and marshes. By precocious zoologists it was commonly held that if one of them caught you with your mouth open it would jump down your throat and refuse to come out again. But that little lizard was lost, had crawled up a drain and through a grating or something and was clearly wondering how he had got there, how he was going to get back to where he came from. Three or four ragamuffins, mouths defensively closed, were on hands and knees poking him with twigs. Their silence added to the oddity of the scene.

Alec and myself rescued him, dropped him down the grating and hoped for the best. We never saw him again, and a lizard lost by lamplight has stayed in my memory as a symbol of loneliness and bewilderment.

The other thing about the Gusset was that one of the four roads that went out from the cross was a private road and led to the house that Valerie lived in. Groups of young aspiring men used to gather at the Gusset to see her cycling past. Or parade in the evenings as far up the private road as was possible which was what Alec and myself had been up to the night we rescued the lizard.

That road, surfaced with a rare sort of red gravel, served three big houses in all, Valerie's house being the biggest and the most remote from the ordinary ways of men. The gravel added an extra touch of fairyland enchantment. At least three stern notices reminded you that the place was private. The house stood on a slope, dark trees behind it, lawns in front sloping down to a bend of the river. Across the water bugles sounded from behind the grey walls of the barracks. It was a fitting place for an enchantress to live in and, naturally and alas, we knew it only from a distance. Like Valerie's smile and her father's nod it was remote. Anything could be going on in that fastness: Craig's despicable, semi-senile infatuation, the tyranny of a martinet of an aunt. In a way we knew so little about her beyond her smile: and the young women who went to the Loreto convent or the Protestant academy couldn't have helped us with information even if we had humiliated ourselves to the point of asking them. She hadn't ever been to convent or academy but to a finishing school in France and to another finishing school in the Isle of Wight. Twice finished, we thought, and oh God, who had had the pleasure. We were vague about what went on in finishing schools.

Bugles sounded across the river. Troops marched to Aldershot and India, and returned. Pipes played the Inniskilling Dragoon and Adieu to Belashanny. It was to be expected that Valerie might fall in love with an officer. Yet it was not a good Saturday morning, with autumn coming on and heavy rains, when Aunt Brigid said: The young officer has gone to see Miss Meredith, the aunt you know.

I hadn't known but I knew now as the Lord God, more or less, said, according to the kirk preacher, to the sinners pleading previous ignorance from the pit of hellfire. Very poorly I felt as I listened. Felt even sorry for Craig as against the unnamed officer. Craig was old and stiff and far down the field, but what hell chance had any of us against a man who, pipes playing, could lead men all the way to India.

—Miss Meredith, of course, is an awful snob. She hardly speaks to

Lady Cromlin because although Lady Cromlin married a lord she was a vulgar person to begin with. The captain . . .

So he was a full captain.

—. . . will need to have his credentials in order. He regards Valerie as a being from another and higher planet suddenly descended upon this weary and desolate world.

So did we all: he was no better than the rest of us.

—Miss Meredith is very stern. Her only true love was killed in the hunting field. She was never in a bus.

The rains passed and were followed by mellow light. One Saturday morning I read out loud: The trees are in their autumn beauty, the woodland paths are dry.

And read the poem all the way to the end: By what lake's edge or pool delight men's eyes when I awake some day to find they have flown away?

She listened to me with more attention than I had ever given to her and I had the decency to feel a little ashamed. With the tiniest of white lace handkerchiefs and the tip of the forefinger of her right hand she picked little drops of moisture from the corners of her eyes. For the first time I noticed that her face, though unwrinkled and bright as a pippin, was very small. On the wall above her where she sat in the corner between the table, at which she had just finished her breakfast, and my four shelves of books, there was a favourite picture of mine: seven highland cattle by a mountain river and, in the background, a great blue shoulder of mountain. My heart's in the highlands, my heart is not here.

—That's a beautiful poem, she said, and you read it very well. It would be lovely to see the lake where the swans were. You see I saw so much of America and so little of Ireland. I never even saw Dublin.

She sipped at another cup of tea. My mother had gone out to somebody's funeral and from the high steeple the dead bell was tolling over the town. The book of poems I closed and went on reading to myself what J. B. Priestley had written about Angel Pavement. Her voice was high up and faraway as if she had taken wings and flown, a tiny black bird glistening with beads, to the top of that blue mountain.

—Dr Haughton, she said or seemed to me to say, has always congratulated Valerie on the roses in her cheeks. But the roses, I fear, may soon be faded. Miss Meredith didn't take to the captain and he thought Miss Meredith was like something out of Charles Dickens or Mrs Henry Wood.

Dickens I knew all about and as for Mrs Henry Wood, well a

travelling company had once brought East Lynne all the way to the drinking and gambling den known as the Hall of the Irish National Foresters, a friendly and benevolent society. Not one of them would ever have been sober enough to recognize a forest if it came at him like Birnam Wood. Dead, dead and never called me mother. That was East Lynne for you.

—Valerie's trouble for a whole week has been to get away from Craig so as to be able to see the captain in secret. One thundery evening she even went to bed with her nightdress on over her clothes, and later slipped out to meet him and got caught in a downpour and drenched.

—All the ladies, Aunt Bee assured me, love a uniform because it makes a man look more like a man.

In so far as J. B. Priestley would allow me, I thought: The hell with Valerie and the gallant captain, their world is not for me, not for us, not for decrepit Craig whoever or wherever he is.

That morning, anyway, my heart was not so much in the highlands as far out on the heaving billow. Vacationing was ended and the grey-eyed, sylph-like cousin of my mountainy schoolfriend had taken ship with her father at Cobh and by that moment must be far beyond the reach of those south-western Irish headlands that stretch out to welcome or to say farewell. In those days of reverie it wasn't all that easy to know exactly who or what one was in love with.

—But love at first sight, said Aunt Brigid, is lightning as the French say. The captain squared up his shoulders in a gesture well known to his fellow-officers and faced up to Miss Meredith. But to no avail. Unalterable hostility. And the minister's daughter has always encouraged her to strike out and make a career for herself. And the inevitable has happened.

At that dramatic moment my eyes and some portion of my mind turned from *Angel Pavement* to Aunt Bee and the wild river, the highland cattle, the blue mountain.

—Valerie, she said, has turned her back on the lot of them and flown to Belgium to distant relatives of her mother.

Well that was that, and it wasn't likely or possible that Alec or myself or the throng who waited with little hope at the crossroads of the Gusset would follow her to brave the opposition of every smiling, scented, bowing-and-scraping man among the Belgians. She was further away than the girl tossing on the Atlantic billow. It never occurred to me that in Belgium or anywhere else there could be a woman the equal of Valerie, that Belgian men might have eyes for other visions. We had lost her forever: the way you see a beautiful girl in a city bus, and you look at her and she looks at you and your eyes meet for a moment, and you know you will never see her again. *Allen's Latin Grammar* told me that pity, remember and forget govern the genitive set. The last word I suppose, was stuck in to make an easily memorizable rhyme. Allen worked that way.

All very wise for my age, except that as, on that blessed morning, I walked to school for a new and my last term she rode her bicycle right under my bows when I was crossing John Street and nerving my thighs and lungs for the steep ascent, under high spires, of Church Hill. She was as large as life, as large and beautiful as herself. No less than three red setters, one of them little more than a pup, tongues out, enjoying the morning as dogs do, trotted behind her. The basket before her overflowed with magazines. The basket behind her was a bright mound of oranges and grapefruit held in place by a sort of netting. She smiled as she passed me by, but I doubt if she saw me. She wore a tweed suit and flat, sensible, expensive, brown shoes. The saddle as always was too low for her. Her splendid knees, one of them quite bare, rotated within easy reach of my hand: making the same motion as the knees of her father, or of any cyclist, made. But it never seemed the same.

One thing was certain: she had not flown to Belgium. Aunt Bee was wrong. Aunt Bee, as Humphrey Bogart might have said, was misinformed. Could it be that Aunt Bee was doting or just clean crazy? She talked too much about euchre and boardwalks in Atlantic City. She was old. All that whiskey. That queasy frozen soup with the bits of chicken in it. That commode which might be all very well on a battlefield, but in a civilized house in a town in Ulster, Ireland? Then another returned American had told my Uncle Owen that there was no part of the States that at some time of the year didn't get too hot, and the sun could have affected Aunt Bee's brain.

Then it dawned on me—so simply that I didn't speak about the matter for a considerable time. The shock of seeing Valerie, followed by the steep slope of Church Hill where the housewives then used to throw the dishwater out the front door into what we called the vennel—and it behoved a man to walk warily—all these may have helped to rouse me from a long dream. The first thing I saw was a Chinese junk, sail spread over a still blue pool. It was on the cover of a missionary magazine that Aunt Brigid read and kept carefully stacked up on a low wide windowsill in her house in Drumgoole. Of course it should have occurred to me to wonder how Aunt Brigid knew so much about Valerie and her people: my mother never mentioned them. But then Aunt Brigid was a travelled woman who would know about such exotics, and she could have heard it all from some knowing person in

Drumgoole: and anyway I hadn't genuinely been listening, I had been thinking of Valerie on her bicycle, the maiden on her throne, boys, would be a maiden still, basket fore, basket aft, red setters trotting behind her, their tongues lolling. I had been thinking of and having my dream of fair women including the American vacationer in the Mountfield mountains, and Valerie and herself between them were, in that bemused season, all the women in the world.

So one free day Alec and myself cycled to Drumgoole and while Alec in the orchard behind the house made talk with Aunt Brigid—he was always a great man for chatting up the ladies, young and old—I had my secret consultation with the files of the magazine. There they all were in the serial story by a gentle sentimental lady novelist: old Craig and the stern Miss Meredith and even a governess called Miss Dundon, and the army officer and his friends who knew him in the squaring of his shoulders, and quite another Valerie who was known as Valerie of Elm Valley which was where she lived, somewhere in the County Cork. It was even another army. And in the latest instalment but one Valerie had run away to Belgium.

All there, and all about somebody else who had never existed except in the imagination of the novelist, and for Aunt Bee and a thousand other readers. But then never had my Valerie existed except in my imagination: and to this day I am never certain as to the degree in which Aunt Bee's mind and my own had mingled. Some of the time we may have been thinking of the same woman. There was that lost lizard blinded by a light high-up, far away and false.

In a mission-shop or Catholic Repository beside our parish church I took to buying the magazine and followed the story to its happy ending. And so we may leave Valerie. In a few days she will have changed her name. But she will always be Valerie of Elm Valley to her husband and to all those who love her.

By which time one Valerie was to me as real as the other. Once only did I speak to either of them. One day fishing along the Drumragh, at a place where the river makes a sweeping triple bend and is crossed by a decrepit but picturesque wooden footbridge, I came on a parked bicycle with two baskets, three barking but friendly red setters, and a beauty seated before an easel and painting. She asked me the name of the place. She wasn't, since she was of the garrison, too familiar with the countryside and the local names. We didn't have a lot to say to each other. She did ask me if I'd had any luck on the river and, as it happened, I hadn't. She seemed to be a practical sort of person and, in so far as I knew the difference, she painted well and she really was, as the man who looked like Rudolf Valentino said, the most beautiful woman in the world even if she was big. She was big, as the Orange song about the Sash me father wore almost says, but she was beautiful and her colours they were fine.

It was the man who looked like Valentino who years later told me that she had married into the Guards. He had kept his hair and the Valentino hairstyle. He was more courageous than another man I knew who won a prize for looking like Charles Laughton—in a prank that began as a dare in a pub—but who afterwards panicked and for the rest of his life took refuge behind a huge bushranger's beard.

—A high-ranking officer in the Coldstreams, Valentino told me. *Cor ad cor loquitur.* But then the Guards are not what they used to be, the empire's gone, pharmacy is in a decline and even the Catholic church is weak at the knees. But I saw her a year ago walking in the Haymarket in London, and she's lovelier now than she was then. She's not even so big. Women with style like that improve with the years.

As for Aunt Brigid, she finished all her whiskey and dollars and did in the end die, which was unusual for her. She was buried in a graveyard on a mountain slope three miles from Drumgoole, and in the parish where she and my mother and Owen the Lilter and the rest of them came from. And buried on the worst day God ever sent: low clouds, drizzle, and a north-east wind would skin an otter. There was a second cousin of mine at the funeral who, when she died, was on a tanker in the Persian Gulf. The company flew him back to pay his respects which was decent of the company. But he neglected to dress for the occasion and there he stood in a tropical suit, shuddering, in a church porch that was cold as a dungeon.

We took him from the churchyard gate and across the road to the public-house and bought him hot whiskey and borrowed for him a topcoat and did our best to keep the life in him. He was the coldest man I ever saw at an Irish funeral.

NEAR BANBRIDGE TOWN

The buffet on the central platform at Portadown where he changes trains always reminds him of the bridge of a ship. Unlike the bridge of a ship it is a great place for meeting people. Nobody, oddly enough, in it at the moment, but they'll come. Trains meet here, people change trains and meet. In 30 years he has passed this way more times than he can remember. Although not now for some years. Yet this very morning in a pub in Dublin at the office breaking-out Christmas party he has said, rather loudly so as to be heard above the unholy noise, that often as he has passed through Portadown, he has never once met a man who came from Portadown.

Reginald with the RAF moustache and the tweeds that will last for ever has just said that for the New Year he will give up smoking: Keep the nostrils clean, Lisney dear fellow, so as in the office to brighten the dull day by smelling the little girls.

In the bank the little girls wear not exactly a uniform, but blouses and skirts of the same colours, yellow for blouses brown for skirts. They look and smell very good. Girls from the best families get jobs in banks, and from the best schools. In the pub for the Christmas party they wear coats of many colours, drink a little more than usual and have flushed faces. Most of the men who are interested in such things know which of them do and which of them don't.

Reggie also says, as he and Lisney and Gubbins huddle in a corner as far as they can from the chaos, that in Ireland it is not commonly possible to have intercourse outside marriage. Lisney says that from his own experience he can state that that is horse-shit. Also that Gubbins here, blond and modest and three years married, has in one fortnight or fourteen days had intercourse with twelve different women not including his lady wife: three of them from the bank, one of them actually taken in the strongroom during business hours with Lisney on sentry-go to prevent interruption; two school-teachers, one fashion model, one housewife, one cinema usherette, one hotel barmaid, one college student, one lady doctor and one civil servant. Reggie admires the stamina of Gubbins and his social adaptability.

—But Gubbins, he says, you must admit that this is most unusual. You struck a pocket.

Gubbins smiles modestly but more to himself than to anybody else and goes on drinking—nourishing stout only. At this moment the six men from the Guinness ships that ferry the stuff to Liverpool come in, invading a room customarily frequented only by bank officials: but hell, it's Christmas Eve. They are big men with blue jerseys, and Guinness written in red on their chests. After a while they begin to sing very loudly: Roll out the barrel.

Reggie says, shouting to be heard: I never could stand chappies who talked shop in pubs.

In a semi-lull in the singing Lisney says that often as he has passed through Portadown he has never met a man who came from Portadown. One of the Guinness men, the biggest and most jovial and with a red moustache, says: I came from Portadown and what's more I'm not going back.

Much laughter. The Guinness men sing: Roll along, covered wagon, roll along.

The voices of the girls become more and more shrill. It is Christmas Eve in the morning. Lisney is thinking of the road ahead of him to his mother and sister in the north-west. Reggie has also recorded, on the tape-recorder in the cash-office, a rallentando of blurts prefacing it with a sennet sounded on a trumpet made from a sheet of stiff ledger paper.

The buffet is still empty except for himself and a white-coated girl behind the counter, and a stout, red-faced grey-haired, bespectacled lady, also white-coated whom, from once, often passing this way he remembers. They talk about the weather and Christmas. She says she hasn't seen him in a long time. She says the next train in won't be here for fifteen minutes. So he bites on the last of his whiskey, belts up his overcoat, says he'll walk the town for twenty minutes, ten away from the station, ten back. His own train isn't due for half an hour.

Near Banbridge town, he hums as he walks down a puddled narrow street of small brown houses, in the County Down one morning last July.

The River Bann is out there somewhere in the darkness, moving sluggishly through marsh and inert meadow, unwilling to lose itself even for a time in the big lake. Banbridge is to the south-east there and the young fellow in the song meeting on a July morning with the Star of the County Down, that sweet colleen, as she tripped down a boreen green and smiled as she passed him by. Every Ulster song should be like that one: love and love and more love and bouncing rustic beauties and none of this shit, turgid as the mud of the Bann marshes, about dying for Ireland or about King Billy on a white horse riding for ever across the River Boyne. She had a nice brown eye and a look so shy and a smile like the sun in June, and when her eye she'd roll she'd coax on me soul a spud from a hungry pig.

Holly and Christmas candles in fanlights and front windows, and here's the main street and lights and bunting for the festive season as we call it, and here's a Chinese restaurant and what did a Chinaman ever do to end up in Portadown? After the warmth of his morning's drink he could do full justice to Roseanne McCann from the banks of the Bann, she's the Star of the County Down. A spud for a hungry pig. He stops to look over a stone bridge but the water is too dark and too far away to teach him anything. No passer-by speaks to him. A dour town, a junction, he has only met one man ever who came from here and he wasn't coming back and was singing: Roll along covered wagon.

Do not use this lavatory while train is standing in station, and the wits would scribble underneath that: Except at Portadown. Yet the first man to make that joke was probably a Portadowner like all Aberdonian jokes are made by Aberdonians. He's back on the platform to the eternal smell of salt herring, and another drink and God send something in the way of amusements on the next train: She looked so sweet from her two bare feet to the crown of her nut-brown hair. Roll along covered wagon, roll along.

The buffet is still empty, even the girl with the white coat has temporarily vanished. But shadowy people are gathering on the platform around the buffet, on the two platforms across the tracks, wearily depositing parcels and suitcases, standing like statues or pacing up and down. The stout lady says that, as you would expect with the season of the year, the trains are running late. He sits on a stool and hums to himself about covered wagons and says to the stout lady: You know the street I lived on at home then led up to the co-operative creamery. It's closed now. Everything goes into a giant milk factory on the river below the town. Articulated trucks go round the country picking up the cans of milk from the farmers. But when I was a boy our road was loud and musical all morning with horse-hooves, cart-wheels, jingling silvery cans, farmboys shouting and even singing. They were great fellows for singing. There was one big chap with the biggest ears I've ever seen and a big mouth gone awry and a wet lip. The ears stuck out. He'd sit on the edge of the cart at the horse's rump, his feet trailing the ground, and sing: Rowl along discovered wagon, rowl along. To the birling of the wheels I'll sing me song. City ladies may be fine but give me Roseanne Devine, rowl along discovered wagon, rowl along. Roseanne Devine was a very bright girl, indeed, friendly with town and country. I often wondered afterwards what sort of a notion your man had of the wild west and the Oregon trail and city ladies and all that. And who in hell discovered the wagon.

The stout lady polishes glasses and listens to him patiently. The coffee cups are ready for the rush. She says: I knew Roseanne Devine. I was in the buffet in your town for two years. She was never out of the station. She met every train, She was hell for the soldiers. Somebody told me she was still alive.

—We should hope so.

He raises his glass: To Roseanne Devine and all the golden girls.

They laugh together. She's a jolly old lady. He wonders should he tell her about Reginald and Gubbins and the twelve city ladies in Dublin in fourteen days, one golden girl in the strong-room, and exclusive of the lady wife. The roar of an incoming train prevents him, which is perhaps just as well. She may not be all that jolly. As the crowd invades he retreats to a corner, secure with elbow on the counter, back to the wall, a post from which he can study the style. The white-coated girl is back and two more of the same with her. The gabble of voices, male and female, particularly female, is delightful, oh human beings were a great invention: cups rattling, steam rising, voices calling for whiskey and coffee and gin and vodka and brandy itself, it's Christmastime in Ireland and nearly everywhere else. A plaster Santa Claus, high on a bracket and up to the hips in holly, looks down on the fun.

The buffet is in two parts, one mob here, another, five paces away, over there: and looking across the two counters and between two white-coated auxiliary girls—one of them has fine shoulders—he sure as Jesus sees Lady Bob in all his glory, bright as a peacock and hasn't aged an hour since last seen ten years ago. And with him is Trooper O'Neill of the North-West Mounted Police, the Mounties always get their man. Let me, unnoticed here, just look at them, let me love them as long ago and always, let me begin with remembering the time when Trooper O'Neill and myself almost became Christian Brothers. This was how that happened. Almost happened.

Too late, though, for remembrance of things past. The trooper has spotted me and raised his right arm. Even at five paces I can't hear him with the din but I know he's shouting: Jim Lisney, Jim Lisney come over here.

Over and around he goes. It's not all that easy. But old friends are old friends and, for their sakes, barriers must be broken and strangers jostled. Glass in hand, out one door of the buffet, through the waiting—

standing or pacing—shadows on the cold central platform, then in through the other door.

—Jim Lisney, Jim Lisney, says Trooper O'Neill, by God it's good to see you. Where, old sod, have you been all these years?

—Dublin.

—All those years in Dublin?

The trooper knows damned well that he has been all those years in Dublin, but what do old friends say to each other when, after long severance, they come together again? The trooper still parts his hair up the middle as he did long ago in honour and admiration of Dixie Dean who was, at that time, centre-forward for Everton. The trooper, without any obvious effort, could then give you like a song the status, scoring averages, points, positions on the League table, hopes for Wembley Stadium and the English Cup, past history and prospects of every team in every division.

—Home for Christmas, Jim? God, we'll have a great time. The old days. What are you drinking, man?

—I'm going.

—Go harder. And further. And fare better.

Reinforcements are rushed up, airborne over the heads of the first line at the counter. Lady Bob has a lime and soda.

—Crippen's dead, says Trooper O'Neill. You'll be sorry to hear.

—I heard. I must have one of the last letters he wrote.

Under a light grey overcoat, tightened at the back with a bit of a belt and a button, Lady Bob, to Lisney's amazement, is wearing a white suit. For a white Christmas. Also a blossoming pure-silk cravat. His teeth glisten. They always did. His auburn toupee might have cost hundreds. And make-up, and rings on his fingers, and bangles on his wrists, and ear-rings and a necklace. Long ago he wouldn't have dared, not even in a garrison town that was tolerant about such matters, about every matter.

—We're the commissariat, says the trooper. What would old Crippen, rest his soul, have called us?

—*Pabulatores.*

—That's it. You took the word out of my mouth. Jim, you were always a hoor for the Latin. We've two women in the guard's van.

—Hostages. Bob, I'm shocked.

—Oh, James Lisney.

A gentle smile, sweet and sad, from Bob, a bellow of laughter from the trooper: Jim, you're a hoor in your heart. The ladies are old friends. One is anyway. Sadie Crawford. Fresh from Soho. She wouldn't face out with the crowds on the platform. And the guard's van is so warm and comfy.

So we're carrying back the booze and sandwiches. Give us a hand. Be with us in the van. It's the only way to travel.

—Sadie Crawford, he says, and Soho. The connection puzzles me.

But the trooper isn't listening. He has burst like a rugby forward through the ranks at the counter and is reaching back parcels and bottles to Lady Bob. When he looks around, the gold rims of his small-lensed egg-shaped spectacles positively sparkle. He is a big man bundled into a bright tweed overcoat. He is an enormous egg, dyed multi-coloured for a Gargantuan Easter and balancing on its end without aid of egg cup. Lisney moves in to help, to fetch and carry, Lady Bob isn't at his or her best in the loose scrum, even if the contiguity might be gratifying. He relays some of the provender back to Lady Bob. Around them the sound is as of the ocean, drink is being gulped down or spilled in memory of the stable of Bethlehem, angels we have heard on high sweetly singing o'er the plain. Sadie Crawford and Soho, what in the name of? But Lisney is really remembering Crippen, who is dead, and Crippen was not, needless to say, his real name.

The primary school then was a two-storeyed granite building on the top of a hill above the playground and tennis-courts and gardens and orchards; and all above the town. Stuck on to it, a three-storeyed house in which the Brothers lived and prayed and suffered. Behind it an ell-shaped modern effort of corrugated iron, lined with wooden panelling and a sort of asbestos, the secondary school, known, until it was pulled down and replaced, as the new school. The playground was vast and triangular, the base towards the town, apex pointing upwards, towards and almost reaching the two schools.

Up that triangle on a fine day in May comes, siren screaming, a police car crowded with men, some in uniform, some in plain clothes, of the local flying-squad. One lieutenant stands on one foot on the running board, prepared to leap and run into battle the moment the car slows to a moderate 50. His pistol is in his left hand, with his right he holds on to the screaming automobile.

Crippen is coming down the four steps from one of the two doors of the secondary school. He wears a pepper-and-salt tweed jacket, an open-necked white shirt and grey flannels which, as is his wont, are hoisted a little higher than is customary above his ankles. Blue socks are visible. He carries a solid brown suitcase full of the books he uses in class. His hair is closely cropped. His face is lean, suntanned, the eyes blue, boyish and excessively intelligent. He halts in dismay and attempts to run back up the steps and regain the refuge of the secondary school. Too late, alas, too late. He is surrounded at gunpoint, frisked and handcuffed. His suitcase is searched for phials of poison. Three are found. As well as Latin he also teaches chemistry. He is taken away. He doesn't struggle. The scream of the siren drops towards the heart of the town.

Nothing of this ever happened. It was all the work of the school fantasist, a man called Gordon, of infinite wit and drollery, inventor of nicknames, the more unlikely the better but with somewhere a little touch of half-zany reason in the choice. It was, anyway, a great town for nicknames and Gordon's inventions passed on from generation to generation to be used by students who never knew how or why they had been invented, or by whom.

Two of the nicknames walk there before me bearing beer and whiskey and sandwiches to two women, Sadie Crawford and A. N. Other, in the guard's van. Trooper O'Neill out of a once-popular novel of the north-west, the great lone hand, author George Goodchild. Lady Bob is quite simply Lady Bob. Apart from chemistry, which includes poisons, and a quiet demeanour, the man called Crippen had little resemblance to his great original.

There are greyhounds in the guard's van but they are, mercifully, muzzled and coralled in boxes and looking out through bars. The proper way to keep them. He has never liked greyhounds. They're not real dogs. They snap. They eat steak and drink brandy and take drugs. They lose your money. In the boxes they whine and patter on delicate feet. Sadie is not to be seen nor is the guard. But a red-headed boy sits in a wheelchair or, at any rate, he sees the back of the head of a red-headed boy, for the wheelchair, to one side of a mountain of bags and parcels, is facing the other way. Then the occupant of the machine, with a twist and a twirl, expertly wheels it around, and it isn't a boy at all but a young woman with a bony boyish face, glistening short curled hair that no treatment could ever straighten, some forehead freckles, bright blue eyes that leap out to meet the stranger and, he has to admit it near Banbridge town, she is very very beautiful. He doesn't know who she is. He can't recall anyone in his town who looked in the least like her, so that he can't have known her father or mother or aunts or uncles. She says: Sadie's in the ladies.

—That's as it should be, says the trooper. Sadie is a lady. And also this is Portadown.

And he sings: Gentlemen will please refrain from passing water while the train is stationary at the station platform.

—But ladies, he says, are different. And so is Portadown. Here, help me Jim, and Bob the Lady and Joan the Boy.

It is the only introduction they get but they are immediately and happily shoulder-to-shoulder as bottles and sandwiches and plastic glasses are laid out on a newspaper tablecloth on the top of a packing-case. Her arms are bare, the elbows dimpled. She wears denims and a white tee-shirt and written in crimson across small pointed breasts: Love my dog.

It is cosily warm in the van, happily cluttered with parcels of all shapes and sizes, Christmas parcels, a living-room in a house used by a large family when somebody has decided to tidy the place and, halfways along, given up in despair. He says: All we need is a Christmas tree.

—We have one in the corner, draped in brown paper.

Hip-bones and shoulders brush together as they help to spread the banquet.

—Welcome stranger, she says, and a happy Christmas.

It is a clear resonant voice with no accent that comes from his part of the country. She smiled as she passed me by. She is very very very beautiful. And she rolled each note from a lily-white throat.

There were two lovely girls in the town when Lisney studied under Crippen. There were many more than two but those two were particularly notable. One was called Madge and the other Dorrie. Madge had flaming red hair, was a tall, loose-limbed, overpowering girl. She was older than himself and had a regular boyfriend of her own age whom she afterwards happily married. But once he had spent two hours kissing her, or being kissed by her, in the darkness of a mild late September, on a wooden footbridge over a brawling mountain stream that came down to join the river a mile outside the town: and those two hours had been better than summer holidays and omnibus paribus, as good as anything that had ever happened to him since.

On the same evening and 40 yards away, and against a five-barred gate in another part of the happy forest, Gordon the Fantasy Man was playing fun and games with Dorrie, a small, plump brunette and very forward. One move in the games was that she snatched from his breast-pocket a Waterman fountain-pen, a present from an American uncle, which he valued more than life itself or honour even, and ran laughing a little way from him and then asked him to find the pen. Correctly he guessed where she had hidden it—Gordon was always ahead of the field and Dorrie was enticing—and lingeringly retrieved it.

She, also, was older than Gordon and had a regular boyfriend of her own age whom she afterwards happily married.

Oh, red Madge and dark Dorrie and Gordon of the Nicknames and a lost happy September, and he thinks of them now when he thinks of

Crippen because one evening Dorrie said to him and Trooper O'Neill and Gordon and the Dead Man McCartney, so-called because he looked like Buster Keaton, that Crippen would be the handsomest man in the town if he would only let his trousers down.

Much coarse laughter and Dorrie even blushed.

She meant merely that he should relax his gallases, braces or suspenders, and cover his ankles. He was, indeed, a very handsome man, clean, clean-living, clean-spoken, just and fair to all mankind, learned and capable of passing on some little of his learning to others: and not in the least like the sad Englishman who dosed the wife and was captured by cable. He lived and died a bachelor and was not thus exposed to the temptations that bedevilled his namesake.

The train is under way. Sadie has returned. She is as brilliant as Lady Bob who in the warmth of the guard's van has taken off his overcoat, folded it carefully, placed it on newspaper on top of one of the barred wooden cells which encloses a malevolent-looking black bitch. No guard is yet to be seen. In a remote corner of the van and behind a mountain-range of parcels two young rug-headed fellows in brown coats are sipping glasses of stout and sorting letters into a rack.

Lady Bob, overcoatless, is now seen to wear, like a matador, a black silk bellyband holding in place, if they need any holding, those skint-tight white pants. Cravatless, and the cravat is laid to rest on top of the overcoat, he displays a short-sleeved tartan shirt, with low, curved not pointed, cleavage, and a smooth white chest, hairless by nature or depilation. Praised be to the Lord of Hosts, but my town has never looked back since the day when, as Gordon used to say, one of the Lyons married into the English royal family. For there was then in the town a clan that went by the name of Lyon, and the old people, who should know about such things, used to say that there were always five generations of the Lyons living at the same time. So to Sadie, by way of greeting and after some years, he says: Who won the war?

And embraces her and kisses both her powdered cheeks.

And Sadie answers: Who but the Lyons?

For a stroller in the dark, on lovers' lanes around the town and in the years between the two wars, might for no reason except hellery or the love of life cry out that question, and be thus answered by some other anonymous voice. To Joan the Boy, Sadie explains: There were so many of them, you see, in the British army and once on a time at the western front. We used to say they won the war. Trust you to remember that, Jim Lisney.

—Old Jamie, the great-grandfather was, they said, in the house in an armchair, stuffed. Your brother, Mick, told me that.

—But once a week, Jim Lisney, he was allowed up and out to walk the greyhounds.

In the noisy swaying van they hold on to each other and laugh at the fantasy, and Lisney nibbles her ear and is conscious that though she has passed 50, her waist and hips are as firm as good rubber. She wears a wine-coloured blazer with white military-style piping. And a dark blue shirt with tartan top, not a blouse. And carries a white plastic shopping-bag ornamented with an enormous brimstone butterfly, also plastic. She has jet-black bobbed hair in memory of Jessie Mathews or Claudette Colbert or somebody, and a wide red mouth and large gentle brown eyes like the Star of the County Down, and a mole with two hairs to the left of her mouth. The singer of the love song said nothing about moles. And a smile like the sun in June.

—And one day Freddy Lyon let me look at the ferret he used to catch all the rabbits with.

When the trap was opened it came out of the dirty wooden box, itself coloured a dirty cream that was almost grey, sinuous as a snake and like a snake, also, in that it didn't seem to have legs or even feet. Not a ferret but a stoat—we don't have true ferrets in Ireland—and we called this monster by the odd name of whitthrit. It looked at nobody. It flowed and looped around again and went back into the box, and Freddy dropped the trap. He said: Nothing here for him to do on that bare ground. They're very intelligent.

He was sitting on the mounting-block, used no longer, never to be used again, at the corner of the smithy, at the entrance to the Back Alley. A thin cadaverous man, never quite shaven, shabby grey jacket, peaked cap, a quite incongruous pair of professorial horn-rimmed spectacles: and very gentle. He had soldiered for a while but the health caught up on him. He hunted with his friend, the ferret, genuinely his friend, they understood each other. Expertly he fished the rivers and lakes, pitying the fish, but food was food. Then he died. He could at times be a philosopher. One day, seated on the mounting block, hands joined, fingers knit between his knees, he said: Jim Lisney, if you don't eat you starve, if you don't shite you bust.

He tells this to Sadie and to Trooper O'Neill but only to them. Screams and roars of laughter in the rocking guard's van. Lady Bob and Joan the Boy are spreading the repast on a shiny blue trunk belonging to somebody who is travelling in more orthodox fashion. Sadie says: The day of Freddy's funeral I was coming out of the church behind two old dames from Fountain Lane. All glorious in black shawls. And scattering holy water over each other. And one of them says, Jesus knows, Maggie, that's the first of the Lyons ever died.

A bellow from Trooper O'Neill, red-coated hero of the white, northwest, the Mounties always get their man. From behind a tree Nelson Eddy bellows: When I'm calling you, hoo-hoo-hoo, hoo-hoo-hoo-hoo-hoo. The boom of the train means that they are going through a tunnel, there's only one on this line, or under a long long bridge of which there are several, going home for a holy Christmas, burrowing deeply into the brown earth that nourished them. A poet he knows in Dublin, a big, gentle, uncouth, splayfooted man touched by God, tells him how he went home for last Christmas, a drink here, a drink there, several (he said several) drinks at Amiens Street Station, seven drinks with old friends at Dundalk, nine drinks with older friends in the roadside pub by oil-lamplight at Blackhorse Halt, then out along the lonely road, suitcase in hand, running at the hills like a horse that knows he's nearing home, like a horse, he said.

The beauty of the guard's van is that you're not haunted by reflections from any windows, ghosts, including your own, travelling with you, bending forwards, leaning back, talking without sound, gesturing, mocking, mimicking. The van is a sealed refuge, a little world apart.

—In that family, Lisney remembers, they had a slew of grandfathers. They had to have or they couldn't all have been there. When I was ten I played street football with Jack and Jimmy Lyon, two little leprechauns even for their age. One day it rained. And Jack and Jimmy said: We'd bring you into the house to play only our oul granda's in and he's crabbed.

—We peeped in through a kitchen window and there he was, a wee man with a beard and a stick, hunched in a low armchair, smoking and spitting.

The trooper says that there was one of the same in every house the Lyons lived in.

The preliminary bombardment eases. Through drifting smoke, with bayonets threatening, a thousand Lyons, little boys and pallid hunters and bearded spitting grandsires with sticks, advance to beat the Germans. These all were part of the furniture of my boyhood. Mons, Mons, Mons, the word keeps ringing like a bell.

—And one day, Sadie, I saw Jack and Jimmy take money out of their mother's purse. To steal money from your mother, I thought, was a bad thing.

—Since then, Jim Lisney, I'd say that you've taken a lot that didn't belong to you or your mother.

—Hoo—hoo—hoo. Hoo—hoo—hoo—hoo—hoo—hoohoo.

—But I'd no scruple helping to eat the proceeds when he spent it in Hop McConnell's sweetie shop.

—My dear father, says Lady Bob.

And Lisney is momentarily but not seriously embarrassed by remembering that Hop McConnell was, indeed, the dear father of Lady Bob, and always a little inclined, as he hopped, to wonder about the son that he and his sainted, slender, Bible-reading wife had brought into the world.

—It was Gordon made us all laugh, Sadie says, when Miss Bowes-Lyon, a commoner, married King George. He said the Lyons were getting up in the world.

It was Gordon said this and Gordon said that and then Gordon is with them in the guard's van, is, in fact, the guard and Lisney is again embarrassed because he should have remembered that after the war Gordon took a job on the railways. We cut the links that bind us or they rust and snap of their own accord. People live on in our memory as they once were. We forget they are living differently now, other times, other places. We even forget that they are dead.

Sleep and philosophy and Christmas Eve are overtaking me.

But Gordon's handgrip is strong and friendly and reassuring. Hands don't change. He says: Jim Lisney, I thought you knew.

The clean-cut face is the same, the sharp exact words. Lisney says that he did know, he had heard: But then I got mixed-up, began to think you never came home again.

—Thinking all the time of himself, Sadie says. He hasn't come up from Dublin in years.

—No Jim, Gordon says, it was Dead Man McCartney never came home. Joined the Palestine police. Went East after that and married a Chinawoman. Lucky man.

Sadie says that it's not true, that Anna May Wong said so. They laugh, even Joan the Boy and Lady Bob, at the hoary joke. They sit to eat and drink. There are two low stools and two tip-up seats on the side of the van, and several boxes, and the two rug-headed stout-sipping sorters join them. Joan the Boy sits down on Gordon's left knee. To Lisney's slight annoyance. Now, as then, Gordon has the way with him, and Gordon, further to increase the annoyance, says: The other knee, Tilly daughter.

She changes her seat to the right knee. Gordon explains: You could sit all night on that knee and it would do nothing for me. Or you. I think.

And Lisney remembers that he had heard that Gordon had lost a leg. He says: Tilly?

She asks him: What is it, stranger?

—Joan?

—Tilly's my name, dear handsome stranger.

Sadie says: She acted in a play. In armour and a sword. A girl would need them nowadays.

Gordon asks: In Soho, Sadie?

—Anywhere. With the likes of you and Jim Lisney groping around.

Gordon's right hand is gently stroking a thigh of Joan the Boy. Lisney is no longer glad to see Gordon again and also he knows now where he saw the Boy before, except that it wasn't her but Siobhán MacKenna or some lesser actress, young lambs crying across the healthy frost, Joan the Boy, for two hours he kissed Madge but down the road, Gordon, ahead of the field, was lingeringly discovering where Dorrie had hidden the fountain-pen and the sandwiches taste like chalk as he studies the pressure of that neat rump on Gordon's living knee, and Gordon asks: Where's the Tec.?

On the authority of the trooper it would seem that the Tec., whoever he is, has met an old friend up the train and is now in the bar and will be along later to sing Noël, Noël, and Christmas Day in the morning: and the long, long booming of the train now certainly indicates that they are in the line's one tunnel and above them in the night is the humped, clenched, sectarian bitterness of Dungannon town.

The trooper excuses himself, gulps the tail-end of a drink and temporarily withdraws.

The two rug-headed sorters return to their rack and refill their stout-glasses. They are silent young men. The train, clear of the tunnel and somewhere on high dark moorland, rattles like castanets. Joan the Boy dismounts from Gordon's knee, the hoyden saint descending from her charger, and sits on one of the tip-up seats. Lady Bob, shivering slightly at the brief sudden draught when the trooper opens the corridor door, rises, restores his overcoat. Sadie on a box cushioned by mail-bags leans back against a larger box, stretches arms and legs, belches, and doesn't bother to excuse herself. They are warm and relaxed and happy and Sadie sings that Christmas is coming and the geese are getting fat, so please put a penny in the poor man's hat. Very quietly the Boy says that Christmas is here.

—A bit sad for you this year Tilly, says Sadie.

And explains to Lisney that the Boy has had a bereavement in the family. He is sorry to hear it but the Boy says that it was only a grandmother and she was as old as sin and grandmothers are sort of expected to die, even if you were very attached to them as she was to this one. So she's back from London for the funeral. Lisney wonders again about Sadie and Soho, but it doesn't seem to be the time to mention any place so remote as the idea or image of Soho is, from the memory of dear dead grandmothers. In the warm silence that follows they grow closer together. Now that the Boy is safely in the saddle on the tip-up seat and away from the threat of the living leg, Lisney finds that his old affection for Gordon is restored: how, anyway, could you hide a fountain-pen in those tight denims? Out of the past he remembers to himself this and that. But it is Gordon who touches the telepathic chord.

—The trooper, he says. Do you remember, Jim, the time the trooper and yourself were going to become Christian Brothers? Being a Protestant, Tilly, you wouldn't know much about things like this.

—I was St Joan.

—She was a class of a Protestant. They burned her, didn't they? But the way it was when we were beginning secondary school, the recruiting officer used to come around.

—For the army?

—No, Tilly. I knew you wouldn't get it. For the Christian Brothers. A smiling elderly brother, seemed elderly to us, from the Headhouse in Dublin.

—The Headhouse? The Nuthouse?

—The Mother House, Tilly.

—Were they mothers or brothers?

—Dear sweetheart, just listen.

Lisney is annoyed again, well at least uneasy.

—This brother would gather around him all the guys between twelve and fifteen and give them a little talk about Jesus.

—His birthday's tomorrow. Even if I'm a Protestant I heard about him.

—So did Joan.

—She heard voices, Gordon.

—Listen Tilly, just listen to my voice, one voice only. Talk to them about Jesus and ask them what they wanted to do with their future life.

—Did any of you ever tell him? Did any of you guess right?

—The way he went about it was to ask us to write an essay, paragraph, half a page. Lisney wrote a great one. Do you recall? To carry the standard of Christ among the peoples of darkest Africa.

—Were you crazy?

She's asking Lisney.

—No, the game was that if you came up with one like that it made life easier. It worked, too. Saved my life once in a Latin class when I was called out, the axe about to descend for work not done, for an interview, the recruiting officer had turned up again for his annual visit, wanted to see how fared the apostle of Africa.

—Hypocrisy, she says. Jim. And Gordon, what did you say you wanted to be?

—A one-legged guard on a railway train. One fellow whose father was a doctor said he wanted to be a butcher. He didn't like his father. He got jail later on for stealing a car and blowing up a customs hut on behalf of the IRA.

—And the trooper?

—A Christian Brother, Lisney says. Just like that. He was straightforward.

—Did he want to?

—Not on your life. The trooper was an expert on the soccer results. We were destined, as they put it, for the English mission. The novitiate was in Liverpool. The trooper said to me: Lisney lad, every second Saturday we'll be able to see Everton playing at home. Dixie Dean, Coulter, Stevenson, Alec Cook the full-back.

—None of you ever became.

—Look around and see, Sadie says. They became something all right. What did you really say, Gordon? In the composition.

—A British soldier, Sadie. Like my father before me. The Dead Man, wrote a sailor. He became that too. Our dreams came true.

—So there you are, says Trooper O'Neill, working moves. Watch out, Sadie. Watch out, Joan.

Heat or no heat he has not unburdened himself of the egg-shaped tweed and there's a faint dew on his high narrow forehead. The Tec. is with him, a small quick-stepping man with a brown hat, a brown moustache, a white rubbery trench-coat: and Lisney remembers the Tec. and the Tec. remembers him. It was years ago, they agree, at Portadown station, and the Tec. explains: You and the man with you were talking Irish. That was why the sergeant, the constable and myself questioned you.

—We were talking Irish to rise you.

—Likely. It wasn't very good Irish. I was born in Connemara and spoke it from the cradle. But the previous day a constable had been shot dead at Dungannon and in this part of Ireland he was more likely to be shot dead by somebody who spoke bad Irish. So we questioned you.

—Quiet times now, Lisney says.

But Sadie, rising to pour drinks, says that the times will be worse before they're better, that when the marching begins the trouble begins but, for God's sake, with Christmas on top of them they've better things to do than talk about politics and, anyway, the tec. is retired now and going away to live in the west of Ireland where he came from and, as well, Jim Lisney was never interested, that she had heard, in anything except women and that, if it hadn't been for the wolfhound by her side he'd have twitched the green gown off Mother Erin herself, and he with one on him like a round tower.

—Oh Sadie dear, says Lady Bob.

They all laugh except Joan the Boy who is stooped tidying-up in the corner of the van and very well she looks in that position.

Then from a newspaper that he has carried with him from Dublin, Lisney reads out that a stallion in a stud-farm in Kildare has got 6,000 guineas for one performance, all that and money too, and that a married woman in England says that a tall dark stranger bewitched his way into her bed, and bewitched her out of £1,100.

—Sadie, he says, I've wasted my golden youth.

I'll follow you, Gordon says, to the First and the Last.

He limps away. He says to Lady Bob: I nicknamed your father Hop, and now I'm hopping myself.

—Dear Gordon, says Lady Bob. My father loved you.

And runs a few paces after Gordon and embraces him: But darling I won't go to the First and the Last. It's so rough and crowded.

—But Bob I thought you liked it rough and crowded. Fifi, Bobby or any name will do.

Lower lips pouting in a parody of Maurice Chevalier, Gordon pinches a cheek and holds on and Bob squeals with delight and goes with the others to the First and the Last: leading the way with the trooper, and Joan the Boy between them, and Sadie and Lisney twenty paces behind. Parcels have appeared like seagulls over a homecoming trawler and the five of them are clumsily burdened, the tec. has gone on to Derry city: and Sadie drops a parcel, and Lisney and herself, stooping together to pick it up, bump skulls as people always do, and laugh and retrieve the parcel and straighten up again, and look ahead under a railway bridge to where the lighted doors of the First and the Last are closing behind the other three. Beyond that, there's a row of white cottages and diminishing street lamps and then the brooding darkness of divided rural Ulster: the town and its life and lights behind them.

—She's a lovely young girl, Sadie says. Treat her well, Jim Lisney.

—I'll buy her all the drink in the house.

—Quite well you know what I mean. She has an eye for you.

—She sat on Gordon's knee.

—Gordon's an uncle to her.

—Uncles can be odd.

—Or a much older brother. Anyway Gordon gave it all up long ago. He married an Englishwoman. Strict. And anyway they're still in love. The wife I mean. And Gordon. She's a fine young one, Tilly I mean, out of the ordinary.

—She is Joan the Boy, Sadie. She doesn't look like a Tilly. She is an able-bodied country-girl of seventeen or eighteen, respectably dressed in red——

—You're colour-blind. Or you're mad. And she was born in Darlington, England.

—With an uncommon face——

—She has an angel's face. Keep it that way, Jim Lisney, you grey-headed bastard. To think that you used to look like Gregory Peck except they say he's a good man. Villainy shows in the end. Too many wrinkles too soon and your face as grey as your hair.

—Her eyes are very wide apart and bulging as they often do in very imaginative people. She has a full-lipped mouth and a handsome fighting chin.

—Why did you say bulging eyes? What's all that about?

—Sadie, it's all in the play. My other name is Ladvenu.

—It's Lad Something, sure enough.

—It was Ladvenu in the play.

—What play?

—The play that Joan was burned in.

—That play didn't mean much to me. Not a laugh in it from start to finish. A dangerous play. All talk. Because Tilly was in it I saw it. But I didn't see you.

—Not the same performance, Sadie girl. My play was in Dublin. The bank official's musical and dramatic society.

—Oh la-dee-da. And you were lad—ee—da.

—Ladvenu, a decent young Dominican friar.

—Christ graciously hear us. You?

—Ladvenu was all for Joan. He took pity on her. He tried to save her from the burning.

—If he was anything to you he wanted to keep her for himself. No offence though, Jim, you always had a bit of a name for the girls. But you weren't the worst, nobody ever found out who was the worst. My brothers were all for you, they said you were the best boy ever to read poetry in the room behind the shop.

He is fascinated by Sadie's hair, spotlighted, as they advance, by a streetlight. It shines so as to dazzle, almost. From much association with women in the bank but, unlike Gubbins, not that way on the sacred premises and certainly not in the strong-room, he knows that her hair has had henna treatment with a sort of wax that the women, or the teevee ads, say gives a gloss, shiny and healthy, the way a thoroughbred would look when well-groomed and curry-combed, or whatever they do to placate and make more perfect four-legged gentlemen who can earn £6,000 by one act of pleasure: and the elder of Sadie's two brothers is running naked up and down a summery riverbank beating his chest with his fists and making noises like Tarzan. Six or so female nurses from the mental hospital are high on a stone bridge that carries the Belfast railway over the river—we crossed it twenty minutes ago. The nurses are laughing so as to be heard by all the men and boys splashing in the river, sunning on the bank.

—They know, Gordon says, that they'll get him in the end if he goes on much longer the way he's going.

He must have been one of the hairiest men in the world, all black and bristling except for his head which was bald and shining white. To get to that cool pool on the river you had to walk two miles along the railway track. By the time you had walked home again to the town on a hot summer day you needed another cold swim. Here and now on Christmas Eve I can smell the tar and the timber of the sleepers, hear the crunch of a careless foot on the ballast, smell the deep warm grass on embankments and cuttings, safe shelters for lovers. That pool was a heavenly place, an all-male heaven, no woman's eye ever looked down on it except those eyes of the strong laughing nurses from the mental which was half a mile downstream. An uproariously funny place, too, and Sadie's brother, the elder of the two, the best part of the fun: hairy body, bald head, horn-rimmed spectacles as big as bicycle lamps, doing his Tarzan act, leaps and runs and somersaults and cartwheels and high yodelling calls for the benefit of the ladies on the bridge. Who did get him in the end but only for a few months out of every year.

—When he's in, Gordon said, the other's out. To run the shop. It's a foolproof system. Lunatic-proof.

But mostly the two of them were out together, running the shop and the wholesale business, at night presiding over a parliament of a dozen or so pals around the range in the kitchen behind the shop, drinking porter, playing twenty-five, reading out loud from the papers, and even poetry by God, or having it read to them like lords and princes in castles and old walled towns: Stand up there, young Lisney, and read out that. Prove to us that your da isn't throwing away good money sending you to school.

Mostly it was Dangerous Dan McGrew and a bunch of the boys were whooping it up in the Malamute saloon, were you ever out in the Great Alone when the moon was awful clear, with only the howl of a timber wolf and you camped out there in the cold, clean mad for the muck called gold, and that night on the marge of Lake Labarge I cremated Sam McGee, and Sadie coming and going, hair then flying and not lacquered down, mostly I remember her in a red dress, moving somnolent boozers or absorbed gamblers out of her way just for the womanly hell of it, and saying to him now: Jim Lisney, are you listening to me at all?

They are standing facing each other and still 30 or so paces from the door of the First and the Last. It's a corner house. It booms, it reverberates, the walls bulge with Christmas merriment. He asks Sadie: Have you gazed on naked grandeur when there's nothing else to gaze on . . .?

—So that's the way your mind's moving.

—Have you known the great White Silence, not a snow-gemmed twig a-quiver? What's this I hear about Sadie and Soho?

Then he is back and Sadie with him in the bedlam, Bethlehem by Jesus, of the morning, all over the world (almost) men are toasting the King of Peace. Toasting him bloody-well brown. In a corner under brown bellying barrels a group of raucous men and demented women are singing out that auld acquaintance should na be forgot, that memories should be brought to mind: and what has he been at every minute since he stood on the bridge of the ship at Portadown, and seeing memories come presently alive before him, and out there in the great dark silence is the brooding countryside, candles of Christmas peace lighted in many windows: and in there is the crowded town his mother and sister are readying the house for the prodigal's homecoming, for auld lang syne, and Sadie, close to him in the crowd, booze and perfume, kohl pencil melting in the heat around serious protruding eyes, has a statement to make about Soho: I'm dead serious Jim Lisney, dead serious now, listen to me.

With Sadie he had waltzed while she sang the Merry Widow and remembered Maurice Chevalier and Jeannette MacDonald until Gordon cut in and brought the house down as he whirled, using his stiff leg to describe a perfect circle. Above the foot of the bed the Queen of England, busby and red jacket, sits on a black horse and pretends not to see them. She has a nice blue eye and a look so shy and, in the small hours and between the sheets and under the queen, she is surprisingly gentle, the tigrish look of youth gone, a gentle face, the resting face of a young mother. She'd coax, upon me soul, a spud from a hungry pig. She says that he is to do her no harm and he tells her that that is not what he came all this way for, all the way back to where he came from: To think that when I saw you first in the van, in the wheelchair, I thought you might be a cripple.

—Would you have loved me less? Or more?

—Can't do any better than I'm doing.

No horse I'll yoke, no corn I'll cut, no sod with the plough turn down——

—What was your nickname?

—. . . till smiling bright by my own fireside sits the Star of the County Down.

—Skinny.

—Were you? You're not now.

—Not that skinny. But Skinny Lisney. You see. Skinny Lizzie. Subtle.

Then after a lull he says: The queen's horse has whinnied.

—That was no horse. That was me.

And when her breath returns she says: Happy Christmas.

And: What was Gordon's nickname?

—He never really had one. But I called him Sir Gordon. He rode so many winners. Gordon Richards, you know, the famous jockey. Sir Gordon.

—From now on I'll call him Sir Gordon.

Is he uneasy again? Not that it really matters. The world is for his wishing. Cold Christmas morning is outside the window. This he knows is their first and last meeting.

—I feel like Nero.

—That's better than Gordon. I'll call you Nero.

His suitcase has been left in the First and the Last and the only luggage he has taken away with him is a bottle of Power's Gold Label, his mother now and then likes a nip in hot milk at bedtime, in a stainless-steel tankard, with a spoonful of honey added to catch the secret of the sun. The bottle, splendid with its golden shield, stands on a tallboy by the bedroom window. Tallboy's a funny word. Together they laugh over it. The tip of her tongue is a butterfly. Next time round she lies back laughing and says that Sadie, since she first heard the going rate in Soho, says that no girl should do all that for nothing, that the girls in Soho make a mint or a mink, that Sadie will get herself arrested preaching that message all over the town.

—I'm dead serious, Jim Lisney, dead serious, now listen to me.

—What's that squeaky noise?

—That was Sadie. Preaching to me. Last night.

—You're no mimic, no actor.

—I was Ladvenu,

—I'll call you Ladvenu. My voices have deceived me. I have been mocked by devils: my faith is broken. I have dared and dared: but only a fool will walk into a fire.

—My lord: what she says is, God knows, very wrong and shocking: but there is a grain of worldly sense in it such as might impose on a simple village maiden.

—Ladvenu, that's Sadie you're talking about. She didn't ask you to strike a rate for making love. Surely to God. Or arbitrate?

—Like the Labour Court in Dublin.

—Labour's a four-letter word.

—Dead serious, Jim Lisney. You talk about wasting your golden youth. Think of all the time the girls in this town waste, misused, abused, manhandled, against five-barred gates, in the corners of fields and the backs of cars, in haystacks, the marks of the iron bars on their backsides forever, hayseed in the hair and not a penny to show for it. Every man, my motto is, should be compelled to pay his way or face a strike. Down tools, Sadie, I said. Jim Lisney, jokes apart, pack up I tell them and head for Soho.

Laugh as much as we may at Sadie, the queen, who sometimes lives quite close to Soho, refused to laugh with us. On the wall beyond the tallboy and beside a wardrobe is a coloured picture-poster of a young girl, round-faced, smiling naked and normal except that a mirror is inset to her middle to give the oddest effect of pain, distortion, screaming.

—The queen up there, he says, on her high horse.

—What about her?

—She's not looking at us.

—Would you expect her to?

—The girl? With the glass belly.

—That's me. My image of me.

—Fragile. This end up. Is this your bedroom?

—They keep it for me.

—They?

—They've gone on to the funeral. I'll follow.

—What does Gordon mean to you?

—We're just good friends. Like film stars. Or yourself and Gordon.

—But we're old friends, boyhood friends, and we're two men.

Cuddling, teasing, no longer Joan the Boy, she asks him is he jealous. He isn't. Or is he? And if so, for what reason? This here, on the bed under the inattentive horse-borne queen, will be the first and the last meeting, and if Gordon has also been here would that not be the real reunion of friends, Madge and Dorrie by the bridge over the mountain stream, this journey to the most secret places, this communion at Christmas, the feast of friends, the candle-fruited tree.

She is asleep again, curled up like a child, turned towards me, hands, very small hands, clutching or resting on my right shoulder, mouth a little open, breathing very lightly. The clock in the far corner ticks away the seconds towards the time when I must leave her and go through the cold empty town and face up to a sorrowful mother and hostile sister in what was once my home, though never quite my home for they moved to a new house after my father died and long after I left the town. The clock ticks away, an answering ticking from the corner behind me, except that if I crush my left ear on the pillow the answering ticking no longer answers. An echo, or the ghost of a clock that may have been there when she was younger or when somebody else who may now be dead slept in this room? An uncanny effect: left ear off the pillow and two clocks tick, muffle the left ear and one clock stops, clocks stop in rooms when people die, she sleeps on.

Then watching her opening eyes he sings softly: Oh, I wish the Queen of England would write to me in time and place me in some regiment all in my youth and prime. . .
—You'd be left with one leg, like Gordon.
—Gordon, Gordon.
—You can't take your eyes off the queen. Look at me instead.
—I'm looking.
—We were loyal Ulster Protestants. That's why she's up there in all her glory, like Joan herself, riding on a horse. I was a brownie, and a girl-guide all dressed in blue, salute to the king, bow to the queen and now I must go to the bathroom.
He lies alone, his eyes closed, wishing he could lie there forever, dreading the cold outside, the frost, the sorrow ahead to which he has contributed his share, the hostility which, perhaps, he helped to create. He remembers on holiday, when he was fourteen, in the town of Enniskillen, the wide waters of the Erne opening out around it, the deep deep meadows and continual corncrakes, most of his time spent bait-fishing for perch and bream under the hill topped by Portora Royal School where Oscar Wilde had been as a boy: deep lake water, lazy days, perch in plenty until Hetty came along and he lost interest in fish and lay with her in the sunny corner behind an abandoned boathouse, Hetty, Hetty, Hetty, a quiet, tall pale-faced girl, the second name has gone for ever; and when he touched her there, just there, she winced and drew her legs together with the strength of a vice and he was staggered to discover that Protestant girls had the same reactions as Catholic girls. Because they didn't have to go to confession they were supposed to be free as the wind and easy. Hetty, Hetty, Hetty, he says it

out loud he is trying so hard to recall that lost surname: and she is back in the room and kneeling naked by a record-player on the floor at the feet of the girl with the glass belly, and Kathleen Ferrier, who died too young from cancer, is filling Christmas with her splendid voice, singing that she has a bonnet trimmed with blue and that now sleeps the crimson petal of the rose, and singing about the stuttering lover and about the fair house of joy to which fond love hath charmed me and, this is it and here it is, he says.

She snuggles. She says: Ladvenu, it's cold outside.

And: Who is Hetty?

—It's who was Hetty. It's a long time ago.

He tells her: And what amazed me, as I tell you, was that she winced and she a Protestant when I touched her there, just there.

—Here's one Protestant girl that will neither wince nor twice nor thrice. How do you say four that way?

—I'd try four times.

—Why not, and five or six or seven if you're fit.

No horse I'll yoke, no corn I'll cut, no sod with the plough turn down. Begod says I to a passer-by who's the maid with the nut-brown hair. She'd coax on me soul a spud from a hungry pig when her eyes she'd roll. That was no horse, that was me. Till smiling bright by my own fireside, sorrowful mother and hostile sister, fair house of joy to which fond love hath charmed me: and wince, she says, and twice and thrice and frice and fice and sice and seven-up sits the Star of the County Down.

There is an old stone bridge over the river, wide and shallow at that point, and right in the middle of the town. On a mellow spring evening he is leaning on the mossy parapet. He is alone. At that moment there is no crossing traffic, none at all. Crippen has become a member of the town council. He wants to beautify the place. In class he talks of amenities, environment, ecology and how every town that has a fine river should have a fine river-walk. From the bridge Lisney looks down at the sun, a perfect undisturbed circular reflection, unquivering, standing quite still although the shallows rattle all around it. He looks down also on a sort of mossy stone shelf where Crippen has planned the beginning of the river-walk. Above the shelf rise high garden walls, grey stone, red brick and brown, and above them a steep slope, gardens and orchards: higher still the backs of the houses of the High Street: three church spires over all. To his left—the parapet runs right into it—is a high house where a man made harness and saddles and also distilled poteen, right in the heart of the town, right under the noses of the police, a quarrelsome man, an old crusty bachelor with a quarrelsome nephew, a young crusty bachelor: and one day, making saddles and sampling their own poteen, the two of them had a set-to that rocked the town, and the nephew went off in fury to another town and, drunk in a pub, told a stranger how his bastard of an uncle was still clever enough to make poteen in the heart of a town and right under the noses of the police. The stranger was a policeman in plain clothes who reached for the 'phone and rang the other policemen to tell them about what was under their noses. The saddler, when he heard them beating on the door, ran the poteen into the river down that black rainspout and it was said that every fish for ten miles downstream was drunk and singing: but the worm and the still he couldn't run down the spout and a good trade was ruined: Lisney looks at the black downspout and wonders how it is that while he is standing on the bridge he knows that Joan the Boy is sleeping beside him, fair house of joy. But on the mossy stony shelf a mother and child are walking, laughing, talking German, he can hear them quite clearly. Then the child falls into the shallow water but continues to laugh and talk German and is kicking about and splashing in high delight. That river-walk never got to any distance. The effluent from a piggery came out over it just down there. The pigman was a power on the town council. Crippen wasn't even a native townsman. Gordon concocted epics about the war of Crippen and the pigman, and the poisoning of the pigs by Crippen, and the drowning of Crippen by the pigman in deep pools of slurry: and Lisney runs to help the German mother to get the child out of the river. He leaves his suitcase on the sidewalk on the bridge. When he comes back one of a crowd of passing schoolboys—they have come out of nowhere, like screaming, swooping gulls—is about to steal the case. He apprehends him, lectures him, forgives him because the boy is himself, but when the boy has gone out of sight he realizes that it isn't his case at all but an abrased battered thing with nothing in it but one boot, a few tattered books, some rusted cutlery, a pair of female underpants, raggedy. So to the still sun in the shallow river he screams and curses about why does he ever carry anything about with him, that he's always losing things everywhere, all his life long, that life is one long process of loss and attrition until life itself is also lost or worn away: and then he is saying all that to an American friend in the lobby of an hotel in New York, that he is always losing things, always leaving things behind him in hotels, and the friend says that New York claims no credit for the loss of his virginity which was on another battlefield and faraway. Yet he knows that she is there beside him and he struggles to awake and does awake in a room in that same hotel in New York, the 'phone ringing and the voice of a Mr

Runciman enquiring for a M. Ladvenu Lisney who has survived an air disaster in Monte Video. He sees that he is in the wrong room. The floor is littered with women's shoes. The wardrobe is stuffed with perfumed clothes of blinding colours. His wife, Madame Lisney, comes into the room. She doesn't recognize him. Joan the Boy is standing by the window stepping into and hooking herself into her underclothes, behind her the naked girl with the glass belly, the tension, the screaming, the pain. Joan tells him that it's frosty outside, Ladvenu, that it looks like a hard north-east wind, that he's not to move, that she'll make some breakfast, that there are five magpies teasing a cat in a pear tree, he can hear their wicked screams of mockery, that what would he like for breakfast, that for herself she can often be content with bread and coffee, that it is no hardship to drink coffee if the coffee be Nescafé: but to shut me from the light of the sky and the sight of the fields and flowers: to chain my feet so that I can never again ride with the soldiers nor climb the hills: to make me breathe foul damp darkness, and keep from me everything that brings me back to the love of God when your wickedness and foolishness tempt me to hate him: all this is worse than the furnace in the Bible that was heated seven times. I could do without my warhorse: I could drag about in a skirt——

She zippers the fly of her crumpled denims, the magpies give one fearful orchestrated scream and fly away and leave the cat to a cold frustrated Christmas around a house that will soon be empty.

—I could let the banners and the trumpets and the knights and soldiers pass me and leave me behind as they leave the other women, if only I could still hear the wind in the trees, the larks in the sunshine, the young lambs crying through the healthy frost, and the blessed blessed church bells that send my angel voices floating to me on the wind . . . Coffee for Ladvenu.

The bells are indeed ringing. Seven-thirty. The morning angelus. The angel of the Lord declared unto Mary and she conceived of the Holy Ghost. His third awakening this morning, and out of the dream of the fair house of joy, will be down there in the frosty, misty valley, in the empty streets.

He steps out into the north-east wind which wakes the sleeping rheum and graces the parting with many tears, and knows where he is or, rather, has his bearings, knows what part of the town he's in, knows the way to go home. This road once was well out on the fringe of the town, clean cottages standing on half-acres, flowers and apple trees and black and red-currant bushes: cottages built for ex-soldiers, the queen might have ridden on many a wall, not seeing many a sight. Very much built up now, blocks of new two-storeyed houses have swamped the cottages, eaten into the gardens. He is quite alone on Christmas morning. The angel of the Lord, the bells said, had declared unto Mary but the bells had not yet said come all to church, good people, good people come and pray. She had given him a Christmas cake to make up for his missing luggage and to go with the whiskey: they wouldn't need the cake at the funeral, he could say he'd left the suitcase on the train.

Over to his left and behind a phalanx of new houses he sees the outline of the Quarries, magnified by the half-light and the frosty mist into Gothic cliffs. Long ago worked-out and abandoned to wilderness and secret lovers. All the wild thoughts and talk that place used to provoke when Gordon and himself, the trooper and the Dead Man and the Dead Man's dog would go rabbiting there on fine mornings and study the traces of the night before: damp crushed mattresses of newspapers in trenches under bushes and briars where lovers had crawled in like badgers except that badgers didn't leave french-letters behind them, scattered like petals on trampled grass. He told her he'd be in touch. He told her how the poet went home: running like a horse at the last hills.

Dressing, stepping into his pants, he said: This teacher we had long ago, Gordon called him Crippen.

—Gordon, Gordon, Gordon.

—He was a good and proper man and religious. If he went to a dress dance he went first to the church and did the Stations of the Cross. You wouldn't know what they were.

—But my head was in the skies and the glory of God was upon me: and man or woman I should have bothered you as long as your noses were in the mud. Ladvenu, have you forgotten who I am?

She poured him strong black coffee.

—And it was a strange sight on a summer evening to see a man in full regimentals, white shirt, bow-tie, claw-hammer coat, following Christ, Simon the Cyrenean, along the Way of the Cross. He was a good man. He never married.

—No wonder.

—He had more to think of. There was a girl in this town, she's a woman now, who said he would be the handsomest man in the town if he would only let his trousers down.

Then he told her about Dorrie and Madge and Gordon and the fountain-pen.

—Gordon, Gordon, Gordon was all she said.

Beyond the ridge of the Quarries there had been, might still be if the growing town had not eaten it up, a pre-Celtic sun-circle of stones. The local people, for no sensible or scholarly reason, called it: The Giant's Grave. Crippen, who is now dead, used to walk his class out to study those stones and, since he was easy-going and innocent and never let his trousers down, half the class would vanish on the way. She said she would call to see Sadie before she followed on to the funeral. He crosses a red metal bridge. The river is high and breathing out mist. Even if there was a river-walk it would be thrice invisible: mist, half-darkness, brown flood-water. Wince, twice, thrice, frice, fice, sice, and seven-up. Repeat. He measures his steps in sevens and remembers joy. He turns a corner and walks on past the long wall of the military barracks. He is in another suburbia, tall old houses as yet undisturbed and unsurrounded. The road rises before him. Later when the town is awake it would be a good idea to pay Sadie a visit: lonely now with the two daft brothers dead. He runs like a horse at the last hill.

He kisses his sister. A cold lifeless kiss. Anyway northern people, apart from lovers and lechers, don't go in much for kissing when they meet and part. Once in happier days coming home, not drunk but merry, he had lifted his mother off the ground, hands under armpits, and danced and whirled her round and kissed her severeal, repeat severeal, times on both cheeks and, although she blushed and protested, he knew that she was delighted. It is not so with his sister. He feels that she shudders. She is tall and dark and with a stern strong profile. She has found him alone in the cold kitchen by a black dead range, his overcoat still on, a glass of whiskey in his hand, the bottle open on the range, Joan's Christmas cake on the table, it is sleeting outside. She is as cold as the kitchen. *Elle a raison, peut-être.* This is not the best way to come home for Christmas. She wears a blue woollen dressing-gown. She tells him that he is late. Or is it early? She waits to be informed. He says that things happened.

—They always do. You haven't favoured us with a visit in a long time. We were surprised when we heard from you. And now you come home like this. But I suppose you did come.

—I suppose I did.

—To meet old friends.

—And make new ones. Make new friends but keep the old: those are silver, these are gold.

—You were always good in company. Better than at home. I suppose you'll want breakfast. Or are you having it?

She brews tea. She tells him that Gordon was asking for him.

Gordon, Gordon, Gordon.

—He was wondering if ever again you'd come home to see us.

—I came.

—You came all right. You're there for all to see. Or only poor me.

—I'll see Gordon tomorrow.

—I daresay you will.

He sips whiskey, looks out at sleet. She goes here and there, rattles cutlery. She says: How is her ladyship?

—Well. I hear. She acknowledges the alimony.

—The separation allowance. And the children.

—Well, too. I see them regularly.

—It's a pity you can't bring them home with you.

—Pity? Is it? Pity, pity. Oh, the pity of it.

—The town would talk.

—So you said. About where is she, where'er she be, the quite impossible she. The town's quiet this morning. For the birth of Christ. Let he who is without sin. And a rock came through the air and clobbered the woman. And Christ said: Oh mother.

—That's a way to talk on a Christmas morning. Are you drunk already?

He may be. Wince, twice, thrice. Bread has no sorrow for me. She sits across from him and sips tea. The house is a tomb above them. His mother sleeps. He says: To communicate. The need, the desire to communicate.

A clock strikes nine.

—What, she asks him, would you have to communicate?

He doesn't tell her but he thinks: a lot, a lot, a boy in a bath-chair, memories of joy, present sorrow, evil greyhounds in cages, a singing man who is never going back to Portadown, an Ulster detective who speaks Connacht Irish, a naked smiling girl with a glass middle, the queen riding straddle above the plains of delight, a horse of a poet running the hills home, a German child falling into shallow water, and all the world and dreams and dreams and dreams.

So as soon as it is decent, and the sleet ended, he walks across the town to see Sadie. He speaks to few people in the awakening streets. Mostly, he is happy to see, they're past and gone before they recognize him. He senses that. He walks fast. He doesn't look back. Were you ever out in the Great Alone? Read that out, young Lisney, and prove that your father isn't wasting his money sending you to school. But the kitchen that was once all light, warmth, company, bottled stout, poetry, poker-schools is now a store-room stuffed with cardboard boxes, the shop is shut for ever, she shows him around, she lives upstairs and lets the ground floor to a man in stationery and light hardware, wholesale. Have you whistled bits of ragtime at the end of all creation and learned to know the desert's little ways. The man should have written: Dusty face. Another man did.

—How was it at home, Jim Lisney?

—Cold, cold. *Sé tá, fuar, fuar.* My mother cried to see me.

—Mothers cry. At least you had a Christmas cake for her.

—She was here so?

—She was.

—And gone?

—And gone. She said to tell you that bread had no sorrow for her and water no affliction. She said to tell you she'd gone to the fire. Like yourself she's not so good at the homecoming or at staying when she gets there. That was what her mother said to me when I went a week to London——

—The sights of Soho. The noblest prospect a likely girl can behold.

—To ask Tilly to come home to see them, and I did, where she works in a shop, typewriters and record-players and things, in Kensington. Your mother says come home and see them. She said, My mother's not my mother.

—Her mother's not her mother. She's Joan the Boy. She's Tilly. She's a boy in a wheelchair. A woman in a bed.

—Did you treat her well?

—To the best of my ability.

—No cheap jokes.

—Sadie, I don't feel like joking.

She stands on her tiptoes and scans him. For Christmas morning the kohl has been removed: No, I don't think you do. As I say, you weren't the worst. How under God did you come to make such a mess of your life? Look at Gordon. The wildest of all of you. Settled.

Gordon, Gordon, Gordon, Sir Gordon, Skinny, Nero, Ladvenu.

—But Sadie, he married an Englishwoman. Direct rule was imposed.

Then: Her mother is not her mother. You said, she said.

—She didn't tell you? Well it's her own business, not yours or mine, and then she said to me, walking in Kensington Gardens: I'll be home for my grandmother's funeral. And I said she isn't dead and she said again: I'll be home for my grandmother's funeral.

—But her grandmother is dead.

—Of course she is. Joan's gone on to the funeral.

—She's gone.

—I told you already. She said to tell you she had gone to the fire. Ten minutes ago in a taxi. But her grandmother wasn't dead when we were walking in Kensington Gardens and she said, and don't tell a soul Jim Lisney, two evenings ago, she said, I saw her standing under that tree.

—Under a tree.

—In Kensington Gardens.

The bells are ringing wild: Come all to church good people. Sadie is dressed to go to Mass. Demure, black coat, black hat and veil, mourning two daft or part-time daft brothers. Far away one of them plays Tarzan on a sunny river-bank and the nurses laugh from the bridge knowing that they'll get him in the end: part-time anyway. Have you swept the visioned valley with the green stream streaking through it?

—The bells are ringing, Jim Lisney. You could come to Mass with me. *Adeste fideles.*

—Her grandmother, you mean, died after that, after Kensington?

—You often find that, Jim, a fierce closeness between grandparents and grandchildren, something we can't see jumps a generation, like green fingers or a taste for music or a sweet tooth, more so in her case, closer than twins, it saved her when they told her, you'll want to know, now I've said so much, when she was fourteen they told her, stupid to bother but somebody else might have told her, that her mother wasn't her mother, her father was her father, if you know what I mean, the grandmother was the father's mother.

—I can guess.

—You've a great brain, Jim Lisney, my brothers always said you were the cleverest boy ever read out loud in the kitchen behind the shop. But. The news distracted her. She was in a home for a bit. Like my brothers. She kept saying she was two people. The granny came and saved her.

—The granny's dead now. Under a tree in Kensington Gardens. Peter Pan and all. But to shut me from the light of the sky and the sight of the fields and flowers.

On the sunny riverbank Tarzan knew he was twenty people.

—Jim Lisney, you're rambling. The bells have stopped. We'll be late walking up the aisle. But, even at that, it would please your mother and sister to see you at Mass.

She takes his arm, the key of the door in her other hand, he carries her handbag.

—I'll look inside for the last time. This room may be gone when I'm here again.

They stand in the doorway. The cardboard boxes have smothered even the range on which so many glasses and black bottles had rested and made rings. He says: I'll say them a poem. They'll hear me wherever they are.

—Jim Lisney, you're crazy. But you're good. They'll hear you.

She is crying. Very quietly.

He stands in the centre of the floor and reaches out his right hand as if he were holding a book and goes, as bold as Demosthenes, into his act: A bunch of the boys were whooping it up in the Malemute Saloon.

A Letter to Peachtree

ETON CROP

I had an uncle once, a man of three score years and three, and when my reason's dawn began he'd take me on his knee, and often talk, whole winter nights, things that seemed strange to me. He was a man of gloomy mood and few his converse sought. But, it was said, in solitude his conscience with him wrought and, there, before his mental eye some hideous vision brought . . .

Here and now I see him in my mental eye. He is in evening dress. He is always in evening dress. Tails. White bow. Silver watchchain. He raises his right hand. He raises it higher. He puts the back of his right hand to his right temple and extends and stiffens his fingers. The hideous vision may at this moment be catching up on him.

The night the big boxer swung at the man who taunted him and missed and, quite by accident, grazed Belinda's beautiful right cheek, established the Eton Crop forever for me as a special sort of hairstyle. Say Eton Crop to anyone under thirty or, perhaps, under forty today and they'll think you mean a sort of a horse-whip in use at a famous public-school, or a haircut administered there as a discipline, something like a crewcut. Or a bit of Swinburnian diversion.

Belinda, though, is part of another story. And Anna belongs to Eugene who was simple and honest and brave, proved to be brave, moreover, in a bloody battle that shook the world. But Maruna of the songs and the elocutions, Maruna of the silken thigh and the disabled electric kettle, Maruna belongs to me. Or the memory of Maruna.

What the man who taunted the big boxer said was: You're better at the dancing than you are at the boxing. What else are you good at?

So the big boxer swung and, being a little boozed and, possibly, also intoxicated by his company, missed and grazed Belinda, and she was in the house for a fortnight until the shiner faded and she could step forth to tell the town her side of the story. She said that he was a perfect gentleman and that she would dance with him again any time he asked her. There were so many girls in the town who envied her even that glancing blow. She said that it would be something to tell her grandchildren about. That was Belinda for you. She was a girl who always looked ahead.

The big boxer was on tour from one town to the next, not boxing, not dancing except for recreation, but singing from the stage. About the dear little town in the old County Down and about his little grey home in the West, and the hills of Donegal, and the tumbledown shack in Athlone. And kindred matters. But that was the only time he ever came our way.

There was not one in all the house who did not fear his, my uncle's frown, save I, a little careless child who gambolled up and down. And often peeped into his room and plucked him by the gown.

No, he is not in a gown now. He is still in evening dress. His head is raised. There is a pained expression on his face. The pain must be in his chest. For the tips of the fingers of both hands are sensitively feeling his breastbone.

For I was an orphan and alone, my father was his brother. And all their lives I knew that they had fondly loved each other. And in my uncle's room there hung the picture of my mother.

My uncle's right hand is pressed strongly against his forehead. He has taken a step forward, leading with the left foot.

There was a curtain over it (that picture of my mother), 'twas in a darkened place, and few, or none, had ever looked upon my mother's face. Or seen her pale, expressive smile of melancholy grace.

One night I do remember well . . .

But hold on a moment, I hear you ask me, who is this uncle and what is he doing in here with Belinda and the big boxer, and Anna and Eugene and Maruna whom we have not yet met.

Later, later, as the sailor said.

Eugene was in love with Anna and kept, not her picture, but a picture of Ginger Rogers pinned underneath the lid of his desk in the last but one year of secondary school. Ginger Rogers for the one time, that I know of, in her lovely life was a proxy or a stand-in. He could not keep Anna pinned underneath the lid of his desk. And for two compelling reasons: she went to the secondary school in the Loreto Convent over the hill and on the other side of the parochial house; and her uncle was a parish priest in a mountainy village ten miles away. If her picture were to be discovered in Eugene's desk, and recognized, life might never be the same again for Anna in the convent or Anna in the village. But Ginger Rogers was just Ginger Rogers, and loved by a lot of people and did not have, as far as any of us knew, an uncle anywhere a parish priest.

Eugene loved long and deeply. No doubt at all about that. Somewhere in the Pennine Chain, or in the Lake District, or somewhere, there's an Inn at the tiptop of a high pass. In the visitor's book a fellow who had cycled or walked up all that way wrote, long ago, that if the girl he loved lived up there he would worship and cherish her, ever and ever, but climb up to visit her, never no never. That wasn't Eugene. At weekends, and all through the holidays, he cycled, or walked and wheeled the bike, five miles up steep roads, free-wheeled five miles down, then, having refreshed his love, pushed or walked up again five miles and, by God's mercy who made the world that way, was enabled to free-wheel home the rest of the road. He gave it up in the end and went to the wars which he may have found easier going. Anyway she was a flirt of a girl even if her uncle was a parish priest and she, an orphan, lived in the parochial house: and she styled her hair in the Eton Crop. As did Belinda. And Maruna. That and some other matters they had in common. Eugene's sister, Pauline, who was marvellous, had her hair in pigtails for a while but she switched to the Eton Crop and was even more marvellous. Eton Crop was the way to be. It was a style that went with youth and beauty and of necessity, you might say, with a well-shaped head. The only comparable thing today might be a sort of Pageboy style, if that's what you call it. Except that Pageboy has a tame, even servile connotation while the Eton Crop had about it the suggestion of daring, you might almost say: Fast. If the word was any longer comprehensible. We have so accelerated. And it also seems to me, conscious as I am of *tempora mutantur et nos mutamur in illis*, and all the rest of it, that the Crop was easier on the eye, male and sexist, than the coloured contemporary Papuan.

One night I do remember well. As I said. Or somebody said.

My uncle is still in evening dress. He has raised his right arm just as if he were a policeman on point duty. Stopped the whole street with one wave of his hand. His left arm is extended, rigid, pointing downwards to the ground at an angle of about thirty degrees.

One night I do remember well, the wind was howling high. And through the ancient corridors it sounded drearily. I sat and read in that old hall. My uncle sat close by.

I read, but little understood, the words upon that book. For with a sidelong glance I marked my uncle's fearful look. And saw how all his quivering frame in strong convulsions shook.

A silent terror o'er me stole, a strange, unusual dread. His lips were white as bone, his eyes sunk far down in his head. He gazed on me, but 'twas the gaze of the unconscious dead.

Then suddenly he turned him round and drew aside the veil which hung before my mother's face. Perchance, my eyes might fail.

Gesture: Be careful not to allow the hands to move apart before the word, face, is uttered. The words in italic indicate where the hands may begin to come together. A slight startled movement is appropriate at: Perchance, my eyes might fail.

And indeed and indeed. I quite agree.

But ne'er before that face to me had seemed so ghastly pale.

— Come hither, boy, my uncle said.

I started at the sound. 'Twas choked and stifled in his throat and hardly utterance found.

— Come hither boy.

Then fearfully he cast his eyes around.

My uncle is sitting down. But on an ordinary kitchen chair, which is odd in that old hall, my uncle's room. The choking is getting the better of him. Again he raises his right arm. Touches his right temple with the back of his right hand. Extends his left leg to a painful rigidity. Leans back in the chair. Will he topple over? But no, by a miracle of cantilevership he is still in the saddle, and still talking.

That lady was thy mother once. Thou wert her only child . . .

Maruna had a pert, birdlike face, a style most attractive to me at that time. She was a very senior girl, all of nineteen, and was not compelled, when off parade and out of the convent-grounds, to wear school uniform. No more than was Belinda who had left school for two years and was as far away from me and my contemporaries as Uranus, or Venus, from the earth. But Maruna was still within reach, or sight, or desire, and because she could wear real clothes was an inspiriting vision of things to come. Out there somewhere was the World and Ginger Rogers and Life. Maruna was the symbol. She also sang like an angel. She sang at school concerts. She sang in the choir in the village she came from. One Christmas morning, it was said, people travelled miles to hear her *Adeste*. She sang at parochial concerts in the village and in the town. She sang at concerts all over the place. And she recited. That was what first brought us together: recitation. And at the same concert in the town hall. She was asking the townspeople about what was he doing, the Great God, Pan, down in the reeds by the river.

As for me: I was telling them, in the words of Patrick Pearse, that the beauty of the world hath made me sad, this beauty that will pass, that sometimes my heart hath shaken with great joy to see a leaping squirrel in a tree or a red ladybird upon a stalk.

At that time I had never seen a squirrel, brown or grey, except in

Bostock and Wombell's travelling menagerie, and thought a ladybird was a bird.

Not a word of the whole thing did I believe. And the hell was frightened out of me. My first public appearance. She was two years older than me and as confident as Gracie Fields and had appeared on every stage within a forty-mile radius and she was as lovely as the doves in the grounds of the parish church. She was on the bill before me and for some reason, unknown to God or man or woman, she kissed me in the darkness of the wings before she stepped into the radiance and the applause. Afterwards she told me that the kiss was to give me confidence. But I doubt if it did. Even in the dark she was as daunting as Cleopatra. Then she was out there before the world and not a bother on her, and there was I, Caliban in the Stygian shades of gloom.

Now there were dirty-minded fellows who went to school with me who had their own notions about what he was doing, the Great God, Pan, down in the reeds by the river: and who were nasty enough to imply that it was nothing for a decent girl to be asking about, or miming on the stage, or anywhere else . . .

That lady was thy mother once, thou wert her only child.

Well, once is enough to be anybody's mother.

My uncle is still balancing perilously on that kitchen chair, his right hand raised high but both feet firmly planted. Pray God he shall not fall.

— Oh boy, I've seen her when she looked on thee and smiled. She smiled upon thy father, boy. 'Twas that which drove me wild.

He may topple.

It must be remembered it is an old man who speaks.

— He was my brother but his form was fairer far than mine. I grudged not that. He was the prop of our ancestral line . . .

Lansdowne Road and Twickenham and all that. Prop? The line?

. . . and manly beauty was of him a token and a sign.

— Boy, I had loved her too. Nay more. 'Twas I that loved her first. For months, for years, the golden thoughts within my soul I nursed. He came. He conquered. They were wed. My airblown bubble burst.

He is still in evening dress. He is still on that chair. But his hands are raised to heaven or the roof.

— Then on my mind a shadow fell and evil hopes grew rife. The damning thought struck in my heart and cut me like a knife: that she, whom all my days I loved, should be another's wife.

—I left my home. I left the land. I crossed the stormy sea. In vain, in vain, where'er I turned my memory went with me . . .

But my uncle has not gone anywhere. He is still before my eyes. He is leaning sideways on that chair, perhaps to indicate the rolling motion of a ship at sea.

And he is still in evening dress.

Can you hazard a guess now as to what was he doing, the Great God, Pan, down in the reeds by the river? He was spreading ruin and scattering ban, and breaking the golden lilies afloat with the dragonfly, and splashing and paddling with hooves of a goat.

She stamped on the stage. Her dainty feet were transformed. She was a marvel as a mimic.

He was tearing out a reed was the Great God, Pan, from the deep cool bed of the river.

Gently, coaxingly she drew it out from the footlights. It was clearly visible.

He was high on the shore was the Great God, Pan, whittling away what leaves the reed had: and from her sleeveless sleeve, or from somewhere sacredly invisible, she had produced a short, shining knife.

He was drawing out the pith of a reed like the heart of a man, and my heart most painfully followed her fingers. He was notching holes was the Great God, Pan, and dropping his mouth to a hole in the reed and blowing in power by the river, and the sun on the hill forgot to die, and the lilies revived, and the dragonfly came back to dream on the river: and the whole town thundered its appreciation and there was I in the darkness paralysed with love or something for that wonder of a girl, and with fear of the ordeal before me.

For when she had disposed of the Great God, Pan, there was nothing or nobody could save me from having to stand out there in the blinding brightness to grapple with Patrick Pearse and the melancholy beauty of the world. If she had not kissed me again, somewhere in the region of the back of the neck, and gently propelled me forward, I'd never have made it: and then there I was, stiff as a post, raising my right arm and then lowering it for the leaping squirrel and the red ladybird, raising my left arm, lowering it, like a bloody railway signal, for little rabbits in a field at evening lit by a slanting sun. The bit about children with bare feet upon the sands of some ebbed sea or playing on the streets of little towns in Connacht, I actually liked and believed in. That, my elder brother said, was the only bit in which I did not sound totally lugubrious, and all honour to the glorious dead and Patrick Pearse. But from the streets of the little towns the road wound downhill all the way and when the poet said that, between one thing and another, he had gone upon his way sorrowful, everybody believed me.

Yet I had a few friends at the back of the hall who contrived to set a cheer going.

On the chaste and protective stairs between the two dressing rooms, one male, one female, she kissed me once, she kissed me twice. And didn't give a damn if the world was watching. As some of it was. She said I was good for a beginner and not to worry, that I could be heard all over the hall. She allowed me to walk hand-in-hand with her to the place where her relatives were waiting to drive her home.

So there sits my uncle, pursued by his memory and roaming the wide world, but still in evening dress, still balanced precariously on that creaking chair. Although I cannot hear it, I know that it must creak.

— My whole existence, he says, night and day in memory seemed to be. I came again, I found them here . . .

The strain of all this is proving too much for him. His mouth is agape. He raises both hands as if somebody were pointing a pistol at him.

— Thou'rt like thy father, boy . . .

Well, why not, nuncle?

His rhyming for the moment has tripped over its feet. Thou'rt, for God sake. Did anybody ever say: Thou'rt?

— Thou'rt like thy father, boy. They doated on that pale face.

Whose pale face?

— I've seen them kiss and toy. I've seen her locked in his strong arms, wrapt in delirious joy.

He simply should not have been peeping.

The tone of his voice now is vindictive to begin with, weakening to the mildly sarcastic. His hands are clenched for a moment and allowed to rest on his knees.

— By heaven it was a fearful sight to see my brother now and mark the placid calm which sat forever on his brow, which seemed in bitter scorn to say: I am more loved than thou.

— He disappeared. Draw nearer, child. He died. No one knew how. The murdered body ne'er was found. The tale is hushed up now. But there was one who rightly guessed the hand that struck the blow. It drove her mad — yet not his death, no, not his death alone, for she had clung to hope when all knew well that there was none.

He is up, with a half-jump, on his feet.

— No boy, it was a sight she saw that froze her into stone.

My uncle makes a long pause in his speaking. He looks fearfully around as if seeking to discover the cause of my, evidently growing, alarm, by following the direction of my glances. Then he's off again:

— I am thy uncle, child, why stare so fearfully aghast?

But, nuncle, why not?

— The arras waves, he says, but know'st thou not 'tis nothing but the blast. I too, have had my fears like these, but such vain fears are past.

But not the rheumatics from sitting in the draughts.

— I'll show you what thy mother saw . . .

Now we're for it.

Eugene really must have been in love with Anna or he never would have cycled over all those mountains. Yet when the impulse, whatever it was, ended, he forgot about it very rapidly. Or so it appeared to us. One night I asked him about it. We were playing football in the dark. That may seem an odd caper to be at. But let me explain. Since Eugene's father was an officer in the British army we had easy access, day or night, to the great river-surrounded halfmoon of playing fields below the greystone barracks. Except to the hockey-pitch which was a sort of sanctuary. The smoothness of it was a wonder to behold and it felt like silk to the fingers, or to the bare feet when on summer nights a few of us would sneak out there, bootless, to play football with a ball painted white. That was away before 1939 and the world was easy. No warning bugles were blown, no rallentandos unloosed over our heads. That was the first white football we ever saw. Footballs in those days were mostly brown.

When, under the protection of darkness, I asked Eugene if he were still in love with Anna, he said he supposed he was but that you couldn't be sure about those things. It took me years to realize that what he meant was that he couldn't be sure about Anna. As for Maruna and myself. Well, I felt her leg once, also in the dark or the half-dark of one of the town's two cinemas. Felt rather her stocking, and that was the height of it. And had a notion for a long time afterwards, and without reasoning about it, that women, or their thighs, were, like the grass on the hockey-pitch, made of silk. Which is not so.

Thomas Moore, now that I think of it, felt the foot of Pauline Bonaparte. Left or right we are not told, but it was then reputed to be the daintiest or something foot in Europe. How did anybody contrive to work that one out? A foot-judging beauty parade? Sponsored by whom? And who felt all the feet?

Did the big boxer, I wonder, remember Belinda for any length of time. Insofar as we knew he had felt only her right cheek and that, and so to speak, only in passing.

— I'll show you what thy mother saw, my uncle repeats.

His tone is hesitating and fearful.

He says: I feel 'twill ease my breast. And this wild tempest-laden night suits with my purpose best.

He raises his arms as if he were about to take off. But instead he goes down on one knee.

— Come hither! Thou hast often sought to open this old chest. It has a secret spring. The touch is known to me alone.

Try as I may, I can see no chest. But my uncle is moving his hands back and forwards over something that clearly isn't there.

— Slowly, he says, the lid is raised and now what see you that you groan so heavily. That Thing . . .

He heavily emphasizes and repeats those two words.

— That Thing is but a bare-ribbed skeleton . . .

He has thrown his hat (metaphorical), at rhyme and/or what the poet called rhythmical animation.

— A sudden crash. The lid fell down. Three strides he backward gave.

He, or the voice of One Invisible, is telling me what is happening, what he is doing. But no crash do I hear. Nor has he stepped backward. He is again standing up but his feet are quite steady in the one place. This you may feel, and I must admit, is most confusing and it also now seems that my uncle is about to throw a fit.

— Oh God, he cries, it is my brother's self returning from the grave. His clutch of lead is on my throat. Will no one help or save.

He clutches his own throat. He collapses backwards on to that unshakeable cane-chair.

Sometime during the summer that followed Pan's invention of the flute and the lamentations of Patrick Pearse on the sadness and transiency of beauty, Maruna came into town one Saturday and in her hand, naked and unashamed, an electric kettle that wouldn't work. It was early days then for electric kettles. Real specialists and diagnosticians in their elemental ailments may have been few. How many elements anyway, in an electric kettle when it is alive and well? Air? Fire? Water? And Earth, if you consider the metal as earth, the bowels of the earth?

We were good friends, but just friends, by that time, Maruna and myself. So I carried the kettle and was proud to, and proud to be seen walking with her. She carried a cord shopping-bag with a handbag in it and, as I recall, three thin books. We walked the town from place to place, hardware stores, building-yards, and one motor-garage, and nowhere found a man to mend the kettle. Until we met Alec who was wise beyond his generation and who had first suggested playing football in the dark, preferably in mixed doubles which we never did achieve:

and who told us that Ernie Murdoch, the photographer, could fix
electric kettles.

— And he can fix more than electric kettles.

— What else can he fix, Maruna asked.

She seemed a little nervous of Alec. He had a grey, level glance and a
well-chiselled, handsome face and a name with the girls, of all sorts.

— Your kettle-carrier, he said, will tell you. The slave of the kettle.
Ali Baba.

But the kettle-carrier pretended ignorance, or innocence, and we left
Alec smiling and Ernie fixed the kettle: and afterwards Maruna and
myself went to the pictures. How could I tell her that Ernie sold rubber
goods and allied products, down in the reeds by the river? She might not
have known what they were about. Explication at the time would have
been beyond me.

Ali Baba and the forty thieves were hard at it in one of the two
cinemas. But after that gibe about the slave of the kettle I preferred the
other palace. It had Virginia Bruce and John Boles and Douglas
Montgomery, and others, and the Swiss Alps and balconies and flowers,
and everybody singing that I've told every little star just how sweet I
think you are, why haven't I told you. I've told the ripples in the brook,
made my heart an open book . . .

She sang with them. She was a bird.

And down in the reeds by the river I once, just once and only for a
moment, touched her silken thigh. That was as far as I ever got or
perhaps, then, had the courage to try to go. There be mysteries. No
golden lilies were trampled on. It was an innocent sort of a world.

Anyway, that was the end of it. She went one way and I went another,
not with conscious deliberation, just went. Early days can be like that.

— Will no one help or save?

No one does.

This you may be glad to hear is positively my uncle's last appearance
on this or any other stage. It might even seem that he has no more to
say. That third person unseen, unknown, sums up for the unfortunate
man who murdered his brother and locked him in a box, and drove his
sister-in-law to lunacy.

— That night they laid him on his bed in raving madness tossed. He
gnashed his teeth and with wild oaths blasphemed the Holy Ghost.

On the page before me the man in evening dress raises his right hand,
bows his head reverently to atone for the blasphemy, and places his left
hand round about where his heart may be presumed to beat.

— And ere the light of morning broke, a sinner's soul was lost.

And here and now, as I turn the last page in this little book, the man in evening dress covers his face with his hands. The instructions or directions in the text that accompanies the verse and the illustrations say that the eyes may be raised at the beginning of this passage and that the attitude given in the accompanying illustration must not be adopted until the final word, and that the reciter may then stand with his face covered for a few seconds, and with great effect.

Then beside that, and in the margin of the page, and in small neat birdlike script, someone has long ago written: Bring electric kettle to town. See musical picture with John Boles and Virginia Bruce.

So this curious little book is all that is left to me of Maruna and her singing and reciting, and of football in the dark and of Eugene who came to be a hero, and of Anna from over the mountains, and Belinda and the big boxer, and Pauline who was marvellous. Was it one of the three thin books that I saw in Maruna's shopping-bag on the day of the electric kettle? Did that gesticulating uncle go round and round the town with us and even into the studio of Ernie Murdoch who had power over life and electric kettles? Did he crouch in the dark when I touched silk and heard Virginia Bruce sing and Maruna sing with her: Friends ask me am I in love, I always answer yes . . .

As for the book. I open it again, for the hundredth time since, the day before yesterday, it came into my possession. A young man stopped me on a road in Donnybrook and handed it to me. He said: You knew my mother. She talked a lot about you. She said to me once that if ever I ran across you I was to pass this little book on to you.

And later, when we had talked for a while: She died a year ago. Singing to the end.

Humming the other day I was, about I've told every little star when a young person said to me that I knew the latest. And genuinely meant it. For a haunting song may return but a lost beauty never. Yet I can seldom look at or use an electric kettle without remembering Maruna. Away back in those days I wrote a poem to her: or about her, for I never had the nerve to show it to her. Here it is. It looks better in prose as most poems would nowadays. It was jampacked with extravagant statements. As that: On a dew-drenched April morning, the sky-assaulting lark, with his rising paean of gladness, to which mortal ears must hark, did never sing so sweetly nor ever praise so meetly as her voice, with full throat vibrant on the starless scented dark.

And wilder still: Never from the lofty steeple did the swinging bells chime down with a note so soul-exalting o'er the morning-misted town, as her voice in trilling rushes, from her lips the soft sound gushes on the air that heaves and dances like a bed of wind-stirred down . . .

Wonderwoman. Up and away.

There was a third verse, pointing a moral.

Sed satis.

Here followeth an exact description of the book.

Five inches by seven. Forty-seven pages, approx.

Cloth, now very much off-white, with green binding. One of a series of Illustrated Recitations by R. C. Buchanan: *The Uncle* by Henry Glassford Bell. Elocution taught by the aid of photography.

That is: Mr Bell wrote the horrendous poem and Mr Buchanan illustrated it with thirty-six photographic reproductions of a man in evening dress elocuting like bedamned. And added an appendix telling you how you also could elocute that poem. There was even a special edition of the poem, with musical background by Sir Julius Benedict and for the especial benefit of Sir Henry Irving when he felt the need to elocute.

How carefully and how often, I wonder, had Maruna studied that book? What secret life did she lead that I knew nothing about? To think that the movements of her body should have been monitored by Henry Glassford Bell who wrote that woeful poem, and by R. C. Buchanan who worked out the gestures, he said, to foster the love of elocution which, he said, was pre-eminently the art whose principles require to be imparted by oral demonstration. That's what the man said. Kissing in the dark wings, kissing on the stairway. Even then, said R. C. Buchanan, this instruction demands ceaseless repetition before it begins to bear fruit.

Should I have simply kissed back? Not felt in the dark for the smoothness of a silk stocking, while everyone suddenly burst out singing about I've told every little star?

But why did the sailor say: Later, later.

Please.

BLOODLESS BYRNE OF A MONDAY

Three tall men excuse themselves politely, close the door gently behind them, hope he doesn't mind. But they are exhausted putting fractious Connemara ponies on a boat for a show and sale in Britain. Odd caper to be at so early on a Monday morning, they admit. And, as well, they're all Dublinmen by accent, and may never have seen the Twelve Bens or Clifden or the plains of Glenbricken.

— Fair enough, they admit.

They are most courteous.

The tallest of the three says he knows the West of Ireland well, and knows the song about Derrylee and the greyhounds and the plains of Glenbricken and about the man who emigrated from Clifden to the other West, the Wild West, to hunt the red man, the panther and the beaver, and to gaze back with pride on the bogs of Shanaheever.

The tallest man also says that from an early age he has been into horses, the big ones, his father drove a four-wheeled dray. Then into hunters with a man on the Curragh of Kildare. Then, on his own and by a lucky break, into ponies. A bleeding goldmine. He is not boasting. The colour of his money is evident in three large whiskeys for himself and his colleagues, and a brandy and ginger for the stranger up from . . .

— Sligo, he says.

— On a bit of a blinder, he adds.

To be civil and companionable. They are three very, civil, companionable men. And he craves company. The need of a world of men for me. And round the corner came the sun.

To the tallest man the fat redheaded man says: Bloodless Byrne was a friend of your father.

The smallest of the three, the man with the peaked cloth-cap, says: Bloodless Byrne of a Monday morning. The brooding terror of the Naas Road. Very vengeful. Bloodless drove a dray for the brewery.

— Bloodless Byrne of a Monday morning, the tallest man repeats.

He wears strong nailed boots and black, well-polished leather leggings.

— It became a sort of a proverb, he explains. Like: Out of the question, as Ronnie Donnegan said. Bloodless. A face on him like Dracula without the teeth. They tried calling him Dracula Byrne. But it didn't stick. He didn't fancy it. He was vengeful. Vindictive. He'd wait a generation to get his own back. He didn't mind being called Bloodless. They say he wrote it when he filled in forms.

— Mad about pigeons, says the stout redheaded man.

— Bloodless Byrne of a Monday. My father told me how that came about.

Carefully the tallest man closes the other door that opens into the public bar, cuts off the morning voices of dockers on the way to work, printers on the way home.

— Bloodless, you see, is backing his horse and dray of a Monday into a gateway in a lane back of the fruit and fish markets in Moore Street. Backs and backs, again and again. Often as he tries, one or other of the back wheels catches on the brick wall. So finally he takes his cap off, throws it down, puts his foot on it, stares the unfortunate horse full in the face, and says: You're always the same of a fuckin' Monday.

— Deep voice he had too. Paul Robeson.

The shortest man removes his cloth cap to reveal utter baldness. A startling transformation, forcing the strange gentleman from Sligo to blink tired eyelids upon tired eyes. The shortest man says: Bloodless Byrne of a Monday.

— Pigeons, says the stout redheaded man.

Bangers, the barman, belying his nickname, steps in most politely, making no din, to gather up empties and hear requests: so the gentleman from Sligo places the relevant order. These men are true companions. And prepared to talk. And what he needs most at the moment is the vibration of the voices of men. And he wants to hear more about those pigeons. And Bloodless Byrne. And why Ronnie Donnegan said it was out of the question, and what it was that was. Drinks paid for, he has five single pound notes to survive on until the banks open and he can acquire a new chequebook.

— Out of the question, he says tentatively.

But the emphasis is on pigeons and the tallest man is talking.

— Fellow in America, Bloodless says to me, wrote a play about a cat on a hot tin roof. Bloodless never saw it. The play. He saw the poster on a wall. Could you imagine Bloodless at a play? Up above in the Gaiety with all the grandees. A play. Bloodless tells me the neighbour has three cats on a black tin roof, hot or cold, and says he wouldn't like to tell me what they're at, night and day. Bloodless has no time for cats.

— Pigeons, says the stout redheaded man.

— No time for the neighbour either. No love lost. No compatibility. No good fences. So one day . . .

— Cats and pigeons, says the stout redheaded man.

— One day the neighbour knocks on the door and says very sorry there's your pigeons, and throws in a potato sack, wet and heavy. Dead birds.

It is difficult not to join in the chant when the stout redheaded man says again: Cats and pigeons.

— What does the bold Bloodless do? Nothing. Simply nothing. He bides his time. He waits and watches. June goes by, July and August and the horse-show, and one day in September he throws a plastic sack, very sanitary, in at the neighbour's door and says sorry mate, them's your cats. Just like that. Them's your cats. In a plastic sack.

There is nobody in the snug, nobody even in the packed and noisy public bar but Bloodless Byrne, nothing to be seriously considered but his vengeance: Sorry mate, them's your cats.

Face like Dracula without the teeth, he broods over the place for the duration of several more drinks which must have been bought by the ponymen: for the five pound notes are still intact and the ponymen are gone, and never in this life may he know what it was that was out of the question. His clothes are creased and rumpled. He needs a bath and a shave and a long rest. The noise outside is of water relaxing from shelving shingle. The snug is silent. The old boozy Belfast lady fell asleep in the confessional and when the priest pulled across the slide, said: Another bottle, Peter, and turn on the light in the snug.

His eyes are moist at the memory of that schoolboy joke.

June, July, August, and then in September: Sorry, mate, them's your cats.

He should telephone his wife and say he is well and happy and sober. Anyway he wouldn't be here and like this if she hadn't been pregnant so that, to some extent, she is at fault: and he laughs aloud at the idea, and rests his head back on old smoke-browned panelling, and dozes for five minutes.

How many years now have we been meeting once a year: Niall and Robert, Eamonn and little Kevin, Anthony and John and Sean and big Kevin, and Arthur, that's me? Count us. Nine in all. Since two years after secondary school ended in good old St Kieran's where nobody, not even the clerical professors, ever talked about anything but hurling and gaelic football, safe topics, no heresies possible although at times you'd wonder a bit about that, only a little blasphemy and/or obscenity might creep in when Kilkenny had lost a game: but no sex, right or wrong, sex did not enter in. No sex, either, on this meditative morning. As you were. That wash of waves retreating in the public bar is now as far away as the high cliffs of Moher on the far western shore of the county Clare.

Day of a big game in Dublin, Kilkenny versus Tipperary who have the hay saved and Cork bet, the nine of us come together by happy accident: a journalist and a banker, a student of law, a civil servant, a student of art and theatre, another journalist, a student of history, an auctioneer and valuer, that's me. There's one missing there somewhere. Count us, as they do with the elephants at bedtime in Duffy's circus. *N'importe.* Bangers looks in and pleasantly smiles, but the glass is still brimming and the five pound notes must be held in reserve until Blucher gets to the bank. Nine old school-friends meet by happy accident and vow to make the meeting annual. Tipperary lost. How many years ago? Ten? More than ten. Twenty? No, not twenty. Then wives crept in. Crept in? Came in battalions, all in one year, mass madness, Gadarene swine, lemmings swarming to the sea: and college reunions and laughter and the love of friends became cocktails and wives who don't much like each other: and dinner dances. So nothing to worry about when this year Marie is expecting, and all I have to do is meet the men and make excuses and slip away, odd man out: which seemed a good idea at the time, late in the afternoon yesterday, or early in the evening, for in this untidy town afternoon melts un-noted into evening and, regrettably and returning as the wheel returns, it is now in a day as we say in the Irish when we say it in the Irish: and here I am, here I am, here I'm alone and the ponymen are gone, and five pound notes is all between now and the opening of the banks . . .

Outside, the translucent stream, as he once heard some wit call it, slithers, green and spitting with pollution, eastwards to the sea. The sun is bright without mercy. His eyes water. His knees wobble. Where had he got to after he left the lads to get with their good, unco guid, wives to the dinner dance? The sequence of events, after their last brandy and backslapping, is a bit befogged.

This town is changing. For the worse. Nothing to lean on any more. Where, said Ulysses, where in hell are the pillars of Hercules. The Scotch House is gone. Called that, I suppose, when a boat went all the way from the North Wall to Glasgow, and came back again, carrying Scotsmen who would look across the river and see the sign and feel they were at home. Scotsmen were great men for feeling at home anywhere, westering home with a song in the air, at home with my ain folk in Islay, home no more home to me whither must I wander, and the Red Bank Restaurant gone, it's a church now, and the brewery barges that

used to bring the booze downstream to the cross-channel cargo boats
gone forever and for a long time. He's just old enough to remember
when he first made a trip to Dublin and saw the frantic puffs of the
barges when they broke funnels to clear the low arch, and the children
leaning over the parapet, just here, and yelling: Hey mister, bring us
back a parrot. A monkey for me, mister. A monkey for me.

And slowly answered Arthur from the barge the old order changeth
yielding place to new. That went with a drawing in a comic magazine at
the time: a man in frock-coat and top-hat standing among the
beerbarrels on a barge, Arthur Guinness of course, immortal father of
the brewery bring me back a monkey, bring me back a parrot. And God
fulfills himself in many ways, over from barges to motor-trucks.

Sorry, mate, them's your cats.

There in that small hotel the nine of us met the day Tipperary lost
the match, and met there every year until the hotel wasn't grand
enough for the assembled ladies. Then it descended lower still to
include a discotheque: and that was that. Nine of us? Dear God, that
was why this morning I counted only eight the second time round, for
Eamonn who discovered that little hotel and liked it, even to the
ultimate of the discotheque, Eamonn up and died on us and that's the
worst change of all.

Somewhere last night I was talking mournfully to somebody about
Eamonn, mournfully remembering him: and God fulfills himself in
many ways.

Out all night, and cannot exactly remember where I was, and did not
get home to my own hotel which, and this is another sign of the times,
is away out somewhere in the suburbs. Once upon a time the best
hotels were always in the centre. Like America now, the automobile
rules okay, the centre of the city dies, and far away in ideal homes all
are happy, and witness a drive-in movie from the comfort and security
of your own automobile: and the gossip and the fevers of the middle-
ages, middle between which and what, fore and aft, I never knew, are no
more: and I am dirty and tired now, and want a bath and a shave and
sleep. Samuel Taylor Coleridge emptied the po out of a first-floor
window. While admiring the lakeland scenery.

But this other hotel outside which he now stands is still, and in spite
of the changing times and the shifting pattern of urban concentrations,
one of the best hotels in town. At this moment he loves it because he
knows it will be clean, as he certainly is not. In the pubs of Dublin the
loos can often be an upset to the delicate in health.

So up the steps here and in through the porch. There is a long porch.
Jack Doyle, the boxer, used to sit here with an Alsatian dog, and read

the papers and be photographed. That was away back in Jack's good days. As a boy he used to study those newspaper photos of handsome Jack and the big dog, and envy Jack because it was said that all the girls in Dublin and elsewhere, were mad about him.

He has heard that a new proprietor of this hotel has napoleonic delusions: and, to prove the point, *l'empereur* in a detail reproduced from David and blown up to monstrosity, is there on the wall on a horse rearing on the hindlegs, pawing with the forelegs. The French must fancy that pose or position: Louis the Sun King on a charger similarly performing is frozen forever in the Place des Victoires.

Tread carefully now, long steps, across the foyer for if that horse should forget himself, I founder.

A porter salutes him, a thin sandy man, going bald. He nods in return.

Were we here last night? Could have been, for the nine of us used to meet here: and the eighteen of us, until that changing city pattern swept the dinner dance away somewhere to the south.

This morning anything is possible. He raises his left hand to reinforce his nod, and passes on. Upstairs or downstairs or to my lady's chamber? Destiny guides him. So he walks upstairs, soft carpets, long corridors, perhaps an open, detached bathroom even if he has no razor to shave with. Afterwards, a barber's shave, oh bliss, oh bliss. He finds the bathroom and washes his face and those tired eyelids and tired eyes, and combs his hair and shakes himself a bit and shakes his crumpled suit, and polishes his shoes with a dampish handtowel. A bit too risky to chance a bath and total exposure, although he has heard and read the oddest stories about deeds performed in hotel bathrooms by people who had no right in the world to be there. Bravely he steps out again. A brandy in the bar, and the road to the bank and his own hotel and sobriety, and home: Bright sun before whose glorious rays.

Sorry, mate, them's your pigeons.

Before him in the corridor a door opens and a man steps out.

This man who steps out is in one hell of a hurry. He swings left so fast that his face has been nothing more than a blur. A black back to be seen as he hares off down the corridor to the stairhead. Hat in one hand, briefcase in the other. Off with quick short steps and down the stairs and away, leaving the door of the room open behind him. His haste rattles me with guilt. That man has somewhere to go and something to do.

To sleep, to die, to sleep, to sleep perchance to dream, and his eyes are half-closed and a mist rolling at him, tumbling tumbleweed, up the corridor from the spot where the man has vanished: and the door is open and the devil dancing ahead of him. There is no luggage in the room, not in wardrobe nor on tables, racks nor floors, no papers except yesterday's evening papers discarded in the waste-basket, no shaving-kit in the bathroom: and the towels, all except one handtowel, all folded as if they have not been used. No empty cups nor glasses nor anything to prove that the robin goodfellows or goodgirls of roomservice have ever passed this way. That's odd. The blackbacked hurrying man must carry all his luggage in that briefcase: but, now that he remembers, it was a big bulging briefcase, brown leather to clash badly with the black suit, big enough to hold pyjamas but scarcely big enough to accommodate anything more bulky than a light silk dressing-gown. Woollen would not fit. *N'importe.* There are two single beds, one pillowless and unused, all the pillows on the other, which is tossed and tumbled. That man must have had a restless night. But who in hell am I supposed to be or what am I playing at? Sherlock Holmes?

The phone on the table on the far side of the rumpled bed would do very well for his expiatory call to Sligo. He reaches across first for it and then, the most natural thing in the world it seems for him to subside, not just to subside but to allow himself to subside, gravity and all that: and to close his eyes. The bed is quite cold even to a man with his clothes on, and that's also odd because the man with the brown briefcase had moved so fast that his couch should not yet have had time to cool. Perhaps he had genuinely passed such a restless night that he had tumbled on the bed for a while, then sat up or walked the floor until dawn. To hell with Holmes and Dr Watson or Nigel Bruce and Basil, Basil, the second name eludes me. Pigeons fly high over a black roof that is crawling with spitting cats.

Opening his eyes again he reads seventeen in the centre of the dial and, with the phone in his hand, says not Sligo but: Room seventeen speaking, room service could I have, please, a glass of brandy and a baby ginger, not too well this morning, a slight dyspepsia, nervous dyspepsia, something I'm liable to.

The explanation perhaps was an error, too long, too apologetic, never apologize, like Sergius in the Shaw play, just barge ahead and hope for the best. Not too late yet to cut and run but, to hell with poverty we'll kill a duck, here's a pound note for a tip on the table between the beds, charge the brandy to the blackbacked man's bill, any man who moves so fast would need a brandy: now down, well down under the bedclothes, nothing to be seen but the crown of my head: and your brandy, sir, the ginger sir, will I pour it sir, do please, mumble but be firm, and thank you, that's for yourself and have one on me, and thank you, sir. It was a man's voice. A porter, not a chambermaid. You can't have everything. And where is the chambermaid, as the commercial traveller said in the Metropole in Cork when his tea was carried to him in the randy morning by, alas, the nightporter. Can't say, sir, about the chamber but the cup and saucer are the best Arklow pottery. Oh God, hoary old jokes: but then my mind is weakening or I wouldn't be here.

The door closes. This is the sweetest brandy he has ever tasted and cheap at a pound. Four notes left. Let me outa here. But gravity strikes again and, eyes closing, he is drifting into dreams when the phone rings and, before he can stop himself, he picks it up and the voice of the female switch says: Call for you, sir.

— Thanking you.

— That you, Mulqueen? Where the hell are you?

A rough, a very rough, male voice.

— Room seventeen.

— Balls. What I mean is what the hell are you up to?

That would by no means be easy to explain to a man I've never seen and on behalf of a man I've never really met.

Mumble: Up to nothing.

— Can't hear you too well. You sound odd. Are you drinking? A bloody pussyfoot like you might get drunk in a crisis.

That's the first time, the reely-reely first time, I was ever called a pussyfoot. Say something. Mumble something. What to say? What to mumble? Have another slow meditative sip. Never gulp brandy, my uncle always told me, it's bad for your brain and an insult to a great nation.

— Mulqueen, are you there? Are you bloody well listening?

— Everything's fine. Not to worry.

— Never heard you say that before, Mulqueen. You that worried the life out of yourself and everybody else. But I should bloodywell hope everything is fine. Although I may as well tell you that's not what the bossman thinks out here in the bloody suburbs. He's called a meeting. You'd better be here. And have the old alibis in order.

— I'll be there. When the roll is called up yonder I'll be there. I'll be . . .

Perhaps he shouldn't have said that, but the brandy, brandy for heroes, is making a new man out of Pussyfoot Mulqueen or whoever he is. Anyway, and God be praised, it put an end to that conversation for the phone at the far end goes down with a dangerous crash that echoes in his ears, if not even in the bedroom. He finishes the brandy, beats time with his left hand and chants: I'll be there, I'll be there, when the roll is called up yonder I'll be there, oh I wonder, yes I wonder do the angels fart like thunder, when the roll is called up yonder I'll be there!

Sips at the empty glass and draws his breath and continues: At the cross, at the cross, where the jockey lost 'is 'oss: send down sal, send down sal, send down salvation from the lord catch my flea, catch my flea, catch my fleeting soul.

And orders another brandy and ginger, and plants another pound, and submerges, and all goes well, and surfaces and drinks the brandy, and realizes that he must not fall asleep, must out and away while the going is good and the great winds westward blow, and is about to get on his feet when the phone is at it again. Here now is a dilemma, emma, emma, emma, to answer or not to answer, dangerous to answer, more dangerous not to answer, the ringing may attract attention, the not answering may bring searchers up. It is a woman's voice.

— Is that you, Arthur.

Arthur is my name.

— Who else?

— You sound odd.

— The line is bad.

— Your hives are flourishing.

My hives? I don't have hives. Good God, the man's a beekeeper, an apywhatisit.

— But Arthur, I'm worried sick about you. What is it? What is wrong?

She is crying.

— O'Leary rang looking for you. I told him where you might be.

— That was unwise.

— I had to. He said things were in a bad way.

— He would.

— Arthur. You sound very peculiar.

— I feel very peculiar.

— What were you up to?

He still doesn't know what he was up to. He says: these things happen. So does Hiroshima. So does the end of the world.

— Arthur, how can you talk like that? You don't sound in the least like yourself. And there is something wrong with your voice.

Best put the phone down gently and run. But she will only ring again before he can get out the door and away.

— Laryngitis. Hoarse as a drake.

He coughs.

— Don't do anything desperate. Promise me.

—Promise.

— In the long run it will be better to face the music. Think of the children.

— I always do.

— You have been a good father. You were never unkind.

She is crying again and he feels like the ruffian he is for bursting in on the sorrows of a woman he has never seen, may never see, pray God. Then his self-respect is restored and his finer feelings dissipated by a male voice, sharp and clear and oh so nasty: You blackguard. Mary is much too soft with you. She always has been.

Nothing better to say than: Who's speaking?

— Very well you know who is speaking, you dishonest automaton, this is your brother-in-law speaking, and a sorry day it was that you ever saw Mary or she ever saw you, or that you brought a black stain, the only one ever, on the name of this family, get over to your office this minute and face the music, it will make a man of you, a term in jail . . .

Christ save the hastening man who has this faceless monster for a brother-in-law. I am shent, or somebody is, Pussyfoot the automaton is shent as in Shakespeare. But what to say? So unable to think of anything better he says: Bugger off.

Somebody must stand up for Mulqueen who is not here to stand up for himself.

— Filthy language now to make a bad job worse, your father and mother were decent people who never used words like that . . .

— They never had to listen to the like of you.

— I'll offer up my mass for you, as a Catholic priest I can think of nothing else.

And slam goes the phone and the gates of hell shall not prevail, and the Lord hath but spoken and chariots and horsemen are sunk in the wave: sound the loud timbrel o'er Egypt's dark sea: and he is halfway to the door when the loud timbrel sounds again. Let it sound. Divide the dark waves and let me outa here. And the bedroom door opens and in steps the thin sandy porter, going bald, with a third brandy and ginger on a tray, and puts the tray down carefully, and picks up the phone and says hello and listens, and cups his hand carefully over the mouthpiece and says: It's for Mr Mulqueen, sir. It might be as well to answer it. Just for the sake of appearances at the switch below.

Sounds, he means. Appearances do not enter into this caper. It's a wonderful world. As the song assures us.

A woman's voice, husky, says: Arthur, this is Emma.

Emma, dilemma, dilemma, dilemma.

He says: Emma.

— Arthur love, don't bother about what they say. Come over here to me.

Which at the moment he feels he might almost do, if he knew where she was. Or who. That voice.

— Arthur, do you read me?

— Loud and clear.

— Are you coming?

— Pronto.

And puts down the phone, and turns to face the porter and the music.

So the porter pours the ginger into the brandy and hands it to him and says: You sat here for a while last night, sir. After the others had gone.

Remembering Eamonn. Now he begins to remember something of the night.

— Nine of you used to meet here.

— Eamonn Murray and the rest of us.

— Poor Mr Murray, God be good to him. One decent man. He thought the world and all of you.

A silence. The phone also is mercifully silent.

— About Mr Mulqueen, sir.

— Who?

— Mulqueen, sir. His room, you know.

— Of course. Face the music, Mulqueen.

— You know him, sir?

— Not too well. A sort of passing acquaintance.

— You'll be glad to hear he's well, sir. They fished him safely out of the river. Nobody here knows a thing about it yet. An errand boy came in the back and told me. I sent him about his business. No harm done.

Another silence. He puts the last three notes on the table between the beds, flattens them down under an ashtray: That's for your trouble, Peter Callanan.

Memory, fond memory brings the light.

— How much do I owe you for the brandy?

— It came out of the dispense, sir.

— The name's Arthur.

— They won't miss it for a while.

— But we can't have that. I'll be back as soon as the banks open.

— No panic. No panic at all. You're old stock. Nine of you. And Mr Murray. The flower of the flock.

— What did he do that for? Jump?

— God knows, sir. He seemed such a quiet orderly man. Never touched a drop. And in broad daylight. Stood up on the wall and jumped with the city watching. He couldn't have meant it. Missed a moored dinghy by inches. But he did miss it.

— He had luck, the dog, 'twas a merry chance.

— What's that, sir?

— Oh, nothing. A bit of an old poem. How they kept the bridge of Athlone.

— Athlone. It's a fine town. I worked there for a summer in the Duke of York. Mr Murray was a great man for the poetry. He could recite all night. Under yonder beechtree. And to sing the parting glass.

He leads the way along the corridor and down the backstairs to the basement, then along a tunnel with store-rooms like treasure-caves to right and left. They shake hands.

— Many thanks, Peter.

— Good luck, sir.

— Them's your cats.

Two cats are wooing in the carpark across the laneway.

— What's that, sir?

— Oh, nothing. Just a sort of a proverb where I come from.

— Like out of the question as Ronnie Donnegan said.

— Something like that.

Bloodless Byrne to the right, Ronnie Donnegan to the left, he walks away along the laneway. He hasn't had the heart to ask Peter Callanan what it was that was out of the question. Ahead of him Eamonn walks, forever reciting: Under yonder beechtree, single on the greensward, couched with her arms beneath her golden head, blank a blank a blanky, blank a blank a blanky, lies my young love sleeping in the shade.

He must ring Sligo and tell her that all is well. All is well. Somewhere poor Pussyfoot Mulqueen is being dried out through the mangle. All may not be well. The music is waiting.

There is a group of seven or eight people by the river-wall. One young fellow points. As if Mulqueen had made a permanent mark on the dark water.

He has never seen the man's face. Shared his life for a bit. Shared it? Lived it.

And he goes on over the bridge to the bank.

MOCK BATTLE

He sings a few lines of the song about blue birds over the white cliffs of Dover. He looks through the downpour at the black face of the stone quarry. It leans like doom over the tiny station. The Belfast-bound train moves on to give them a clear view of the quarry's brute ugliness. Nobody working there today, no bewildered rooks fluttering before that formidable face. No sensible bird would be out of the house in such weather.

He says that all his life he seems to have been looking at that quarry, in all weathers: going south, going north, ever since he first went to Dublin when he was ten, on an excursion train and that was twenty-one years ago.

She says: If the photographer doesn't fish why does he always carry a fishing-rod in the back of the car?

— Only when he's travelling in the country.

— But why? Even in the country. If he doesn't fish. You wouldn't expect him to drive round and round Belfast with a fishing-rod.

— It's quite simple.

He is, and he knows it, painfully flippant. He knows that she also knows. The air is gelid in the wooden shelter. Although outside, even in the downpour, it must be hot and sticky. It is the middle of July.

— You didn't explain how simple.

— He has good contacts with that sort of magazine, in London and in the States, *Field and Stream, Over the Hills and Faraway, Up the Aery Mountain and down the Rushy Glen, Beyond the East the Sunrise beyond the West the Sea, Come Hear the Woodland Linnet, Wander Lust, Stand and Stare*, and all that sort of thing. You can imagine.

— I can quite easily imagine.

Twenty-one years ago, going south, he had passed along here, not more than twenty paces from where he now sits sheltering. Not another soul now to be seen on the drenched pitiable platforms (only two) of the junction or station or halt or what you will. The brutal quarry over all. The few people who have disembarked with them from the northbound train have departed in automobiles, leaving them to wait in that wooden box of a shelter for the cameraman driving from Belfast with his fishing-rod and, it is to be assumed, his camera. But twenty-one years ago the sun had been shining. He sat beside his father, a travelled man and proud of it. Jamie Kyle, the town-crier from his own home-town, sat across from them. Now, as a much-travelled journalist, he knows that there are only two town-criers left in Ireland, one in Listowel in Kerry, one somewhere in Connacht. He has told her about that journey: how Jamie, looking out the window, had misnamed every landmark they passed, and been patiently corrected by his father. The town-crier was not a travelled man. His duties did not demand it. That was the first time he himself had seen the Mourne mountains, the Carlingford hills, the Irish Sea.

She takes one step into the rain, stands shivering for a moment, steps back again. She says that it's a great day for a battle or a pageant or whatever. She says that she can quite easily imagine but she still can't understand about the fishing-rod. If he doesn't fish.

— A day like this, she says, will destroy Alison's service. She'll rust.

He ignores that one. He tells her about the fishing-rod.

— He likes to take photographs of people fishing. Preferably with an old humpy stone bridge in the background. So wherever and whenever he sees a fine old stream and a pleasant bridge . . .

— A railway bridge wouldn't do.

. . . he ambushes the first passing stranger, what George Moore would have called a chance shepherd . . .

— The apt literary reference.

. . . and mounts the rod, puts it in the stranger's hand, asks him to stand on the bank and be photographed. He's made some masterly pictures that way. The *Observer* once used a whole page of them. He's a first-class man.

She has lost interest. She touches, with those elegant hands, her slightly-hollow cheeks. Those hands were the first things he had noticed, at rest, swans on a lake, on a desk at a German class in college. A sideways kick of the wind scatters rain around them. In such a place, on such a day, the white Parisian net, binding or ornamenting her dark hair, is to him aggravatingly absurd. She says: Weather like this must be bad for the guts, I mean of tennis racquets. Alison will wilt.

Coatless he stands in the rain and looks south towards Dublin: and there on the platform, and praised be to Jesus, is the photographer proudly advancing, stepping in through a gateway in the white wooden railings, normally a tall greyheaded, bespectacled, professorial sort of a man, but now, with an overcoat and a pacamac over it, an enormous egg, or an elongated, bloated french-letter: Princely O'Neill, and that isn't his name, to my aid is advancing with many a chieftain and warrior clan: he carries no rod, he carries no tripod, he carries no cross and he carries no stone but he stops when he comes to the grave of Wolfe Tone.

The rain has eased somewhat. One solitary stupid rook is peering and picking around the face of the quarry. The ghosts of twenty-one years ago go south down the line.

The fishing-rod, the camera and more besides are in the boot of the car. In their company he places his briefcase and overnight bag. He explains to the photographer that, after the mock-battle, they will leave his wife, Dublin-bound, back to the station. Then the two of them will go on to Belfast to cover the opening of that new theatre. She explains that she must go back to Dublin to relieve the baby-sitter and look after the children. There is one child. She says that Anthony's favourite sport is tennis, not fishing: You couldn't keep him away from Fitzwilliam. Even when he's supposed to be working.

Innocently the photographer responds: I played there once myself. In a club competition. I have relations in Donnybrook, quite close to Fitzwilliam.

— Then you'd understand perfectly.

They pass over a canal bridge, old and narrow, with a high arch. Nobody around to be conscripted or pressed into fishing. Then through a village where the sun is shining and the photographer says that it may be a good day after all. She is in the back seat, half-reclining, her hands locked around her knees, gracefully raised. She says: Anthony says that life begins every day you waken up. Isn't that a beautiful thought?

From a rise in the road they see to the east a small handsome pear-shaped lake. It glistens under a brightening sky. Beyond the lake a broad slope of parkland. On the crest of the slope a great house with a backdrop of high trees.

— That's the field, the photographer says.

With a childish curiosity, subtly planned, and in a most gentle voice, she asks: What field, Mr Lockhart?

— Where the mock battle's held. What else? The two armies get ready in the yards behind the house.

— That must be fascinating. Two armies. They have to be very big yards.

He is a simple man and notices nothing, Anthony hopes, in the style of her talk, slightly elevated, carefully picking and pronouncing the words, a missionary lady speaking English to a black baby. When he was a boy the missionary propaganda urged you to buy a black baby.

Somewhere in Africa he now must own six or seven, grown-up and bouncing. Male or female? He laughs at the idea.

— Anthony, she says, is amused. He has secret jokes.

— It's good fun, Lockhart says. And, unlike a lot of what goes on here in Ulster, it's harmless. Just a pageant. Orange and Green. King James and King William. Year after year. Celebrating the battle of the Boyne in 1690, you know. Not a shot fired in anger. You crossed the Boyne today on the way up from Dublin. Over the big viaduct at Drogheda.

She has lost interest: a trick she has. She says: There's a chap Anthony knows, a printer, a rather coarse fellow. He goes to all the tournaments in Fitzwilliam. He says tennis brings out the woman in a woman. I wonder what he means.

— Pageants, says Lockhart.

He is speaking into a long silence. Outside the sun is making a brave effort.

— Pageants, he says, have a way of going aft agley.

— Ah, she says, like the best-laid plans of mice and men. Burns sounds so much better in an Ulster accent. Anthony reads Burns so well.

It doesn't seem necessary to acknowledge the compliment.

— There was a chronic pageant at Carrickfergus in County Antrim. I got a good picture of the actual incident. Right under the big Norman castle. It must be the biggest castle in Ireland.

— Trim, Anthony says. I mean Trim Castle. In County Meath. Or perhaps Liscarrol by Buttevant in North Cork. Except that Liscarrol's only a shell now. Goats depredating within the empty walls.

— Anthony, she says, is very good on castles.

— I was lucky to get that picture. The actual incident. Chronic. It made a holy laugh out of the whole business. You see it was meant to be the landing of King William of Orange. That actually was where he landed. Carrickfergus. Before 1690 and the battle of the Boyne. The sea was choppy that day. And at the very moment when the king was to step on to the quayside the boat bucked and King William landed on his backside in the briny.

— The real King William.

She asks so innocently.

— No, of course not. The man in the pageant.

Lockhart seems, for the moment, taken aback. Anthony is annoyed. All very well to play this game with or on your familiars, meaning your erring if suffering husband, but not with or on strangers. So with great determination, and knowing that she feels she may have gone too far, he caps the story of what happened at Carrickfergus with the story of what happened on the Boyne at Drogheda. The great resonant Shakespearean actor, Anew McMaster, was involved: playing St Patrick in a pageant for a Patrician jubilee year. That, they say, was where St Patrick landed. Drogheda. McMaster dressed in a long white linen robe. Stepped out on what he thought was solid ground and went up to the hips in mud. Floundered out, cursing blue, went into a riverside pub, squelching and dripping, and proclaimed: *Ego Patricius, filius diaconi Calpurnii, servus servorum Dei*, and in the name of Christ crucified who rose again even for the redemption of the citizens of Drogheda, serve me a large glass of Irish whiskey.

Lockhart thinks that is a very funny story and goes to prove what he always thought about pageants. The Dutch King goes forever, and seat first, into the salt water. The Britoroman Saint resurrects, orating and cursing, out of the mud of the sacred river, Boyne. The brave effort of the sun is weakening. The woman is silent. Anthony hums a tune. They drive on towards the mock-up of an ancient battle.

In a barn behind the Big House and gathered all around a silent resting tractor, the young fellows are dressing for the mock battle. King William sits high on a tractor studying the style of both armies. He is the only one to wear a crown. He has a grey moustache. King James wears a bowler. Anthony thinks of Oberammergau. He has never been there.

Back in the village the one hilly street has been crowded. This is a rural festival, a market-day as well as a pageant. Stalls on the streets and the rain beginning again. Loud singing from public houses. Men wearing orange sashes and blue sashes and black sashes all glittering with metal insignia. And bowler hats by the billion. Like London stockbrokers. Men staggering two by two and three by three out of one pub and into another, defying the weather, friends greeting friends. On one market stall a splendid display of delph chamberpots, brightly beflowered.

— Twenty yards long if it's an inch, Lockhart says. Sixty feet of Charleys.

He is lost in wonder. He is a tall grey, gentle, inoffensive man. He takes several photographs. He asks the man who owns the stock and the stall to hold two of the bright objects aloft and takes two more photographs.

— No happy home, the man says, should be without at least one.

— All rural comforts, Lockhart says. And repeats: All rural comforts.

She walks on through the mizzling rain. Anthony follows. From the boot of the parked car Lockhart takes one of those large coloured umbrellas you see at racecourses. All along the avenue from the village to the field of battle patient people shelter under dripping trees. Steam rises from a tea-tent. Three pipers, all in Stuart tartan, drone in meditative preparation in a corner of the barn. They have to be brothers. They look like bloody-well triplets. They disregard the bucolic warriors. They greet Lockhart as an old friend.

— Brothers from Belfast, he says. In Scotland once they piped for the queen.

He takes their picture: for the twentieth time, he says. But this is special. They will lead two kings and two armies to the watery field. They stand and pipe under a picture of the queen on the wall of the barn. She sits on her horse. She wears a busby and a crimson jacket and looks very well. The warriors, some of them, cheer. For Lockhart or the pipers or the queen in the saddle? Does she know that if it hadn't been for what's going to happen today she mightn't be sitting there? Anthony opens his notebook and begins to ask questions. She says: Record it all for posterity. A day to remember. Another day out of our lives. I'll go to the tea-tent and the loo if there is one.

She walks away, swaying with style, stepping well in black, glittering, well-fitting kneeboots. No sodden wrinkles or furrows there. She knows how to wear those things. The warriors show some interest and for a moment Anthony is, nostalgically, compelled to admire. But why, oh why, had she ever said that she wished to come?

It isn't all that easy to distinguish one army from the other. Berets, and cocked hats plumed with esparto grass, brown corduroy breeches and white canvas breeches, and wellingtons, and hobnails and leggings are all over the place. And braided jackets, some red, some blue, some green, whimsically distributed it would seem. More greens than reds or blues, which is odd. No orange jackets. Which is odder.

— Collect our swords, King James says, and we'll fight you in front of the house.

Asking around so as to fill his notebook Anthony discovers that every man is a bit vague about the exact origins of the battle. Nothing in that to wonder at. Three hundred years ago did the poor bloody footsloggers who marched down to the Boyne water at Oldbridge, or defended the last ditch at the defile of Duleek, know what in hell it was all about? King William himself, a stout cheerful purple-faced man and well able to handle his unhistoric but traditional off-white horse, is non-committal: It's a day out, you see. It's a day out for the local people. The weather's seldom as bad as it is today. We should have held it over by Poyntzpass.

— Why so?

— When it rains in Scarva the sun shines in Poyntzpass. That's what you'd call a proverb.

A young man who admits to being a Jacobite says cheerily as he gathers up his blanks: We'll riddle ye.

Another voice says: Where's Morrison till I get a rattle at him.

King James says: No shouting, boys. No language. Remember there are ladies on the platform. Real ladies.

Over a loudspeaker, and away round at the front of the house, somebody is making a speech: but a gusty wind and the strengthening rain make mockery of all oratory. Croaking rattles, minor explosions, a few scrambled words get as far as the farmyard, words you'd expect anyway and readily recognize: loyal, the Queen, the Union and the United Kingdom, No Surrender, Derry, Aughrim and the Boyne, No Popery, the Pious and Immortal Memory.

With a hey-ho, the wind and the rain.

A Williamite, also self-confessed, says: Put all your bullets in at wance and you'll have a machine-gun.

And another voice and another and another: How many bullets do we get? Do they let a bang? They wouldn't be much good if they didn't . . .

Babel of voices and several bangs and somebody shouts: Save your bullets for the battle.

And a voice that most certainly belongs to a horsetrooper ignores the regal veto on language and wants to know what hoorin' bastard stole his gun.

King William commands: Boys, no firing in the farmyard.

King James in the hayshed retreats up a haystack to get out of the rain and, after a while, calls down, voice muffled by warm hay, to know if the service is over. From outside, rising and falling with the wind and the rain, comes the sound of the singing of hymns: the human voice, unlike the crackles of the loudspeaker, riding easily on the elements. Lockhart sings along: Awake, sweet harp of Judah, wake, retune thy strings for Jesus sake. When God's right arm is bared for war, the thunders clothe his cloudy car, where, where, oh, where shall man retire to escape the horrors of his ire?

Lockhart reckons that that's a good question. He suggests the tea-tent. He says he has enough pictures of idiots to fill a *Mad* comic. A Jacobite whose gun won't work holds up for a while the march to Armageddon and King William takes him behind the lines, into the hayshed, to make the weapon battleworthy. King James descends from the haystack and slowly and stiffly mounts a bay cart-horse, a tank of a horse. He is a cadaverous Quixote of a man. One voice cries: Foward March.

Another voice responds: We can't be out there galloping around in the middle of God Save the Queen.

One young man tells Anthony that he's dying for a drink but the rule is no booze before the battle. Another, more academic, tells him that in former times they used to take the royal prisoner, meaning King James, back to the barn with his hands bound behind him. Anthony is about to say that King James wasn't captured at the Boyne, that he was halfways to Cork or Waterford or somewhere on the road to gallant France before the bloody day was well begun. But who cares and what's the point? The hymn-singing is ended. On distant brass the anthem has been played. King James in his stirrups stands up and cries: Follow on, boys, follow on.

Anthony notes: If he had only been so forward at the original battle history might have been altered.

So they march to the field and their banners, they have several, are so gay, defying even the brutal downpour: the Jacobites in the lead: but before and foremost of all the three famous pipers, the three McCoys, all splendid in the battle-plaid of the royal Stuarts. They play the piobaireacht of Domhnall Dhu and Lord Mansfield's march, and the Munster battle-song (Rosc Catha na Mhumhan) to which, depending on your politics, you can also sing the words of the Boyne Water: July the first in Oldbridge town there was a grievous battle, where many a man lay on the ground by the canons that did rattle. King James he pitched his tents between the lines for to retire. But King William threw his bomballs in and set them all on fire.

The dating is old-style in the old verse. Anthony is writing like mad. He notes: Today, unlike in the past, it is an ecumenical sort of a battle.

And: If the only guns ever heard in the north of Ireland were the guns of Scarva then the north of Ireland would be a happy place.

In her absence his genius is unrebuked.

With Lockhart beside him, or half a pace ahead, he brings up the rear leaving a desolate dripping farmyard behind them. Oddly enough no animals are to be seen. Hidden in an upland booley while the marauding soldiery passes? Lockhart's pacamac glistens with a thousand jewels. Somewhere out in the rain, on the sodden slope going down to the pearl-shaped lake, the battle is joined.

— There was a fellow there, says Lockhart, who told me that one year King James won the battle.

— Kidding. You must be.

— No. The same King James is here today. The gloomy fellow. Settled and sober now. He took religion. But a wild one when he was young. Got roaring drunk and cleared the field.

Anthony has his lead par: Here on the historic field of Scarva, where year after year the battle of the Boyne is replayed in pageant, the course of history was, on one celebrated occasion, dramatically reversed . . .

Lockhart is laughing. He has a helpless silent laugh that shakes his body and contorts his lined, amiable face and, just at the moment, showers raindrops all around him: That's pageants for you. Essentially ridiculous. All end up in mockery. Pageants are preposterous. The pipers told me that if they played all the Roman hymns and Irish rebel songs ever heard of these rustics wouldn't know the difference. Still it's a day out. A day out for the country people. Pos and all.

Anthony writes: In days to come a man from these places may proudly hold up a delph domestic utensil and say to his son: My great greatgrandfather brought that home from the mock battle of Scarva.

Heirlooms. Tradition. The meaning of history.

All the way to the tea-tent Lockhart is singing in the rain: Then pure, immortal, sinless, freed, we, through the Lamb, shall be decreed: Shall meet the Father face to face and need no more a dwelling-place.

All Anthony can think of saying is: And all day long the noise of battle rolled.

In the tea-tent she is seated, legs elegantly crossed: and it's not all that easy for a lady in long boots to sit cross-legged with elegance. She sips tea and talks with two women in blue overall coats. They are the supervisors of the six girls who serve the tea and they have suspended their own serving and supervising to talk with the handsome stranger. She is very gracious. She is always gracious to other women, even to Alison when they meet. Which hasn't been often. She says she admires young girls who play tennis well: such fine leg-muscles so well displayed by those short white skirts, gorgeous Gussie, frills on her panties. Or is that passé: and do they, perhaps, go to tennis in dungarees, like the young ones you see on the streets nowadays, all dressed up for the shipyards?

One of the blue ladies brings tea to Lockhart and Anthony. Then the two of them excuse themselves and go back to their work. She says: Anthony, they're so polite. One of them told me she saw the Queen speaking to Roman Catholics. At an army parade in London. She says the Queen doesn't mind Roman Catholics. That's the way she put it. The Queen doesn't mind Roman Catholics.

Lockhart says that in his local in Belfast there's a little Orangeman in a bright-check cloth cap who sits on his own in a corner of the snug and laughs into his pint and at intervals says to himself: Roman Catholics make me laugh.

— You have strange ways up here, Mr Lockhart. Anthony comes from up here. He often tells me so. Even if the Queen never spoke to him. But then he's only a lapsed Roman Catholic.

Passing with a tray of steaming cups of tea, one of the blue women says: The wasps would worry you. There must be a nest of them here where we planted the tent. They're thick around the sandwiches.

But she seems quite cheerful about it. Even more cheerful when Lockhart tells her that the wasps are half-Orange and have every right to be there: and then he demonstrates to her that a few spoonfuls of strawberry jam dissolved in a big jar of boiling water, and cunningly placed in a corner of the tent where she suspects the nest may be, will draw the wasps from the sandwiches to a warm, sweet doom.

Wasps and tents. Wasps in a tent. Even a single wasp in a tent. Anthony first met Alison in a tent. At night when you're asleep into your tent I'll creep, bleep-bleep-bleep, for I'm the Shake of Awrabee and your love belongs to me. That was at a charity tennis-tournament in a village in the Wicklow mountains, and how he found his way there or what he was doing there he cannot exactly remember. It was a warm day and the trestle-table holding the teacups and sandwiches was out in the open air. But the honey-coloured, blonde, young girl, short white skirt, legs well-made yet by no means trunks of trees, had withdrawn to the tent to sip tea in the shade. They sat beside each other on an upturned, wooden packing-case. They laughed a lot. Her forehead perspired from the tennis and the tea, and bore the faint thin line left behind by the green eye-shade. Nobody in the tent except the two of them and a single wasp buzzing somewhere unseen. So he told her about another tent and time, and even about another wasp: when he was ten or thereabouts, on a bright day at a sports-meeting just outside his home-town. A pileup on the track in a cycle-race and one of the cyclists, a big golden haired man, had an injured leg.

— He was helped into this bell-tent, you see, and I peeped in and there he was, sitting on the ground, dribbling whiskey into tea and sipping it. He saw me peeping and called me in. He had sandwiches, too, the thinnest sandwiches I've ever seen. He offered me a sandwich. But this one wasp kept buzzing around it. His hair was nearly the colour of the yellow or golden bits of the wasp. There was a smell of whiskey from the tea. But it was nothing to the smell of embrocation, so thick in the tent you could nearly see it. It put me off. I didn't know what it was.

At that time. So I refused the sandwich and I can still see the look of hurt and puzzlement on his face. He seemed to be a gentle sort of fellow. And all the time that one bloody wasp kept buzzing.

Alison listened to all that and seemed to take him seriously. Not the brightest girl in the world, perhaps, and with none of the style of somebody with a French mother. But she listened to that story as if it meant something to her. Then they searched for that one wasp but, although they could hear it buzzing as merrily as a bird sings, they never did find out where it was.

From the field where fame is lost and/or won, wet people come in, really dripping, to be warmed by cups of tea. The tent is filling.

— Anthony, she says, is at his dreams again. He's smiling to himself.

Yet he feels that he detects, just for an instant, the echo of affection in her voice.

At Poyntzpass, as Lockhart puts it, the sun is splitting the stones. But she points out that while the sun is shining and no rain falling the stones are unperturbed. Nobody, just or unjust, to be seen. They're all back at the battle, or the aftermath of the battle, and the rain, most likely, lashing merrily down.

— It was always assumed by me, Anthony says.

— A statement, Mr Lockhart. Anthony is about to make a statement.

— That when my decent Orange neighbours had a day out they were blessed with good weather. Nobody ever heard that it rained on the great day, the twelfth of July. So why should it rain all day in Scarva on the thirteenth.

She suggests that the reason may be that the sun shone on Scarva all day yesterday.

Sharp and clear the quarry stands up like a monstrous desert fortress on the rim of the ridge ahead of them. A long freight train goes South.

— It's a mystery, Lockhart says, that we may never understand.

— Don't bother to wait with me, she says. You must get to Belfast. You have a play to cover. It might be a scoop. It might be a hot story.

The rooks have left the quarry-face and flown off homeward to join their own chapel.

— Won't you come with me?

He is doing his best, he thinks, to settle the row that blew up on the train from Dublin. But she doesn't answer him. She says to Lockhart: I've things to do in Dublin. More or less urgently. And early in the morning. And there are the children.

596 · A LETTER TO PEACHTREE

One child. And a housemaid. There was one miscarriage.

Lockhart says that he knows, he knows. That children are a problem. She raises her right hand and opens and closes it in farewell to Lockhart, and walks away from them along the empty platform.

For the people of this new theatre a local poet has written a fine celebratory poem. To players everywhere, he says, he owes much thanks. Such circumstances, he says, they have set before his mind that he has shed his momentary care. Anthony's care seems more than momentary. She's in Dublin now, finding a taxi to take her home. At the first interval Lockhart and himself slip out for a whiskey. It has been a long, wet, disheartening day. To the mad King and his fool the poet sends his thanks, to the broken man who sees flame make a saint, to the peevish pair who wait beside the tree, to the harridan who urges her cracking wheels beyond despair, to all who have given him rapt occasion of a richer kind, O'Casey's humours, Lorca's sultry rage, the Theban monarch's terror, gouged and blind. A fine poet, but at the moment doing nothing for Anthony. She is opening the hall-door now, entering the house they had once entered so happily. At the second interval Lockhart and himself go out for another whiskey. During the third act he dozes for a while. Grotesque yokels march out to do mock battle. Alison and himself fail again and again to find that wasp.

In the foyer when all is quiet a few of the theatre people are drowsily chatting. He sits by the telephone in the manager's office which opens off the foyer. He sips a third and very large whiskey, courtesy of the house. Lockhart, similarly sipping and quite content, stands in the doorway. In Dublin the telephone rings for a long time: is answered at last by a sleepy housemaid. She isn't home yet. But he can hear her voice out there in the foyer, talking to and being welcomed by a tall actress, an old friend: But you're so late. I should be in Dublin. It's so lovely to see you. The Dublin train I missed. Nothing for it but to come to Belfast. But we didn't know you were coming. Anthony didn't tell us. Anthony didn't know. He will be so surprised to see me.

She is in the doorway beside Lockhart. He replaces the telephone. She says: Surprise, surprise, surprise.

She says: Is Alison not here? Or there?

Then: There may be a dance in the club. The mirth may be so high that none of them can hear the phone.

Lockhart is trying not to listen, trying to shuffle away.

— Or is she not there, where and when you expected her to be. An awful thought. She may be fickle. La donna etcetera.

Lockhart has moved out of sight, far enough away to meet and briefly prevent the tall actress and the manager's wife.

— You were phoning her.

— Who's her?

— Bouncing little Alison, playing bat and ball. You were phoning her.

— No I wasn't. I wasn't phoning Alison, bat or ball or bouncing.

— Who then were you phoning?

Nobody could better answer that question than herself, but she's not in Dublin to answer it. Which is absurd. He is very tired. He gulps his whiskey: hot but tasteless. The tall actress, the manager and his wife, and Lockhart playing a hopeless delaying game, are at the doorway. The manager wears a crimson shirt. He says: A most unexpected pleasure. You must kip with us. We'll have a ball.

— We wouldn't dream. Would we Anthony? Anthony has had a most tiring and disappointing day.

He picks up the telephone. He says: My wife missed the Dublin train and came on here.

Lockhart smiles at everybody in turn. All over Ireland and the neighbouring island and France and Germany and Spain, all over the bloody world, there are wonderful rivers and bridges and passing strangers who will readily pose as anglers. Anthony fingers the dial: There's the Royal Avenue hotel and the Grand Central and the Union.

— The Union let it be. You could call it symbolic. Anthony sees symbolism all over the place.

— I stayed there when I was a boy.

— What happy associations it will have. For Anthony.

The tall actress has felt the cool wind and is talking and acting as she never did on the stage. The doorway is suddenly crowded with people. The manager pours drink for all, large glasses and a steady hand: it's a solution of a sort. The ball is on. So from memory he dials the number and says: Is that the Union hotel?

And, as it so happens, it is.

THROUGH THE FIELDS IN GLOVES

He never will forget the face of the first of the sixteen girls he assaulted. Of the lot of them perhaps she appealed to him most. Light on her feet. Bouncing. Miniskirted. Minnehaha. Auburn hair in little kinky curls that looked as if you strummed them they'd play a tune. She was so surprised she couldn't say a sound. Her mouth opened in a perfect O. A perfect pink O, and little teeth showed and a flickering tongue, but no sound came out. Blue jacket with brass buttons. White silk flouncey scarf. White skirt, and so little of it that he had free play with her fragile legs. She raised her arms, hands drooping, as if she was about to fly. Her white small handbag fell to the ground and he was sorely tempted to grab it as a souvenir: there's nothing left for me of days that used to be, there's just a memory among my souvenirs. She wore no gloves. She was up on tiptoe for a while, really about to take off. But he flew instead, his work well done, her white skirt splashed with red. He could run like a hare, quick round the corner past the big, rich red-brick houses, high spiked iron railings, high privet hedges, a road on which you seldom met moving people. Then across the park by the lakeside walk, high hedges again, God himself can scarcely see what's going on down here. Out on the bank of the river, across the bridge by the bakery, down along the riverwalk: on the opposite side of the roadway a chain of small, poor cottages, a different world. No one would ever expect to find you in two such different places on the same day: then sit on a bench and watch the river widening towards the sea. A pity about the white handbag. The wife woulda loved it, even if she couldn't show it off. But perhaps it was safer that way. No evidence of his deed. No souvenirs. There's nothing left for me when Mama's had her tea, she eats as much in hours as I could do in years. He doesn't like that song. Some fellow who thought he was funny made up the words all over again and all wrong, just as if he knew about what wasn't his business.

As quiet here as in a church when there's nothing going on. There's a bit of a green park and a few benches. The river's very wide and slow now. Brown and green blobs of scum floating on it. A few ducks. A man said to him one day do you ever go up to evening devotions in that church in that convent in Drumcondra, you should you know, all the nuts in Dublin go there, who's a nut, but he meant no offence, all the nuts do go there, why he doesn't know, hopping from one foot to the other, sticking their thumbs in their mouths, but very quiet most of the time, that's the way to keep them: quiet. If the river and the city were not so dirty you could smell the salt from the sea.

The second girl was beautiful, but beauties can sometimes have no character, nothing you'd talk about or remember. Perfect complexion. Oh, a lot of bottles went into the making of that. Nose, a bit long. Long blonde hair. Light brown costume, a sort of fluffy hairy material. And nursing in her arms a packed plastic shopping-bag. So that she couldn't defend herself or her costume. She didn't scream. She said: Fuck you. You shit. Fuck you.

She was no lady. But he was gone like a flash before she could do fuck all about anything. It was oil that time.

The third girl: but how could you expect any man to remember everyone of sixteen girls. Or who would want to hear about them. But the fifth girl now was odd because she had a lame leg and ran after him and almost caught him. She could run like the black streak or the brown bomber or whoever it was. Something very abnormal about that and she lame. He felt sorry for her. In a sort of a way. She wasn't as well-dressed and fancypants and slim as the others.

Nobody to be seen in any direction but a few children playing by the edge of the water, and a wisp of a girl wheeling a pram, somebody else's pram, not her fault. A jet roars up from Collinstown, roars over the city, roars off to the south, roars and roars like a madman: at home, when they fly over, he can't hear his ears, or Martha whispering and sighing in her big chair, or Julia, who has goitre, rattling on forever about the Children of the Atom. They have a bloody nerve making that much noise. What he'd like to know is who gave them the right; packed full of slim bitches, that one still roaring, off south to Paris or Turkey or Torremolinos. He sweats at the thought of it, and shivers with the cold even though the sun is shining on the dirty water. The roar dies away. It's over Wexford by now: and he can again hear the children, little voices like birds. One of the Fatima ones was called Jacinta, but you don't say it like that, but with a hawk and a ha as if you were clearing phlegm. Julia and the goitre and the Children of the Atom. She can pronounce nothing. Some people were born with no brains.

Carefully he picks up his blue airlines zipper-bag: and walks home, thinking it's the funniest way to get to know people, women especially.

You see them before. You see them during. You see them after: and sometimes you can even read what they say about you. He keeps the clippings, carefully hidden away. Poor Martha can't move and never would find them, but Julia's a curious hawk. And women get things wrong. And they tell lies. That one with the thin spike-heels, and pink pyjamas on her, out in the bright light of day: and a bundle of black hair, fuzzed out and blowing, and a face all painted, a bit of a tart and no better than she might be. When she saw the weapon she tried to run, but the left spike broke and down she went, and was at his mercy, covering her face with her hands and crying to the ground: and she was purple, hair and all, not pink, when he was finished with her. But the liar, she told the guards she fought like a tiger and might have marked his face. You couldn't trust their bible oath. Moreover she should have said tigress.

His cottage is number four in the last block of seven brown-brick cottages. Across the narrow roadway and over the low wall the tidal flow has held the greasy river to a standstill. Beyond number seven there's an acre of sparse salty grass, then sand and the flat sea. The sea-wind and sometimes even the spray or a flooding high-tide burn the grass. He turns to the right at number one, then left up the back laneway to the collapsing old garage at the rear of number four: his happy home. You could hide a corpse here, let alone a blue zipper bag: and if it didn't stink nobody would ever find it: old mattresses and old tea chests, the chassis of a dismantled motor, two broken lawnmowers, a discarded dresser. The landlord, who has houses out at rent all over the place, dumps everything here and removes nothing. But we can't complain, can we, he doesn't push for the rent, and he was always most considerate about Martha's misery, and he never minds us running the bit of a shop on the premises?

Here in an old wooden meat-safe that got woodworm is the perfect place for the bag of tricks, as secure as in the Bank of Ireland in College Green: Julia calls it the Bank of the Island, she can pronounce nothing. Nothing. Then out again and around the front of the cottages, approaching this time from the side of the sea: and down two stone steps and into the shop, alarm-bell ringing, and through the shop, Julia gulping with the goitre behind the scales and the counter: and into the kitchen behind the shop, and Martha in her chair, God help us all.

He lives on eggs most of the time, henfood out of their own shop. Julia isn't much of a cook and Martha can't rise out of the chair, a big rocking-chair that because of her weight won't rock. So he cooks his own eggs, boiled, fried, poached, scrambled, but not omelettes, he was never any good at omelettes, it's just as well that he doesn't like them: and the bin on the day before the dustbinmen call is always so full of eggshells that he fears that when he lifts the lid to put in more eggshells there'll be nothing more or less to be heard but chirping chickens. Martha lives on slops and milkfoods, stuff for toothless children, that Julia cooks for her, if you could call anything that Julia does cookery: and the bell rings from above the shopdoor, and Julia runs in and out, gobbling like a turkey, between the scullery and kitchen and the shop: mostly children sent out on messages by lazy parents, small orders, eggs, loaves, bottles of milk, tins of stuff, on and on long after the big shops have closed, the thin ones in white coats won't work after six, out walking with idlers who'll get them all in the family way and that'll fatten them. That's the advantage we have, charging high when the other shops are closed and the public can't get it anywhere else. He'd spoil their whiteness for them, only you couldn't very well go into a crowded shop in broad daylight on a commando: he had thought, off and on, of wearing white, white overalls like a painter, when he was out on a raid, but then you'd be too easily seen from a long distance, either advancing to attack or retreating, mission accomplished, in good order.

No, the best disguise was the old cloth cap, the old reliable: although he had thought of blackening his face like a paratrooper. The trouble was how would you get it washed again in time: in the lake in the park with the ducks quacking at you and the water thick as treacle from those Muscovy monsters? Too pass-remarkable. Once when he was a young fellow and sneaking out at night to try to pick up the dirty young ones that hung around a certain chipshop on the Northside, Martha had always been a decent girl and hadn't hung around like that and look at the thanks the goodness of God gave her, he had walked right under the nose of his own father, and a fine long nose he had, he takes after his father in that, who didn't know him from Adam because he was wearing a cloth cap he always kept hidden in a secret place of his own in the house: nobody at home knew he had it and it wasn't much of a cap but it was as good as a mask. In Belfast, a plumber's mate once told him, they called cloth caps dunchers, neither he nor the plumber's mate who worked for a while for his own father with the nose, knew why: and in Glasgow, hookerdoons, because you hooked them doon over one eye. He often laughed to himself at that joke, Scotchmen were funny like Harry Lauder, when he was a boy he had seen Harry Lauder in the old Royal, laughed his sides sore.

Julia is sitting there as she always sits on the very rim of a round-bottomed cane chair, the sort you see in bootshops, always on the rim as if she hadn't enough backside to fill a chair: and reading out of the evening paper and saying Peter the Painter strikes again. Every time she reads out about Peter the Painter she tells over and over again what the Raid Indian did to the girl in Summerhill on the Northside, she means Red Indian, she never gets anything right. She says she knew the girl and the Raid Indian but with Julia, who's as thin as a broomstick except for the goitre God pity her, you never can credit a word.

The Raid Indian, she says, wasn't a proper Indian at all but a fellow from Ballybough on his way to a Francy Dress Ball in the Mansion House, and in Summerhill he stabbed a young one with a knife.

And Martha stirs and the chair strains and she says what did he want to do that for.

As if she hadn't heard it all before.

Julia says that the young one was sixteen and as bold as brass.

But why, Martha goes on, did he stab her.

He pays no attention. Julia's slim, fairenough, but it doesn't do her much good, she's able to walk but she's not out there on the streets, dressed to the ninetynines.

Julia says that the fellow was all dressed up you see for the francy dress, feathers on his head and things hanging out of him of all colours like the bend of the rainbow, and a knife in a bag, like the pictures, and two more with him, and a crowd after them, jeering, and the young one caught and pulled out a handful of his feathers and the next thing she knows a stab in the back.

Martha says the dirty brute.

Little she knows: but how would she know anything and she too heavy to get out of the chair and too afraid of choking to lie down. He could weep. And all those others free to come and go as they please.

But Julia says the judge said the fellow didn't mean it, and he was carried away and thought he was a real Raid Indian and the young one was tormenting and jeering and pulling his feathers. The cut was an inch and a half long and on the left side of her back bleeding and the fellow said he was doing a wardance and waving the knife and the young one hit against him and he didn't know he cut her until somebody told him, case dismissed. She had only two stitches.

Martha says that wonders never cease. She always says that.

Julia says pray, pray to Our Lady and the Children of the Atom, Russia will be converted and the sun started to roll from one place to another and changed colours, blue and yellow and everything, and came down nearly to the ground, and the people all crying and telling their sins out loud and there wasn't a priest anywhere, and then it jumped up again into the sky as cute as a coolcumber.

Julia's crazy: Julia says but this Peter the Painter must know he's doing it, he's done it before and he'll do it again.

Martha asks who was it this time, and points to the evening paper; and two of them, Julia says, photographs and all, they look as if they're pregnant: and the shopbell rings and Julia is up and out like a greyhound, so fast that he hasn't time even to ask her to bring him back a handful of eggs, all that running and excitement is good for the appetite, jogging.

Right well he knew but nearly too late that they were not pregnant. It was the funny clothes they were wearing. Julia never walks about on those swanky streets and roads, and knows nothing about the latest fashions. They looked like twins, short, bright, blonde hair, rimless glasses, little turneduppity noses: dressed like twins in blue-and-white smocks that made him make his mistake and use the spray, women who were up the pole couldn't run, spray one, spray two, red white and blue for England's glory, he mightn't have bothered about them only for that, red, white and blue like the Union Jack: and the way they looked at him as if he was of no account. But light white runner-shoes and bobbysox like John McEnroe and that should have warned him: took after him with the speed of light, saying nothing, just racing quiet like bad dogs, bitches, but no brains, no teamwork, no co-ordination. Tripped over each other and came down with a crash like a house falling, glasses flying east and west, and one of them was so winded that she couldn't get up or see where she was and the other stopped to help her, twins. The holy show of tangled legs and petticoats he saw when he looked back tempted him to give it another go and spray their legs so well that they'd be stuck together for a month of Sundays. But they might be only foxing, so he outfoxed them and vanished in the bushes.

But the lies they told. When Martha was asleep in the chair and Julia was busy in the shop with the late customers he cutely slipped the evening paper under his jacket so that later he could clip the clipping. Said he struck them and knocked them down, and that was a bloody lie because it was completely against his principles to touch a woman, slim or thin or fat or obese the doctors said, with his hands: and poor Martha, Julia says, has a gross of obesity. But, just like Julia, there never was a woman who could get anything right, except about the cap, in every clipping it said that Peter the Painter wore a cloth cap, but could never tell the colour, they didn't know he had three hookerdoons, that was as funny as Harry Lauder's red kilt, all three of different colours: and he'd buy a few more only it might be dangerous now to be seen in a shop looking for cloth caps: and they didn't know how easy it was to slip a cloth cap into a zipper bag and walk away, as cute as a coolcumber as Julia says, a tall bald man with a long nose. No woman or no clipping ever noticed that he had his father's nose but how could they since they had never known his father.

As he had known him when his father took him with him to help on jobs, and paid him a helper's wage, and he only a boy in short pants: his father was a decent man and fond of poetry. On the northside the father was a plumber, was no more, was long gone and resting in the faraway end of Glasnevin cemetery where all the patriots are buried. In the middle of the meadows, his father used to say, beside or behind Glasnevin or something, the corncrakes cry or creak all night long, or something like that, it was part of a poem: and his mother was a thin, quickwalking, brownfaced woman, hat pinned on one side, sixpence each way, never more and you couldn't have less, up and down the street all day long to the bookies, she could run like a hare: whatever happened to poor Martha to be there night and day like that in the chair: and the place that as a boy he liked best with his father was up on the roofs of the houses between the Strand Road and the northern railway, low houses and low roofs but with great gullies like mountain valleys and all sorts of treasures there that the kids would throw up from below, tennis balls, glassy marbles, yoyos, toys and once, believe it or not, a full-blown football: he had a world of his own up on those roofs and could think of all sorts of things: and the big black engine would go north on the same level as the roofs, and the people waving, and his father saying they'll be in Derry or Belfast before we're home for tea, and that you could write poetry and books about trains, the big wheels and the stories of all the people passing. Up on the lead of those gullies he learned to use the blowlamp, dead easy and the paintspray on the same principle, change the nozzle, one for paint, one for oil, and easy to come by for any man in the trade, and any God's amount of paint, he doesn't need much. As for poetry he was never much for that: but once in a pub, he could remember exactly when, because it wasn't often he darkened the door of a pub, redfaced bastards on whiskey and overdressed bitches drinking gins and tonics that cost the moon and sixpence, and a fat woman walked past to the loo as they called it nowadays and a drunk at the counter said why do you walk through the fields in gloves fat white woman whom nobody loves: and then said to the barman that that was a poem, as if anybody wouldn't have known, even if it wasn't much of a poem.

Misery Martha can't walk through the fields but she loves nice gloves. She has lovely small hands, not too pudgy about the knuckles and how did that drunk know that nobody loved the fat woman who walked out to the loo?

Julia doesn't like Peter the Painter. Julia says that if a girl works hard and saves up to buy good clothes, she ought to be allowed to wear them in peace and not to have some madman spraying her with paint and easel oil. How does Julia know they work hard: and the worst thing is that Martha agrees with her, creaking in her chair and saying yes, wonders will never cease, to everything Julia says: and Martha says the dirty brute where does he get all the paint, and he thinks that's all the thanks he gets.

Julia's a sort of a farout cousin to Martha and not too clean, and, sitting with the two of them in the kitchen, he often thinks that she could make a better fist of keeping Martha comfortable in her chair: and if it hadn't been for Julia and her tongue going like a hambell Martha would lie down at night, much better than sitting all the time except for the usual, and he always leaves the house then, and the two of them to work it out between them. He would never have shown Martha in the paper about the case of the woman choking, but Julia, no, nothing, nothing could stop her, a forty-stone woman crushed to her death by her own bulk while firemen, all in the evening paper, tried to widen the doors of her home to take her to the hospital: and the doctor said that she had recently developed influenza and began lying down in bed, and that that wasn't good for her and the fat around her chest crushed her to death: and for years before that she had slept sitting up, and that way, the weight didn't press on her. Eight men carried her on mattress-covered plywood boards and a whole other slew of men sawing the doors wider but she died before she could be put in the pickup truck that was waiting in front of the house: and all that, faraway in sunny California, full of slim stars dressed to kill and married forty times. But one girl, now that he thinks of it or that the clippings remind him, and the only thing she said she noticed was that Peter the Painter had a long nose: but he can remember nothing at all about her.

Does Julia ever wonder why the evening paper vanishes every time there's a piece in it about Peter the Painter: you'd never know with Julia, and thin people are hell for curiosity, and he must remember to take the evening paper away all the time, and not just now and then.

This particular morning the first one he notices is a girl in red tights and a long red thing halfways between a jacket and a proper coat: not much sense in spraying her with red paint. That was a sort of funny, and he should have said miss, can you wait here for a while and I'll run home and change to white or green: the green above the red as the song says. The evening before that Martha was watching teevee and Julia getting ready to go out to her sodality and rattling on about the Children of the Atom: and about how Lucia, Looseyah Julia says, had asked the lady about two girls who had died recently, from some place with a funny name, and how the lady said that one of them was already in heaven but that the other one would be in purgatory until the end of the world: and that was a long time to be in purgatory or anywhere else: Looseyah mustn't have liked the other one: and the little boy, Francisco, said that he saw God and God looked so sad that Francisco said that he would like to console him, and Lucia said that many many would be lost: not much point in being God and lord of all if you have to lose so many and to look so mournful about it, although to have to listen to the like of Julia and to look at poor Martha like a mountain in the chair would put a long face on Harry Lauder, keep right on to the end of the road, keep right on to the end: and Jesus wept and would weep again if he saw the way Julia washes herself, a dip to the tips of her fingers and a stab of the comb to her hair, and the hat cocked on her head and trotting off to her prayers with a regiment of pious ones the like of herself. For himself he washes long and hard, not that he needs it but his father was a clean man and he likes to take after his father: as fancy as those slim ones are they mightn't be any better at the washing than Julia, and a spray of paint might do them a good turn by forcing them into the bathtub. He had worked in bathrooms in swanky houses and it wouldn't do you good to look at some of them: and working by night in the cellarage of some fancy lounge bars, you couldn't work there by day because you and the staff would be falling over each other, the rats were as big as cats or calves, if people only knew what they were drinking or where it was stored: and a man once told him that nuns never washed below the navel, it was the rule, but he supposes it would be a sort of a sacrilege to go in for spraying nuns with paint, or even oil.

But keep right on to the end of the road, keep right on to the end, though the way be long let your heart be strong, keep right on round the bend: and round the bend is bloody well right and you can say that again or sing it, and plenty more where that came from, and you're breaking my heart all over again oh why should we part all over again, and poor Martha used to love that song: and perhaps this is the day that he should pack it: for that one in the red tights gives him a very hard look but he goes on his way and pays her no attention. How can she know what he has in his mind or what he has in the zipper: and the next girl is a tall one with canary-yellow trousers and a blue sleeveless sweater, and the half-sleeves of a white blouse: all crying out for a splash of red. Thinfaced, redheaded, chewing, tightly pulled-in at the waist: her backside, though, when she falls and it's looking up at him, is fat and flabby and he feels that he may have made a mistake, and then he goes and makes a mistake for he stoops and hesitates and with one wipe she claws the cap off his head and nearly takes the head with it: and there he is, bald as a hoot as Julia says, and to make a bad job worse he isn't near the park that day but in a long quiet road at the back of the football grandstand and not a bush within miles: if you're tired and weary still journey on till you've come to your happy abode, and as he runs his feet hammer out the tune, and the road quiet and nobody to be seen: with a big stout heart to a long steep hill you may get there with a smile: freedom to run to the sound of your own hoofbeats like the bighorn sheep on the wild prairie and springtime in the Rockies on the teevee. Nobody to be seen but that one with the red tights fifty yards away along a side-road and waving her red arms at somebody in an upstairs window and shouting out allahakbar: he should have let her have it in the first place.

After that mishap he wears a hat: but some bloody burglar breaks into the old garage and breaks this and that and all round them, and steals the old mattress he keeps the clippings in. Julia says there are people around this place who would steal the grace out of the Hail Mary but, leaving all sides ajoke as she puts it, time it is and more than time that somebody put a stop to that Peter the Painter: and that one girl got a good look at him and that she had seen him before when he poured paint all over her, and that he was a bald man with a long nose. Martha says that wonders will never cease, it could be you, but he says I'm not the only one in the world: but, anyway, caution from now on and a nod's as good as a wink.

But the glooms and the restlessness when he looks at Martha in the chair and listens to Julia talking about Martha and Mary, and the Lord himself sitting in his chair, but well able to rise up out of it when he takes the notion, and ascend into heaven when the day comes round: and the Lord's Martha was able to move, not that she got much thanks for it, killing herself cleaning the house and Mary sitting on her ass at the Lord's feet getting all the kudos: a hell of a house it would be for the Lord or anybody else if Martha sat down and refused to get up and left the dishes in the sink.

On top of the hollum oak, says Julia to Martha, and Julia is always busy about many things and Martha, like Mary, sits and sits but not at the Lord's feet and, God of Almighty, she has not chosen the better part:

on top of the hollum oak, the lady came from where the sun rises and places herself on top of the hollum oaktree, like the big trees in the park, that's what Francisco said when the Canon asked him: does she come slowly or quickly, she always comes quickly, do you hear what she says to Looseyah, no, do you ever speak to the lady, no, does the lady on the hollum oak ever speak to you, no I never asked her anything and she only speaks to Looseyah: and who does she look at, says the Canon, you and Jack Hinta or does she only look at Looseyah: no she looks at the three of us but she looks longer at Looseyah.

Whoever it was that robbed the old garage they wouldn't be able to make head or tail out of the clippings in the thin cardboard box in the old mattress, if they ever found them, or even, if they did find them, they'd just throw them away and never know that they were of any importance to anybody.

Martha says to Julia that the lady was very beautiful as if Martha was asking Julia a question and as if Martha hadn't heard this rigmarole twenty times over.

A hat isn't as good as a duncher or a hookerdoon: it doesn't sit so steady on the head.

Julia says that Francisco said that the lady on the tree was very beautiful, more beautiful than anybody Francisco had ever seen, with a long dress and over it a veil which covers her head and falls down to the edge of her dress which is all white except for gold lines, and she stands like somebody praying, her hands joined up to the height of her chin, and a rosary around the back of the palm of her right hand and hanging down over her dress, and the rosary as white as the dress: and if she had the misfortune to meet that Peter the Painter fellow she'd regret it.

He says before he can stop himself that Francisco never heard of Peter the Painter, and regrets that he said anything: but Julia, rattling on, has noticed nothing and is scattering the evening paper all around her, sheets all over the floor, and reading out about this man who owned a restaurant somewhere in England: and come from the east like the majors, Julia says, who came to King Herald who killed all the babies: or like the lady in white herself coming from the east to roost like a white bird on the hollum oaktree. But the wife of that man from the east could no more get out of the chair than Martha here, says Julia, and the poor man got depressed and made up his mind to burn the whole place down, and all in it: he went beresk, Julia says, and put the torch to the house and poured so much paraffin that he might have wiped out half the town except that it didn't catch right, and the floor was so slippy that when the eggspector of police walked in he slipped and measured his length and ruined his good uniform, and was so mad he hit the man:

and the woman in the chair threw a bowl at the eggspector and cut his face, and it's all up in court, a holy show.

Oh lady, mother of Christ, on the hollum oaktree, get me out of here, away from the rattling-on of Julia, and Martha saying that wonders will never cease: and keep my head in the state of grace, that's what my mother used to say when the ways of the world were too much for her: and I'll say nothing lest I offend the Lord with my tongue. Then she would curse like a trooper and my father would laugh.

Great white gulls drift in the windy day, or strut like boxers on the seawall, like the white lady on what Julia calls the hollum oaktree. The hat does not sit easy, but it looks well and it looks different, and that's important, it isn't so easy to change your nose, that's funny: and he carries the machinery now in a white plastic shopping-bag with the name of the shop written on it: and he crosses the street if he sees a woman wearing anything red, a stitch in time saves nine. The playing children on the flat place by the widening river do not so much madden him as halt him, with not a pain exactly but a cold weakness, and memories of the happy days spent on the gullies of the roofs, treasure island, with his father: and the train with all the people puffing off to the north.

Sometimes he thinks as he walks across that flat place that burning the whole caboodle up or down might not be such a bad idea: the shop and Julia, and Martha in her chair, the garage and mattresses and all, and himself as well.

The park this day seems to have more children in it than he ever saw in one place in his life before. Where do they all come from? Not that he doesn't know. They congregate mostly in one corner around seesaws and swings and chutes and the like: and the big joke is that at that corner and just outside the red park-railings some cute builder has put up a block of fancy expensive flats, or apartments as they call them, or service flats who do they serve and with what, every modern this, that and the other, view of the park and the river and the mountains away faraway, alone all alone by the wavewashed shore, and not a bloody word about the view of the playground, and the children squalling all day long Maryanne outside your wide solar window. Crowd of crooks today in the building business, as much as a tradesman can do to get his money out of them: it wasn't that way in my father's time: but nothing now is on the mend: and Martha will never move out of that chair except to be carried, and crazy Julia can rattle on forever about the white lady and the Children of the Atom, and pray, pray, pray and Russia will be converted, and the sun jumped out of the sky, and the cow jumped over the moon, a likely story, if it jumped out there in Portugal it would have jumped out everywhere else, even here.

He does not come this way often: small streets of redbrick houses around the corner from the block of francy flats, he is beginning to talk like crazy Julia, and the sun jumped out of the sky: he doesn't like these streets, narrow, no gardens before the houses, the little windows too close to you, every Tom, Dick and Harry, and Biddy and Bridget, and Jack, Sam and Pete, and Sexton Blake, and Buffalo Bill, and Laurel and Hardy, can see you little old lady passing-by: and there she is in a blue sweater with a Mickey Mouse on each breast, and black hair pulled back in a bun and parted distinctly up the middle, and tight blue levis as thin as sticks, and her little backside bouncing out, and as quick on her feet as a sparrow in a bush of bridesblossom or mock-orange: and he goes for the glasses and the dromedary Mickey Mice, for those bloody skintight levis would be no loss, one way or the other: and his hat blows off and the bloody street is full of Children of the Atom, and there he is as bald as a hoot, as Julia says, and dropping the shopping-bag and no time to pick it up, nor his hat even wherever it may be: and keep right on to the end of the road, keep right on to the end, though you're tired and weary, still journey on till you've come to your happy abode: and racing for the park and the bushes: and the children after him shouting, and he clips one of them on the ear: and across the grass of the soccer pitches, and a car in the park against all regulations, a bloody squadcar across the grass and no park-keeper to stop them: and the children around him like bluebottles, jeering: and he goes beresk, as Julia says, and kicks three of them and knocks another down with his fist: and so here we have you in the heel of the hunt, me bold Peter the Painter, says the fat man with the moustache as he leaps out of the squadcar, and two guards with him, and your painting days are over as the tattooed lady said when she killed her husband: and beyond the bushes there is Julia, darting like a rabbit.

For a minute he thinks it is his mother, hat cocked and pinned-on, and up and down the street, sixpence each way, never more and you couldn't have less: but no, it is Julia, and the children cheering, and the squadcar going back across the park and, swear to God, driving clean through a flowerbed: nothing these days is on the mend.

YOUR LEFT FOOT IS CRAZY

The stout man whose wife and two daughters run the school of ballroom-dancing doesn't sleep with his wife and tells me so almost every Monday and Thursday. Can I be the only man he confides in? He wears an expensive dark-brown suit with a darker stripe. And wide-toed, handsewn brown shoes. He is bald but with dark tufts at the ears. He has thick blackrimmed spectacles with golden arms, three rectangular perforations in each arm. All this gives him a scholarly appearance. He doesn't dance. He's the business manager. Or perhaps the clerk. His wife, stout and motherly but in an authoritative sort of way, doesn't dance but she supervises the dancing while he seldom or never puts a foot on the dancing-floor. He sits behind a desk in a sort of ante-room but it isn't too easy to see what exactly he does beyond just sitting behind the desk: he smokes, he reads, he shuffles sheets of paper with lists of names but the fees are paid in advance at the beginning of a season and paid to his wife on the dancing-floor after a brusque lecture about the rules of the Academy; the rules are brief, no booze, no big boots or hobnails, proper dancing pumps and formal clothes, no sweaters, no denims, this is a dancing academy not a shipyard, not tails exactly, although they're not prohibited, nor tuxedos nor claw-hammer coats or what you will, but respectable suits, preferably dark-brown or navy-blue and, for the ladies, long dresses not all the way to the waxed floor but well-below the knee, no slacks, no summer shorts, no mini-skirts, no disorderly behaviour. This is a very civilized dancing-school.

Who is the maid on the dancing-floor, he hums to himself, and since I know that song, which Sydney McEwan has sung so well, I can go on with the words in my mind and wonder what he's really thinking of and why he doesn't sleep with his wife. He never tells me why. Like foam on the wavetop, foam on the wavetop, who is the maid on the dancing-floor, who but the bride who came sailing. Is that what's in his mind as he hums?

The two daughters demonstrate and teach, God of the dance do they demonstrate, and their two young men in impeccable tails to help them. The ante-room glitters with the cups the four of them have won in competitions in Ireland, England, Scotland, Wales and the Isle of Man. One of the daughters is a brunette who mostly wears whites and greens, the other, a blonde, favours pinks and mauves. Mostly they demonstrate tangoes because most of the cups are tributes to their undeniable ability to tango, but tangoes are very advanced stuff for students and far beyond the powers of Peter who dances as if he had two wooden legs or was a little snubnosed bear doing his paces on a hot plate: and it is Peter's plight and his falling in love that have me in a dancing academy for the first and, I promise myself, the last time in my life. Tangoes are not for me, so I sit in the ante-room with the father of those female dervishes and he tells me that he doesn't sleep with his wife, but never tells me why or why not, and I tell him about Buckramback who taught dancing in South Tyrone in the early part of the nineteenth century. We also talk about football and fishing and women. We are at the back part of the fourth floor of a corner-house on the quays above the Liffey. At the front the music plays and the dancers dance, and who are the maids on the dancing-floor? Nobody pays the least attention to us: nobody ever pays any attention, that I notice, to him, and my fees are paid for the term or season and nobody gives a fiddler's flute whether I tango or trot or fly through the air with the greatest of ease.

It was the time in the history of Europe when American troops in large numbers and in uniform appeared on the streets of Dublin for the first and, so far, the only time. British soldiers did not so appear. Even, or especially, Irishmen in British uniform. Because of history? Because of the hardness of our hearts? But American troops were different. General Mark Clark was Irish, wasn't he? Most American troops were Irish, weren't they? This was Spencer Tracy and the Fighting 69th alive and well and walking about in Dublin. So they were to be seen all over the place and everybody was very glad to see them, and glad they were to be there to be seen, and glad that the war was over. Peter and myself used to watch them out of the high corner-window at which we spent a lot of our time. We were minor civil-servants, which is a nice way of putting it, and had an easy-going boss who spent a lot of his time in a pub across the street, the door of which was visible from the high window, so we sat and smoked and watched the door and the street and the traffic and the people, and the American troops because there were so many of them about, and one day Peter said: I want to dance. I must dance.

And I said: Dance and be damned and enjoy yourself. He's over in the pub.

And he said: But I can't put a foot under me.

Which in a way wasn't to be wondered at.

Peter was just out of a seminary, having made up his mind that he wasn't fit for martyrdom, red or white, on the foreign missions. Or had his mind made up for him: he was hesitant in speech and action. There are priests and nuns, postulants, neophytes and novices who can dance like David. Peter wasn't one of them. He had entered the seminary from a strict home where dancing had been discouraged. Dancing meant drink and women and dark corners. As well as which he wasn't made for dancing. To glide was not in his nature. He hopped. In a later style of dancing, if you could call it that, he might have managed. He was also shy: the strict home and the seminary had made their marks. A small snub-nosed man with close-cropped hair and a tight jacket.

The brass-ornamented swing-doors of the pub across the street opened and our boss stepped out. A poet I know wrote that ancient Celtic monks prayed in dark stone cells so that when they came out into the sunlight they really knew whether God was. He blinked. Rubbed his eyes. Stretched himself, actually stretched himself, a senior civil servant, on the public street, and yawned, then placed his right hand round or about his navel and, I'd say, belched. We stubbed our cigarettes, buttoned our jackets. Peter always had some difficulty with that operation. Not because of corpulence but because the jacket, brown tweed, must have predated the black, now discarded, jacket or jackets he had worn in the seminary. We prepared ourselves for our desks. But wait. He's not making a move to cross the street towards the office. He's facing right, staring with interest. Seeing God? He was a very stout man.

— Running on oil, Peter said.

Then into our field of vision, as they call it, came the tall, strong, blackhaired whore, one of two wild-eyed sisters from the County Roscommon who had taken off for town when they heard of, or sensed, the passing of a part of the great army. By her side and with his arm around her waist (a man may allow himself a few liberties when away from his own home town: that's a quotation) walked a tall, thin, blond, American soldier. He looked shaken. Drink, perhaps, and a wild night with that wild woman in one of the lodging-houses opposite the railway station up the street. He could have been embracing her just to keep himself from collapsing. Harder on him, I thought, than the Battle of the Bulge. But, because of Peter, I didn't say that out loud. She smiled at the boss. She and her sister were friendly girls and had a wide acquaintance. He stood to attention and gave a fair imitation of a military salute. Which the soldier courteously returned. That must have cost him an effort. They walked on out of our field of vision. He looked after them and smiled at nothing and rubbed the back of his head, then disappeared again through the swinging doors. We lit two more cigarettes.

— Peter, I said, beware of the women.

— That's it. That's the trouble. The way it is I'm walking out with one of a set of twins and she dances.

— Let her dance with her twin.

— She's a girl, too.

— It has been known to happen. I'm told you see them at it in all the dance-halls.

— It's no joke. You've no notion how awkward I feel.

— I'll give your condition deep thought.

— If I take Brenda out Joan comes too. They link each other and smile sideways at me. Like meeting yourself twice in a mirror. If I was able to dance I'd get one of them on her own.

— Which is which?

— Brenda is which.

— You've no complaint. Two for the price of one.

— If you would help out.

— Anything for a friend.

— And if you'd come with me to a school of ballroom dancing, on the quiet like, not telling the twins, I want to surprise Brenda some night by taking her to a ballroom.

— And I'll surprise Joan.

— You're a friend indeed.

— Is a friend in need.

The boss resurfaced, looked east and west expecting another vision. Not finding one he began to cross the street. We went back to work.

From the far side of the river Liffey the Room or School of Ballroom Dancing, high in a fine red-brick building and with wide windows looks, in the dusk or the dark, like a garden of delights; coloured paper lampshades like kingsize concertinas, swaying, undulating shadow-shapes that must be something nobler than men and women, and, on warm evenings, the sound of music on the waters.

— An oriental garden, I say.

We are very young. We lean with our backs against the parapet of the bridge and look up at the coloured windows, the dancing shadows, and he sings, a daring song for a modest man: There's a soldier in the garden and with him I will run for my heart's filled with pleasure and I won't be a nun, I won't be a nun and I shan't be a nun . . .

— They wouldn't have you, one of the girls says. You're the wrong shape.

They have come up beside us, crossing the bridge on their way to the tango which they are quite capable of performing in a robust, rural fashion. They are not the twins nor yet the wild sisters, the courtesans from Roscommon. They most certainly do not look like twins, they are not even sisters and one of them comes from Ballyvourney in West Cork, and the other from Nenagh in Tipperary. They dance together when they feel like it, although not quite with the approval of the lady of the house. But they'll dance with anybody and they dance well, would even dare to match their style with the two elegant boyfriends of the beautiful dervishes: and why they bother coming to the school at all we cannot well make out. One is small and dark and round as a pudding, a very tasty pudding. The other tall and redheaded and you'd see her if you closed your eyes and for a long time after, and that evening on the bridge she says to me: Why don't you dance? I'd like to dance with you. I fancy you.

Admittedly, that's flattering. But somewhat to the amazement of Peter, who has never heard the story before, I tell her about the broken ankle that has never properly set; limp a little to prove it too as we climb the stairs and the beat of the music grows louder. It's a lie, not the music but the spiel about the ankle. Because even from Peter I have to conceal that I know as much about the theory of dancing as he does, and as for the practice . . . Well in that as in other things I may be a disgrace to my family, for while they are all elegant dancers I'm no better at it than the renowned Clarence McFadden who, in a song my mother used to sing, went to a dancing-academy to study the waltz: One, two, three, come balance like me, you're a fairy but you have your faults. When your right-foot is lazy your left one is crazy, but don't be unaisy I'll larn you to waltz.

And in the summer Gaelic College in the Rosses of Donegal the whirls and thuds of the dusty stampedes of the Irish dances, the Walls of Limerick, the Siege of Ennis, the High Caul Cap, have simply made me dizzy, when I had the nerve to join them at all: so that my talks with the good man who never tells me why he doesn't sleep with his wife are for me a refuge and a haven. They keep me from being out on that there waxy floor making a bloody fool of myself. On which dangerous floor the daughters and the boy friends go round and round like seraphim on the wing and sway backward and forward like the saplings bent double by the gale when the wood is in trouble on Wenlock Edge.

We get on splendidly together. He seems to be happy when we talk and, because of that, his wife who is kindly, if authoritative, leaves both of us at peace and, as Dr Johnson might have put it, compels me to no gyrations. That is, doesn't force me to dance nor try to, and I am at ease. Or was until the tall redhead told me she fancied me. Her company would be most desirable. But, oh God, at what a price: and inside the dance goes on and outside the two of us sit, heads together, cigarette smoke rising, two veterans in an ingle talking of lost wars.

— I'm going to write a book, I tell him, about William Carleton. He wrote novels in the nineteenth century.

To write that book is my honest intention.

— Bully for you, he says. I look forward to reading it. Why Carleton, more than anybody else?

— Well for one thing he was a novelist and so am I. I mean I will be.

— 'Tis in reversion that you do possess.

The quotation takes the harm out of it. We roar laughter into our cloud of smoke. It is an odd place for Shakespeare, or perhaps it isn't. Beatrice was born under a dancing star. The tall redhead who fancies me comes out from the music and movement of the inner room, stands in the doorway and looks at us for a while, then says to us that some people have all the fun.

— Join us, he says, and make the fun better.

She does. That doesn't make me teetotally happy. She has told me that she fancies me and she's lovely to look at: it's the sort of thing that sooner or later affects a young fellow. But to respond to her may mean that I'll end up in agony out there on the slippery floor and, unlike Peter, I am not as yet goaded on by the desperation of love.

— For another thing, he came from Tyrone and so do I.

She asks me who I'm talking about but with the din from the dancing-floor I can pretend not to hear her and still be polite.

— For a third thing, I was as good as reared on him. I'm deeply devoted to him and his people. They're my own people, not much changed over a century.

Looking at his most professorial, he says that that's the best reason yet: and again she asks me who I'm talking about. This time I allow myself to hear her. The flattery of her open-mouthed interest is pleasant. Not open-mouthed exactly. She's too beautiful to gape. Just lips a little moist and slightly parted. Othello felt the way I feel, in the early stages that is, when he charmed her ears and all with tales of antres vast and deserts idle, and cannibals that eat each other, the Anthropophagi, and men whose heads do grow beneath their shoulders. But look, oh Lord, where the flattery of an open mouthed attention led Othello.

— And one of the great experiences of my early boyhood was to read his novel *Fardorougha the Miser* in serial form in the *Ulster Herald*. It was more exciting to read it that way. You had to wait a week for the next movement. As people used to wait for the next of Dickens.

She blinks a little: well, I am talking to impress. A civil servant can be as learned and literary as any professor and, moreover, it is my intention, when I have enough money stashed, to get out of that job and back to college.

— And one of the funniest characters he ever wrote about was a teacher of ballroom-dancing. Buckramback. That was his name.

— Buckramback, he says. Fancy that.

He laughs until he chokes and coughs and has to take off his glasses to wipe his eyes.

What, I wonder, is he thinking of.

— But Buckramback, she says, that's a comical name.

Thereafter there's a fourth person with us while, with the help of William Carleton, I try to explain to them about Buckramback, to set him curtseying and prancing on the floor before us: while inside the music sounds and the tango goes round and round and Peter hops and hops towards the wild moment when he will have Brenda cut off from the herd and all on his very own.

— They called him Buckramback because he had been for a time a drummer in the British Army. He didn't like soldiering. He deserted so often and was caught so often and flogged so often that his back was cartaliginous. As hard as buckram, that is.

But they know what I mean.

— He was a dapper light little fellow with a Tipperary accent crossed by a lofty strain of illegitimate English he had picked up in the army.

— Tipperary, she hums, never more will I roam from my dear native home, Tipperary, so far away.

He compliments her on her singing voice and she is obviously pleased: he has such a way of humouring the ladies that it's a continual wonder to me why he doesn't sleep with his wife: she's not as young as she used to be but she goes out and round in all the right places. And is well perfumed.

— He wore tight secondhand clothes, shabby-genteel, and his face was as secondhand and tight-skinned and wrinkled as his clothes. And tight breeches, and high, brightly-polished high boots, also cracked, and white stockings, and a tall hat and coloured gloves: and small as he was he would take on to fight any man. But he was also and always a gentleman to the ladies.

— The image of yourself, she says.

And sounds as if she means it, the bit, that is, about being a gentleman to the ladies, and I try not too well to pretend that I haven't heard.

— He kept his dancing-school in a roadside cabin, and the country-girls around him in all their frocks and ribbons, and the young fellows in knee-breeches and green-tailed coats.

— Like a postcard for St Patrick's Day, she says, Paddy and the pig, and the pig running wild and twisting the rope round Paddy's legs.

— But dancing was the least part of what Buckramback had to teach. He could teach the country boys and girls how to enter a drawingroom in the most fashionable manner alive. They that never saw or would see a drawingroom.

— You never know, she says. You should see me at work. Even if it's not my own drawingroom.

— He taught the whole art of courtship with all politeness and success as it was practised in Paris during the last season.

She says that she would give her heart and soul to see Paris and Gene Kelly and Leslie Caron and all the dancing. And singing.

— And how to write valentines and love-letters as Napoleon wrote them to his wife or his two wives.

He says that Buckramback would be a useful little man to have about any well-ordered house: and, if I hadn't been swept away by my own eloquence and learning and the elation of owning an audience, I would have known that the mention of valentines would set her humming: I'll be your sweetheart if you will be mine.

— And teach the ladies how to curchy and the young gentlemen how to shiloote the ladies.

Curchy, she knew, was curtsey.

— But shiloote, she says. Did he mean salute? I've heard old countrymen say shiloote.

— He meant salute.

— Like soldiers in the army. All present and correct.

She stands up, our four eyes fixed on her, and performs in a way to warm the heart of any sergeant-major, or any other man.

— No, he meant kissing. To shiloote was to kiss.

— Amo, amas, amat he says. Followed by osculo, osculas, osculat. Or perhaps osculo comes before amo.

— Amo I know, she says. L'amour.

Her eyes glow. This is perilous country. This could lead me out there, and in the company of this maid, to the dancing-floor where she, but not her spavindy partner, would move like foam on the wavetop, foam on the wavetop.

In my secret and poltroon's heart I knew that I wanted to be her partner. But not out there under coloured lights, in jostling crowds and perpetual motion, and contrasting comically with the prizewinning boyfriends. Or even with Peter who must by now be picking up something. The shadows I craved, green secrecy and silence: and I didn't need a man who didn't sleep with his wife to tell me (which he did politely when she had left us for a while to do a routine tango with her tasty pudding of a friend), didn't need him to tell me, I repeat, that it was an odd way to make love to a girl, to talk on and on about a character from an author dead and at rest in Mount Jerome cemetery for the better part of a century. And what young fellow in love was ever afraid to go dancing with the loved one? The primitive country-boys in caubeens, knee-breeches and green-tailed coats, were more daring. Clarence MacFadden, awkward and all, was a better man than I was: he tried. Peter was a better man: he was trying. And this was the middle of the twentieth century and the streets full of heroes returning from an ended war: and faint heart never won, and all the rest of it. My friend and confidant was kindly and fatherly. It wasn't in him to be otherwise. But in the cloud of smoke that bound us together he was concerned and critical. It would have been no satisfaction to me, even if I had had the gall to do it, to *tu quoque* him and tell him that he didn't even sleep etc. For my own good he was talking, I knew. He was telling the truth. At every stage of development or decline, love, it occurred to me, had its special problems.

But I want to tell you about the twins, Peter's twins. Brenda and Joan.

They lived in Donnybrook in a quiet side-street of bay-windowed houses built at the turn of the century out of good red brick from Somerset. The Joycean ship that came into Dublin out of Bridgewater with bricks carried across the Irish Sea the walls of most of those houses. The side-street led to, still leads to, the beauty of Herbert Park. So on a bright Sunday morning after Mass the four of us met for the first time between the lake and the bandstand in the corner of the park by the Ballsbridge bakery wall. All very pure and proper, and shaded and pleasantly fanned by noble trees: the faint odour of fresh bread an added intimacy. The band would not be out until the afternoon.

It was the season in which the ducks walked the grass, parading their ducklings. Two Muscovy ducks, like boozed geese with the whiskey-drinker's crimson horse's-collar round their necks, stood on the concrete rim of a small leafy island and scowled at the water and the world. They always kept the same place and everybody, the other ducks I mean, left them alone. They looked both dirty and dangerous.

One of them affected, as we'd have said in another century, bright colours. I'm talking now about the twins. The other went abroad in more demure shades. Brenda was the bright one. They were handsome girls, both of them: if one was the other almost had to be. They spoke well, the good, clear, unaccented (almost) English of the Dublin middle-class: as in Bernard Shaw. They had dark-blue berets and brown eyes that were always smiling. They were good-humoured but never laughed out loud, not, at any rate, while we were with them. They were self-assured, capable I'd say, good managers, good housekeepers, the pride and joy of their parents, and rightaway I could see how they had Peter rattled. One of them would have rattled a veteran. Two was, or were, by much too much or too many.

Twice round the entire park we walked slowly. That, roughly, would be three miles.

First we headed north across the lime-lined road that cuts the park into two portions. By the happy corner where there's a toy railway for children, seesaws, a long-armed tree that God grew to pleasure pygmy climbers. By the back of the tennis-courts: where, out of respect for Peter's pure passion, I looked ahead, keeping my eyes from the strong thighs of the girls leaping about in short skirts. Brenda went on Peter's arm, Joan went on mine, and with such military force and precision that those who met with us were forced unto the grass. By the bowling-green where stout ladies and elderly gentlemen in white peaked caps were doing the Francis Drake. Where do they come from, the good people who join bowling-clubs? Four-deep, we looked at them over the precisely-clipped hedge and I made the inevitable remark about my bias running against the bowl, then had to explain what the hell I was talking about.

Diagonalwise across grass that was half-white with fluff from the maples. Back again across the dividing roadway and along a pillared walk that showed us the splendid planned vista of the lake. All around the sporting-grounds where roaring youths were engaged at soccer, Gaelic football and hurling. In another happy corner there was a whirligig for children, and chutes, and twenty little girls on twenty swings were rising and falling in rhythm and singing the same chirping song. To our right was the river Dodder, then high trees and big houses and, a few miles away, the blue Dublin-Wicklow mountains to which, Peter wildly proposed, we would some Sunday go cycling. But also cunningly: it isn't so easy to maintain on bicycles the four-deep flying formation. Somewhere in Wicklow heather he meant to have his will, whatever it was.

But back for now to the empty bandstand and the corner by the

Ballsbridge bakery wall. Then round the course once again, clockwise, except that the second time round we didn't stop to look over the hedge at the bowlers and I did peep sideways at the stout thighs of the girls playing tennis: as I was riding on the outside, if you follow me, and could pretend to be looking at Peter who was hugging the rails. Four deep all the time. Four at a table we had poisonous coffee at a lounge-bar in Ballsbridge. Then Peter and myself took a bus into town. The two young ladies walked home across the park. Because their parents mightn't like to see them escorted home so early on a Sunday morning. Better, I savagely thought, than late and drunk on a Saturday night. Not one word can I now remember that anybody said on the walk or at the coffee-table. Nor could remember even on the very next day. Apart from that bit about the bias and the bowl.

Only pity kept me from telling Peter what I thought. Only sheer force of friendship brought me out again on safari: second-time to a cinema where we sat four abreast and no scuffling took place. Chocolates were consumed. The twins didn't smoke and didn't fancy the smell of smoke. There was much whispering and crinkling of tinfoil. An elderly gentleman in the row in front asked us, loudly, to be quiet, and the usherette shone her lamp on the elderly gentleman and asked him to be quiet, and voices all over the place asked everybody else to be quiet: this was long before the days when cinemas became so infested with riotous ten-year-olds that you couldn't even hear the uproar of Star Wars.

Afterwards, we had coffee and sweet-cakes in a green-walled green-carpeted restaurant where I knew all the waitresses: principally Josie who was tall, wide-mouthed, most affable always to me; and Marie who was only gorgeous and had a married lover who wore a fur-coat and walked the streets leading a big dog on a silver chain. Something odd about chaps who wear fur-coats and lead big dogs on silver chains. He and the dog came in that evening and were introduced to Peter and the twins. Who liked style and dogs. Who were so impressed that on the way home we walked two-by-two at a distance of almost twenty paces. And hand-in-hand. Peter held Brenda's hand. Joan held my hand. My heart, I now knew, was elsewhere. Off the bus at Ballsbridge. Along the river-walk to Donnybrook. The Dodder, ten feet below us, whispered of all sorts of things.

To Joan I told how somewhere in the mountains and along the upper waters of that river, perhaps in Glenasmole or the Glen of the Thrushes, might be the spot where, in mythology, had stood the hostelry of Da Derga. How the King, Conaire the good, had been murdered there by Irish outlaws and marauding sea-rovers: and the hostelry burnt. How the murdering marauders or the marauding murderers had camped on

Lambay island and sailed in, under darkness, to Merrion or Sandymount strand where James Joyce had set Stephen Dedalus walking between the markings of high and low tide. How Conaire went to his doom because he had had the ill-luck on the way to the hostelry to break all his geasa or taboos. How one of those geasa was: Do not let two reds [redheads] go before you to the house of a red.

She listened with exemplary, if obvious, patience. Somewhere else, I said to myself, and to the sound of music and dancing, I would find a livelier, more loveable listener for one of the greatest of all stories. Yet that thing about the taboo got to wherever her head was. She repeated it over and over again: Do not let two reds go before you to the house of a red.

We leaned against the park railings, the park closed and the dark behind us. Across the narrow water great trees stood up like clouds: the lights of the mansions on Anglesea Road shone through them. Music came to us over the water from the dance-pavilion in the grounds of the rugby-football club. We whispered and kissed. Peter kissed Brenda: believe it or not, but I saw him at it. Joan kissed me and I kissed her in return: fair's fair. The thin red line had been broken by the symbolism of a man in a fur-coat, with a gorgeous, only gorgeous, mistress, and a big dog on a silver chain.

On the Dodder bridge at Donnybrook Peter stood as proud as a turkey-cock, and said: Have the rothar [bicycle] oiled for next Sunday. We're off for the mountains. Brenda wants to see the Devil's Glen.

Looking out of high city-windows any more you don't see as much as you used to, for the odd reason that the streets and sidewalks are more crowded. More people, in Dublin at any rate, more cars, too much wood, fewer distinctive trees. People I saw then from our spy-window and smoking-room I can see quite clearly to this day. As well as that there was a darkhaired young woman who worked in our office: lonely, hollow-cheeked, slightly sallow but lovely, who sometimes when the boss was across in the pub used to stand with us at the window and, while we smoked, sip tea. A cup held delicately between finger and thumb, never a saucer, and we never saw her brew the tea nor knew where. She brooded. She was mysterious. She went away to be a nun and it pains me a little still to think that, in her presence and all unwittingly, Peter used to sing his daring song: There's a soldier in the garden, etc.

His daring song! Far below us the soldiers from the war returning walked up and down. She sipped her tea and talked little and was one of those people I can see as clearly now as I did then.

Gobnait, the red, comes out to us. She is flushed from the dance. Through rings of smoke like the rings round Saturn we contemplate her beauty. She is, I am now convinced, the most beautiful woman I have ever seen. She is called Gobnait because, as I've said, she comes from Ballyvourney and that odd name (say it with a vee) is the name of the patron saint of that place: a consecrated virgin, Gobnait of the Bees, who cooled the ardour of a chieftain, who would have explored her virginity, by unleashing at him a hive of honeybees: sweets to the sweet, farewell. She stands in stone, cut by the great sculptor Seamus Murphy, above the holy well at that place, and bees, cut in stone, circle forever around her chaste feet.

Gobnait knows all about Gobnait and can stand still and mime the statue and with pursed lips make a noise so like swarming bees that you'd run for cover. Nobody but a born actress could compress such a mouth to a thin colourless line. Through the smoke two sour chieftains look at her and, speaking for myself, lust and wonder: foam on the wavetop, foam on the wavetop. Her tasty plump little pudding of a friend sits at a distance and is clearly very happy. She's a jolly girl, would be most attractive if Gobnait were not standing there and the bees buzzing around her. They are very fond of each other, Gobnait and the jolly girl.

Gobnait has absorbed every word I've said about Buckramback. One evening she mimes him. It's uncanny, even a little alarming, how a tall redhead with so much about her that you can't take your eyes off even when your eyes are shut, can become a dapper light little fellow with secondhand clothes, shabby-genteel, tight breeches, brightly-polished high boots, white stockings, a tall hat, coloured gloves. She bows and scrapes to the ladies and in a roadside cabin, long-gone, kisses laughing rural beauties, long-dead. He lilts: One, two, three, come balance like me.

She, or Buckramback or Clarence McFadden, waltzes to the lilting. Marcel Marceau himself couldn't do better. The music in the inner room has ceased. Peter is standing in the doorway wiping his brow. Behind him the crowd is gathering, even the motherly lady herself and the dervishes and their boyfriends, tails and all: and when the lilting and miming stop, the applause and laughter begin, and one of the boyfriends waltzes Gobnait round the room, her red hair flying. For the only time in my life I feel weak and sick because I'm a disgrace to a family who are all good dancers.

Peter and myself walk Gobnait and her friend to the last Enniskerry bus. They work in a big house there and that's twelve miles away. There's no time for coffee in the green restaurant. She takes my arm, holds it close to her, she is very warm and my knees are weak. She says: I'd love to have seen him. Buckramback. I'd love to have gone to those dancing classes.

So I tell her that while I'm not able to enable her to see Buckramback I can bring her and her friend some Thursday afternoon, which is afternoon-off for domestics, to the national gallery to show her the portrait of the man who created or remembered Buckramback. The friend's name is Pauline which I don't know until that moment. She is one of those amiable girls who don't seem to need a name: I ask her also to come to the gallery because through sudden fright I crave the safety of numbers. In contrast to Peter.

It is the first time that I have looked real love in the face.

When the last bus has gone off towards Enniskerry and the dark mountains Peter says to me: Tonight I danced my first tango.

Christ keep Brenda when he gets her in the mountains, and if he finds her in the glen her blood will stain the heather.

No, we never did get as far as the Devil's Glen. It was a windy day with showers blowing up all the way from Ballyvourney, a place I now thought of all the time. No matter in what direction you faced, that wind was against you. Cycling was slavery. The best we could do was make the secrecy of Calary lake to the right of the high road from Enniskerry to Roundwood. To the east the Sugarloaf stood up sharply over the moor. To the west, and high above us, the gloom of the woods and Djouce mountain into which, about that time, a French plane had crashed because the pilot hadn't been speaking to the navigator. Down there in the woods the long lake hugged itself, arms tightly folded.

We walked along the west of it, then across at the dam and sluicegate, then along the east of it and back again, and across again and back along the west of it: you could sing that. Joan and myself in the lead and hand-in-hand, Brenda and Peter ten paces in the rear and stepping well. On a carpet of damp pine-needles we picnicked. Neither God nor St Patrick intended Ireland for picnics. Murderous midges came around us in the damp and fed on us. We fed on ham sandwiches and lukewarm tea. Then halfway up Djouce mountain, searching for and not finding the wreck of the French plane: and talking about nothing else. Those girls were dull and so was Peter. Not their fault that day, perhaps. For as we walked I kept repeating: Bosomed high in tufted trees, bosomed high in tufted trees.

To the wonderment of all.

Because on the far side of Enniskerry, where the road falls steeply to the bridge over the Dargle, was the mansion in which Gobnait worked. And Joan. Just like that: bosomed high in tufted trees.

To the dripping woods I proclaimed: Where perhaps some beauty lies, the cynosure of neighbouring eyes.

They were used to me now. They made no comment.

No bums disturbed, no blood stained the damp pine-needles. Segregation went only so far.

But the sun came out in the evening and, homeward bound, we could see, faint and faraway, the outline in Ulster of the Mourne mountains.

In Enniskerry I sneaked a secret half-whiskey and a pint. Badly needed. Those girls were deadly. Courage for the dreary walk, pushing bicycles up that hill.

Halfway up the wonder happened. Two on one bike they came down like the wind. A man's bike. Pauline on the bar, Gobnait in the saddle, hair flying. They called my name. And Peter's name. They didn't stop. Out of sight round a corner and down to the bridge and the village. Bosomed high in tufted trees.

Brenda asked what was that.

— Girls from the office, I told her.

For Peter's sake: to preserve the secret of the school of ballroom dancing. That first fine careless tango.

The mizzling rain came on again and kept us company all the way to Donnybrook.

Peter never could have been described as passionate and I had only gone with him to balance the boat, as I take care to explain to Gobnait on the following Thursday afternoon.

— Pushing up the hill, she says, you all looked so woebegone it was funny.

She laughs so happily, right before the portrait of the man who had created or remembered Buckramback. There he sits: a long, strong, heavy, northern face, hair going grey and thinning over the temples, a respectable black coat, a quill in the right hand, an elbow resting solidly on a copy of *The Traits and Stories of the Irish Peasantry*.

— And a fine man indeed, she says. Very like my father. A fine countryman. You might look like that when you're growing old. You might look distinguished. We'll wait and see.

She has come without Joan. We walk hand-in-hand on the polished slippery floor. We stand for a long time before the battle of the Boyne, and the merriment and mayhem and writhing limbs around the nuptials of Eva and Strongbow: my arm is around her waist; the gallery is as secret as the woods of Djouce mountain to which some day when the sun is shining we will go together. Her hair is on my shoulder.

The zoological museum is noisy with school-children.

— But, she says, children I love and all these things are better than just pictures.

Skeletons of whales, apes, male and female, with all found and every hair numbered: and the Rathcannon elk about which I am the greatest living authority as, on that day and being inspired, I am about many other things: no longer even has the dancing-floor any terrors for me, foam on the wavetop, foam on the wavetop, and I tell her that my father's father and the Rathcannon elk came from the same place. She says that there's a definite family resemblance. She stands back and studies me and the high proud skeleton.

— Your father's father wasn't so tall. What was he?

— A policeman.

— They made them bigger then.

— They found him in a marsh in 1824.

— Your father's father?

— And dug him up.

— Not a pick on his bones.

— From his toes to the tip of his antlers he's ten feet and four inches.

— Your father's father's people were a fine body of men. You take after them.

We kiss to clinch our happiness in the presence of the Rathcannon elk and his two skeletal companions, one female. Passing children giggle. The man at the turnstile bar scratches his old beard. We are past caring. We aren't laughing any more. Round the corner then to Stephen's Green to sit on a bench in the sun and look at the lake. We talk little, we don't need to. Then to tea in the Country Shop with all the delicacies a minor civil servant can afford. She laughs again when I tell her about the ham sandwiches and lukewarm tea in the wood under Djouce mountain. When we go there together the fare will be better. She promises.

Even to please Peter there was little point in pretending much longer with the twins: Joan or Brenda. For a while we went on parading in the park, cuddling mildly at the movies, sipping coffee in the all-green restaurant, chatting to the affable Josie and the gorgeous Marie who was having some trouble with the lover with the fur-coat and the big dog on a silver chain. We stood regularly in the shadows on the river-walk by the Dodder, and kissed a bit and whispered. Peter may have been well content. His ambitions went no further. Joan and myself stood here.

Brenda and Peter stood there, twenty paces away, regulation distance. Or did they? For I had begun to suspect something peculiar. That the twins changed their clothes, swapped I mean, and their colours. Was it taste, was it touch, was it odour?

It couldn't have been sight. They looked alike. Or hearing. They talked alike. Poor Peter I thought: and tested and tricked them with the magic formula from the tale of the death of King Conaire the Good: Do not let two reds go before you to the house of a red.

Joan couldn't remember the words. It wasn't Joan. For three nights later she was word-perfect, and without prompting. That was Joan. Three nights later she hadn't a clue. That was Brenda. Poor Peter. They tasted the same. And sounded and looked etc. They were playing a game and the stakes weren't high, they hadn't even bothered to do their homework, they stood to lose nothing and we, sure as God, had nothing to gain. Never knew if Peter ever knew and, as in two little girls in blue, we drifted apart: and Gobnait and Pauline made the newspapers, not the headlines exactly but not a brief paragraph neither.

They got two and a quarter inches, single-column, provincial papers please copy, and I kept the clipping for a long time. And that was that, the man's bicycle one in the saddle one on the bar, brakes that snapped and the stone bridge at the foot of that precipice of a hill: foam on the wavetop.

On my last visit to the dancing-academy we talked about it through the smoke.

Now and again I communed with the Rathcannon elk and thought of Buckramback and Clarence McFadden.

Peter and myself never did take Brenda and Joan to a dance: and four years later I met Brenda, or so she said, on a street near Ballsbridge. She was married and happy and wheeling a pram and halfways to filling another, and I wondered, but was too polite to ask, was her sister similarly situated. Of course it could have been Joan. How was I to know? They tell me there's only one sure way for a man to find out.

THE JEWELLER'S BOY

The first day the boys from Gallows Hill paid any attention to Robbie, the barefooted son of Jamie the Jeweller, was the day Shorty Morgan's watch got broken in a wrestling match. It was an Ingersoll watch with a black face on it, and phosphorescent digits you could see in the dark, and a phosphorescent railway engine puffing across the centre of the black face. It had cost five shillings. It was Shorty's favourite Christmas present ever. The glass of it got broken when Lanty Cassidy fell on Shorty in this wrestling match in which we were supposed to be Finn MacCool and his Fenians. Lanty was Finn. He was a born leader.

Shorty picked himself up when he heard the crunch and reached frenziedly for a patch watch-pocket that a fond mother had stitched on to the front of his trousers. Then he sat down and began to cry. It was poor behaviour for a follower of the great Finn, captain of the warriors and hunters of ancient Erin. Yet we felt too deeply for him, and for the magnitude of the tragedy, to speak any word of reproof. Nobody else owned a watch. Shorty was a spoiled child. We sat in council in a circle around the Big Tree on the top of Gallows Hill. Just as the men of Finn might, according to the story-books, have sat in council, after a hunt or a foray, on the Hill of Allen in the County Kildare. The Big Tree was only the stump of a tree. Somebody with nothing better to do or, perhaps, to make a tethering base for straying cattle or goats, had once driven deep into the trunk two iron bars with hooked ends. That was enough to make us think that people had been hanged from that tree, thus giving the hill its grisly name, and the area around the tree-stump a special awe and sanctity suitable for our council meetings.

We assessed the damage. The glass was gone. The hands were miraculously preserved, but paralysed. The back was dented and bent and refused to open. So it was no longer possible to view with fascination what was going on in the very soul of the machine. The railway engine that gleamed so splendidly by night was a sad thing in the harsh daylight of ruin. Pathetically, soundlessly it puffed on, going nowhere forever and forever.

Shorty ceased to sob. He was a blond, squinty, shortsighted little boy with thick, oval-shaped, silver-rimmed spectacles and close-cropped hair. He gulped and tried to be brave.

— There's nothing for it, said Finn McCool, but Jamie the Jeweller. They say he can bring the dead to life.

— That means, somebody said, going all the way down to John Street.

— The police are down there, said yet another Fenian.

— They're after the whip-fighters still.

— They're only after Tall John.

— They're after the jingbang lot of us.

— It's a big risk to take.

— Well, Finn MacCool said, if you're all feared to ride into town I'll go myself. Give me the watch, Shorty.

But we couldn't let our captain shame us. Nor could we let him go down on his own into the suspect world of orderly, police-patrolled society.

So, led by Lanty, we descended, crossed the Fair Green, clattered in nailed boots along the staid blue pavements of John Street, shops and offices all around us. Past the Methodist meeting house where the air was always fluttering with pigeons: and to Jamie the Jeweller's where John MacBride who was musical said he could stand all day listening to the ticking and the chimes.

Bearing the wounded watch Lanty entered. The rest of us, awe-struck, looked through the window at the dumb-show going on inside. Jamie was a short, grizzled gentle stump of a man and he had something like a miniature telescope stuck in his left eye. Expertly, he opened the watch as we had not been able to do. There was a sad saintly little smile on his face. It was also a giggle but we couldn't hear that part of it. He switched on a light that was under a green shade on the counter. He applied the light and the telescope to the watch. Then he ceased to smile. Or giggle. He shook his head sadly. He handed the wounded thing back to Lanty and with a cry of agony Shorty was in through the door to gather to himself his beloved engine. We followed like chief mourners.

— Not Tompion himself, said Jamie, and he was the greatest clockmaker that ever lived, could make that engine move again.

He groped under the counter, came up with a silvery pocket-watch, shook it, wound it, set it, held it to his ear and nodded with satisfaction.

— How about a swap, young Morgan, he said with great kindliness. Your watch for one that goes. I might get a spare part or two out of yours. Here, take this one.

He held it out towards Shorty who backed away suspiciously.

— Can you see it in the dark?

— Well no, said Jamie. But I reckon you could always strike a light.

— It's no good, said Shorty, if you can't see it in the dark. And there's no railway engine on it.

— No. But the works work.

— It's not a fair swap, Shorty said.

Jamie smiled sadly, accepting the stubborn obtuseness of the young.

Then a voice spoke from the shadowy, chiming, ticking sanctuary at the back of the shop. Since, for the moment and until the speaker stepped forward a little, we could see nobody, it almost seemed as if Jamie, the Magician, possessed a clock that could speak. The voice said: Give him his own watch too, dad. That way, at night, he can look at one and listen to the other.

— Son, said Jamie, that sounds like a mighty fine compromise.

Then the voice stepped forward. We looked in gratitude and awe at this Daniel come to judgement. We already knew him by sight but, for several reasons, he didn't belong in our world. The first of the many extraordinary things about him was that he had been born in America and, away back before jets and Lindberg, America was a long way from Gallows Hill. Jamie, a native of our town, had gone to Boston as a young man, married there and lived there until his wife died, then sadly and quietly came home bringing with him his one rare child, a boy about fourteen years of age. But what a boy. He went bootless and bare-legged, from the knees down, except in deep winter. Not from poverty, for Jamie the Jeweller made real money. But the mild little man with the telescope to his eye could never force that beloved son to wear shoes against his will: and in those days the police minded their own business, like murder, robbery, rebellion and poteen, and left social welfare to the few old ladies who cared. The wild boys from the Hill envied Robbie. They were never allowed to go barefoot. There was too much broken glass left over in that part of the town from the Saturday night homeward courses of drunken men. To add to their envy, Robbie, since his father brought him to the town twelve months previously, had successfully resisted any attempt to send him to school.

So the Hill boys, myself among them, assuaged their feelings by referring to Robbie as Girly Girly. He wore a velvet corduroy zipper jacket and knickerbockers, which looked to us like long bloomers, of the same material. He had a pale oval face, large liquid blue eyes, a wide forehead and brown curling hair: the sort of face that I saw long afterwards in an early portrait of Rupert Brooke. It was said that he was delicate and needed nine different colours of pills. Yet for the sake of

Shorty we were grateful to him that day. Even if embarrassed by the necessity for being grateful.

He followed us as we went, shuffling and bumping against each other, into the street.

— Hillbillies, he said.

Not with contempt but with curiosity. He was rationally considering us.

— Do you still fight with whips up there on the Hill?

He spoke to us as if we came from some interesting place. Like the moon. And not from a suburb five hundred yards away. He was the urban man. We were a little in awe of him because he had crossed the Atlantic in a liner and seen buildings higher than the church steeple which was all of two hundred feet.

Shamefacedly we admitted that the whipfights were no more.

— Tall John and the razor fixed you, he said.

But with pride we said: The police fixed us.

It pleased us to consider ourselves as wanted men.

The whipfights had taken place between the boys of the Hill and the boys of Brook Street, another suburb at the far end of the town. Nobody paid much attention to these mass and manly conflicts until Tall John, a broad muscular dwarf of a Hill boy with a curious sense of humour, tied a cut-throat razor to the end of his whip and drove both armies before him into the staid streets where professional people and merchants worked and lived. Shop windows were broken. And old ladies knocked down. And the police appealed to. No arrests were made. But terror descended on Brook Street and the Hill. Whips were confiscated, or hidden as, in days of ancient rebellion, steel pikes were hidden in cornstacks in haggards or in the thatched roofs of mountain cabins.

— A pity, Robbie said to us, you had to stop. It was a fun thing. This town needs excitement. I'll give you some. As from tomorrow.

With patience and with scepticism we asked him how?

— I've got this job. Driving the van from the railroad to the post office. Look out for sparks. Always wanted to drive a horse and van.

Then he said that he hoped Shorty's new watch would go. Then left us with the feeling that we had been dismissed as soon as he had made his pronouncement. He went back into the ticking, chiming shop and, as we went, all the clocks began in chorus to tell us that it was teatime.

We didn't believe what he had told us. Yet the coincidence of his departure to all those chimes left us with an odd feeling that he might readily turn out to be a wonder. So we were only half-reassured when John MacBride who was musical said: That fellow's the greatest liar under heaven. Who'd ever trust him out of the house with a horse and van.

At that time the town possessed only one demon driver and he was a ghost. Few people had seen him. Those who claimed to have done so were not the most trustworthy of the community. Sam Mullan, for instance. Sam thought he was a Scotland Yard man. So he hid behind walls peeping at people. Or in Sunday dusk darted from lampost to lampost tailing people who generally ended up by turning into the cinema or into the Sacred Heart church for evening devotions. But Sam swore that he had seen the headless ghost of Adam Tait, an evil landlord of the past, flog his four spectral horses down from Gallows Hill where so many of his victims had gasped their last. The horses dragged a flaming coach down John Street and High Street and Market Street to vanish, still galloping but rising into the air, over the County Hospital. There were imaginative young people, Shorty Morgan was one of them, who swore that by night they heard the passing of headless Adam and his wheels and horses.

But when Robbie, a uniform cap on his head according to regulations, took over the mail van we forgot about ghosts and headless monsters.

Goaded by an ashplant and excited by shrill nasal cries the old bay horse that pulled the two-wheeled covered wagon was galvanized into a gallop. The top half of the van was of red wickerwork with the royal insignia done crudely in black. Twice a day like a crimson flash it swept from the post office to the railway station and back again. As green with envy as the van was red with paint, we sat on the top of a high wall by the Station Brae, and watched the wild fellow pass, and raised a cheer that we hoped was ironical. Then John MacBride who was musical would say: He'll kill himself. That's what he'll do.

— He'll wreck the town, said Lanty. But, God, you have to hand it to him. He has go in him. Wherever he's going.

On his return journey Robbie was merciful enough to allow the tavered horse to walk up the Station Brae. Then he'd wave his ashplant at us and call us hillbillies. But with a laugh and in a voice that nobody could resent. And when he came to John Street off he'd go with a slap of the plant and a wild drumming of hooves. In Jamie's chiming shop old ladies clutching ailing clocks under shawls shuddered as the demon driver went past. On one occasion Mrs Gormley's alarm-clock, a new-fangled effort that had stopped the week after she bought it, started again and rang at the reverberation. But Jamie, helpless before the uncanny wildness of the girl of a boy, never looked up. He simply smiled, or giggled, and peered more intently through his glass at the intestines of watches and clocks.

— In America, said Lanty, I'd say his mother's father drove a stagecoach. Or a runaway covered wagon.

We had seen the film about the covered wagon and the film about the thundering herd. It was Robbie's genius to bring them to three-dimensional life, off the screen, right in the heart of our town.

Once a month the shopkeepers barricaded themselves against cattle. Because, on the monthly fairday, buying and selling of cattle overflowed from the Fairgreen at the butt of Gallows Hill and all along the level of John Street: and even on to the High Street and the steep hill before the Court-house. The oldfashioned Irish fairday, driven out by orderly marts conducted in large concrete buildings, has gone nowadays. Except from towns like Drumshanbo in the County Leitrim where you can buy a good blackthorn for seventeen old pence or a small hairy donkey for five old shillings. Or from Killorglin in the County Kerry where once in a year the local people worship not God but a gentleman goat, raised up on a platform: and where tinkers and tourists flock to the fair of Puck, and where a tall fashion model from London once slipped on the steep street and measured her elegant length in liquid cowdung.

But in our youth and in our town the old ways still survived. Merchants were forced to put up wooden palisades to protect plateglass from the buttocks of bullocks. Cattle heaved, jostled and relieved themselves on the pavements. Dealers bargained and spat and slapped hands. Sheep stood in sad, terrified semi-circles, heads together and to the wall, trollopy tailends turned to the incomprehensible world. It could have been the crowds, or the smell of dung. Or the suggestion, brought with them by drovers and cattle, of wide pastures remote from the treadmill of post office to station and back again. Or it could have been the accumulation of torment he had already endured at the hands and ashplant of Robbie. Or all those things together. But this fairday the old bay horse transmogrified into a raging Bucephalus and went running wild through a herd of red bullocks on the Courthouse Hill. Foaming at the mouth he circled three times the black female figures on the Boer War monument. Bullocks went right and bullocks went left. One drunken drover climbed the monument for safety and hid, a child again, in the sheltering arms of the big-bosomed Victory who presided over her lesser sisters: Peace, Prosperity, Love and Industry.

Seated behind the glasscase counter in his shop of glass and glossy tiles Mick Jones, the deaf tobacconist, lifted his eyes from the morning paper to find himself confronted by a whitehead bullock who had wandered in to escape from the tumult. The counter had to be removed before the animal could be coaxed, tail first, out of a confined space in which one twist or sideways shuffle would have caused ruin.

Then, on the fourth time round the monument, the horse tired, slipped, came panting to rest on his belly. Robbie and the Royal Mail rolled out on to a street exactly like the one that had befouled the fair figure of the London model.

It was a miserable end to his first ambition.

— To drive a horsedrawn vehicle to the danger of the public is in itself a heinous offence.

That, in due process of law, was Captain Flower, the magistrate.

He had more to say: But to carry His Majesty's Mails is an honourable responsibility of which even the youngest should be aware. Or, if not already aware, they should be instantaneously and in no uncertain fashion made aware.

Shod for the occasion, and wearing a new cloth suit, spectacles, and a patch of sticking plaster on his wide forehead, Robbie stood at the bar of justice. No longer had he that fey appearance of a magic creature that he had when he emerged, barefooted and knickerbockered, from the melodious shadows at the back of his father's shop.

— But for your youth and extreme inexperience, said Captain Flower, and the respectable standing of your father in the community, I would impose on you a heavy fine or even commit you to prison or a reform school.

Then with a roar that rent the musty, scribbling silence of the courtroom: Attend to me, young man. What in the name of heaven are you staring at?

— Your honour, at the doodles Mr O'Neill is making in his little book. They fascinate me.

Captain Flower was a redfaced frog of a man who had fought both Boers and Germans.

Eddy O'Neill, one of the town's two reporters, made on his pad the doodles that meant: Laughter in Court.

Captain Flower was a renowned salmon-fisherman and the president of a rose-growers' association. He lived in a big countryhouse by a bridge over the Drumragh river at a place where, it was said, Red Hugh O'Donnell watered his horse when he was escaping back to his native Donegal from durance in Dublin Castle and the power of the first Elizabeth. In the gardens, ranked with roses of all colours, before the captain's house, were white marble statues of heathen goddesses, of vast interest to the growing boys of the town. But it was always risky to encounter the captain, who considered that even to peep over the hedge was a form of trespass. He was a man of the utmost wrath.

So Eddy O'Neill doodled his most vivid descriptive writing as the captain's gavel rapped the bench, and the captain's red face turned purple, and the laughter died away in the courtroom.

— What age are you, young man?

— Fifteen, your honour.

— Look at me, young man. Not at Mr O'Neill.

— Certainly, your honour.

But his eyes could not keep away from the point of the magic pencil touching the reporter's pad, scraping, twisting, darting, making curves, recording words and thoughts as a seismograph records the tremors of an earthquake. This was something more wonderful than horses and wagons or the insides of his father's clocks.

— You are an American citizen, young man.

— Yes, your honour.

— In that land of the free and the home of the brave they may never have told you about contempt of court.

— Never saw the inside of court before, your honour. It's mighty interesting.

Having narrowly missed apoplexy the captain was settling down, the purple slowly fading into the grey of the face of an ironic man who had been everywhere and seen everything.

— The court is overjoyed that you find something here to interest you. For the benefit of our young visitor you will, Mr O'Neill, doodle this on your paper: Bound to the peace for two years to be of orderly behaviour.

— It's not law.

Said the lawyer who had been engaged by Jamie to make a formal appearance on behalf of the son.

— In this Court my learned friend should be aware that what I say is law. With motor machines becoming a greater menace on the road every day. With tractors ousting from the land the beneficial horse. With all that and more, the public must be protected from speed maniacs. Doodle all that down, Mr O'Neill, for the instruction, edification and benefit of our young friend from the New World.

Eddy O'Neill doodled down a lot more than the words spoken or the sentence passed in that comic court. Comic: because the world knew that any decision made by Captain Flower would be, if challenged, automatically upset in any higher court.

Eddy's brown overcoat trailed its tails. It was never buttoned: was frayed at the cuffs and stained with porter. His black felt hat had once been walked on in a scuffle at a political meeting and retained concertina wrinkles. In the snug of Broderick's pub, halfways between the courthouse and his office, he reigned as lord of all discussions, did most of his work, a share of his sleeping: and sipped good malt and hollowed his cheeks as he rolled the first sip round and round his mouth giving, as he said, full benefit and blessing to the remotest cavern of every hollow tooth. He wrote with a pencil stub in a sweeping, curving long-hand: The only factor that has this latterday Jehu, born in Boston city, like the burglar renowned in song, still walking at liberty among us, is that it was not in the power of our esteemed magistrate, Captain Flower, to impose any more severe penalty.

Then raising his eyes as the door of the snug opened he saw Robbie before him, again barefooted and knickerbockered, wearing no spectacles but identifiable by the brown curls, broad forehead and the sticking plaster.

— Your pleasure, young man.

— Pardon me, sir.

— I would offer you a drink. But the law forbids. The law we must respect. As today you learned from our choleric captain.

— The redfaced gentleman, sir, who has all the statues in his rose garden.

— Young Uncle Sam, you are observant. You have a sense of style. What book are you in?

— Book, sir?

— Class, form, grade? Grade you call it.

— I don't go to school, sir.

— Why not?

— Never could see the point in it, sir. I wanted to drive horses.

— Your horse-driving days are over. Thanks to the ukase of Flower, the grower of roses. What do you aim to do now?

— Be a reporter, sir. Just like you.

— Just like me. Vaulting ambition. Have you looked closely at me?

— Yes, sir. Saw you making the signs. The doodles, sir. Cutest thing I ever saw.

— Young man, when I used to tell my mother that I wanted to be a reporter. Or a journalist. As I grandiloquently put it. Do you know what she used to do?

— No, sir.

— She would go to the dresser where she kept her prayerbook. A big Key of Heaven with coloured ribbons hanging out of it. Behind a willow pattern plate. And forthwith she would launch into the Thirty Days Prayer.

— Why, sir?

— You see, I thought being a journalist was something like being fat and rich like G. K. Chesterton. And taking part in debates with George Bernard Shaw and talking philosophy and whittling bits of stick and impressing the people. And writing essays once a week in the *Daily News* for princely sums, and collecting the essays later into little red books to be published by Methuen of London, with your signature done in gilt on the cover. And being honoured by the Pope and all.

— Yes, sir, Robbie said.

He rubbed his bare feet sensitively on the floor.

— But my mother thought that being a journalist was having nothing but dirty overcoats. And sitting most of the day in the snug of a pub. And reporting cases of serious offences by army recruiting officers against young girls. That was why she made the Thirty Days Prayer. Not that it did her much good. Except that the Lord spared her and she didn't live long enough to know how right she was.

— I still want to be a reporter, sir. I like the idea.

— O. Henry, a gentleman in your country, was of the opinion that a journalist was a man with dandruff on his coat collar and a whiskey bottle in his hip pocket. And not so far wrong. And Bernard Shaw, a fellow from Dublin, said he never met a journalist who owned a pencil or could spell. But then he was a perfectionist.

So Robbie said he owned several pencils.

— But my barefooted, brownheaded young man, do you put them to any use?

Shifting on his seat, surveying with a gleam in his eye the other inhabitants of the snug, his faithful audience, drawing his ancient brown coat around him as if it were a patrician toga, taking a longer than usual sip of the yellow malt, painstakingly blessing every hollow sucking tooth, then swallowing with one quick warming gulp, Eddy said: But Robbie, son of Jamie of the gems and jewels, you're a hero any man would take to. I'll make you a reporter if you do three things for me. I'll put you under three geasa or three taboos the way the daughter of a King did with an ancient hero. Do you understand?

— I reckon I do, sir.

— The first thing is you will go to school and study above all things the King's English. Which, at the moment, you speak with variagations. As Biddy Mulligan, the Pride of the Coombe, in the city of Dublin, would put it. Then to the technical school to study shorthand. The magic doodles, you know. The dots, strokes and curves that mean mouthfuls. That can record both Captain Flower and the thoughts of Socrates.

— Yes sir, said Robbie.

Obedience in his drooping shoulders he turned sadly away.

— And the third thing, Robbie, is to go home and put on your boots and keep them on. Because, while from here to Ludgate Circus and the Rose and Crown on Dorset Rise, I've seen gentlemen of the Press in many's the sore condition, I've never yet seen one in his bare feet. Then come to me in a year with your pencils sharpened.

— Yes, sir, said Robbie.

He went home, his naked soles kissing farewell forever to the smooth sidewalk, blue as the pigeons, of John Street.

Aleel, the swineherd, who was bid by Forgaill's daughter, Emer, go dwell among the seacliffs, vapour-hid, did as he was told. And came back faithfully when his days of waiting were no more. So did Robbie, and Eddy O'Neill made him a reporter.

Men find their calling in the oddest ways. When Robbie came to us from the big city of Boston he rejoiced in the cool freedom of quiet, blue pavements where you could run barefooted and clap your hands, startling feeding pigeons from the grain that scattered from the nosebags of farmers' horses. In those days a boy could earn twopence holding a farmer's horse while the owner went into the bank or the post office or the public house. Robbie grew to love the smell of horses and their long, serious heads. Then, above all the methods of transport he had seen across the ocean, nothing equalled the style and colouring of the red wagon. If he hadn't driven the red wagon to ruin, he might never have discovered the magic of Eddy O'Neill's pencil. If he and his father on that day had not been so kind to Shorty Morgan, the boys of the Hill might not have been so ready to oblige him with his first story as a war-correspondent.

Dressed in new tweeds and well-shod, he came to where we sat in council under the ghost of the Big Tree and the ghost of the gallows it had been: the writhing victims of Adam Tait swinging from every branch. To Lanty he said: Here's a proposition. I need something exciting to write about. Something with Go in it. A war-story.

— War, we said.

— Whip fights, he said. The next best thing.

Speaking to the man in his own language, Lanty said: The heat's on.

— You're not scared of the heat.

Which, of course, with his taunting encouragement and with our liking for him, we were not. So, complete with Tall John's razor and police intervention, and several charges in court for breaches of the peace, giving rise to oratory that almost burst Captain Flower's bubbling bloodvessels, the noble game of whip-battle between the Hill and Brook Street was played for the last time. There are people in the town who still have preserved in wallets or scrapbooks or in boxes of knick-knacks his description of that battle. It was the last piece of writing he did under the tutelage of Eddy O'Neill. After that he moved on to bigger things. Hitler and Hirohito ultimately provided him with better opportunities than we, with the best will in the world, could ever have managed. He was in all sorts of places and survived to write about them. We were proud of him because we had, even Captain Flower aiding, helped him to find his way and provided him with his first battle.

Shorty Morgan, a man now and not much shorter than anybody else, still has the two watches. He was always a great man for keeping things. He has, also, a pair of cufflinks purloined from an elder brother who had them from an Irish-American who was in the milk business, as they called it, in Albany, N.Y. The cufflinks are illustrated with coloured miniatures of the liner on which the milkman crossed the Atlantic for the Eucharistic Congress in Dublin in 1932. For Shorty, still as imaginative as when by night he heard the passing of the ghostly demon coachman, they are, when he shows them off, always an excuse for talking about the life and times and sudden death of Legs Diamond.

A WALK IN THE WHEAT

Three swans flew above us, very high and swift for swans, before we turned off the highway. They flew northeast towards the big, islanded, windy trout-lake that fused the borders of three counties. We followed a byroad towards the village in the lost valley. The old man who had been reared in that valley shaded his eyes and looked up at the swans. Looked after them until they were no longer white magic birds but black specks drifting in the haze of a Spring morning. We thought of reeds and water over shore-stones and dirty grey cygnets growing into snowy beauty. He said: In my boyhood here it was a saying that it was a lucky day you saw three swans flying.

We marched down the red byway: the American woman in green slacks and white Aran sweater, the old man and myself.

I love red roads where basic sandstone glows up through the thin surface of tar or, better still, untarred roads in mountain valleys where the rain-puddles are the colour of rich chocolate.

In blue, morning mist this was no midland country of lakes and low green hills. For the lakes were steaming cauldrons and the hills were elevated by haze into floating Gothic palaces the height of the Rocky Mountains. Four miles we had walked from the fishing hotel in the triangular market-town where draughty gusts of Spring wind set the pictures dancing on the walls: where all the photographs in the hotel lounge and dining-room were of a lavish white wedding that had happened in Buenos Aires.

— From these parts, said the old man returning to his native place, they emigrated mostly to the Argentine. Not to New York or Boston or Chicago. There was a reason for that. A famous Irish missionary priest who had gone ahead of them to the pampas. They mingled Spanish and Irish names and blood.

The panelling in the hallway of the hotel had been damaged when a terrified whitehead bullock had invaded the place on the last fairday. We were surrounded by good, midland grass building beef into red cattle. Behind hedges and orchard trees, chickens sheltered from the ruffling wind.

— There was a man in these parts in my youth, he said, was reputed to own a hen laid three times a day. And one of the three eggs was invariably three-cornered. But I must myself admit that I never saw one of those miraculous eggs.

The gloss of the strengthening sun was on the young hawthorn leaves. Clipped tree-stumps were phosphorescently white. Ash trees, slim as young girls, stood up on their own above the ranked hawthorns.

— My father had green fingers, he said. I'll show to you strangers an avenue of trees he planted.

The old woman with the silvery can in her hand met us just where the narrow road twisted, dipped suddenly, and we had our first sight of the wall and tower of the ancient abbey-ruin. She was tiny, with brown wrinkled face and blue eyes: and the eyes brightened and the face came to life when she saw our guide. She reached out her hand to him. She wore a black shawl with tassels and trimmings, a black skirt, an apron made out of a well-washed potato-sack, a pair of men's boots. She held his hand for a long time. She said: Dermot, you're welcome back to your own place.

— If it was still my own place.

— The ground doesn't change, she said.

The silvery can held goats' milk, and if we stepped with her into her cottage by the side of the road we could share the midmorning tea with herself and her husband. She explained, not to Dermot but to the woman and myself: If you haven't supped tea with goats' milk then you don't know what tea is.

So we went with her to help her carry the milk and, ourselves, to break the morning. Her husband, not quite as old as herself, gillied on the lakes for visiting fishermen, and the rafters under the thatched roof of the cottage were laced with rods and the handles of gaffs and nets. She sang for us, standing with her back to the hearth fire, her hands tightly locked behind her back, her eyes raised but tightly closed, and a young smile on her face. So sweetly, too, she sang a song about the lakes and hills, the valley, the ancient abbey, the monks who once upon a time had chanted and prayed there, the miracles wrought by the patron of the place, the holiness of the last hermit who had lived in the valley: and about a tyrant king who, after the manner of Holofernes, had been tricked and killed by the decent people. The words went haltingly to Tom Moore's melody about the harp that once through Tara's halls. Those words had been written by an old flame of hers who had long since emigrated to the land of the gauchos. When he had been gone for ten years and was showing no sign of returning she married another and tried to forget the song-writer: who afterwards married a half-Spanish woman and died among strangers.

Her husband tapped his pipe on the hob and said: I never did think much of it as a song. There was a young schoolmaster by Granard in the County Longford made a song was twice as good. There was more history in it. And a tune he didn't borrow but made it up out of his own head.

She said, sadly enough, yet still with the sauciness of a young girl: The old tunes were the best.

She put some of the goat's milk in an empty whiskey-bottle and gave it to the green-legged woman. With her blessing hovering about us, and the taste of strong tea flavoured with goats' milk in our mouths, we went down into the valley.

— That song she sang, Dermot said, was a fair resumé of the history of the locality. The people of this place were breastfed on legends and wonders. Miracle springs and miracle mills. Wood that won't burn. Water that won't boil. Water that flows uphill. There now is the wood that won't burn.

Ten yards from the road, in a marshy field, yellow with mayflowers, stood a bare, three-armed thorn bush. We crossed a shaky stone stile and went towards it. Rags and rosary beads hung from the withered arms. A small well, spotted with green scum, nestled down at the twisted roots, and through the shallow, particoloured water we could see coins and holy medals lying on the bottom. Abandoned sticks and crutches decayed with age, and one metal-and-leather leg-brace, were piled to one side.

— Three arms to the bush, he said. For the Father, the Son and the Holy Ghost. The water of the well won't boil. The wood of the bush won't burn.

The woman, sceptical and literary, quoted: Said the wicked, crooked, hawthorn-tree.

— By all accounts the saint wanted it so, he said. It was his holy well.

He had his hat in his hand. He was a big man, still handsome. But the fair locks of youth had gone and his clean, well-shaven chin and shiny, washed baldness, and around his eyes some freckles that lingered from boyhood summers, gave him at times the glow of childish, innocent enthusiasm.

— Did anybody ever try, said the woman. I mean boiling and burning.

— Oh woman, he said, of green shanks and little faith and foreign origins.

Then he covered his head and laughed loudly. He said: Not to my personal knowledge and belief. But the tradition is that anyone who ever tried to boil the water or burn the wood regretted it. And the sick were cured here. Faith made the dry bush blossom.

Faith it was, too, that made the water run uphill and confounded the sceptical miller.

— Look to the right hand now, he said.

We had regained the road.

— That there is the Hermit's Rock. Beyond that rock and the steep hill it stands on, there's one of the loveliest of the lakes of Ireland. And look to the left now.

The width of two fields away and close to the ruined abbey was a shapeless heap of grey stones.

— Over there, the saint built a mill. And no sign of water next or near it. A miller passing the way mocked him. In the legends millers were always mockers.

The water will come, said the Saint. And he blessed the mill and the millstones. And here where we stand by the side of the road the water burst out and flowed past the mill as you see it to this day. It leaves the lake on a lower level. Flows under the earth and under the hermit's rock. Comes back here to the daylight. The story says the mocking miller died of shock.

— You could see his point, she said.

The water fountained up by the roadside, spread out in a weedy shallow pool, then narrowed to make a stream. A man watered a horse in the miracle pool. Geese paddled by the horse's head. Lambs with black noses grazed on the steep slope that went up to the hermit's rock.

— Before God, said Dermot, it's my old friend, the Stone Man. I thought he was dead and gone years ago.

Together the daughter and myself said: Another miracle. A man of stone.

He came towards us, leading the horse. Small, hunched and lame-legged, he splashed through the shallow water, scattering the paddling geese.

— Dermot, he said. I couldn't mistake you. You've come back at last. To see the old places.

— No longer mine, said Dermot. But I've brought a visitor from Dublin. And my daughter.

— So I see. So I see.

The horse grazed the roadside grass. The geese, again at peace, returned to the weedy water. A poet's words came into my head, a lazy description of a Connacht village: Where seven crooked crones are tied all day to the tops of seven listening halfdoors, and nothing to be heard or seen but the drowsy dropping of water and the ganders on the green.

— You're welcome, girl, said the Stone Man. You're also a sort of a wonder. The first woman, I'd say, ever to wear trousers in this valley. Three thousand shaven celibate men once chanted prayers here. They wouldn't have welcomed the likes of you.

— But they might have, she said. As a change from chanting.

We walked through the village of seven houses and a pub, and a small village-green with an old worn stone cross. The place was still asleep. To the right hand the Hermit's Rock towered above us. To the left, across the valley and beyond the ruins of the abbey, was a graceful conical hill, green of grass, gold of furze, topped by a head of stone.

— My hill, Dermot said. If it hadn't been for an aging man in love and a designing young woman. My father's first family were left with nothing.

— I'll walk with you to the summit, said the Stone Man. If you wait till I hand the horse to the servant-boy.

He led the horse down an entry by the side of one of the seven houses.

— He has a name I suppose, she said. A real name.

— He has the name he got at the font. But nobody ever uses it. Old as I am, he's older. He came to this valley, a journeyman stonecutter, when I was sixteen. The year my father married again. The year before he died and the new woman put us out. A local landlord and the parish priest and the Protestant rector paid him to come to restore the abbey. So that the occasional learned visitor could look at it in some comfort. Up to that it was all weeds and dead scaldy jackdaws and stones scattered all over the place. Morning to night he was there like a leprechaun, hammer and chisel tinkling, working by the light of a hurricane lamp in old cloisters that nobody here would go near after dusk. Then he married a woman of the place and stayed here. And was a journeyman no longer. But the jokers said it wasn't the woman he married but the old stones of the abbey.

— Will we walk by the abbey path, the Stone Man said. Or by the church and the schoolhouse?

He had ornamented himself with a grey tailed coat and an ancient bowler. He supported his limp on a varnished blackthorn.

— By the church and the schoolhouse, Dermot said. That's the path I knew best as a boy.

The low, grey, cruciform church had a separate bell tower. To ring the bell you swung on a huge iron wheel. The whitewashed, oblong box of a schoolhouse had narrow, latticed windows.

— My uncle taught there, Dermot said. A tyrant with black

sidewhiskers. And more severe on me than on any boy in the valley. He was a cattledealer, too, and thought more of bullocks than of boys. He had a gold watchchain thick as a ship's cable. And a green velveteen waistcoat. He went every week to the cattlemarket in Dublin. Once he came back and by my father's hearth solemnly told us how a young woman. A daring hussy with paint on her face, he said. How she had had the temerity to address him, outside the City Hotel on the northside. Where the cattlelairs were. But, he said, with one glance I froze her to silence. Listening to him I thought sadly of a poor painted Red Indian squaw petrified like Lot's wife. So I asked him, uncle, why did you freeze her with a glance. Dermot, he said, she was a loud woman. Or that was what I thought I heard. Long after I realized he said lewd. But it puzzled me at the time.

— Mayhap she was loud, too, said Greenshanks. Singing. Or swearing. Or playing the guitar.

— Yet I will say this for my uncle. He did his damnedest to fight when my father died. And that woman took the land from us. And threw my brothers and sisters and myself out on the ways of the world.

— Jack Dempsey, said the Stone Man, nor the best counsellor ever took snuff or wore a wig could not fight the sort of marriage agreement they make in this part of Ireland. They could teach lessons to the French.

By a masspath that went under blossoming hawthorn and skirted the edge of a field of young oats we began to ascend. Then, crossing a wooden stile, we were on another narrow road, going up steeply, screening stones loose under our feet. In his boyhood the children used to gather at the foot of the hill and, with cheers, help the horse with the peat-cart, heavy from the bog, to make the grade. His step quickened, his shoulders bent, he was a child among cheering children, digging heel-and-toe in the pebbles, approaching home in the evening. As we ascended we saw more and more of the sights that had remained with him when, faraway in exile, he'd close his eyes and recall beginnings: white crosses in a graveyard above a small lake: the sheen of clipped horses, free and running, manes flying, in the fields: the pebbly way going between red beech hedges: the sun gold on the little lake like a path you could walk on: scrubby, wintry, hillside land beginning to flame with blossoming furze: slopes holy and haunted by the shadows of monk and hermit.

— A tireless wonder to quote both poetry and prose your uncle was. That was the Stone Man.

— We knew the Readamedaisy by heart, Dermot said. The name of the book as written was *Reading Made Easy*. He had the stonebreakers by the roadside quoting Byron and Burke. Stop, for thy tread is on an empire's dust. It is now seventeen years since I saw the queen of France. And the impeachment of Warren Hastings.

Suddenly the Stone Man is standing up like an orator, asking us to look down from this height on the beauty of his abbey, the square tower, the round columbarium to the left. And, in a voice grating like rusty metal, reciting from the repertoire of the dead schoolmaster: Where the ivy clings to the ruin and the moss to the fallen stones, where the wild ash guards the crumbling gable and the brook goes babbling, where the quiet of ages has settled down on green fields and purple hills, there is the faithfulest memorial of a past that is dead.

Paying no heed to him Dermot strides onward. He opens one half of a creaking iron gate. He says: My father planted that avenue of trees. I told you he was a green-fingered man.

The reverent breathing of the trees, the devotion of a dead man who had digged and planted and loved, for a second time foolishly and late, was with us. Green beech, copper beech, ash coming tardily to leaf, they whispered to us of the man who had helped to give them life. They were, also, his children. Rooted in the ground. Not to be cast out.

— Her one son lives in that bungalow on the slope, he said. He never married. We won't call on him.

I ventured. He's your half-brother.

— He may be. But I'm no brother of his. Half nor whole.

He strode on heavily, leading us between the trees.

— He might have the gall to tell me I was a trespasser. He has the land, legally, that rightfully belongs to us. But it always half-consoled me that he never had the harvest of son or daughter to leave it to. The sheaves in the field wouldn't feel the same in his hands, as in mine. He wouldn't know how ready and willing the ground is to yield. He wouldn't know what these trees are saying.

The road began slightly to descend. Older trees, giant oaks and sycamores, were among the ash and beech his father had planted. From a branch of one of the sycamores a thrush had sung to the good days of his boyhood. Always he had thought, the same brave cock guarding his territory with music. One bird to one tree. A propertied male proud on his own land. That bird would be long gone, his place taken by a younger cock, and another, and another. The trees, the green silence, deepened around us. We were on what had once been a clear cobbled square, now badly weedgrown, in front of a long, low cottage, the old abandoned farmhouse in which he had been born.

— She grew grand, he said, and left the old place to the cattle and hens.

— No, it wasn't that, the Stone Man said. She claimed she smothered living among trees. Some people are like that. So the new house was built up the hillside.

Chickens picked and fluttered and squawked around us. Close to the sagging doorway cattle had softened and muddied the ground. We followed him into the shadowy dung-smelling room that had once been a large kitchen. He had his hat in his hand again. He didn't speak for a long time. The woman took a ballpoint from the bag she carried and wrote her name on one white speck of wall. Then handed me the ballpoint so that I could sign myself beside her.

— Outside there, he said. That garden hedge gone wild. It made a magic circle around my childhood. It spread its leaves and shade over me on mornings like this. I'd peep out through it and see the world. I've seen a lot of the world since then. But nothing as sad to me as the spectacle of this house. This day.

— Things change, dad, the woman said.

— Every rafter in this kitchen had a special name I'd given it. And the polished mantel beam was King of them all.

The woman said again that things change.

— I was born in that bedroom below, he said. And when I was small and in bed, the moon would shine in on me through that door. When I lost the door I lost the moon.

— It's somewhere still, she said.

— And outside in the evening the rocktop of the hill above was a giant's head. Eyes and all. And the green slope was the giant's cloak floating off towards the west.

— We'll go to the summit, the Stone Man said. And study the view. Five counties you can see from the crown of the giant's head.

We could feel his anger, or pain, growing as he led us up to the summit. The Stone Man, to ease the strain, talked of the view we could see, the coloured prospect of five counties and a dozen lakes: and talked of the tyrant of a Dane who had been killed by the decent people. And of the hermit who had lived in the valley. He joked at the woman about her green legs. And about the three thousand celibate men who wouldn't have allowed her into the valley.

— You'd have shattered all the rules of cloisura, he said. Why; women weren't allowed into the saint's mill. It was reckoned to be as holy as any church he ever built.

— It could be, she said, that he was afraid they'd find fault with his baking. If he could bake his own flour that is. Old bachelors never like women near their kitchens.

— Two miles away, said Dermot, there's a place called Hangman's Hollow. A landlord in the eighteenth century had a man hanged there for stealing a loaf of bread.

— The tyrant Dane, said the Stone Man, had a more subtle method. Every year he exacted from every house in his territory an ounce of gold. If he didn't get it he cut off the nose of the defaulter. So they called it Nose Money. But he had a weakness for the girls.

— Green legs, she said.

— History is silent. He demanded that a local chieftain should send him his daughter for diversion. So she came. And with her twelve beardless youths wearing skirts. And when the poor man was drunk they stuffed him in a barrel and drowned him in a lake.

— If he had been a bible-reading Christian, she said, he'd never have fallen for the old beardless youth trick.

On top of the hill we sat down and drank the goats' milk that the singing woman had given us.

— There's a man walking over there, Greenshanks said.

She pointed across the valley to the slope below the Hermit's Rock. But try as we might we could see nobody.

— The ghost of the last hermit, the Stone Man said. Visible only to a woman who has tasted the magic milk of the white goat. They say he broke his vow in the end. He was a hunting gentleman who gave up the world. And lay in a hole in that rock. With his proctors, as they were called, ranging the country for him. Bringing back corn and eggs, geese, turkeys, hens and sheep. He ate like the quality. It was the chief part of his holiness that he was never to stir out of the cave. But this fatal day he heard the hounds and the horn. Too much for him it proved to be. Off he went on a neighbour's mount. Broke his neck at the first stone wall.

— The man's gone now, she said.

She stood up hurriedly.

— There are ticks in the grass.

White marl fringed the two small lakes at the foot of the hill and shone up at us like silver from underneath the water.

Surveying the carpet of counties Dermot said: My father used to walk a lot around the rock. He said it was holy ground.

— This entire valley is holy, the Stone Man said. Look through the chancel arch of the abbey when the furze blossom is out in all its glory. It's as if you were looking at the light of the heaven.

He led us down by another path so that he could display to us the arches, the cloisters, the cool stones of the love of his heart. We crossed a whole field of clover and yellow pimpernel, then followed a gravelly, slippery goatpath through the furze. The blue air above us was cut by the whinnying sound of flying snipe. Far below, where the stream went on from the saint's mill to join the great lake the swans had flown to, three boys and a dog followed the twisting course of the water. The boys threw sticks and stones. They crossed and recrossed the narrow stream. The dog barked and leaped in the air, plunged in to rescue floating sticks. Their actions had a happiness isolated from time.

— Spring was always a glory in this place, he said.

Then, loudly enough to be heard four fields away, he shouted a verse of a poem: Tomorrow Spring will laugh in many waters, ever the ancient promise she fulfills. Tomorrow she will set the furzebloom burning along my father's hills.

Where the furze ended we crossed a stile, the woman leading. Before us lay a broad flat field bursting with the promise of young wheat.

— Walk round the edge, I called to her. Don't trample the man's crop.

— Sink him to the pit, Dermot roared. Who owns this land?

He went across the field, sinking his heels deeply for purchase and possession. Soft clay spurted up behind him. Tender green shoots lay crushed on his path. With savage steps he wrote out on the land the story of his long-thwarted passion for the lost thing of his own. We followed him, stepping carefully, as if we feared that the stalks might cry out.

That was a late year for the ash. So there were four great ash trees, still bare, but proud and defiantly independent of decoration, on the green in the triangular market-town. Within the square they formed, stood the old collapsing market-house built by an eighteenth-century landlord to resemble a miniature St Paul's. In its cellars, rebels in 1798 had been flogged and otherwise tortured before the dragging-out to death. Or so the Stone Man told us. He had come with us for a farewell night of drink and talk and song.

The rough Spring wind of the morning had died. The pictures no longer danced in draughts on the walls of the hotel's hallway. During the day a carpenter had repaired the damage done by the whitehead bullock. The gentle lady who owned the hotel told us about that white wedding she had attended in Buenos Aires, about the fantastic length of the bride's train. She showed us some sombre religious prints she had brought back with her. Spanish and Irish faces looked at us from the walls of the dining-room.

Then out in the public bar the people were gathered to say welcome to the returned exile and his daughter. A girl in a red dress, without urging or invitation, sang a song about a Donegal beauty called the Rose of Arranmore. There was a great willingness in the people to sing. The Stone Man, elevated, threw his blackthorn and bowler into a corner, roared to the barmaid: Give me, girl, as the tinkers used to say, a glass of Geneva wine and a wisp for the ass.

Then in a voice like the sawing of old branches he sang the song the woman of the goats' milk had sung that morning.

Greenshanks whispered to me: My father loved that hill.

— One tiger to one hill, I said. One singing cockthrush to one sycamore.

We left the crowded bar and walked down the long yard between byres and stables at the back of the hotel. A pig nosed at a cartchain. There were nettles and abandoned motor-tyres, rusty lengths of corrugated iron, the twitter of evening birds. And slow sparse raindrops. In the bar behind us Dermot had raised his voice and was singing that his boat could lightly float in the teeth of wind and weather and outrace the smartest hooker between Galway and Kinsale.

She said: Since I was a child I always liked him to sing. That was always his favourite song.

She said that he had hurt himself when he hurt the wheat and the ground: And I felt nothing. Nothing at all. Except that it might be cute to have a summer cottage in such a heavenly place. To get away from New York in the heat. That worries me that I felt nothing. That he was a stranger to me.

— He never spoke to me much about this place, she said. As you'd think a father might.

— The subject was too painful. The dispossession. Diaspora.

— He had one funny story, though. About a funeral. And the mourners stopped at a pub and left the coffin and corpse on a stone wall outside. They said, sure God rest him, what would be the point in bringing him in. 'Twould only vex him.

She was laughing and crying.

— But I did see a man walking round the Hermit's Rock. The hunting hermit? Or my grandfather walking on holy ground: Or the shadow of a cloud on the grass? But I saw something that nobody else could see. One woman in a valley with the ghosts of three thousand celibate men. Wasn't it a sign to show that, in spite of them, I belonged to the place?

THE PYTHON

When the wine and the after-dinner cognac dies he wakes from the glutton's stupor, sniffs the dark room, knows exactly who has stopped in the place before him. The air-conditioning makes for most of the time like the noises of a Gipsy Moth: then, every four or five minutes, clanks as if a chained man inside were trying to get out. It pumps humid air into an atmosphere already oozing: and odorous. The man who has left that odour behind him has not slept here on his own. Not even in this easygoing hotel do tomcats sign the register on their own. But pets are permissible and somewhere in the world there is a noseless man or woman, or a pair without noses and thinking that a tomcat is a pretty pet.

In the odorous dark he listens to the little man from Paris who says that it is an octopus, so the little man pulls out his knife and opens his eyes, then thinks it's a dream, then thinks that it isn't, that the octopus is reality and is draining him with its suckers: but, no, it is simply the dreadful humid heat: he is sweating, he says, he had gone to sleep about one o'clock, then at two the heat had waked him, he had plunged into a cold bath and back into bed without drying himself and right away the furnace roars again under his skin, and he is sweating again, and he dreams the house is on fire and says that this is more than mere heat, this is a sickness of the atmosphere, the air is in a fever, the air is sweating: and more of the same.

The little man from Paris is writing about humid heat.

At four in the morning the telephone begins to ring, and rings and rings. The crazy woman will just now be leaving the hotel-bar. She calls him from the payphone outside the door of the gents. That woman could clear a bar-counter quicker than the Black Death. But he answers the phone in the end. And will go to her room to get away from the smell of the tomcat. Also: her air-conditioner works. And there may be other reasons. She has long dark glossy hair, and prominent glistening American teeth: and her craziness is not menacing, only gentle and amorous.

When he switches on the light he finds it hard to believe that there is no cat to be seen: yet if a cat may vanish and leave a smile behind it, then another cat may vanish and leave a smell. The book in which the little man from Paris laments about the humid heat lies open on the other, unused, bed. He checks his memory against the text. Not bad, not bad at all: for this clinging, sticky, smelly heat might very well affect a man's memory. But that cold plunge and that crawling back untowelled on to the bed was a bloody bad idea: the little man, a philosopher too, might have killed or crippled himself with rheumatics.

A quick shower now, a quick brisk towelling, helps and cannot harm: go glistening to the gentle crazy woman with the glistening teeth and the glossy hair: and as he combs his hair he thinks that the week that has just passed has been, the papers say, the bloodiest week of this warm season in little old New York. The paper is there on the dressing-table and still saying it: Fiftyeight murders, three young drug-addicts executed on a rooftop, they get a few lines on a backpage: Mafia boss murdered, that makes the front page for Mafia murders are as popular as baseball: and a most poetic policeman says take a poor guy, it's sweltering, he don't have an air-conditioner, he takes a few beers, there's no place to go, he gets mad at something, then all of a sudden it bursts out, he grabs a knife.

The knife is farandaway the most favoured weapon for warm nights.

He does have an air-conditioner. Puff, puff, puff, a wonderful breath of foul air. Clank, clank, clank, jealous Vulcan is trapped in the crater, let me outa here. Dear dark woman with such hair too, I come, I come my heart's delight.

He has never carried a knife.

Or if he had been carrying a knife he would have attacked the python yesterday when the musician draped it around Judith's neck. Young women should not wear pythons around the neck. He recalled then with a shudder a story he had read about an Irish lord who when he was a young man in Oxford kept a python as a pet. He does not trust pythons. He, that is, not the noble lord who was lunatic enough to keep in his lodgings on the High a python fourteen feet long. Tame, he thought. Tame? But didn't like strangers. Nothing is tame that doesn't like strangers. So the landlady's daughter opens the box that the python lives in, and the python coils round and round the landlady's daughter, bruising her to the extent of thirty-five pounds sterling which was big money in the year of the Franco-Prussian war: and the python is banished to the zoo, a proper place for pythons.

All of which he tells the musician who laughs at him and says: Landladies' daughters in Oxford, England, should know better than to poke pythons.

He is not content until Judith and the two girls in her company are away from that python and out of that zany penthouse: all fixed up with blooms and screaming birds like a tropical jungle, and with fish in glass tanks that dance, the fish not the tanks, when the musician plays the piano. A sort of dance: swishing round and round, Boccaccio's seven young ladies and three young gentlemen barefoot in the crystal water and with naked arms engaging in various games. What games? But the piranha fish do not dance. Four of them in a tank which they share with a small black shark, all so dangerous to each other that they leave each other alone. The shark seems to sleep. The piranha deliberately, like the Eleventh Hussars, do not dance. They are small fellows with buck teeth. They stare out through the glass wall and say: If we had you in the Amazon.

Being fair judges of fleshmeat it is to be assumed that they stare hardest at Judith and Marion and Barbara, blooming American belles just turned twenty, fit any morning to play games in Boccaccian streams: not at myself, nor at Murtagh, lean, longjawed sports writer over from Dublin to witness and comment on an ancient Celtic stickball game in a field in the Bronx: nor, by God, at the musician, tough and brown and bald and wrinkled. Even piranha fish may prefer tender meat.

Life is much more liveable in the bar and restaurant on the ground floor. And tolerably cool, too. No puffs, no clanks, but currents of real air reminding me again of Boccaccio in the Italian mornings, and the middle-ages dead and done with, and love and laughter in the air: and cool water fringed by smooth round stones and verdant grasses.

To the three young women Murtagh explains the nature of the stickball game; No, not curling. Hurling. Curling is something you do on ice. Like sliding a flatiron along ice. We don't have enough ice in Ireland. No, this is hurling. And it's not at all like the stickball I saw the Puerto Rican kids play around the corner there in an alley off Seventh. That's a sort of pelota or handball with a broomstick. No, hurling is hurling. Hurling is different. There's an Irish, Gaelic, word for it, but that wouldn't interest you. It goes back into history. It's the most natural thing in the world, for a man to hit a ball with a stick. There's something like it in Japan, I've heard. Though perhaps I'm confusing shinto and shinty. That's what they call it in Scotland. Shinty. Something like hurling. But then the Scots would have borrowed it from us. Great men to borrow, the Scots. Two teams. Fifteen a side. On one pitch, just like American football. The stick's about three feet long with a smooth curving blade. The best ash, cut with skill. The clash of the ash, they say. The ball's the size of two fists clasped. Like that. . .

He shapes the delicate white hands of Marion to resemble the ball. Cute man Murtagh. He is pleased with these young American women to whom last night I introduced him.

— That's the way the game is organized nowadays. Long ago it used to be played by mobs. All the men of one clan or parish against all the men of another clan or parish. And the pitch was unconfined. Over hedges and ditches and bogs they were bound, as the song said. But in the game, nowadays, we have rules and limits. Even in Ireland we have rules and limits. Anyway, you'll see it all in the Bronx. Tipperary vee New York. And what are you all having to drink?

In honour of the heat outside it is mostly cold white wine. Manolo, the Spanish barman, brings the drinks and olives and celery stalks, and impeccable good manners. Piped music, but very mildly, plays a flamenco tune. The musician has stayed aloft, playing to the toucans and the python, and the black shark and the staring piranha.

— Some night, Murtagh says, the piranha will come out and get him. You couldn't feel easy with those brutes about the house. Not a laugh in them from start to finish.

The young ladies from Boccaccio, Pampinea, Fiammetta, Filomena laugh into their cool tinkling drinks. Faraway in the sunny south and in a women's college he has sat with the three of them and nine hundred and ninety-seven others, in the great dining-hall and over his Hawaiian salad (cherry), reflected that Lord Byron could never stand, or sit, to see a woman eat. That sad-crazy mother of his must have been sloppy over her soup. Or it may just have been that Byron preferred his women otherwise engaged: at falconry, or the careful stitching of samplers, or at the dance, or at playing on the virginals.

— But what, saith the fair Pampinea from Tennessee, did you expect to find in a women's college if not women.

— A point well made. But knowing from faraway, from the far side of the Atlantic, that a women's college is full of women, and finding yourself at dinner, one man among a thousand women, are two different things. Not that I object. Now that the first shock is over, I rather like it.

The three young women who have asked him to sit with him at their circular table thank him merrily.

— Sometimes, they say, the chaplain joins us.

— Let us hope we never need a chaplain.

Lord Byron, he reflects again and with increasing wonder, could not have endured to be in that fine, old, southern, circular, timbered dining-hall watching and listening-to one thousand healthy females, hungry and unashamed, by no means walking in beauty like the night. Noble lord and all as he was, one thousand pairs of parents might have had qualms to hear that he was aprowl on the campus and, on faculty row, in possession of his own private lair into which he might entice or drag his prey.

— Belshazzar, from thy banquet turn he says, nor in thy sensual fullness fall.

And has to explain himself at some length. These are serious women. And curious.

Between bites and sups Fiametta talked of St Exupéry and Kafka and wonders, God bless the girl's digestion, what effect Schopenhauer and Kierkegaard had on Kafka. She was, and is, a thin, intense, freckled girl with spectacles and, in those days, she did most of her study in the reading-room attached to the chapel.

— Because, she said, there is always the crucifix on the wall. You can look at it when you are depressed.

Filomena, who was then plump and writing a paper on American pragmatism, said: There is always tea.

She is trying to slim but she found that strict dieting interfered with her ability to write papers.

Fiammetta said that the chaplain was a devout Calvinist and that one could talk to him about anything except religion. To most questions he returned as answer one and the same question: Cannot we know God.

Filomena said that she had been detailed in the forenoon to cheer up three depressed freshmen. The cause of their depression was not homesickness. But that so far they had had no dates. So she said: Consider, sisters, that somewhere there must be three or thirty young men with the same problem. That cheered them up.

— Hope, she said, there is always hope. Don't I know. Fat girls always know.

That was four to five years away back from this day of the python and hurling and humid heat: and heat or no heat, Murtagh says, duty calls him to the Bronx and we don't have to go with him unless we want to see the hurling. So to hell with the heat and the five of us head for the Gaelic Park in the Bronx.

— Filomena has problems, Fiammetta says. She has a situation. She has three situations. I've asked her to ask you about them. You were once so helpful to me.

This is in the subway to the Bronx: which, the subway, is nothing more nor less than a noisy putrid horror. She shrieks the message into my ear. Her voice has become as thin and shrill as herself. But because of the surrounding noise nobody except myself hears her. Nobody bothers to hear her because of the heat. Murtagh has fallen in love or something with Pampinea. All this is so strange to him. The other day on Lexington Avenue he looked up in boyish wonder and said that never again would he mention Liberty Hall which is Dublin's one skyscraper, lopsided and all of seventeen floors: skies are low, mostly, over the islands. Even the heat is, to Murtagh, a happening. Then to crown it all he has met a genuine belle from Tennessee: Boccaccio himself had never by any crystal Italian stream imagined better. Murtagh whispers into the ear of Pampinea who listens, enchanted, to his brogue. He is as exotic to her as she is to him: and somewhere there may be the prospect of a room with an air-conditioner where they may gather even closer without dissolving into a dew. Filomena is asleep or feigns sleep. Even if she hears, it doesn't matter, for Fiammetta is consulting me, the wiseman, with her permission. What was it that I ever did or said to help Fiammetta? With the heat and the noise I cannot remember: and the situation is, or the situations are, three men, two of them married and all contestants for the hand, by metonymy, of Filomena who, now that she has slimmed, is a mighty attractive proposition.

Next Sunday the pattern at home will be keeping and the young active hurlers the field will be sweeping . . .

It is some time in the eighteenth century and in the prison in the town of Clonmel in the county Tipperary a young man sits and waits to be hanged.

How sad is my fortune and vain my repining, the strong rope of fate for this young neck is twining . . .

And he remembers his home and the boys at the hurling in some sunlit pasture on the lovely sweet banks of the Suir. Who was he? What deed had he done? Who wrote the sad song about him? Burning with enthusiasm to explain the nature of hurling, and much else, to Pampinea, Murtagh sings the old song in the over-crowded cab that carries them, sweating, from the train to the playing-pitch: and far far from green Suirside grass is the rectangle of American scorched earth on which fifteen men from Tipperary, sticks in hand, do battle with fifteen Irish expatriates who, similarly armed, have taken it upon themselves to represent the city of New York. The game itself, and not just its finer points, is lost in clouds of acrid American dust. Every time a hoof or a stick or a ball or a body strikes the earth a spiralling sandstorm, devil of the desert, arises.

But back of the stands and terraces, in bars and in restaurants, several vintages of Irish-America have thrown their hats at the invisible game and are making certain sure that the heat will not dry nor the dust choke their throttles. Joining them, I find that I am among my own and far away from those awe-inspiring moments when the sun catches the tops of the buildings on, say, Seventh and I am shaken into asking myself why did man ever challenge the heavens by building such Babylonian towers.

Out on the pitch the desert devils move here and there. Here in the tents the corks pop and the stout and whiskey flow. The jovial din is only stupendous and, in the middle of it all, two nuns, one young, one old, sit on chairs and confidently shake collection boxes: and Filomena snuggles close and tells me of her three situations, two of them married, one Irish and single and works in a bank, one an airlines' pilot and English, one an American academic, all for one and one for all, and all together in New York on this warm day.

— And to think, she says, that once upon a time I counselled freshmen who were hardup for dates.

To think, indeed. The years and dieting have made her most desirable, and one solution for three situations is to find a fourth that will cancel out the other three. So he turns the topic by talking to her about poetry, about that same convict of Clonmel pining in his prison, and how nobody knows who he was, nor who the poet was who wrote about him in the Irish. Which he quotes mellifluously, and in full, in the cab on the way back to Manhattan. And how the Irish was translated into English in the nineteenth century by a lonely sort of a poet called Jeremiah J. Callanan whose spirit responded to that cry from the past: At my bedfoot decaying my hurlbat is lying, through the boys of the village the goal-ball is flying. My horse 'mong the neighbours neglected may fallow, while I languish in chains in the jail of Cluainmeala.

Which he tells her means Honeymeadow, a lovely name, a handsome town, a lovely river valley, romantic Ireland is not dead and gone but alive and well in the back of a cab in the humid heat in New York: and back in Manolo's Spanish bar and restaurant they are mysteriously alone or together, and Murtagh is somewhere with Pampinea, and Fiammetta has gone somewhere else alone so as to be able to catch an early morning flight to somewhere: and the three situations have been for the moment forgotten about for the poetic sake of the young man pining in the deathcell and sadly remembering his horse and the hurling in green meadows: With the dance of fair maidens the evening they'll hallow, while this heart once so warm will be cold in Cluainmeala.

But during dinner the vision fades and the situations relentlessly return, as later they are expected to do for drink and a discussion.

Her father is an episcopalian clergyman in Detroit.

— But it is not because I feel that life should be sinless. Or can be. Life should be simpler. Or plain simple.

He is prepared to agree. They hold hands across the table. She sips a tiny sip of his wine: then kisses the glass. One, two, three add up to complications. Four is as simple as a May morning. True love is an even number.

— Some things I want to buy, she says, in the supermarket.

So, after dinner, she goes for a while, leaving him gloating like a sultan, and returns with a plastic bag full of the things.

— My studio isn't fifty yards away.

They walk the fifty yards. He carries the plastic bag. It is a long walk in the sweating heat and the things in the bag are surprisingly heavy. Cans grind against each other. Somewhere on Sixth they find a doorway and one of those straight New York stairways. There is no elevator. The studio is on the fifth floor. He grunt and sweats. He fardels bears. Green meadows are forgotten, and crystal streams. Boccaccio was a liar.

She paints. He has already known that. There is something on the easel. An Andy Warhol prospect of a can of Sprite. There are other things on the walls. But even before the door opens he smells them. Not the Andy Warhol nor the things on the walls, but three of the largest cats it has ever been his misfortune to, he was about to think, see. A Manx, near neighbour to a Dublinman, tabby and tiger-striped. An Iranian: long hair sweeping the floor, tail like a living bush. A Thailander: slender as a snake, not sweet as a pawpaw in May nor lovely as a poppy, but mean and snarling behind a black mask. She takes from him the plastic bag. The cans are cans of catfood. He sits and watches while she feeds the jealous brutes on three separate willow-pattern platters and from different cans. She loves them. They love her. There is a camp-bed in the corner. For the cats or Filomena, or all in together this humid weather? She sits on it and they talk, he and Filomena, across a room crowded by cats. The cats stare at him. Could they outstare the musician's piranha fish? After a while Filomena and himself go back to the Spanish bar.

On the way to which he tells her the tale of Big Joe who played the clarinet. In the orchestra in a mammoth cinevariety theatre in Dublin. He was very handsome. He could run like Ronnie Delaney. He had need. He had seven mistresses.

— Knew three of them to talk to and two more by sight.

Because Big Joe was married the most he could manage was to see one of the girls one night each week after the late show. Told each girl he could manage only one night a week because his wife was jealous. Told his wife, to explain about the two hours, that he was having a drink with the boys. Which worked. He possessed man's greatest blessing: a complacent wife. Anyway she had him the rest of the time, when he wasn't playing the clarinet. Satisfactory. All present and correct.

There was one problem. In the interval between the second show and the late show, and when the movie was on the screen, every one of the seven wished to meet Joe somewhere or other for a chat and a drink or a cup of tea. He couldn't have them all in the same place so he, like a general, stationed one here, one there, around the central city, sentries, single spies, redoubts; and ran on foot, the quickest method of transport in crowded places, and sat and sipped and talked and kissed, and so on and on, and then back to the pit to blow the clarinet.

— Joe, I said, rationalize, rationalize. Not the breath of Leviathan could stand the strain.

— And I worried about him.

— What happened? What happened?

She must wash and perfume more than she paints or even makes love: There is no odour of cats.

He tells her that the last time he was back in Ireland he met the man who had played the saxophone in that same pit. And asked him how was Big Joe. And heard: Poor Joe, he went to London and dropped one day running along Shaftesbury Avenue.

— He took on too much territory. Alexander knew when and where to stop. Rationalize, Filomena, rationalize.

But no use in talking to her. She is surrounded, possessed, coiled around by pythons, and perhaps the only man who could be all the world to her would be that odd Egyptian officer mentioned by Thomas Mann whom she read so carefully in college: Weser-ke-bastet, what a bloody name, on imperial duty in the city of Shechem. But known to the Schechemites, wise guys, simply as Beset.

He mentions to her the name of that gentleman. But if in the course of her college reading she had ever noticed the fellow she has long forgotten him.

— What was about him?

— His two passions in life were flowers and cats. The local divinity of his home-town was guess what?

— A cat.

— Bright girl.

— Scarcely a flower.

— A cat-headed goddess called Bastet.

— What a fun idea. I'll paint her.

— Everywhere he went, and morning noon and night, he was surrounded by cats. All colours. All ages. All breeds and sexes. Not only living ones. But mummies. Before whom he placed offerings of mice and milk. And wept as he did so.

— Another fun idea. Could I decorate my studio like that?

He does not remind her that Beset was what used to be called a pansy: and Filomena's nature, it might seem, cries out for more than cats.

— Tarry with me.

She has actually used that word. Tarry.

Perhaps it is that old usages, old words survive in the south. Or is it just remembered from her reading?

— Tarry with me, she says, until they come.

— Tarry with us, he says, for already it is late and a perverted world seeks to blot Thee out of sight by the darkness of its denials.

— What is the man saying?

— That's part of a prayer my mother used to read out loud. At night prayers. With the Rosary. On the first of every month. Consecrating the household once again to the Sacred Heart of Jesus. The reference is to the disciples on the road to Emmaus.

— Wow!

No, it was not Judith here beside him and waiting for her men, it was Fiammetta, Marion, who did most of her study in the reading-room attached to the chapel because the crucifix was on the wall and she could look at it when she was depressed. Judith who was plump and into pragmatism, and who said there was always hope, and that fat girls always knew, is now beautiful and the desired of all or, at any rate, of four men. Correction: three. Four, only for a very brief moment.

— Tarry with us for the drink and the discussion.

— Would I not be, to coin a phrase, *de trop*? Four's company, five's a . . .

— Quorum. Be our chairperson. My master.

— And they knew him in the breaking of the bread.

— Be then my saviour. Marion used to say: Cannot we know God.

— The chaplain used to say.

Her nervous laughter. Three men arrive. All together. He feels that it would be apt if they paralleled the cats: one Manxman, one Persian, one Siamese. But that would be too much to hope for. They are as he heard they would be: two of them married although that doesn't show, one of them Irish which is obvious, one of them quite as obviously English, one of them an American academic: and how would you guess? Not one of them is of any particular interest. That is not just because they have come between himself and Filomena: Judith. No, the cats have already done that, those three cats, that invisible tomcat, that humid heat. Jean-Paul Sartre's octopus, that python.

If there was to have been a discussion my presence has put an end to that. Nothing above or beyond uneasy badinage. What a word. What does it mean? Nothing to do with badminton? Or shuttlecock?

— Hope, she had once said, there is always hope. Fat girls always know.

Fat girls hope that some day they may be slim. For what?

She leaves us for a while to go to the loo. It is the Irishman who says: Gentlemen, let us settle this. Once and for all.

No pistols, no swords are to be seen.

Carefully he takes from his wallet a small airmail envelope with green, white and gold trimmings. The Irish Republic. He shakes it. It rattles. He says: This envelope that you see in my hand contains three quarters. One of them is marked with a cross.

To me he says: Sir, as an impartial member of the audience inspect this envelope and the coins therein to see that there is no deception. It contains three quarters, coins peculiar to the United States of America, one of them marked with a cross clearly cut. When you have made your inspection and assured yourself of my veracity and bona fides, kindly pass the bag along, keep it moving, look, inspect, satisfy yourselves that all is fair and square, ladies and gentlemen, in for a penny in for a pound, come in your bare feet, go home in a Studebaker . . .

All is fair and square. The coins are restored, the envelope rattled, and he who finds the cross takes the woman. The Englishman finds the cross. They shake hands all round. And also with me. Fair field and no favour. The Englishman buys a round of drinks. All smiling, yet perhaps nervous, she returns from the loo. My advice or chairmanship is never needed. Later on the Englishman takes her by the elbow and gently leads her away. Quite uncomplainingly she goes: insofar as I can tell. Snarling cats stand there to prevent me from doing anything about it. A drink with the losers, perhaps myself a loser. A friendly goodnight.

That was all yesterday and late last night and now it is four in the morning, and the phone rings and rings, and the daft dark woman with the glistening teeth will be waiting, air-conditioner working: no cats.

I come, I come my heart's delight.

What do I mourn for? Lost innocence? Lost opportunity? The crowded condition of the world? The fury and the mire of human veins?

In the penthouse the python sleeps and the piranha stare into the darkness.

SECONDARY TOP

We come up from the river and watch him playing darts with young fellows in the alcove off the public bar in the fishing-hotel. Young fellows are tolerated there: just about. Darts and rings and baby-billiards, but no juke-box. A side-door opens to what has once been the stable-yard so that the fishermen won't be disturbed by through traffic. We sit where we can see and consider him. An atracap of a man with tight trousers, too small even for his small legs. He hasn't, the poor devil, the least idea of who we are. Or who I am. He could have seen Dale's picture in the papers. Or listened to him at an annual conference. Or passed him on the street in Dublin. Or observed him playing golf at Lahinch, the tough old bastard. Or heard about the way he forever jingles loose change in both pockets of his plus-fours. Plus-fours, anyway, have lived long enough or died long enough ago to be unusual. But the heart of the atracap is with the noisy boys. His eyes are on the dart-board. He notices nothing else.

— I am the Martian Marksman, he screams in fake falsetto.

And dances upon his little feet and scores a bullseye.

— I am the Black Wizard of Blue Mountain.

Stepping high he goes round and round the green baize of the baby-billiards. Bent double and moaning low, the half-dozen boys follow him.

— He plays darts with the boys, I say.

— An unnecessary comment, young man.

Dale jingles, but only in one pocket. He has a glass in his right hand. He says: With the girls too. Darts.

— I'm O'Driscoll the rover, the little man says in a startlingly profound baritone. That's me. Fineen O'Driscoll the rover, Fineen O'Driscoll the free.

He darts and, to applause, has another bull's eye. He is popular among the boys. He dances from one little foot-full of turned-up toes to another and chants, really chants: I am the Seawolf. I am Blackbeard Teach. I am old bold Henry Morgan. I am Captain Blood. I am the fastest gun in the West.

— In this secondary top, old Dale jingles, do they do everything through Irish.

He seldom or never now comes out of headquarters and has to be enlightened on details.

— Everything, I tell him. Every single thing.

Although, under the circumstances, it may be conduct unbecoming inspectors of the Department we laugh right heartily: and next morning study the girls the Seawolf plays darts with. Which is easy because the back or business entrance to the secondary school is right across the sleepy street from the fishing-hotel. Not exactly a complete secondary school but the smaller establishment we call a secondary top. The toddlers and under-twelves go in by the front door which looks down over lawns and flowerbeds to the river widening out into the lake.

The first letter of complaint had come to the Department from Worried Mother, no other identification. She had heard rumours and she had suspicions. No hard facts, no fingerprints. The letter was filed away but not forgotten. When Worried Mother wrote again she signed her name and had three other worried mothers to support her. Still no hard facts. No little girl had talked. There was a slight suggestion that the mothers were thinking of the law and that if the fathers knew and also worried, the remedy might overstep the law. Like tar and feathers. Then there was a scrawled letter from the parish priest to say that he was too old and his two curates too young to handle such a case.

— The church is done, Dale said. Ecumenism. Truckling to Protestants. Guitars on the high altar. In the old days the parish priest's blackthorn would have settled the case in five minutes. But I'll be glad to go with you, young man. You'll need a guide, counsellor and friend. Bloody maniac poking at the little girls. And I'll fish that river again. Fished it before you were born. With the long Castle Connell rod that you won't see the like of nowadays. Spliced with waxend made up of many strands of shoemaker's thread spun together by hand. The line running through the rings. Soak the cast in the pool . . .

He jingled, and rambled on for a long time about the way gentlemen fished before glass-fibre or Japan were heard of.

— I'll show you fishing, young man. We'll combine pleasure with our painful duty. Also the rods will be a sort of disguise. Incogniti.

Incogniti here we sit, girl-watching from the bay-window of the residents' lounge on the first floor. Green skirts, bare knees, green jerseys, white open-necked shirts: mostly. Some daring spirits have their own styles.

— They say, I say, that you're in trouble when you begin to look at your daughter's schoolfriends.

— Worse trouble if you begin to look at your grand-daughter's schoolfriends.

That jolts me a bit. He has a name for being a puritan. He says: They eat a lot of toffee.

A sweet little redhead, thirteen or so, goes by, cheeks swollen by an iced lolly, the stick of the lolly standing out white and stiff. Does the manikin hold their lollies while they suck?

— Atracap's a funny word, Dale says.

For our man has come into view, alone amid the lightsome throng, wearing, startlingly, a flat black Mexican hat, taking short steps, carrying a bundle of books.

Dale says: Texas Jack.

For no reason that I can think of: and, anyway, I am meditating on that word atracap. Never, I tell Dale, did I find it in any dictionary.

— For the good reason, young man, that it's not there to be found. A rural corruption of apricot, I'd say, and meaning something like arc or arcan which Father Dineen's dictionary will tell you means a chest or a coffer, or the last little pig in a litter. Or a dwarf. Or a lizard. Or a diminutive creature of any kind.

— Or simply an ark. As in Noah. How about acrobat?

— Or if you spell it eeayarcee, the heavenly arch or vault. Or a rainbow. Or water. Or honey. Or, as an adjective, bloody or blood-red.

— Like the poet, Whitman, Father Dineen contained multitudes.

— Or knew that our native language did.

We are talking pedantic nonsense because we feel, uneasily, that it's a mean thing to come sneaking up and spying on the little man. We have our orders. Fair enough. The Department is the Department. What else? But still!

Inside the building the warning bell sounds: five minutes to go. The flow of green girls strengthens, is blocked for a minute or two at the narrow doorway to form a green living pool. Shrill voices rising. Laughter. A teacher, or two or three or four, patiently, pressing through. Our quarry has vanished. Where did he get that hat? Old Dale says that in the cowboys and Injuns he read when he was a boy, Texas Jack always wore a flat black hat. He stands up. He steps forward into the bay of the window. He says two or three times: They came like swallows and like swallows went.

He tells me that he is moved to tears by all those light voices, by all that innocence. But he weeps no tear: and because we know what we know, or suspect what we have been led to suspect, the girls, twelve to seventeen, don't seem like that to me at all. Not all of them: several of them, by heaven, very well developed indeed. But how, merely by sight and a distant prospect at that, are we to know which of the young ladies are involved. Look now at that beauty: an Italianate sort of a girl, dark glossy hair blowing in the wind, shining back at the sun, turning and turning her head like a tennis umpire. No, that simile's trivial. Like an exotic bird that would spring and fly. Then thoughtfully, solemnly, with her left hand pushing her hair back, smoothing her forehead. She is also an original: she wears a red cardigan and levis. But she is by no means old enough to be a teacher. Dale says: Pitiful to think of them all growing up to be harridans, scolds, barges.

So touching, I think, the way they fold their arms over growing breasts: a discovery, an embarrassment, something to hide. Or protect. Look at that one now, stepping stoutly forward, schoolbag like knapsack on shoulders, spectacles, a sullen face, tails of hair in her eyes, the heavy green skirt clinging and making a valley, a coom, a gougane, up and up the coom until the mountain splits and the stream comes down from the sacred source. Old Dale and myself may not see eye to eye on these matters so I keep my poetic thoughts to myself and say tentatively: Such a leprechaun of a man to be engaged in such astronomical deeds.

— Atracap, he says.

And jingles.

But so far, he reminds me, we have no proof of anything. It may be merely gossip. Nasty matrons. With dirty minds. Who may have some other reason for disliking him. We must get some reliable information.

Going the other way along the street are three young women in blue jerseys and skirts, white shirts, precise blue neckties. They're a bit older than any we saw in the flight of swallows, now all gone through the gateway. Their age, difference in direction and slight difference in style puzzles Dale. He doesn't notice that they're blue and not green. The old walrus is colour-blind.

— In a place in England, he tells me as we go out into the morning, two young ones got up a charge against a teacher. A popular fellow. Handsome. Thirteen years of age. The young ladies, as you may guess, not the teacher.

Dale would be a striking figure to meet in the early morning in Paris, France, or London, England, or New York, N.Y. On the main street of a small town in the West of Ireland he is a wonder to behold and a problem to walk with. He attracts attention: six feet three, shining high-domed bald head, strong bright roughcast pebble-dashed tweeds, no plus-fours this morning, just normal trousers, but even at that. And the walrus moustache, and the bright yellow-brogued feet stamping to shake the earth, and the jingling in the pockets: the sheep are coming home in Greece, hark the bells on every hill. The walrus moustache: red, gone grey at the tips, not yet drooping. When the scholar and poet, Douglas Hyde, was President of Ireland, his secretary, a Mr Dunphy, up there in the Phoenix Park, wrote a book about the office of the presidency and was known as the Keeper of the Great Seal because Douglas Hyde had a Dale moustache, or Dale, here stamping like a warhorse beside me, has a Hyde moustache. He confuses me. He talks down to me: from his altitude, from his experience, down to my five feet nine, dark suit gone a little shiny, dark featureless hair combed straight back. Everyone in the town, if anyone of them ever was anywhere, must recognize him. The management of the school will as soon as they see him: he need scarcely identify himself. Anyway he was here before, fishing that river, and over the years he can't have changed much except for the worse. Incognito my backside. But, as he explains to me, it's not that we're here. It's what we're here for. That's the incognito, young man.

The town stirs sleepily around us. Towns like this don't rise early in the morning.

— The trouble began when the young English ladies heard that the teacher was plotting matrimony. To a grown woman. The girls followed him around. Not only the two who made the claims. But the whole school. Like the children after the Pied Piper. One of the two kept a diary full of fantasy.

— Three in a bed and all, I say.

That's to irritate him. Anyone can read the Sunday newspapers. All human life is there. Or even the *Daily Telegraph*.

— He must have had something, I say.

— He had, young man. He had a lot of trouble. One of them had the gall to ask him why had he got to get married. Women can be demons, you know. Big or little. Worse even than little boys. That sensible English poet said he never liked children. Even when he was a child. Read the Sunday newspapers, young man. Not *The Times* or the *Observer*. All opinions and no news. But the other papers.

It is one of the many aggravating things about him that he constantly repeats your own opinions and statements to you, without copyright acknowledgement. There are people like that. From me he heard about the poet who didn't like children. That also is the sort of thing that, rightly or wrongly, I am always saying about the Sunday papers.

Searching for that reliable information we are on our way to the parish priest. For even after the advent of the twenty-third John, the Venetian joker who put the whole establishment on a skater-board, the parish priest in Ireland may still be the man, and the master of morals. But this one isn't where he should be: in the parochial house at a mahogany table as wide as Wembley stadium, and eating his breakfast of bacon, egg and sausage. The table's there, fair enough. We can see it from where we stand in the wide linoleumed hallway. It's in there in the dining-room where it should be, and the door is open. But the dining-room, the hallway and the table have about them a desolate and abandoned air. Even though the place smells most diligently of polish and the table shines and glimmers. The housekeeper says: He's in his office.

— Tell him we're here, young woman.

Dale shows a card.

— His office is below, sir. Down in the town. I'll phone him and say you're here.

She picks up the telephone from a hall-table. From the first landing on the stairway a clock chimes ten. Most solemnly. Against the booms she speaks her message. She is most noticeably a young woman, early twenties, brunette, excellently formed. Dale is so astounded that he jingles with a new fury. As I said he hasn't been out of cold storage for a long time: and only the river and the lake it flows into drew him out. He has expected the door to be opened by the traditional dragon, over canonical or any desirable age. She tells us, lisping a little, rising on her toes to look up into Dale's face, that her master, if not her man, has a delegation with him below: that he can't come up but, perhaps, we could come down. Dale stops jingling. Is the Department being lightly treated? To steady himself he massages his high dome with both hands. She lisps and politely smiles us out. The door closes behind us. We stand for a while looking down on the town.

— We may only hope, he says, that she's a nun in disguise.

— Incognita, Mr Dale, I say.

And with some slight satisfaction.

From the high hill the house stands on there is a splendid view of the town: the big eighteenth-century mansion that became the convent and the school, the lawns sloping down to the river, the beechwood through which, after leaving the lawns, the river disappears and reappears. Beyond the beechwood the morning glitter of the lake. The avenue going back down to the town goes round and round the conical hill.

— A sacerdos, I say, seated on a high mountain.

Dale snorts.

The parish priest tells us that he got rid of them before we came in. He says: It was excellent or lucky that you went to the wrong place first. I never no more use the parochial house for bidnis. I'd sell it if the bish would allow me. It would make a better hotel than the one you're staying in. But it doesn't seem fair to ask my parishioners to walk up that dangerous hill if they want to see me. It wouldn't be good for the hearts of the old. Unless they could drive or be driven. And the young would do it on autocycles. A danger to themselves and everybody else. The young actually do come to see me. Mr Dale you're welcome.

He also welcomes me. And by name. He did say bish. And bidnis. He may have been for a while on the American mission. As they may still call it. To the heathen. But even that may be no longer necessary when every boy from an Irish bog can make singing or something noises like any boy from Memphis. He has met us in a narrow hallway opening off the main street and beside a butcher shop. His office is on the first floor above the shop. We go up a stairway narrower than the passage.

— I'm not a king or God himself that people should have to go up a high hill to see me.

— Or, Dale says, up a high hill not to see you.

— Sorry about that.

Since he seems a little in awe of Dale, and may be talking fast to reassure himself, I mumble that no harm was done, that the climbing exercise was better than jogging. Dale jingles menacingly: How did you know we were in the hotel? And our names?

— Eyes and ears. It's a small town. Like also, I was expecting you. So was the delegation I got rid of before you could get here. The three afflicted mothers. Not so much afflicted as ready to rend the poor fellow limb from limb. These young ones are a menace. The kittens entice you in. The tigresses pounce.

To demonstrate a pounce he opens the door of his office with a whoosh. No jingles from Dale. Which indicates that he is momentarily off-balance, malfunctioning. He stoops to enter. The sergeant is there waiting for us: and a lot more that's odd in a priest's cell or office or sanctum or what-you-will. The odour is of oil, but not of chrism. Through the one of the two windows that is open comes the sound of a male baritone, a good one, proclaiming that the moon hath raised her lamp above: then the sounds of chopping and what may well be the sharpening of the knife on the steel. In high summer the window would be, pray God, barred and bolted or closed with gauze against the butcher's bluebottles.

The sergeant sits on what, because of its position between the desk and the closed window, has to be the priest's chair: a faded cane with wobbly legs. For it creaks pitiably as he stands up and reaches out a strong hand to Dale and myself. With the other hand he steadies and gentles the restive chair. A big, obviously jovial man who carries his uniform with splendour, stripes shining like the distant lakewater in the morning. He says: Mr Dale, they tell me you have the rods with you. We met a while ago on Lough Derg, Dromineer, for the mayfly.

So Dale tells him that his intelligence service is working well. But he is gratified, laughs happily for the first time since he left Dublin. We help him with the laughter. In various keys. And sit down on an assortment of seats: the priest on an upturned wooden box, Dale in a well-preserved oaken desk-chair that stands apart in a corner, myself on an abbreviated bench on part of which somebody has placed a folded newspaper, almost certainly to prevent the backsides of trousers from sticking to the greasy surface. Dale says: You're interested in machinery.

The sergeant explains: Motorbike, Mr Dale. His reverence here thinks the clergy shouldn't go in cars. The new Church, Pope John, you know.

The bits of the bike are all over the place: cleaning, confession, is in process.

— When I was in the States, the priest says, I read a New Zealand poet who wrote oh wouldn't you laugh at the top of your voice if ever it came to pass that Christ went by in a big Rolls Royce and the bishop went on his ass. That changed my outlook.

I venture: The road to Damascus.

Dale jingles: and glowers across at me as if I had stolen his thunder. But sometime in the future he'll tell the story and claim my remark as his own. He says that we were expecting to meet an older man: and, sure as God, this is not the man who wrote to the Department to say that he was too old and his curates too young to handle such a case. This is a live-wire of a man somewhere in his forties. He wears a sailor's gansey or polo-necked sweater: clerical black, though. He is small. His hands move all the time. His dark, tousled, curly hair is oily but still straggles down over his forehead. Deep-brown eyes burn out at us from behind thick spectacles, rimmed also in clerical black. What has come over Rome and the bishops and where did they get him? A name, perhaps, for building churches.

— My predecessor, he says. Gone to glory. Full of years and merits. He wrote to you three months ago.

The sergeant tells us that the first thing is that the law, if it can help it, doesn't want to have anything to do with this business.

— Nor, says the priest, does the Church. Much.

— And I'll tell you why, says the sergeant.

— Playing doctors, says the priest.

— Will we ever forget it, says the sergeant.

They must have rehearsed that bit. At any moment they may rise and go up and down, singing, soft-footing, on the littered floor, like Byng Hope and Bob Crosby.

— It was in all the papers, says the sergeant. The shame of the locality. The world was pointing the finger at us. We don't want that again.

We wait. Neither of us have in any papers, Sunday or Monday or any other day, ever read a damned thing about this place. The singing down below has changed to: I come, I come my heart's delight.

And there is the demented scream of a disordered mincing machine.

— The long and the short of it is, Dale says, that they're passing the buck to the Department.

— Buck is correct. The Department. That's us.

— No. We are but delegates. Lords lieutenant. Viceroys. The Department is the king.

And later: Young man, that was a deplorable pun.

We have finished the soup and the sole, and are finishing the white, and breathing before the meat, and allowing the red to breathe. It can be said for him that he sees to it that we lunch and dine like viceroys. He picks his teeth. He repeats: Viceroys.

Then to my amazement and, possibly, also to the amazement of the few people in the hotel dining-room, he stands up, raises his right hand and proclaims: Upon the king! Let us our lives, our souls, our debts, our careful wives, our children and our sins lay on the king! We must bear all.

And sits down and bellows with laughter: and I am somewhat shocked even to suspect that an oldtimer like Dale could seem in any way to mock the Department: and in the presence of a subordinate. But he has been in an odd mood ever since the motorcycle priest told him that he, Dale, had been a close friend of the priest's father: and that discovery had come at the end of the sergeant's solemn narration of the scandal that had rocked the town, and, unseen by either of us, reached the newspapers.

— We'd never have moved, the sergeant said, if two of the little blackguards hadn't attacked a married woman. Five months' pregnant.

In broad daylight. In the middle of the convent meadow. There's a
public footpath, you see, across the meadow from the bottom of the
marketyard to the Mullinagowan Road. A rightaway. From time
immemorial. And even then we shouldn't have moved. Publicity's the
worst possible thing. If somebody, not the guards, had just taken the
brats aside and beaten their backsides sore. But we had a Super then
who was all for law. And we can't even beat backsides to settle this one.
And whose backside? His or theirs?

The historic right-of-way had only been the proximate cause of the
outrage and attempted assault: frustrated by the screams of an aged nun
who was watching from a convent window.

— No. Two families under one roof. Always a risky thing. Cousins.
Sort of. In and out through each other. You couldn't count them. Male
and female. It began with tickling and what they called playing doctors.
And after a while you wouldn't know who was up to what. Or with
whom, as the rhyme says.

The sergeant wrinkled and wiped his brow and was genuinely
embarrassed: perhaps not so much at what had happened as at where it
had happened: in his jurisdiction. Two of the boys, he said, real cousins,
legitimate as the Four Courts, were thirteen and fourteen. They called
the tune, made up the games. Anyway they were thirteen and fourteen
when they got too big for their boots and attacked the woman. The
capers were going on for twelve months and nobody any the wiser.
Strange thing was that once it was well started the girls took over.

— Not so strange.

That was Dale. Jingling. But slowly. Meditatively: A case in the
Sunday papers a few weeks ago. A fifteen-year-old spent a night with an
Arab student. In a most respectable English city. So far so good. But the
next night she was back for more, bringing her eleven-year-old friend
with her. Broke into the fellow's flat where he was with two other
students. Students, indeed. And there they all were, happy, until the
police came. The police inspector said: They obviously went with the
intention of receiving attention.

He had stolen the story from me and it was necessary to fight back: In
the same paper it said that in Saudi Arabia nine men were beheaded for
murder and sexual offences, three for rape, three for sexual assault, and
three for having sex during the holy month of Ramadan.

— Ram is right, said the sergeant. The Arabs may have the answer.
Beg your pardon, father.

Father, laughing heartily, did not seem in the least offended.

— And outside the courthouse, the sergeant said.

He was speaking only to Dale. Courtesy? Respect for rank?

— Outside the courthouse, on the day the case was heard, three of the worst of them were there in white socks and skipping ropes and butterfly ribbons in their pigtails. Skipping and playing hopball. The defence put them up to it.

— That, said the priest, was the picture that made the Sunday papers. Our image.

— One, two, three O'Leary, said the sergeant. Ten O'Leary catch the ball. A rhyme, he explained, the children used to sing, hopping the ball.

After that there was a long silence. Except for the singing and the slashing from the shop below. The song now was: *Funiculi, Funicula*.

— He has a fine voice, Dale said.

He stood up. He said: We'll do what we can. And as quick and quietly as we can.

The priest thanked him: I've looked forward to meeting you, Mr Dale. My father used to talk a lot about you.

— Who was your father?

A name was mentioned. And recognized. With emotion.

— He went to the States, Dale said. A good man. He died there. God rest him.

— I was born there. When he died my mother brought me back here to go to school. A chaplain in the navy for a bit. Small men get on well in the navy. They don't hit their heads so often. But I was seasick most of the time. You couldn't get me into a ship now for love of God or man.

— Or women, I said.

Uproarious laughter.

By that time we were down the narrow stairs and out again into the street.

A pert, redcheeked face and a fluffy white scarf and a shoulderbag. Followed by a little mouth simultaneously pouting and trying to suck the last drop out of an orange. Three steps behind the orangesucker that unusual Italianate girl with the cardigan, patterned fairisle today though, and the levis. Never may I know why she dresses differently. No, she looks too adult, too self-controlled to be part of any group, even, by heavens, of a hockey-team: there are certain women who always walk alone: she would be more than a match for the little man, homunculus with a beard and a flat black hat, now dancing and dartplaying down below in the alcove off the public bar and giving himself, with bright imagination indeed, comic names. School is over early for this day. Dale is off somewhere with the parish priest, sentimentalizing about the priest's father or something: and his absence is an ease and a chance to read, and to study the girls emerging, and to speculate. There's a girl with a sort of German helmet hairstyle, a fringe, the classically-proud pale face of a king's mistress, courtesan, made beautiful by the painter's sycophancy and skill: but real and alive out there in the crowd at the side-gate. A man might easily be tempted. Or set to thinking. She carries a brown leather violin case. Above green stockings her bare knees seem very large. Perhaps later on in life knees may slim or lessen of their own accord. There's a blonde with fine thoughtful features walking arm-in-arm with a tall, pimply, darkhaired, bespectacled girl who, cool as a breeze, produces cigarette-case and lighter, and lights up, with a skill that any schoolboy of the thirties might have envied. Arm-in-arm again, they proceed, a fragrant cloud above them.

But most of them favour the chewing of toffee, or the chewing of something: most unlikely that it could be tobacco twist. Perhaps the way of it is that he has fallen for the odour of toffee on dew-fresh lips. Where the bee sucks there suck I. Or down in the house of the funeral, the wakehouse with the mourners all assembled and rejoicing, I first put eolas, knowledge, on my brownhaired girl: her cheeks were like the roses and her little mouth like the brown sugar: there was sweetness on the tips of the branches and honeycombs at the roots of the bushes, and the fish in the waves were leaping with pleasure because she was alive. That's my memory of a song I heard an old woman sing in Donegal Irish and a poet I know who heard the song at the same time improvised a sort of New Orleans rhythm: Honey with the mouth like brown sugar.

Repeated over and over to the stamping of feet and clapping of hands: Honey with the mouth like brown sugar.

How tall they are. Vitamins. Orange juice. Young people in the States get taller and taller. Perhaps our laws should take that into account. And they learn so much so soon: magazines, discotheques, television programmes that would have set our greatgrandmothers running out of the room. Or would they? Mysteries, mysteries, mysteries, masks in green jerseys and skirts and blazers: except for that daughter of Italy in levis and patterned fairisle cardigan: all bound for homes where so far they have kept their secrets, those of them who have secrets to keep.

One last straggler: a sideways look, long dark hair, white stockings, long loose green coat. Honey with the mouth. And the fish in the wave are leaping with pleasure because she is alive: and two of the blue young women, one with vivid red hair, cross the street and disappear from my view. Into this building, perhaps. Now that the parade is over I'll descend to the public bar and find better company than my own thoughts: or Dale who tomorrow, God be praised, goes to the lake with the sergeant. Even in a place like this there must be somebody.

There is, too. There is Fineen O'Driscoll the Rover, Fineen O'Driscoll the free, as straight as the mast of his galley, as strong as a wave of the sea. His name is not O'Driscoll: his mother's name was. We have made a study of his papers, his record, up to the moment faultless. Up to what they call, here and there in Munster, this little weakness. To what might, in any other part of the world, be regarded as a sign of strength. He is a dab hand at the darts. With the boys or with the girls. With no effort in the world and with, in succession, an underhand and an overhand, he notches two triples. The enthusiasm of the boys shows that they really like him. He hops on his two little feet. He wears those boxer's coloured boots that have ruined the walk-style of half the world. He chants: I'm Fineen O'Driscoll the Rover, Fineen O'Driscoll the free.

He teaches while he plays: The O'Driscolls of the southwest were famous sea-rovers. Or pirates the Saxons would have called them. As if their own greatest hero at the time wasn't the greatest pirate who ever sailed a ship. What was his name, Jimmy?

A sallow-faced boy who could be the brother of the girl in the cardigan and levis answers: Drake, sir. Drake he's in his hammock and a thousand miles away.

The features and colouring don't suit so well on a boy.

— Correct, Jimmy. Sometime you should see his statue on Plymouth Hoe. It's alive. He played bowls, though. Not darts. Do you know why he went on playing? Even when the Spaniards were in sight.

— No, sir.

— Tide. The tide, man. He couldn't get out until the tide rose. But we had our own pirates. Who was the greatest of them all?

— Granuaile O'Malley of Westport, sir. Grania of the Ships.

— True, Jimmy. A queen among men. But a tough woman. Too tough for any of you.

He picks up the darts that the inferior aims of two boys have scattered broadcast. He says: Fineen isn't frightening. There's a great ballad about Fineen. An old castle towers o'er the billows that thunder by Cleena's green land, and there dwelt as gallant a rover as ever grasped hilt in the hand. Eight stately towers of the waters lie anchored in Baltimore Bay . . .

Is this the way he talks to the girls?

— Does that remind you of anything, Tommy?

— The other poem, sir. The sack of Baltimore. About the Barbary corsairs kidnapping the Cork people. She only smiled, O'Driscoll's child, she thought of Baltimore.

— Nifty, Tommy. You are the flower of the flock. You will be a writer someday.

He scores a bull's eye. He doffs that odd hat to mop his brow. This mannikin is good for these boys. Wisdom and learning and poetry at the dartboard.

Without the hat he is different, thoughtful, melancholy, a lonely little frightened man, good for the boys and hiding in their company. But what about the girls and what do the boys know about the girls and Fineen the Rover? Ah well, screw the girls I was unfortunately about to think. Yet sitting here spying I feel like a . . . What? A spy, and how does it feel to be a spy? It depends, it depends, as the strong farmer said about his prize bull's pizzle. So to Gehenna with the whole pathetic business and let Dale, the old departmental windbag, do his own moral dirty work. This is not why my sainted parents sent me to college. Carry my drink to the far end of the bar. Sit with my back to the wall that separates the bar from the entrance hall and reception. Look around for company: and hope to find it. Virtue is its own reward but no man would refuse a few fringe benefits.

It is the east and Juliet is the sun. It is the blue girl with the red hair. She enters through door on my left, walks the length of the bar, and what a walk, exits by door at far end. Beyond that there's a narrow hallway and, perhaps, a powder-room. No youthful whinnies or whistles or snickers. The presence of the master? Or the overwhelming style of the girl? The master speaketh not. But the boy who might be the brother of the Italianate girl is a cool cookie and also, perhaps, inured to beauty, and ventures: Miss Moynihan, may we go with you?

Briefly she pauses, swivels, smiles, snaps her fingers, says: Follow on, boys, follow on.

And leaves an awed silence behind her and an air warm and crimsoned with things unspoken, the game for a few moments forgotten, the master meditating, his hat in one hand, a few darts in the other: myself turning my glass in my hand and looking into its depths and suspecting that away down there something may be made manifest, a sunken city, a mermaid, anything. The barman, polishing glasses, taps one of them on the counter and when I raise my head he winks and smiles and clicks his tongue as you would to a horse, and I raise my glass to him and to all the memories of all the queens that ever were. We are brothers akin, guesting awhile in the rooms of a beautiful inn.

The jet-trail of her perfume is still in the air when she is back. For the sake of good manners my eyes are cast down as she advances, *oculis dimissis, omnia videns*, as the Jesuit said about the pensive nun, devout and pure: and what I do see just across my table is her blue skirt, cunningly filled. The blue girls, I know, work in the bank: and God be thanked that I am not like Dale, the old walrus, colour-blind: and thanked again because association with the bank-girls can't leave a man on the windy side of the law. She speaks to me by name. She says: There's a small private bar behind reception. Where you might be more comfortable.

So, like the gentleman that I am, I take her word for it and go with her. To find that she told me no lie, and to meet the other girl in a discreet little pine-panelled room with fire in the grate, hunting-prints on the walls and, in a glass-case in the corner, the biggest pike that ever against his will came out of the lake. The other girl is dark and quiet and coy. They are engaged at sausages and toast and tea. Nothing coy about this redheaded woman: because for God's sake let us sit upon our rumps and forget about girls, greenwood that smokes and weeps, Elvis Presley yahooing I'm a redblooded fellow and I can't help thinking of girls, girls, girls, good enough for the likes of Elvis or Fineen: and let's talk about women, the something dame rejoicing and crackling in the flame.

More to the dark girl than to me she says: We might as well be blunt.

Waiting seems to be in order. So I read from the hunting-prints that Aiken etched and Sutherland aquatinted. The dark girl says that this room is used mostly by lawyers from the courthouse. Nothing very blunt about that. Continue to wait. There are no lawyers visible. Miss Moynihan says: It isn't their day. So the place is quiet. That's why we enticed you in.

— Am I in danger?

Laughter.

— We can talk, she says.

— We can tell you, says the dark girl.

— Tell me what?

But, Ireland being Ireland, I know. They know my name and status, they know my business, they know more about it than I do or Dale does, half the town must know and be at this moment passing the glad tidings on to the other half: and the quicker Dale and myself and Fineen are up and away the better. No scandal, the sergeant said. No bobbysoxers playing hopball at the Courthouse steps. No pictures in the papers.

— We watched Mr Dale and yourself watching him playing darts with the boys.

— We didn't see you watching us watching him.

No point in pretending ignorance. Had they also watched us at the first-floor window watching the little, not so little girls, and not exactly thanking God for them. But no. She demonstrates. In the wall behind one elongated hunting-print there's a peephole from which the affairs of the public bar and the alcove are visible.

— He's a good little fellow, she says. He's happy with the boys. But he's afraid of women.

— Not according to report.

— I mean women.

— They know that, the dark girl says. So they surrounded him. They're a ring of little demons. They make jokes about him.

— He's afraid of women, Miss Moynihan repeats. Grown women. And who are we to say that we blame him. We work with ten of them. And the young ones can be worse. Or every bit as bad. Or not so well able to hide it. They'd giggle at the separating of the sheep and the goats. Then he drifted into it gradually. Through teaching, you know, holding their hands when they draw a map.

The dark girl says: Geography, how are you? Tell what you know about the River Ganges. The river Ganges in this way resembles the river Shannon. He teaches geography and history.

— Where, I ask, did he get that hat.

— Amateur acting, the dark girl says. He's very good at that. As you might imagine. He wore that hat in Blood Wedding and liked it and wouldn't surrender it.

Through a hatch beside the peephole I order another drink. They abandon tea for vodka, just one, and back to the bank, and no odour, and no one the wiser. They come in here often at this time. Marie is engaged to a solicitor but he's away today.

— The talk of those girls, she says. Shameless. One of them I hear shouting to another, shouting, the town and the reverend mother could have heard every word. Shouting can you keep a secret, cross my heart and hope to die, Mary Sherlock in the fifth has had her monthlies. We didn't talk like that in our time.

— Marie, can you remember that far back?

Laughter.

Angela says: The curse has come upon me cried the Lady of Shalott.

— Angela, you're shocking Mr . . .

Again I'm mentioned by surname.

— My name, I say, is Larry.

— The night, says Angela, before Larry was stretched.

Laughter from all three of us.

— What the little man needs, Marie says, is a good gentle woman to mother him.

— Somebody just like me, Angela says.

Marie crows like a rooster. Then she says: They talk about him to each other. Naturally. Women do talk. And especially little women. I've heard them. One of them said, you know that little redhead, Mona something, she said he's a funny little man, he'd cry for anything, like a baby, he'd make you tired looking at him crying: and the other said why does he cry and she got her answer, he cries if you don't, then he cries if you do. That, as sure as God, I overheard here one day in the powder-room, two of them slipping in to smoke where they had no right in the world to be.

— Did they talk to anyone else?

Miss Moynihan enlightens me: One of them did. To me. For a reason. You may not believe it. Love. She fell in love. And jealousy. He was giving too much attention to her best friend.

With mock profundity Marie says: Eternal triangle. Too many strings to his bow. Getting his lines crossed. He's a good fisherman and should know better.

To my horror the two of them laugh quite merrily. Well: not absolutely to my horror. The wrong, or whatever it is, may be mixed.

— Which reminds me, says Angela. There are worse things afoot.

— The mothers, I say. The law.

— The fathers, Marie says. Lynch law.

— Word gets around, Angela says. Tarring and feathering. I heard it mentioned. And the cat of ninetails.

— And worse, Marie says, I heard suggested.

Angela nibbles the last fragment of sausage and sips the last sip of vodka. She hums. But our good times all are gone and I'm bound for moving on.

And I cap the quotation: I'll look for you if I'm ever back this way.

Then back to the bank with them and back with me to my balcony, *id est*, that window on the first floor: to watch the street and the convent gate and to wait for Dale. To hear that he and the sergeant have made all their plans for a day on the lake, and Fineen the Rover to go with them. So all I know I keep to myself, for the present, let old Dale have his swink to him reserved: and I telephone the bank the next morning and make my own plans for better things and thrills than the hooking of harmless fish.

Suddenly I am surrounded by girls, little women, no longer in school uniform, no longer chewing, no longer smoking as they step daintily along, the clothes have changed them, this could be a dream, if I try to escape they surround me they seem to be everywhere, grave Alice and laughing Allegra and Edith with golden hair. They wear skimpy jackets, all colours, and flimsy jeans, more like pyjamas, all colours, and perfumes and hairstyles. They smile and speak politely as they pass along the corridor, Dale holding the door for them, a most impressive figure. A school-party on a trip to Dublin: and the last in the line that Italianate girl, brown eyes studying Dale gravely, even sparing a glance for his curate.

— Pygmy women, Dale says.

As we relax into our own compartment.

— Not so pygmy. Anyway pygmies, I hear, have some odd customs.

— Yet, he says, that parade should help you to realize how a man might wobble, waver, go astray. Might even be inclined to forget that the law, not nature, makes a difference between seventeen and fifteen. You were yourself talking about vitamins and orange juice. And those tall American teenagers.

To Dale, back in his plus-fours and monstrous as anyone may imagine, my mind and heart, if not my eyes and ears, are closed, are back in a lakeside wood with Angela, are leaping forward to meeting her again when she comes to Dublin. People meet, the mountains never. Fineen the Rover, pointing darts with the boys, weeping over the girls, has brought us to that meeting the mountains may never enjoy. Sunlit landscape drifts happily past. Ireland has never been so beautiful. Dale talks on from the top of a faraway mountain. As futile as Jehovah. As ignorant. Fineen is the fellow who has made things happen.

— But the Department, Dale says, might make some of it up in expenses. That is if the Department wasn't aware that it was so doing. Did you ever hear the story of the Bad Linnane's hat?

That may well be the only one of Dale's stories that I have never heard.

Then he says oddly: He's lucky. He has neither wife nor family. Neither chick nor child, he said. It was necessary to query that. Should the phrase not be check nor child?

The western mountains fall away behind. We cross the big river. In the lull at Athlone we can hear the girls singing.

— His father and mother died young, Dale says. An aunt somewhere is the only relative. He's free to run. He won't be missed. The sergeant didn't intrude. A discreet, considerate man.

Then, after a pause: A good wrist and a great man for the Red Butcher.

— The sergeant?

— No. Fineen, as you call him. The Red Butcher is a fly. I'm not so sure he's right in that. On that water. But it worked. And he knows every ripple by name. No man with an eye and wrist like that should be confined.

— Worried Mother would be overjoyed to hear you.

Flat fields and dark bogland slumber all around us. With the renewed rattle of the train, we can no longer hear the girls singing.

— He ties his own flies. He has very nimble fingers.

— Daresay he has. At the darts too.

— Young man?

But, oddly again, he laughs.

— Texas Jack, as I prefer to call him. Canada's the place for him. Or Oregon. The Far West. Great rushing rivers. I fished some of them. The Rogue river. Zane Grey, you know.

A brief pause at a small halt to allow a westbound train to proceed. No sound of singing. What are they up to now?

— Texas Jack. Fineen the Rover. He's three men or more. The Martian marksman. The Black Wizard of Blue Mountain.

— The cat among the pigeons.

— Advised him to work only at university level and to pray to St Joseph every night to keep him from screwing the freshmen.

Astounded I am. Has he picked up that one from associating with the motorbike padre, heaven's angel?

— He hadn't his fare, you see. But without knowing, or anonst to itself, the Department might make up to me some of the money. That's the Irish i ngan fhios do. Without his being aware of it. In the north, English-speakers in rural places used to corrupt it to anonst. They were, in fact, speaking Irish anonst to themselves.

— I know.

— That's why I was thinking of the Bad Linnane's hat.

No invitation will he get to bore me with another story but he's in the mood for it, needs neither invitation nor encouragement: In my days there were two brothers on the reporting staff of a certain Dublin newspaper, the Good Linnane, the Bad Linnane, both good men, gentlemen, but one was a strict sober disciplined man, the other a humorous fellow, God's good company in a bar or on a journey.

A pause. A long stare. At me. Two girls pass along the corridor, one a chubby, freckled, bespectacled redhead. They smile at us. He waves a hand.

— He was reporting, the Bad that is, an open-air political meeting when a scuffle began. His hat was knocked off and trampled in the mud. And at the end of the week he added to his expenses, item one hat, and the cashier told him that it was no part of the policy of that paper to provide its reporters with hats: and at the end of the next week said, with a sneer, no hat this week and the humorous man said it's there but you don't see it.

— The invisible hat.

— It became proverbial. Invisible like the Bad Linnane's hat. So the Department may never know the good it helped to do.

— You astound me.

He really does. How all along we have misjudged this man.

— I thought I might. You're young yet, he says. And easily astounded.

In the corridor six more young ladies file past, demurely, on some private business.

— He'll make out all right in Canada. We're all entitled to one mistake.

— One?

The redhead and her companion, still smiling, go back the way they came. He waves again.

— Throw no stones, he says. Throw no stones.

Two of the six returning, meet another two. There is some giggling in the corridor. The city is not far away. Giggling, that is, from three of them. The fourth is that daughter of Italy. Or could it be Egypt? She doesn't giggle.

— There was a young one when I was a boy, Dale says. Something like that sallow girl. The same eyes. My first love. Made an assault on her one day. Went wild. Wrestled with her for a long time.

The girls have moved on. He stands up and looks out the window. He goes, jingle, jangle, jingle.

— Crazy with curiosity I was. Nothing much transpired. Fortunately. She cried a lot. But she never told. She was twelve. I fourteen. I might have made the newspapers.

— Few of us haven't some secret, I say.

The corridor is crowded with laughing girls, a sudden rush from the stairway, a sudden raid from the hall, such an old moustache as he is might be a match for you all.

— Young man, I'm not hearing confessions.

— Father Abraham, you're not getting any.

— But how did we miss it, he says. How did we miss that picture in the papers? Three girls in pigtails and skipping ropes and playing hopball before the Courthouse.

Still wondering we walk the platform. Marshalled by two teachers, female, a crocodile of young ladies goes before us.

A LETTER TO PEACHTREE

Always I prefer not to begin a sentence with an I, so I'm beginning this sentence and letter with the word Always. Which can be a beautiful or a terrible word, all depending on where you are, how you feel, who you are with, what you are doing, or what is being done to you. Days may not be bright always and I'll be loving you always. That last bit I really do mean, you, over there, soaking in the Atlantan sun on Peachtree.

Do you know that there was an Irish poet and novelist, a decent man who, as they would say over here, never laid his hand on a woman, and who tore up his mss. and died a Christian Brother, and who wrote a lovesong to say that he loved his love in the morning, he loved his love at noon, he loved his love in the morning for she like the morn was fair. He loved his love in the morning, he loved his love at noon, for She was bright as the Lord of Light yet mild as Autumn's moon. He loved his love in the morning, he loved his love at Even. Her smile's soft play was like the ray that lights the western heaven. He loved her when the Sun was high. He loved her when He rose. But best of all when evening's sigh was murmuring at its close.

Clear, godamned clear that he knew nothing about it. How could he keep it up, always?

Howandever, as Patrick Lagan says, here we are on this crowded train, the cameraman called Conall, and Patrick and Brendan and Niall and myself, and this plump girl in jodhpurs, well, and a red sweater as well, and good horsey boots to walk about in. And a mob of people, a jampacked train, dozens standing in the corridors, and going towards the wide open spaces of the Curragh of Kildare where the great horses run. There's a man with a melodeon sitting on the seat in the john, merely because he has nowhere else to sit, his big, square-toed boots nonchalantly over the threshold, the melodeon tacit, the man sucking an orange. Jodhpurs leans her right shoulder, her round cheeks flushed, against my necktie spreading like the Shannon between Limerick and the sea, the tie you gave me when I took off for Ireland, a tie wide, I say, as the Shannon, a basic blue and green and, floating on that, slices of orange, a bloodred cherry and a branch of blossoming dogwood. Some tie. The tie that binds us.

This all about Jodhpurs I tell you not to make you jealous but to explain to you how crowded the train is and to give you a general idea of the style and spirit of the journey. Conall the cameraman has asked Jodhpurs to pose against my tie, your tie. She has been on the train with some friends on the way to the races. But when she sees Conall she drops out and joins us. She has the hots for Conall. He is quite a guy. Italianate handsome, dark wavy hair, quick gestures, good tweeds, and style, and as tough as a hawser and, to add the little dusting of pimento, a slight stutter, only noticeable when he's sober. But good-humoured and talking all the time.

Now let me tell you something.

My grandmother came from Ballintubber in the county of Mayo. She had the old belief about how it was ill-luck to meet a redheaded woman on the way to market. Jodhpurs is sure as hell redheaded. But howabout, for added value, a redheaded man, big as Carnera, dressed in rustcoloured chainmail tweed, whose too-tight trousers betray him and burst wide-open between the legs when he is strap-hanging in this crowded train? What would you do on an occasion like that? Walk the other way? Look the other way? As any lady would or should.

One little railway-station, two, three, four little railway-stations whip by, then wide-rolling, green spaces with racing-stables, a silhouetted water-tower, a line of exercising horses. Conall says that over there in the national stud by Kildare town he once did a set of pictures of a famous stallion, and he, the stallion, was the smallest thing you ever saw, everywhere and every way no bigger than a pony, Conall says, and says that he, Conall, was himself better hung and I'm prepared to take his word for it. But he is clearly meditating on the goodness of God to the big man who burst. Who has had to borrow a mac from somebody to cover his glory, or his shame. Which it just about does. He is a very big man. Seems to me that that earthquake or revelation, or whatever, just about sets the tone for all that is to follow. Conall puts his curse on crowded trains and on the sharp corners of the leather case he carries his camera in, and says that if there isn't a fight at the play tonight his time will have gone astray. Because of the crowd on the train he missed a proper, or improper, shot of the red man who burst: at the actual instant of bursting, that is. But he knows the red man and the red man's two comrades. Three army officers, out of uniform for a day at the races. The big red man has not, say the other two, been out of uniform, except when in bed, for years. So they have almost forcibly fitted him, or stuffed him into that tweed which, under strain, has not proved a perfect fit from Brooks Brothers.

Then the crowd leaves us at the railway halt, one platform and a tin hut, out on the great plain of Kildare: and off with them all to the races. Conall, who already has had some drink taken, must have sucked it out of the air, no jug visible at any time since Dublin, sings after the racegoers that the cheeks of his Nelly are jolting like jelly as she joggles along up to Bellewstown hill. Which Lagan assures me is a bit of a ballad about another race-meeting somewhere to the north. He promises Jodhpurs, whose cheeks, fore and aft, are firm and by no means jolting like jelly, that he will sing it for her later on. He's a good man to sing a ballad or quote a poem. She latches on to us, and to hell with the races, and we are elsewhere bound, and not to any market.

But how did we all come to be on that there train when the red man was unseamed from the nave to chaps? Listen! The previous evening, a lovely May evening, Dublin looking almost like one of those elegant eighteenth-century prints, I walked over the Liffey at O'Connell Bridge, then along Eden Quay and for once, the name seemed apt: and into the Abbey bar to meet Patrick Lagan, a man I've mentioned in previous letters. Like, when I went to Brinsley MacNamara to talk to him about his novels and my dissertation, he passed me on to Patrick Lagan. He said that Lagan had more of his books than he had himself, all autographed by me, I mean all autographed by Brinsley. He said that Lagan knew more about his books than he himself did. Curious thing, he said. Brinsley begins many statements with those two words: Curious thing.

Life seems to him almost always absurd and he may well be right about that. He even made a collection of some of his short stories and called it: *Some Curious People.*

Along Eden Quay, then, and left round the corner at the Sailors' Home, and past the burned-out shell of the old Abbey Theatre. Which has recently gone up in smoke taking all sorts of legends and memories with it. With Brinsley I walked through the rubble, a big man, Brinsley, once a great walker by the river Boyne, but now moving slowly, arthritic feet, and leaning on a stick, and remembering and remembering many curious people.

But the Abbey Bar, round yet another corner, still survives, and Lagan was there in all his glory and a few of his friends with him. There was a lawyer and a professor of history, and a bank-manager, who is also a music critic and who plays the organ in a church, and two actors from the Abbey Theatre, and two reporters from the paper Lagan works on, and one cameraman from same: a mixed and merry throng. And Brinsley, dominating all in physical size and mental dignity, and being treated by all with the respect which is only his due.

Curious thing, he says, how landscape, buildings, environment, physical surroundings can affect the character of people. Take, for instance, your average Dublin workingman. A rough type. A man with a young family, he goes out to the pub in the evening. He drinks a pint, two pints, three, four, five, six, perhaps ten pints. He's a noisy fellow. He sings. He talks loud. He argues. He may even quarrel. He staggers, singing, home to the bosom of his family, in tenement apartment or corporation house, goes to bed quietly and, soundly, sleeps it off. But down in the so soft midlands of Meath and Westmeath, where I come from, things are different. The heavy heifers graze quietly, and the bullocks, all beef to the ankles. The deep rivers flow quietly. Your average workingman there is a bachelor. Living most likely with his maiden aunt, and in a labourer's cottage. In the quiet, green evening he cycles six or so miles into the village of Delvin for a drink. He drinks quietly. One pint, two, three, anything up to ten or more. In the dusk he cycles quietly home and murders his maiden aunt with a hatchet.

Curious thing, environment. Curious thing.

The name of Conall, the cameraman, is also Lagan, but no relation to Patrick. Patrick says that Patrick was a saint but that Conall Cearnach was a murderous bloody buff out of the mythologies before Christ. There's a poem about the fellow, Lagan says, you'll hear it from me sometime, as I feel we will, he's a helluva man to quote poetry. In a booming base barreltone that would put Ariel to sleep.

Then, when I tell Conall that I am over here from Harvard to write about Brinsley's novel, *The Valley of the Squinting Windows*, about village and small town hatreds, and in relation to Sinclair Lewis and the main street of Gopher Prairie . . .

How are you over there on Peachtree Street in sunny Atlanta? Think of me in the Margaret Mitchell museum.

And in relation to Edgar Lee Masters and all the tombstones on the Spoon River, and Sherwood Anderson away out there in Winesburg, Ohio, and a Scotsman called George Douglas Brown and his House with the Green Shutters, about whom and which Brinsley has put me wise, and about all the dead life of small places . . .

Well, then, Conall Cearnach he says to me, but, man, you have to come with us to where we are going. You'll be missing copy if you don't. This is going to be it.

At this stage Brinsley leaves us but only briefly and only to travel as far as the john and back again. We are sitting in a nook or corner of the bar. The door of the john is right in there. For the reason that his feet give him some discomfort Brinsley doesn't stand up rightaway but slithers, sitting, right up to the door of the locus. Niall of the Nine Hostages, ancient Irish King, and Brendan the Navigator, ancient Irish saint, who sailed an open boat all the way almost to Peachtree, who are sitting between Brinsley and the holy door, stand respectfully out of his way. Then he stands up finally to his most majestic height.

Curious thing, he says. This reminds me of the only good parody I ever heard on the style of John Millington Synge. It was the work of that great player, J. M. Kerrigan, and it began like this. Was it on your feet you came this way, man of the roads? No, 'twas not, but on my arse surely, woman of the house. As in the Shadow of the Glen.

Then with an amazing agility for a man so big, he dives into the john and we laugh at the joke and respectfully hold our conversation until he returns. When Conall tells me that there is this company of travelling players and that, in this country town, they are planning to put on in the parochial hall this play, says Conall, by a French jailbird about a Roman Catholic cardinal taking off his clothes in a kip. Or worse still, says Conall, about two women, a madame and a hoor, (anglice: whore), disrobing or disvesting or devestmentizing a peacock of a cardinal, and think of that, for fun, in an Irish country town. So the parish priest naturally, or supernaturally, prohibits the use of the parochial hall and, having done so, takes off for the Eucharistic Congress in Antananarivo, or somewheres east of Suez. He didn't have to read that play to know it was no go, and the players have booked another, non-sectarian hall and are going ahead and, Conall says, the man who owns that hall must fear not God nor regard the parish priest, and must be so rich and powerful that he needn't give a fuck about King, Kaiser or cardinal.

But there is this organization called Maria Duce, like the Mother of God up there with Mussolini, which will picket the hall to keep the clothes on the cardinal, and a riot is confidently expected, says Conall, and if you want to see what life is like in an Irish country-town, man, you gotta be there.

Conall lowers his voice.

Even Brinsley himself at his worst and wildest, he says, never thought of that one. A cardinal in a kip. In the buff.

For kip, here read brothel. Not kip as in England where it may mean merely a place to sleep in.

So here we are on the train, Patrick and Conall and his camera, and myself, and Brendan and Niall and Jodhpurs: and the world and his mother are off to the races: and, somewhere ahead, a red cardinal is roosting and waiting to be depilated: and the priest of the parish is awa, like the deil with the tailor in Robert Burns, to Antananarivo: and Patrick is singing that on the broad road we dash on, rank, beauty and fashion, it Banagher bangs by the table of war. From the couch of the quality down to the jollity, bouncing along on an old lowbacked car. Though straw cushions are placed, two foot thick at the laste, its concussive motion to mollify, still, the cheeks of my Nelly are jolting like jelly as she joggles along up to Bellewstown hill.

Onwards and upwards. The play's the thing.

Eighty miles from Dublin town.

The poet Cowper points out, as I would have you know, that not rural sights alone but rural sounds exhilarate the spirit and restore the tone of languid nature, that ten thousand warblers cheer the day and one the livelong night.

He means the nightingale. I reckon.

What lies ahead of us is not going to be exactly like that.

The gallant lady who leads the strolling players holds back the raising of the curtain for our arrival. But with the best or the worst intentions in the world, or with no godamned niggering intentions whatsoever, we succeed in being late and the play is well advanced when we get there. We have been delayed in the bar in one of the town's two hotels. Not drinking has detained us but a sudden attack of love, or something, not on me, already, as you know, wounded and possessed, but on Conall the fickle, the flaky, the volatile, the twotimer of all time, who wouldn't even curb his bronc until Jodhpurs had gone for a moment and what else to the powder-room. No, just one look over the bar-rail at the barmaid and he was hogtied, and said so out loud, very very loud. Like I love my love in the ginmill, I love her in the lounge. A mighty handsome brunette she is.

Jodhpurs, though, takes it all mighty cool. She is by no means in love with Conall, just lust, and she tells me that he does this everywhere and all the time, and Lagan intones like a monk of Solesmes: O'er Slieve Few with noiseless trampling through the heavy, drifted snow, Bealcú, Connachia's champion, in his chariot tracks the foe: and, anon, far-off discerneth in the mountain hollow white, Slinger Keth and Conall Cearnach mingling hand-to-hand in fight.

Prophetic?

Wait and see.

That's the beginning of the poem about the ancient hero or whatever.

Lagan explains in considerable detail that Slieve Few is a mountain in the heroic north, and in the mythologies. A few notes I make. Research? You never can tell.

For Connachia read Connacht.

Conall is now behind the bar. He went over it, not through it. He's a pretty agile guy. His arm is around the barmaid's waist. She is laughing most merrily. Nobody by now in the place except the four of us. For Brendan and Niall have really gone ahead to the theatre. But when Conall had first attempted to go over the top, Lagan and myself decided it might be wiser to stick around and keep a snaffle, Lagan said spancell, on him. That may be not all that easy.

Jodhpurs, I may tell you, has the same surname as myself. Except that she spells it differently. Carney, not Karney. So much I found out by standing beside her when she was filling in the hotel register. Waiting my turn I was. With the register.

We are now at last in the theatre. Or in the substitute hall. Which is by no means in the most elegant part of the town. There are no praying pickets. Conall is outraged. No pickets, no picture.

Perhaps they have prayed and picketed and departed before we got here. But no. Later we are to hear that they were never there. Also flown to Antananarivo?

To get to the hall we go through a dark entryway. Seventeenth century at the least. Footpads? Stilettos? Christopher Marlowe? No. Bludgeons? Newgate calendar? No. Nothing but bad lighting and potholed ground underfoot. Easy here to sprain an ankle. We are in an ancient market-place, long ago forsaken by markets and by everything and everybody else. A hideyhole for Art? A last refuge for strolling players? Then up a covered and creaking wooden stairway that climbs the wall, then down four shaky wooden steps and here we are, and where is the kip and where is the cardinal?

But there is no kip. There is no cardinal at the moment to be seen.

Conall, as is his custom, has got it wrong. Or so Lagan later booms.

What we are looking at is a weeping broad in a long, black dress, kneeling down before a roaring Franciscan friar. Or a fellow roaring, and wearing what might be a Franciscan habit except that it's so badly battered from strolling with the players that it's hard to tell. He could be Guy Fawkes or Johnny Appleseed or Planters' Peanuts or the man who broke the bank at Monte Carlo. But whoever or whatever he is, he sure as hell is giving that broad hell. Boy, is he giving her hell. What I mean is, he is telling her in considerable detail where she will find herself if she doesn't mend her ways and get smart, and get real smart and give up that old wop trick of screwing her brother. If you can tell by a slight protuberance she seems to be in the family way by her brother.

Curious thing, Brinsley is later to say, but there was always a soupçon of that in the midlands where I come from. John Ford, not the man who makes the cowboys, seems to have been much possessed by the idea. As T. S. Eliot said Webster was by death. Curious fellow, Ford. And Webster. And Eliot.

Brinsley met Eliot when Eliot was round the corner from the Abbey Bar to give a lecture in the Abbey Theatre that was. My research proceeds. Curious thing.

But listen to the friar as the broad is listening or pretending to listen.

He is telling her about a black and hollow vault where day is never seen, where shines no sun but flaming horror of consuming fires, a lightless sulphur choked with smoky fogs in an infected darkness: and in that place dwell many thousand thousand sundry sorts of never-dying deaths, and damned souls roar without pity, gluttons are fed with toads and adders, and burning oil poured down the drunkard's throat, and the usurer is forced to sip whole draughts of molten gold, and the murderer is forever stabbed yet never can he die, and the wanton lies on racks of burning steel.

Watch it, chick, watch it.

The friar also wises her up about lawless sheets and secret incests. About which, we may reckon, she knows more than he does. And tells her that when she parks her ass in that black and gloomy vault she will wish that each kiss her brother gave her had been a dagger's point.

Jasus Christ, says Conall, this is worse than any sermon I ever heard at any mission. What was the parish priest beefing about? He couldn't do better himself.

He says all that out quite aloud and several people hush him up, and the friar thinks they mean him and gets rattled, and, to my high delight, the incestuous broad giggles. For her it is mighty obvious that hell hath no furies.

To you, down there on Peachtree, a mission would be a sort of a tent-meeting, hellfire a-plenty, the Baptist tabernacle in Marietta, yeah Lord Amen, and washed, when the time is ripe, in the blood of the Lamb or the Chatahoochie river. What has the Good Lawd done for you, as the preacher roared and pointed by mistake at the harelipped, hunchbacked cripple, and the harelipped, hunchbacked cripple, in so far as his cleft palate would allow him to articulate, whistled back that the Good Lawd damn near roont me.

Then when the curtain creaks down to separate the scenes, something has to separate them, and the lights come up in the body of the house, Conall stands up to take pictures and to make a speech.

Jesus and Amen!

We are, *in tempore opportuno*, to find out that the valiant woman, far and from the furthest coasts, who leads the strolling players was so annoyed with the parish-priest that she cancelled the kip and the cardinal for something in which, when most of the cast has been massacred, another cardinal and the Pope get any loot that's left.

For we're off to Anarivo in the morning.

Then and thereafter Conall has bad luck with his photographs. For why? He keeps dropping the camera. The audience love it. Light relief. Charlie Chaplin. The audience need it. Some of them know Conall very well. He has been around. They cheer when he drops the camera. But in a mild, friendly, appreciative sort of way and not so as to disturb the players. Overmuch.

Conall's speech begins by thanking the audience on behalf of the valiant woman and the strolling players. Then he thanks the players and the woman on behalf of the audience. Then he sits down where his seat is not, or a place to put it. He has a standing ovation for that one. Then Brendan and Niall and Jodhpurs persuade him into a corner at the back of the hall and hold him there, good old Jodhpurs, and the curtain creaks up again, it sure as God creaks, and here we are back in Renaissance Parma and nothing worse going on than incest and multiple murder.

Not one picture all night long did Conall capture.

Up on the stage, Grimaldi, a Roman gentleman, has just knocked somebody off, the wrong person, as it so happens, or, at any rate, not the person he means to knock off. The cardinal, when the matter is drawn to his attention by the citizens of Parma, is inclined to take a lenient view. For why? See text. The cardinal, in brief, argues that Grimaldi is no common man even if he is somewhat inclined to first-degree homicide. Grimaldi is nobly born and of the blood of princes and he, the cardinal, has received Grimaldi into the protection of the Holy Father.

Hip, hip hurrah, cries Conall, for the Holy Father. Send Grimaldi to the Eucharistic Congress.

There are some murmurs but more laughs among the audience. Stands to reason they're the laughing rather than the murmuring sort of audience. Otherwise they wouldn't be here.

Then Soranzo who is a nobleman, who wishes to marry Annabella and who thinks he has all the boys in line, is raising his glass which he has filled from the weighty bowl (see text), to Giovanni who is screwing Annabella, but not just then and there, who is, as I may have already explained, Giovanni's sister, and Soranzo, in all innocence or something, is saying: Here, Brother Grimaldi, here's to you, your turn comes next though now a bachelor.

Then to Annabella Soranzo says: Cheer up, my love.

Conall repeats that, and shouts something that sounds like: Tighten up there, M'Chesney.

Lagan basebarrelltones: Gag him, for God's sake.

And the house is hilarious.

Then enter Hippolita, masked, followed by several ladies in white robes, also masked and bearing garlands of willow. Music offstage. They do a dance. Not the Charleston, you may safely speculate. Soranzo says: Thanks, lovely virgins.

Conall says: How do you know.

The house rocks.

You see the joke, such as it may be, is that Soranzo has been having it off with Hippolita and now wishes to jettison cargo, and she, knowing this, is out to waste him but, before she can do so, Vasquez, a low type and no nobleman, slips her the old trick of the poisoned cup, and the friar, wise guy, says, fairly enough, that he fears the event, that a marriage is seldom good when the bride banquet so begins in blood. He sure is the greatest living authority on hell and matrimony.

Curious thing.

Read the rest of it for yourself.

Enter Soranzo, unbraced, and dragging in Annabella, and calling out: Come strumpet, famous whore.

Conall: Give the girl a break. She'll come on her own.

Soranzo: Wilt thou confess and I will spare thy life?

Annabella: My life. I will not buy my life so dear.

Soranzo: I will not slack my vengeance.

Conall: They're not getting on. There's a rift in the flute.

Soranzo: Had'st thou been virtuous, fair, wicked woman.

Conall: Thou can'st not have everything.

Soranzo: My reason tells me now that 'tis as common to err in frailty as to be a woman. Go to your chamber.

Conall: Politeness is all. Carry the chamber to her, sir.

Conall seems to know his Shakespeare.

Curious thing.

Three pictures are taken.

Not by Conall Cearnach of whom, the original warrior I mean, more hereafter. But by Brendan the Navigator who proves to be a good man in a crisis. He is a blond block of a man in a brown, serge suit. He is a Fingallian. That means that he comes from the north of the County Dublin, or Fingal, the land of the fairhaired foreigners where, Lagan assures me, some of the old farmhouses still preserve the high, pointed, Scandinavian gables, a style brought in there a thousand or so years ago by sea-rovers who settled.

One picture Brendan takes of Giovanni entering from left with his sister's heart impaled on a dagger, and dripping. A red sponge, I'd say, soaked, for additional effect, in some reasonably-inexpensive red wine.

All hearts that love should be like that. Mayhap, they are.

One picture he takes when the banditti rush in and the stage is strewn with corpses, and Vasquez, I told you he was a low type, tells the banditti that the way to deal with an old dame called Putana, whose name's a clue to character, is to carry her closely into the coalhouse and, instantly, put out her eyes and, if she should be so unappreciative as to scream, to slit her nose for laughs.

Exeunt banditti with Putana.

And that's about the next best thing to the riot that didn't arise.

The survivors are the cardinal, and Richardetto, a supposed physician, and Donado, a citizen of Parma, and Vasquez, the villain, who rejoices that a Spaniard can, in vengeance, outgo an Italian. Giovanni has just cashed in his chips. So the cardinal wisely advises those who are still able to stand up, that they should take up those slaughtered bodies and see them buried: and as for the gold and jewels, or whatsoever, since they are confiscate to the canons of the church, he, the cardinal, or we, as he calls himself, will seize them all for the Pope's proper use.

Conall: To pay for the . . .

But Jodhpurs has put her strong hand over his mouth.

Hautboys.

Sennet sounded.

Curtain.

The third picture Brendan takes is of the valiant lady making her curtain speech, and all the players, to the relief and felicity of all of us, resurrected and reunited. She thanks the audience. She thanks the gentlemen of the press. She thanks Conall personally and as Conall Lagan and not, as Patrick says she should have done, as Conall Carnage. To loud applause. Even I am astounded. Ireland is a more wonderful place than I ever thought it could be. Later I find out that Conall and the valiant woman are firm friends, that she even loves Conall as a mother

might love a wayward son. Also I find out that to make absolutely
certain of a good house, she took no money at the door: and that the
picketers did not bother their ass picketing because the priest was far
awa, far awa, and the weather was raining.

Up to that moment none of us have noticed or mentioned the
weather.

And the next act opens back in the bar in the hotel.

The night is in full swing.

We return to our festivity and do our best to put the corpses of Parma
out of our thoughts. We manage to do so.

To tell you the whole truth as I have promised always to do, well to
tell as much of the whole truth as a lady should hear or wish to hear, we
sit drinking, slowly, sipping, no gulping, spilling or slobbering, and the
talk is good. We sit for several hours after official closing time and in
the learned company of two uniformed police-officers and two detectives in plain clothes. One of the detectives has been among the
audience and thinks the play the funniest thing he ever laid eyes or ears
on since he saw Jimmy O'Dea, a famous comedian, in the Olympia
theatre in Dublin when he, the detective, was in training in the Phoenix
Park.

Jasus, the detective keeps saying, I tought dey'd never stop. And de
lad coming in wit her heart on a breadknife. I could have taken me oat
'twas a pig's kidney. And Himself dere was de best part of de play.

The detective comes from a fairly widespread part of Ireland where
they have problems with a certain dipthong.

By Himself he means Conall whose constancy and endurance is
astounding, for talking and dancing and singing and telling the women
he loves them: Jodhpurs in one breath, the barmaid in the next, with a
few words to spare for any woman in the place, under or over sixty. He
sits with us for a space. Then he is up at the bar or behind the bar and
occasionally kissing the barmaid who objects, but mildly. To much
general laughter. He is, believe it or not, most courteous. He knows
tout le monde and it knows and likes him, and I do notice that he
seldom renews his drink, and I wonder is it booze that sets him going or
is he just that way by nature. Outgoing. Extrovert. You could say all
that again. He can dance. He can sing. He does both at intervals. He
even wears a wedding ring. He uses all his talents to the full.

We may be forced, Lagan says, to hogtie Conall as his namesake,
Conall Cearnach, was hogtied by Bealcú, or Houndmouth, from Ballina,
the champion of Connacht before Christ was in it. Not that Christ ever
had much influence in certain parts of Connacht.

Nothing I know can stop Lagan. He will boom and drone on now until the sergeant and the guard and the two men in plain clothes, and anybody else who cares to listen, will know all about the wounding and healing of the ancient hero. But, hell, what am I here for? Research is research. And where is my notebook?

Lagan explains to the plain-clothes men and the guard that when Bealcú urges his charger and, ergo, his chariot across the snow to the place where he has seen the two warriors in combat, Slinger Keth lies dead and Conall Cearnach, wounded, lies at point to die. The guard and the plain-clothes men show every evidence of interest. The sergeant is up to something else. He has the ear of Brendan, the Viking sea-rover or the sanctified navigator, what you will. He, the sergeant, is saying slowly, spacing out the words carefully: Soap . . . necktie . . . chocolates . . . cigarettes . . . pipe and tobacco-pouch . . . book or book token . . . shaving-cream or aftershave . . . socks . . . record or record-player . . . pen . . . handkerchiefs . . .

Or rather he is reading those mystic words out of the newspaper that employs Lagan, Conall, Brendan and Niall. He asks Brendan what he thinks of all that. Brendan says: Aunt Miriam is a very good friend of mine. And a most considerate and efficient colleague.

This is extremely curious. Niall is, for the moment, at the far end of the bar, engaged at conversation with some friends he has encountered.

Lagan says: Put jockstrap on the list. For Conall over there.

Seems Lagan can narrate to four men and simultaneously listen to a fifth. There is much general laughter at mention of the jockstrap. Over at the bar, but on this side of it, Conall has one arm around the barmaid and the other around Jodhpurs. All seem happy. Am I losing contact? Events mingle and move too fast for me. It is a long way from here to Spoon River.

But aside from all that: When Houndmouth sees Cearnach flat on his ass on the snow he proceeds to badmouth him. Calling him a ravening wolf of Ulster which is where Conall, hereinafter to be known as Cearnach, comes from. Who answers: Taunts are for reviling women.

That's pretty good.

— Hush up, he says, to Bealcú, and finish me off.

But no, Bealcú will not have it noised abroad that it took two Connachtmen to knock off one Ulsterman. His game is to bring Cearnach home with him to Ballina or wherever, to have him patched up by the Connacht medicos and then, for the glory of Bealcú, and whatever gods may be in Connacht, to kill him in single combat. So Bealcú binds Cearnach in five-fold fetters, which is what Lagan thinks we should do with our Conall, then heaves him up or has him heaved up on the chariot, to be somewhat cheesed when he tries to lift the Ulsterman's war-mace.

What a weight it was to raise!

Brendan interrupts, reading out aloud from the newspaper. This is what he reads: The girl in the picture is playing with her white mice. Do you have a pet mouse? If so what colour is it? Do you like mice? If not, write and say why. Could you write a poem about a mouse? Try.

— Christ of Almighty, says Lagan. What are you all up to?

And the sergeant says that his sixteen-year-old daughter is a magician all-out at the painting and drawing, and can turn out a poem should be printed.

Brendan explains. Mostly or totally for my benefit. The others know all about Aunt Miriam. Which is the name of the mythical lady who edits the page from which the sergeant and Brendan have been reading: Aunt Miriam's Campfire Club.

The sergeant's daughter and a slew (sluagh, in the Irish) of her schoolfriends wish to join. Brendan says that he will look after all that. He reads further to explain to me about that odd list of objects: Choosing birthday presents for fathers, uncles or older brothers can sometimes be quite difficult. So what about carrying out a birthday survey? Ask your father, brother, uncle, teacher or any man over twenty-fiveish to put the birthday presents on this list in order of their choice. Bring your completed list into class next week. Check the answers and count up in class how many men put socks or soap . . .

Or de jockstraps, says one of de plain-clothes men.

Let joy be unconfined.

It is early in de morning. Am I losing my diptongs?

Brendan later admits, blushingly, that Aunt Miriam is his beloved wife. That is not true. Aunt Miriam, in fact, is a somewhat eccentric and retired clergyman. That is supposed to be a wellkept secret. But Brendan writes down the names and addresses of the sergeant's daughter and all her friends. He says that he will see to it that Aunt Miriam's secretary, who doesn't exist, will send to each and every one of those young enthusiasts the Campfire Crest, a sort of badge. He promises that the letters they write to Aunt Miriam will be printed in the paper. And the poetical works of the sergeant's daughter. All this, for sure, he looks after when back in Dublin. But the entente he sets up between us and the sergeant is to prove real precious some hours later when Brendan and Niall are on the road, by automobile, to Limerick city where they have something else to report. Or on which to report. Even in Ireland, English is English.

Action stations!

The clock strikes three.

Jodhpurs says she will hit the hay. A challenging thought. The barmaid has vanished. Brendan and Niall have taken the road for Limerick city. Conall and Lagan and myself would seem to be the only living people left. One of those corrugated things has been pulled down and the bar is closed. Lagan and myself set sail for the bottom of the main stairway. But is that good enough for Conall? No, no, by no means no. He says that he wants one more drink. But he is a lot more sober than he pretends to be and he has something else, as you may imagine, in his calculating mind. We try to reason with him. To talk him into calling it a night, or a day. No use, no use. Down a long corridor that leads towards the back of the building he sees, and so do we, a light burning. That, it may appear, is where the barmaid has found covert. So hitching his wagon to that star, Conall Carnage steams (block that metaphor), down the corridor and through the heavy-drifted snow, and thunders on the door of the room of the light as if he owned the world, and barges in, and finds . . .

Two young clergymen drinking-up. The curates, or assistants, or lootenants of the parish. The mice relaxing while the tomcat is farawa, farawa in Antananarivo. One of them turns angry-nasty. Through embarrassment, it may be, at being found out. Tells Conall, and in a clear shrill voice, that this is a private room. The barmaid is nowhere to be seen. So Conall demands to know what in heaven, or hell, two clerics are doing drinking-up and being merry in a private room in a public house at three o'clock in the morning. And why are they not at home writing sermons and banning plays as any zealous sacerdotes should be. Cleric Number Two asks him, politely enough, to leave. Then Lagan grabs Conall and begins to urge him out and Lagan, although an anti-clerical of the old style, apologizes to the polite priest, explaining that Conall has a drop too many taken. Out of nowhere the proprietress appears, a tough sort of a lady in late middle-age. She exhorts Conall to have some respect for the cloth. From halfways up the stairs Conall intones: Bless me, fathers, for I have sinned.

Lagan chants, but only so as to be heard by Conall and myself: *Dies irae, dies illa, solvet saeclum in favilla* . . .

We propel Conall as far as and into his room. That day, we reckon, has been called a day.

So Bealcú urges charger and chariot westward through the borders of Breffny. Bearing with him the corpse of Keth the Slinger and the wounded and captive Cearnach. They come to a place called Moy

Slaught where the ancient Irish used to worship a pretty formidable idol called Crom Cruach. He was a hunk of stone or something and his twelve apostles, twelve lesser hunks, sat round him in a ring. Along came Jones, meaning St Patrick, and thumps old Crom with his Bachall Iosa, or the staff of Christ, and Crom bears forever the mark of the bachall, and the earth swallows the twelve lesser idols: and, just at that moment in Lagan's narration, all hell breaks loose in the street outside the hotel.

Lagan and myself are sharing a room. Where Jodhpurs has vanished to, we do not know. Jealousy, at last, may have driven that tolerant girl to roost in some faraway place. The hotel is a corner house. Our room is right on the corner and right above the main door. On which door Crom Cruach and his sub-gods twelve seem at this moment to be beating. Where, cries Lagan, is the staff of Jesus.

He looks out one of our two windows but the angle is awkward and he can see nothing. The beating at the door lessens. Then ceases. But there is a frenzy and a babel of voices. Then the door of our room opens and the sergeant steps in. And says most modestly: Mr Lagan, as the eldest member here present of the press-party, could you please come down and put a tether on this young fellow before he wrecks the town.

For Carnage is off on the warpath again, with or without benefit of chariot. Meantime, back at the ranch, Cearnach has been unceremoniously dumped on the fairgreen of Moy Slaught where he is getting a poor press from all the widows he, in happier times, has made in the West of Ireland.

And Bealcú says: Let Lee, the leech, be brought.

And Lee, the gentlefaced, is brought from his plot of healing herbs. Like Lagan walking down the stairs to see what healing he can bring to Conall Carnage in the hall below. Followed, at a safe distance, by myself and the sergeant who gives me a brief breakdown on what has caused the brouhaha. Seems Conall made down again to the door of the lighted room. To find it locked and bolted. To Carnage that presented no problem. He bangs on the door and roars out that he wants somebody to hear his confession. Lest he die in sin. Then comes a-running the lady of the house and with her a big guy she has somewhere drafted so as to throw Conall out. This big guy is a mighty-big big guy. So he pushes our Conall back as far as the main hall where Conall, who is nifty, steps backwards up two rungs of the stairs, so as to gain purchase, and throws a hard, roundhouse swing at the big guy, who is also nifty. And ducks. And Conall knocks down the lady, and the lady screams bloody murder, and the big guy and the clerics just about manage to heave Conall out the front door and lock it, and Conall goes to work with fists and feet, raising holy hell on the oak, three inches thick, and ringing the bell, and roaring Bless me, fathers, for I have sinned, and lights going on and children crying all over the town as if, says the sergeant, Jesus had come again, and the lady phones the fuzz, and here we are again, happy as can be, and Jodhpurs, neat girl, and one of the plain-clothes men are holding Conall, and Lagan is saying that Conall is a good kid, and the lady is shouting that he's a pup, a pup, a pup.

Lagan shows himself to be some diplomat. M. de Norpois. Hit the Guermantes trail. The matronly presence of Aunt Miriam is still there to aid him. He and the sergeant mutter together in one corner. Conall calms down. Jodhpurs is good for him. Like Hector in Homer she is well known as a tamer of horses. Then Lagan and the sergeant come to this arrangement. That Conall will go for the night to the calaboose with the lawmen. For no way in hell will the lady have him for the night in her hotel. What, she says, will my husband say when he comes home and hears that I was assaulted under my own roof. What, says Lagan, will the parish priest say when he comes home from wherever in heaven he is and I tell him that his two curates were drinking in your office at three o'clock in the morning.

Détente.

The lady screams that rightaway she wants to prefer charges. The Sergeant, gently but firmly, says that she must wait until the next day or, to be exact, daylight of the same day. She screams again that Conall's swipe has smashed her spectacles. For corroboration, the big guy has already gathered up the fragments, *colligite fragmenta ne pereant*, into a brown paper-bag. Evidence? Or second-class relics? Jodhpurs, gallant girl, offers to go with Conall. To burn on his pyre. But Conall, like a hero going into transportation, kisses her farewell, several times, advises her to catch a few hours sleep, she may need them: that the night to come, and still so far ahead, is yet another night. The lady of the house is about to have a fit. So the big guy leads her away. The clerics have vanished. Up the chimney? Then Conall marches off, taking the lead with the sergeant, the plain-clothes man bringing up the rear. But halfways across the street, the plain-clothes man stops, shakes hands with Conall and goes off another way. Home to his bed and his wife, if he has one. Conall marches on, under escort, to his lonely prison cell. Or so I sadly and foolishly think.

Carnage now lies in the hoosegow. Cearnach lies under the care of Lee the Leech. Who, gentlefaced as he is, still strikes a hard bargain with the victorious and vengeful Bealcú. Has Lee, like the sergeant, a soft, melancholy voice and a moustache that droops as if the humid heat had gotten to it?

— Do you know what he said to me, Lagan says.

Not Lee the Leech, but the sergeant.

When the two of them, Lagan and the sergeant, were muttering in the corner.

— He said to me, Lagan says, that if the lad never did worse than knock that damsel down, he won't do much wrong in the world. She would skin a flea. (For the price of its hide: a native colloquialism.) 'Tis well known, says the sergeant, that she adulterates the whiskey. Anyway, the lad never hit her.

No direct hit. The wind of his passing, like that of a godamned archangel, simply flattened her.

— Anyway, the sergeant said. The lad struck out in self-defence. And missed. The only bruise would be on her backside where she sat down with a thump. He that cares to feel that way may find it.

— But keep an eye on things here, the sergeant said. You and the Yank. And I'll watch the young fellow. We want no trouble. Nor capers in the courtroom. We're overworked as it is. And that's the true.

Then Jodhpurs kisses us goodnight.

And that's the true, as the sergeant says.

And we rest our weary heads. And somewhere in gardens, and on the fringe of the town, and all over Ireland, the birds are beginning to sing.

— Curious thing, Brinsley says to me through my tumbling half-sleep.

— Curious thing. Georgia is famous for peaches. Or that's what the Irish Christian Brothers told me.

Once I had told him that there was a dame on Peachtree Street, Atlanta, Georgia. Meaning you. Well aware I am that there are many and various dames on Peachtree.

He capped my statement by telling me that there was once, he had heard or read, a dame in Belmont, richly left, and she was fair . . .

Then he went on about the peaches.

Seems there is or was a geography compiled by an Irish Christian Brother for use in schools run by the Irish Christian Brothers. It lists or listed the chief products of various places. Inchicore, a portion of Dublin, has rolling-stock. Georgia has peaches.

It is the dawn. The summer dark, the poet said, is but the dawn of day. That's Lagan quoting. He is up and shaving at the handbasin. No rooms with bath here. Rise up, he says, and do begin the day's adorning. He is a healthy man. He needs no cure. He tells me that Lee the Leech says that healing is with God's permission, health for life's enjoyment made. My American head is a purple glow and my belly full of the linnet's wings: and Lee the Leech agrees to heal Cearnach but insists that when the healing is perfected there shall be a fair fight and no favour, and that if Conall is triumphant he is to have safe conduct back to the Fews, his native part of Ulster. Also: that while the healing is in process no man shall steal through fences to work the patient mischief or surprise. He demands an oath on the matter: to Crom the God, to the sun, to the wind.

Lagan pulls open the heavy window-curtains and the sun comes through with a scream.

All quiet on the street outside. The good folk here do not arise betimes.

What healing is there for my hapless head?

My eyes I close and see viscous, bubbling peaches.

What healing for Carnage in his dungeon drear?

Lee the Leech has unlocked Cearnach's fetters.

Valiantly I face the razor.

— Curious thing, Brinsley says, Plato never bothered his barney about anachronisms. Curious thing.

But I swear by God and Abraham Lincoln, and by the body of Pocahontas, lovely as a poppy, sweet as a pawpaw in May, he is there in the dining-room and leathering-in (as Jodhpurs says), to his breakfast when she, me and Lagan get downstairs to the dining-room. He? Who? Brinsley? Plato? Bealcú? Lee the Leech? Conall Cearnach? Crom the God? No, but our own dear Conall Carnage for it is he. Eating egg and bacon and sausage and black pudding and drinking black coffee by the bucket. And eating butter, putting it into his mouth in great globs. Lubrication, he tells me. Oil the wheels. And the big end. Never did I see the like. Almost threw up to watch him. The lady of the house hovers in the background. Out of arm's reach and the swing of the sea. Amazed me that they served him anything. But he's a hell of a hard man to resist. Jodhpurs is all joy. Growing boys need food, she says. She glows. She is, I blush to say it, looking ahead to the night ahead.

Then while Carnage roisters and we nibble he tells us about the night or the remnants of a night just passed. Seems he never had it so good. Here is what happened. Conall and the sergeant walked back to the barracks. Who should be there but the second plain-clothes man (as in Shakespeare), and the garda or guard who had been drinking with us earlier in the night. Conall asked if they were going to lock him up and they said no way. Then another garda appeared with a tray and teapot and bread and jam. Everybody was, as Conall put it, fierce polite. Then the lot went home except Conall and one man or guard or garda, or what-in-the-hell, who was on night-duty. Who placed six chairs in strategic positions. Then produced a spring and a mattress which he balanced on the chairs. Then the all-night man said hop in and the two of them, and the town and the cattle in the fields and the birds in the bushes, slept until the sergeant came in at dawn, and with a bottle of wine from faraway Oporto. There were drinks and handshaking all round and that was that. Curious thing. Curious country, Ireland.

The healing of Conall Cearnach is, by now, well under way. He is still on his bed or on the scratcher (a Dublin usage), and he heaves thereon, Lagan quotes, as on reef of rock the ocean wildly tosses. Don't quite get that. The bed, the ocean, should be tossing, not Cearnach, the Rock. And the sons of Bealcú are worried. What is Lee the Leech up to? How fares the Ulsterman, the man from the Fews? So from a distance the sons of Bealcú spy, as best as they can, on the medical treatment. The patient no longer tosses on the bed nor does the bed toss under him. Now he is up and about even if he is pallid as a winding-sheet. Swear I do to Edgar Allen Poe that I do not know, nor could wildly guess at the pallidity of a winding-sheet.

Now Cearnach is out of his chamber. This isle of is full of chambers.

Cearnach is walking on his feet. What else?

We have paid our bill to the barmaid who is doubling in reception and who has the giggles. She giggles beautifully. All over. She kisses Carnage a fond farewell. The lady of the house is not there to be seen. Nor to see. We walk on our feet, all four of us, on eight feet, through the town to the other of the two hotels. It is an ancient and historic town. And looks the part. But I have a hunch that we have become part of the history. For the people on the pleasant side-walks are peeping at us and trying to pretend that they are not peeping. As are the sons of Bealcú peeping away out west, not in Kansas, but on the fair green of Moy Slaught. To see Cearnach, a ghastly figure, on his javelin propped he goes. But day follows day and Cearnach convalesces and convalesces, and with herbs and healing balsams he burgeons like a sere oak under summer showers and dew, and the sons of Bealcú are fearful for the future of their father.

Or the Dazee, as Carnage puts it.

Another Dublin usage.

Carnage is beginning to show some interest in the story of the healing of his namesake.

We have reached the other hotel. A mighty handsome place. But it is now bright morning and, after last night and all that happened where we were, even a roominghouse on Ponce de Leon, which flows into and out of the street of the Peachtrees, as you know, could be a mighty handsome place.

The valiant woman is here, having her morning gin, and some of her players around her. She is a widow. Her husband, who was a playwright, had a long enmity with Brinsley who is, also, a playwright. But valiantly she did her best to keep the peace between them. She tells me a lot. Research, research, research. The hardships of strolling players in rural Ireland. The money she is losing. Seán O'Casey, she tells me, is a cantankerous bastard when it comes to giving permission to anyone to put on his plays in Ireland. He wants money, for God's sake, money. Ah well. To make him madder still the Maria Mussolini Duce people picketed a play of his in the Gaiety in Dublin, and the Sinn Féiners, long ago, nearly wrecked the old Abbey over *The Plough and the Stars*, and one old nut of a theatregoer roared at O'Casey that there were no prostitutes in Dublin, and O'Casey said, mildly, in return, that he had been accosted three times on his way to the theatre and the old nut cracked back that if there were prostitutes in Dublin it was the British army put them there.

— Good on the army, Carnage says.

Lagan hushes him up.

But all that about O'Casey is history. Away back in the 1920s.

Return to the here and now.

We have one hell of a lunch. The valiant lady pays.

Then honking in the street and shouting at the door come Niall and Brendan, all bright and glittering in the lunchtime air, and all the way from Limerick city, and all ready to drive you all back to Dublin town.

They have had their own adventures.

For on the way to Limerick city they rested for a while in a roadside tavern. Not a roadhouse. Just an Irish pub, open day and night and to hell with the law. Niall had driven that far. And in the tavern they got to talking with this elderly farmer who lived back in the boondocks in mountains called the Silvermines. He sang songs. He hobbled on a stick. So kindhearted Brendan reckoned that the old-timer was too old and too hirpled (an Ulster usage) to walk home. Off with the three of them, and a bottle of whiskey, through a network of mountain roads to a shack where Senex lived alone. Brendan uncorked the whiskey. Senex produced three cracked and yellowing mugs. Out with Niall to the henhouse to rob the nests. Shall it be my lot, he thought, in the screeching and fluttering dark, to be beaten to death by the wings of hens in a cró, or hutment, on the slopes of the Silvermine mountains. Then out of all the eggs he could find he made, he says, the world's biggest-ever bloody omelette, chopped it into three fair halves, and they ate the lot and drank the whiskey, and Senex staggered safely to bed and, with Brendan the Navigator at the wheel, the pair of them set out to try to escape from the mountains. Which does not prove to be all that easy. For the dustroads go round and round about to find the town of Roundabout that makes the world go round. Nor is an overdose of whiskey the best navigational aid. In the chill dawn, with Brendan asleep and Niall at the wheel, they stumble on Limerick city which is beautiful, as everybody knows, the river Shannon, full of fish, beside that city flows: and Niall, shaking Brendan awake, says where is Hanratty's hotel, and Brendan sings out: You find Hanratty's. I discovered Limerick.

Then they find the hotel and are no sooner asleep than the phone rings from the Dublin office to say that it has heard that a pressman has assaulted a woman during or after the performance of the banned play, and would somebody please tell the other end of the phone what in hell is going on down there.

Enter now the garda of the previous night.

Not into Limerick city but into that handsome hotel in which we are washing down our lunch. Seems the lady of the other hotel has called the Dublin office to report the disorderly behaviour of two cameramen, Patrick Lagan and John Karney, meaning me. Now I have become a cameraman and a knockerdown of ladies. She has threatened legal action. The old blackmail — settle-out-of-court trick. The office disowns both of us. Lagan is on holidays and I was never there, and even Conall Carnage is under semi-suspension for some previous misdemeanour and, anyway, he hasn't been mentioned. So Lagan calls the lady and says that if she wants legal action or counteraction she is more than welcome any time, and that those two young clergymen would sure smile to be subpoenaed, and about the hell there would be to pay when the boss gets back from Antananarivo.

Enter the sergeant.

To approve of Lagan's diplomacy, or whatever. To bid us godspeed and a safe journey, and to say that things will surely settle if we see Carnage safely back to Dublin.

Exeunt omnes.

One little town. Two little towns. Three little towns.

No stops, Niall says, until we're safe in Dublin. Or, at any rate, as far as Roche's of Rathcoole.

Meaning a famous singing public-house about twenty-five miles from the city centre. The public-house does not sing. Only the people in it. Well, they try. A master of ceremonies at the piano. Ladies and gentlemen, one voice only, please. And the saddest man in the house stands up and wails: Caan, I forget you, when every night reminds me . . .

Well you know that I cannot forget you. Accept this letter in lieu of vows.

Anyway, Lagan is quoting: Forbaid was a master-slinger. Maev, when in her bath she sank, felt the presence of his finger from the further Shannon bank . . .

— That guy, says Carnage, had a mighty, long finger.

Jodhpurs smacks him. But gently. She is sitting on his knee. It is a small auto. We are six people. We are counted, Brendan says, like the elephants, after they are washed, at bedtime in Duffy's circus.

Lagan annotates his quotation. Research.

Conall Cearnach, do you follow me, had killed Aleel, the last husband of Maev, queen of Connacht. Aleel and Maev started a war when they quarrelled in their bed because he had a bull and she hadn't.

— So, Carnage says, that we don't have to be professors or literary editors to know what that was about.

Again Jodhpurs smacks him. Then they kiss. Niall who is at the wheel says that somebody or something is rocking the boat.

Then, after the killing of Aleel, Maev retires to an island on Lough Ree in the river Shannon. Once a day and at dawn she takes her bath in a springwell on that island. Vain woman, she thinks there isn't a peeper in Ireland dare peep on a queen. But Forbaid of Ulster has long sight as well as a long finger, and spots her from afar, and comes in the dusk secretly to the well and, with a linen thread, measures the distance back to the far shore. Then he stretches the thread on the ground, in a safe and secret place, plants a wooden fence-pole at each end of it, puts an apple atop of one pole, stands at the other, practises with his sling or handbow until he can take the apple ten times out of ten. Then one fine morning he stands where the river Shannon's flowing and the three-leaved shamrock grows and, across the wide water, where my heart is I am going to my native Irish rose, he clobbers the queen between the eyes with a two-pound rock, and she falls into the well, and that is the end of a queen who was longer in the bidnis than Queen Victoria: and the moment that I meet her with a hug an' kiss I'll greet her, for there's not a colleen (cáilín), sweeter where the river Shannon flows.

— Smart guy, Carnage says. But he hadn't much to peep at. She must have been a hundred if she was a day.

More smacks and kisses. Niall heaves to. Threatens irons for mutiny. Jodhpurs kisses back of Niall's neck. On we go.

Then more kisses, did I stop them when a million seemed so few?

That was Lagan. Courtesy of Mr Browning.

Wait for it, Carnage says

Then we get the entire spiel about Oh, Galuppi, Baldassaro, this is very hard to find, I can scarcely misconceive you it would prove me deaf and blind, but although I take your meaning 'tis with such a heavy mind . . .

And much more of the same.

That's Lagan's party piece. Or one of them.

We know now, Carnage says, who broke up the party in Fitzwilliam Square.

Much laughter. For the benefit of the visitor Lagan explains: It is, John, one of the many afflictions of my life to have the same surname as our dear friend, Carnage. Here and now happily restored to us, through my, shall we say, diplomacy, and the friendship of the sergeant. Although, if the case had gone to court, even the most humane District Justice would have felt compelled to give him six months without the option. For last night's performance and, furthermore, for his previous record. That gold ring he so proudly wears. Consider it.

Carnage raises and swivels an elegant right hand. The ring glows.

That ring is by no means his ring, Lagan informs me. He is not married. Do not think it. Not a woman in Ireland would have him. In wedded bliss, that is. No, that ring belongs to a lady with whom he is, shall we say, familiar. Who received it from her husband. From whom she is now sundered.

Life, life, says Carnage.

And twists the ring on his finger.

Who to support herself, Lagan says, ventures out occasionally on the scented and sacred sidewalks of Dublin.

We all, says Jodhpurs, have to do our best. Poor Maryanne.

Jodhpurs has a lot of heart.

So Carnage has a friend, Lagan explains. Odd as it may seem, he still has friends. This friend lives in an apartment in Fitzwilliam Square. A select area. And invites Carnage and Maryanne to a party. Invitation instantly accepted. Conall Carnage is hell for parties. And two or three or four, accounts and authorities differ as in Edward Scribble Gibbon, two or three or four cabloads arrive somewhat noisily in the elegant Square, Carnage and Maryanne, and some of Maryanne's business colleagues, and some of their friends, and create such immortal havoc that the gardai or the guards or the guards or the police or the coppers or the bobbies or the peelers or the fuzz or the pigs or the gendarmes or the effing Royal Irish Constabulary or whatever in hell you visiting American scholar, or embryo scholar, may care so to describe them, are called by the startled and highly-respectable neighbours, and the unfortunate man is evicted from his apartment in Fitzwilliam Square . . .

With more kisses, who could stop them, Jodhpurs is keeping Carnage quiet.

Does that sentence, or does it not, need a question mark. This one does????

Niall is singing about the sash his father wore.

Brendan, his voyaging o'er, is asleep.

The green countryside flows past.

And the great and much-appreciated joke, Lagan says, was that the news went round the town that I was the Lagan responsible.

More green countryside. Beautifully sunlit. One more small town.

How lucky, Lagan says, was Conall Cearnach to live so long ago.

But the sons of Bealcú are on the warpath and one of them reminds the other of the method by which Forbaid, the master-slinger, had fingered Maev, the Queen. Every morning from afar they watch Cearnach grow stronger and they fear for their father, and watch Cearnach coming at dawn to the fountain or well-margin to drink: while Cearnach is thinking, in the words of the poet, how a noble virgin, by a like green fountain's brink, heard his own pure vows one morning, faraway and long ago, all his heart to home was turning and the tears began to flow . . .

Jodhpurs likes that bit.

Not many pure vows, she says, do I hear. Nor Maryanne, in the course of her career.

So Lagan explains that Cearnach is thinking, while he weeps, of the wife and the weans (children, to you), back home in Ulster in Dunseverick's windy tower. Then up he leaps in a fit, runs round like a whirlwind, swings the war-mace, hurls the spear, and Bealcú, also peeping, but from another point of vantage and unseen by his sons, has the crap frightened out of him.

Cearnach, Carnage opines, has had his morning gin-and-tonic. There must be good stuff in that there fountain. Mayo poteen? Mountain dew? Georgia Moon Cawn whiskey?

Which may be more-or-less what Bealcú thinks. Not in relation to booze but about a god who, Bealcú thinks, may be in the fountain and to whom Cearnach prays, and Bealcú reckons he might just sneak in and, himself, mention the matter to the god.

But what about his vow, cries Jodhpurs. His vow to Crom Cruach and the sun and the wind.

She seems to know more about the story than a man might imagine.

She and Carnage are cheek-to-cheek.

Even if not dancing.

Has she tamed him?

Briefly we pause at Roche's of Rathcoole. Just long enough to hear six times on the jukebox one of Niall's favourite songs. Idaho, Idaho, I lost her and I found her at the Idaho State Fair, he broke twenty broncos and one grizzly bear, but she broke one cowpoke at the Idaho State Fair, Idaho, Idaho . . .

Once in my life I passed, by Greyhound, through Boise, Idaho.

No singing customers are present in Roche's of Rathcoole. It is too early in the evening.

Caan I forget you . . .

No questionmark here needed.

But this is not Dunseverick's windy tower. No, we are back somewhere in the environs of Dublin and we are in a tower, one of four, and one of them at each corner of an ancient castle. For Lagan, Patrick, has been invited to a party in this tower. A friend of his rents it. Just the one tower. He is a prominent painter, this friend. We get there about midnight. There is a tree in the courtyard that was planted there more than five hundred years ago. At Lagan's suggestion Carnage tears off a bit of the bark and some leaves to send to you. They are safely in a small box and I will bear them with me across the broad Atlantic. There is a tradition that Edmund Spenser ate his first meal in Ireland in this castle. As for myself I ate there what, but for the grace of God, might have been my last meal on earth: the ghost of the poet, perhaps, looking over my shoulder and babbling of a goodly bosom like a strawberry bed, a breast like lilies e'er their leaves be shed, and all her body rising like a stayre, and you know the rest of it, and I love my love in the morning, I love my love at noon . . .

Poor fellow. No wonder he entered the Christian Brothers. Not Spenser. But that other gentle poet.

But speaking of ghosts, this castle is haunted by a peculiar shade. Or by peculiar footsteps that are heard going up the winding stairs. But never coming down. Steps only. No person. No wraith.

Carnage says: Don't blame me.

The Castle has other associations which I will enumerate when I see you. And a pleasant seat which I was unable to see. For it is now past midnight. We enter the great hall. Not of the castle. But we enter a pretty commodious room halfways up the tower. To see a fine throng, glasses in hands. And to be welcomed. And to see a distinguished-looking, elderly, moustachioed gentleman trying to climb the wall. Uttering foul oaths the while. Seems that he has been attempting to climb the wall for several hours. Nor is he alone at that caper. Several of the guests are having a go. A hop, step and jump across the room. Then a roar and a run and a leap at the wall. Does not make sense at first. Then it dawns on me. The aim of the game is to leap higher than the door, turn round in mid-air and end up seated on the wide lintel shelf. Solid oak. Only one guest succeeds. A small man with a Chaplinesque moustache. A painter. Or, also, a circus acrobat. He is rewarded by a bottle of champagne. Which he drinks while sitting on the shelf.

Lacking the long finger of Forbaid, the master-slinger I stay safely on the carpet. For the wear and tear of the journey to renaissance Parma and back is beginning to tell, and all I want to do is to lie down. So up with me, up the haunted, twisting stairway, up two more floors, the furore dying away below me. No rough men-at-arms do I meet, cross-gartered to the knees or shod in iron. No footfalls do I hear but mine own. A small room I find and, joy of joys, a bed. On which, fully clothed, I collapse with a crash. Then down below in the Hall of Pandemonium, Carnage becomes aware of my absence and is worried. Believe it or not, but Carnage is a real human being. He begins searching all over for me. He runs downstairs and looks all around. All around the grounds and in the pouring rain. Checking all the cars. Climbing the ancient tree. Then, systematically, he begins to search the tower from the ground up. Where, at the end of an hour, he, inevitably, finds me. Shakes me awake to find out if I am still alive. Puts a pillow under my head. Tucks blankets around me. All the while assuring me that I should come downstairs and have another drink to help me to sleep. He is very concerned about me. He says that he mainly worries because I seem so tall, blond, thin and innocent, and mild-mannered, that I can only come to harm among the rougher Irish. Even the women are hard, he assures me, and you have got to be tough to stand up to them. He is taking care of me all the time, talking to me like a worried father to a not-too-bright, not-too-strong son. He is twenty-one. As you know I am twenty-five and have survived even the army.

At four in the morning I arise to begin the day's adorning. Still slightly stupefied. Go down the haunted stairway. My host gives me coffee and sandwiches and tells me that I should write not about

Brinsley but about Joyce. He is actually a relation. Not of Brinsley. But of Joyce.

So in honour of James Joyce we go for a morning swim off the Bull Wall where Stephen Dedalus walked and saw the wading girl and cried out heavenly god and all the rest of it. Research, research! Oh, the delights of a dawn plunge in the nude in the dirty water of Dublin Bay. Jodhpurs and all, or Jodhpurs without her jodhpurs. My eyes I modestly avert. Credit that if you can. She swims well. Not Dedalus himself, when he walked into that epiphany, ever saw the like. So strip I do and clamber down the rocks. Brendan, who has more sense, stays clothed and warm and holds my spectacles for me. The water is colder than ice and about as comfortable as broken glass. But it almost restores us to sobriety. We splash around there for thirty minutes or so and nobody, praise the Lord and hand me down my bible, is cramped or drowned. Then we sit on the rocks and watch the day coming up over Dublin city, and over the bay, and over Clontarf where Brian Boru bate the Danes, the dacent people, Lagan had said, without whom there never would have been a Dublin. For Brian, Lagan had argued, was a wild man from Limerick or thereabouts, as bad as or worse than Carnage or Bealcú . . .

Now Lagan has gone. For unlike the rest of us he has a home and a family to attend to, and Jodhpurs tells to the end the tale of the killing of Bealcú, another sore case of mistaken identity. She has read the poem, or has had it read to her, at school. Seems hard to believe that a strong broad like Jodhpurs ever went to school or to anywhere except the racing-stables. But Carnage says she was very bright at school, prizes and scholarships, and still is, and in all sort of places and ways, and can hold her own in talk on such topics even with the learned Lagan himself who is, says Carnage, as you have noticed, a sound man, and he will have my suspension lifted, he has the decency, he has the influence and he doesn't really mind being mistaken for me, it gives him stories to tell, and you may have noticed that he has a weakness for telling stories.

It is now the intention of Carnage to finally (Lagan would violently object to the split infinitive but since he's not here to hear me I'll split it wider still), get in the sack with Jodhpurs, when she will be once again divested of her jodhpurs, and Jodhpurs is raising no objection. As for me, I walk alone because to tell you the truth I am lonely, I don't mind being lonely when my heart tells me you're lonely too . . .

Then Karnage who is Kind, forgive that one, says come home with him to his apartment, he has a spare room and Maryanne is not, at the moment, in it, and he wants me to sleep for eight hours while he and

Jodhpurs do what they have to do, and he loves his love in the morning and all the way to noon. So he hits the gas and speeds back towards Dublin city. Only the three of us left. The roads are wet and slippery. They almost always are in Ireland. We turn a corner. We approach a bridge. We go into a spin, an all-out spin. To you I pray. We ram the brick wall of the bridge. It rams us. Karnage is thrown out of the Kar. The front windshield kisses me, my only kiss since I left Atlanta. But it holds up under the strain and Jodhpurs gets the reins, the wheel, and tames the horse and all is almost well. What I sustain, you may be glad to hear, is, merely a stunned elbow, a bruised black-and-white forearm and a cut finger. They will be perfect again when I get to Peachtree.

We are now somewhere on the outskirts of Dublin city. It is very early on a Sunday morning and nobody to be seen and, to top it all, it begins once again to pour rain. We try to push the car over off the road into a vacant lot. But the front right fender is crushed into the tyre and will not allow the wheel to move. We pull, we push, we grunt, we strain. No deal. Well, we make twenty-five yards but that gets us nowhere except into the middle of the road. But, God a mercy, along comes a big milk-truck, ties a rope to the battered bumper or fender, drags the wreck into the vacant lot. The rain continues. We start to walk downtown. The truck is going the other way. Another truck. Going my way. Offers us a ride. Do we accept? You're goddamn right we do. And gratefully settle back. To travel half a block when Truck Number Two cranks out. Oh Gawd! We walk on. The rain continues.

In the north of Dublin city there stands a small hotel. More than one, but one will do. It's not the Ritz nor the Savoy but the door is open and the coffee hot and strong. Karnage has left his Kamera in the Kastle. Now we krack. Karnage and I. Not Jodhpurs. She pours the koffee. We sit in the lounge. Just the three of us. But when Karnage talks to me I hear instead the booming voice of Lagan. Not imagination. Really, the booming voice of Lagan. He sings about the sash my father wore. He sings in Irish about a maiden in Donegal whose cheeks were like the roses and her little mouth like brown sugar. Honey with the mouth like brown sugar. A good beat for a black combo. He recites about dear Pádraic of the wise and seacold eyes, so loveable, so courteous and so noble, the very West was in his soft replies. But Lagan is nowhere to be seen. He says that free speech shivered on the pikes of Macedonia and later on the swords of Rome. He says Love that had robbed us of immortal things, and I rise to protest, but he is not there.

This is ghastly and I tell Karnage who says that, Good God, he hears him too.

We search the lounge. But he is nowhere to be found. Nobody anywhere to be seen except an unconcerned and bored female clerk. We pay for our coffee. We depart.

In the spare room of Karnage I lie down and try to sleep, remembering Thee, oh Peachtree. But rightaway the room is full of voices and above them all the voice of Lagan intoning that by Douglas Bridge he met a man who lived adjacent to Strabane before the English hung him high for riding with O'Hanlon.

Then up I leap up and dress, and tiptoe, almost running, out of the house to walk, in a daze, the awakening streets and find a restaurant, and eggs and coffee. Then I go to my lodgings.

I might not have bothered to tiptoe. Karnage later tells me that when he has done the gentleman by Jodhpurs they sleep, off and on, for thirty-six hours. You may have noticed that I have just broken one of my rules.

Stretched out again on a bed and sleeping, I suppose, I have this strange dream. This poem I have written and I am reciting it to a group of Roman citizens. It ends like this: A wooden sagging is in my shoulders and wood is dogma to an infidel.

Those words I take from my dream exactly as dreamt. No meaning. No connection with anything. But in my dream they made sense. Houseman said that each man travails with a skeleton. Lagan had been booming about Wenlock Edge and the wood in trouble and then 'twas the Roman now 'tis I. Perhaps I was trying to say that each man carries within himself a cross, the shoulders the crossbar, the spine the upright.

Damned if I know. Or care.

Time passes.

We are back in the Abbey, the bar not the theatre. A lawyer, or professor of history, a bank-manager who is also a music-critic and who plays the organ in a church, two actors from the theatre, and Niall and Brendan and Karnage and Lagan. No Jodhpurs. No Maryanne. Maryanne I am never to meet. But Brinsley honours us by his entrance. Huge, stately, brown overcoat, wide-brimmed hat. Leaning on stick.

Karnage has confiscated your, or my, necktie of many colours which he is wearing with wild ostentation. Cleverly he conceals the coloured body or expanse of it under a modest pullover, then whips it out like a lightning flash to startle and dazzle each and every newcomer. Lagan says that he and Karnage will wear your necktie, week about, so that they will never forget me nor the voyage to Parma. I am touched. (For a second time I have broken one of my rules.) Leaving that resplendent necktie with them I know that as long as it lasts, and the material is strong and well-chosen, I will be remembered and spoken of in the land of my forefathers.

And Lagan has used his influence and Karnage is no longer suspended. They go off to work together.

Time passes.

Curious thing, Brinsley says to me, but there are young fellows who say about me that I belong to a past time. I don't mean a pastime. But a previous period in history. But there is no time that is absolutely past, and little time in the present, it passes so quickly and, for all you or I or anybody knows, there may be no time in the future. Only eternity, we have been told. A most dismal idea. Imagine listening to (he mentions a well-known name), and God help and preserve him and lead him to a better and happier way of life, but imagine listening to him forever. So here's to the young fellows who think they know more than their elders. The total sum or aggregate or whatever you call it of knowledge, or whatever, in the human brain is always about the same. You might as well listen to your elders. You'll end up like them and nothing much accomplished. Lagan, though, is different. He raises his cap, mentally, to men older than himself. He admits that we have been here first and he knows that he is on the way to join us. Curious thing.

Time passes.

But whatever exactly did happen to Bealcú who broke his vows to the god, to the sun, to the wind. The poem I will read to you when I meet you, as arranged, in Washington D.C. My vows I have kept and will keep. All of the forty-one verses of four lines each I will read to you when you have the leisure to listen.

Conall Cearnach is safely back in Ulster.

Time passes.

If anybody in time to come ever reads this letter, found in a tin box in a hole in the ground on Kennesaw mountain, it may be said that it is merely a zany folktale from an island that once was, way out in the eastern sea. All parish priests and all that. And drink. Well, there are a lot of parish priests in Ireland and there is an amount of drink consumed. Apart from a curious crowd called the Pioneers. Not a damn thing to do with Dan'l Boone and the New River that runs west where so many rivers run east.

Here I give you a genuine slice, or bottle, of old Ireland, as I ate, or drank, it.

There may yet be worse things than parish priests in store for the new Ireland.

Time passes.

My money from home has arrived.

To Lagan I owe ten pounds. Not that he would remind me. In an envelope I fold the notes, and leave them, no message enclosed, at the counter in the front-office of his office. Way back behind, the machines are rattling for the morning paper.

Farewells I abhor.

So from the far shore of the Liffey I salute his lighted window and walk home to pack.

Peachtree, here I come.

By way of Cork city and Cobb and a liner over the wide Atlantic.

Look for my ghost on Eden Quay. Round the corner from the Sailors' Home ... ...

PROXOPERA

S ea-lions and sharks, *alligators and whales with mouths that would swallow a truck* . . .

That lake would never be the same again.

. . . oh the sights that we saw as we waited for death on the treacherous waves of Lough Muck.

Yet the birds, they say, sang around Dachau.

The waterfowl now swim on the still surface or fly around and cry around the circle of hills, harvest-coloured. The holidays are over and the dry rustle this year is early in the leaves. A dozen or more waterhens are in convention in a reedy corner near a sagging black boathouse. Only in one bay on the far shore is the silence disturbed by two black boats, moving slowly, men just barely using the oars or standing up and sitting down again. The sound of voices comes faintly across the water. He says to his son: the lake will never be the same again.

—The water never knew what was happening.

—I doubt that. Water may know more than we think. And grass. And old rocks. Think of all those old rocks that were around us in Donegal for the last three weeks. The lake looked as if it knew what was happening on the day of the water-skiing.

His son's wife who is a tall handsome red-headed girl with slightly prominent teeth, daring breasts and the faintest hint of an incipient double chin – very voluptuous, although he shouldn't be thinking along those lines – says that on the day of the water-skiing the lake was bright and dancing. On the night that thing happened the lake was dark and still. Wouldn't that make a difference?

He pats her on the shoulder affectionately as he climbs out from the back of the car where he has been sitting with the two children and a large glass jar containing two morose crabs rudely torn away from their homes on the Donegal shore.

She is an amusing imaginative girl.

—But no, he says, still waters run deep and all that. Water doesn't need light in order to see. Water is a sort of god. Or at any rate a goddess. That's what people thought long ago, they called rivers after goddesses.

The lake for sure had been a goddess on the day of the water-skiing. Never had he thought that he would see on his own lake the sort of thing you saw on the movies or television: Californian or Hawaiian beaches, galloping rollers, bouncing speed-boats, naked young women on surfboards, Arion on the dolphin's back, rising and falling, vanishing, reappearing through jewels of flying spray, spirits at one moment of the air and the water, marred by no speck of sordid earth. Was it better or worse to be young now than it was, say, forty-five years ago?

For him in his boyhood that lake had always been asleep. He lived in those days in the town three miles away. The walk from the town to the lake switchbacked over rolling farmland, root crops and oats, heavy black soil, solid square slated farmhouses, a well-planted Presbyterian countryside. After the first mile it was the custom for himself and his comrades to slither down an embankment where the road crossed the railway to the west and the ocean, to walk a hundred yards into a dank rock-cutting, to drink there from a spring that came on an iron spout out of the naked rock. That, for him, had been the well at the world's end mentioned in the old stories. No water had ever tasted like that water. One of the best meals he had ever eaten had been eaten there: raw turnips taken from a neighbouring field, cleaned at the spring and sliced, washed down by the clear ice-cold water. There was also the delight and danger of being caught there by a train, of crushing close to the dripping rock until the roaring belching monster passed.

Half a mile further on, the road went up a steep hill and into a tunnel of tall beeches. In the autumn and right on into January the leaves stayed so russet the road seemed warm. On the hilltop to the right hand and dominating the countryside stood a square, white, three-storeyed house inhabited then by an amazing family: strong, red-cheeked, flaxen-haired brothers and sisters, a dozen or more of them, he was never quite sure how many. They came, carrying bibles, to church in the town but never all of them at the same time. The popular report was that under that roof brothers and sisters knew each other as brothers and sisters conventionally shouldn't: it was a fascinating idea.

From the top of the hill you had a choice of routes: to the right the longer one, uphill, down dale, passing a place where there was a wooden bridge over the bend of a river, going round the world for sport, by fifty farms, a corrugated-iron-roofed Orange hall where there had been a bloody row one night because some guileless, love-deludhered young Orangeman had brought a Catholic girl to a dance, and by half-a-hundred ridges and bridges to rejoin the shorter route at a crossroads and go on the level to the lakeshore.

The shorter road ran straight along a spine of sandy, heathery, eskerland where once the glaciers had stopped. Below, in a hollow of quaking bog was a small lake, surrounded by sallies and bog-birch, in which demented old ladies and others were continually drowning themselves. There was an almost vocal sadness about the place. Association? Or had it been melancholy to begin with: right from the beginning of time, from the melting of the glaciers? That little lake as far as he knew had never had a name.

From the crossroads where the two routes rejoined, the road went again under splendid beech trees, the lake, a white light, widening and brightening at the end of a tunnel until it burst on you in all its delight, only a few miles all round but an almost perfect oval, a black boathouse to the right and boats dancing attendance in a semi-circle in front of it, a half-mile around the gravelly lakeshore road the bright red timber of the jetty and diving-boards at the swimming-club.

These dark days the swimming-club didn't function any more. The water-skiing had been a heroic attempt to give that sort of life back to the lake. The last attempt? The lake would never be the same again.

The murmur of voices still comes across the water from the men searching and searching in a bay among the reeds, in a bay that had been the best place of all for perch on those long-lost sunny days.

July was the best month for perch and the best day was the twelfth. It was folklore that the Orangemen always got a sunny day for their procession of bands and banners in honour of King William of Orange and the Battle of the Boyne. Up to the age of twelve or so the band and the banners were what the Americans called fun things: fifes and pipes and brass and melodeons, kettle drums, big drums, and giant drums beaten – merely to make a rolling rhythmical bedlam that might bring down rain on the Sahara – with bamboo canes by sweating coatless men with bleeding knuckles. Often it took two men to carry one of those drums, one fore, the actual drummer (naturally) aft. The best drummer was the man who smashed the most canes, even the most hides. Odd as the jungle it all was, bongo, bongo, bongo, I don't want to leave the Congo! but what the hell? The marching men wore coloured sashes. On the silken picture-banners King William on a white horse went splashing across the Boyne, or Queen Victoria sat on a throne and handed a bible to a kneeling negress and the legend said: The secret of England's greatness.

Then after twelve or so you began to think and the thing wasn't funny any more, wasn't just parade and pantomime, and the giant drums were actually saying something. Like: To hell with the Pope, Croppies Lie Down, We'll kick Ten Thousand Papishes right over Dolly's Brae, Slewter, slaughter, holy water, harry the Papishes every one, drive them under and cut them asunder the Protestant boys will carry the drum.

What it was all about was hate which, as always, bred hate, and suddenly you were sick of the town on that day and the lake was paradise.

Like the Orangemen the perch shoaled and were lively in the heat and the sunshine – and hungry for bait. Heat haze clouded the sun. Ripening oats on hills around the lake stood motionless as sheets of bronze. From green hills cattle stampeded to the shore to wade in until the water lipped their bellies, to stand lashing hopelessly with their tails against relentless clegs. The surface of the lake was dark and quiet except that once in a while an arc of little ripples would move on it, coming from nowhere, vanishing suddenly; and a breeze like a quick kiss from a ghost would touch a sweaty forehead and be gone again; and after that the perch would move, mad as mackerel, tearing the water as if the low hot skies were raining rocks, and all you had to do was pull them in, big and little, striped black and green and orange, fine fighters, big dorsal fins opening and closing, in outrage and despair, like Japanese fans.

The best corners in the lake were in there beyond the boathouse where the reeds were so high you were almost but not quite cut off from the rest of the world: or over there where men in black boats were still probing and dredging. Almost but not quite. For through a gap in the reeds you could, as you waited for the perch, look across the waters at the white house. Reeds made one frame for the picture. Beech trees set back from the avenue that led up to the house made another. There were other houses, Orange and Green or Protestant and Catholic, on the hills around the lakeshore, but they were simple thatched cottages and nothing at all in the bay-windowed, wide-fronted style of the white house. He had always envied the people who owned it, the lawn and flower-beds before it, the barns and varied outbuildings behind it. He had missed strikes and earned mockery from his companions by sitting heedlessly, absorbed in envy of the people who lived in that house, long and white, an air of aristocratic age about it: and, the most beautiful thing of all, cutting across a corner of the lawn a small brook tumbling down to join the lake. To have your own stream on the lawn was the height of everything.

In reveries now between sleeping and waking, relaxed in a deck chair on a sunny lawn and looking at the lake through half-closed eyes, he liked to tell himself that he had always known he would own and live in that house. That wasn't so. He may have wished that he one day would, but however could he have known. Premonitions were notions you had after the event.

Here they all were now, his son and son's wife and their two children, all happy after their Donegal holiday, the children tired but still talkative, the displaced crabs motionless as the rocks they came from: and himself. All being driven slowly by his daughter-in-law between deep banks and hedges into the farmyard, home again, and out of the car now, the children suddenly energetic again and racing in circles around the yard like hounds released from kennels, running to this and that corner to see if everything is as they had left it.

Behind the hayshed the three great sycamores are dark and motionless in the evening. Not one of the party seems as yet to have a premonition about anything. Well, perhaps the sycamores, perhaps the crabs.

All the way back from Dungloe in Donegal the streams they crossed had been in a brown foaming fresh. The rains and tempest of last week, the Lammas floods coming early this year; and now sunshine that by the texture of it would last until Christmas. Countless bees are still hard at it in the pink-oxalis borders that his son's wife loves so well because of the radiance that opens to the sun, because she has her flourishing apiary in the orchard beyond the hayshed. And the benefit of heather-blossom into the bargain from a small patch of turbary within beesflight and on the lakeshore.

The bees in the pink blossoms, the breeze in the sycamores make the only sound. There is suddenly something too much about the silence.

The pink borders, living with bees, go all round the yard, backed by the white barns and byres and stables, doors and windows outlined in red. Nothing moves but the bees. He stands alone, ten paces from the car, and breathes in the peace and is inexplicably perturbed.

The little boy runs towards the hayshed where three weeks ago there was a litter of cocker pups. The little girl dances towards the back porch of the house. She calls: Minnie, Minnie Brown, we're home again from Dungloe town.

On the journey home he has composed that rhyme for her. Minnie is the housekeeper and it is odd in a way that she hasn't been out in the yard to meet them.

His broadbacked son walks towards the red half-door of one of the stables. The harriers ride no more in these times but he still keeps and pastures two amiable hacks. A stout quick-tempered man who too early, and much to his own chagrin, has gone completely bald and whose jacket never buttons without obvious strain. The back of his egg-shaped head is comic.

His wife, a full-bodied red wine, goes gracefully after her little daughter.

He stands where he is, simply looking at his house, at his people, at the sycamores, at the last fifty years. Time stands still. The little boy comes running back from the hayshed. Trotting rather. His head down and sideways as if he were playing ponies. He pulls, pulling a bellrope, at his granda's jacket. He says: Granda, there's a funny man in the hayshed.

Granda already knows. The man has stepped out into the open. He has a shotgun. He wears a felt-brimmed hat and a gasmask. The mask has been slashed at the mouth for the sake of sound but the effect still is as if somebody with laryngitis were trying to talk through tissue paper and a comb. He says: Freeze. Everybody freeze.

As in the best or the worst gangster films except that the hoodlums talk and act cool and this fellow seems to be nervous: All of you freeze.

Granda says: Including the children?

He picks the boy up in his arms. The man advances, pointing the shotgun. The wheezes say, almost as if the creator of the wheezes had a cleft palate: One false step. Into the house. All of you. We're all inside.

They walk towards the house. He comes behind them. Not all inside the house. Because another masked man steps out from the laurels and rhododendrons to the right. He has a sock or something over his face. Carries a pistol. Wears a workman's tin hat.

His son walks before him, the back of his neck now red with anger. Even his egghead seems to be changing colour. He says: Who are you? What the hell is this?

—We'll let you know a chara, the second man says.

He has a sharp clear voice and something like a Cork accent: Inside, everybody inside.

This is the first time that I have ever been ordered into my own house. He is for a moment paralysed with anger. He watches his daughter-in-law carrying her daughter and bending under the lintel, the doorway is low, then his son, the back of his neck on fire with fury and the mark of Donegal sunburn, then Gasmask waving the shotgun. The ass of Gasmask's trousers is shiny and hangs low. There's something familiar-looking about his feet. Holding the little boy whose heart beats like the heart of a captive bird he stands stiffly on his own threshold.

—Keep it moving, old man.

That's Corkman speaking.

—Why should I? What hell right has a lout like you to order me about in my own house?

—This right.

It is, of course, the gun poking into the small of his back. This is cowboy country.

—I'm hardly worth shooting. Or kneecapping. The knees anyway aren't working as well as they used to.

—You're an old fellow, we know. But don't make things hard for anybody else. Children can be kneecapped.

—You would too. All for Ireland. Or is it Orange Ulster? But then you're from Cork.

—Less talk. Inside. Deliver the goods. That's all you have to do.

With a child in his arms and a pistol at his back he hasn't much choice. From the kitchen, as he walks a tiled corridor and across the wide scullery, he hears the sound of the television: whizzes, bangs, the clanking of machinery. So that the coloured screen is, ludicrously, the first thing to catch his eye. Against a blue sky a fighter-plane is falling, twisting, leaving behind it a spiral of black smoke. The Battle of Britain. Then he sees Minnie, stiff as a stick in a high wooden armchair. Gagged and bound. In a rough Belfast accent the third man says: Wizard prangs. And the bastards of Brits wouldn't even give us the credit for Paddy Finnucane. They say no Irishman was killed in the Battle of Britain.

Corkman says: Fuck you and Paddy Finnucane. Turn that bloody thing off. What do you think you're on? Your holidays?

Gasmask twists the knob. The plane hasn't yet touched earth. What is it about Gasmask's feet?

—Uncork the old dame. She can't do any damage now.

The third man, wearing a black felt mask that covers all his face, and an old-style British soldier's peaked cap, steps forward from the window bay: with no gun showing but with a hunting-knife at his belt. He unsheathes the knife, hacks away the gag, and the ropes that bind Minnie to the chair. They lie where they fall. Minnie moves her arms stiffly. Given time her tongue will get going. Not even the odd terrifying feeling of talking to a mask will keep Minnie mute.

—You're welcome home all of you and God bless you, she says, even if it wasn't much of a reception you got.

She slobbers a little. Her jaws and tongue are still stiff from the gag. She is a tall, brown-faced, wrinkled witch of a woman who always dresses in black for the husband who deserted her when they were three years married and that was forty years ago. The story as she tells it at Christmastime, or on the few other occasions when her memory is unfrozen by festivity, always follows the same formula: We tracked him everywhere, even as far as Newcastle-on-Tyne where he vanished without trace. We heard he joined the British army under a false name. But I know to God that even if he called himself Montgomery he wouldn't be taken in the Coldcream Gurkhas.

She stands up stiffly. She says: You'll want some refreshment after the long journey. At any rate you had a happy holiday. I got all the postcards you sent me. And Catherine, how are you? and Gary boy, don't be frightened. It's just that I wasn't that well able to greet ye when ye came in. But I'll make it up to ye when these blackguards are gone.

The children go to her silently and stand holding on to the long black skirt that recalls treachery and desertion and a man too worthless to be taken in an imaginary regiment, named contemptuously.

—Sit down old lady, Corkman says. Keep the children with you if you like.

—Thank you for nothing, Paddy from Cork. And who are you to tell me to sit down in my own kitchen?

—Sit down, for Christ's sake, and don't try my patience. You can cook everything in the house in half an hour. First, I've something to say.

—If you speak as well as you look you should be worth listening to.

—If you don't sit down we'll knock you on the head and tie you up again.

The voice behind the sock has risen an octave. She says: You're a hero. A grown man with a gun in his fist isn't afraid of any old woman.

But she is herself afraid and the children sense it. They cling to her. Catherine begins to sob.

—Oh Jesus, says Gasmask, I hate to hear children cry.

Corkman says: You should be running a creche. Suffer the little children. Sit down, you old hag, while your kneecaps still allow you to bend your knees.

—Wait a minute, his son says.

And takes a step forward. But Corkman tilts the pistol upwards and there is a silence broken only by the little girl's sobs; and that seems to last for a long time until Corkman laughs, a rich, hearty, surprisingly good-natured laugh. He says: There's many a fat farmer whose heart would break in two if he could see the townland that we are riding to. Dear gracious old lady would you for the last time, and for the love and honour of Almighty God, sit down and shut up and keep the children quiet?

She's frightened, more by the masks he'd say than by any horrors that she, at her age and coming out of another time, can readily imagine. Even though she reads the papers every day and clucks her tongue and says Sacred Heart of Jesus over outrage after outrage she has not yet fully realised the nature of the deeds now being done – for Ireland or what they call Ulster. Masks and queer faces and painted devils she can understand and she knows that they are evil: Lucifer looked like that once upon a time with the addition of horns and tail and a cow's foot. Yet, frightened or not, she does not give up easily: I'll sit down when Mr Binchey asks me to sit down. Either of them. They are the masters in this house. And gentlemen into the bargain.

Under the sock Corkman hisses like a serpent. Binchey senior realises with guilt that he has been enjoying or at least studying this struggle of wills between an old woman and a madman in a mask. Binchey junior, isolated and furious and helpless where the pistol has halted him in the middle of the floor, says hoarsely and so unexpectedly that it sounds like a startled shout: Sit down, Minnie. We'll hear what the man has to say.

The hissing ceases. It has been a most deliberate performance. Corkman says: Well said, Mr Binchey Two. *Ex ore infantium* or out of the mouths of babes and sucklings. Thanks for consenting to listen. I don't want to be forced to show you who for the moment is master in this house. But I want you two men to listen carefully. If everybody plays ball nobody will get hurt.

The children, silent again, are together between Minnie's long legs, faces to her midriff like frightened sheep at a fair.

—If the three of you would sit together on that couch for the sake of concentration like, we could get down to business. What time is it now?

Gasmask tells him. He pulls a chair close to the couch and sits looking at an angle at father and son and the woman between them. He says: We'll have a wait but it can't be helped. The stuff isn't here yet. We can't move until light, tomorrow morning, when the good people are going to Sunday mass.

—What in hell do you mean? You're telling us nothing.

That was Binchey Two.

—Patience brother. I'll explain. I want Binchey One here to do a little milk delivery. To one of two spots in the town. He'll even have a choice. This is a free democratic society.

—My father-in-law, she says, can't drive any more.

Binchey Two says: I'll do it.

Corkman is hissing again, steam escaping. What sort of a mind is in there behind the sock?

—Jesus, give us credit for some savvy. We know you're suspended for dangerous and drunken driving. The first Royal Ulster cunt of a constable that saw you would pull you in. The town wouldn't get its milk delivery.

—It's a proxy bomb.

—How bright you are, fat farmer.

—Afraid to do your own dirty work.

—Stuff it. Too many pigs spoil the breath. They say that when you were in college you used to go to the cattle-market in the morning to get dung on your boots to let the world know you were doing agriculture.

Soldier's Cap, who sits straddle on a chair, his back to the low bay-window, the light fading through the blood-red leaves of Virginia creeper, and who is honing his hunting knife on the heel of his hand, laughs hoarsely, Gasmask stands by the door, butt of his shotgun grounded, at attention almost, a soldier of the Republic. What the hell is it about his feet? Gasmask says nothing. Binchey Two is very red in the face and in the bald head: The smell was better in the cattle-market, and that goes for you. Put down the gun and step outside and we'll see how much pigshit you contain.

—Easy, easy, fat man. We're here on business.

—Keep it that way.

Minnie whoops and cackles: It was a fair gentleman's challenge.

The hissing must make the sock uncomfortably damp. Gasmask shifts his feet and gun-butt: behind the mask he could be alarmed. The woman says: Take it easy, everybody. My father-in-law has been forbidden to drive. He has a heart condition.

—The police don't know that.

—He could drop at the wheel.

—He can drive carefully. Lady, we all have heart conditions.

Binchey senior says that nowadays a man is lucky to have any sort of a condition, or a heart to tick or a knee to bend: What do you want me to drive and where?

—You'll do it.

—I don't have much choice.

—You're a reasonable man.

—I wouldn't count on it.

The woman says: The people will wonder if they see him driving.

—They will like fuck, Soldier's Cap says. They'll just think he's so mean he can't keep his hands off the wheel.

Again the coarse laugh. He has a gravelly recognisable voice. With the exception of Corkman these are local people, for Gasmask's feet are as familiar as fireirons. Soldier's Cap knows that he still has an interest in the hackney-car business that his father, who was also a saddler,

founded. Corkman walks slowly, blowing into his pistol, to where
Soldier's Cap sits straddle in the bay of the window. They wait uneasily
for blows and discipline. The children have not moved. Minnie
murmurs to them and strokes their heads. Corkman stoops and
whispers, hissing, and Soldier's Cap leaps up as if he had been
electrocuted, sheaths the hunting-knife, stands rigid as a guardsman.
The last light is dying behind the red creepers. Binchey Two sullenly
repeats to Corkman: I can easily do the driving. Who'll stop me on a
Sunday morning?

—Your license is suspended.

—Like you don't want to do anything illegal. My father has bad sight
as well as a weak heart.

—He can drive slow and wear his glasses. Look, farmer boy, we've
been over this.

The woman says: I drove back from Donegal.

—Lady, we can't send a woman out with the goods.

—Chivalry, says Binchey One.

—Dear Christ, Corkman hisses, we have enough to do fighting the
Brits, without listening to your bullshit.

—Fight the Brits, says Binchey Two, to the last Catholic shop in the
village of Belleek or the town of Strabane. Man, you love the Brits, you
couldn't exist without them. The nickname is affectionate. They give
you the chance to be Irish heroes. They give you targets you can easily
see.

In a low strained voice, controlling hysteria, the woman says: Stop it,
all of you. Let's get this over with. There are the children.

—Sense, lady, says Corkman. I could do biz with you.

Before her man can again explode, she says: The occasion won't arise.
But tell us, for God's sake, what the drill is.

—Simple. Sometime during the night a creamery can will be
delivered here. All you have to do is drive it into the town and leave it
in one of two places.

—What happens to the car?

—You're well insured, farmer boy.

Soldier's Cap says: Commandeered by the freedom fighters.

But the silence that Corkman allows to settle for a while after that
remark indicates to Soldier's Cap that his words are unwanted.

—Suppose, says Binchey One, that we all refuse to do it.

—You won't. There are children. And the women. We don't want to
be rough.

There's an even longer silence and then Minnie's voice, low and hoarse: Harm a hair on their heads and I'll pray prayers on you and yours.

—Jesus, Gasmask says.

But Corkman tells the old woman to be quiet: Pray not for me nor on me but for yourselves and for your children.

—You mock God's words, Minnie says.

—Jesus, Gasmask says, I don't like this.

He shuffles uneasily from one familiar foot to another.

—It'll be a nice quiet time, says Corkman. But plenty people on the roads going to mass and meeting. The Brits and the R.U. cunts will be keeping a low profile. Put the children to bed, old woman. You (he means Soldier's Cap) go with her and keep your big mouth shut. One place is the entryway between the town hall and the post office. But if the security there is too tight the next best place is the avenue between Judge Flynn's house and the golf-club. Very close to the Judge. We have the women and the children and your fine fat son. Remember that.

—I'll remember. I'll remember it for a long time.

—No threats, old man. You're in no fucking position.

—Judge Flynn is one of the best men in the north.

—The more reason he shouldn't be where he is. He lends credit to the system.

Soldier's Cap, who has returned, ventures to say that Judge Flynn is a tool of imperialism. No comment from Corkman.

—So you kill a man more readily because he's a good man. And blow up the town hall and post office. What's the point?

—You could call it a reprisal, Corkman says, for what they found in the lake.

And the lake would never be the same again.

The undulating movement of the skiers, the sweeping curves made by the speed-boats, the wash and the perturbation of the waters could have brought the body up from the depths. Over there in that corner where, now that twilight has fallen, the men in the black boats have suspended their search for the murder weapon.

The body was badly decomposed. Forensic scientists said that it had been in the water for some time. You'd hardly need to be a forensic scientist to guess that much. Never knew before that we had a forensic scientist in the town or district. They could, though, have brought them from Belfast. Or the army may bring a truckload of them with it wherever it goes. Badly needed nowadays.

But with or without them it was a fair guess that the body might have been in the lake from the night of the evening on which the man who owned it didn't come home from work. Lying weighted down there in the dark until the movement of life on the day of the water-skiing drew it up from the mud at the roots of the reeds.

That water-skiing would be the lake's last effort to laugh. *Sea-lions and sharks, alligators and whales.* A man I know wrote a good comic song about that lake and that line was part of the chorus.

An early-morning fisherman, idling in one of those black boats, saw the floating body in that quiet corner among the reeds. A wire that had come unwound led to a fifty-six pound weight sunk deep in the mud. The man had been in his thirties and was the father of four children. Last seen alive when he locked his public-house in the town to drive his white Mazda car the three miles to his rural home. When he didn't get home at his usual time his wife raised the alarm. Bloodstains and shirt-buttons were discovered in the laneway leading to his house. A neighbour said he had heard five shots fired in the dusk.

For two weeks after, hundreds of people walked with the police and their tracker dogs scouring the country. Nobody seemed to suspect the lake because it was far away in another direction. So the water-skiing went happily ahead. But murderers in the dark had made the sleeping lake their accomplice. The innocent lake had been forced to share the guilt. The lake, out there and fading into another dusk, the lake knew. It could never be the same again.

Corkman is speaking: They killed him because some of us used his pub. He wasn't one of us. But he was with us. We'll get them.

—They say ye shot him because he spoke against murder gangs at a town council meeting.

—Mind your manners, old man.

—Manners, says Binchey Two.

—Anyway, it's a fucking lie. We'll get them.

—You'll get who, Binchey One asks. The town hall. The post office? Judge Flynn who sure as God had nothing to do with it?

—We'll show them we're active. That we can plant bombs where we like.

—Big deal. When my father does it for you.

—Stuff it, farmer.

His hand, a long bony pale hand, has tightened on the pistol. It could also be a damp hand.

The women and children have been locked into Minnie's basement bedroom. They have been told that their men's lives depend on their conduct. But as an extra precaution Soldier's Cap has been ordered outside to watch the bedroom window, to watch the world around them. He clearly doesn't like the detail but he goes. The dishonoured lake lies uneasily in the darkness: *Oh the sights that we saw as we waited for death on the treacherous waves of Lough Muck.*

Binchey One says: Judge Flynn stands for justice and peace.

—Old man, for an old man who was a famous teacher you've no head on your shoulders. They'll blame the people who put the body in the lake. Who wants peace?

—Logic, says Binchey Two. We. They. Them. Us. Who, in Christ's name, is who? Everybody wants peace except the madmen.

—Big words, farmer boy. We're not dealing with logicians. Let me tell you a story.

Seated on a chair by the door that leads to the night outside, and the lake and the town, Gasmask crosses his legs and, dear God, I know now what's familiar about his feet, his father's feet, poor civil shambling sod. In the corner on the floor behind him there's a child's tricycle, red with green wheels, and a doll's pram, the doll sitting upright and staring, lonely for three weeks while her playmate was in Donegal, still lonely, and surprised that no hugs and kisses have come her way for the homecoming.

—The little girl, he says, may need her doll.

—See to it, Corkman says.

And Gasmask stands up on his father's awkward feet and, with his shotgun trailing, wheels the pram out the other door and along the corridor to Minnie's room. The severed ropes and gag still lie where they fell. What has happened to the two crabs in the jar? The dead have peace but they don't know it.

—Let me tell both of you a story to show you the sort of animals we're dealing with.

Binchey Two says: Public relations.

Corkman ignores him. He tells his story.

—There were three U.V.F. men came over from the murder triangle by Portadown to kill a Catholic in Newtownstewart. Two hit men and one man to finger the subject. When they got there the man's away in Dublin. They go into a pub in Newtownstewart and start to drink. Then the fingerman says he knows another papish who would be better dead. They set out to get him. But he has emigrated to Canada. Feeling very bad they go back to the pub in Newtownstewart. On the way home, well drunk, they stop in Gortin Gap for a piss and the gunmen shoot the fingerman because he couldn't find anybody for them to shoot. One of their own. Think of that, old man.

—Quite right they were, says Binchey Two. He wasted a whole day on them. Time's money in your business.

—You'll push me too far, farmer boy.

—Go out and tar and feather a few girls. To keep your hand in.

—Jesus, I'll kneecap you just for the fun of it.

—Kneecaps are up in the Tam Ratings, the popularity polls. You don't know who you are until you look at your knees. I made you a fair offer. Put down the gun and step outside.

—Jesus.

Corkman is on his feet, the pistol coming up. Binchey One steps in front of him.

—Enough. Both of you. One shot and I'm through.

And to his son: Keep it cool. This will all be over by noon. Think of the women.

Corkman says: You should have whipped sense into him before he went bald. Men have been shot for less.

They are all seated again except Gasmask who stands shifting from one awkward foot to the other, his back to the wide window. Corkman orders him to pull the curtains. And to Binchey One: Get what rest you can. I want you fresh for the morning.

The curtains are drawn. Gasmask hisses: The shades of night are falling fast.

—A poet, says Binchey Two, by God a poet.

—As regards the men in Gortin Gap, Binchey One says, it makes more sense than to murder Judge Flynn because he's a good man. More of you should kill each other. Go to the Greenland Cap and settle whatever it is between ye and leave normal people alone.

Bearing the bomb, an angel of death, he will in the morning drive past the graveyard in which his wife is buried. *Soles occidere possunt et redire.* The back of the couch is hard against his spine. This is a rare way to keep a vigil. St. Ignatius, turning his back on the sword and vowing himself to Christ and to Christ his mother, had, in the mad manner of the man from La Mancha, watched all night over his armour. *Nobis cum semel occidit brevis lux.* There would be no time to stop to say a prayer at the graveside. The urgent business of Ireland did not nowadays allow time for prayer. *Nox est perpetua, una dormienda. Da mihi basia mille.*

No time to walk crunching up the gravel path, past the graves of men and women who were still alive in his memory. The tall tweedy jeweller, a great man to fish trout and salmon, prematurely bald like my pugnacious son, who had married such a handsome brunette, much younger than himself, from another town, that he was the envy of every man. Mysteriously, she died young and the tall lean man fished no more, spoke little and only to few and, among his jewels and trinkets and chimney clocks, withered away.

The two main paths in the graveyard are cruciform, Protestants to the left as you enter, Catholics to the right, the cross that had divided them in life divided them also in death: on one arm of the cross the grave of my father and mother and beside it my wife, a controversial placing perhaps, since she had been born and died a Protestant; and beside her the grave of that big happy companion of my youth, six years older than me, with whom I used to go shooting and fishing. He taught me the ways of guns and the ways of women, and became a military doctor and, in some dark night in the early days of the Hitler war, shot himself in his rooms in Aldershot camp in Britain. *Soles occidere possunt et redire.* Catullus also was a great friend to me in those days, when I, as people used to say, wooed her and won her, one day in the High Street her father halting me, at the beginning of my summer holidays in my second year in college, and asking me would I grind his daughter in Latin for her senior certificate.

That lovely old thatched farmhouse, pointed eaves, and dormer windows cowled in the thatch, apple-orchards all around it, at a crossroads a mile north-east of the town: can't remember who lives in it now. Happy hours, heads together over Allen's Latin grammar or Ritchie's Latin composition, and Livy and Tacitus and Virgil and Horace, and Catullus, my favourite, who naturally was not on any secondary-school course but, *da mihi basia mille.* I could even quote a lot of Catullus in those days and I had a good voice. The evening the hem of her school uniform skirt caught on her case of books as she lifted it from the floor to the table, and the skirt came up with the case and my breath caught a bit as I saw for the first time the perfections of that body, her burning innocence. Standing behind her where she sat and quoting Catullus and looking down on the white northern slopes of her breasts and thinking of the warm south, the true, the blushful Hippocrene: and one breast in time was to be cut away for cancer leaving behind it a strange, chaste champain about which she used to make jokes, almost lewd for her. But even that sacrifice could not halt the cancer.

The evening I asked her father could I marry her, and he said yes, he walked with me to the edge of the town where the roads meet and he talked with melancholy about what was to come on Europe and the world. A tall handsome man with a Roman profile and dark hair, not a rib of grey in it, parted up the middle. He was a tea and whiskey salesman, and ineluctable war would ruin his livelihood. He said: We lived through one big war. We won't be able to stand a second. The world will never be the same again.

He was dead in six months. Coronary? Melancholy? He lies buried with his wife and a son who died of wounds after Dunkirk. On the other arm of the cross. There will be no time, either, to pray at his grave.

Corkman sits, his elbows on the kitchen table, the pistol on the board before him. He is silent but very much awake. His son, with his head in his hands, seems asleep – but restlessly. Gasmask is snoring in Minnie's rocking-chair. Through the slit in the mask the snores make a sound that was never heard before. For sure and certain these distorted faces are out of a nightmare. Soldier's Cap is making out as well as he may in the shrubbery, with the cold promise that the watch will be changed at three in the morning. Corkman's tin hat has tilted and the sock-or-something, misshapen over his face, makes him like a Guy Fawkes or that Colonel Lundy the Orangemen used to burn annually in effigy in happy memory of the siege of Derry. *From Antrim crossing over in sixteen eighty-eight, a plumed and belted lover came to the Ferry Gate.* That was the Earl of Tyrconnel. *She summoned to defend her, our sires, a beardless race. With shouts of No Surrender, they slammed it in his face.*

The Apprentice Boys of Protestant Derry, the Maiden City, close the gate before Tyrconnel and the troops of James Stuart. The long memory lives on. With riots and ructions and bombs and bloody Sundays as much a maiden now as Dresden on the morning after.

All this he says to Corkman. No comment. Gasmask creaks and rocks in the chair. The snores ride on like advancing shingly waves.

—The Cambridge rapist, he says, had a better mask than any of you. More imagination. You must have seen a picture of it in the papers. Like a great black pointy bonnet with a long zipper where the mouth should be. He had sewn hair all around the bottom of it so that it looked as if he had long hair and a beard.

No comment from Corkman.

—And white eyebrows painted above the eye-holes. And painted in white on the forehead or what covered it the simple word: Rapist. He wasn't, do you see, ashamed of his craft, trade or profession. When a girl woke up and looked up and read that in the middle of the night she knew right away what was in store for her.

No comment.

—What could you write on your forehead?

From behind his cupped clutched hands Binchey Two says: Cain.

No comment.

—The chief constable in Cambridge blamed the case on the prevalence of unchecked porn. A dangerous word to use. It could have been misprinted.

—Old man, you talk too much.

—It's an old man's privilege.

—You don't have any privileges until you deliver the goods.

—After that, says Binchey Two, you could send him a 1916 medal. No comment.

Binchey One says that according to Irenaeus in Edmund Spenser's Viewe of the State of Ireland the kerns and gallowglasses oppressed all men, spoiled their own people as well as the enemy, stole, were cruel and bloody and full of revenge, delighted in deadly execution, were licentious, swearers and blasphemers, common ravishers of women and murderers of children.

—He didn't like the Irish, old man. We know you taught Latin and history and English literature. It had to be English. We know what your history was like.

—You know a lot for a stranger to these parts.

—I do my homework.

Gasmask's snores trample onwards towards a gravelly coast.

He is wandering through London streets with his wife. They are planning a trip by water to the country but they fall asleep in a pub or in a flat and can't get to the boat. We meet a young official who asks me to telephone Mary Cluskey that in my youth I rolled in the ditches with, on the expert advice of that big happy man who died in Aldershot by his own hand. And when I'm talking to Mary on the 'phone I can still hear my wife's voice in the background. I keep asking Mary to pass the 'phone on to her but when she tries to, my wife is gone. Then she reappears, walking along Kensington High Street and carrying two travelling bags. She says she won't go to wherever it was we were going because I would only torment myself and her. Kensington High Street becomes a clay road between shambles of outhouses. We meet a crowd of boys playing with dogs and ask them the way to Hampstead. We have been going the wrong way, and an adult, a dwarf, Dickens' Daniel Quilp, redirects us. We sit down to eat at a rough wooden table and in the open air. My son is there as a boy, and his sister, grown-up, the image of her mother. In a dry, deep-sunken dyke to my left are bundles of antique books, weather-stained, mouldering. Then a girl at a little table, also to my left, produces tickets for a raffle and I am sharing a room with an Old Christian Brother who taught me in secondary school and had slight homosexual tendencies. There are two beds in the room, hospital screens, the floor slopes steeply down from one wall to the other, my bed is behind a screen in the corner farthest from the door. The old brother's pupils are doing exams and doing badly and in the dusk there is the slapping of buttock-flogging (he was an adept) and wailing from an adjacent building. In his bed I fall asleep but, perhaps wisely, go to my own bed when he comes in, and Mary Cluskey is there. Then the room is full of autumn leaves blown in through a window and the door, which is swinging open in the wind. Mary is picking up the leaves. She is pleasantly naked. The door slams shut.

And Gasmask has snored and rocked himself out of the chair and is picking himself up from the floor. The whole room is awake. Corkman says: Go out, for God's sake, and relieve Charlie Chaplin. Keep awake. Don't frighten the birds.

He has for a long time had recurrent nightmares about books left to rot and decay in the open air, sometimes in heaps or bound bundles, sometimes, even more crazily, on orderly shelves. He was also at the deathbed of that old Christian Brother in Baldoyle in Dublin. The old man had had a happy and holy death. On the Chinese mission he had picked up the passion for boys and buttock-whipping. He had had two brothers in the flesh who committed suicide and to the end, almost, he had a fear that he would go that way.

His son, yawning, stretching himself, says out of nowhere: It was simply that I preferred the cattle-market, to the college. There was more brains there. And, believe it or not, less shit.

No comment from Corkman.

Then knocks and footsteps round the house, whistles after dark. Corkman gives his pistol to Soldier's Cap: Watch this pair. Your life's on it. That's the milk delivery.

There has been no sound of a car engine. That could mean that the milk delivery has been prepared in and carried from somewhere close by. Or did the car stop a distance away so as not to draw attention to the house? It would be odd to think that somebody in a neighbouring cottage could all the time have been plotting and preparing this. His son says: One day when I was in primary school I was walking home through Fountain Lane where the soldiers' girls lived. Two of them were having an argy-bargy and one of them called the other a hoor. So being all of eight years of age I went right home and asked my mother what was a hoor? She laughed until she cried. She said: You'll find out soon enough. There's a fair share of them in this town.

—Next morning I'm on my way back through Fountain Lane and one of the pair is leaning out over the half-door, red in the face, hair in the eyes. She shouted at me: Wee fella, did you pass many worms this morning?

—That puzzled me for a long time. You see I couldn't recall seeing or overtaking any worms.

Something's going on outside. The gentlemen go by. Five and twenty ponies trotting through the dark, brandy for the parson, baccy for the clerk, laces for a lady, letters for a spy, watch the wall my darling . . .

—That's life for you, his son says. Or a lot of it. Hoors and worms. Worms and hoors.

No comment from Soldier's Cap. Corkman has come back. He says: That was the milk delivery, the creamery can. Brace yourself old man. You might yet be the first of your breed to die for Ireland.

Standing with one foot in the stone-flagged corridor and one in the basement bathroom, holding his shotgun as if he were behind a covered wagon and waiting for Indians, Gasmask hisses: Be careful Mr. Binchey. And good luck.

Binchey One is in shirt and trousers, and washing and shaving. This is a job he needs to be fresh for: Oh weep, my own town, for after all these years of love I carry death to your threshold.

Carefully he combs back his plentiful silver hair. It changed colour after she died but it stayed with me. When he was younger and drank more than was good for him he always had a fancy that if your hair was combed you looked sober. He soaks a facecloth in cold water and swabs his face, particular attention to the ears so that I'll hear the bomb if it goes off prematurely. Do you hear the bomb that kills you? On the western front the old sweats said that you didn't hear the whistle of the shell that had your name on it. Yet how could anybody know if nobody lived to tell the tale? He says: That's the oddest bloody wish I ever heard, Bertie.

He hadn't meant to use the name but the harm's done now, if it is harm. Gasmask doesn't move. Or Bertie. He may be seeing Indians. He hisses: Search me. Silence is golden.

With those temporary speech-defects he should eschew sibilants.

—Your father's feet, Bertie.

—I'm saying nothing.

—I'd know them anywhere.

—For God's sake don't let him know you know me.

—Are you afraid of him?

—He's hell on wheels. He might hear us.

—He can't with the sound of the rashers frying.

And also the voices of children who seem blessedly to have adapted, accepted painted devils and funny faces so as now in the morning to be able to dance around Minnie, Minnie Brown, we're home again from Dungloe town, and to tell her in a pattering hail-shower of words in two voices about Donegal and the ocean and the crabs in the glass-jars and the golden and white strands of the Rosses. Soldier's Cap has been detailed to carry the crabs into the kitchen. Corkman says: Anything to keep them quiet.

He sits by the outer door, pistol in hand, back to the wall. Soldier's Cap has been sent out again to watch the world and the loaded car. Binchey Two sits on the couch, his head in his hands, brooding, his father fears, violence. The two women cook breakfast. It is Sunday morning and callers are unlikely and it is the custom of the house to pick up the Sunday papers in the town after mass. So there will be no newsboy. For all the townspeople know, they are still in Donegal.

—He's all ears, Gasmask hisses. He's one of the big ones.

—Who? That half-educated gutty from Cork. He's big when he's out like the prick of a jackass.

—Holy God, Mr. Bee, be careful. Keep your voice down.

—In my own house.

—It's his house now. For the cause. You were good to my father, Mr. Bee, my father always says.

—The son repays me.

—It's the cause, Mr. Bee. We must get the Brits out of Ireland. They want our oil.

—Our hairoil. I never knew we had oil.

—We will have offshore oil.

—You won't see much of it, Bertie boy, where you're going. You'll have more need of luck than I'll have.

—Not my name, Mr. Bee. Walls have ears. The trees outside have ears.

—You really are a poet, Bertie. Your father was a decent man. Your father's son shouldn't be mixed up in this.

—I'm a soldier of the Republic.

—You're an ass. You could give me that gun. Mad Eyes Minahan has only a knife.

—Jesus, Mr. Bee, you know him too.

—No mask could hide those mad eyes.

He hadn't recognised the eyes. He had just guessed. If I survive this, will I pass the names to the police?

Carefully he knots his dark-green tie, Dublin poplin. He could do with a clean shirt: and suddenly his care for such things at such a time seems crazily comic. Yet he dusts the broad shoulders of his pin-striped jacket, carefully polishes and sets his pince-nez: she had always liked them.

—You could give me that gun.

—Dear God, Mr. Bee, talk sense. You were a teacher. He'd kill us all. Even if he didn't get me, they would. There's no way out. Sorry, Mr. Bee.

The elbow of his left arm, slightly crooked, pains a little as it has done most mornings since he broke it in a boxing bout in college and, after my time, my son was shaping well on the college team but he lost interest and gave all his heart to farming: and perhaps Bertie, as stupid as his father before him, is right and there's no way out, and Corkman is calling from the kitchen to say that time is ticking away and the milk may be boiled over.

His son still sits with his head in his hands. The empty doll's pram is under the table. The doll is asleep in Minnie's bed. The crabs stare out from their jar on the wide windowsill. Rashers and eggs and tea laced with brandy, good for the ticking of the heart. There's a double naggin of brandy in the back of the car and he hopes they haven't found out about that. The family sit and eat, and Corkman and Bertie guard the doors, they'll eat, Corkman says, when the milk is safely on the road. His son's strong hands, now marmalading bread for the children, are matted with dark hair, none on his head, the fingers are thick and flat-tipped, brutal. He is dangerously silent. Could have been a champion in the ring but it was nature for him to find his content on the land, among cattle and horses, behind him generations of strong farmers who had survived the famine of the 1840s and grown stronger in a new and better world. Branching out into saddlery which also belonged to the land, then into a fleet of hackney cars which seemed to be a natural successor to saddlery. Or unnatural? Over the tea laced with brandy, Franco-Irish courage, gallant France, indomitable Ireland, the noble name of Hennessy, he sniffs the wax-end and leather and daubing in the saddlery, then the gasolene in the garages, another new world, old Ford cars, tin lizzies, that stood high and stilted and quivered like thorough-breds when you set the engine running, and had never been perverted to carry bombs. Proxy or otherwise. Looking back at it now it was a lost lyrical innocent place in which gasolene smelled sweet as the rose and droppings of spilled gasolene reflected all the colours of the rainbow. Corkman says: Let's take a look at the goods.

His son's wife picks up from the floor the severed ropes and gag, puts them in a plastic trash-bag and hopes out loud that they'll never be used in this house again. Then sits on the couch, her arms around her children. The little girl, golden as her mother with the promise of wine, wears a leprechaun's navy-blue jacket and slacks, remembers, and hides her face against her mother and whimpers a little. It could, except for the whimpering, be an idyllic picture. They look at her in silence. But do masks or the minds in them really look? What can they see but other masks? Not men or women or children. Not the shadows of God.

There is a low sky and gentle mizzling rain but a promise in the light wind that the sun will shine before long. The red tricycle with green wheels has somehow or other found its way out to the yard. Lacking the sun the borders of oxalis are closed and colourless. Bertie is a poet and the trees have ears. And the lake. And eyes too. There it is, silent as if nothing had happened. But you can't fool me. The treacherous waves. You know what happened. You helped it to happen. The searchers in the black boats have not yet started work. Or do men search for murder weapons on the seventh day? Lough Muck, Loch no Muice, the lake of the pig. Pig's lake, what pig? *Me and Andy one evening was strolling, we were happy and gay you can bet, and when passing by Drumragh new graveyard, a young Loughmuck sailor we met.* She sleeps forever in new Drumragh on the wrong arm of the cross. *He brought us along to his liner that was breasting the lake like a duck. And that was the start of our ill-fated cruise on the treacherous waves of Loughmuck.* That now was the first verse of the comic song: two drunks from the town astray in these rural parts, falling footless in a dyke, suffering alcoholic comas about an ocean cruise on the oval inland lake, a comic laughing lake, sea-lions, sharks, alligators, whales, shipwreck, and a pity it was that the name of death, *oh the sights that we saw as we waited for death,* had to be mentioned in the chorus of the song: *There we lay on that beach quite exhausted till a man with a big dog drew near. He shouted out, Hey, clear away out of this, we want no drunk towney boys here.* Laughter and innocence were gone. The shadow of the monstrous mythological pig brooded over a landscape that could never free itself from vengeance and old wrongs. A pig of an island, an island changed by the magic of the Tuatha-de-Danaan into that mammoth of a black pig crouching on the sea, so as to try to prevent the Milesian wandering heroes from coming safely to haven on their isle of destiny. What a destiny, to consort with murderers in the valley of the black pig.

Corkman opens the boot of the car which has been reversed or pushed back to the hayshed, in which there is another car, a Ford Cortina. But it didn't come there during the night. No noise. Must have been there before we drove from the happiness of Donegal into the haunted farmyard.

—You're a learned man, Corkman says.

Bertie, like a statue of the Rifleman, stands in the shrubbery away at the gable of the house.

—There she is. You'll like to know what's in her.

She is a stout squat creamery can, shining silver.

—One hundred pounds of ammonium nitrate mixed with fuel oil and about three pounds of gelignite.

—A sweet cocktail.

—She'll do the job. Watch her. Technologically we've made big advances.

Carefully he closes the boot: Don't bump her, old man.

—Advances? Towards what?

—That's the way we'll bugger the Brits. Technology.

The town hall, the post office, any innocent person who might be in them or walking the street past them, Judge Flynn doomed because of his virtue: a madman spoke behind the mask, the man in the mask was mad.

—Some American says that shortly any fool will be able to make a hydrogen bomb in his own backyard.

—You read too much, old man.

Once upon a time a creamery can had been a harmless or lovely, even a musical object. Up and down the street in the town in which he was reared, the horses and carts from the farms would travel, bright with jingling cans, taking fresh milk to the creamery, taking away the skim milk for cattlefood. In Hamilton's smithy where three gigantic Presbyterian men, a father and two sons, swung their hammers and reddened the forge, the horses and the cartwheels were shod when the need arose: Presbyterian iron, and across the street his father and his helpers, all Catholics, including Bertie's poor fool of a father, provided the leather. Genuine co-operation: the horses had no sectarian prejudices. One large red-faced farmer-boy would sit sideways on his cart, outsized hobnailed feet trailing the ground and, fancying himself perhaps on the Oregon trail, would sing in the rural dialect: Rowl along, covered wagon, rowl along.

No shuddering shattering death in those bright cans.

Nowadays motor-trucks took the cans to a modern factory.

—Time's ticking away, Corkman says.

He agrees. What else is new? Corkman is a bore: and suddenly the brutal effrontery of the whole business freezes his blood and sets him shivering. What right have these brainless bastards with their half-baked ideas to crash in on the lives of better people, to bind and gag old women, set children whimpering, and himself bearing death and ruin to the town he loves. Ireland? What Ireland? Ulster? What Ulster? Multiplying like body-lice, the other crabs, in the hairy undergrowth, one madman produces another. He says to Corkman that, indeed, time is ticking away, that they're all closer to the grave than they were yesterday morning. He says: I heard of a man who defied a gang like you . . .

—Gang? Watch it, old man.

—And said: Murder me now. What would you do, Corkman?

—Try me and see. Nobody would miss your son, for starters. But listen to me now and listen good and no codacting. You can't take the short way into the town. They may be easy on a Sunday morning at the roadblock but you might bump her on the ramps. She's as delicate as a virgin.

Then the backdoor of the house slams thunderously. Soldier's Cap has come backwards out through the doorway like a rocket and is flat on his ass and roaring. Bertie the imbecile, soldier of the legion of the rearguard like his father before him, is also flat but on his belly, shotgun aimed on the backdoor. Corkman says: Don't move, old man. Charlie Chaplin couldn't guard a henhouse. Has farmer boy a gun?

—He has the 'phone.

—It's small use to him. We fixed that. Be your age. Has he a gun?

—He has a shotgun somewhere.

—In the house?

Soldier's Cap rises, falls again over the green-wheeled red tricycle, comes crawling crabwise across the yard towards the hayshed and his master and the loaded car and the concealed can. Corkman calmly raises the pistol: Jesus, I could shoot him where he creeps. Only it wouldn't be worth the noise. The dung I have to work with. Where's the shotgun, old man?

Soldier's Cap crawls closer. Bertie leaps to his feet and, in a perfect imitation of a British paratrooper shooting down civilians in Derry on Bloody Sunday, races round the corner of the house, goes down, shotgun ready, on one knee, under a windowsill and close to the backdoor. Bertie has studied the art of war, or whatever it is, on the teevee.

—You may as well spill, old man. It's not in the house.

He may as well spill. His son hasn't a hope. He says: No shooting then. If so, no driving. The gun's up on hooks in the stable-loft.

—It's safe there. We'll get it later. And no conditions, old man. Who in hell do you think is boss around here?

Soldier's Cap has crawled into what he thinks is the shelter of the hayshed. He moans what seems to mean that his jaw is broken. He rises to his knees: and, fair enough, if his jaw isn't broken it, and his mask, are in some disarray: my son still has a good right, and it is mad Minahan. Then Corkman with care and deliberation kicks Soldier's Cap in the privates and the creature goes down again howling.

—A lesson in discipline, soldier. And now, old man. Into battle.

The pistol is pressed against the back of his head.

—Walk slowly across to within twenty paces of the door. Tell the idiot farmer boy to step out backwards, hands behind back. Women and children in kitchen and quiet. If not I'll shoot you in one knee-cap. Also we'll run the milk delivery up the back-door and leave it there. Time's ticking away. The virgin's in the boot. Waiting to be bust. Fed-up fooling, old man. Soldier-boy on your feet. You stupid fucker. The Battle of Britain and Paddy Finnucane. And get the cuffs out of the Cortina.

He stirs mad Minahan more than briskly with his foot and the creature rises and hobbles, doubled-up and moaning, towards the hidden car. They pace across the yard. Quasimodo Minahan lurches behind. The borders of oxalis are stirring in expectation of the sun. The birds are busy. The birds sang around Dachau. The mouth of the pistol is not touching his head but he feels that it is. Cold shivering anger at outrage is not enough. You need guns and bombs and swinging ropes and the shooting of hostages. But here and now there's no help for it, no way out. If the milk has to be delivered anywhere, better not at your own door. So his son steps out backwards, hands behind his back, and Quasimodo, hobbling sideways and groaning, snaps the cuffs on him in a flash and a click and, for better value, kicks him viciously on the shins. Corkman laughs again that astoundingly good-natured laugh and says: Chained in the market-place he stood, a man of giant frame

Then: To the wheel, old man, to the wheel.

—Will my son be safe?

The humiliation, oh heart of Jesus, the humiliation, hoors, whores and worms.

—If he minds himself, and if you deliver the goods. He can't masturbate the way he is. He won't grow hair on the palms of his hands. To the wheel, old man.

—The women? My daughter-in-law? The children?

Bertie's father's awkward feet have walked into the house.

—No time, old man, for tearful farewells. Kiss them all you want when you come back. If you ever do. Time's ticking away.

The pistol, really touching his head, pushes him towards the car. His son stands silent, chained in the market-place amid the gathering multitude that shrank to hear his name, men without hands, girls without legs in restaurants in Belfast, images of Ireland Gaelic and free, never till the latest day shall the memory pass away of the gallant lives thus given for our land, images of Ulster or of a miserable withdrawn corner of O'Neill's Irish Ulster safe from popery and brass money and wooden shoes. These mad dogs have made outrage a way of life. To the wheel, to the wheel, to the wheel, time's ticking away, in the town the churchbells are ringing, Catholic, Church of Ireland, Presbyterian, Methodist, Baptist, all calling people away from each other to get them in the end by various routes, *variis itineribus* to the home in the heavens of the same omnipotent, omniscient, omnipresent Great Father with a long white beard, but why not unite here and now and not wait for then, come all to church good people good people come and pray, and the angel of death is at the wheel or on the wing, and ye know neither the day nor the hour.

Before him like a blood-red flag the bright flamingoes flew. The bright evil lake is behind him. The car runs well. To look at it, nobody would have a notion. This now is the crossroads and the longest way round is the shortest way home. And his still-silent, silvery passenger, glutted with fuel oil and gelignite and ammonium nitrate, might be discommoded into burping by the bumps of the ramps. Beloved, may your sleep be sound. She sleeps in New Drumragh. Death sleeps in the silver can. In Dublin long ago he had gone with her to see that movie about Venezuela and the wages of fear. A friend of his had even introduced them to the Frenchman who had written the novel: a tall man, visiting Dublin at the time, who wrote about dead-beats in a vile South American town, island of lost souls, taking perilous jobs, only the lost would take them, that was a pothole and a bad bump, driving nitro-glycerine or something to mines or quarries or was it oil-wells: the occupational hazard, a blinding flash over the ridge, scarcely an explosion, just a blinding flash and that was that.

But at least those wrecks of men were paid to carry the stuff. More or less they went willingly. If they won through they had their ticket to somewhere out of hell. If they didn't, they felt no more pain. While I ferry murder to my town and its people so as to save my children, my children's children, an old deserted woman, a long white house. And on the cause must go, through joy or weal or woe, till we make Ireland a nation free and grand. Not even the Mafia thought of the proxy bomb, operation proxy, proxopera for gallant Irish patriots fighting imaginary empires by murdering the neighbours. Could Pearse in the post office have, by proxy, summoned Cuchulain to his side, could the wild geese have, by proxy, spread the grey wing on the bitter tide, could all that delirium of the brave not have died by proxy, Edward Fitzgerald, and Robert Emmet and Wolfe Tone? Corkman seemed semi-educated, and must know that poem, and also, let me carry your cross for Ireland, Lord, but let some other unfortunate fucker carry the bomb for me.

Proxopera, he says, and likes the sound of the word.

Proxopera Binchey, fit foe for the Red Baron, zooming in to attack, and dear God there was a bump that nearly stopped my faulty heart, my palms are sweating, my crotch is scourged and where in God's name is the brandy that was under the cushion in the back of the car? He finds it, and blessed be God, blessed be His holy name and blessed forever be the holy name of Hennessy, and stands on the roadway sipping, and breathing in the living morning. This is a quiet place, and a good place to drive the accursed thing into a field and be shut of it forever, except that he knows that some of them, not Corkman, not Bertie, not mad Minahan, but some fourth monster, and unmasked and like an ordinary human being, is watching him from somewhere, hedgerow, hilltop, to see does he truly deliver the goods.

Six weeks ago that man near Kesh, by the Erne in County Fermanagh, was ordered to take a loaded bomb into the town and simply drove it at sixty into a field and jumped out and scuttled for his life and the gunmen took off in panic, like shit off a shovel, in his car and didn't stop for twenty miles and abandoned his car beyond Ballyshannon: real true Irish heroes, they were, when their own yellow hides were in peril. Like the way they were all to stand and fight if the Brits went ahead with Operation Motorman and went into the Bogside in Derry, but on the day and night of Operation Motorman the heroes were safe across the Border getting heroically drunk in Bundoran on the ocean, a health resort of high renown. But at Kesh there were no hostages: and what would that Corkman and mad Minahan do to his son and his wife and children: soldiers of the Republic in their own eyes, knee-cappers, murderers, arsonists, protection racketeers, decorators of young girls with tar and feathers, God, the oddities that in times like these crawled out from under the stones.

The green rolling landscape is happy all around him. Where are the watchers hiding?

Brandy breaks out in sweat on his brow. Time's ticking away. He's as lonely as Alexander Selkirk, lord of the fowl and the brute, lord of destruction and the day of doom. Into battle then. To the wheel. To the wheel. Get a good grip on myself. Another sip. More sweat, but the heart seems easy. A man of my age in Belfast was forced to drive a bomb to the Europa hotel, already bombed seventeen times, and had a heart attack and died, and the bomb didn't even go off: the cursed murderous cretins, and all the happy days I passed along this road on my way to the innocent lake and the vision of the white house of destiny: and now, out of humanity's reach, I Alexander Selkirk, on my own island and passing her holy grave without time for a prayer, must finish my journey alone.

Traffic is slight for a Sunday morning. Have the men of blood frightened the people from going to mass or meeting? Three cars overtake him and hoot at him in salute, and in the noise and reverberation of their passing he grips the wheel until his sweating palms hurt. He doesn't hoot back. They'll all be surprised to see me driving. God preserve any of them from stopping to make enquiries. An old woman – oddly enough he doesn't recognise her although he thought he knew everybody on this road – thumbs a lift and, out of habit, he is almost about to respond. She'll be amazed and annoyed that he hasn't. People in these parts were always generous about giving lifts. These morons have blighted the landscape, corrupted custom, blackened memory, drawn nothing from history but hatred and poison. Proxopera, proxopera lift up your voice and sing. So he sings, but softly: Going to mass last Sunday my true love passed me by. I knew her mind was altered by the rolling of her eye. And when I stood in God's dark light, my tongue could word no prayer, knowing my saint had fled and left her reliquary bare.

My true love passed me by. No, but I passed her by, in fear and without a prayer, when I passed the green spiked railings of new Drumragh. He sings again, this is as close to prayer as I can come: Ringleted youth of my love with your bright golden tresses behind thee, you passed on the road up above but you never came in to find me.

How dear to me now, doomed to solitude, a murderer by proxy, are my memories, how dear the ordinary details of life, a red tricycle with green wheels, a doll's pram, the rocks of Donegal, two crabs in a glass jar, the wrinkled face of an old woman, the winy body of a young woman, the bald head of my angry son, the voices of his children, the sound of the hooves of his horses, the oxalis opening to the sun now breaking out splendidly beyond my doomed town.

Spiked green railings surround the dead, the gravelled cross divides them.

Outside a Wesleyan hall in Belfast a woman has been found impaled on the railings. Foul play is not suspected. She fell from a window. Of a Wesleyan hall? Odd, very odd. And in Belfast, where for six years there has been nothing but foul play. Christ, there I went bump bump over a bridge over a small stream out of which, with the humble worm, I took my first ever brown trout. Has the creamery can moved? Rattled? How do you fall from the window of a Wesleyan hall and impale yourself on the railings? Shades of Shaka, the great Zulu, who amused himself by seating his enemies on pointed stakes and letting them sink to find their own level. A very painful happening, buggery by proxy, proxbuggery. But the Turks had more finesse with a slender, pliable, tough rod tapped gently in at the anus and up and up, an expert job, and out at the back of the neck and one end of the rod lashed securely to the other and the victim raised on a pole to perish as soon or as slowly as he pleased. With their hammers and nails and carpentered crosses the ancient Romans were a crude bloody crowd. Proxopera in the highest, hosanna to the king.

Long ago she said in all innocence: Take my cherry.

They were sitting in an ice-cream parlour in O'Connell Street in Dublin.

He picked the cherry from the top of her phallic Bombe Cardinale, blunted multi-coloured obelisk of ice-cream, and told her what she had just said, and she blushed and laughed and laughed and blushed, and still I remember the first touch of the tip of my finger on the fragile membrane.

—She's as delicate, Corkman said, as a virgin.

Or was that what the bastard had said?

And that, God above, was another bad bump. St. Christopher, pray for me, who carried Christ on your back, I carry Lucifer, evil and a blinding light.

Once in an old churchyard that must have been in some eighteenth-century engraving, and beside a high Norman earth-work, a friend of mine and myself came on a Sunday on a newly-opened grave, opened to receive its guest on the Monday morning. Down, deep-down in the next door grave reposed a skeleton, not a bone out of place, but bed-clothes temporarily disturbed for the reception of the new guest. Inlaid to the brown clay, head tilted restfully back, hands joined together a little above where manhood or membrane might have been. She sleeps for the life of the world in new Drumragh where soon, perhaps, I may join her but, also perhaps, not with my bones in their proper positions. Before the city hall in Belfast people kneel around more than a thousand small white crosses, one cross for every person murdered in the name of Ireland or the name of Protestant Ulster. Bertie of the blundering hereditary feet talks of the Republic, Corkman the crazy talks of technology, and I drive on, sick with fear and an awful resignation, to bring death to my own, to keep death from my own.

My father was a great man for bananas, treaclebread and oatmeal porridge. Three hundred and sixty-five days of the year, three hundred and sixty-six in Leap Year, even on Christmas day and after the Christmas dinner, he would prepare and sup his own oatmeal.

Once upon a time the country people held that human skulls had healing properties, chiefly for the healing of epilepsy. You broke off a little bit of the skull, ground it into powder and drank it. That is, if you were an epileptic. Also, milk could be boiled in the skull and given to the patient. Over there near Keadue on the shores of Lough Key in the west of Ireland, the skull of Turlough O'Carolan, the last of the bards, was so used until somebody stole it from his tomb. To preserve the bard's skull? Or to make a corner in the curing of epilepsy? In new Drumragh she sleeps forever, her skull on a pillow and under a canopy of Ulster clay. Goldsmith, Thackeray said, could have heard O'Carolan and God of Almighty what am I thinking of, broken-down pedant sitting on a volcano, Empedocles on Aetna, and that was a bump and a bump and an 'alf and my hands are so slippy they can hardly hold the wheel till the vessel strikes with a shivering shock, even the roads have gone to blazes since the troubles began, Good Heavens it is the Inchcape Rock, as our ship glided over the water we all gazed at the landscape we knew, we passed Clanabogan's big lighthouse and the Pigeon Top faded from view: but, alas, as we sped o'er the waters, we were all soon with horror dumbstruck, for without any warning a big storm arose on the treacherous waves of Lough Muck, and Sacred Heart of Jesus what now is happening in my white house that I first saw and loved across the waters of the lake that have been polluted forever: and Bertie's father was a born fool for this night, when my father was cooking the porridge, he steps into our kitchen with a collection box, and all round his left bicep a tricoloured ribbon oh, collecting cash for Caithlin Ni Houlihan, the Hag of Beare and Caith Ni Dhuibhir, and Patrick Pearse and the sainted dead who died for Ireland. Nowadays people die for Ireland in the oddest ways.

—And what will you do with the money, says my father and he carefully watching the bubbling oatmeal.

—Elect members to Stormont and Westminster, Mr. Binchey.

—And what will you do then, Brian boy?

—The members will then abstain from attendance, Mr. Binchey. They'll be abstentionist members.

—Bully for them. That'll save train and boatfare. And what will you do then, Brian?

—Spread our propaganda among the Orangemen, Mr. Binchey. Bring them round to our way of thinking.

—A laudable intention. And what then, Brian?

—Declare a republic, Mr. Binchey.

—Oh la dee da, says my father and goes on stirring the porridge.

But how could Brian help it and the way he was reared, with an uncle that was forever in and out of jail for Ireland and an aunt that blew herself up making bombs for Ireland and a mother that ran a restaurant and lodging-house always as full of republicans as Rome before the Caesars, so that it was regularly being raided by the Royal Ulster Constabulary, and one night Brian's mother and Bertie's grandmother poured from a second-floor window, and all for Ireland, the contents of a chamber-pot from under the bed of a drunken journeyman-carpenter, over the shoulders of a police sergeant who came knock knocking at the door: and the sergeant's name was Poxy Thompson because of the pock marks on his face and for no worse reason, and one of his shoulders was lower or higher than the other. A family that was fierce Irish, as they'd say in irony in Dublin; and now Bertie on his father's feet and with a face like a faceless monster goes plodding unbidden around the house of my boyhood dreams.

But Kyrie Eleison what is this on the road on a Sunday morning, smoke rising from the smouldering stump of what's left of the Orange Hall where once that love-bewildered young Protestant provoked a riot by footing the light fantastic with a papist girl. In this present Ulster world there's little place for the light fantastic: close to Newry town the U.V.F. or was it the U.D.A. murdered a showband.

My road drops down, doing a double bend, into a saucer of a valley. High, green, terraced banks, no turn left or right, no turning back, no way out except straight through: *There we were like two Robinson Crusoes far away from Fireagh Orange Hall. Though we starved on that rock for a fortnight, not a ship ever came within call.* Fireagh, here I come. And the Orange Hall has just gone. Up in smoke. Thirty or so people are in and around what's left of it. As close to the smouldering ruins as they dare to go. The flames have blackened the bushes on the high bank above. Sweet sight for a Sunday in a good autumn. No soldiers around. This is a fire. Not a fight. Thank God for that. But for what? One policeman raises his blue-black arm. What can I do but stop? No use to say to him halt me at your peril. And the peril of everybody in this little valley. And of my son and his wife and Gary and Catherine and Minnie, Minnie Brown we're home again from Dungloe town.

—Good morning, Mr. Binchey. Bit of a surprise to see you at the wheel.

A decent fellow. I drank with his father. Also in the force. And a brother of his, a plain-clothes man, murdered in the town, twelve months ago. Sitting reading the paper at a barcounter when two gunmen walked in. Into a pub in which he had had his first drink. And in which on my way from teaching I used to drink with his father, at the same counter at the same place. Tried to pull his gun. They shot him once. Crawled into the gents. They followed him and finished the job and shouted: We have you in the right place on the shithouse floor.

That pub would never be the same again.

—Good morning, constable. I wouldn't be at the wheel only necessity knows no law.

How true, how bloody true.

—We got back from Donegal last night. Margaret wasn't feeling too well. Robert's on the suspended list. As you know. So old grandad has to head off to the chemist. But I'm taking it easy.

—It's the best thing to do these days, Mr. Binchey. If you can. What do you think of that on a Sunday morning?

The engine purrs. He's afraid to cut it off. God only knows what restarting might do. The constable is a squat solid civil fellow with a squint, and his face smudged from the fire the way the soldiers, now and in this place, smudge their faces on night patrol, in my own town, dear God, battledress and camouflage in my own town. Could I tell him that time is ticking away? Could I tell him that someone in the crowd is watching?

—What happened, constable?

—I.R.A. I'd say, a reprisal for the Catholic Church at Altamuskin. The U.V.F. tossed a bomb into that.

—Oh, what a wonderful war.

—So now the U.V.F. will bomb another Catholic church. Or a Catholic pub. Then the I.R.A. will shoot a policeman or bomb a Protestant pub. And then the U.V.F. . .

—Was the brigade here?

—Couldn't make it. Fires everywhere this bloody morning. All a few miles outside town. Cornstacks. Barns. Anything.

Aha, the grand strategy, get the brigade away from the town, make straight the path for Binchey the Burner. Time's ticking away.

—They could be up to something else, Mr. Binchey. All this could be a diversion.

It sure as God could, except that diversion is not the word that Mr. Binchey, his ass squelching in a pool of sweat, his stomach frozen with fear, his mind running crazily on irrelevancies, would have chosen. What at the moment is relevant? Time's ticking away. Time's relevant. How long have I left? How long has anybody left? Half an hour after I place the bomb even at the remoter place, the Judge's house, say fifty minutes to an hour, constable, constable let me pass or I'll wet my pants or my heart will stop.

—These are queer times, Mr. Binchey, pubs and churches, women and children, my own brother, the Tower of London, and in London too the Ideal Homes Exhibition, a bomb by the escalator, sixty-five mutilated and eleven of them Irish, bad, mad times.

With utterly resigned terror Mr. Binchey recalls that the constable's father was an amiable long-winded man. In the smouldering wreckage another constable has discovered something and the crowd has gathered around him. So if I go up I'll only bring this boy with me. The watcher, whoever he is, will be watching from a safe distance. That's the name of the game. Proxopera. Proxopera. He spells it to himself as a sort of charm to move the man to let him pass. But, hands on the door of the car, stooping down, square head half in the window, smudged face still smelling of good aftershave lotion, the young man in blue-black uniform one of the last surviving symbols of an empire gone forever into the shadows, is prepared to talk to Mr. Binchey, as venerable, as respectable, as comforting as the face of the town clock: this is an historic moment and I was a teacher of history and Latin and English literature, and time is ticking away.

—But one of the worst things of all, Mr. Binchey, was that business in the Catholic graveyard at Lisnagarda on the outskirts of Scarva in County Down. Even in the bloody graveyard nothing's sacred.

She sleeps, waiting for me, in new Drumragh, I come, I come, my heart's delight.

—I didn't hear about that.

—It happened, I'd say, when you were in Donegal. The caretaker of the graveyard, sixty-one years of age, a woman, walking in the graveyard in the morning, sees a wreath lying on the path. Purple plastic chrysanthemums and white roses. Thinks it was blown from a new grave. Picks it up. Boom. Boobytrapped. Sure as Jesus. Could you beat that, Mr. Binchey?

An awkward question, in the silvery can, constable my constable, time is ticking away, I'm booby-trapped like the white roses and purple plastic chrysanthemums, we may boom and go aloft together.

—Only a part of it went off or the poor woman was done for. As it was, hands, legs and body severely injured. An old lady. Sixty-one. In a consecrated graveyard. Blood running out of her, she staggered three hundred yards to the nearest cottage, rapped on the window and collapsed. Only one shoe and stocking on, blood everywhere. Something, she said, hit me on the foot when I lifted the wreath. God in heaven, wouldn't you think an old woman would be safe in a graveyard?

Every spring we lay on her grave a bunch of daffodils, a branch of green and golden whin.

—Nothing's sacred, Mr Binchey. But I'd better not hold you up.

You'd better not indeed.

—And the odd thing, Mr Binchey, is that a lot of these fellows, IRA or UVF or UDA, or ABCDEXYZ, if left alone wouldn't hurt a cat or a child. But get a few of them together and give them what they think is a leader or an ideal and they'd destroy Asia and themselves and their nearest and dearest.

A military truck comes from the direction of the town.

—Good luck, Mr Binchey. And I hope young Mrs Binchey will be well soon.

—Thank you, constable. And so do I.

Two soldiers walk towards them. They wave casually at Mr Binchey as he goes on his way towards the town he was reared in.

Those two soldiers looked like lizards, protective colouring to be worn in the emerald isle, Ireland of the welcomes and the bomb in the pub and the bullet in the back. He remembers a time when the soldiers in the town dressed smartly, pipeclayed belts and shining brass badges, polished nailed boots, puttees rolled with precision, peaked caps at an exact angle, walking cane under the oxter the way you'd truss a chicken. They were part of the town then, too, even if they were also part of the far-flung empire: the Royal Irish, the Royal Inniskillings, the pipes playing Adieu to Bellashanny and the Inniskilling Dragoon as they marched from the barracks to the railway station and thence to Aldershot and India or Egypt or the West Indies or Hong Kong or the Burma Road itself. A soldier out for the evening could talk to friends on the street although regulations did not encourage them to loiter at street corners. They drank with the people in the pubs and no madman gloried in shooting them dead in the shithouse. They relaxed with the girls in and around a public park. Or, better still, in whatever private place a poor man could find. Nobody thought of them as an invading hostile army. No girl had her head shaved or was tarred and feathered.

But then we always had with us Bertie's father and the like of him. Curious thing, but the only book I ever saw in the hands of Bertie's father was a copy of *Mein Kampf*. Not in his hands exactly, but under the oxter where the soldiers kept the canes. He had a stiff left leg and always wore a brown belted overcoat, and had no brains, and through 1939 and 1940 he was never without that book. Never did I see him open it to peek at the treasures within. Was he like the vagrant who was washed and treated at a delousing centre and was delighted to discover, buried under alluvial mud in his navel, a collar-stud he had lost six years before? Yet he carried, even if he didn't read, *Mein Kampf*, because since the Jerries were marching against and going to invade England, Hitler had to be a republican. Declare a republic, Mr. Binchey. Oh la dee da, says my father, and goes on stirring the porridge. And about the same time there was a crazy missionary father going around, a roaring beanpole of a man, preaching missions in rural and even urban churches, the purest Goebbels who had noebbels at all, and all about the Jews and the Freemasons, and the real names of the rulers of Russia, all ending in ski, until his religious superiors had to put a stop to his gallop and lock him up or something. Oh never fear for Ireland, boys, for she has soldiers still.

No pipeclayed belts, no shining brass badges, no girls in the park, no drinks with the people in the pubs. But soldier boys like lizards on a sunny Irish Sunday against a background of scorched hedgerows and a burned-out Orange Hall, black wicked guns carried at an angle, pointing upwards, Martian antennae. They hold on to their guns as if they might rocket into space. They whistle through their teeth so as to seem carefree. Young fellows from the other island who scarcely know where they are or what they're doing here or what in hell it's all about. Their boots are dull-black, rubber-soled. They can move as quietly as cats round corners or along alleys. In the old days you could hear the clatter of the nailed boots half a mile away: evil secrecies of the world we have lived into. Forty shades of green, ironically, the green above the red, over trousers and combat jacket. And over the bullet-proof vest, a life-jacket for very dry land, and tied down back and front. But only a black beret protects the head and where have all the tin hats and helmets gone?

Christ hear us, Christ graciously hear us, I'm gripping the wheel so hard that my left arm has gone completely numb, it's not there, it's amputated, I've only one arm remaining and the road is empty and the sun bright and high and I swelch in sweat but I'll make the bridge where the railway used to be before I rest long enough to shake and rub and exercise that arm back into existence. In Jefferson County jail in Alabama there's a prisoner who's in for using an artificial arm to kill a man—like the joker who killed Miss Kilmannsegg with and for her precious golden leg. He has two artificial arms and he complains that the people who run the prison won't let him wear them so that he can't eat, shave, brush his teeth, change his clothes or clean himself after crapping: but the prison people say that if he had his arms he'd hurt somebody, and there you are, like Ulster, an insoluble problem, and my left arm now hurts like hell so it must still be there but, *exaudi nos domine*, there's the bridge around a pastoral corner, lambs on the green hills gazing at me and many a strawberry grows by the salt sea and many a ship sails the ocean, and up a slight slope, and once up there I can survey the morning smoke of my own town.

There below me as I lean on the parapet and puff and sweat and sip the last of the brandy, the blood of Hennessy the God, is the Grand Canyon of my boyhood, now a choked-up formidable dyke where weeds and wild trailing brambles have smothered the magic well at the world's end. No train will ever again go through there bringing noisy happy summer crowds to the breakers at Bundoran. The world is in wreckage and these madmen would force me to extend that wreckage to my town below, half-asleep in the valley, my town, asleep like a loved woman on a morning pillow, my town, my town, my town. Declare a republic, Mr. Binchey, destroy the town, Mr. Binchey. Who's watching me now? Where are they? And down in the Grand Canyon I ate sweet raw turnips and drank, from the rock, water as cool as Moselle. That spring will never be the same again, yet for what civilisation, my town, is now worth, we still have inherited something, we have many good memories. Now I see. Let them watch and damn them to the lowest pit.

Here where I lean, the parapet was once shattered by a runaway truck and during the repairs a boy wrote in the soft concrete the name he imagined himself by: Black Wolf. And I'm the man who was the boy who wrote Black Wolf, and the concrete hardened, as is its nature, and there the name still is, and would Black Wolf ever submit to what the madmen are now trying to force on me, and go on for the rest of his life remembering that to save his own family he had planted death in his own town which is also his family? And even if every blade of grass were an eye watching me, to hell with them, let the grass wither in the deepest Stygian pits of gloom, and blast and blind the bastards and Bertie Bigboots and Mad Minahan and that creepy half-literate Corkman. Now I see. Mud in the eyes is a help and, more than my son and his son, or the bees in the pink oxalis, I see there my town and all its people, Orange and Green, and the post office with all its clerks and postmen and red mail vans, and the town hall and its glass dome and everybody in it — from that fine man, my friend, town clerk, or mayor, for forty-odd years, down to the decent tobacco-chewing man who swabs out the public jakes in the basement, my people, my people. Under that glass dome I played as a young man in amateur theatricals, the Coming of the Magi, the Plough and the Stars, the Shadow, God help us, of a Gunman, and the return of Professor Tim and the Monkey's Paw and the shop at Sly Corner and Look at the Heffernans, and all the talk and all the harmless posturing and laughter, my people. Hissing into a sock or something Corkman couldn't know what a town is. Even by consenting for a moment to drive this load of death I've given these rotten bastards some sort of a devil's right over the lives of my people. What, after my death, will they say about me in the local papers, what would they remember: that I carried a bomb on a sunny Sunday to the town hall and the post office or to the door of Judge Flynn who's one of the best men in the north and who goes every day in danger: they've already murdered a good Judge at his door in the morning and in the presence of his seven-year-old daughter, and now I see and there she is, the virgin, the sleeping beauty inaccessible in a sleeping wood, and thorns and thorns around her and the cries of night? Did she stir in her sleep? Did her guts rumble? My left arm stings but it is alive again.

He places his left hand, palm flat, on the creamery can. He strokes her as if she were a cat. He recalls harmless tricks of boyhood, putting carbide in tins, boring holes in the tins, clamping down the lids, dripping water through the holes, listening for the hiss, putting matches to the holes, and delighting in the bangs and the soaring tins: or tossing squibs over the garden fences of crabbed old men. Down in the valley his town is at peace and blue peace is on the hills beyond. This may be farewell forever, the end of my ill-fated cruise on the treacherous waves of Lough Muck. He says to the can that, daughter of Satan, you'll never get to where you were sent. The beleaguered white house is far away in another world, her grave is very near. He closes the boot carelessly, turns the car sharply on the road, and drives back towards the nameless lake of the mad old women.

That pillar of smoke, of cloud, ahead of me cannot, surely to God, be still coming from the corpse of the Orange Hall. The smoke had died down before I left the place. Where does it come from? Up the steep hill and into the tunnel of tall beeches. Not yet russet enough to make the road seem warm. Up and down this hill, through this tunnel, walked so often that amazing family of strong, red-cheeked, flaxen-haired brothers and sisters, a dozen or more of them, clutching their bibles and meditating, perhaps, on Lot's daughters and the night before. All gone

now. Where to? Somewhere in England? Lost in the last war? Did they
separate or stay together? House and place went to a stronger farmer
who lives elsewhere. The house, a barn now like the barns behind it,
and out of the tunnel and close to the hilltop and the checkpoint
Charley and, under God, it's the barns are on fire, not smoke only but
fine dancing flames, another diversion, all the fun of the fair, to keep
the army and police away from Binchey the Bomber! They'd burn all
Ireland so as I could plant one bomb to burn what was left and get the
Brits on the run. Who'd want to stay? The Irish have to. Some of them.

Only two soldiers, lizards, at the checkpoint. One looking one way,
one another, for the enemy, for fire-bugs, for the brigade if it ever gets
here.

Careful and slow, the ramp might bust the virgin.

So he says to one soldier, and is amazed at the cold steadiness of his
own voice, many an old woman walked along this road to a lonely end:
There's a bomb in this car, I want to dump it in the bog beyond,
proxopera, a proxy bomb.

The first soldier says: Fuck.

Involuntarily goes back a step.

The second soldier says: Let me take the wheel, dad.

The first soldier says: I'll phone the squad. Is gone.

—The wheel, dad.

—Why should you? It isn't your town.

—Hurry, dad.

—They have my house and family. The white house by the lake.

—Dad.

—Follow me. Keep far away.

He drives on. More rapidly. Fuck: to quote the first soldier.

Far behind he hears the siren of the brigade. Fuck, again. What does it
matter? This road that I drive on is Suicide Road. Wages of fear. Many
an old woman. Now an old, an aging, man. Dad, indeed. Grandad. A boy
walked along this road to see a vision of his white house. Up and down
on esker land, sandy humps, that the icebergs left behind. The lake is
below, bog birch and sally bushes, nobody ever fished there, nothing
there ever but death, the still water glistens, shimmers, dances, for a
moment he sees two lakes, then one lake as large as the ocean,
boundaries fading and undefined. Now here, where old withered women
stumbled to meet the dark lover, should, surely to Satan, be the place
for the virgin to awake, relax, open legs, abandon the membrane. A dry
season, thank God, and wheels don't sink on the turf-cutter's path that
goes through bog and birches, but bump, bump, bump, he goes, and
branches crack against the windows and sides of the car and on and on,

and why not now go on and on and the spirits of old dead women, with such hair too, shriek around him. The car stops. The front wheels sink. That's that. Out and away. Which way? To the lake? The road is back there, and the soldiers, some of them, he hears coming carefully after him. He, carefully also, goes towards them, not stumbling. It's not over. Every step is a step towards the white house. The harvest colours are splendid on the hills above and around the bog. Beech leaves will soon begin to redden. He walks between two soldiers. And the elder of Lot's daughters said to the younger: Come let us make him drunk with wine and let us lie with him that we may preserve the seed of our father, for our father is old, and there is no man left on the earth to come in unto us after the manner of the whole earth.

A voice, the second soldier, says: Dad, you're raving. Shock.

Somewhere behind there's a muffled boom. His feet are on the hard road. Strong arms are holding him.

—Let me see. Now I see.

They turn him round. The pillar of cloud rises out of the bog, birches and sally bushes. There's some flame and crackling. Judge Flynn is at home. The town goes about its Sunday business. He tells them about the old women who committed suicide in that nameless lake. The first soldier says effing lucky you weren't a suicide yourself.

—Careful, dad, says the second soldier. Here, lean on me.

There's a crowd on the road, around a Land Rover.

—All this, says the first soldier, is what my dad used to call a real Irish fuck-up. My dad, you see, was Irish, from Liverpool.

But the only thing he can see is a grainfield, red for the reaper. Beyond it somewhere is a white house.

—Home, he says.

—Careful, dad, says the second soldier. Some of us are on the way. You need a rest.

—Good news this morning, Mr. Binchey. Two of them blew themselves up in a car driving into the town of Keady. A loaded handgun was found in the wreckage of the car and police deduced that the men, one already dead in the garden of a roadside house . . .

You're nearer God's heart in a garden.

. . . and the second dying in the wreckage, had either been on their way to leave the bomb in Keady or to deliver it to someone else.

—The police could be correct in their deductions.

—When they go out to harm other people it's always to me a happy sight to see the harm come back to their own doors. God is just.

—Or to their own cars, Minnie. Or to other people's gardens. Once upon a time we used to talk of misguided youths.

—Who guided them or misguided them?

—Ireland. A long history. England. Empire. King William. The Pope. Ian Paisley. Myself. I was a teacher of history.

—With all due respect, Mr. Binchey, we all had the same history. How many people now in your time did you blow up and you as good an Irishman as the next?

—Two weeks ago I came close to it.

—But you didn't do it. You were a hero.

The treetops billow around his third-floor window, three shades of green, beeches turning russet. Through gaps made now and again by the billowing he glimpses a bright suburban road, a bend of a river, a bridge, his town, Venice, for the present preserved.

From the white house and the lakeshore Minnie Brown has come to him with fruit and flowers and the Sunday papers from Dublin and London: his son and daughter-in-law and grandchildren will follow later. The newspapers are filled with the most wonderful reading for an ageing man whose heart is not in the best condition. The crabs from Donegal are still alive and seemingly doing well. Minnie has survived the rascals and the blackguards and her long wrinkled face has the glow of a girl. A forty-eight-year-old father of six children, ranging in age from six to thirteen, has been killed instantly when gunmen burst into his brother's pub at Aughamullen on the shores of Lough Neagh and sprayed the public bar with bullets. The dead man is Patrick Falls, a chemist and a native of the area, but he has been residing in Birmingham for the past four years. He had previously a pharmacy business in Belfast, for sixteen years, but was forced to go to England when his shop was destroyed in an explosion. He had returned to his native Aughamullen a week previously to make arrangements for the building of a house for his wife and family and himself. On the night of his murder he had gone into the bar to allow his brother, Joseph, to have a tea-break. Only one customer was in the public bar when the gunmen entered. One of them killed Mr. Falls instantly. A second opened fire on the customer, seventy-year-old Alphonsus Quinn of Ardboe, wounding him in the arm. The gunmen fled to a waiting car and sped off in the direction of the Protestant area of Tamnamore . . .

Home is the sailor, home from the sea . . .

But on the other hand . . .

A sixteen-year-old boy who moved to Australia from Glasgow with his parents eight years ago has been murdered in rugged country near Adelaide. Police say the boy was clubbed to death. His body was found lying beside his new car. His father said the family had left Glasgow to escape violence in the streets.

And thus the whole round earth is every way bound by the gold chains about the feet of God.

—Now here's a hussy and a half, says Minnie.

She reads slowly, pointing, peering, asking for help with the more rugged words: Susan Shaw is the blonde who puts sheer enjoyment into Manikin cigars. Her abundant sex appeal has helped advertise everything from car-polish to riding saddles. She has nakedly graced the pages of the popular press . . .

—Look at her, Mr. Binchey, tearing her shirt off and her mouth open. No wonder the world is the way it is.

Mr. Binchey looks and is not displeased and makes no verbal comment. But to please Minnie he clucks a little.

—She gets twelve pounds a picture with her clothes on and two hundred and fifty in her pelt. Mr. Binchey, did you ever?

—Never, says Mr. Binchey.

Surprisingly Minnie, who hasn't much respect for sex, laughs until the tears flow down the gullies of her cheeks.

—Well now, says Mr. Binchey.

His father might have said: Boysaboys.

Or Ladeeda.

Or was Ladeeda only for politics and republics? He is tired, he cannot remember, the billowing movement of the treetops is lulling him asleep. But again to please Minnie he makes a heroic effort to keep awake and to listen to her and to go on reading the papers. He is after all a hero. Also: he feels she is hiding something. If he lets her talk she may betray herself.

—It says here, Mr. Binchey, that the I.R.A. blew up a young private soldier of the Ulster Defence Regiment as he was making a regular call on a sixty-eight-year-old house-bound widow. He was off duty and on a tractor and going to chop wood, a daily task to help the aged widow. All U.D.R. men have been warned (Mr. Binchey has had to help her with some of the words) to exercise caution in carrying out spare-time errands of mercy to help the aged and infirm.

—It's in an English newspaper, Minnie.

—Still.

The gullies of her cheeks are again wet but not, this time, with laughter.

—For all those blackguards care, Mr. Binchey, all of us old people could starve or freeze in our houses. If we had a house left to starve in.

She has betrayed herself. He is wide awake. The tree-tops are still, or seem to be. The town below is still unviolated. The gun attack which killed three men in the Belfast pub owned by former Stormont minister, Roy Bradford, is believed to have been the work of a Republican group seeking vengeance for the bombing of the White Fort Inn in Andersonstown in which two men died and six were seriously injured. Come landlord fill the flowing bowl, and an Irishman's pub is no longer his castle: it was all so unexpected, in seconds men who had been enjoying themselves and watching athletics on the teevee were slumped dead or wounded at the counter.

—What was that you said, Minnie?

He is still reading the paper.

—Sacred Heart of Jesus, they'll murder me, Mr. Binchey. You weren't supposed to know until you were up and about.

—Know what, Minnie?

—They burned the house, Mr. Binchey.

—They burned the house.

—Since then we've been living in Judge Flynn's.

—In Judge Flynn's.

—All except Mr. Binchey, Mr. Binchey. He's living in the barn to get the repairs going.

—Repairs. Judge Flynn is a good man.

—He is, Mr. Binchey. And his wife's a lovely woman, too.

—She is.

—It was the fellow with the gasmask. And the shotgun. He said they should burn the house to destroy fingerprints. And the Corkman laughed and said he thought that was the funniest thing he ever heard.

—Fingerprints.

—Mr. Binchey tried to get at them. It was then they shot him in the left knee.

—But Minnie, they can't destroy footprints.

—No, Mr. Binchey.

She doesn't know what he's talking about.

Convert the Orangemen, Mr. Binchey. Declare a Republic, Mr. Binchey. Burn the house, Mr. Binchey, to destroy fingerprints.

—They burned Portrush too, Mr. Binchey.

—They did indeed, Minnie. So why should we worry. I read in the papers about Portrush.

Eight buildings in the centre of Portrush, County Antrim, one of the major holiday resorts in Northern Ireland, were destroyed after a telephone warning that ten bombs had been placed in the town by the Provisional I.R.A.

You may talk of Bundoran, of Warrenpoint and Bangor, but come to

Portrush if you want to be gay. Yes, Billy me boy, put your hand in your pocket, just spend a few ha'pence and come to the say.

That was in a comic song about the seaside resorts of Ulster.

Bracing breezes, silvery sands, booming breakers, lovely lands, come to . . .

No, that was about Bundoran where the Catholics go, not Portrush where the Protestants go.

But the Orangemen could now, couldn't they, burn Bundoran? Or pubs in Dublin? Or the Ark of the Covenant if they could find it, or the Pearly Gates or Uncle Tom's Cabin or the tumbledown shack in Athlone or the house that Jack built or the little old mud cabin on the hill? What anyway do people want with pubs, or all those houses, or hotels or churches or schools or libraries or happy holidays? Burn the bloody lot. Wipe out all the world's fingerprints.

The papers slither on to the floor and he falls half-asleep and Minnie sits there and cries silently.

There is a place in the lake called the Blue Stones. Twenty feet out from the shore and in shallow water two conical blue rocks stand up a few feet above the surface and look at each other as if they were in love, lovers turned to stone and unable for all eternity to touch or taste.

When he was twelve years old he owned a Brownie camera, a birthday present. His pal, Tony, and himself, both trouserless, waded out to the Blue Stones. Tony balanced on one, he on the other. He peered and clicked and snapped Tony balancing, bare-legged, shirt-tail fluttering, and the snapshot was no sooner taken than Tony fell off into the water. Sitting on the shore in the July sunshine, Tony naked, his clothes spread out on a bush, they laughed and dried themselves and ate toffee and drank lemonade.

He can't now in his half-sleep remember when exactly it was that he had the terrible dream about Tony.

He, not Tony, is, in the dream, sitting alone by the great glowing range where his father used to stir the porridge. He is reading a book. Out in a scullery a voice keeps chanting, like the voice of a schoolboy learning something by rote. He listens more carefully. It is Tony's voice. He tiptoes to the door of the scullery. Tony is standing by a blackboard with chalk markings on it. He has in his hand a long, yellow, wooden pointer. He is spelling out something but it makes no sense. Then, as he watches, black hair grows on Tony's face and his upper teeth protrude like fangs: and he awakes screaming that Tony's going mad, Tony's going mad.

The odd thing is that at the age of eighteen Tony did go mad. A premonition? Or was the dream before or after the event? Either way, that was the end of the laughter of the water and the Blue Stones. A dream, like the dream of the white house. Somewhere, somewhere he still has that snapshot.

His eyes open again. Minnie has dried her tears. When I was a teacher, pin-stripe and pince-nez, my jokes in class were well-known, even became proverbial, so I may have given something to my town to be remembered as long as the last of my students live, then to be forgotten or attributed to someone else. Cathy comes in and runs to Minnie. At least my body will go intact to lie beside her, membrane by member, ghosts, to the final, far beyond this partial, day of doom. Gary comes in and runs to his grandfather's bedside. But by the living Jesus they should not have touched my house, my living dream seen across water and through tall reeds and beech trees, they should not, they should not have touched my living dream, mad Minahan, Bertie Bigfeet, Creepy Corkman whoever you are, I will see you all in hell. Her son comes in hobbling on a half-crutch. Followed by his wife, as rich a red wine as ever, carrying parcels and grandfather's clothes.

—Minnie, Minnie Brown, Cathy sings, we're home again from Dungloe town.

The crabs are dead within the last hour. The oxalis is past its best. The house is burned. There is no laughter around the Blue Stones. The lake will never be the same again. Tony the madman roars through his dreams. Oh, the sights that we see as we wait here for death on the treacherous waves.

—But not destroyed, his son says.

More than my town, more than my family, my dream of a white house.

—They did their worst, his son says. But they should have brought a professional pyromaniac with them. We kept it out of the papers.

—You could have told me.

By the living Jesus they should not have tampered with my dream.

—You had enough to recover from. We thought it better.

Minnie and his daughter-in-law and the children are by the window laughing at the antics of a crew of magpies in the swaying treetops. The town, still undisturbed, is far below. His son gathers the newspapers from the carpet, stooping and rising again with some difficulty. He says: You knew them.

—Two of them. That'll do to begin with.

—I felt you might know them.

—Oh, I've been watching people in this town for a long time. Their faces. Their families. The books they read. Even their feet. If you looked at little else but the way people walk you could write a history of a place. Boots, boots, boots marching up and down again. Kipling, you know.

Patiently his son says: I know.

And through a gap in the reeds he looks, as he waits for the perch, across the water at the white house. Reeds make one frame for the picture. Beech trees, set back from the avenue that leads up to the house, make another. He envies the people who own it, the lawn and flower-beds before it, the barns and varied outbuildings behind it. He has missed a strike. Tony is laughing. And the most beautiful thing of all, cutting across a corner of the lawn, a small brook tumbling down to join the lake. To have your own stream on your own lawn is the height of everything.

ABOUT THE AUTHOR

BENEDICT KIELY was born in 1919 in Dromore, County Tyrone, and raised in nearby Omagh. After graduating from University College, Dublin, in 1943, he settled in the city and began his career as a writer. By 1945 he was a full-time critic for *The Irish Independent* and had published his first book, *Counties of Contention*, a nonfiction account of the partition of Ireland. His first book-length fiction, *Land Without Stars*, appeared soon afterwards, and was followed by eight further novels, a novella, and several story collections. Many of his stories first appeared in *The New Yorker*, and in 1980 a selection was published by Godine under the title *The State of Ireland*.

Mr. Kiely has lectured widely in Ireland and the United States, was literary editor of *The Irish Press*, published dozens of 'Letters from America' in *The Irish Times*, and has become, over the decades, one of Ireland's best-known broadcasters. He has also written travel books, several important studies in Irish literature and politics, a story for children, and, most recently, two volumes of memoirs.

In 1980 Mr. Kiely received the award in literature from the Irish Academy of Letters, and in 1996 was named Saoi of Aosdána, the highest honor bestowed by the Arts Council of Ireland. He lives in Donnybrook, Dublin.